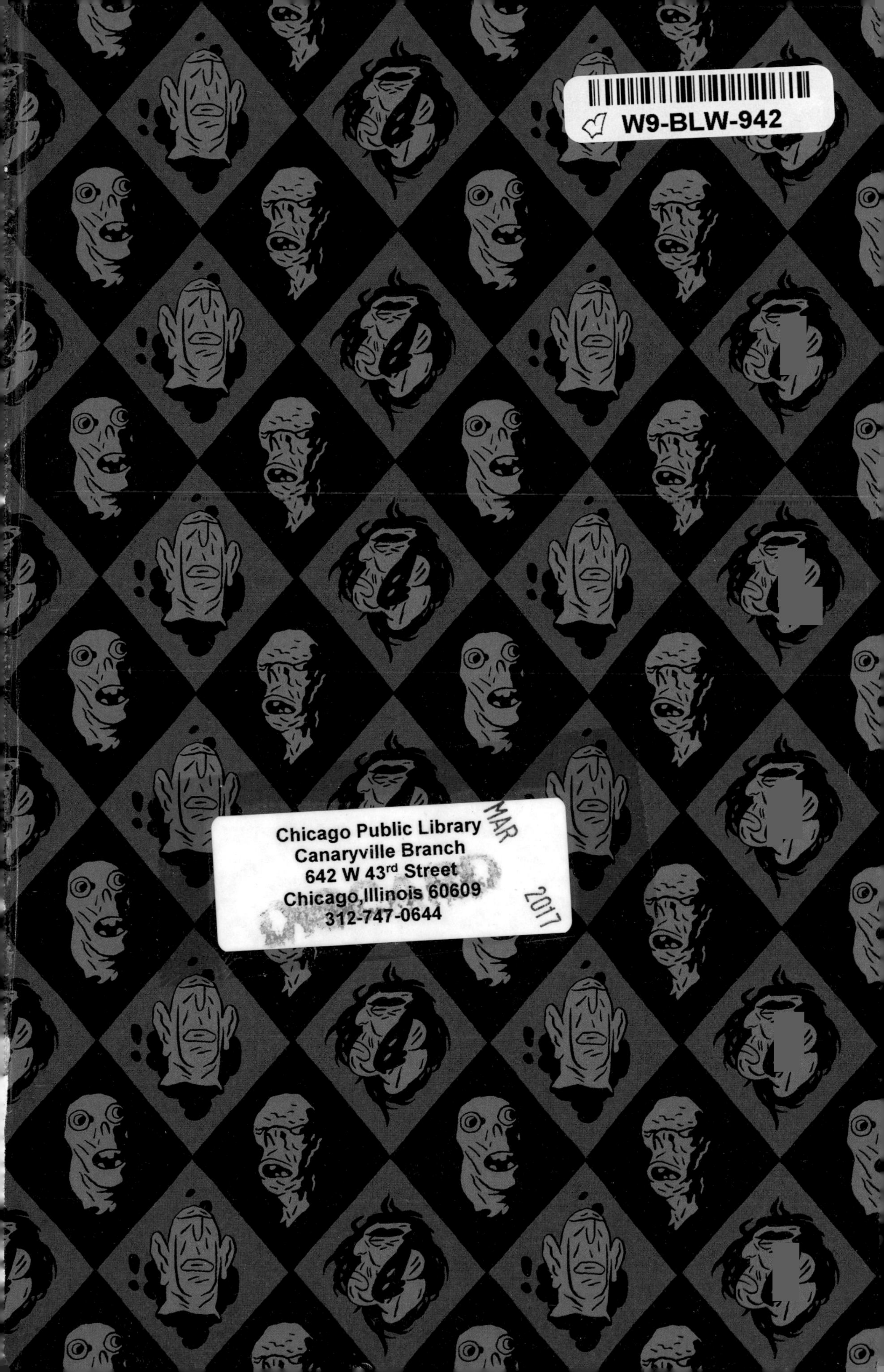

IMAGE COMICS, INC.

Robert Kirkman - Chief Operating Officer
Erik Larsen - Chief Financial Officer
Todd McFarlane - President
Marc Silvestri - Chief Executive Officer
Jim Valentino - Vice-President

Eric Stephenson - Publisher
Corey Murphy - Director of Sales
Jeff Boison - Director of Publishing Planning & Book Trade Sales
Jeremy Sullivan - Director of Digital Sales
Kat Salazar - Director of PR & Marketing
Branwyn Bigglestone - Controller
Drew Gill - Art Director
Jonathan Chan - Production Manager
Meredith Wallace - Print Manager
Briah Skelly - Publicist
Sasha Head - Sales & Marketing Production Designer
Randy Okamura - Digital Production Designer
David Brothers - Branding Manager
Olivia Ngai - Content Manager
Addison Duke - Production Artist
Vincent Kukua - Production Artist
Tricia Ramos - Production Artist
Jeff Stang - Direct Market Sales Representative
Emilio Bautista - Digital Sales Associate
Leanna Caunter - Accounting Assistant
Chloe Ramos-Peterson - Library Market Sales Representative

IMAGECOMICS.COM

HEAD LOPPER, VOL. 1: THE ISLAND OR A PLAGUE OF BEASTS TP
SECOND PRINTING. DECEMBER 2016.
ISBN : 978-1-63215-886-4

HEAD LOPPER

& THE ISLAND
or
A PLAGUE OF BEASTS

Written and Drawn by
ANDREW MACLEAN

Colored by
MIKE SPICER

Chapter 3 Colored by
ANDREW MACLEAN

Epilogue Colored by
LIN VISEL & JOSEPH BERGIN III

Designed and Lettered by
ANDREW MACLEAN

CHAPTER ONE

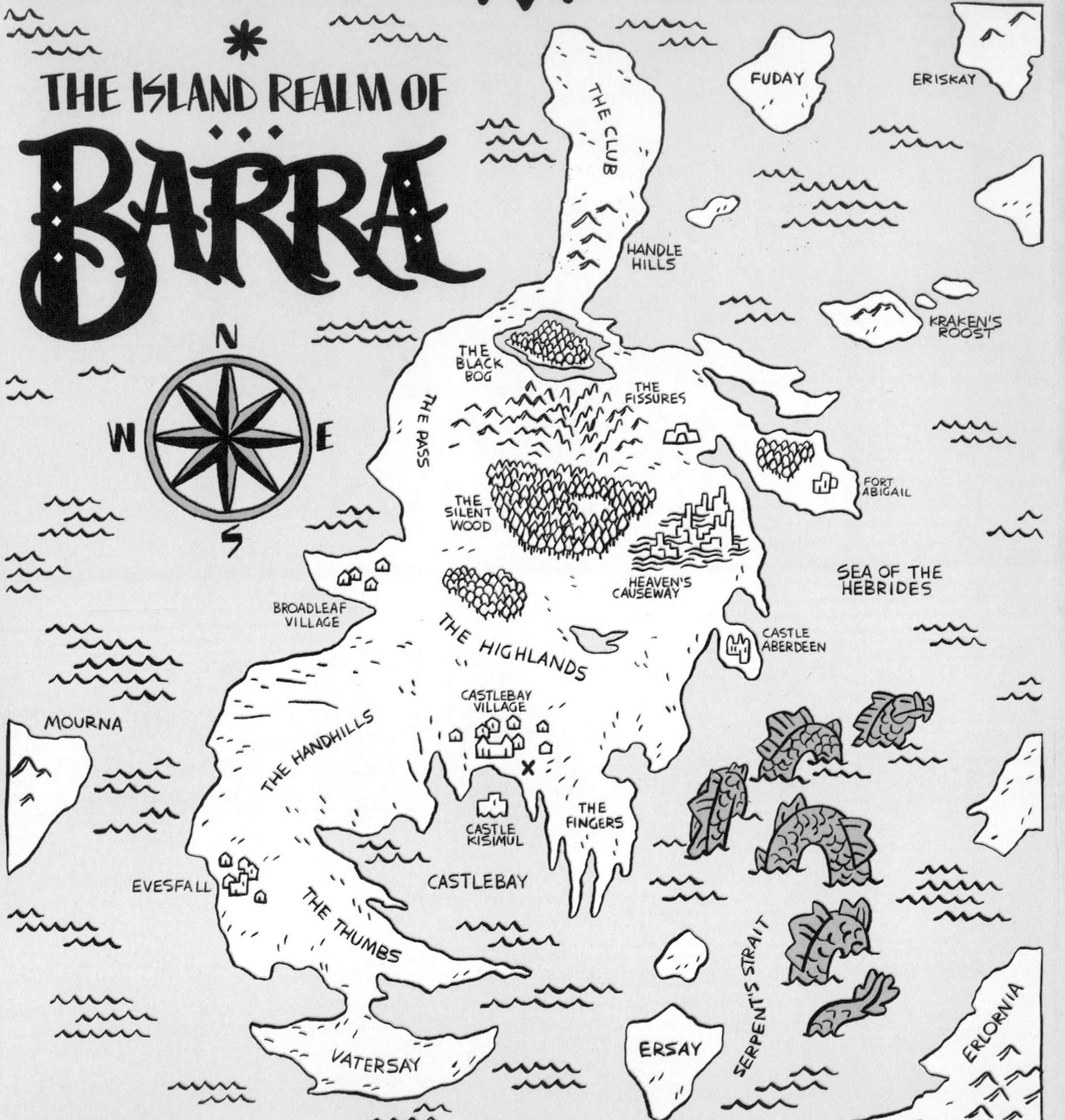
THE ISLAND REALM OF
BARRA
N
W
E
S
THE CLUB
HANDLE HILLS
FUDAY
ERISKAY
KRAKEN'S ROOST
THE BLACK BOG
THE FISSURES
THE PASS
FORT ABIGAIL
THE SILENT WOOD
HEAVEN'S CAUSEWAY
SEA OF THE HEBRIDES
BROADLEAF VILLAGE
THE HIGHLANDS
CASTLE ABERDEEN
CASTLEBAY VILLAGE
MOURNA
THE HANDHILLS
THE FINGERS
CASTLE KISIMUL
EVESFALL
CASTLEBAY
THE THUMBS
SERPENT'S STRAIT
ERLORNIA
VATERSAY
ERSAY
X=NORGAL & AGATHA

BLOOD AND WATER

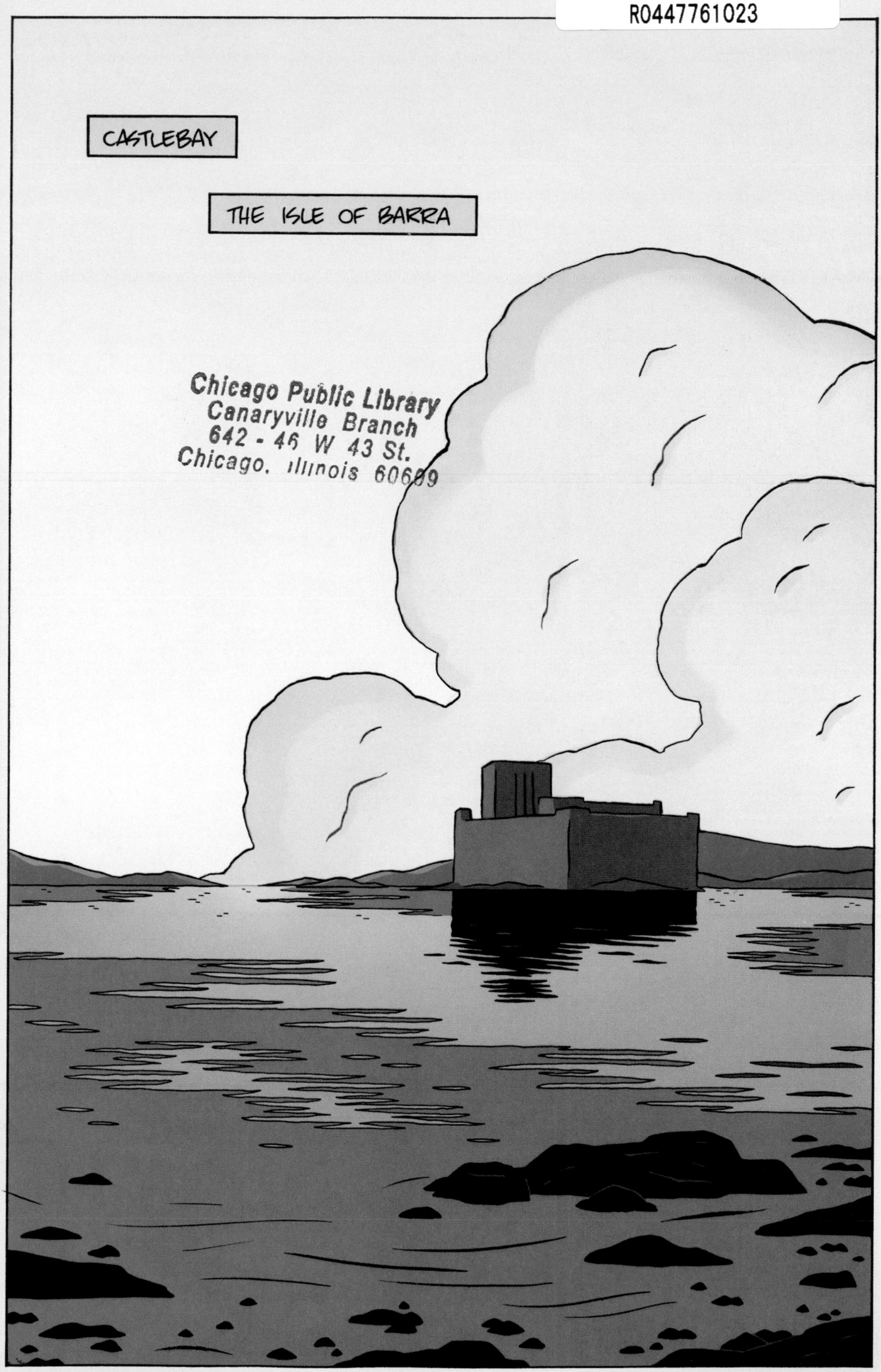
CASTLEBAY
THE ISLE OF BARRA

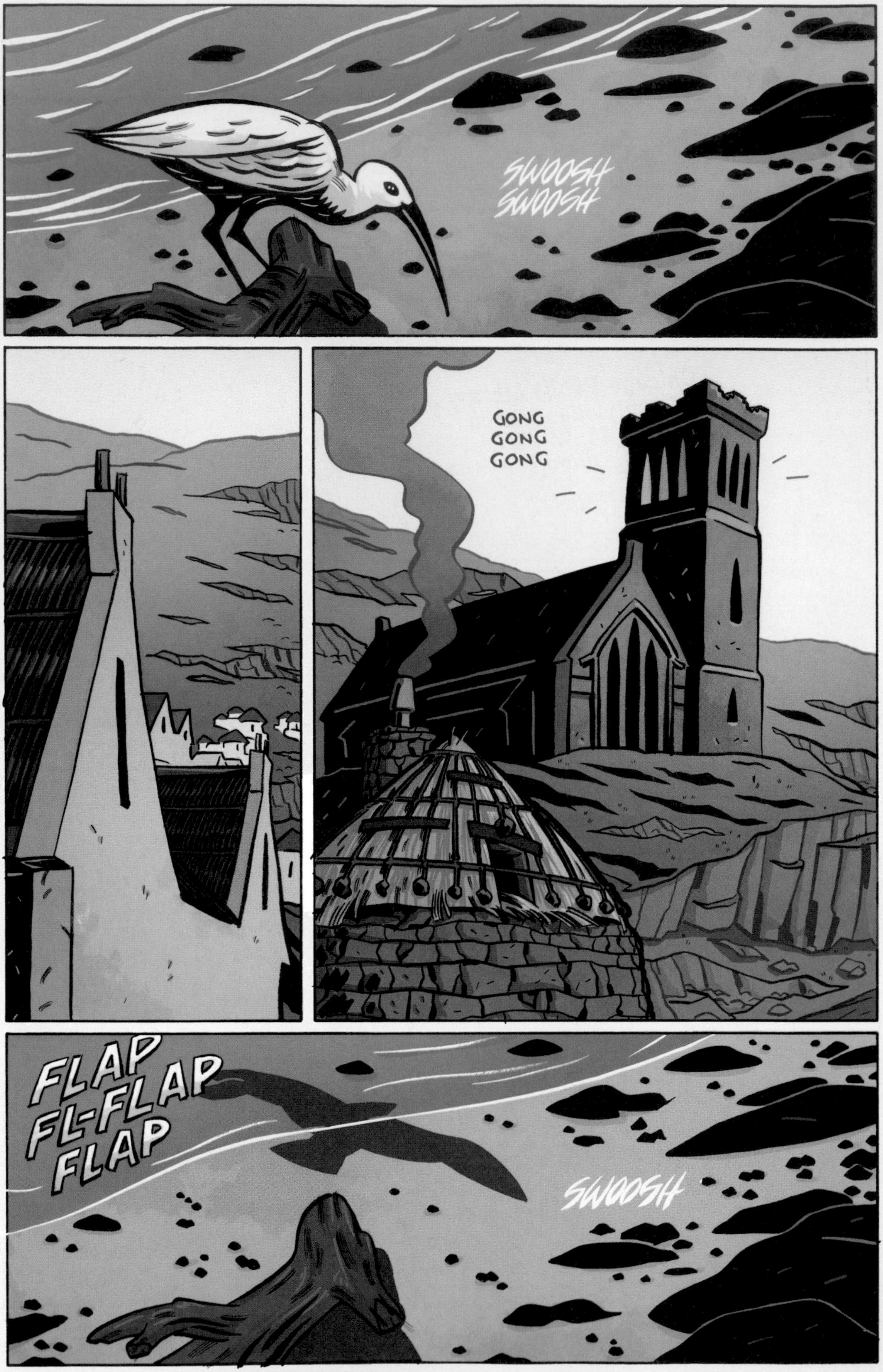
SWOOSH
SWOOSH
GONG
GONG
GONG
FLAP
FL-FLAP
FLAP
SWOOSH

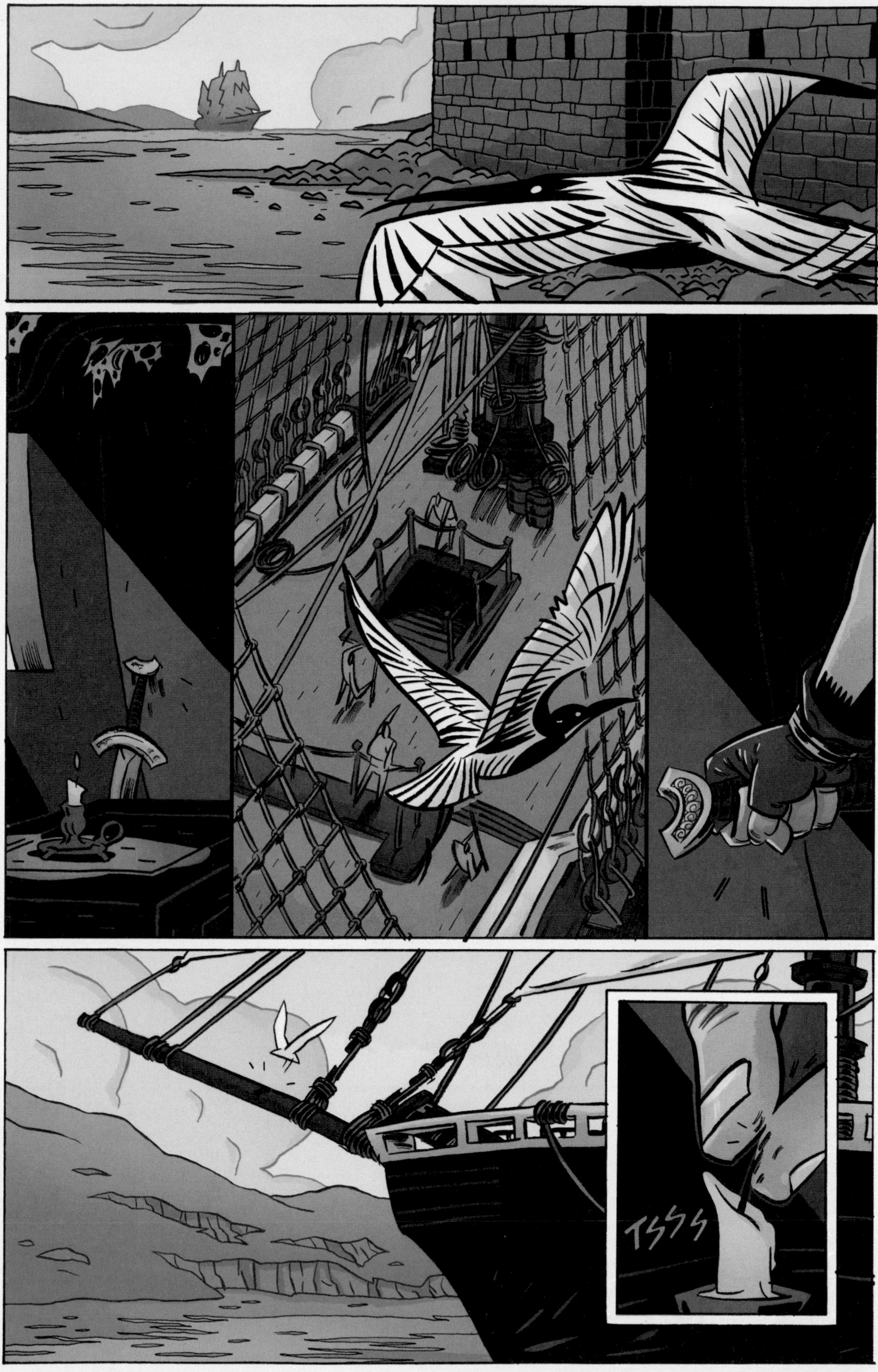
TSSS

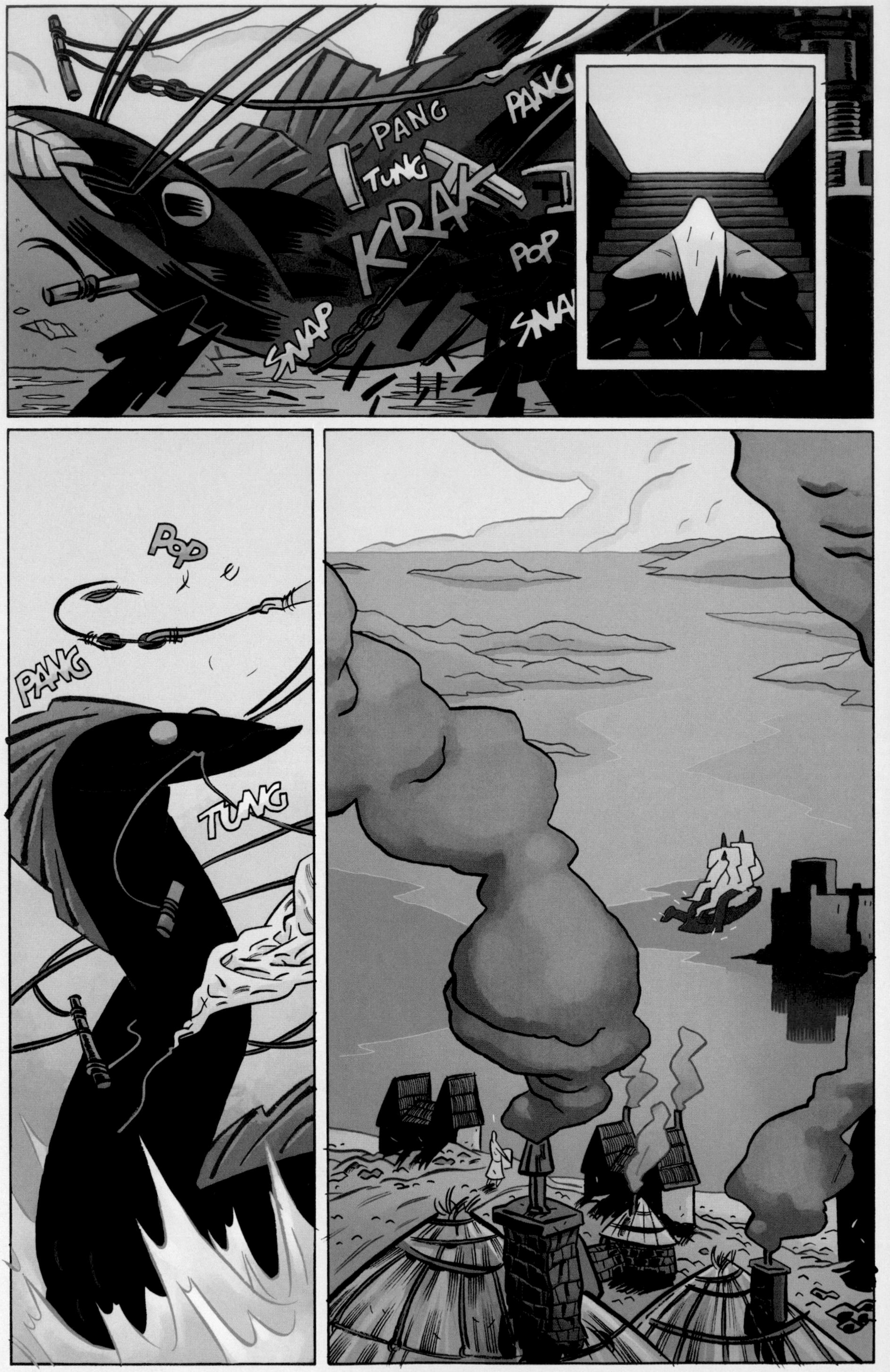
PANG
TUNG
KRAK
PANG
POP
SNAP
POP
PANG
TUNG

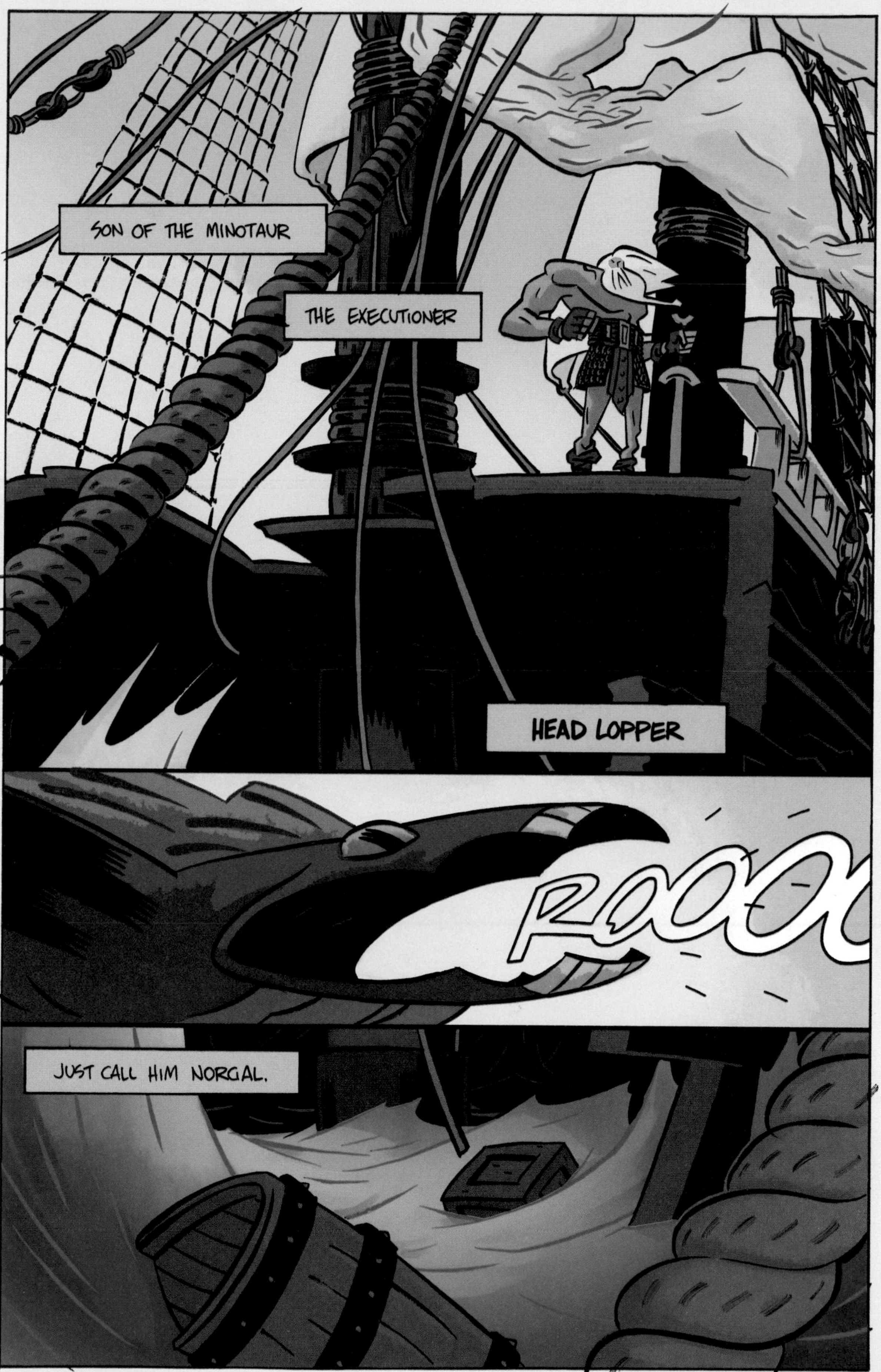
SON OF THE MINOTAUR
THE EXECUTIONER
HEAD LOPPER
ROOOO
JUST CALL HIM NORGAL.

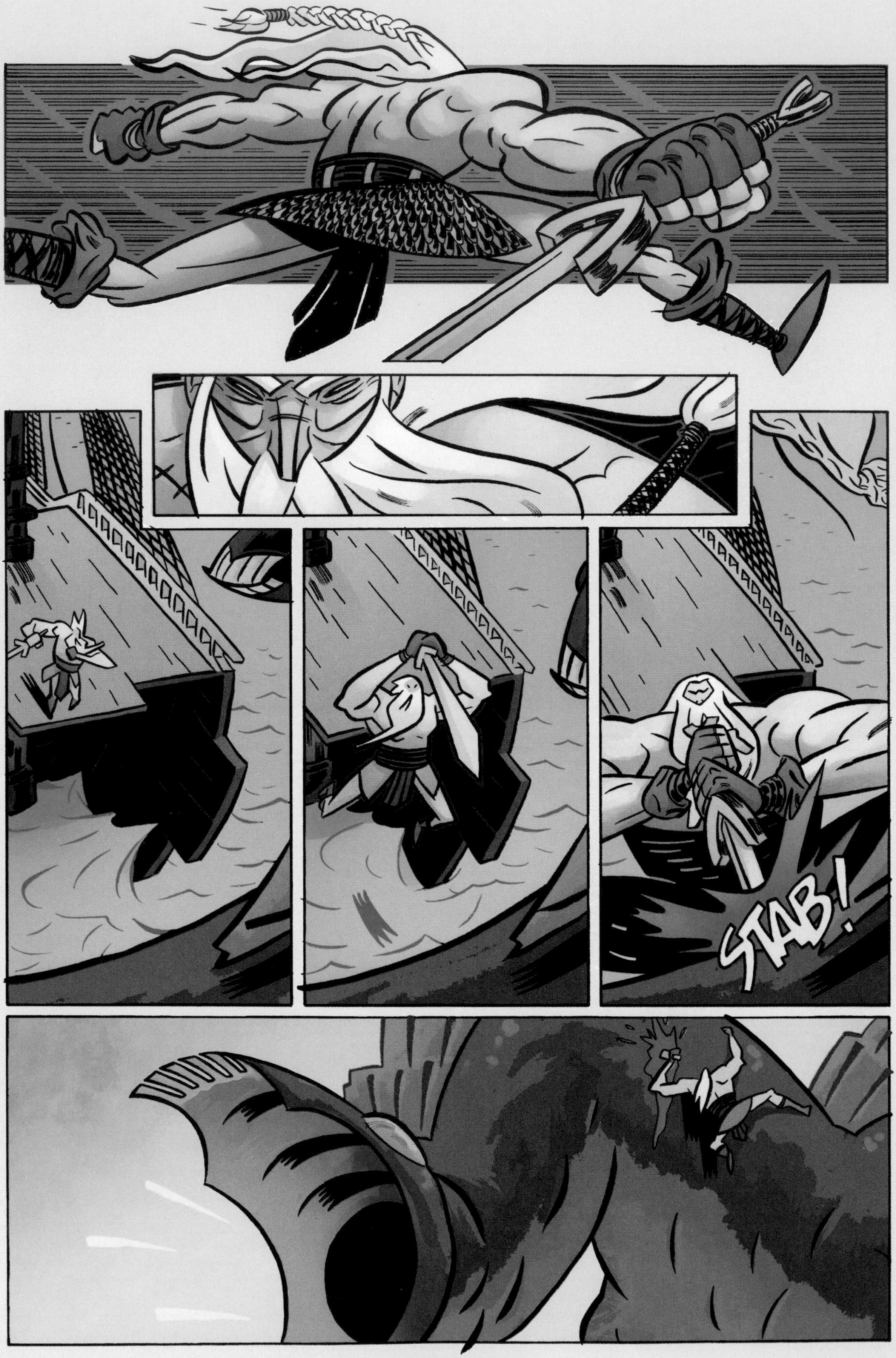
STAB!

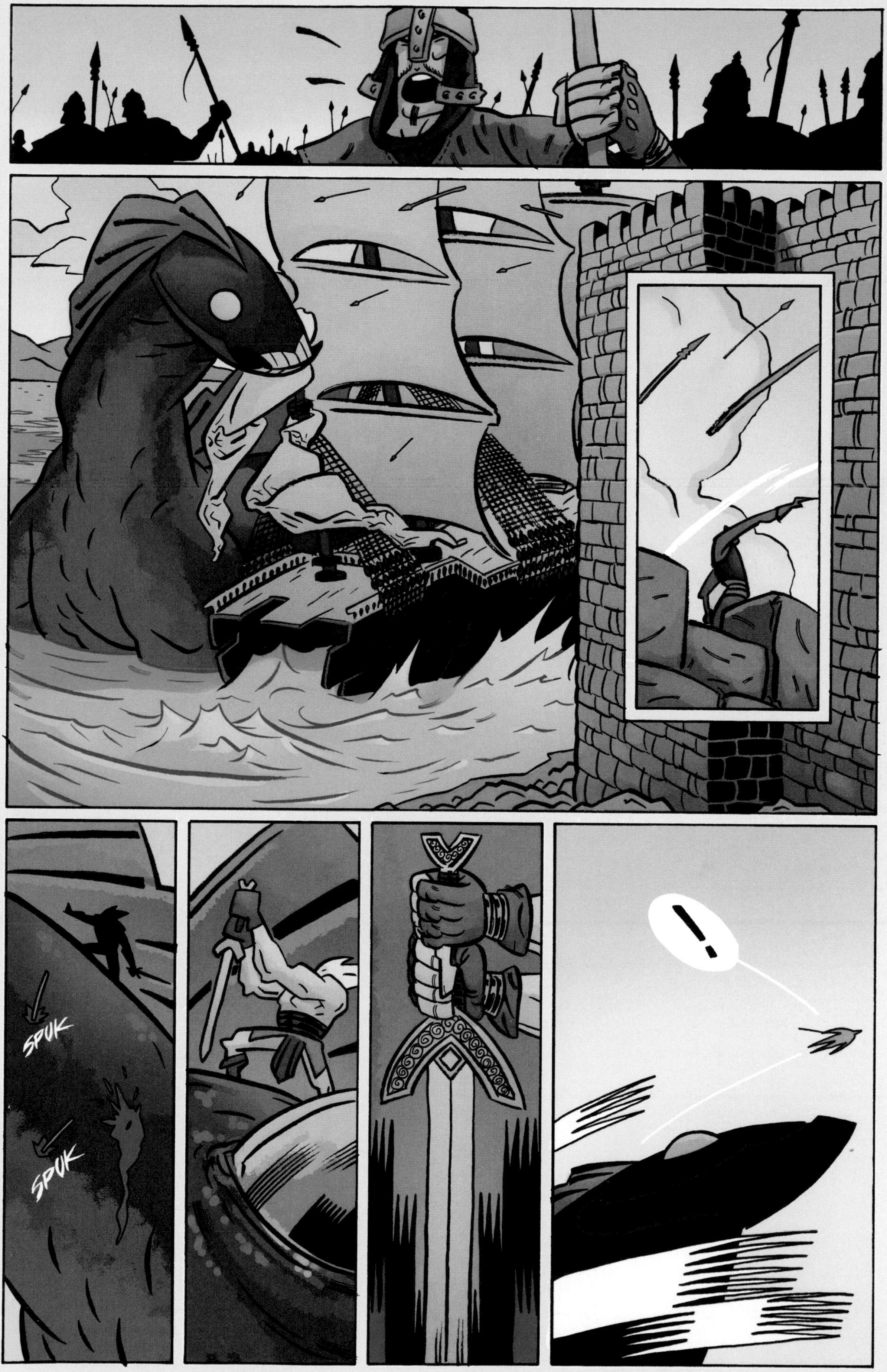
SPUK
SPUK
!

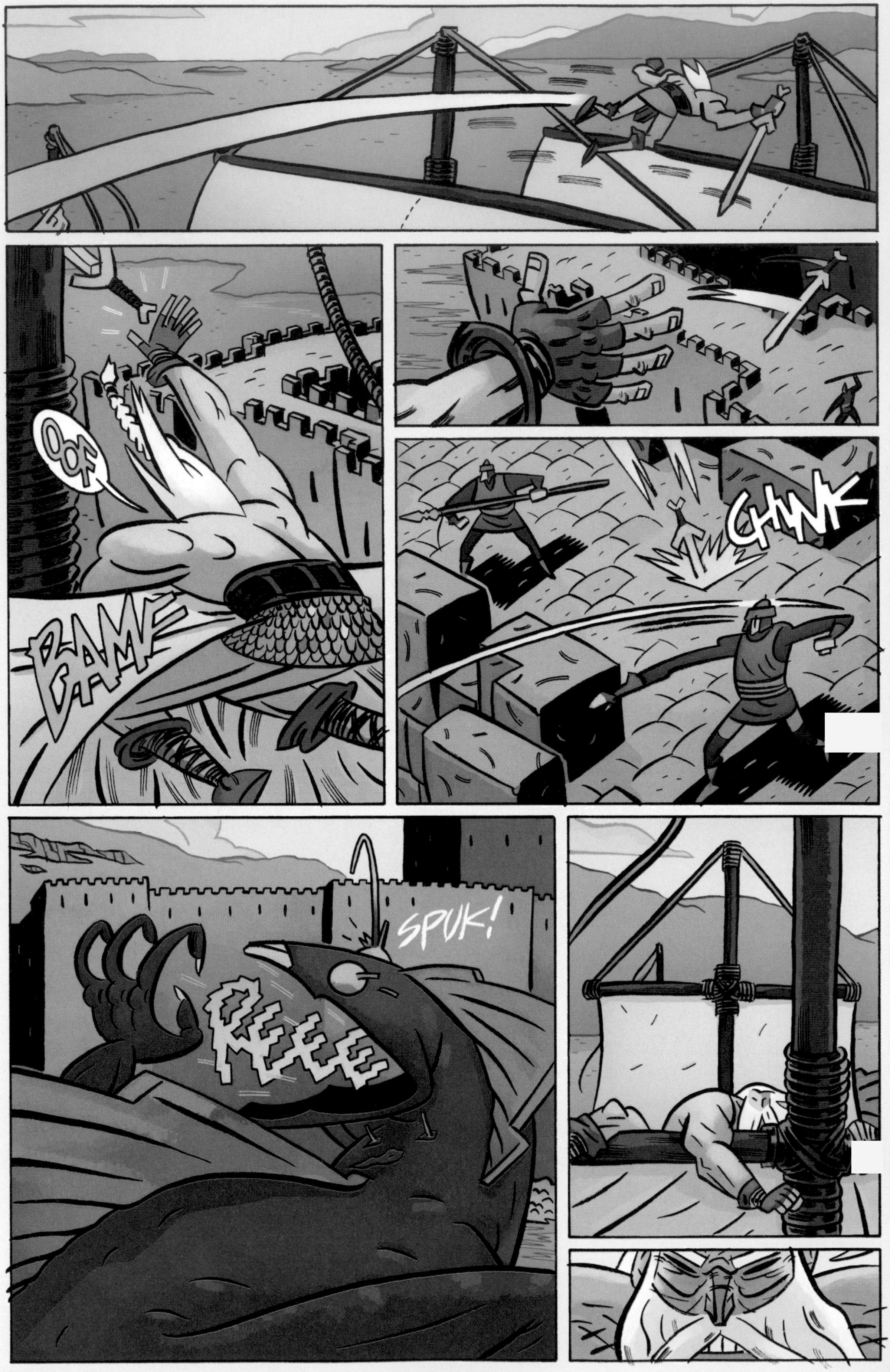
OOF
BAMF
CHINK
SPUK!
REEEE

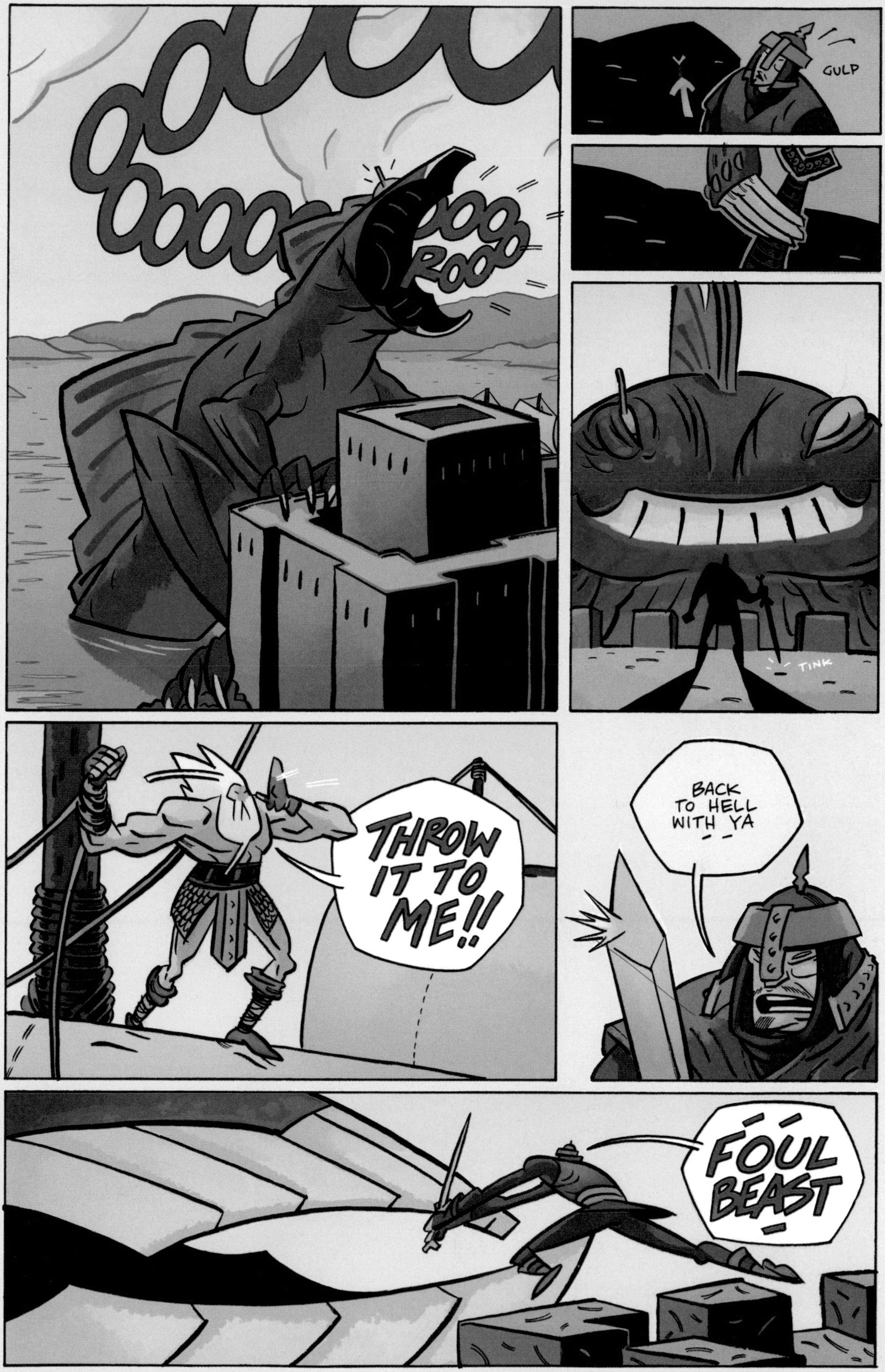
OOOOOOOOOOOOOOOOO
ROOO
GULP
TINK
THROW IT TO ME!!
BACK TO HELL WITH YA
FOUL BEAST

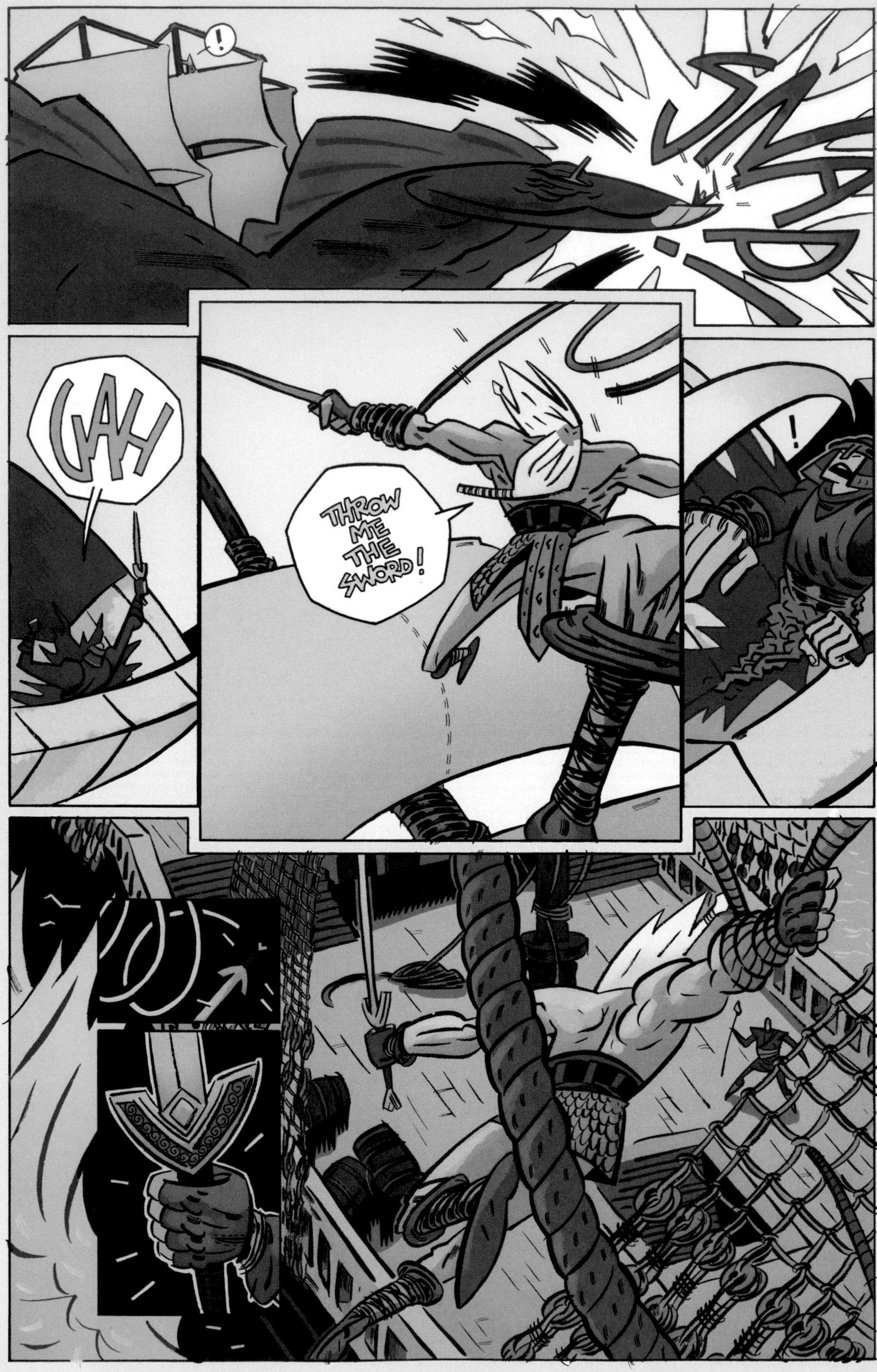
!
SNAP!
GAH
THROW ME THE SWORD!
!

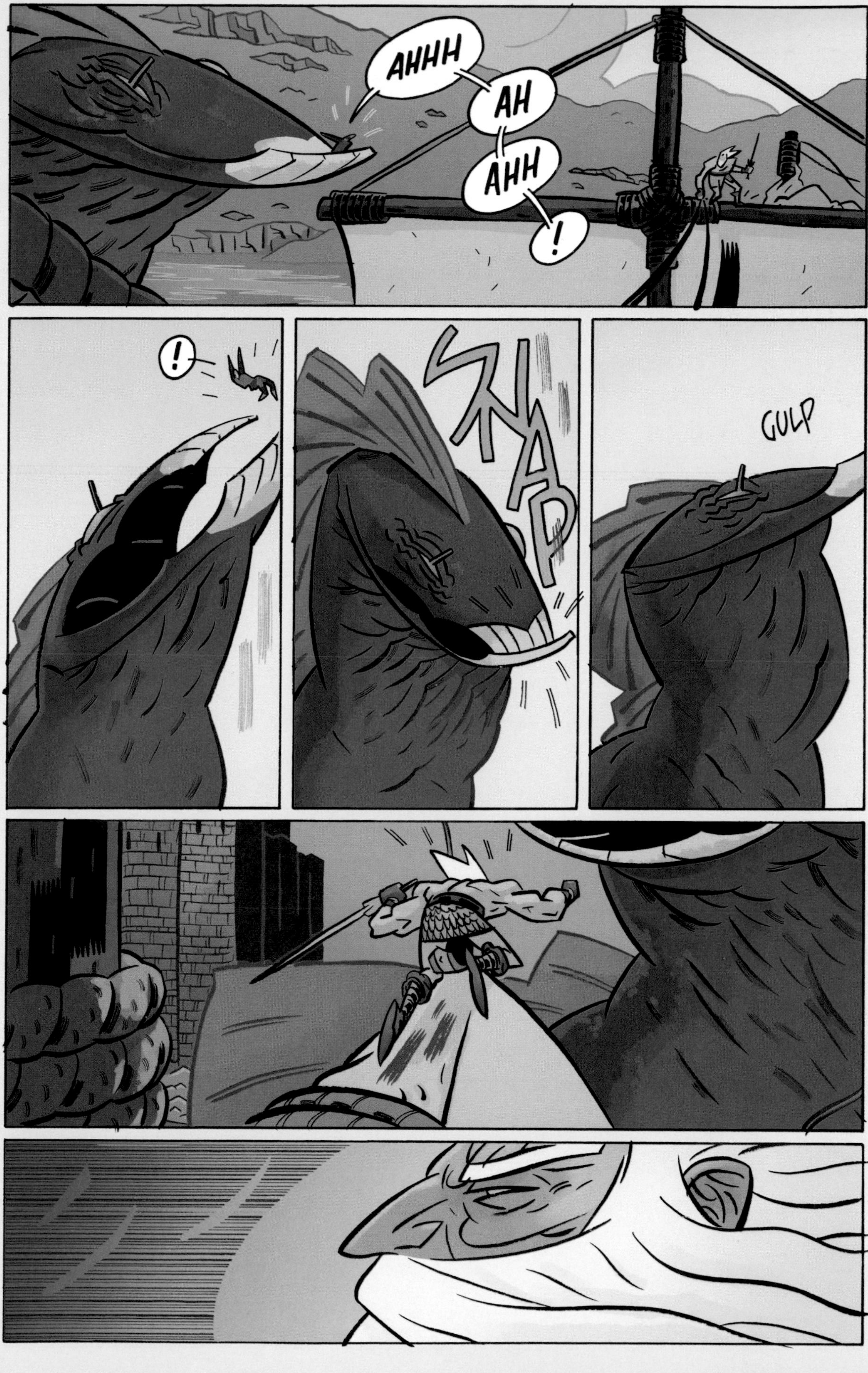
AHHH
AH
AHH
!
!
SNAP
GULP

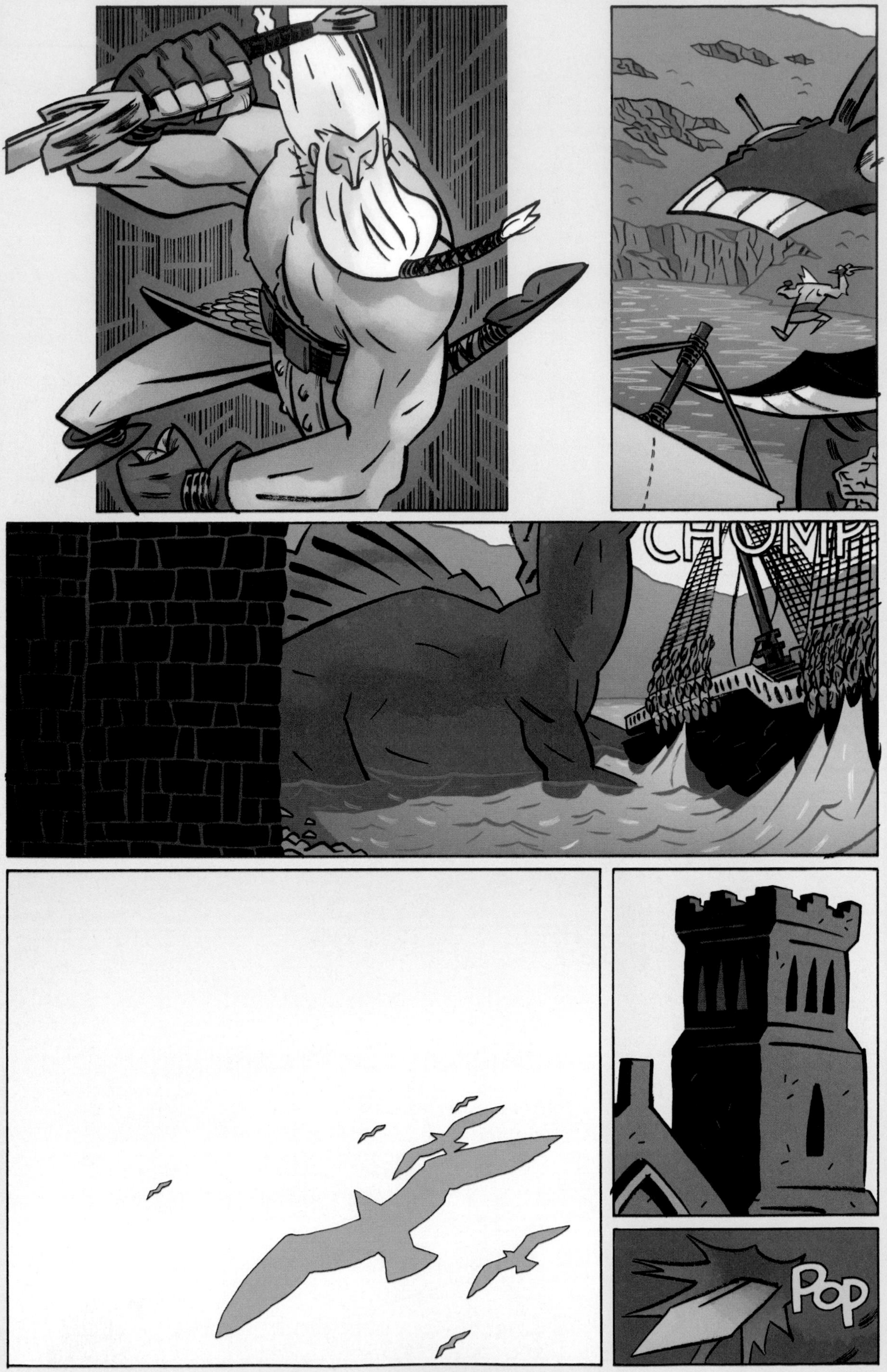
CHOMP
POP

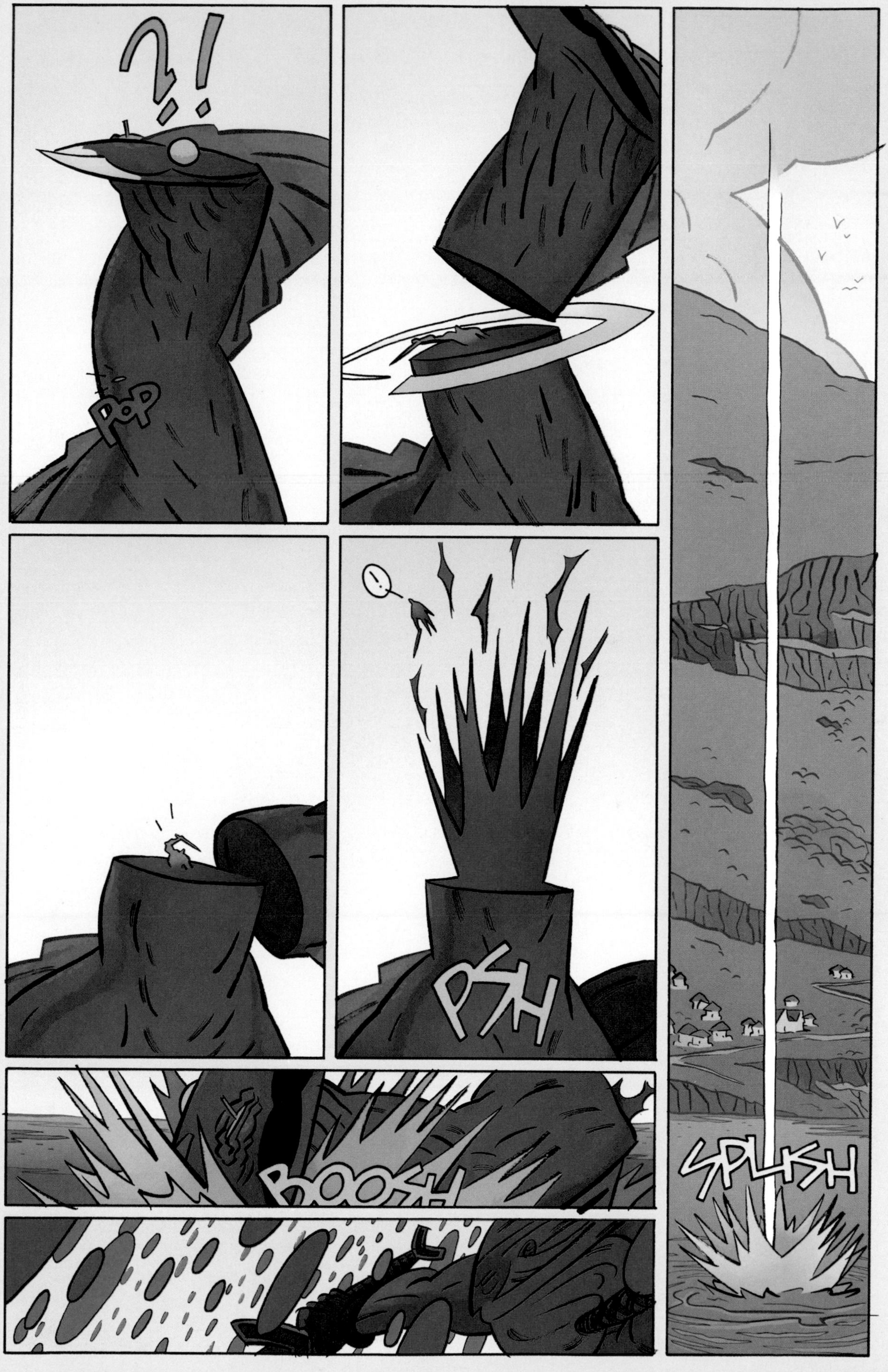
?!
POP
PSH
BOOSH
SPLISH

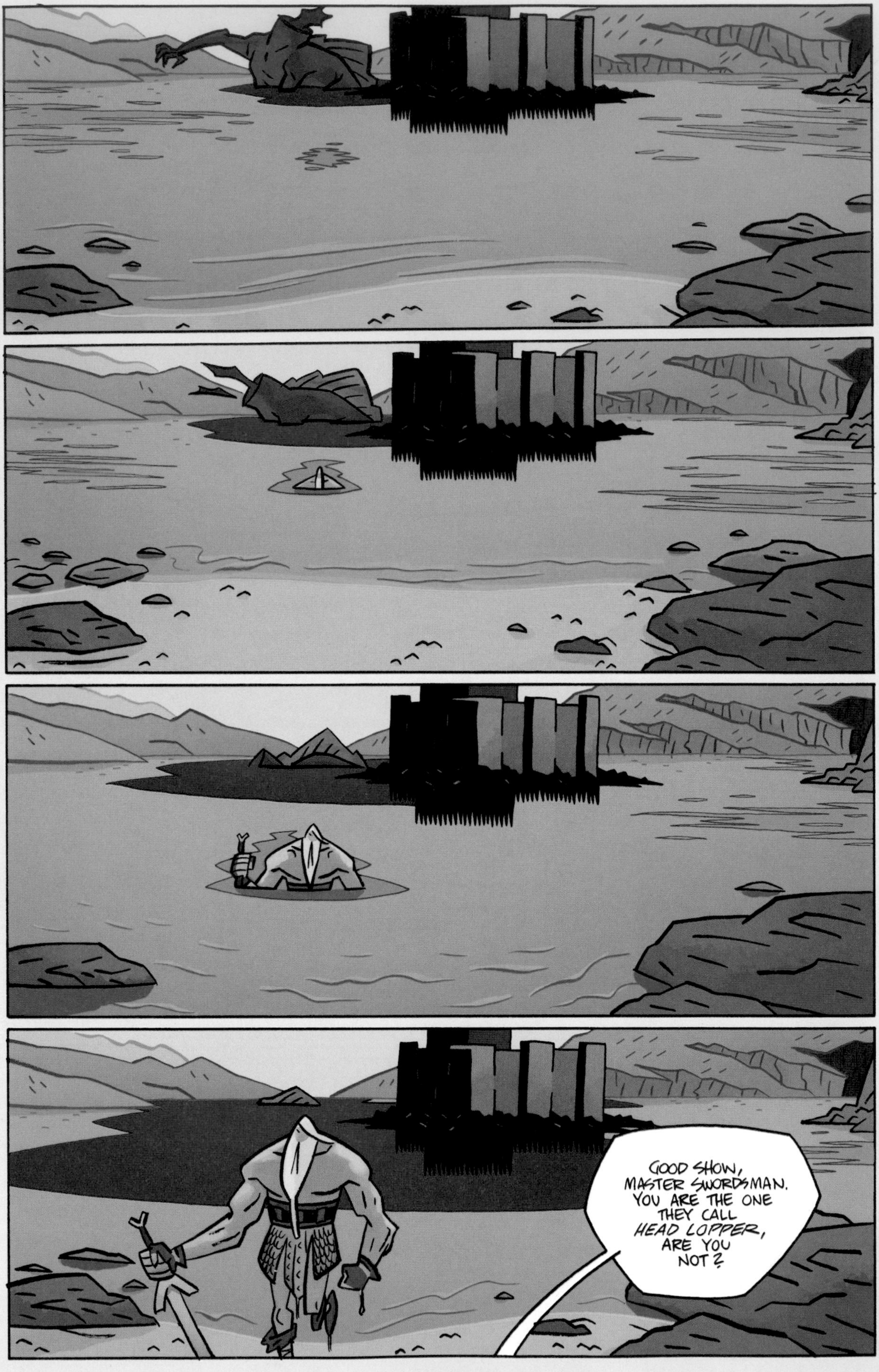
GOOD SHOW, MASTER SWORDSMAN. YOU ARE THE ONE THEY CALL HEAD LOPPER, ARE YOU NOT?

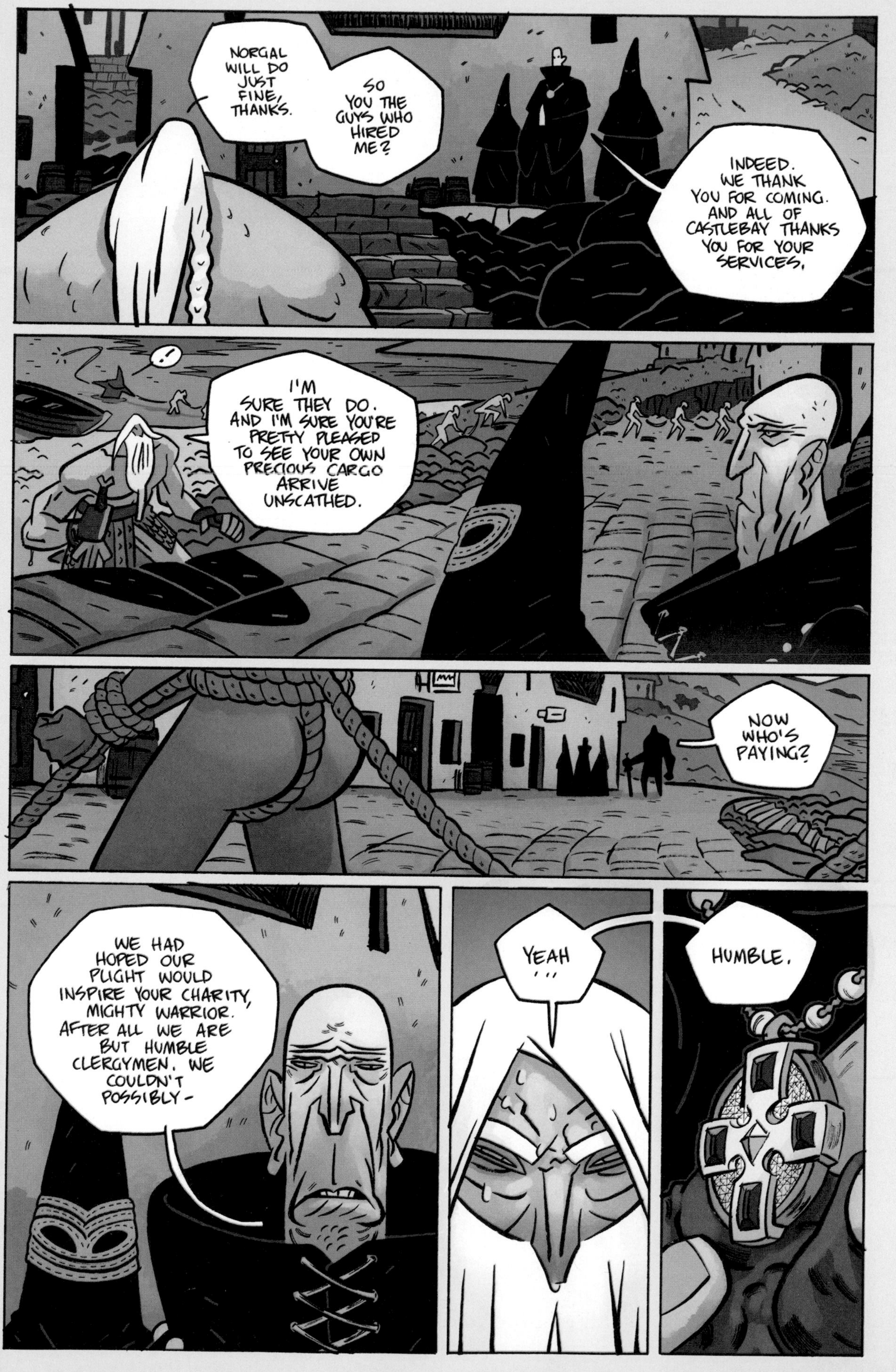
NORGAL WILL DO JUST FINE, THANKS.
SO YOU THE GUYS WHO HIRED ME?
INDEED. WE THANK YOU FOR COMING. AND ALL OF CASTLEBAY THANKS YOU FOR YOUR SERVICES.
!
I'M SURE THEY DO. AND I'M SURE YOU'RE PRETTY PLEASED TO SEE YOUR OWN PRECIOUS CARGO ARRIVE UNSCATHED.
NOW WHO'S PAYING?
WE HAD HOPED OUR PLIGHT WOULD INSPIRE YOUR CHARITY, MIGHTY WARRIOR. AFTER ALL WE ARE BUT HUMBLE CLERGYMEN. WE COULDN'T POSSIBLY-
YEAH ...
HUMBLE.

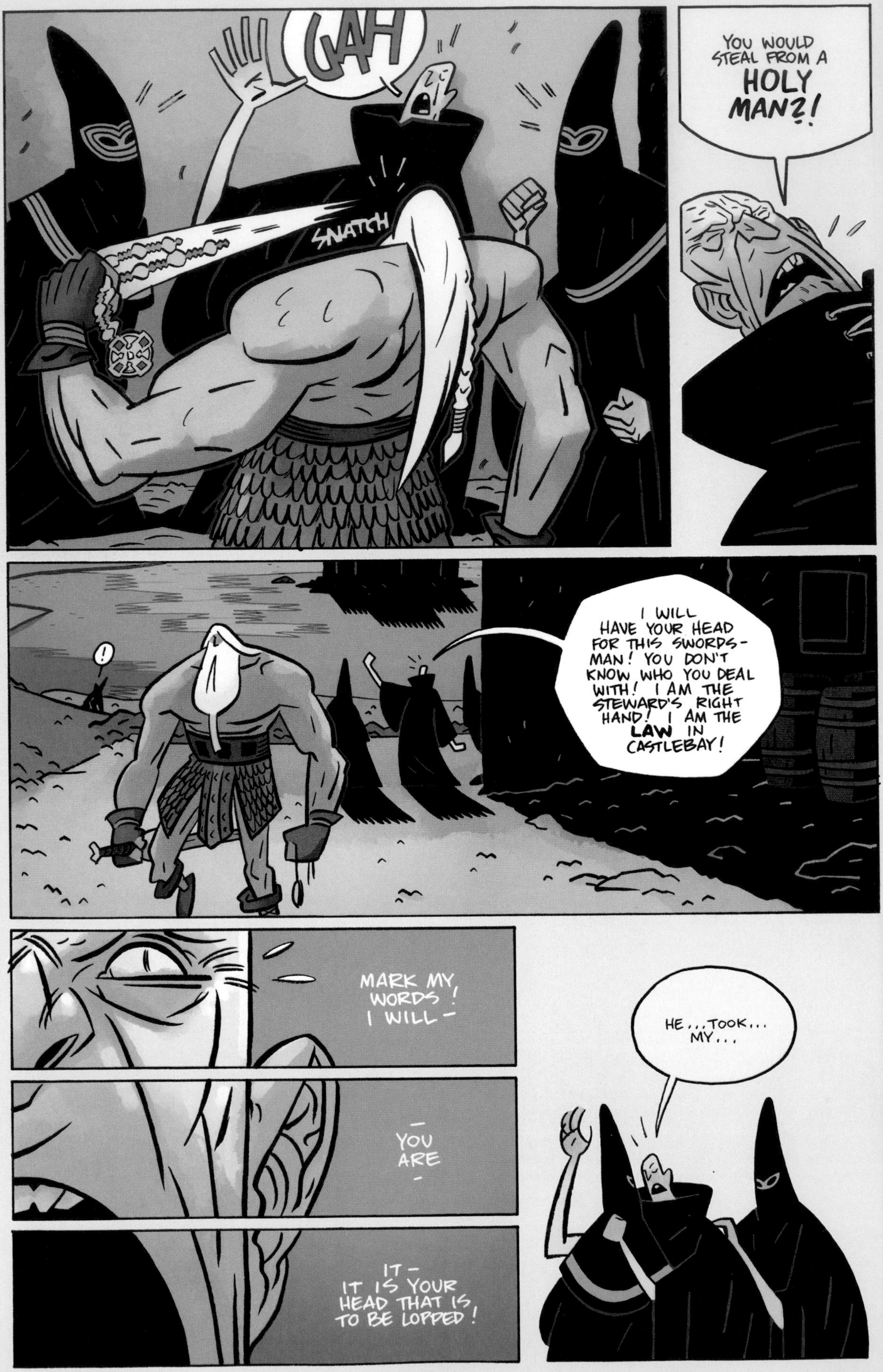
GAH
SNATCH
YOU WOULD STEAL FROM A HOLY MAN?!
!
I WILL HAVE YOUR HEAD FOR THIS SWORDSMAN! YOU DON'T KNOW WHO YOU DEAL WITH! I AM THE STEWARD'S RIGHT HAND! I AM THE LAW IN CASTLEBAY!
MARK MY WORDS! I WILL-
-YOU ARE-
IT- IT IS YOUR HEAD THAT IS TO BE LOPPED!
HE...TOOK... MY...

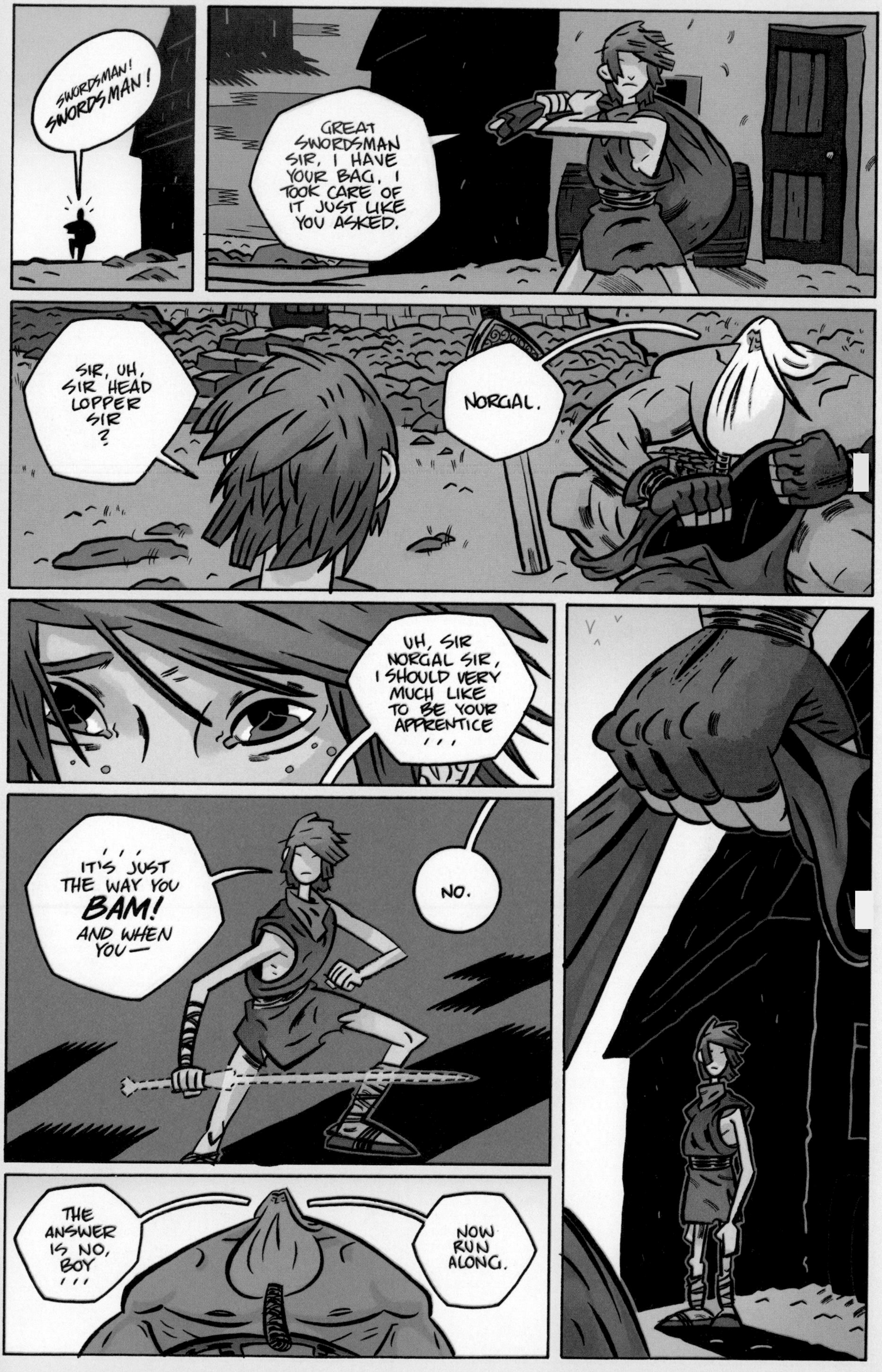

SWORDSMAN! SWORDSMAN!
GREAT SWORDSMAN SIR, I HAVE YOUR BAG, I TOOK CARE OF IT JUST LIKE YOU ASKED.
SIR, UH, SIR HEAD LOPPER SIR?
NORGAL.
UH, SIR NORGAL SIR, I SHOULD VERY MUCH LIKE TO BE YOUR APPRENTICE...
...IT'S JUST THE WAY YOU BAM! AND WHEN YOU—
NO.
THE ANSWER IS NO, BOY...
NOW RUN ALONG.

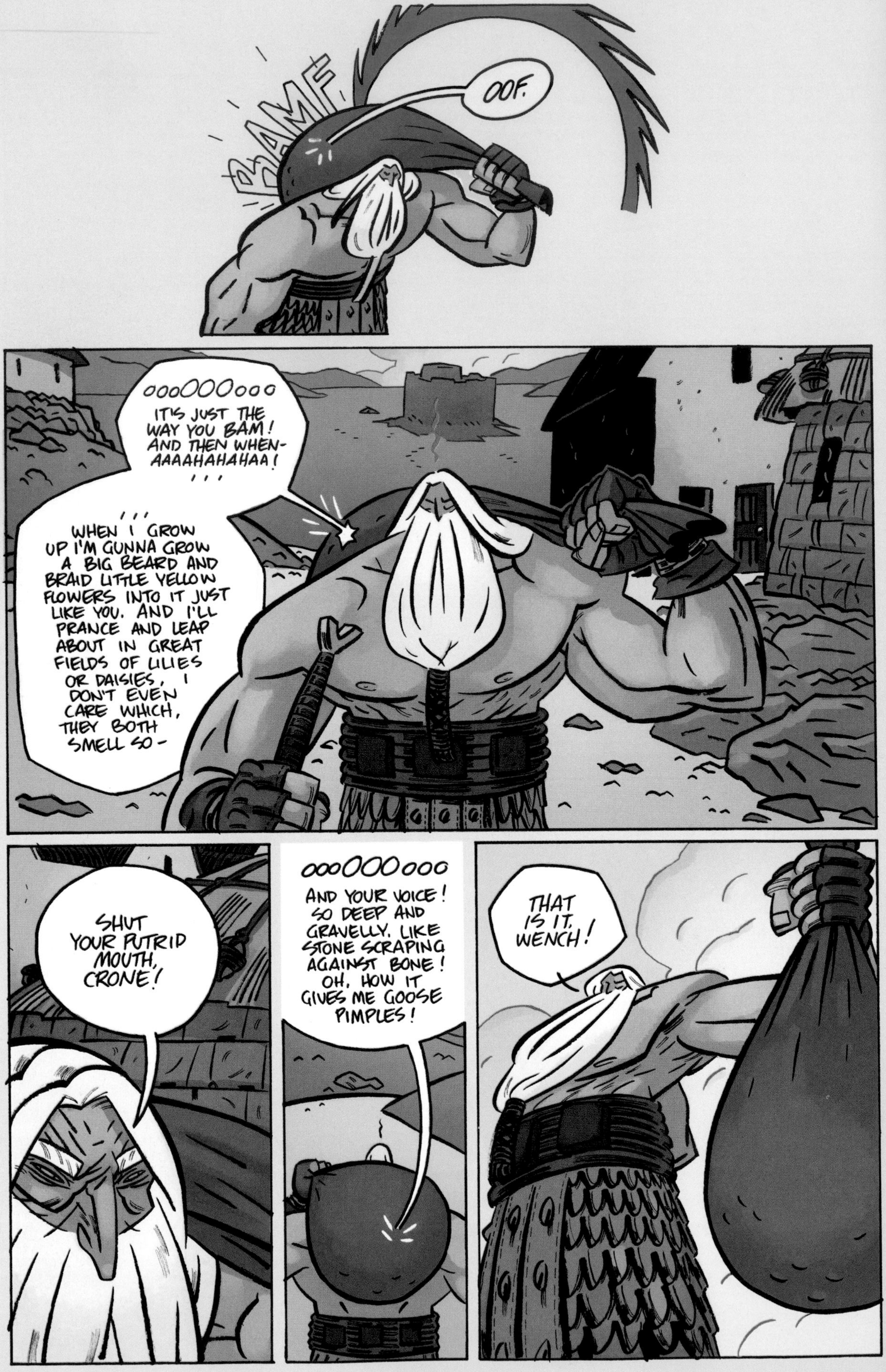
BAMF
OOF.
oooOOOooo IT'S JUST THE WAY YOU BAM! AND THEN WHEN- AAAAHAHAHAA!
WHEN I GROW UP I'M GUNNA GROW A BIG BEARD AND BRAID LITTLE YELLOW FLOWERS INTO IT JUST LIKE YOU. AND I'LL PRANCE AND LEAP ABOUT IN GREAT FIELDS OF LILIES OR DAISIES, I DON'T EVEN CARE WHICH, THEY BOTH SMELL SO-
SHUT YOUR PUTRID MOUTH, CRONE!
oooOOOooo AND YOUR VOICE! SO DEEP AND GRAVELLY, LIKE STONE SCRAPING AGAINST BONE! OH, HOW IT GIVES ME GOOSE PIMPLES!
THAT IS IT, WENCH!

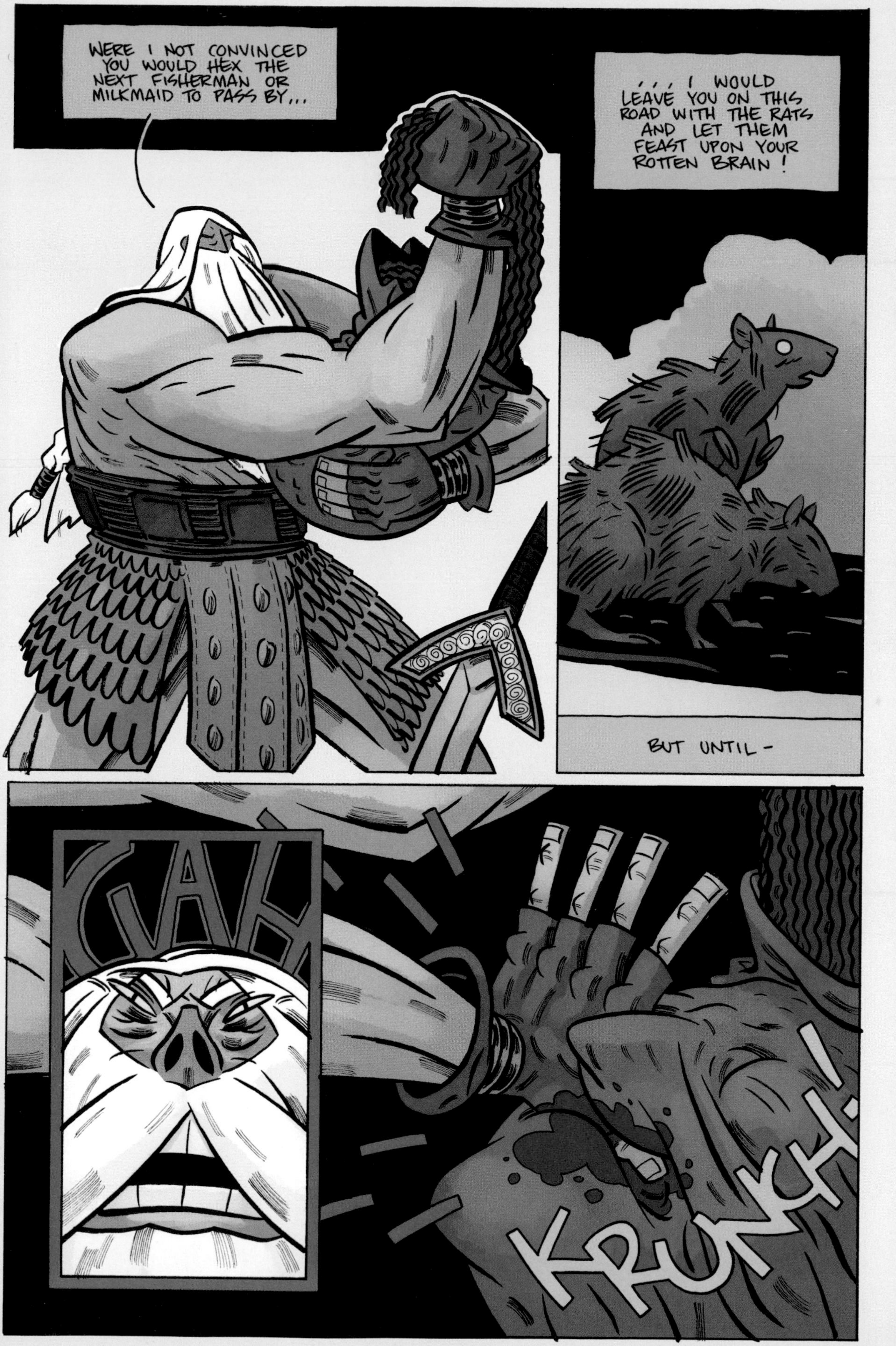
WERE I NOT CONVINCED YOU WOULD HEX THE NEXT FISHERMAN OR MILKMAID TO PASS BY...
...I WOULD LEAVE YOU ON THIS ROAD WITH THE RATS AND LET THEM FEAST UPON YOUR ROTTEN BRAIN!
BUT UNTIL-
GAH
KRUNKH!

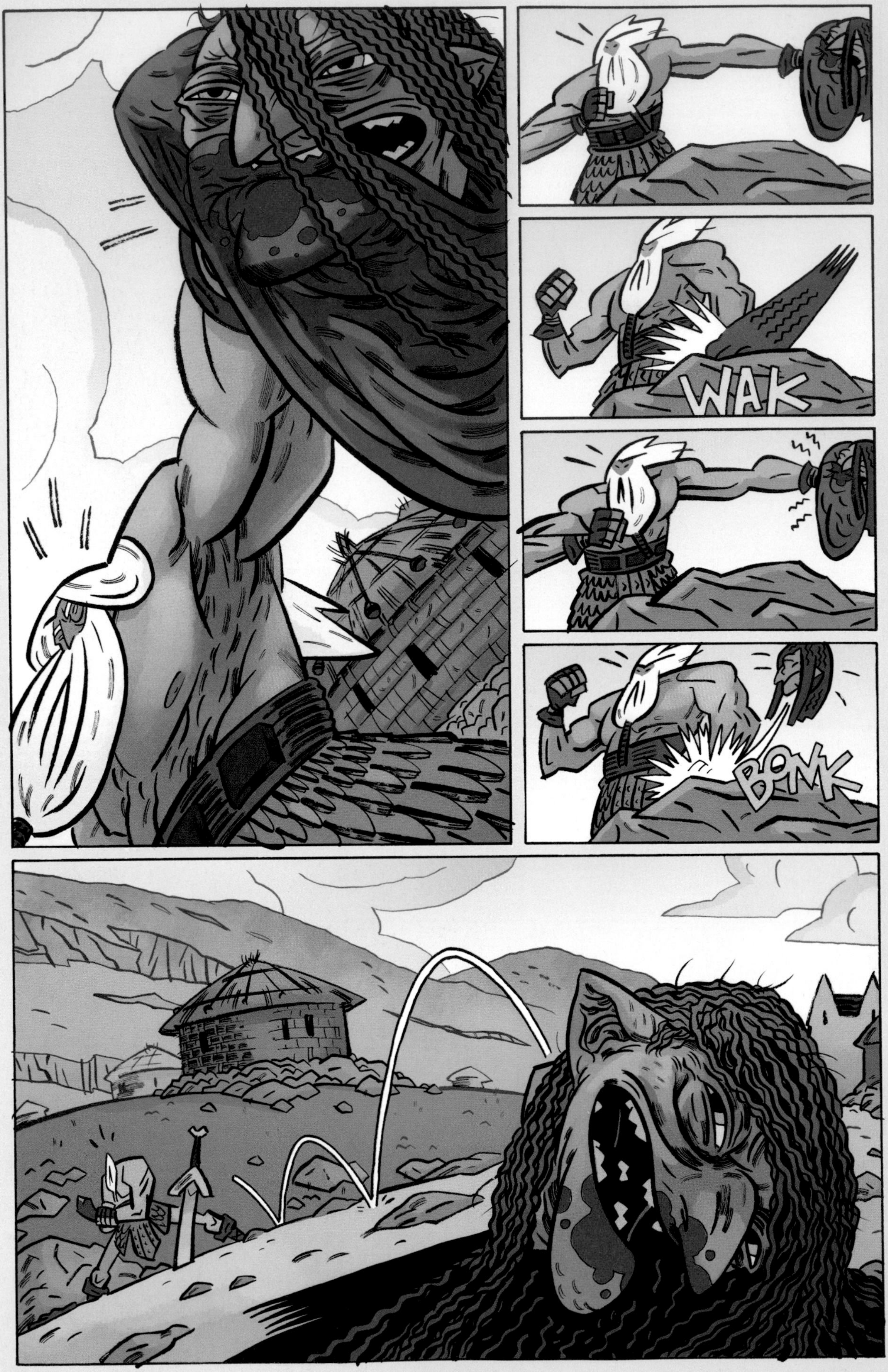
WAK
BONK

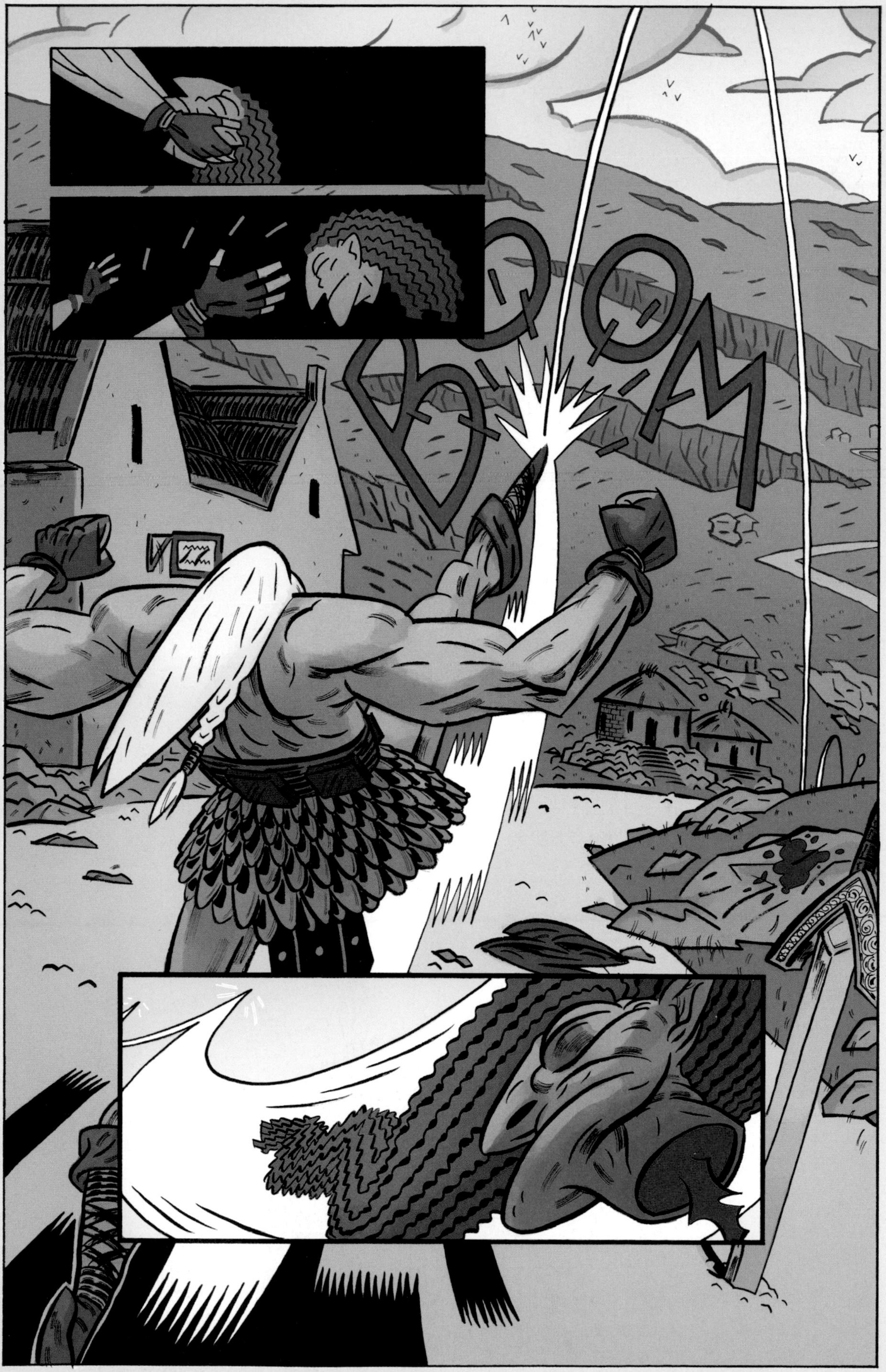
BOOM

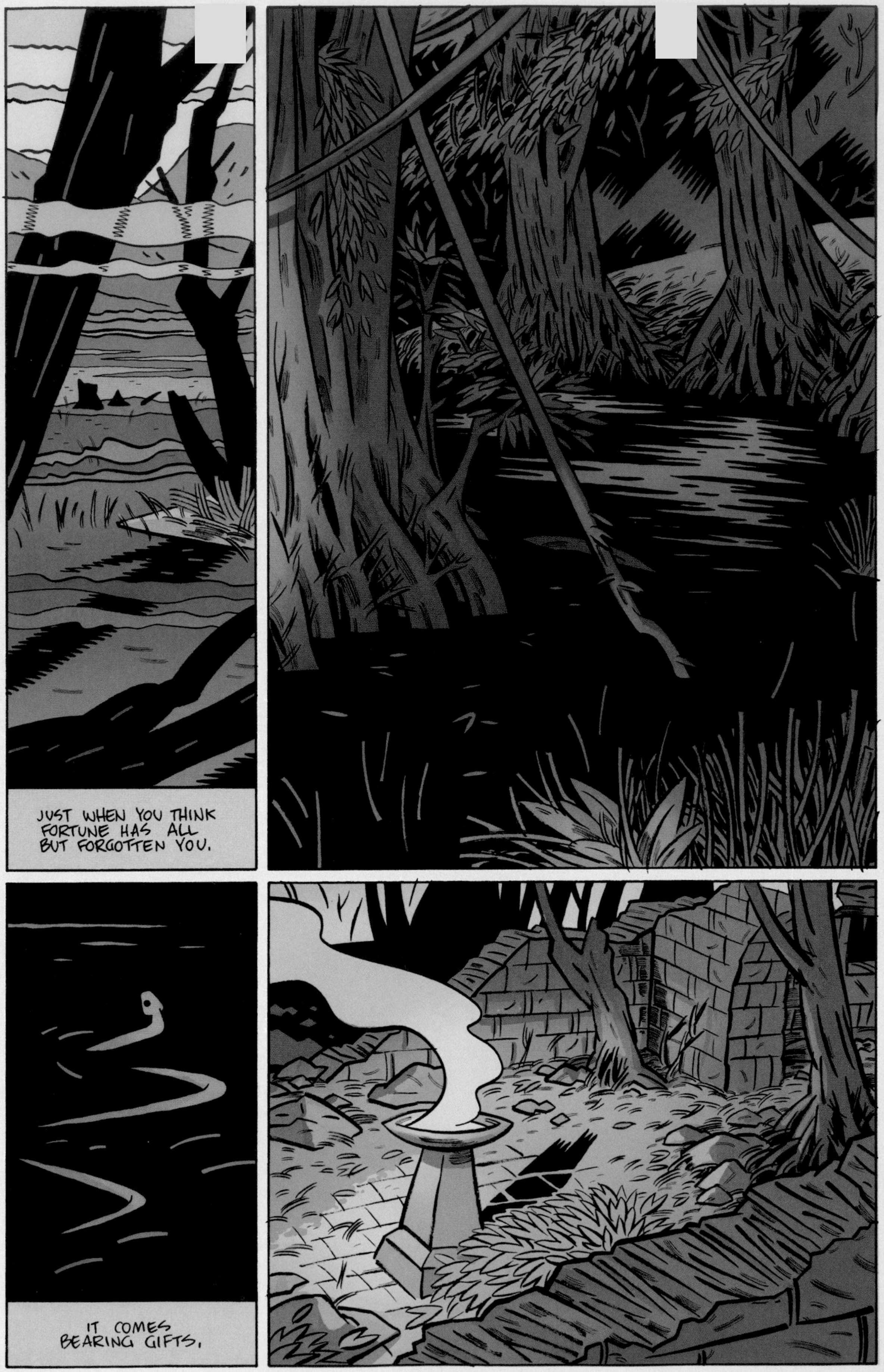
JUST WHEN YOU THINK FORTUNE HAS ALL BUT FORGOTTEN YOU.
IT COMES BEARING GIFTS.

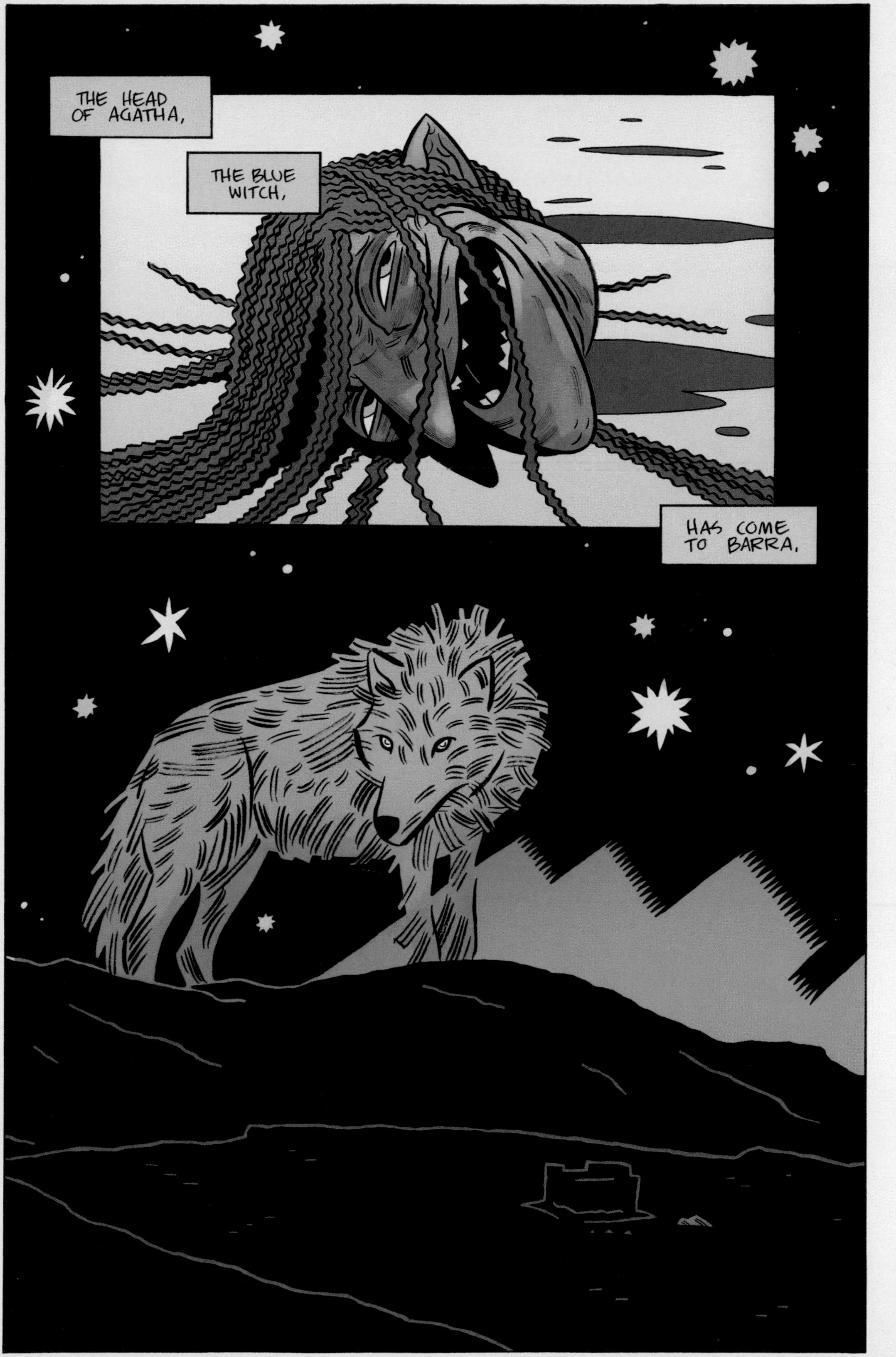
THE HEAD OF AGATHA,
THE BLUE WITCH,
HAS COME TO BARRA.

CHAPTER TWO

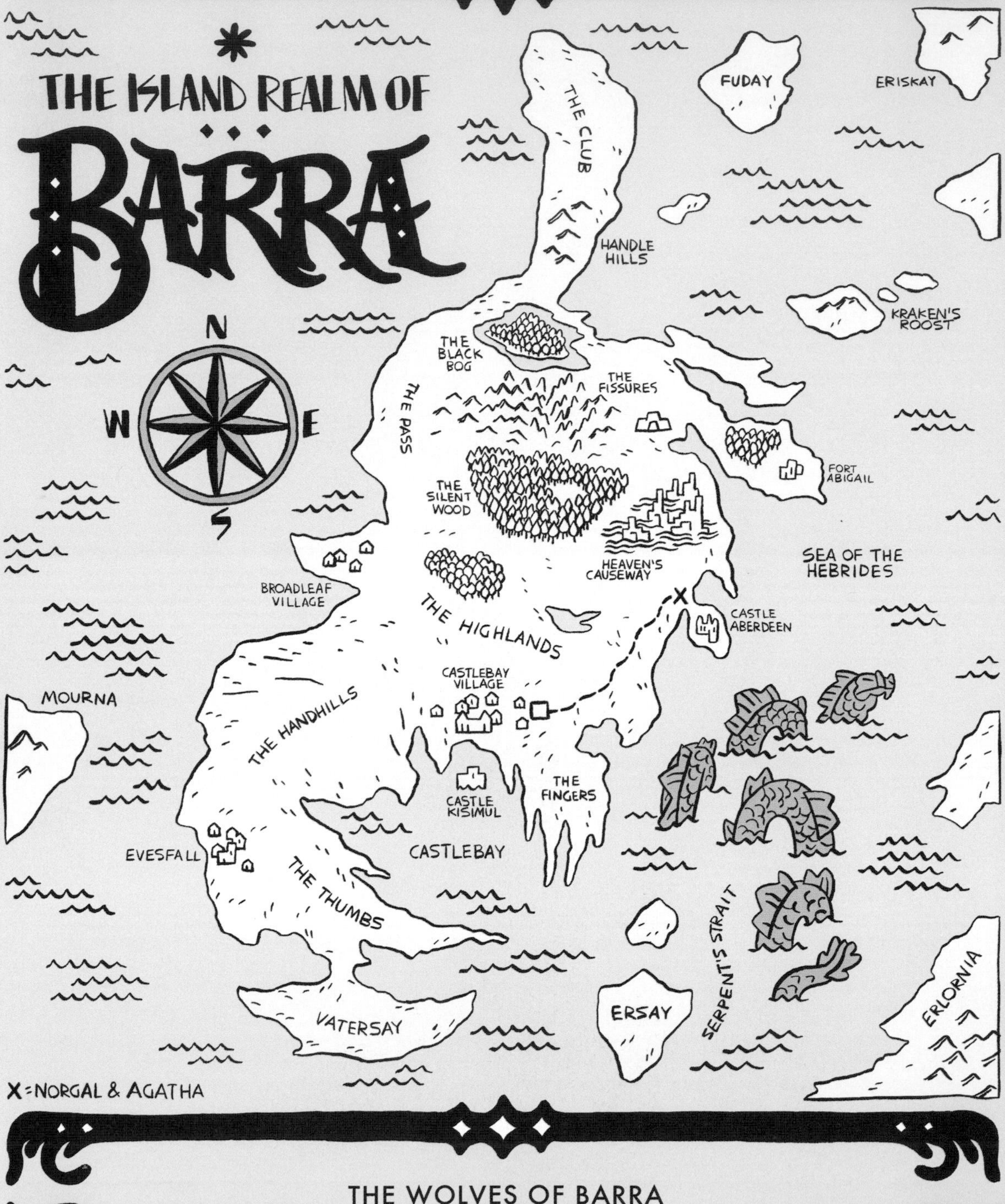
THE ISLAND REALM OF
BARRA
N
W
E
S
THE CLUB
HANDLE HILLS
FUDAY
ERISKAY
KRAKEN'S ROOST
THE BLACK BOG
THE FISSURES
THE PASS
FORT ABIGAIL
THE SILENT WOOD
HEAVEN'S CAUSEWAY
SEA OF THE HEBRIDES
BROADLEAF VILLAGE
THE HIGHLANDS
CASTLE ABERDEEN
CASTLEBAY VILLAGE
MOURNA
THE HANDHILLS
THE FINGERS
CASTLE KISIMUL
EVESFALL
CASTLEBAY
THE THUMBS
SERPENT'S STRAIT
VATERSAY
ERSAY
ERLORNIA
X=NORGAL & AGATHA

THE WOLVES OF BARRA

COLD IS THE WIND WHEN THE HOWL IS BORN,
A TRUMPET TO CHILL THE BLOOD AND BONE.
SHADOWS SLIDE AND RAISE THE DUST,
AND OLD CRONES SPEAK THEIR WARNINGS THUS,

"THE WOLVES HAVE COME, CHILD.
THE WOLVES HAVE COME."

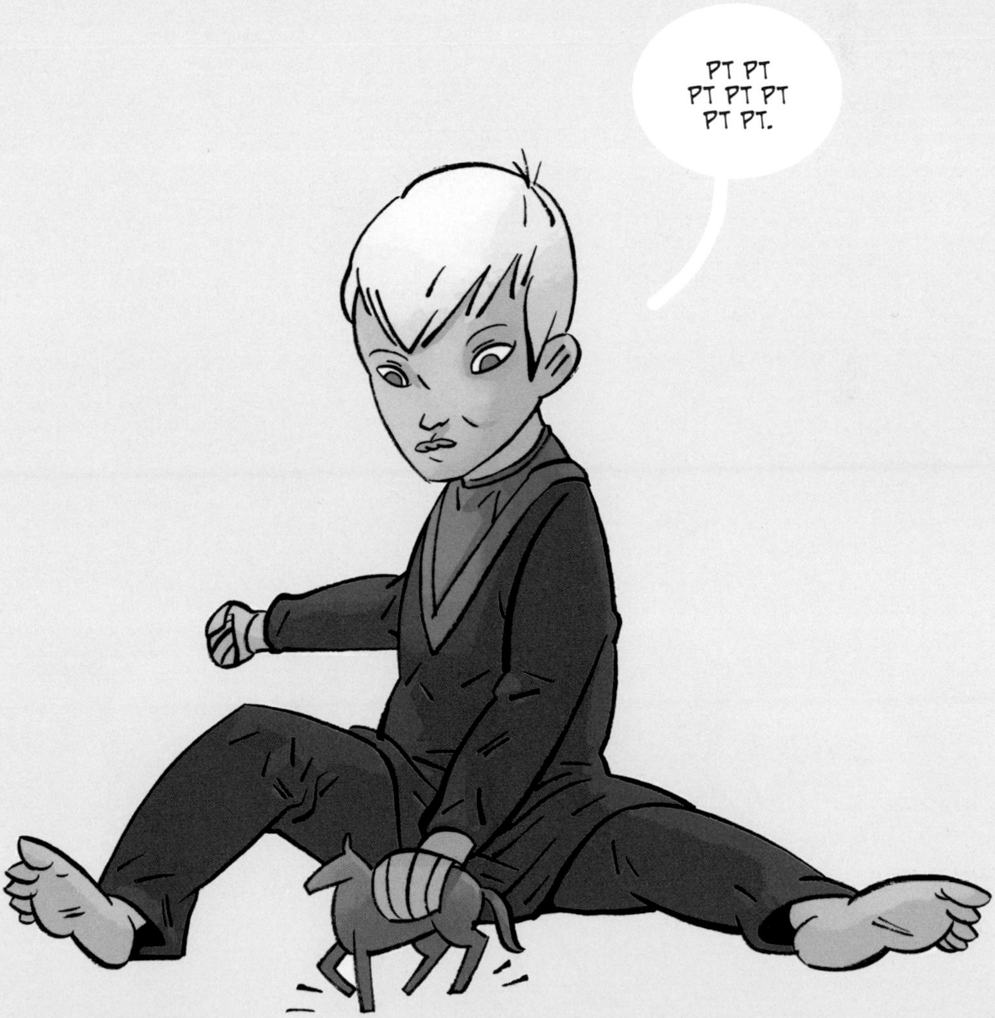
PT PT
PT PT PT
PT PT.

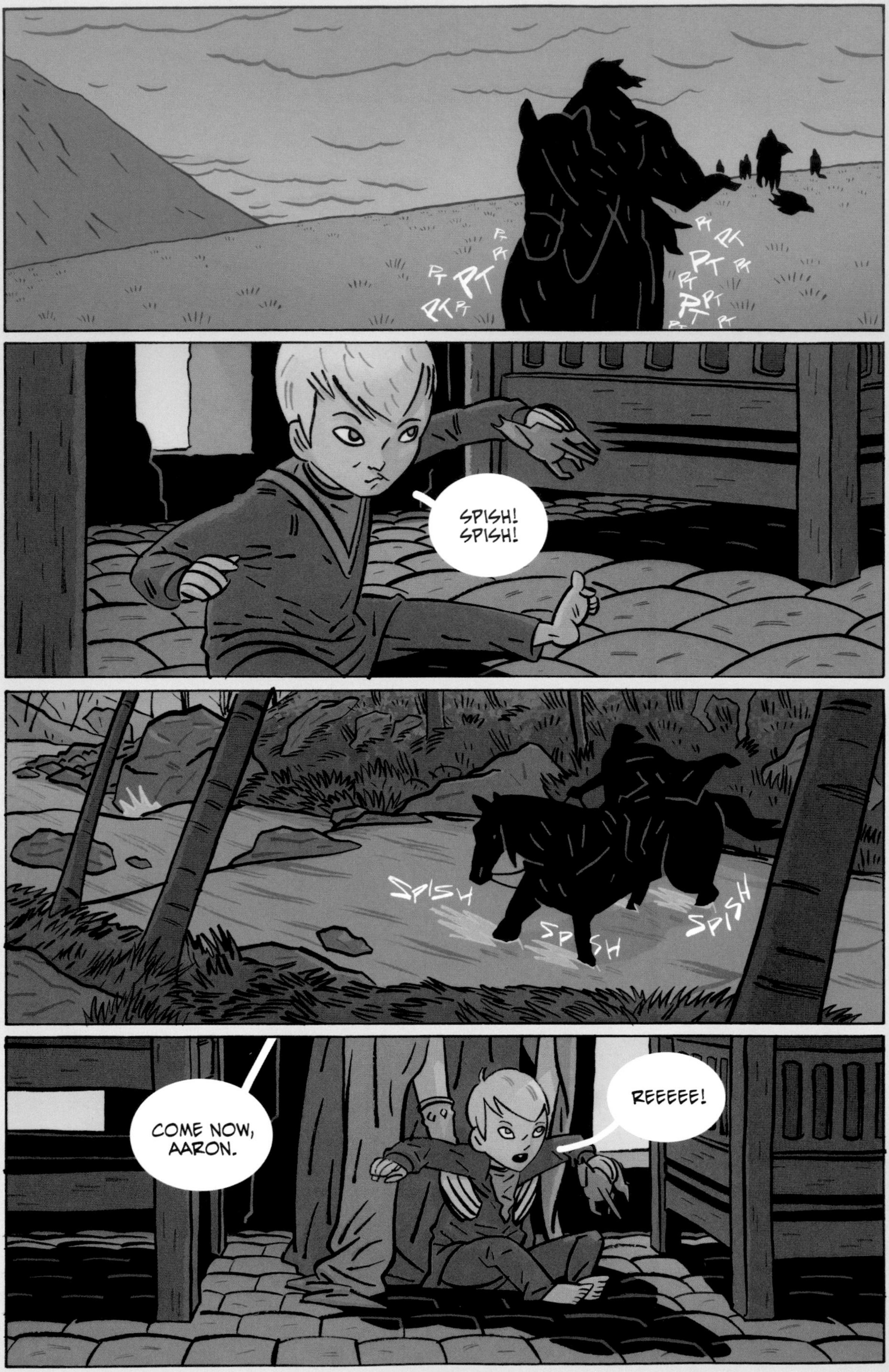
PT PT PT PT PT PT PT PT PT PT PT PT PT PT PT
SPISH! SPISH!
SPISH SPISH SPISH
COME NOW, AARON.
REEEEE!

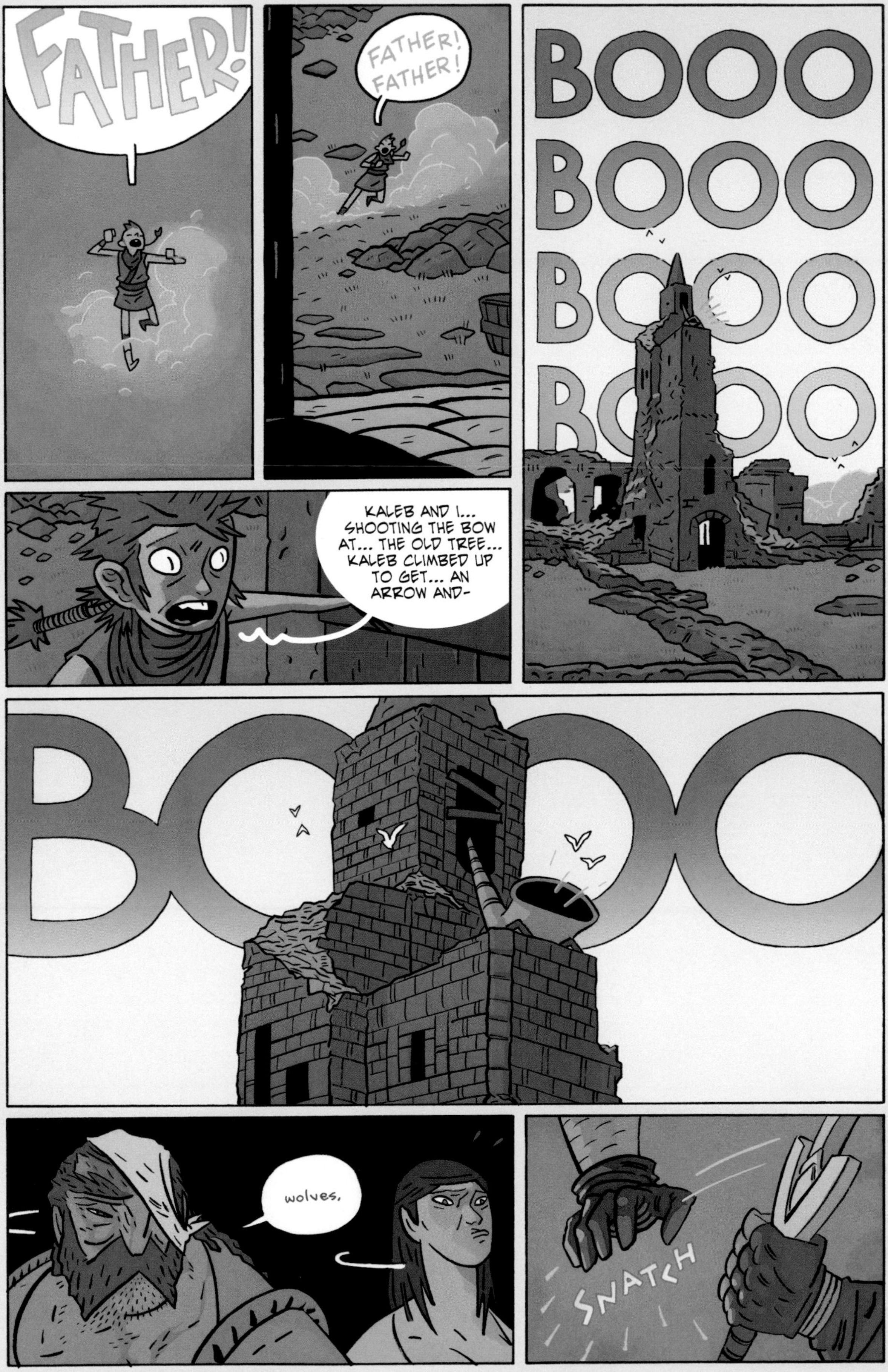
FATHER!
FATHER! FATHER!
BOOO BOOO BOOO BOOO
KALEB AND I... SHOOTING THE BOW AT... THE OLD TREE... KALEB CLIMBED UP TO GET... AN ARROW AND-
BOOO
wolves.
SNATCH

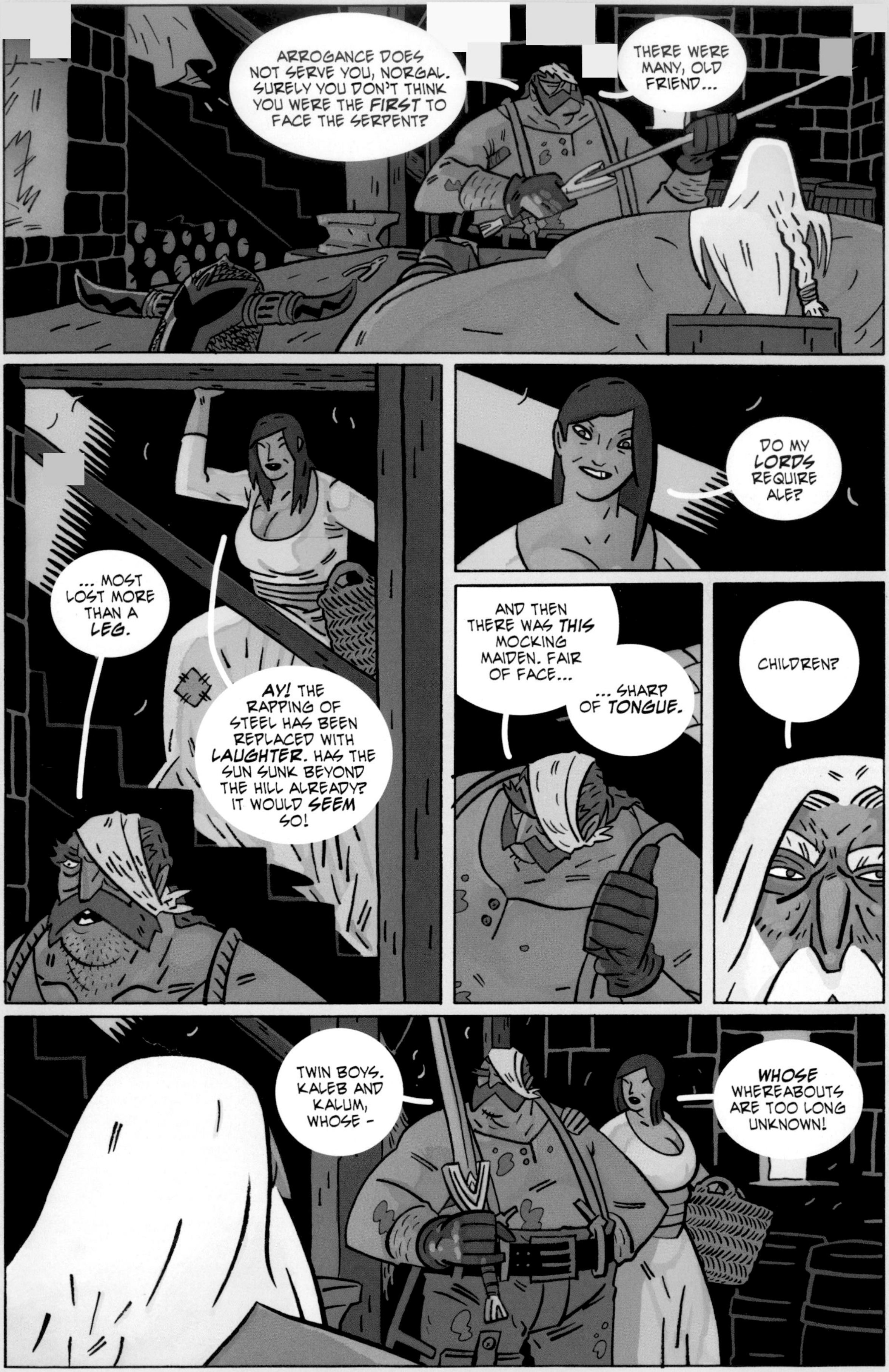

ARROGANCE DOES NOT SERVE YOU, NORGAL. SURELY YOU DON'T THINK YOU WERE THE FIRST TO FACE THE SERPENT?
THERE WERE MANY, OLD FRIEND...
... MOST LOST MORE THAN A LEG.
AY! THE RAPPING OF STEEL HAS BEEN REPLACED WITH LAUGHTER. HAS THE SUN SUNK BEYOND THE HILL ALREADY? IT WOULD SEEM SO!
DO MY LORDS REQUIRE ALE?
AND THEN THERE WAS THIS MOCKING MAIDEN. FAIR OF FACE...
... SHARP OF TONGUE.
CHILDREN?
TWIN BOYS. KALEB AND KALUM, WHOSE -
WHOSE WHEREABOUTS ARE TOO LONG UNKNOWN!

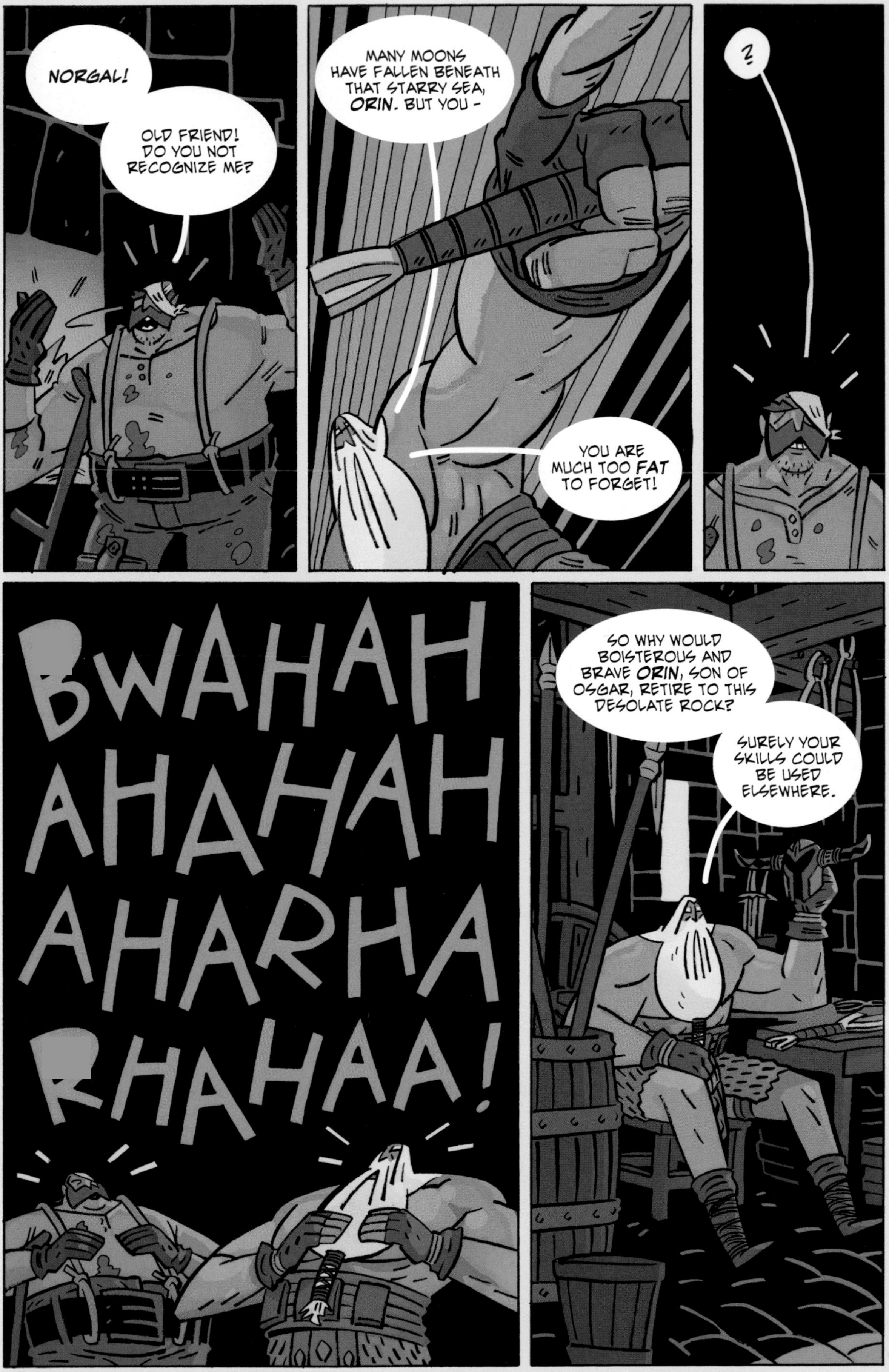
NORGAL!
OLD FRIEND! DO YOU NOT RECOGNIZE ME?
MANY MOONS HAVE FALLEN BENEATH THAT STARRY SEA, ORIN. BUT YOU -
YOU ARE MUCH TOO FAT TO FORGET!
?
BWAHAH AHAHAH AHARHA RHAHAA!
SO WHY WOULD BOISTEROUS AND BRAVE ORIN, SON OF OSGAR, RETIRE TO THIS DESOLATE ROCK?
SURELY YOUR SKILLS COULD BE USED ELSEWHERE.

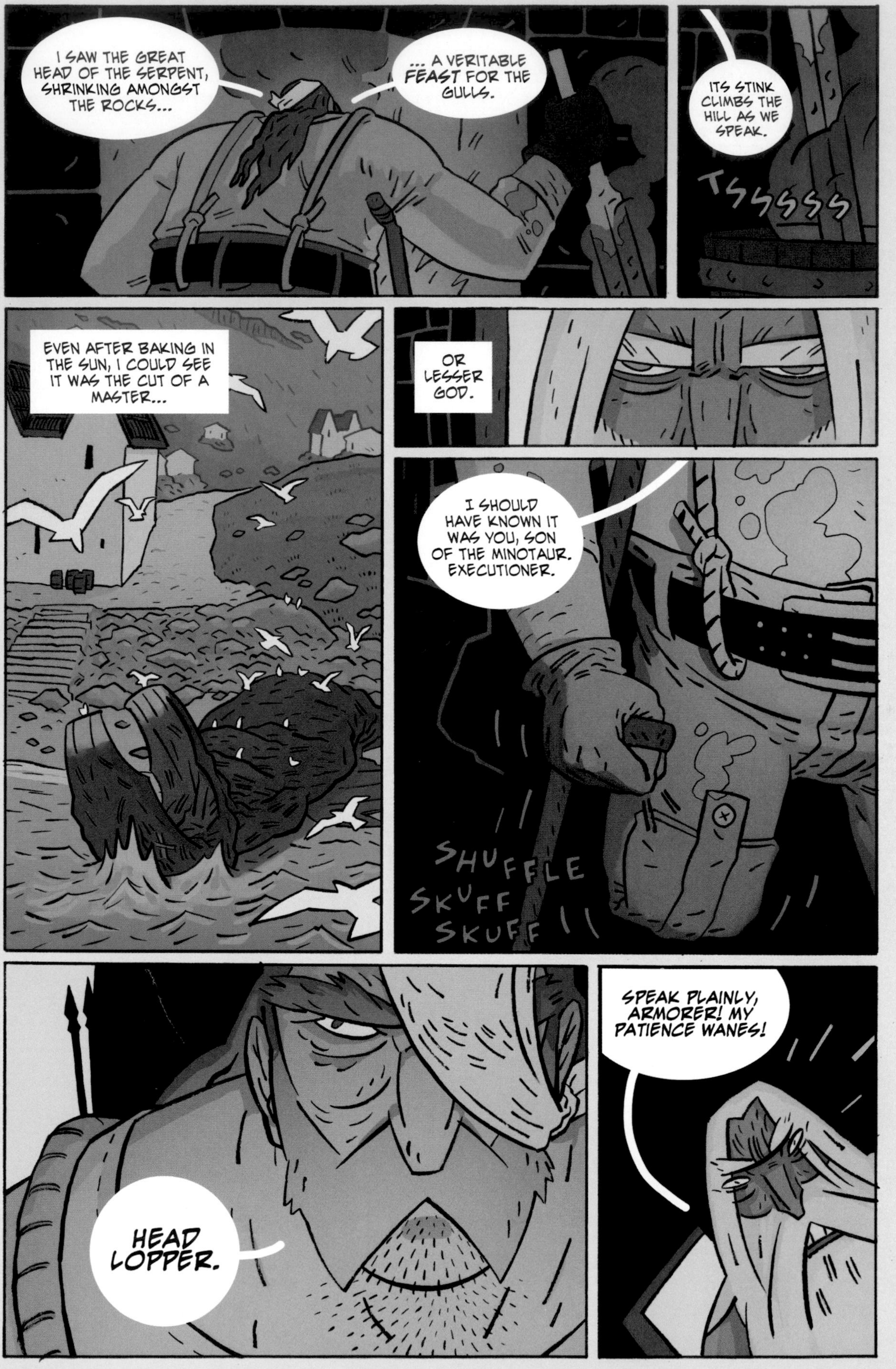
I SAW THE GREAT HEAD OF THE SERPENT, SHRINKING AMONGST THE ROCKS...
... A VERITABLE FEAST FOR THE GULLS.
ITS STINK CLIMBS THE HILL AS WE SPEAK.
TSSSSSS
EVEN AFTER BAKING IN THE SUN, I COULD SEE IT WAS THE CUT OF A MASTER...
OR LESSER GOD.
I SHOULD HAVE KNOWN IT WAS YOU, SON OF THE MINOTAUR. EXECUTIONER.
SHUFFLE
SKUFF
SKUFF
HEAD LOPPER.
SPEAK PLAINLY, ARMORER! MY PATIENCE WANES!

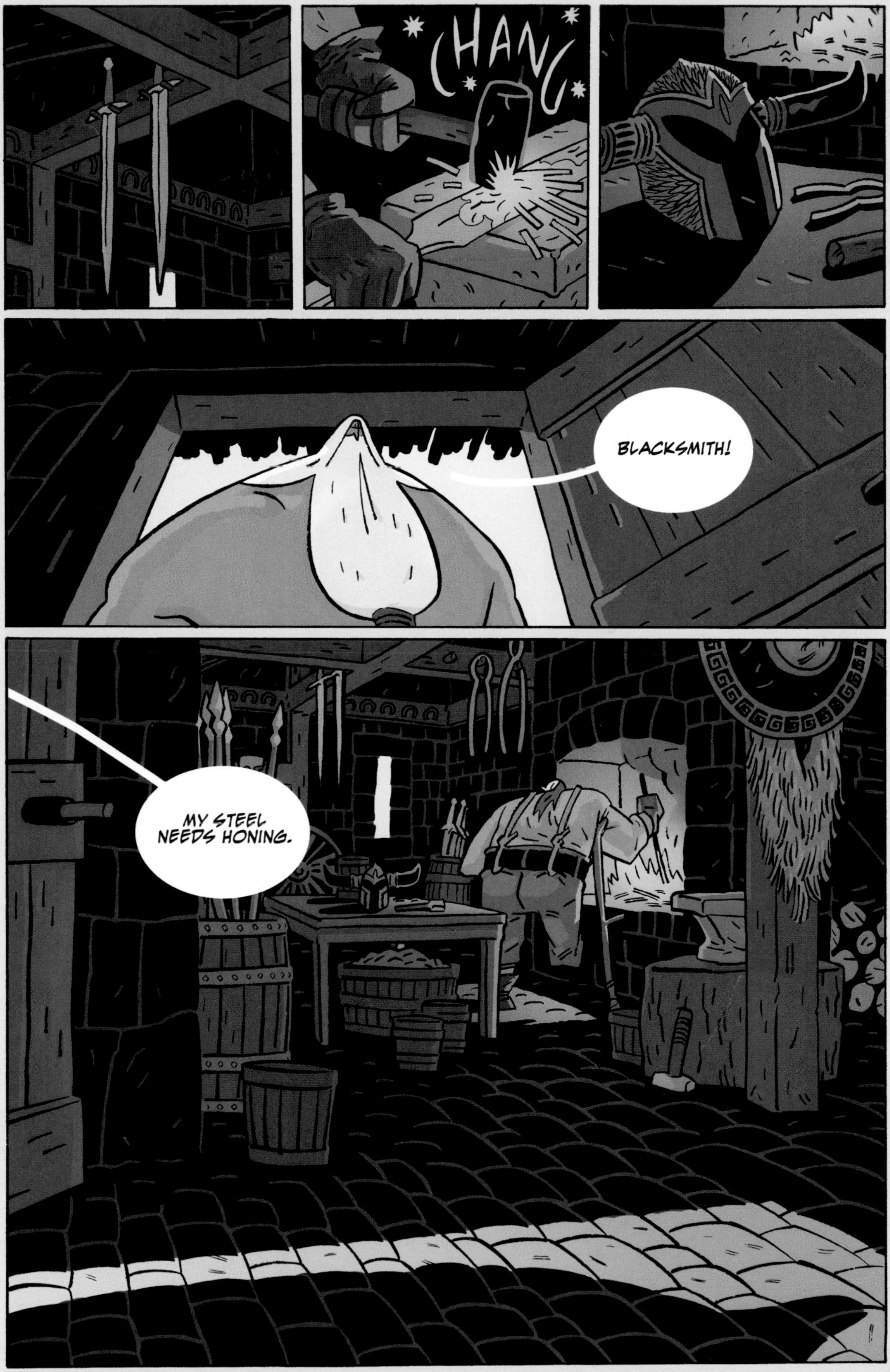
CHANG
BLACKSMITH!
MY STEEL NEEDS HONING.

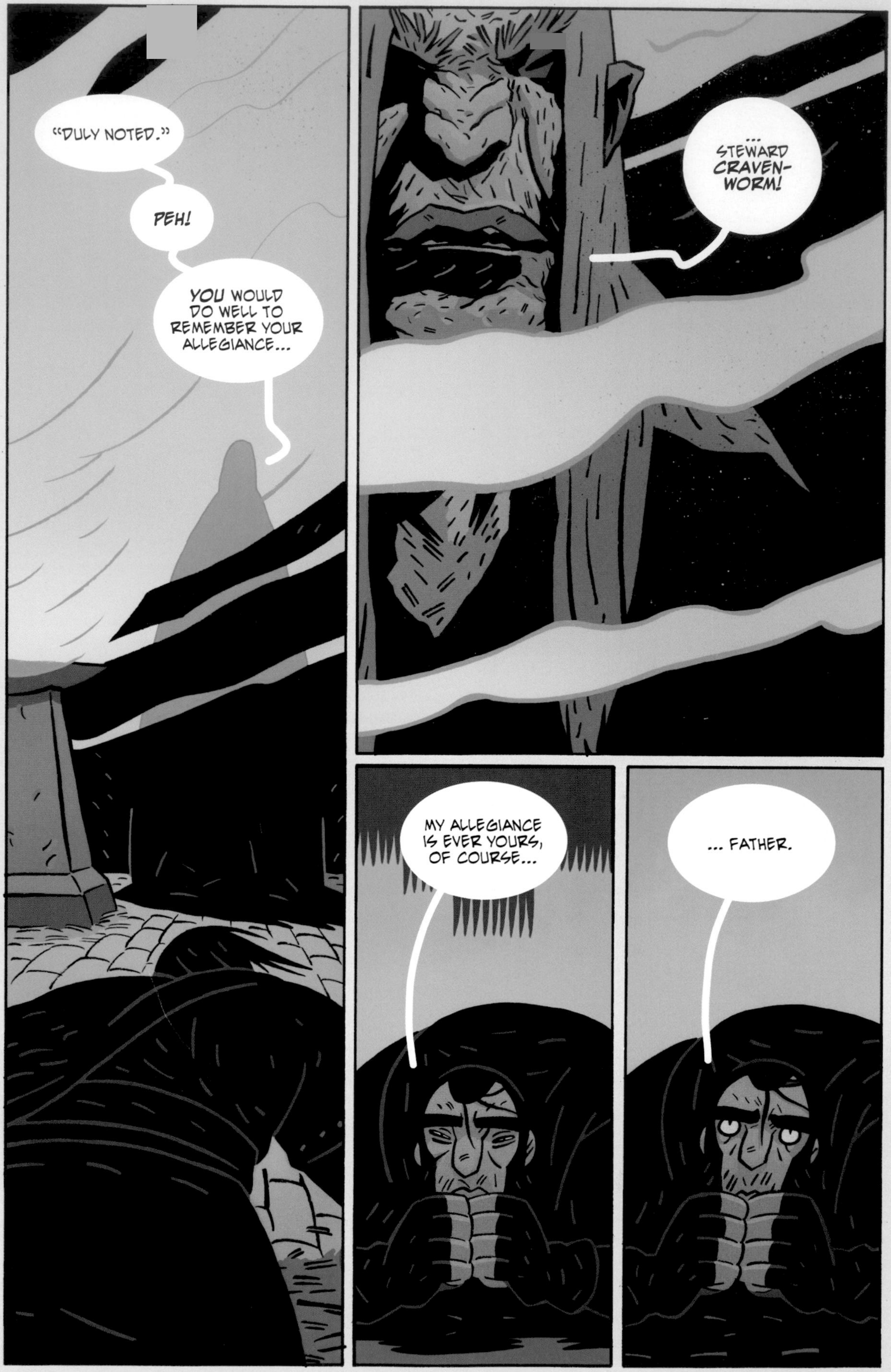
"DULY NOTED."
PEH!
YOU WOULD DO WELL TO REMEMBER YOUR ALLEGIANCE...
... STEWARD CRAVEN-WORM!
MY ALLEGIANCE IS EVER YOURS, OF COURSE...
... FATHER.

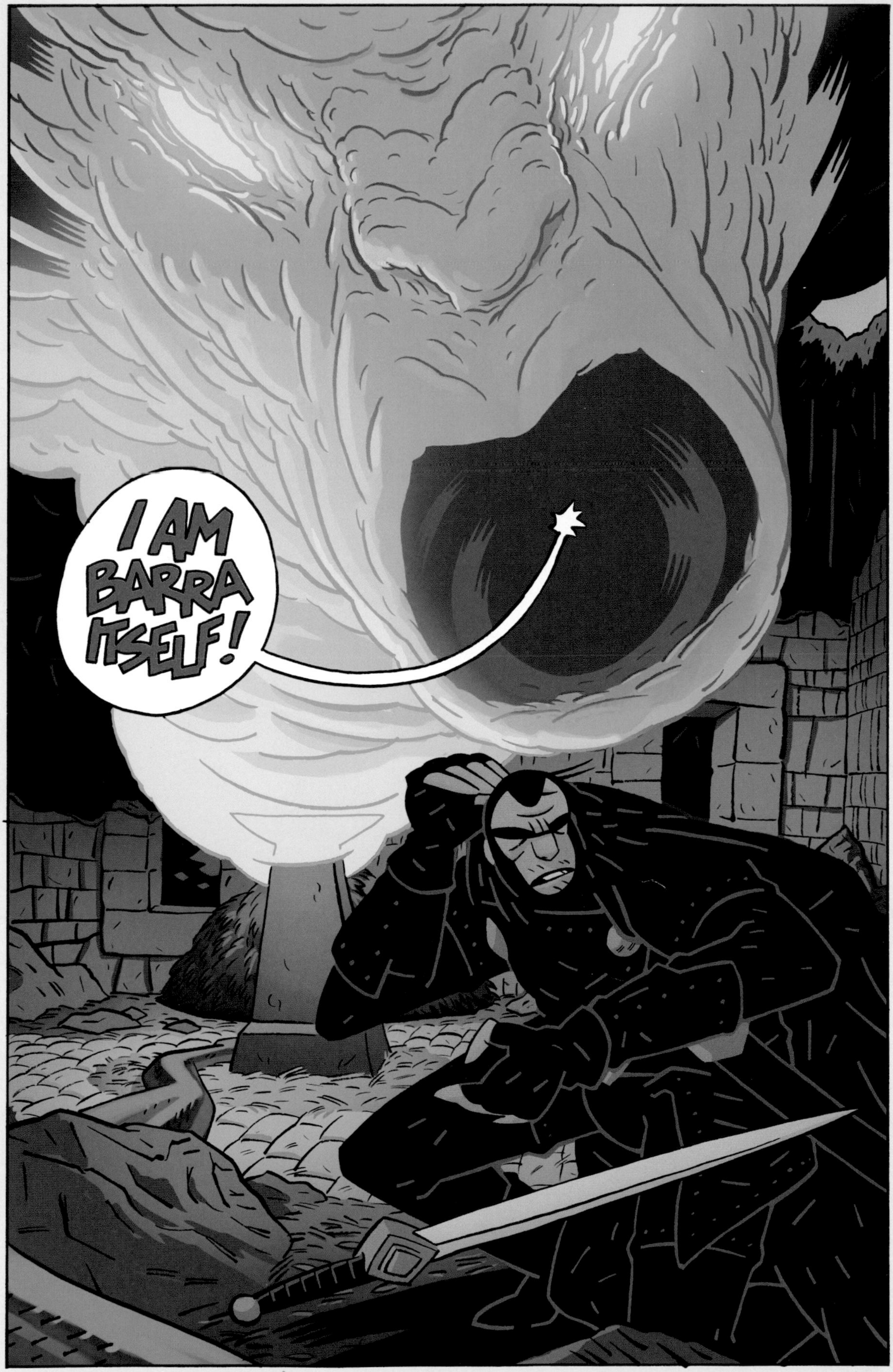
I AM BARRA ITSELF!

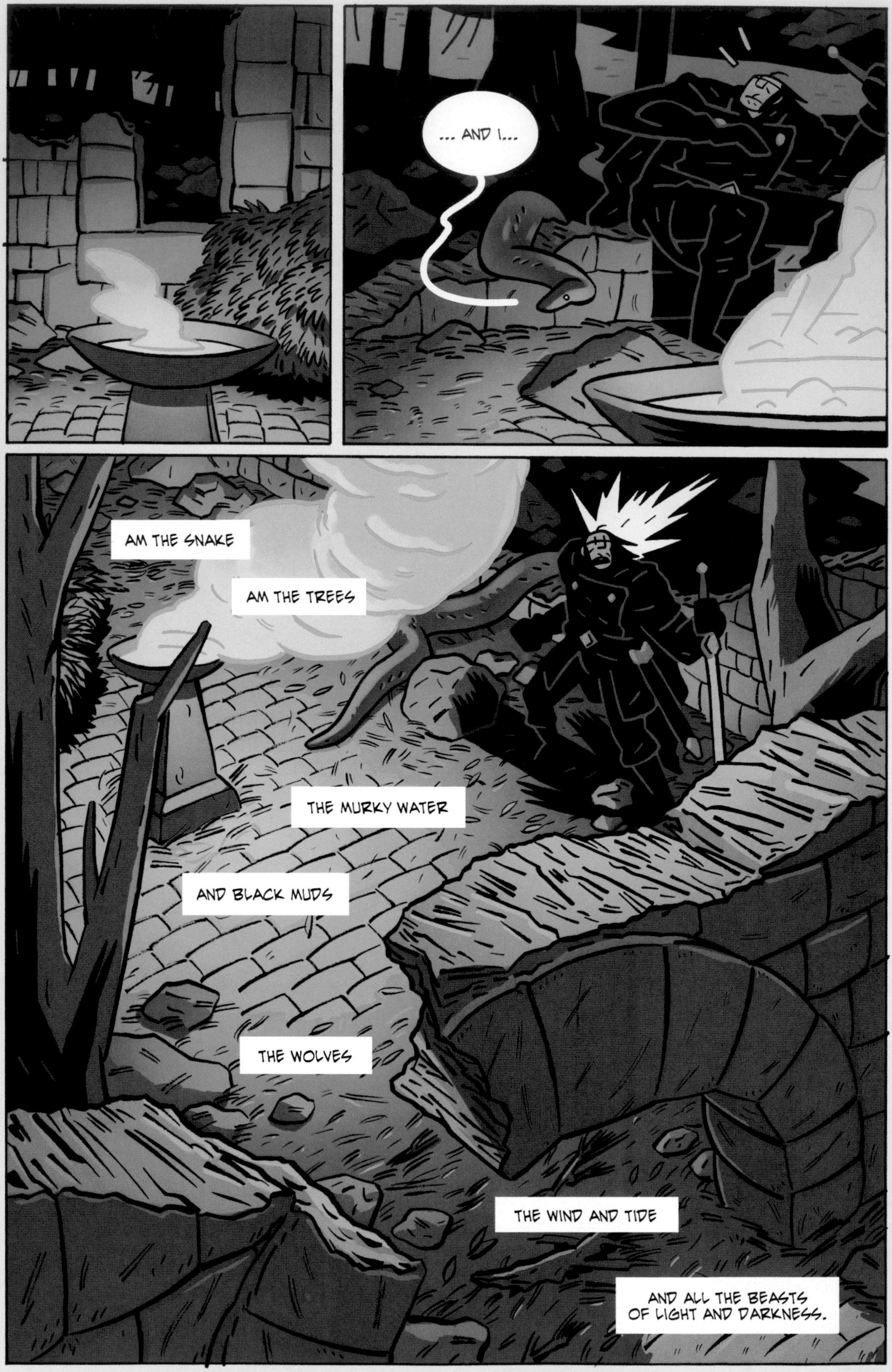
... AND I...
AM THE SNAKE
AM THE TREES
THE MURKY WATER
AND BLACK MUDS
THE WOLVES
THE WIND AND TIDE
AND ALL THE BEASTS OF LIGHT AND DARKNESS.

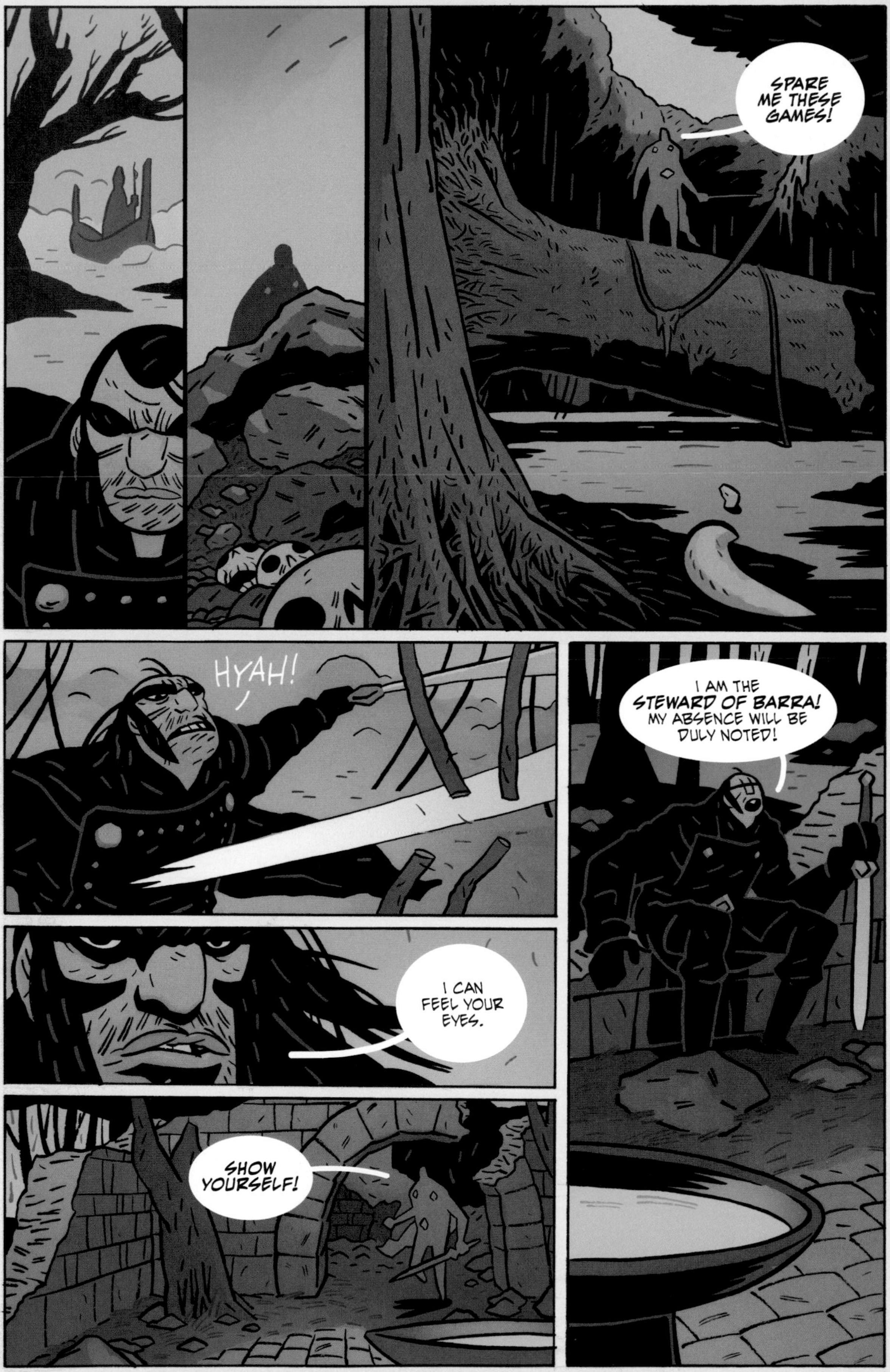
SPARE ME THESE GAMES!
HYAH!
I CAN FEEL YOUR EYES.
SHOW YOURSELF!
I AM THE STEWARD OF BARRA! MY ABSENCE WILL BE DULY NOTED!

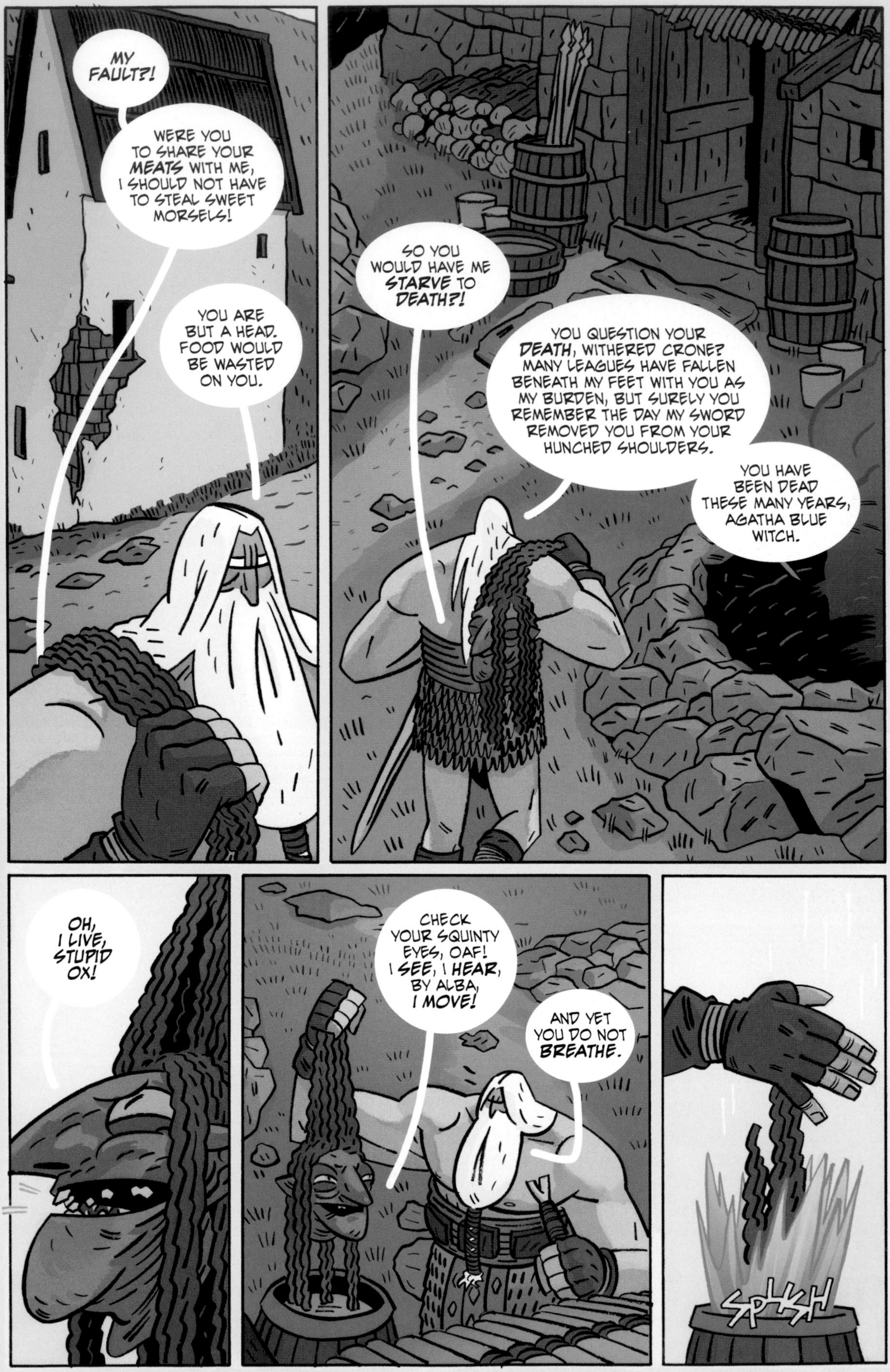
MY FAULT?!
WERE YOU TO SHARE YOUR MEATS WITH ME, I SHOULD NOT HAVE TO STEAL SWEET MORSELS!
YOU ARE BUT A HEAD. FOOD WOULD BE WASTED ON YOU.
SO YOU WOULD HAVE ME STARVE TO DEATH?!
YOU QUESTION YOUR DEATH, WITHERED CRONE? MANY LEAGUES HAVE FALLEN BENEATH MY FEET WITH YOU AS MY BURDEN, BUT SURELY YOU REMEMBER THE DAY MY SWORD REMOVED YOU FROM YOUR HUNCHED SHOULDERS.
YOU HAVE BEEN DEAD THESE MANY YEARS, AGATHA BLUE WITCH.
OH, I LIVE, STUPID OX!
CHECK YOUR SQUINTY EYES, OAF! I SEE, I HEAR, BY ALBA, I MOVE!
AND YET YOU DO NOT BREATHE.
SPLISH

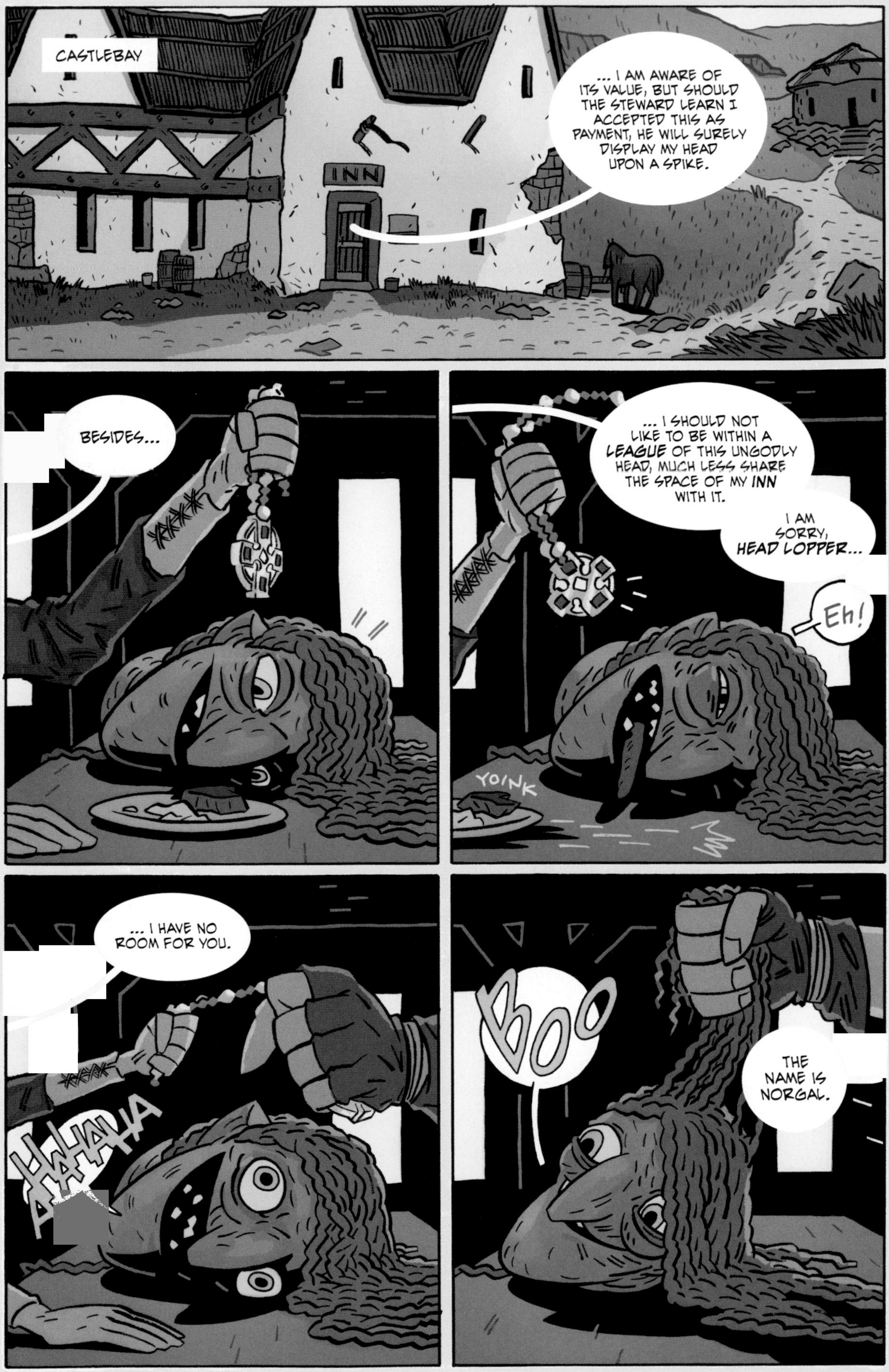
CASTLEBAY
... I AM AWARE OF ITS VALUE, BUT SHOULD THE STEWARD LEARN I ACCEPTED THIS AS PAYMENT, HE WILL SURELY DISPLAY MY HEAD UPON A SPIKE.
INN
BESIDES...
... I SHOULD NOT LIKE TO BE WITHIN A LEAGUE OF THIS UNGODLY HEAD, MUCH LESS SHARE THE SPACE OF MY INN WITH IT.
I AM SORRY, HEAD LOPPER...
Eh!
YOINK
... I HAVE NO ROOM FOR YOU.
HAHAHA
BOO
THE NAME IS NORGAL.

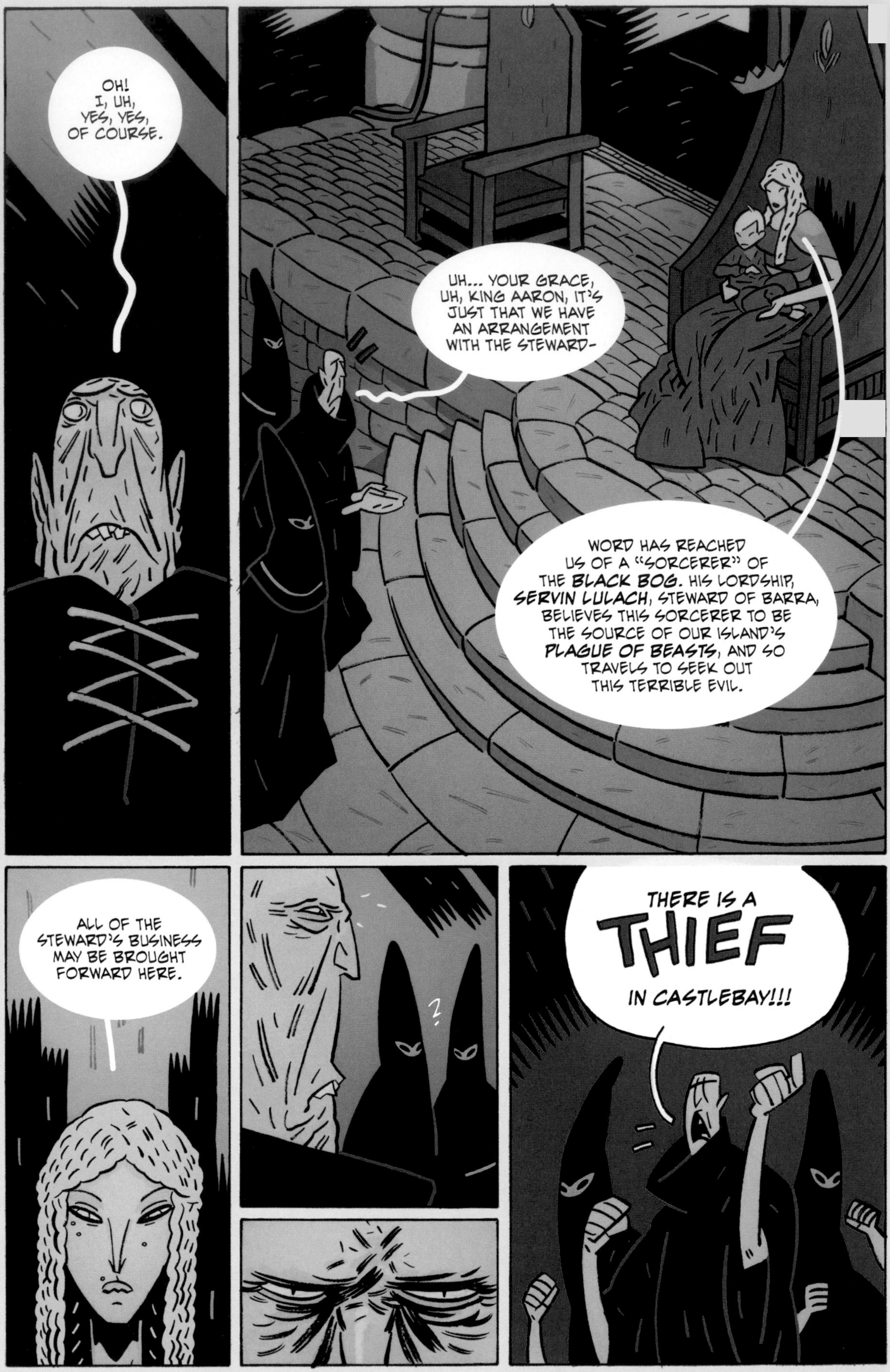
OH! I, UH, YES, YES, OF COURSE.
UH... YOUR GRACE, UH, KING AARON, IT'S JUST THAT WE HAVE AN ARRANGEMENT WITH THE STEWARD-
WORD HAS REACHED US OF A "SORCERER" OF THE BLACK BOG. HIS LORDSHIP, SERVIN LULACH, STEWARD OF BARRA, BELIEVES THIS SORCERER TO BE THE SOURCE OF OUR ISLAND'S PLAGUE OF BEASTS, AND SO TRAVELS TO SEEK OUT THIS TERRIBLE EVIL.
ALL OF THE STEWARD'S BUSINESS MAY BE BROUGHT FORWARD HERE.
?
THERE IS A THIEF IN CASTLEBAY!!!

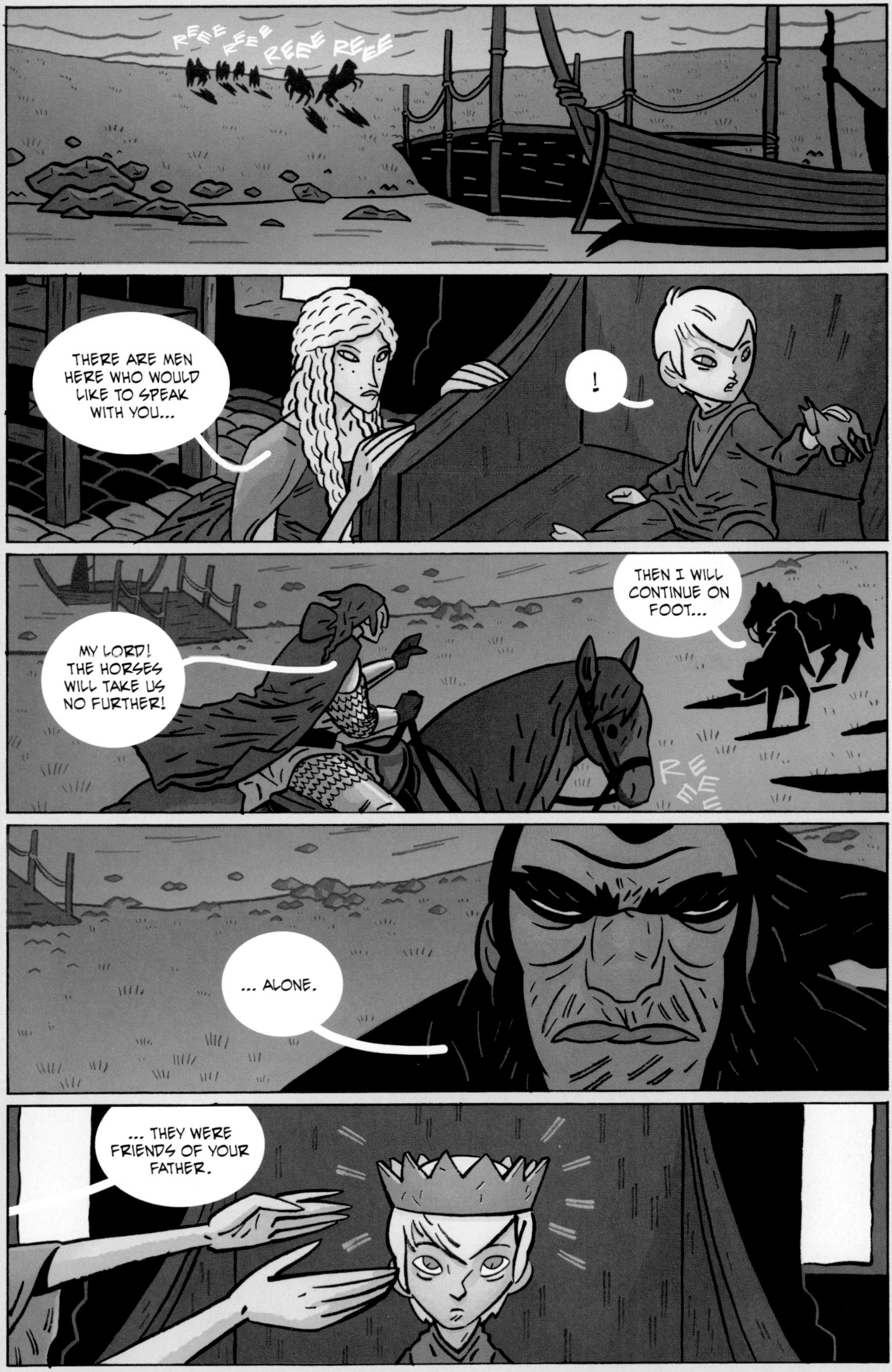
REEE REEE REEE REEE
THERE ARE MEN HERE WHO WOULD LIKE TO SPEAK WITH YOU...
!
MY LORD! THE HORSES WILL TAKE US NO FURTHER!
THEN I WILL CONTINUE ON FOOT...
REEE
... ALONE.
... THEY WERE FRIENDS OF YOUR FATHER.

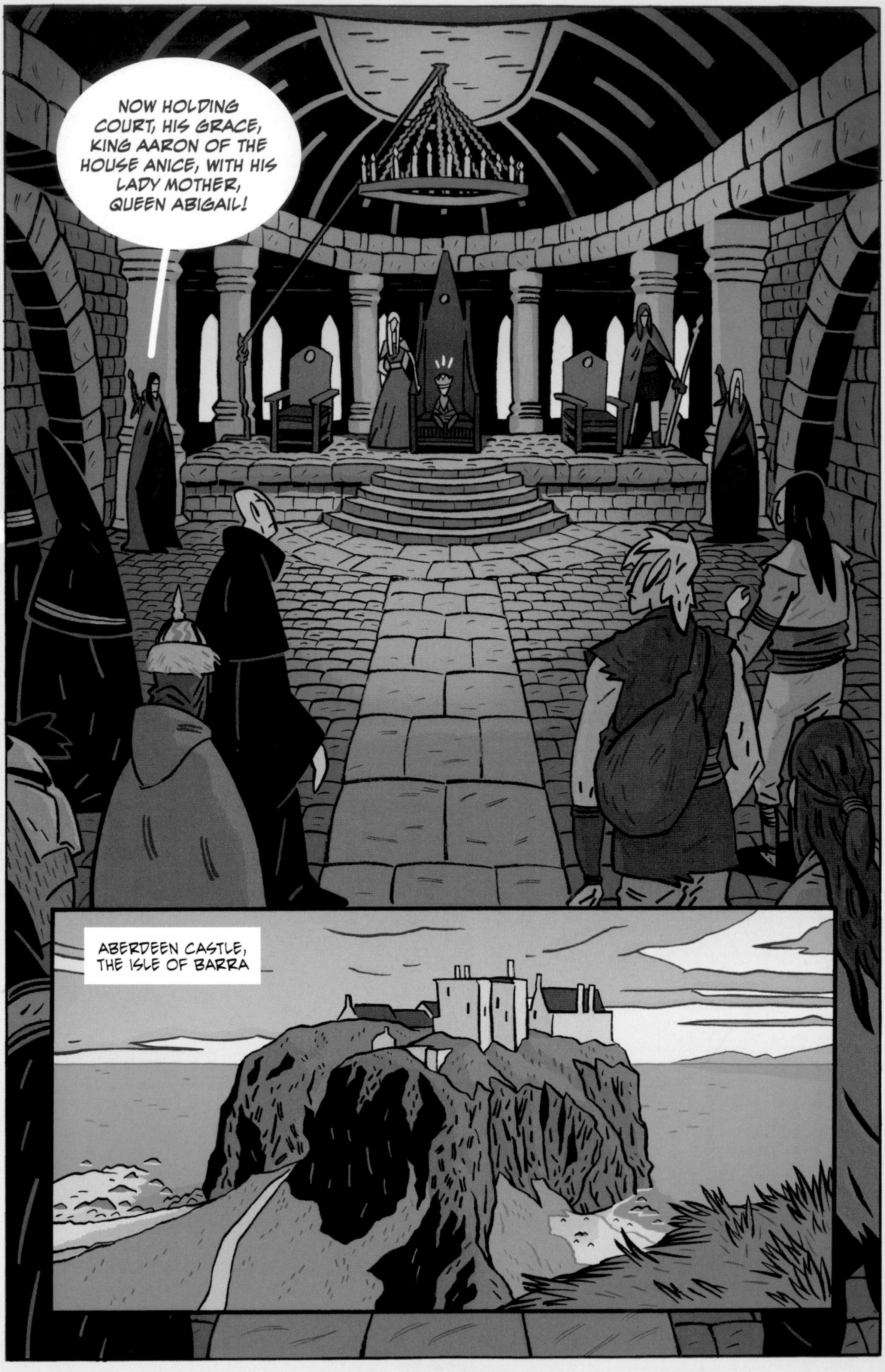
NOW HOLDING COURT, HIS GRACE, KING AARON OF THE HOUSE ANICE, WITH HIS LADY MOTHER, QUEEN ABIGAIL!
ABERDEEN CASTLE, THE ISLE OF BARRA

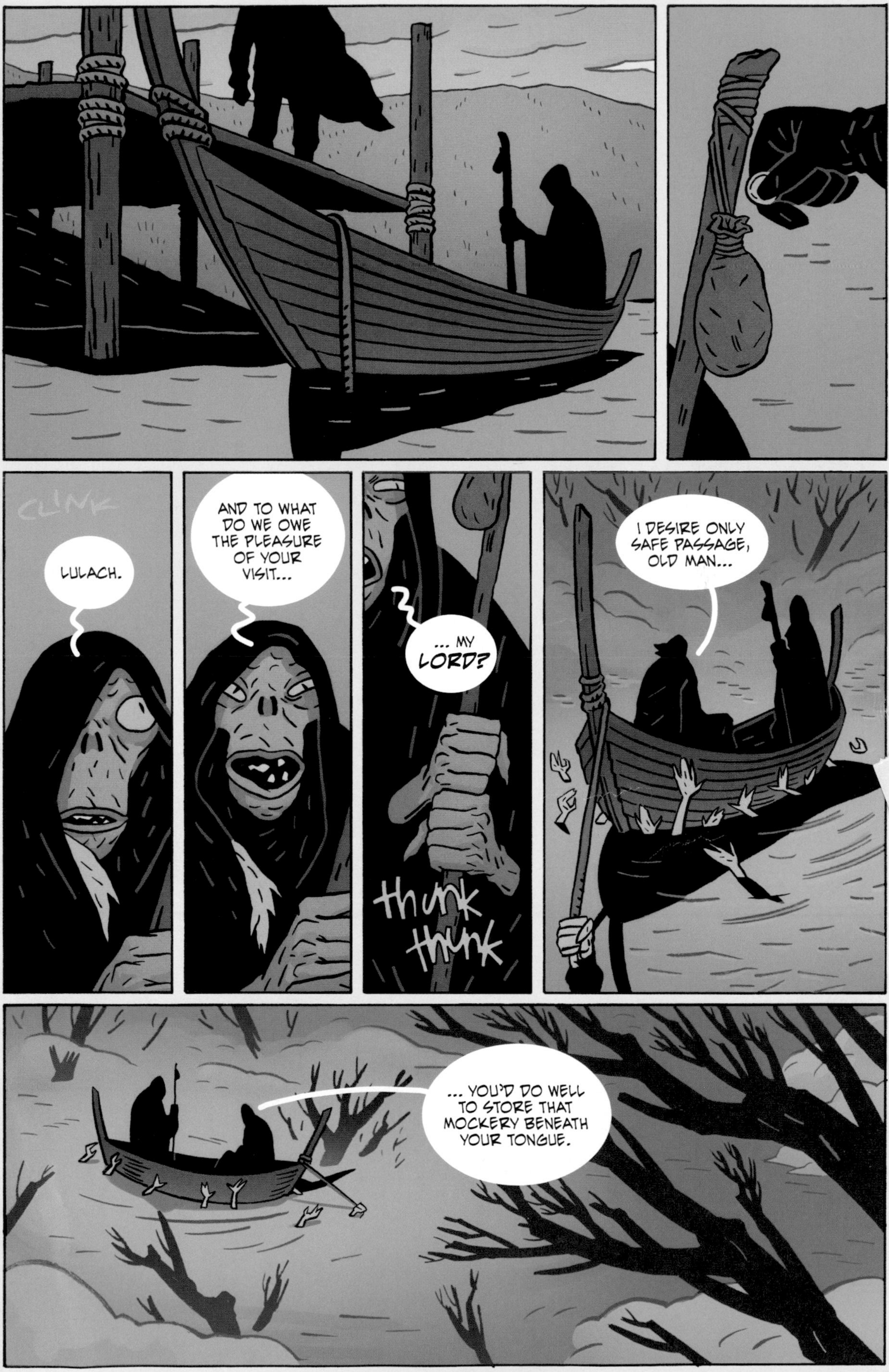
CLINK
LULACH.
AND TO WHAT DO WE OWE THE PLEASURE OF YOUR VISIT...
... MY LORD?
thunk thunk
I DESIRE ONLY SAFE PASSAGE, OLD MAN...
... YOU'D DO WELL TO STORE THAT MOCKERY BENEATH YOUR TONGUE.

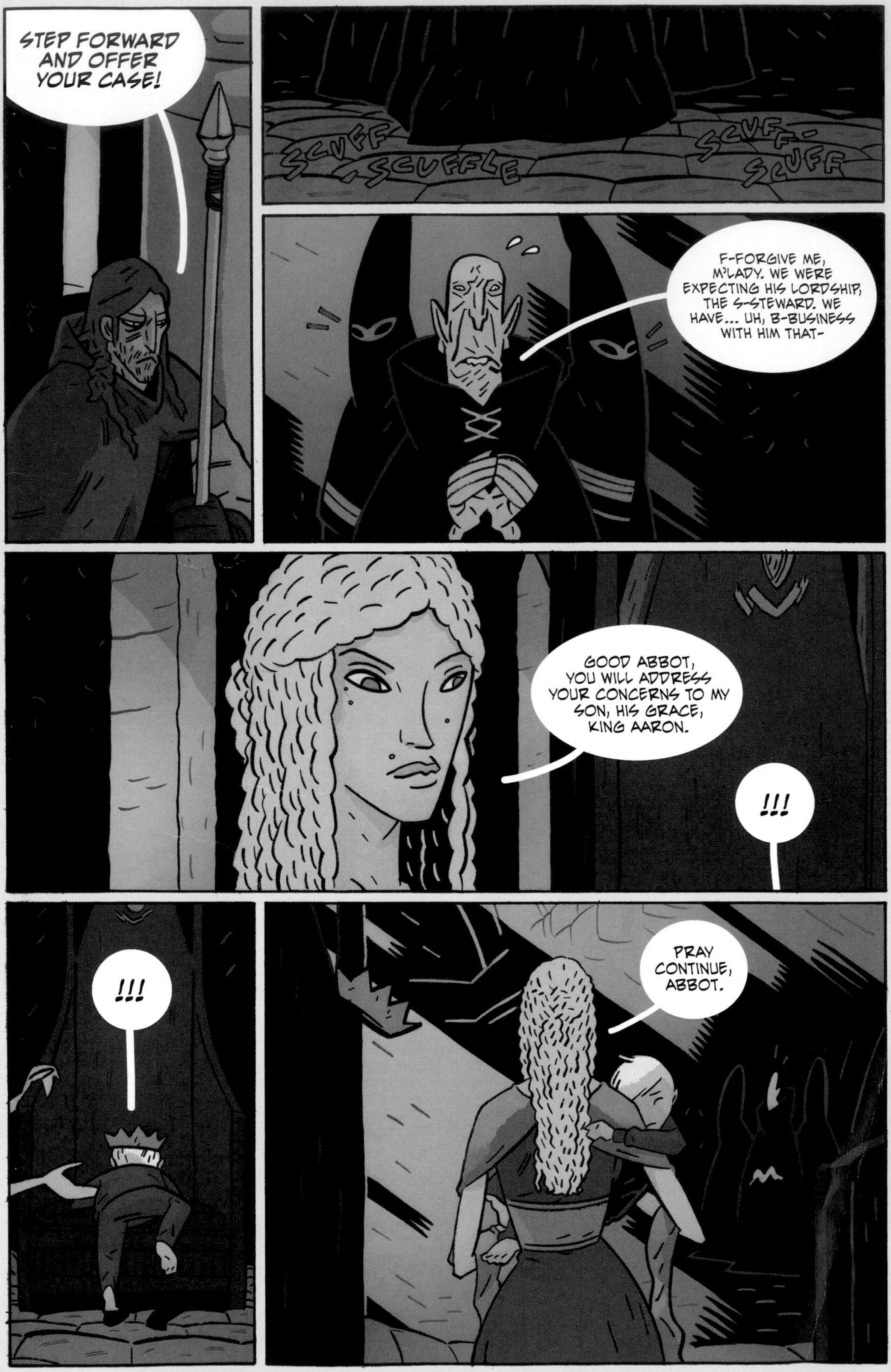
STEP FORWARD AND OFFER YOUR CASE!
SCUFF-SCUFFLE
SCUFF-SCUFF
F-FORGIVE ME, M'LADY. WE WERE EXPECTING HIS LORDSHIP, THE S-STEWARD. WE HAVE... UH, B-BUSINESS WITH HIM THAT-
GOOD ABBOT, YOU WILL ADDRESS YOUR CONCERNS TO MY SON, HIS GRACE, KING AARON.
!!!
!!!
PRAY CONTINUE, ABBOT.

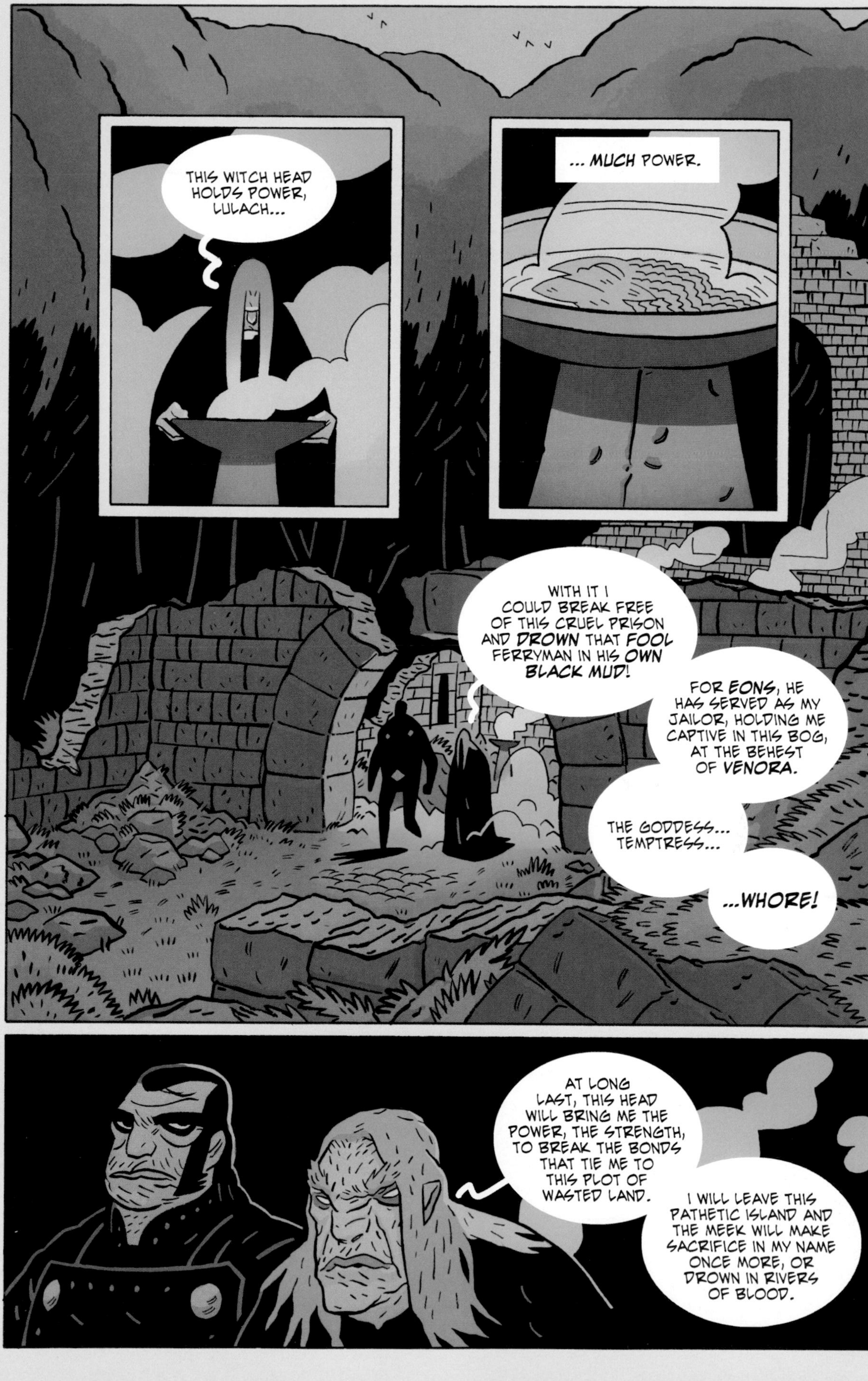
THIS WITCH HEAD HOLDS POWER, LULACH...
... MUCH POWER.
WITH IT I COULD BREAK FREE OF THIS CRUEL PRISON AND DROWN THAT FOOL FERRYMAN IN HIS OWN BLACK MUD!
FOR EONS, HE HAS SERVED AS MY JAILOR, HOLDING ME CAPTIVE IN THIS BOG, AT THE BEHEST OF VENORA.
THE GODDESS... TEMPTRESS...
...WHORE!
AT LONG LAST, THIS HEAD WILL BRING ME THE POWER, THE STRENGTH, TO BREAK THE BONDS THAT TIE ME TO THIS PLOT OF WASTED LAND.
I WILL LEAVE THIS PATHETIC ISLAND AND THE MEEK WILL MAKE SACRIFICE IN MY NAME ONCE MORE, OR DROWN IN RIVERS OF BLOOD.

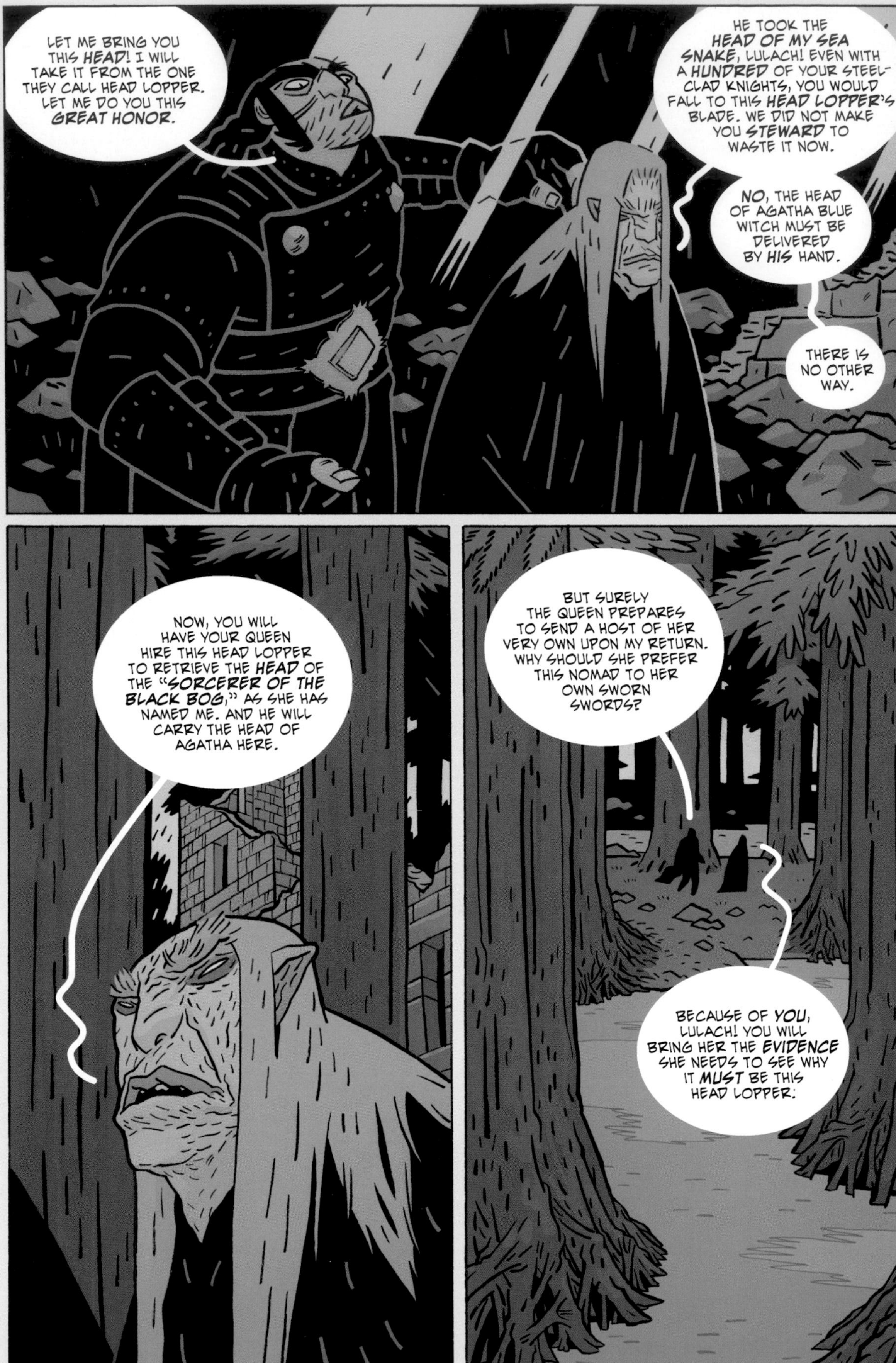
LET ME BRING YOU THIS HEAD! I WILL TAKE IT FROM THE ONE THEY CALL HEAD LOPPER. LET ME DO YOU THIS GREAT HONOR.
HE TOOK THE HEAD OF MY SEA SNAKE, LULACH! EVEN WITH A HUNDRED OF YOUR STEEL-CLAD KNIGHTS, YOU WOULD FALL TO THIS HEAD LOPPER'S BLADE. WE DID NOT MAKE YOU STEWARD TO WASTE IT NOW.
NO, THE HEAD OF AGATHA BLUE WITCH MUST BE DELIVERED BY HIS HAND.
THERE IS NO OTHER WAY.
NOW, YOU WILL HAVE YOUR QUEEN HIRE THIS HEAD LOPPER TO RETRIEVE THE HEAD OF THE "SORCERER OF THE BLACK BOG," AS SHE HAS NAMED ME. AND HE WILL CARRY THE HEAD OF AGATHA HERE.
BUT SURELY THE QUEEN PREPARES TO SEND A HOST OF HER VERY OWN UPON MY RETURN. WHY SHOULD SHE PREFER THIS NOMAD TO HER OWN SWORN SWORDS?
BECAUSE OF YOU, LULACH! YOU WILL BRING HER THE EVIDENCE SHE NEEDS TO SEE WHY IT MUST BE THIS HEAD LOPPER.

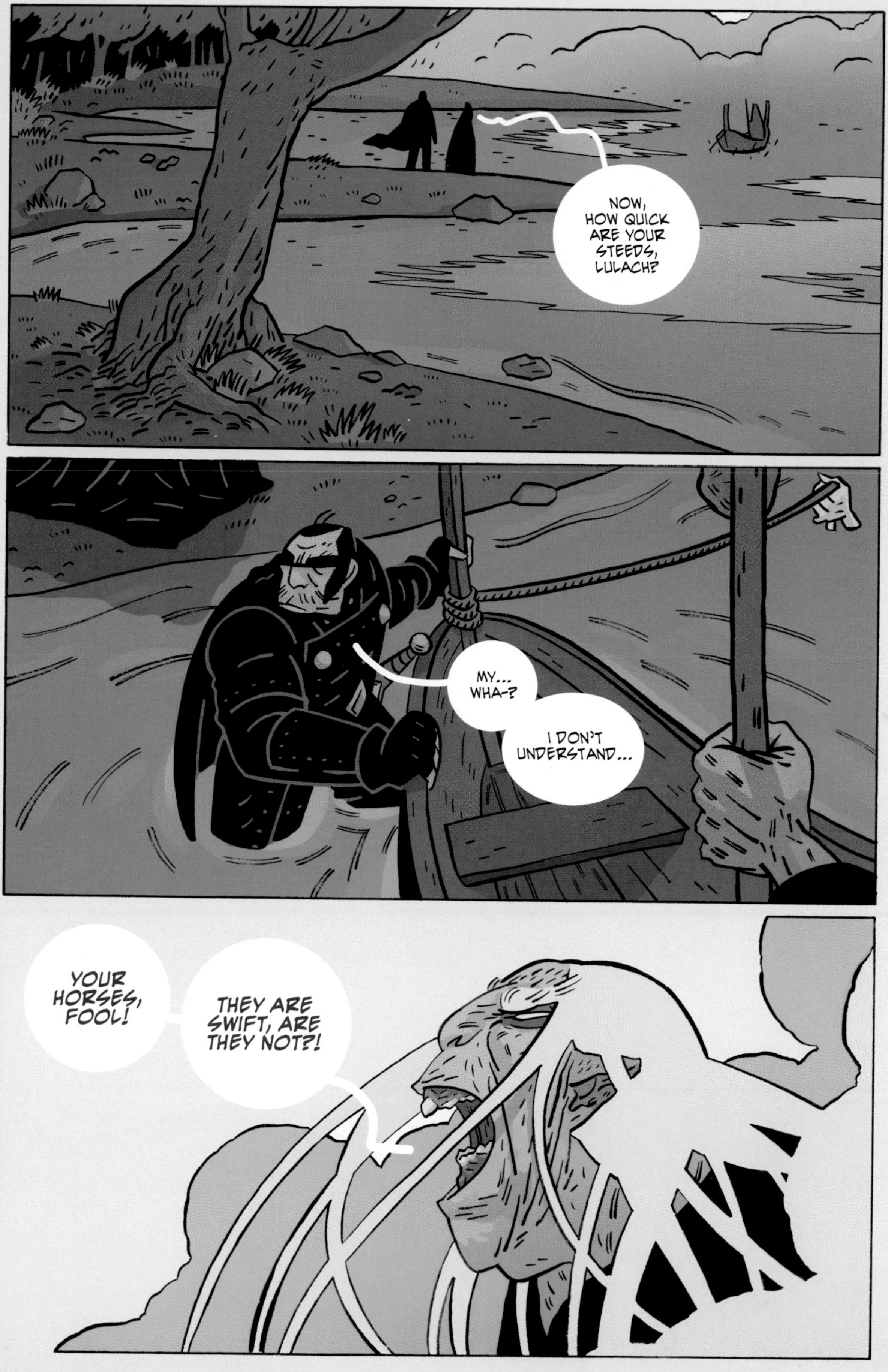
NOW, HOW QUICK ARE YOUR STEEDS, LULACH?
MY... WHA-?
I DON'T UNDERSTAND...
YOUR HORSES, FOOL!
THEY ARE SWIFT, ARE THEY NOT?!

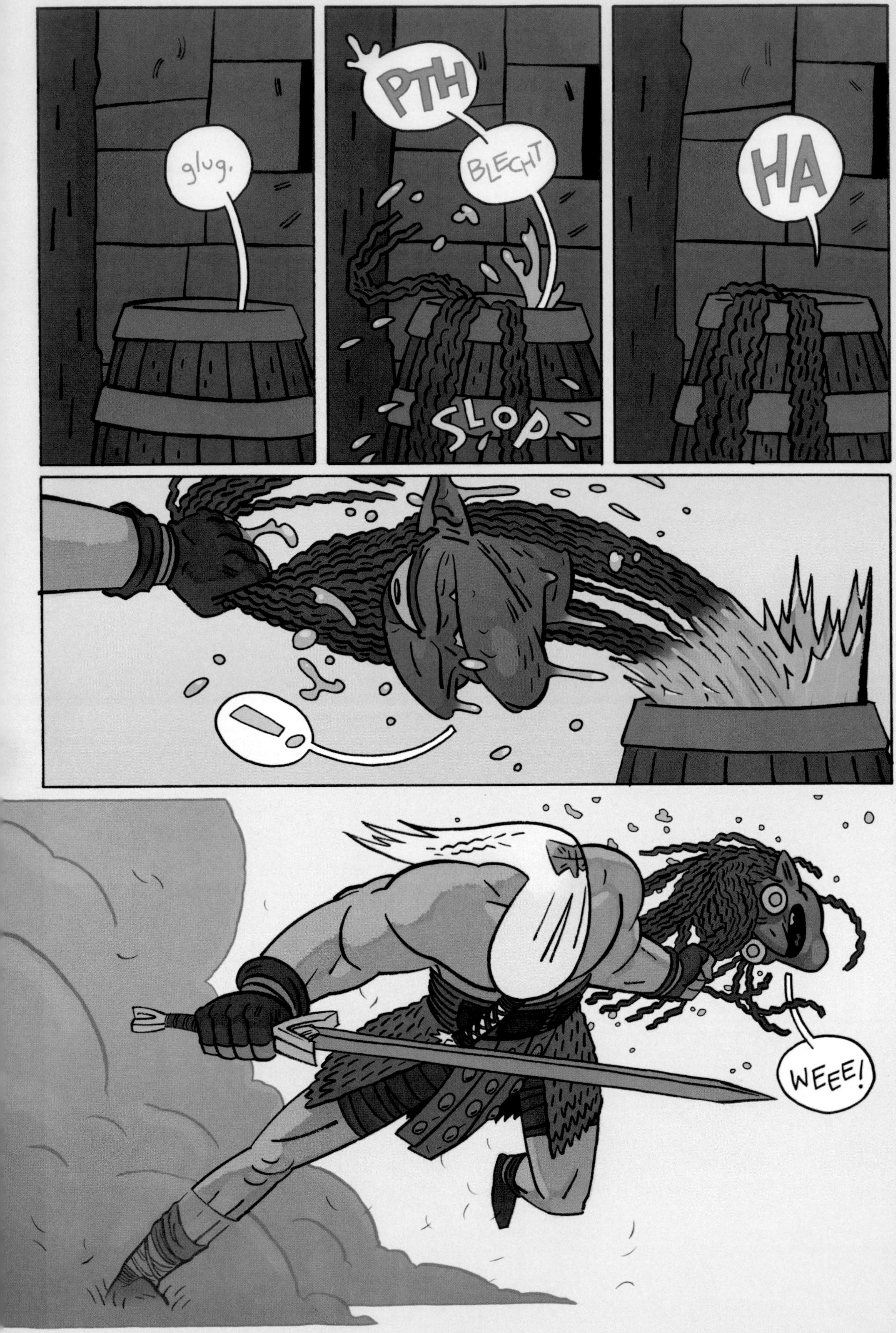
glug,
PTH
BLECHT
SLOP
HA
!
WEEE!

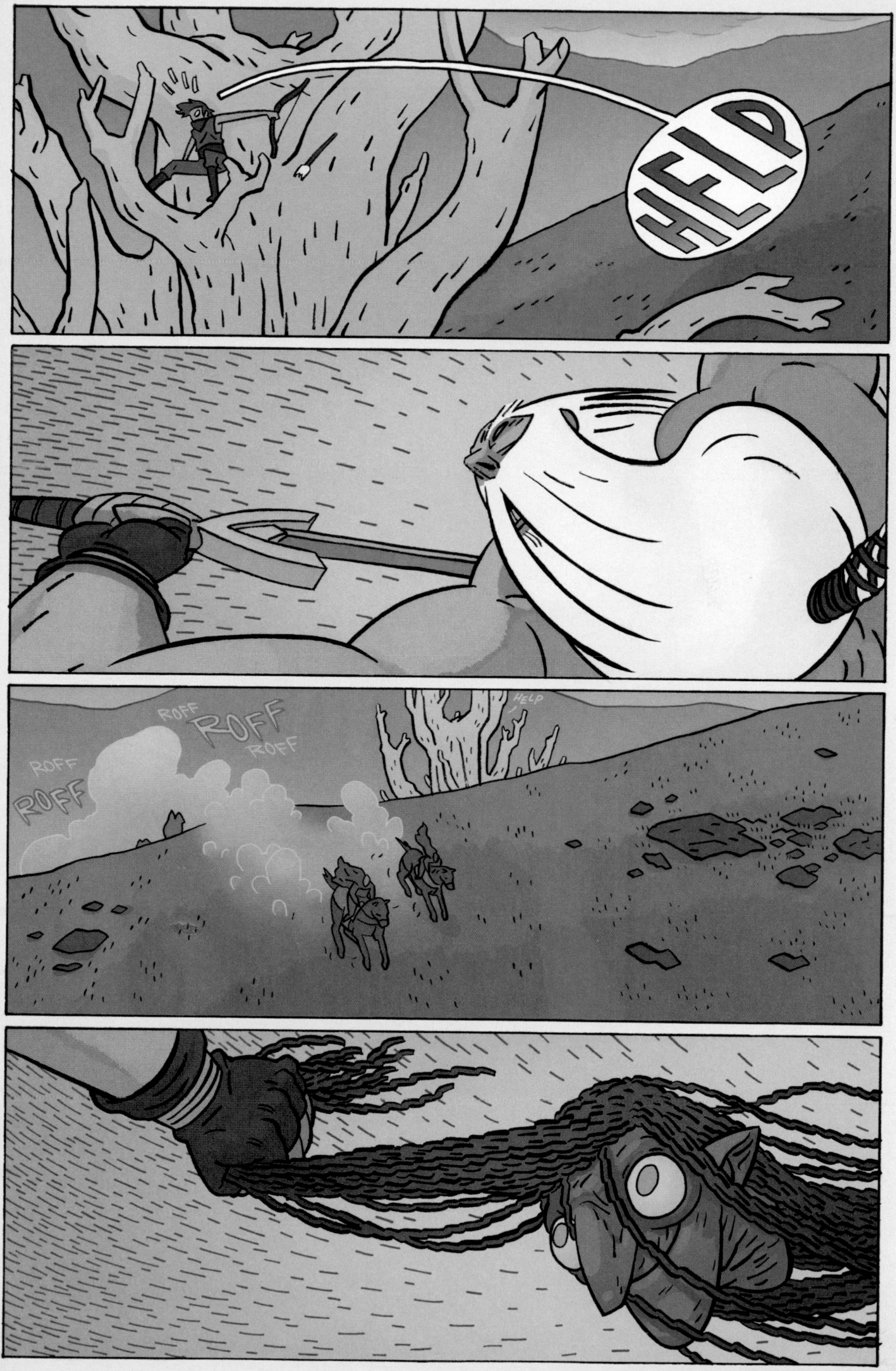
HELP
ROFF
ROFF
ROFF
ROFF
ROFF
HELP

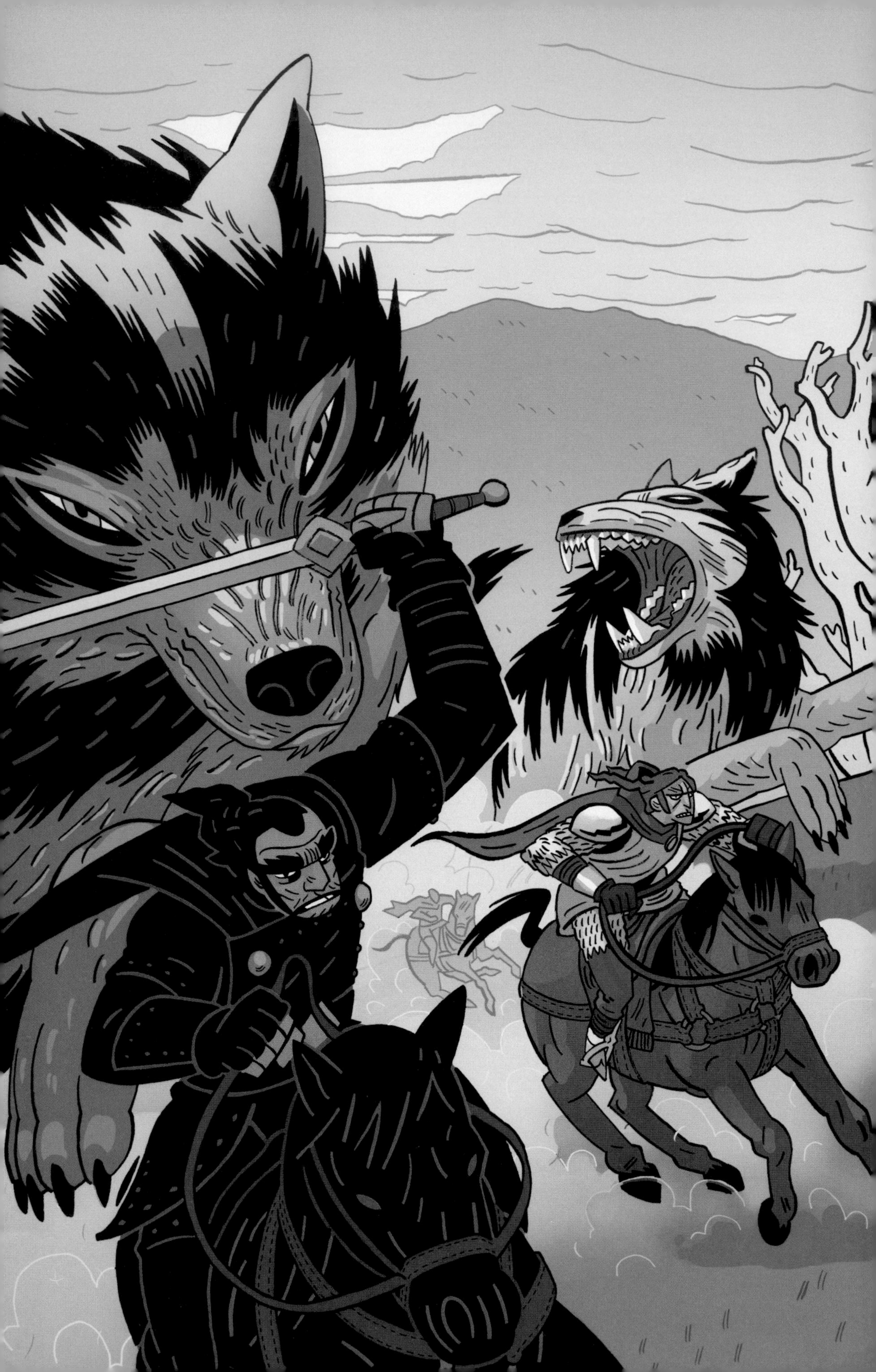

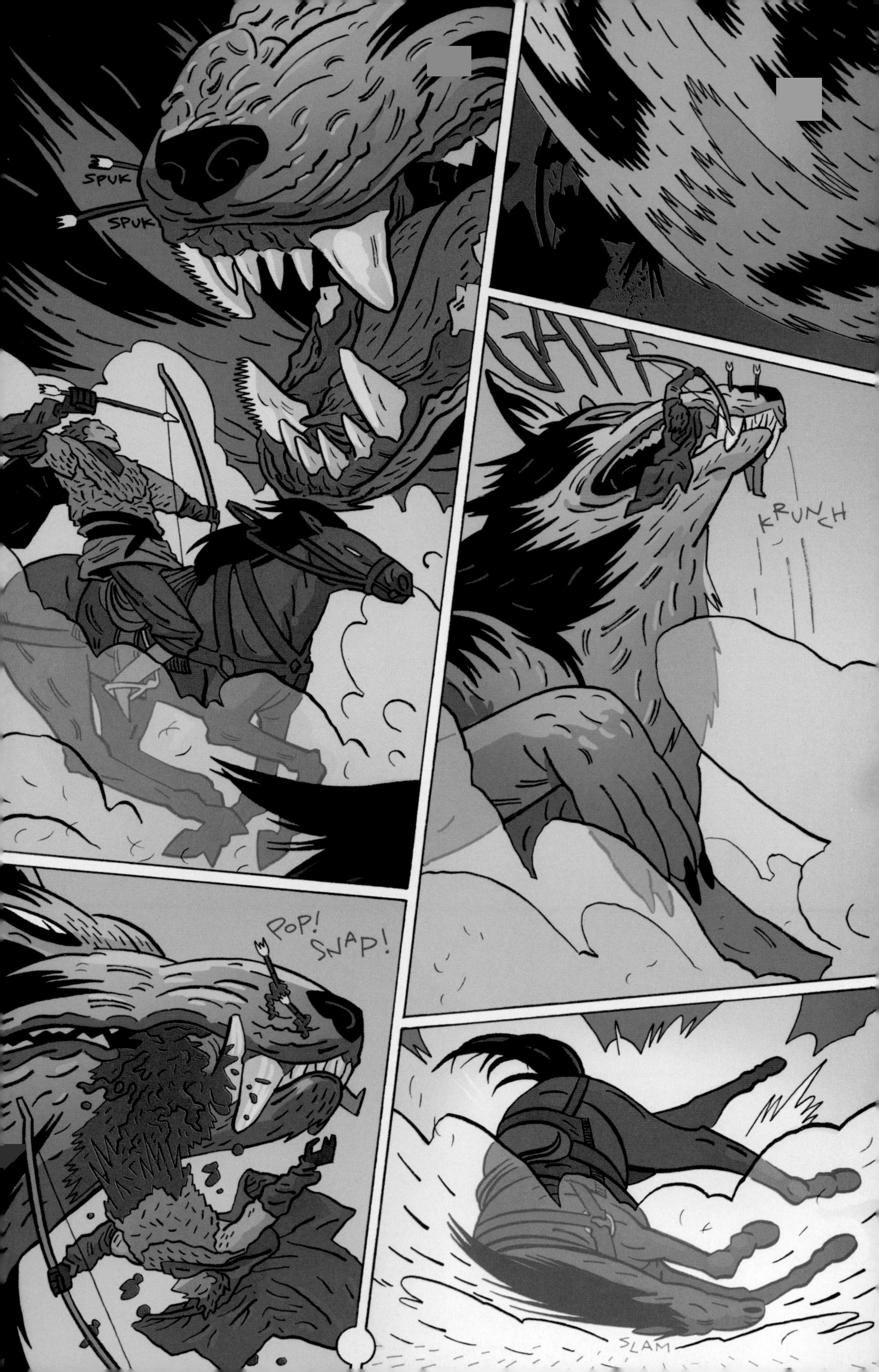
SPUK
SPUK
GAHH
KRUNCH
POP!
SNAP!
SLAM

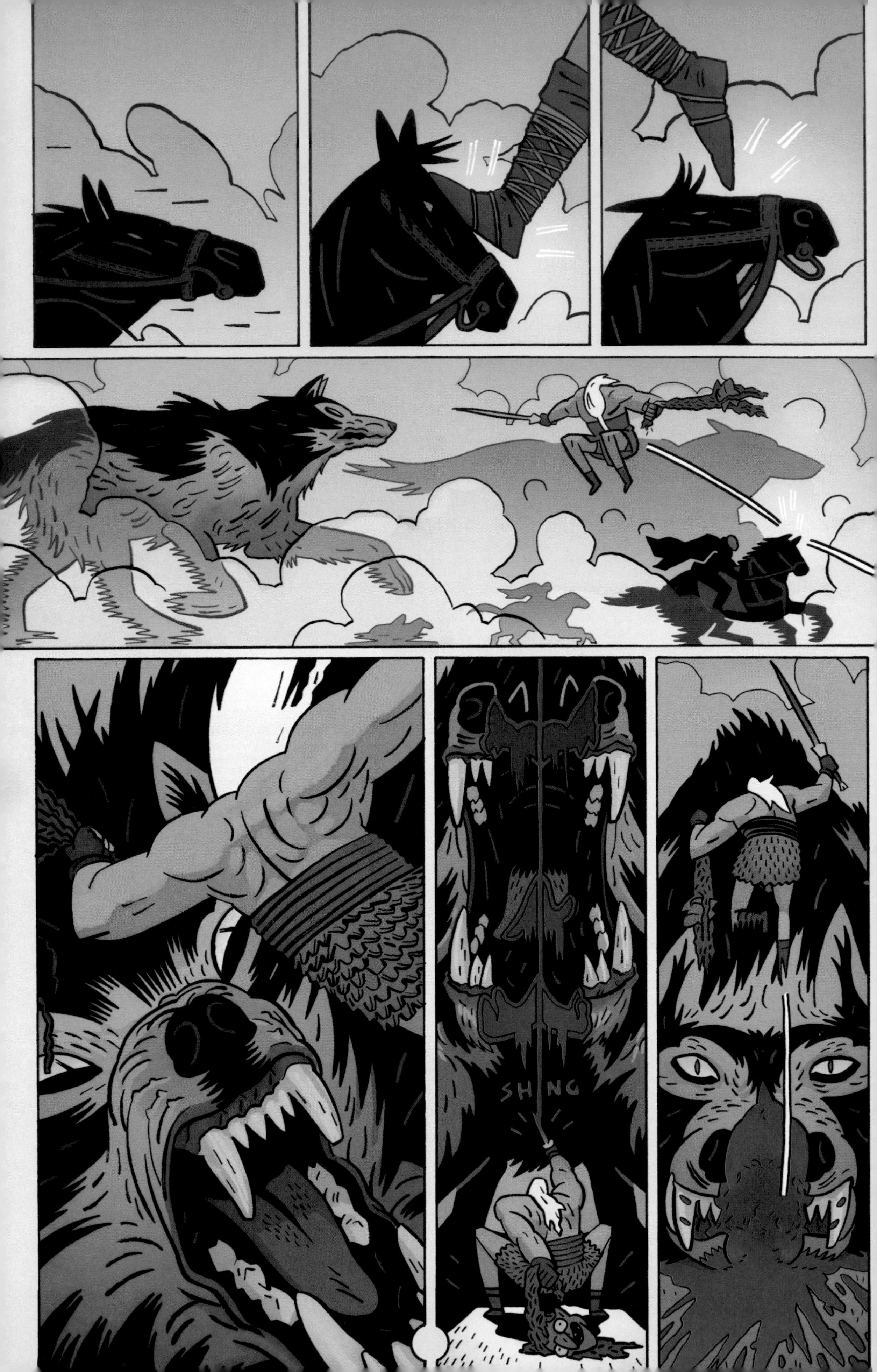
SHING

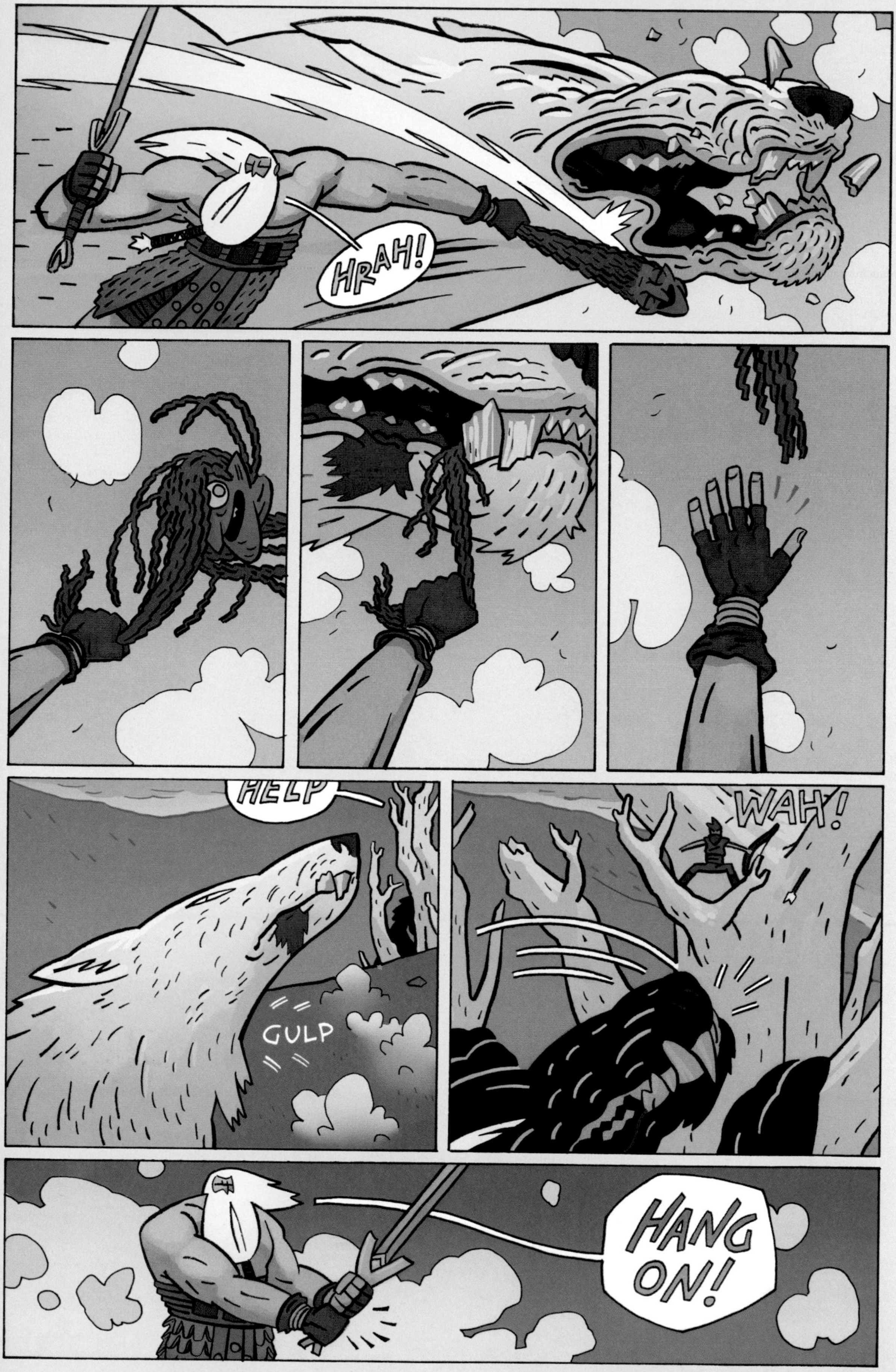
HRAH!
HELP
GULP
WAH!
HANG ON!

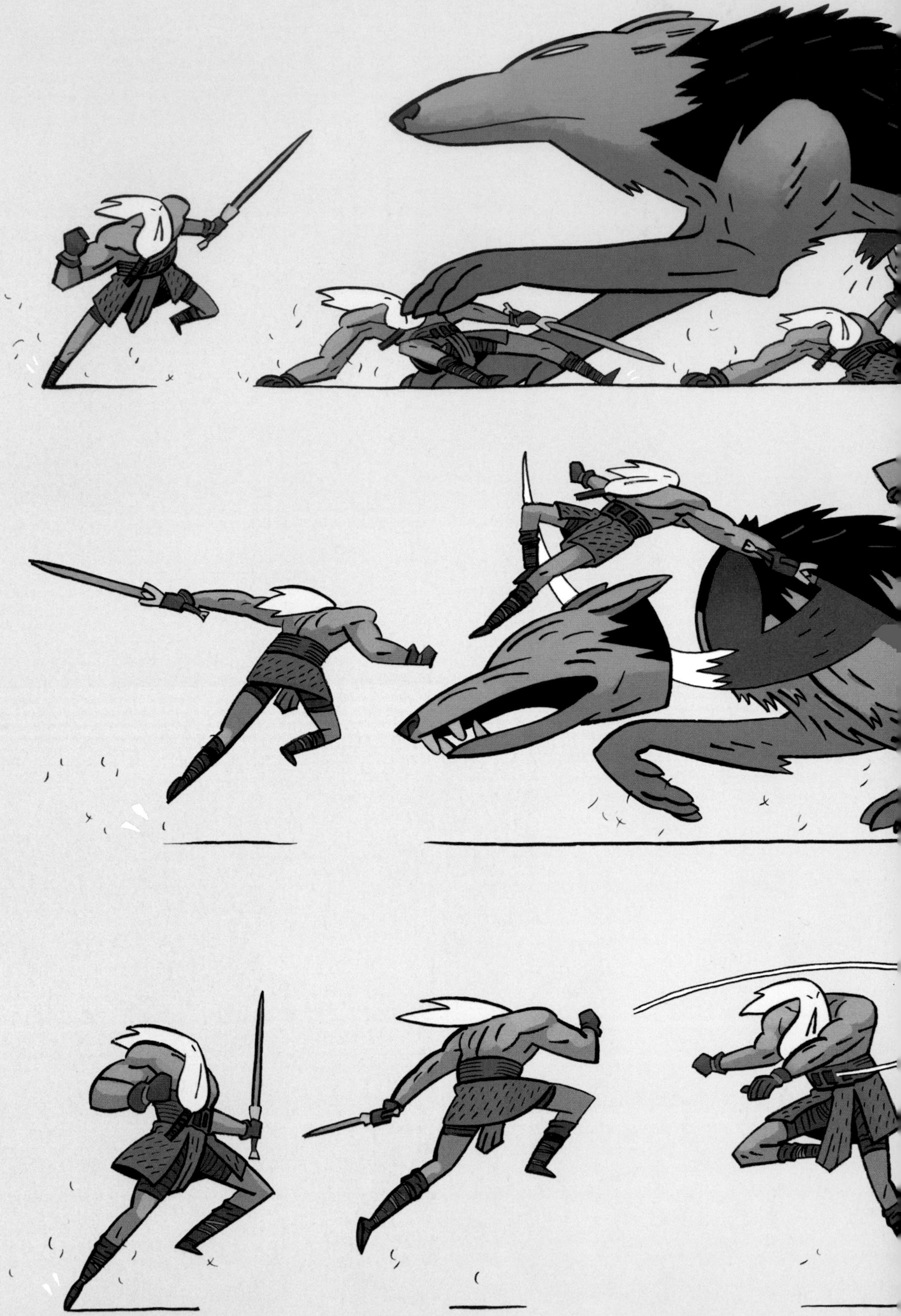

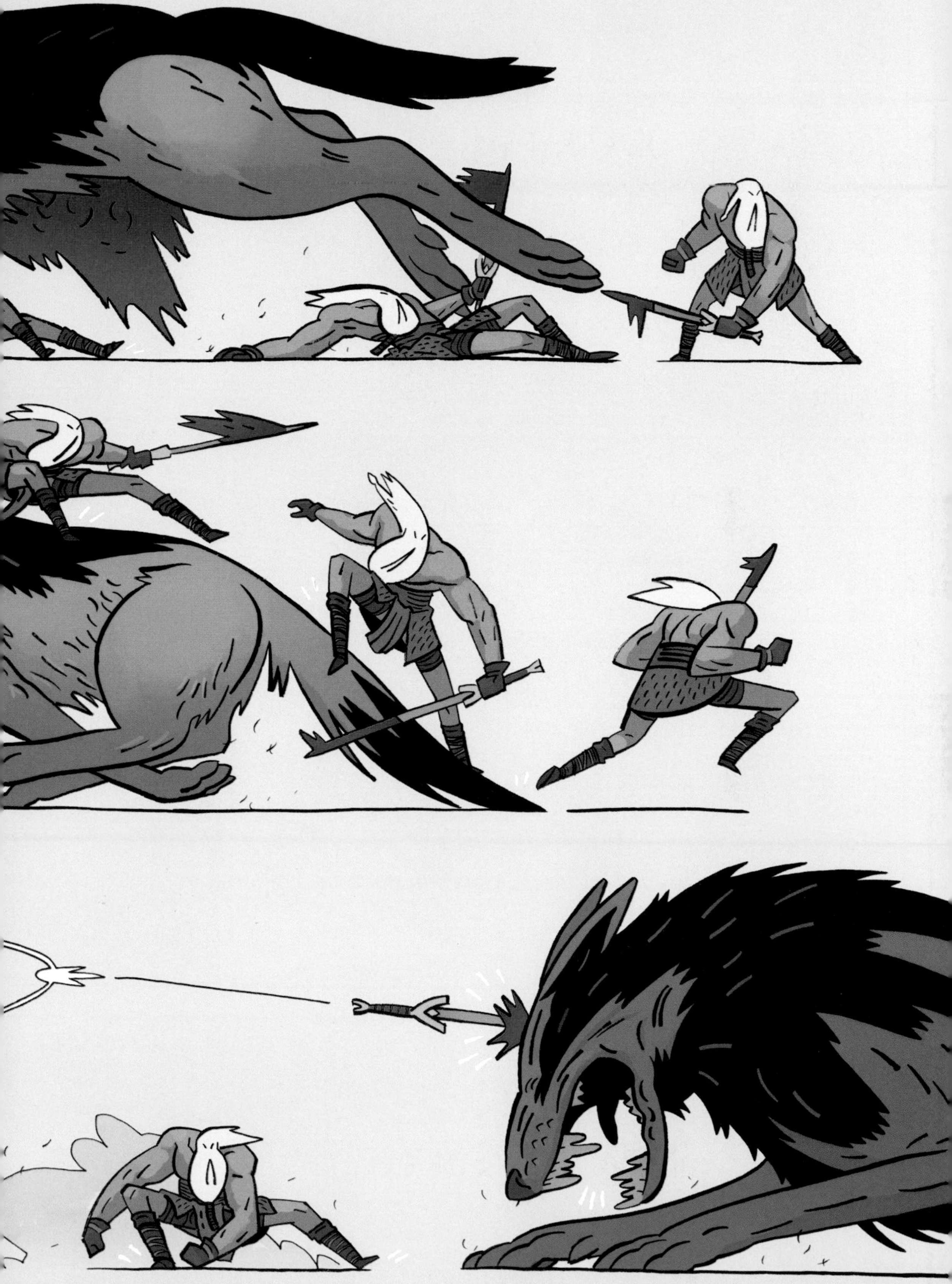

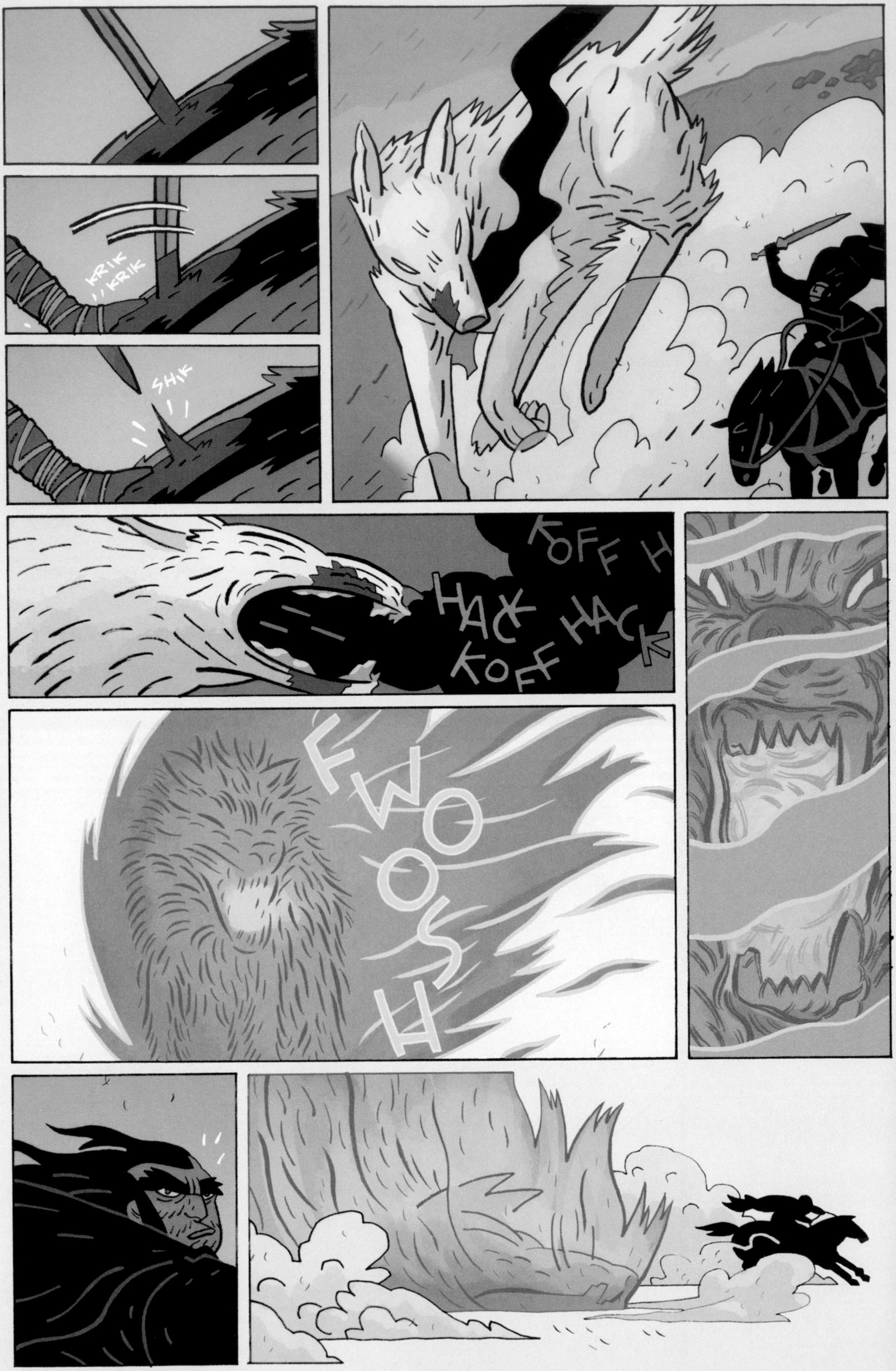
KRIK KRIK
SHIK
KOFF HACK HACK KOFF HACK
FWOOSH

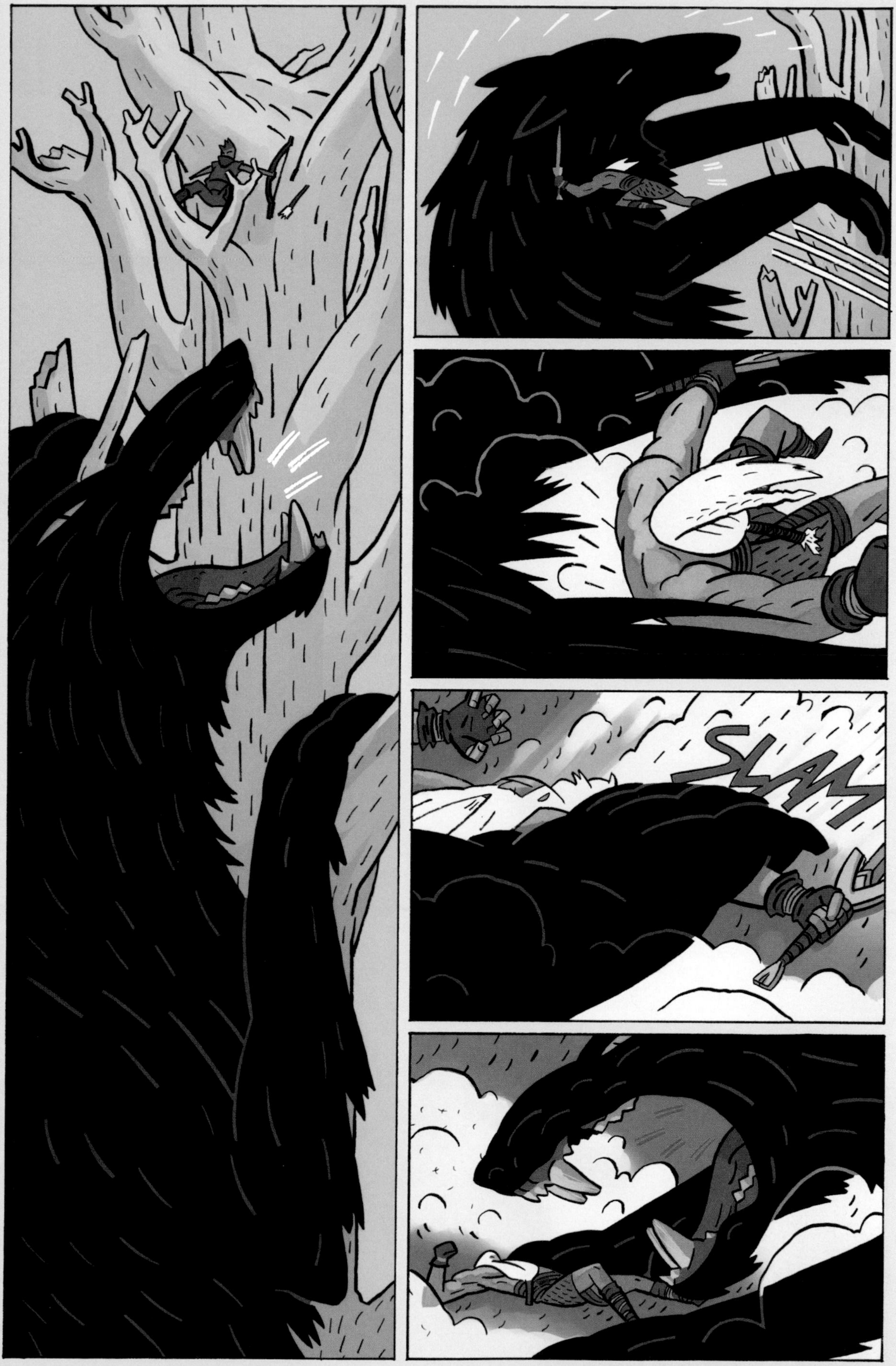
SLAM

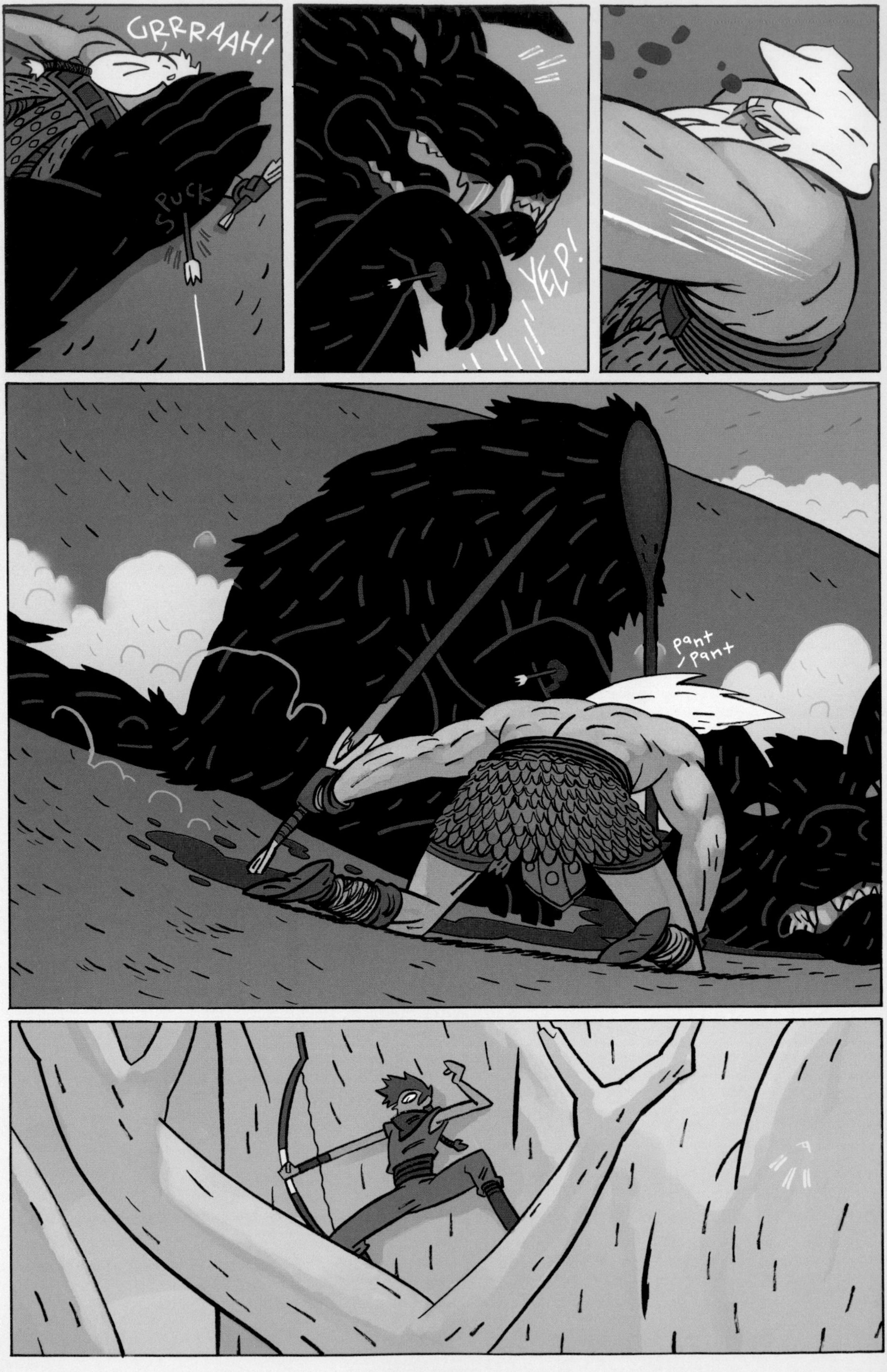
GRRRAAH!
SPUCK
YELP!
pant
pant

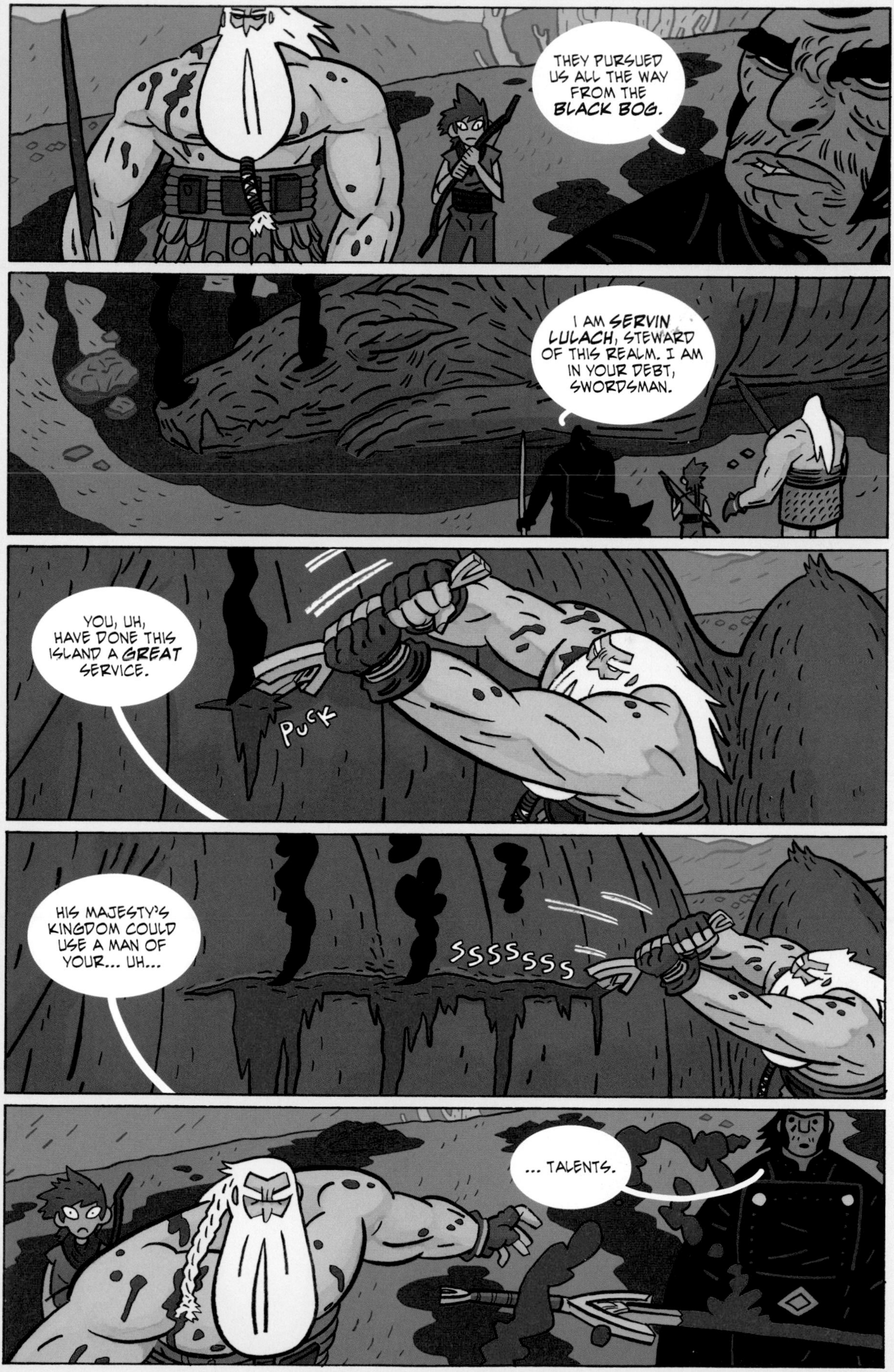
THEY PURSUED US ALL THE WAY FROM THE BLACK BOG.
I AM SERVIN LULACH, STEWARD OF THIS REALM. I AM IN YOUR DEBT, SWORDSMAN.
YOU, UH, HAVE DONE THIS ISLAND A GREAT SERVICE.
PUCK
HIS MAJESTY'S KINGDOM COULD USE A MAN OF YOUR... UH...
SSSSSSS
... TALENTS.

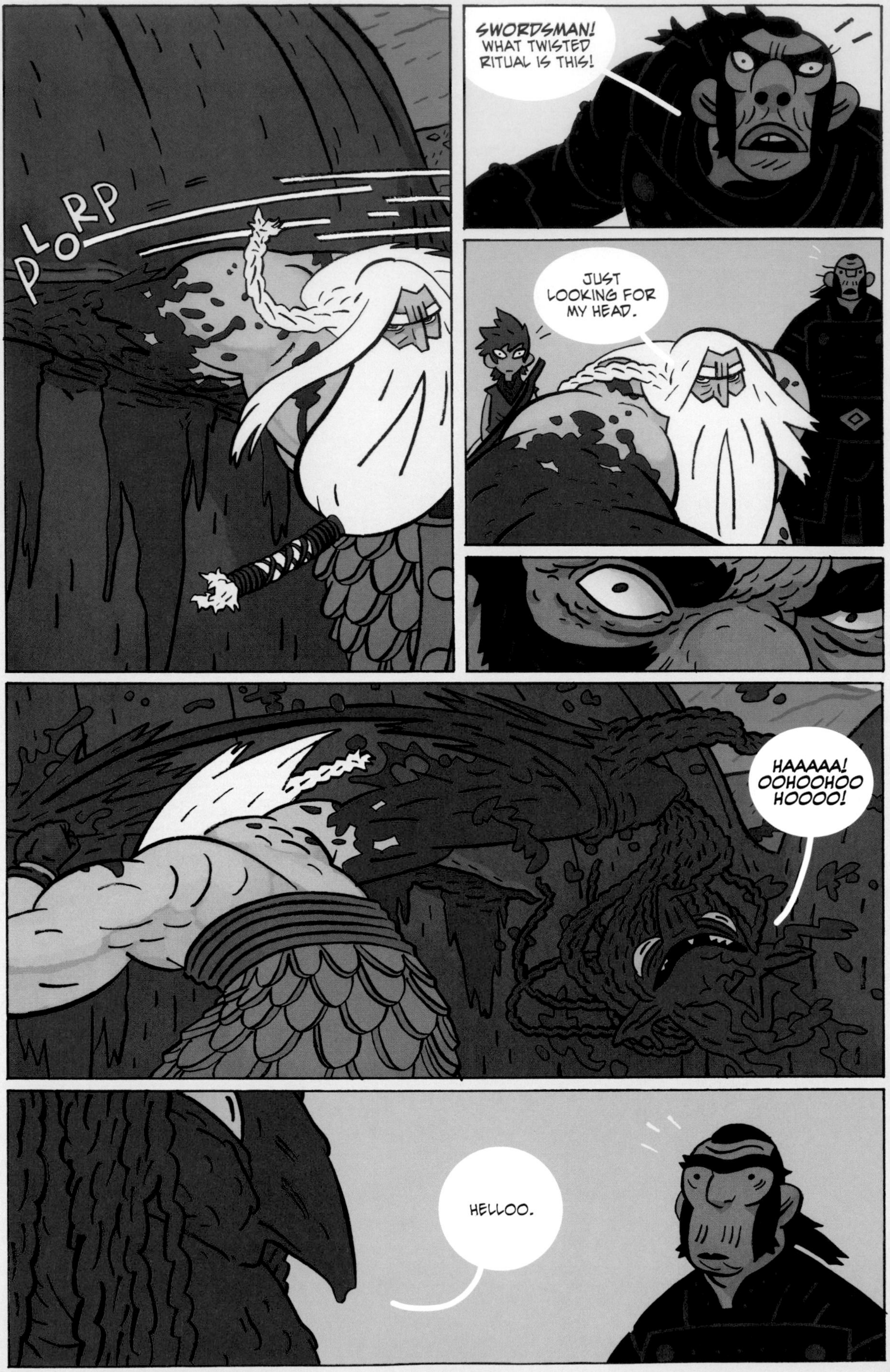
PLORP
SWORDSMAN! WHAT TWISTED RITUAL IS THIS!
JUST LOOKING FOR MY HEAD.
HAAAAA! OOHOOHOO HOOOO!
HELLOO.

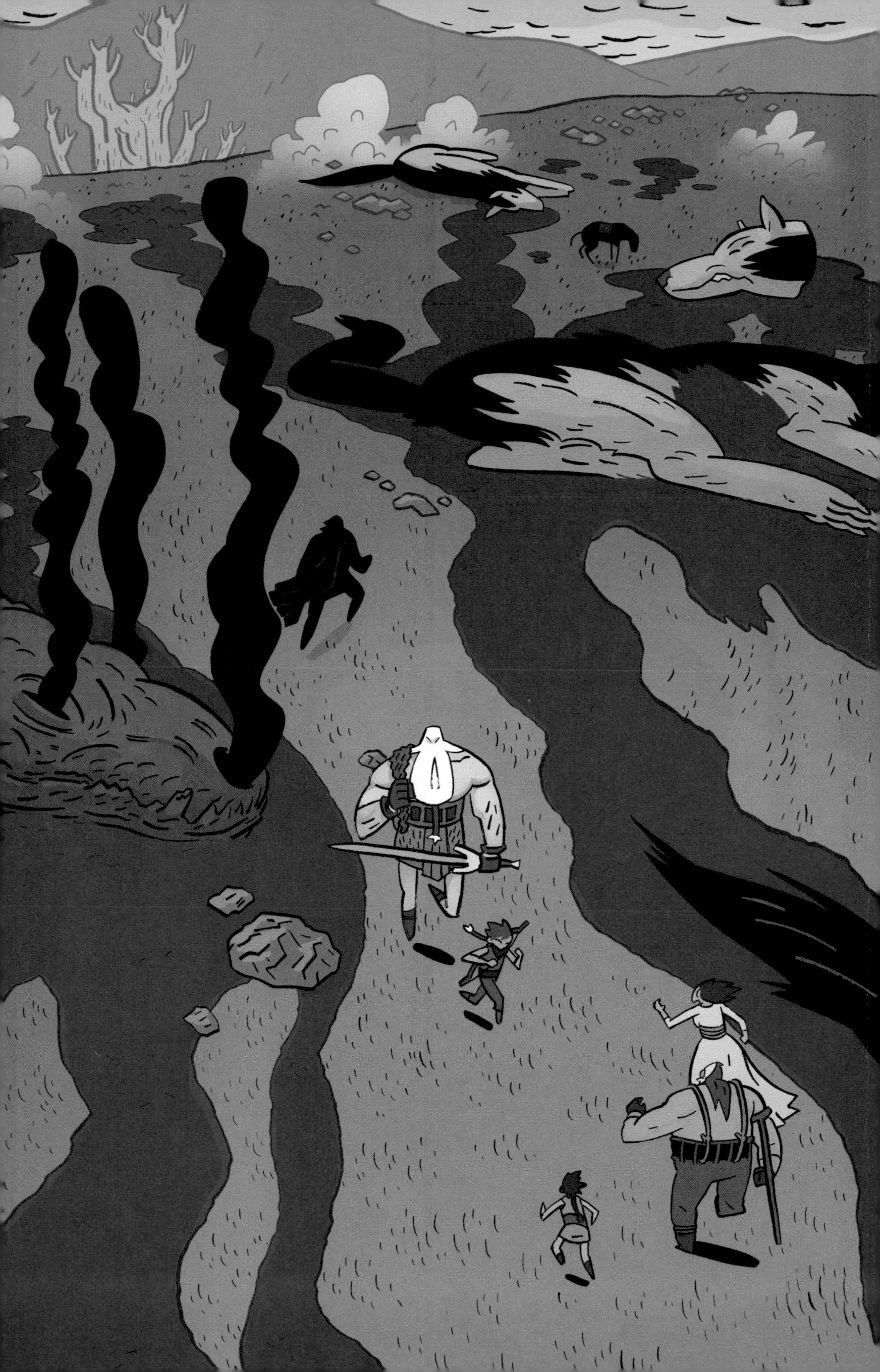

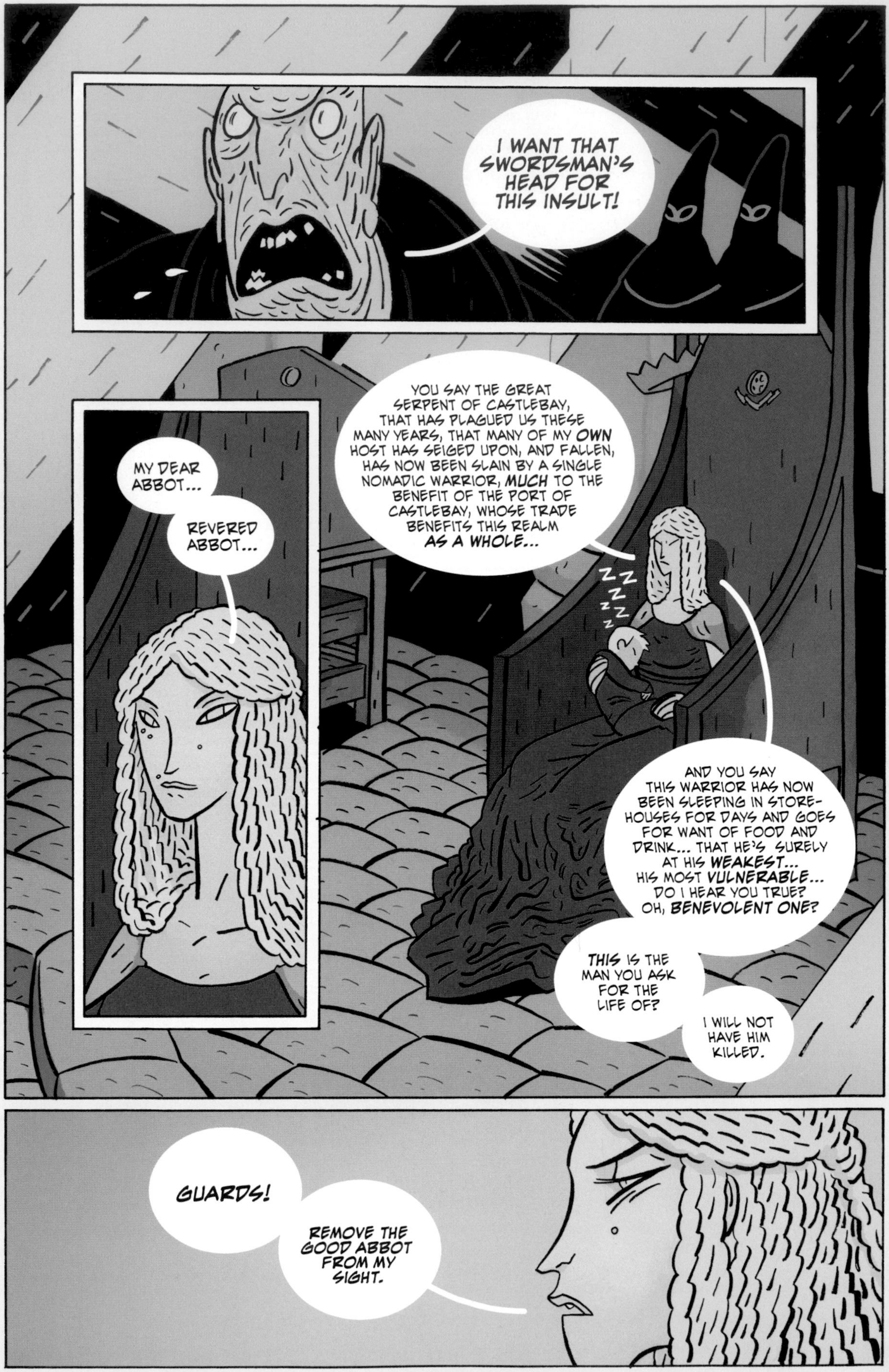
I WANT THAT SWORDSMAN'S HEAD FOR THIS INSULT!
MY DEAR ABBOT...
REVERED ABBOT...
YOU SAY THE GREAT SERPENT OF CASTLEBAY, THAT HAS PLAGUED US THESE MANY YEARS, THAT MANY OF MY OWN HOST HAS SEIGED UPON, AND FALLEN, HAS NOW BEEN SLAIN BY A SINGLE NOMADIC WARRIOR, MUCH TO THE BENEFIT OF THE PORT OF CASTLEBAY, WHOSE TRADE BENEFITS THIS REALM AS A WHOLE...
ZZZ
AND YOU SAY THIS WARRIOR HAS NOW BEEN SLEEPING IN STORE-HOUSES FOR DAYS AND GOES FOR WANT OF FOOD AND DRINK... THAT HE'S SURELY AT HIS WEAKEST... HIS MOST VULNERABLE... DO I HEAR YOU TRUE? OH, BENEVOLENT ONE?
THIS IS THE MAN YOU ASK FOR THE LIFE OF?
I WILL NOT HAVE HIM KILLED.
GUARDS!
REMOVE THE GOOD ABBOT FROM MY SIGHT.

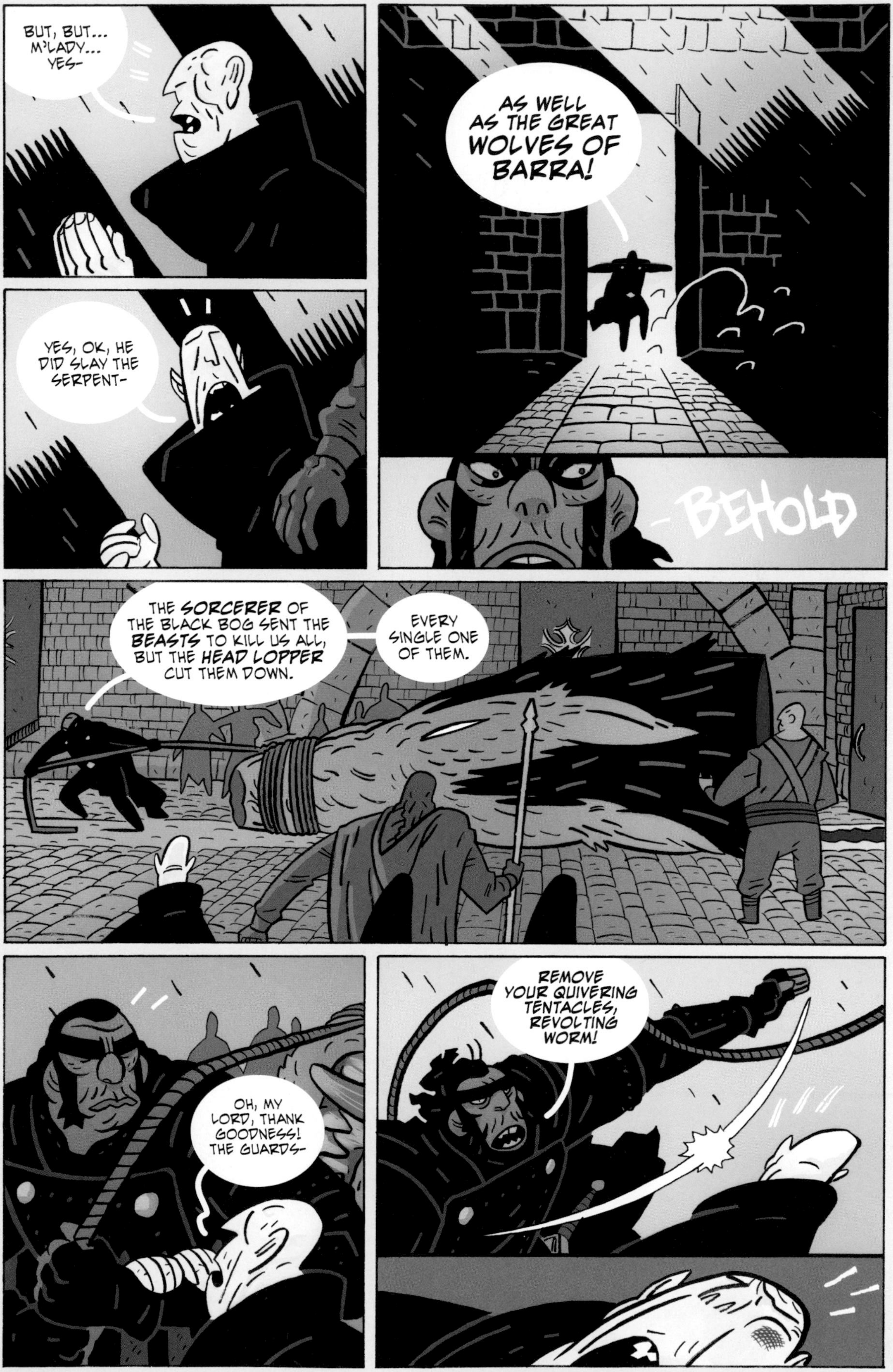
BUT, BUT... M'LADY... YES-
AS WELL AS THE GREAT WOLVES OF BARRA!
YES, OK, HE DID SLAY THE SERPENT-
-BEHOLD
THE SORCERER OF THE BLACK BOG SENT THE BEASTS TO KILL US ALL, BUT THE HEAD LOPPER CUT THEM DOWN.
EVERY SINGLE ONE OF THEM.
OH, MY LORD, THANK GOODNESS! THE GUARDS-
REMOVE YOUR QUIVERING TENTACLES, REVOLTING WORM!

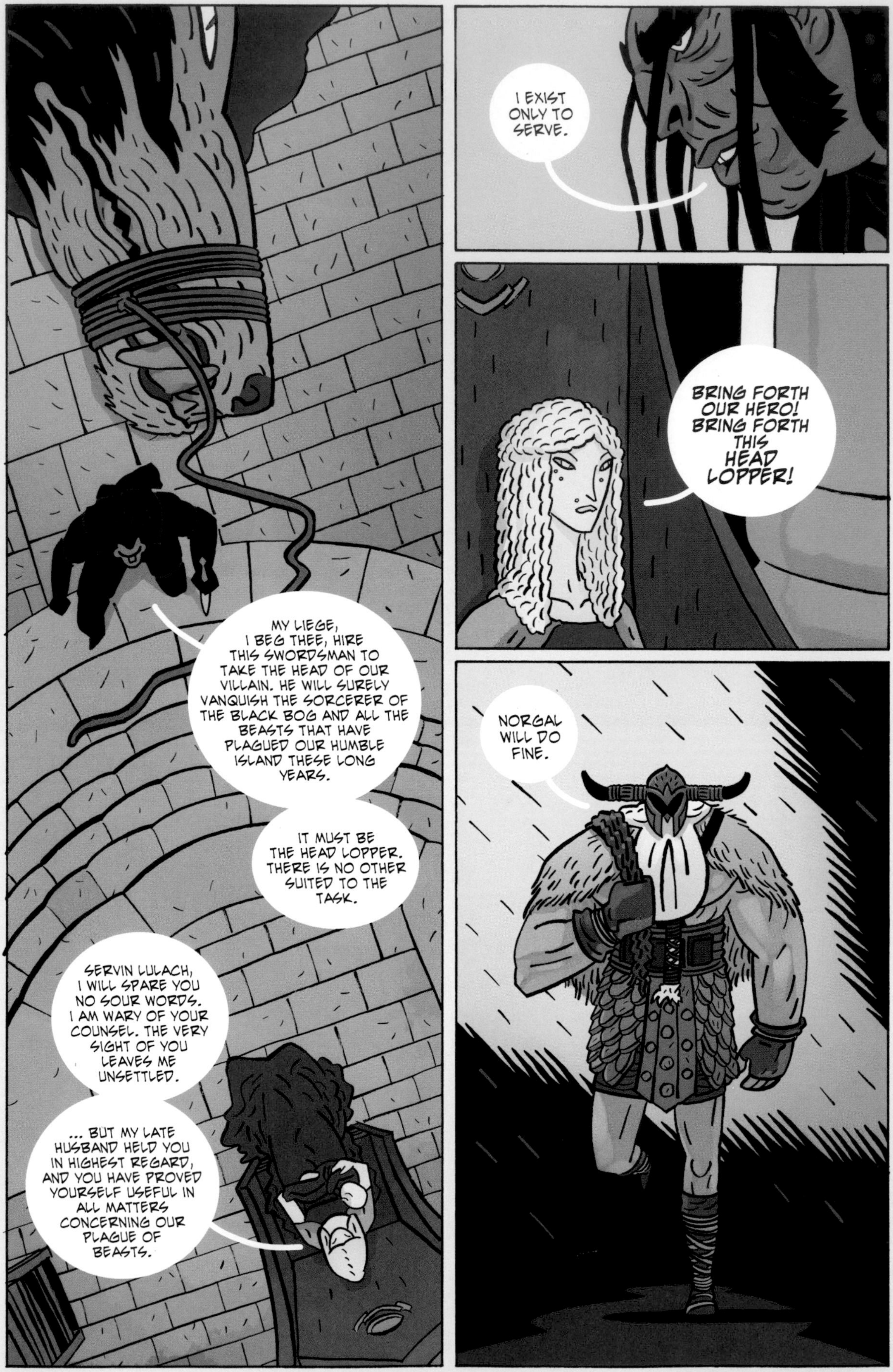

MY LIEGE, I BEG THEE, HIRE THIS SWORDSMAN TO TAKE THE HEAD OF OUR VILLAIN. HE WILL SURELY VANQUISH THE SORCERER OF THE BLACK BOG AND ALL THE BEASTS THAT HAVE PLAGUED OUR HUMBLE ISLAND THESE LONG YEARS.
IT MUST BE THE HEAD LOPPER. THERE IS NO OTHER SUITED TO THE TASK.
SERVIN LULACH, I WILL SPARE YOU NO SOUR WORDS. I AM WARY OF YOUR COUNSEL. THE VERY SIGHT OF YOU LEAVES ME UNSETTLED.
... BUT MY LATE HUSBAND HELD YOU IN HIGHEST REGARD, AND YOU HAVE PROVED YOURSELF USEFUL IN ALL MATTERS CONCERNING OUR PLAGUE OF BEASTS.
I EXIST ONLY TO SERVE.
BRING FORTH OUR HERO! BRING FORTH THIS HEAD LOPPER!
NORGAL WILL DO FINE.

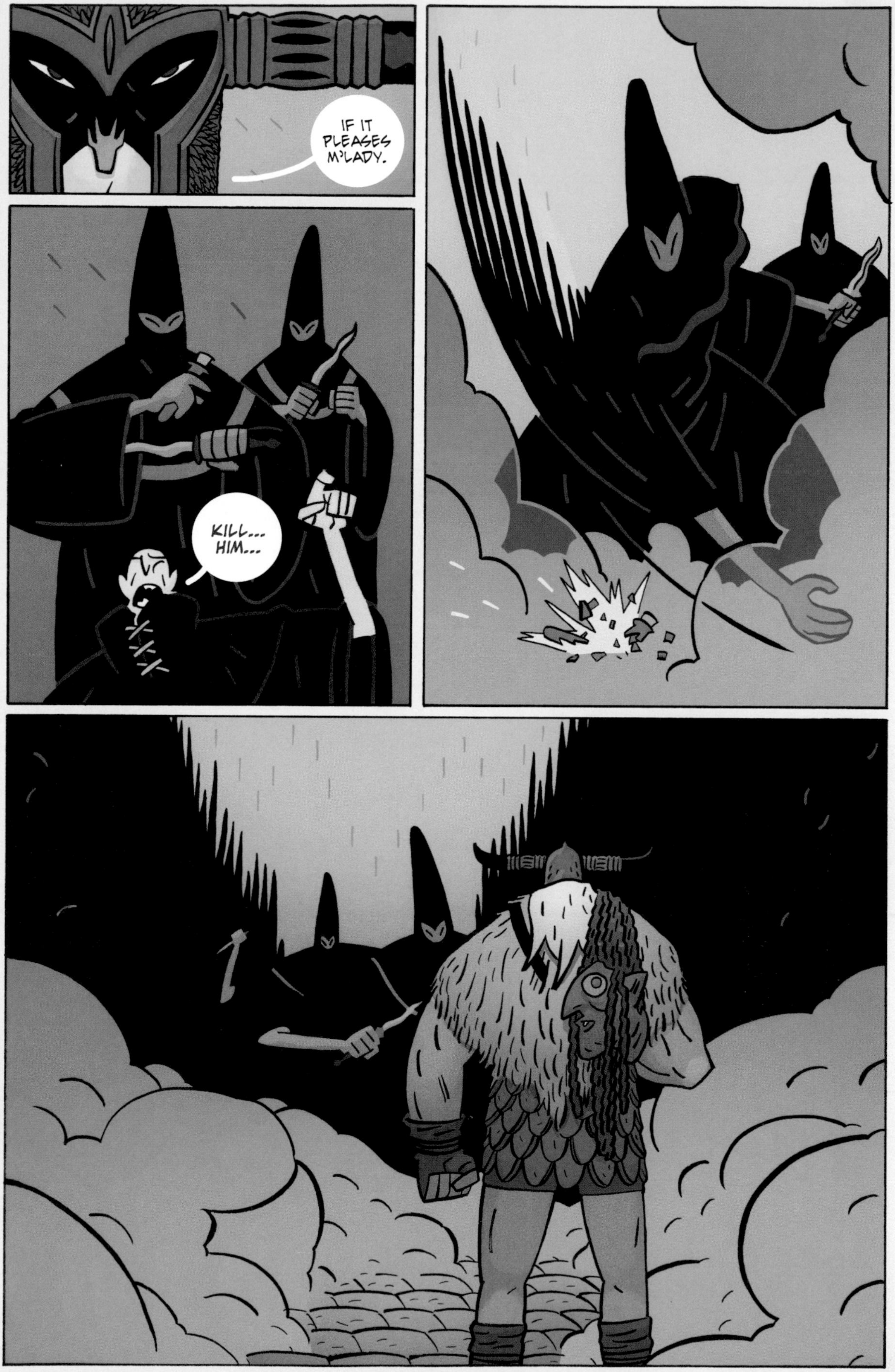
IF IT PLEASES M'LADY.
KILL... HIM...

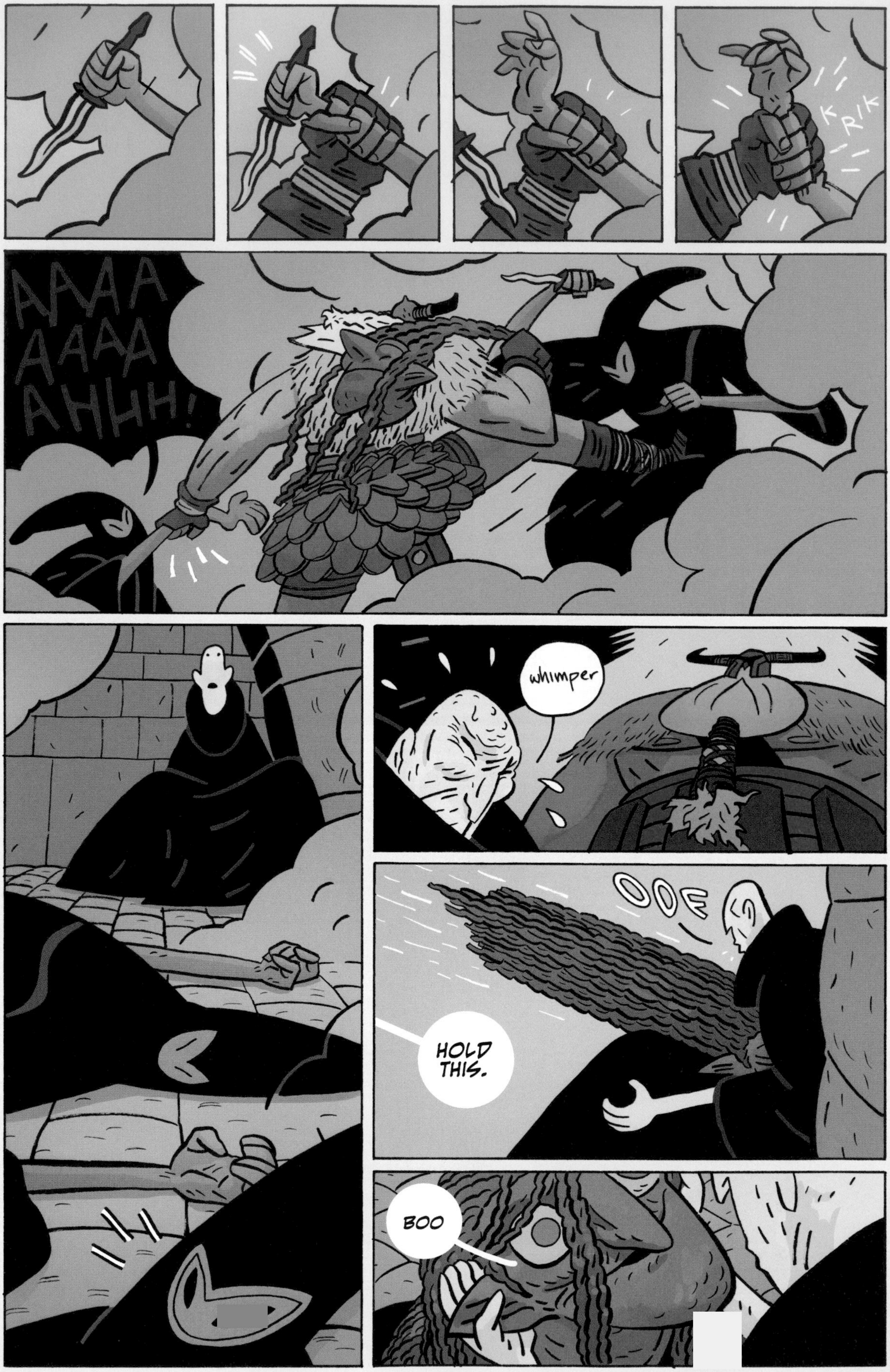

KRIK
AAAA AAAA AHHH!
whimper
OOF
HOLD THIS.
BOO

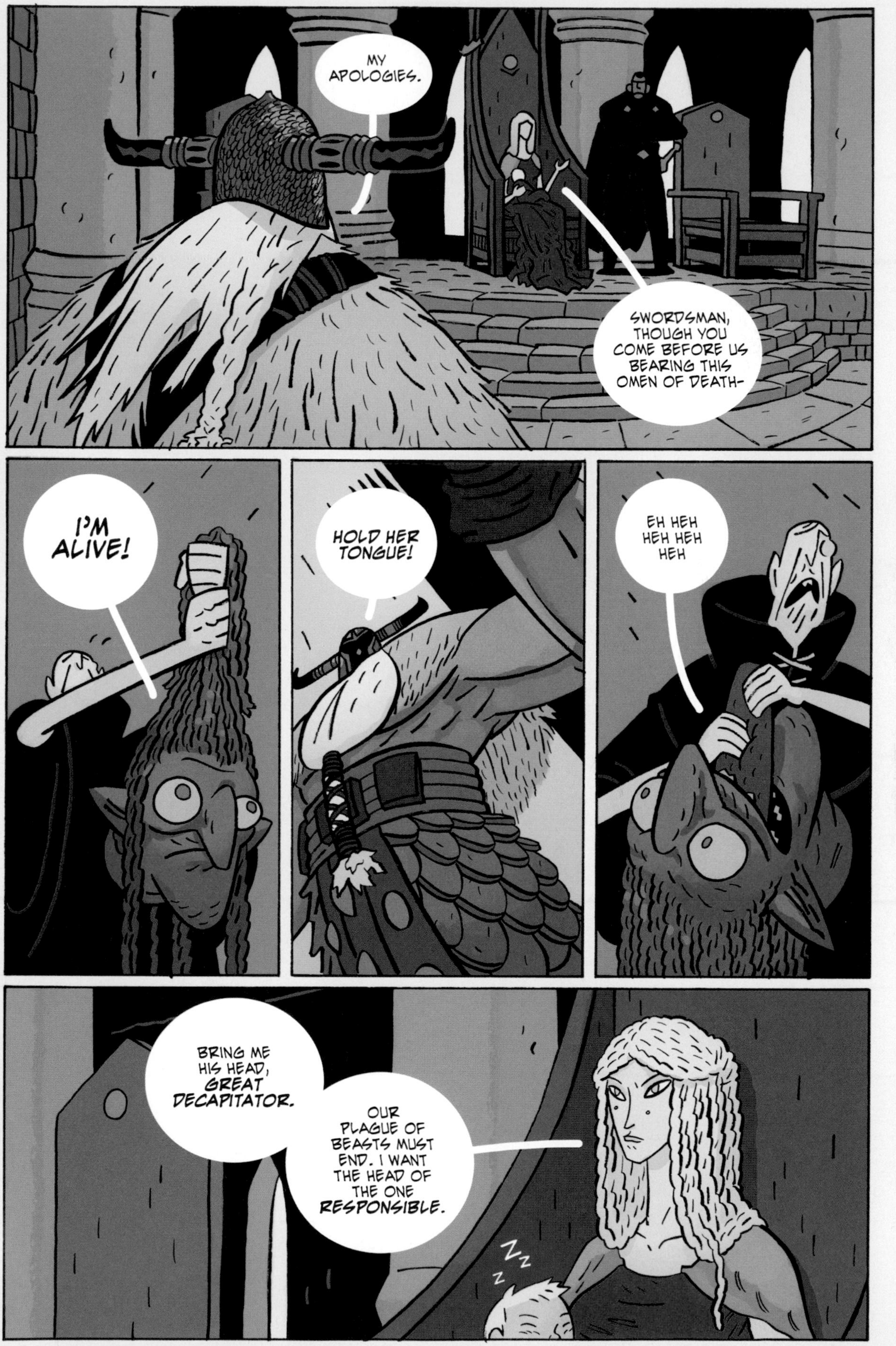
MY APOLOGIES.
SWORDSMAN, THOUGH YOU COME BEFORE US BEARING THIS OMEN OF DEATH-
I'M ALIVE!
HOLD HER TONGUE!
EH HEH HEH HEH HEH
BRING ME HIS HEAD, GREAT DECAPITATOR.
OUR PLAGUE OF BEASTS MUST END. I WANT THE HEAD OF THE ONE RESPONSIBLE.
Z Z Z

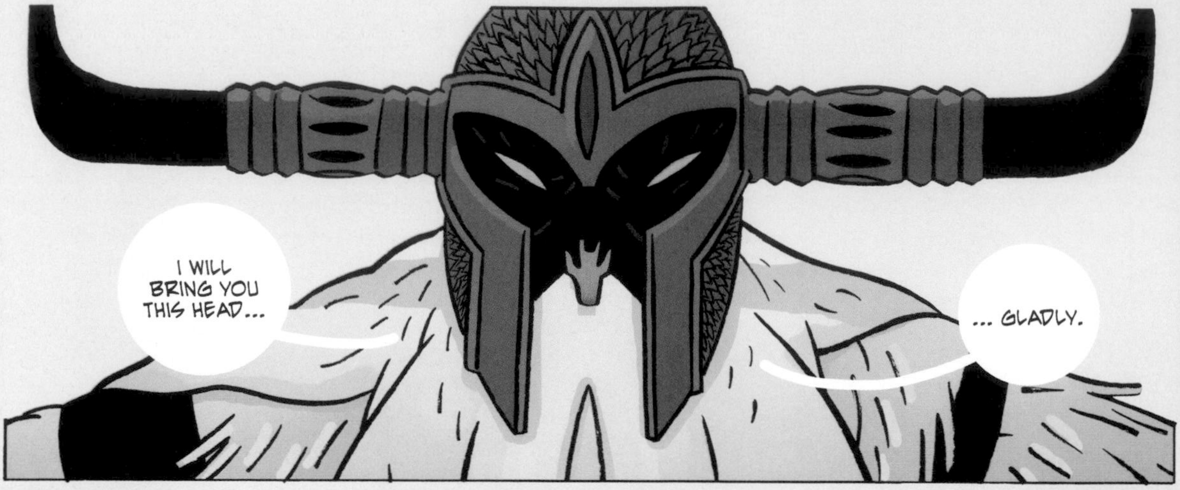
I WILL BRING YOU THIS HEAD...
... GLADLY.

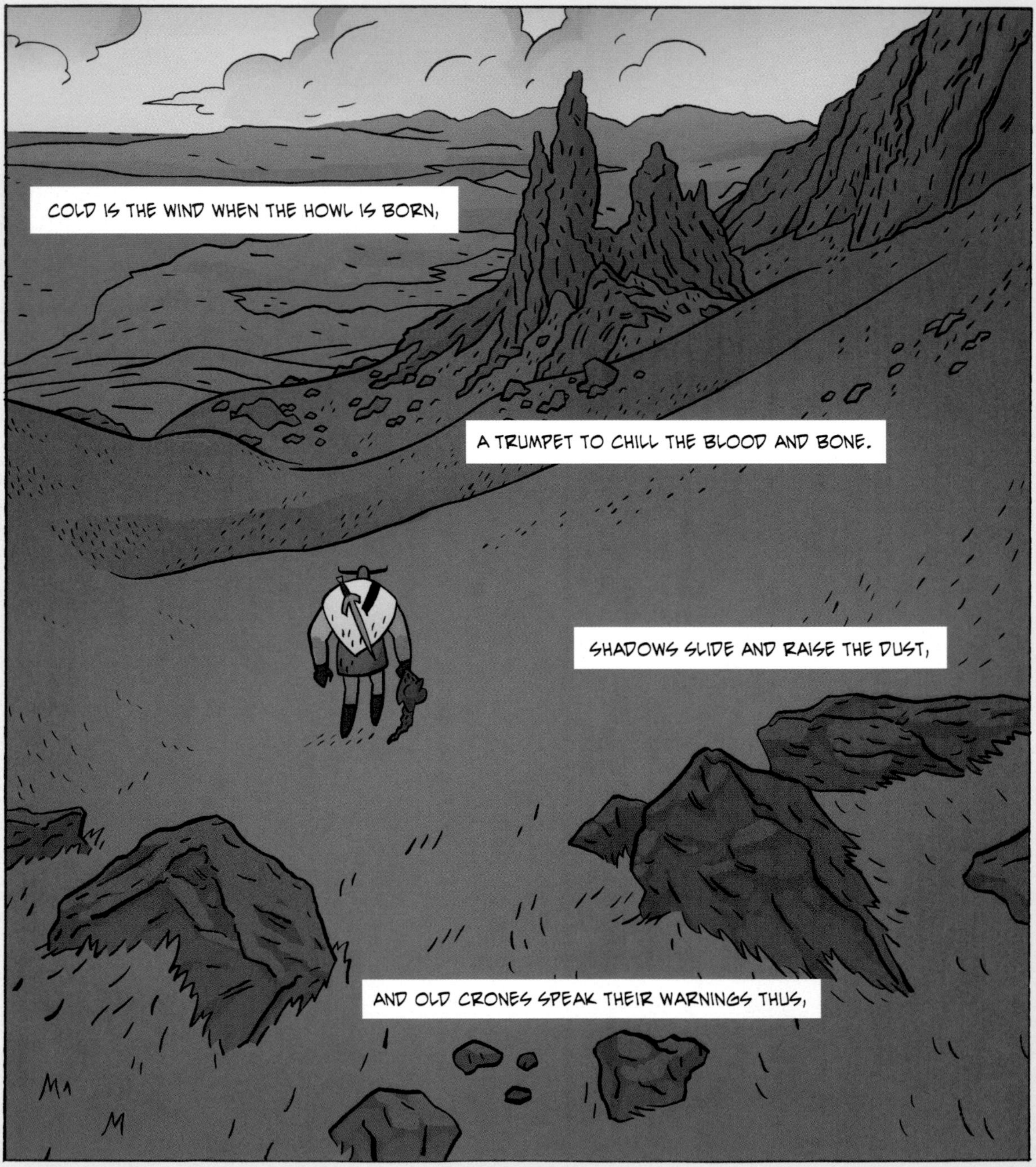
COLD IS THE WIND WHEN THE HOWL IS BORN,
A TRUMPET TO CHILL THE BLOOD AND BONE.
SHADOWS SLIDE AND RAISE THE DUST,
AND OLD CRONES SPEAK THEIR WARNINGS THUS,

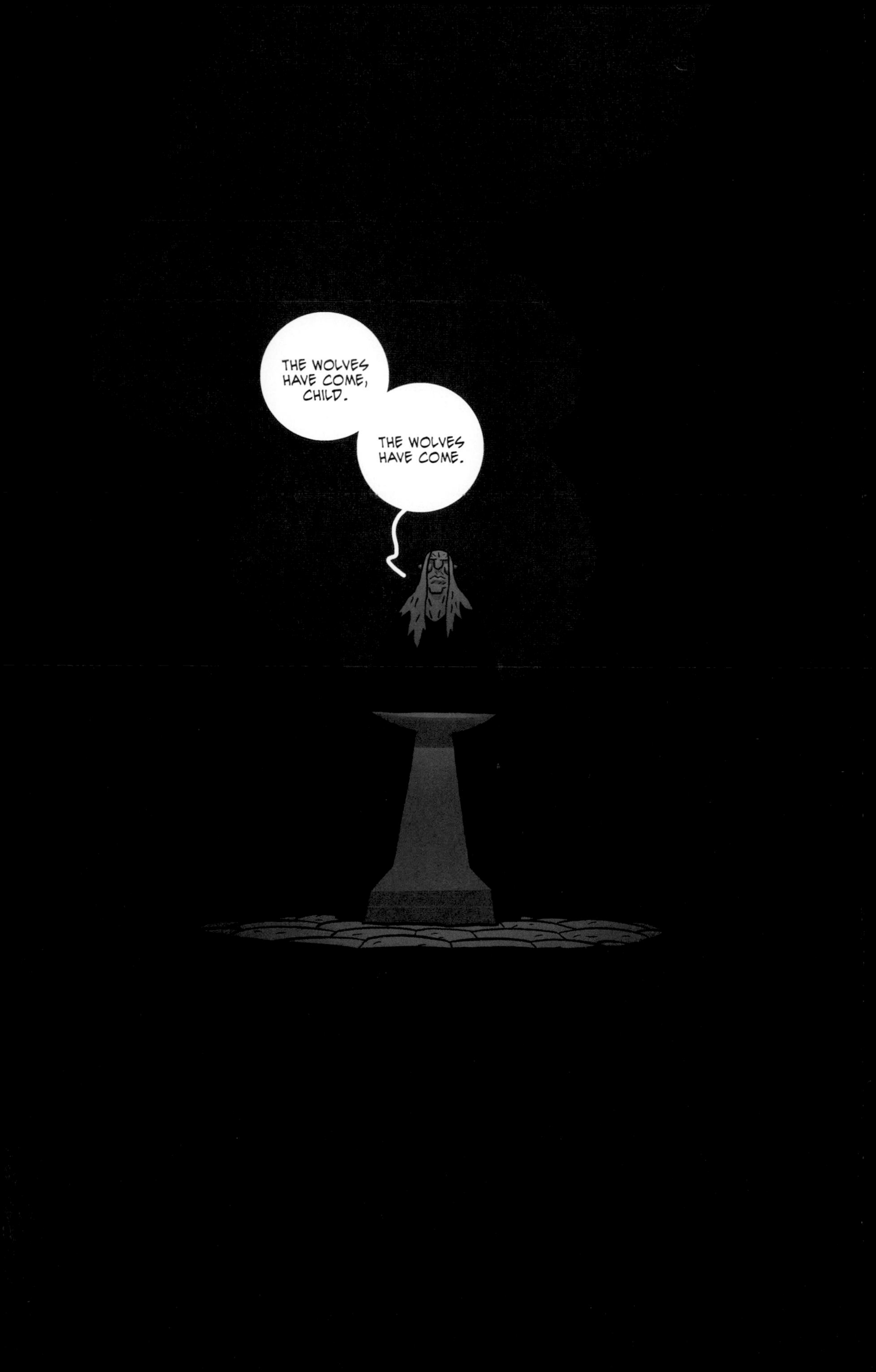
THE WOLVES HAVE COME, CHILD.
THE WOLVES HAVE COME.

CHAPTER THREE

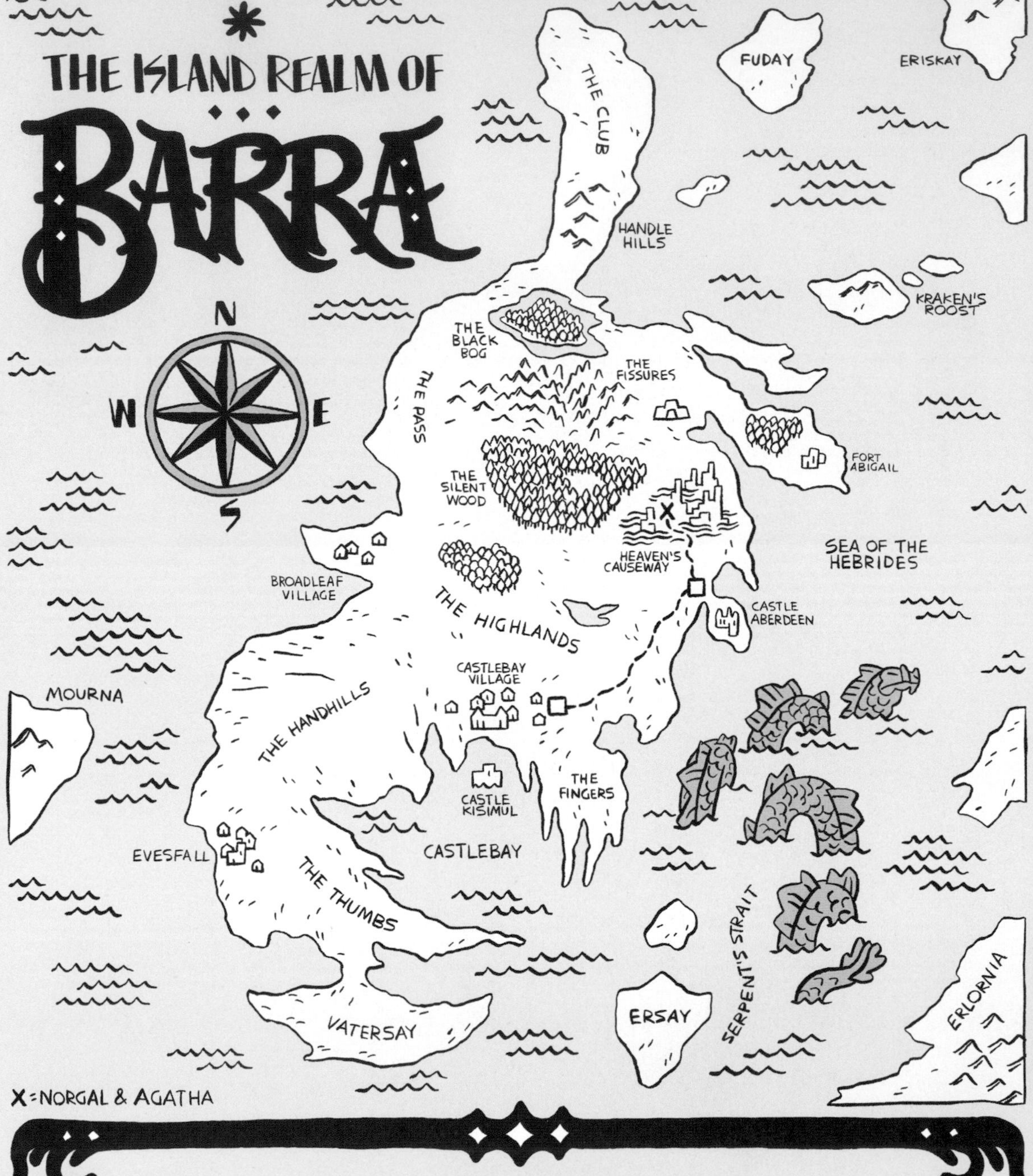
THE ISLAND REALM OF
BARRA
N
W
E
S
THE CLUB
HANDLE HILLS
FUDAY
ERISKAY
KRAKEN'S ROOST
THE BLACK BOG
THE FISSURES
THE PASS
FORT ABIGAIL
THE SILENT WOOD
HEAVEN'S CAUSEWAY
SEA OF THE HEBRIDES
BROADLEAF VILLAGE
THE HIGHLANDS
CASTLE ABERDEEN
CASTLEBAY VILLAGE
MOURNA
THE HANDHILLS
THE FINGERS
CASTLE KISIMUL
EVESFALL
CASTLEBAY
THE THUMBS
SERPENT'S STRAIT
ERLORNIA
ERSAY
VATERSAY
X=NORGAL & AGATHA

THAT WHICH LURKS IN THE MIST

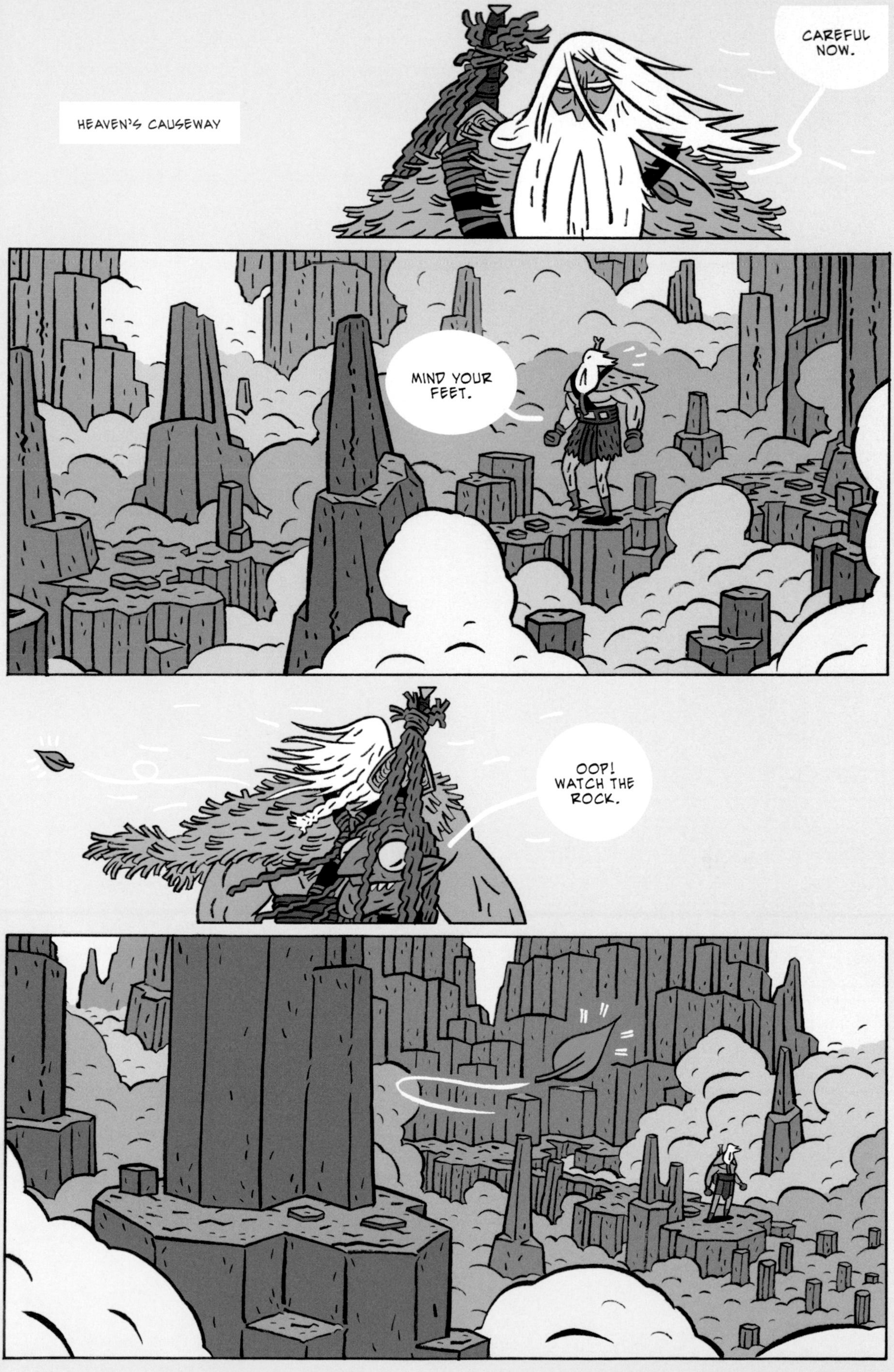
HEAVEN'S CAUSEWAY
CAREFUL NOW.
MIND YOUR FEET.
OOP! WATCH THE ROCK.

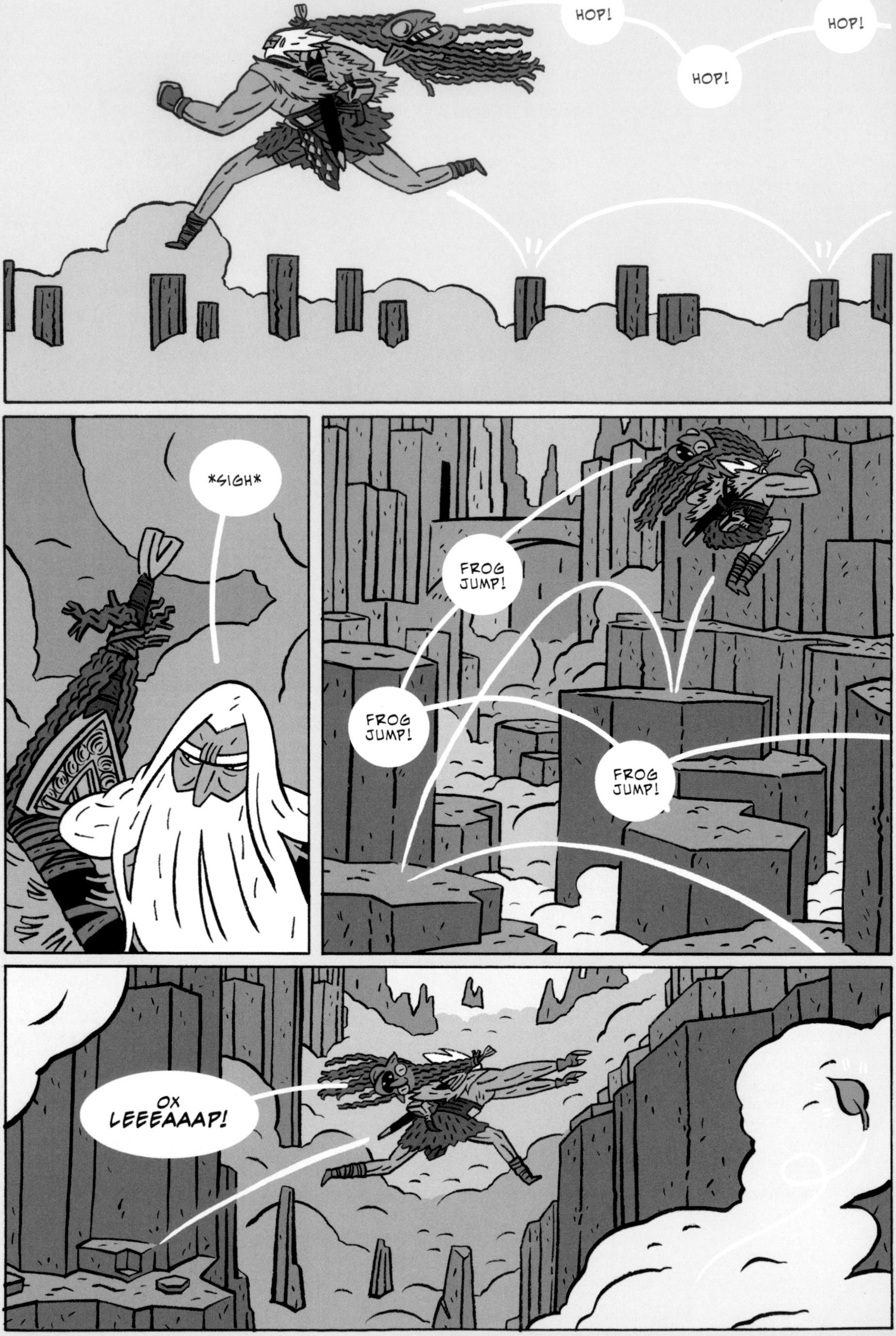
HOP!
HOP!
HOP!
SIGH
FROG JUMP!
FROG JUMP!
FROG JUMP!
OX LEEEAAAP!

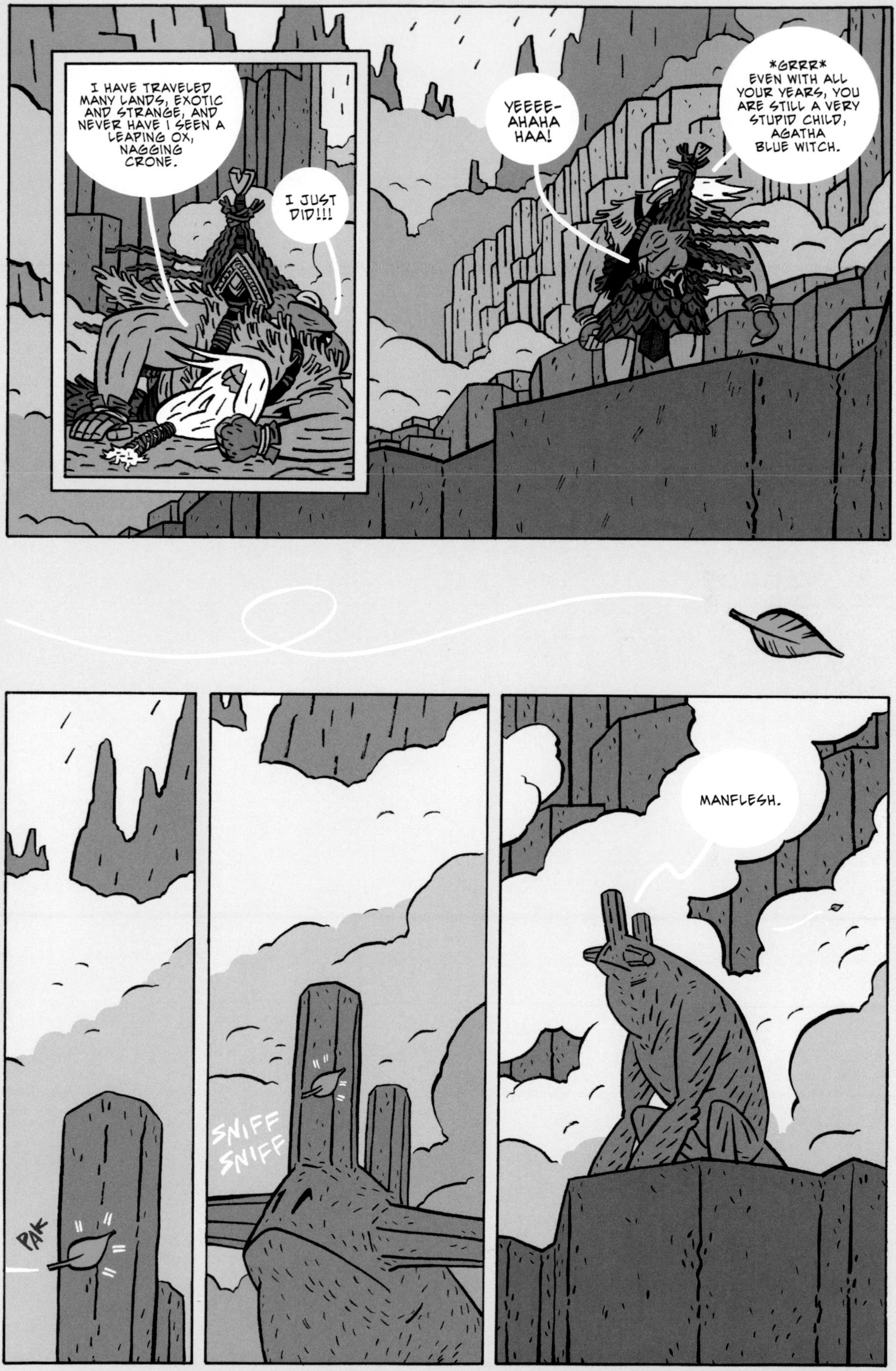
I HAVE TRAVELED MANY LANDS, EXOTIC AND STRANGE, AND NEVER HAVE I SEEN A LEAPING OX, NAGGING CRONE.
I JUST DID!!!
YEEEE-AHAHA HAA!
GRRR EVEN WITH ALL YOUR YEARS, YOU ARE STILL A VERY STUPID CHILD, AGATHA BLUE WITCH.
PAK
SNIFF SNIFF
MANFLESH.

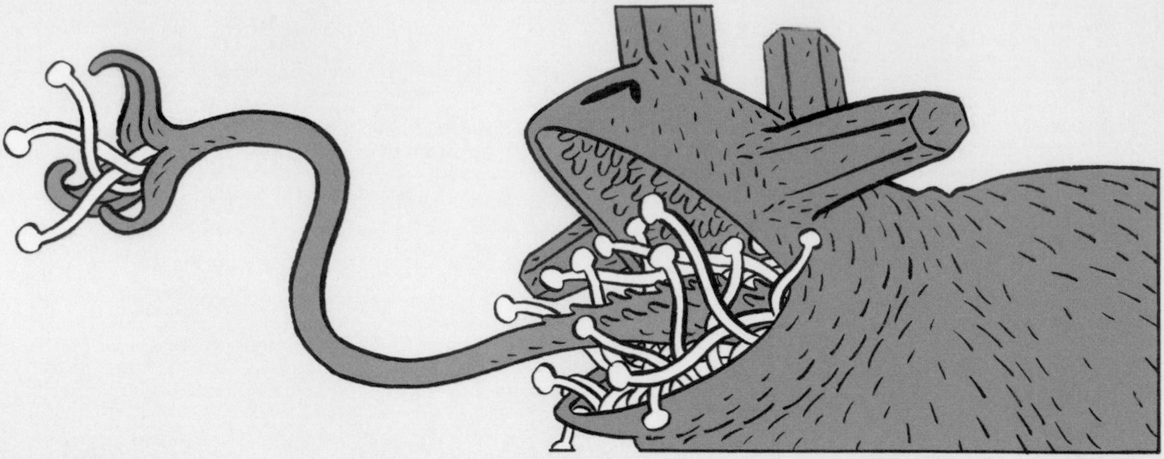

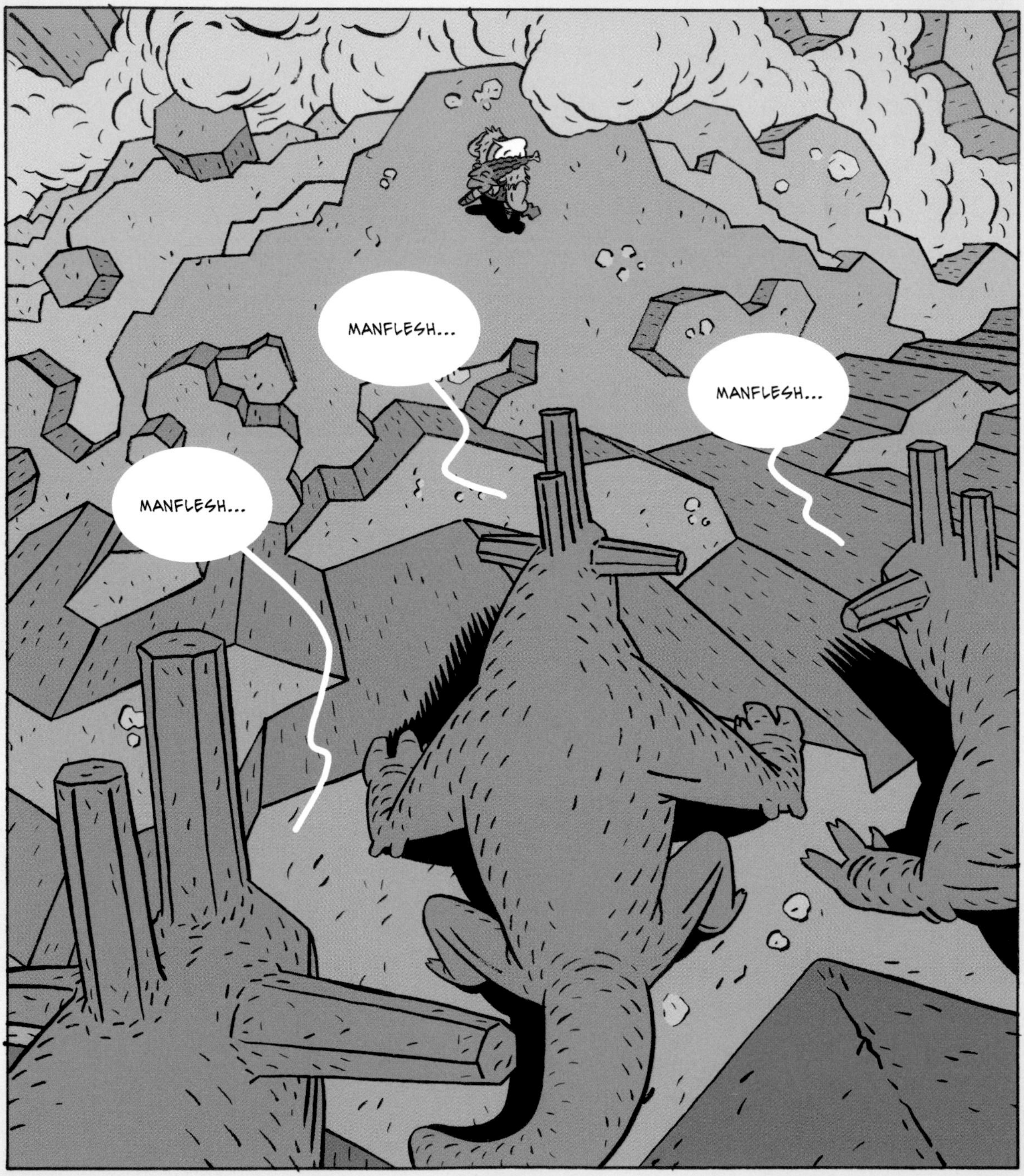
MANFLESH...
MANFLESH...
MANFLESH...

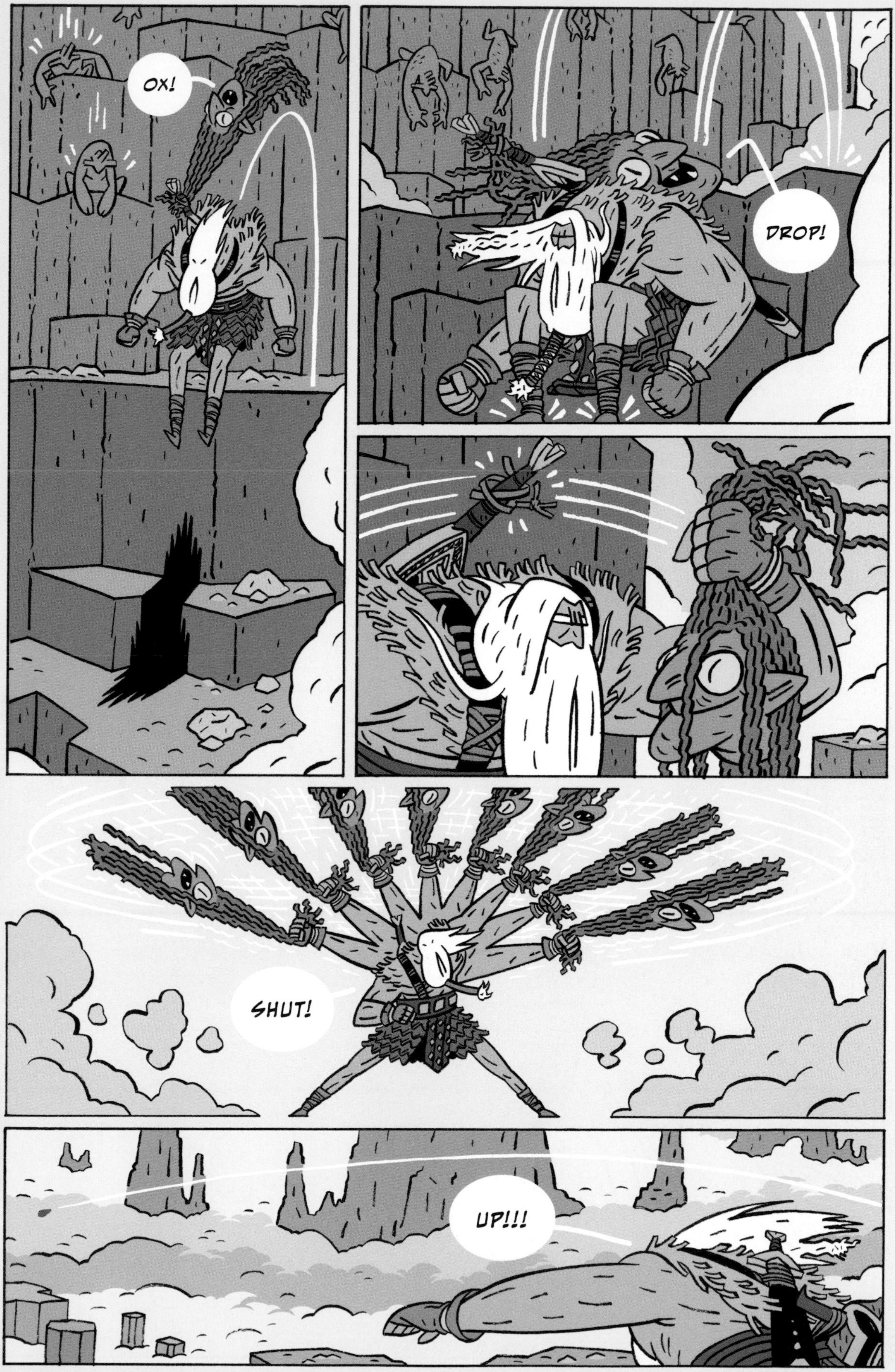
OX!
DROP!
SHUT!
UP!!!

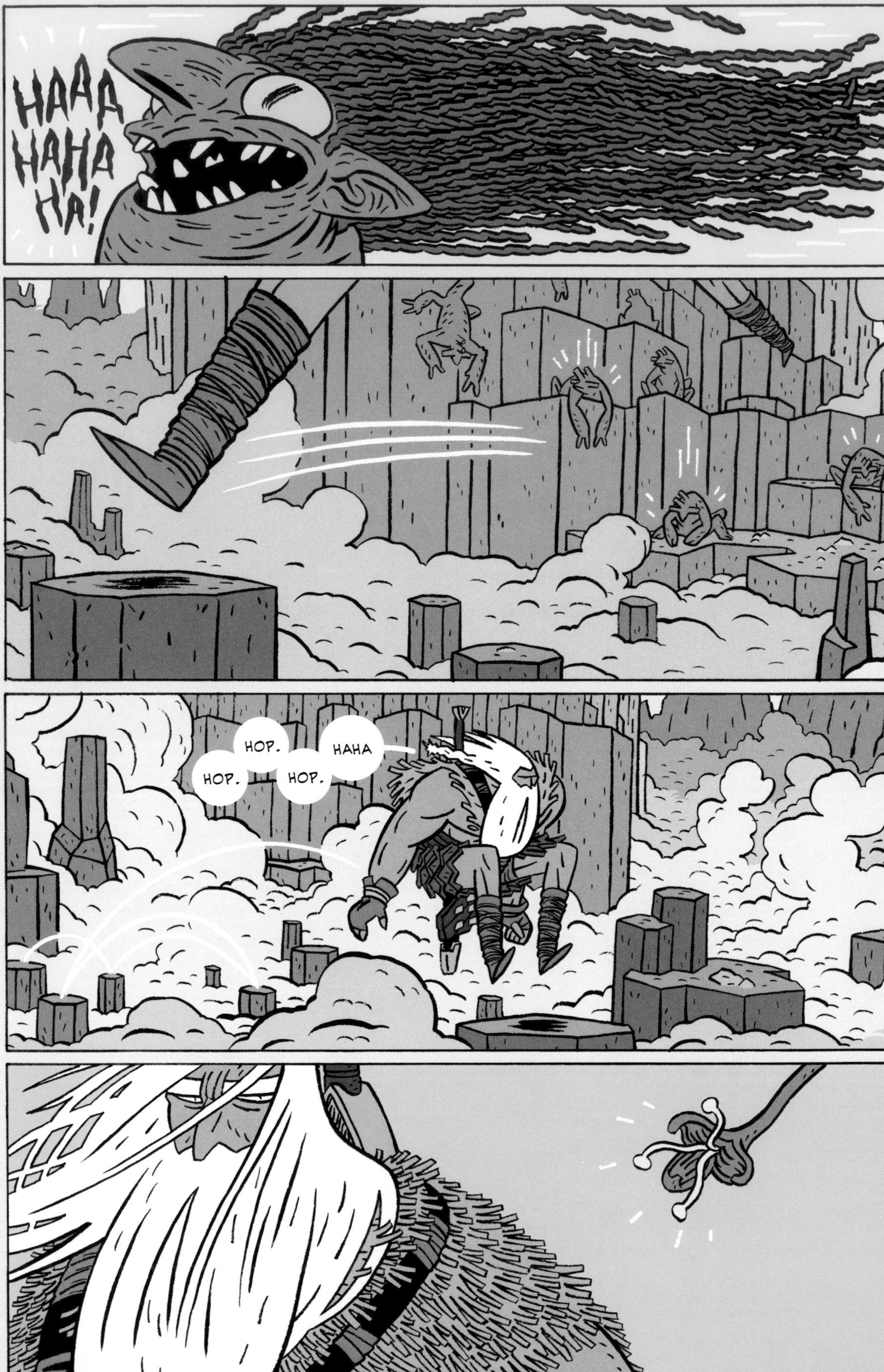
HAAA HAHA HA!
HOP.
HOP.
HOP.
HAHA

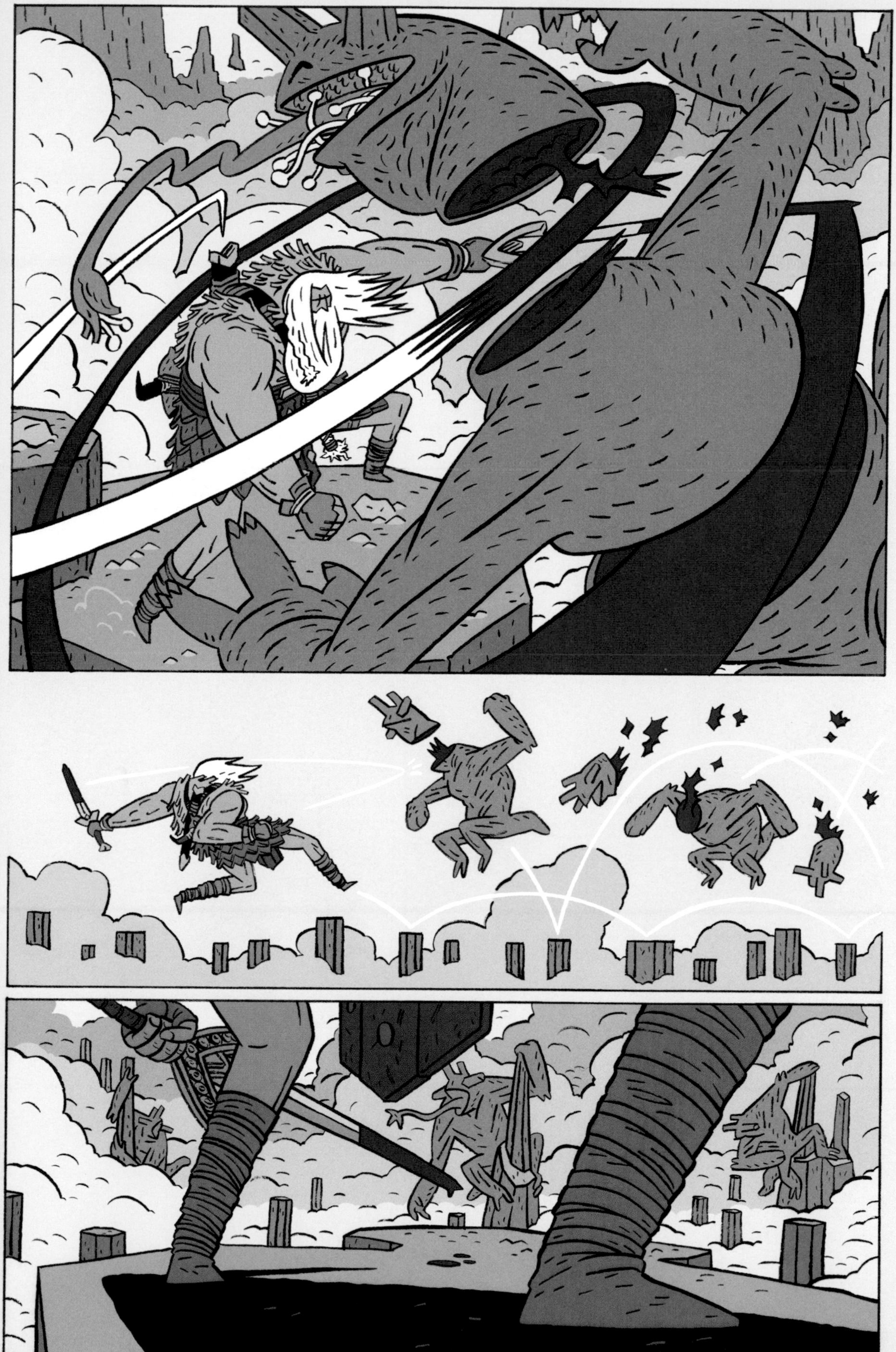

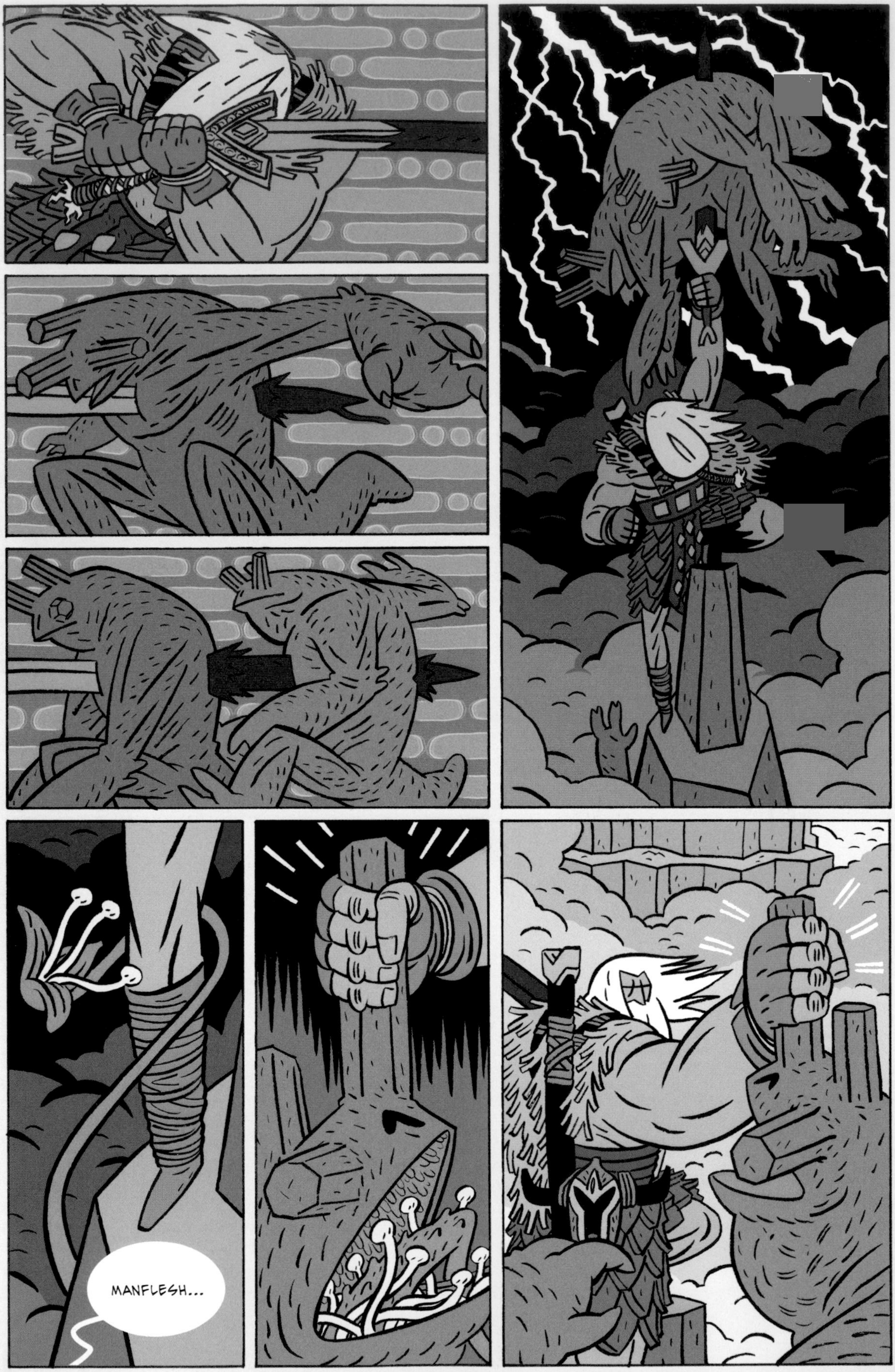
MANFLESH...

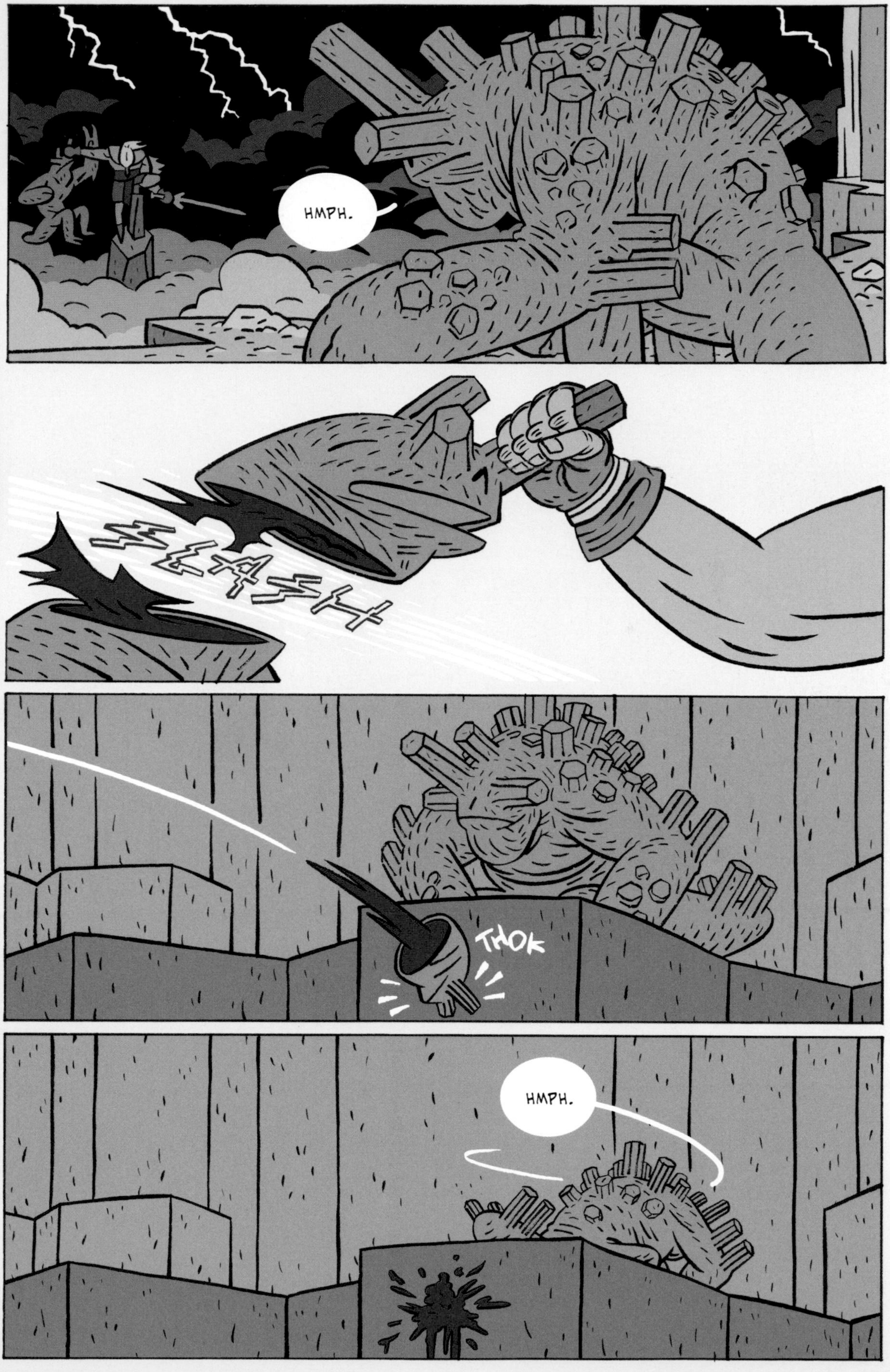
HMPH.
SLASH
THOK
HMPH.

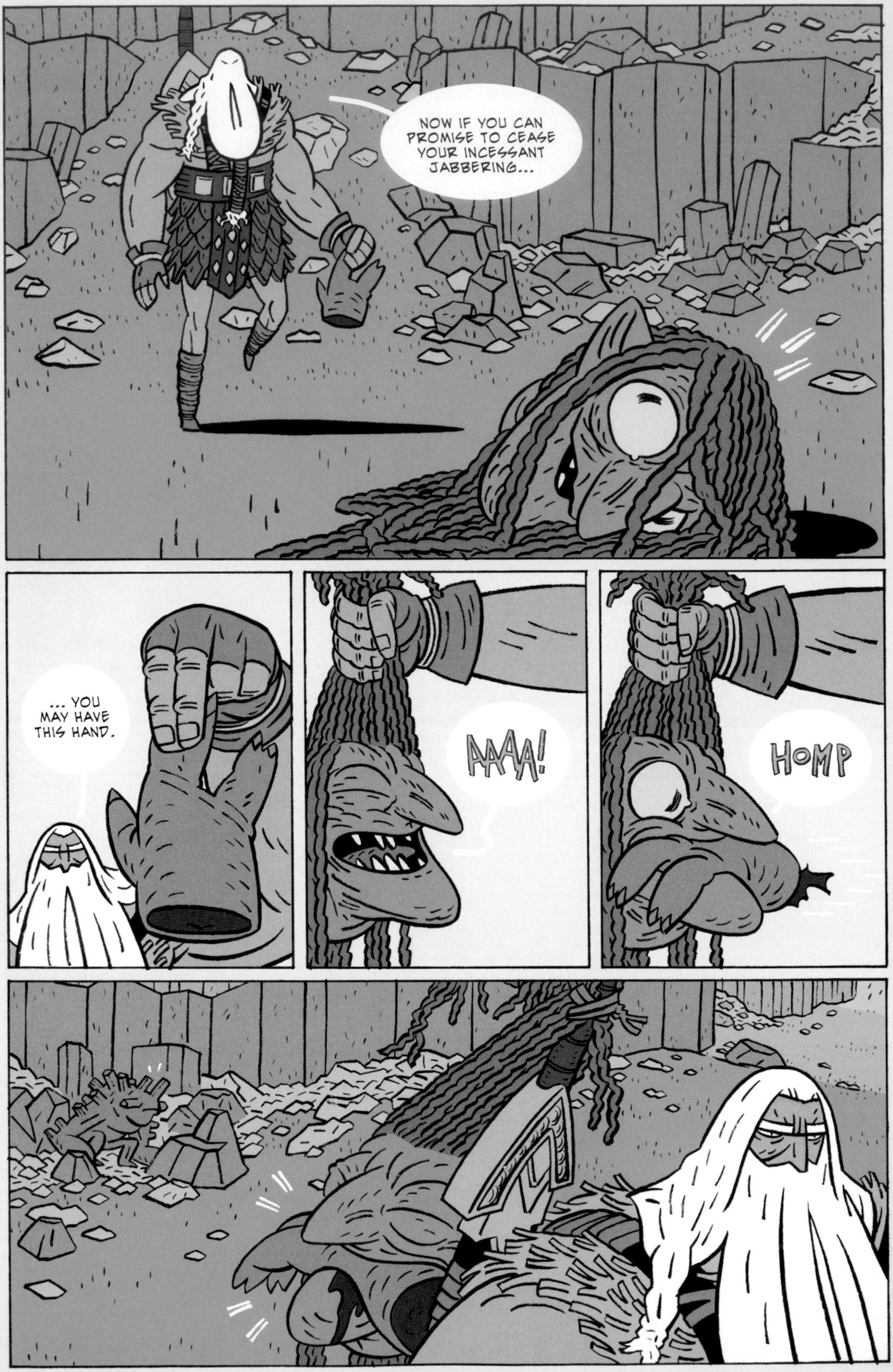
NOW IF YOU CAN PROMISE TO CEASE YOUR INCESSANT JABBERING...
... YOU MAY HAVE THIS HAND.
AAAA!
HOMP

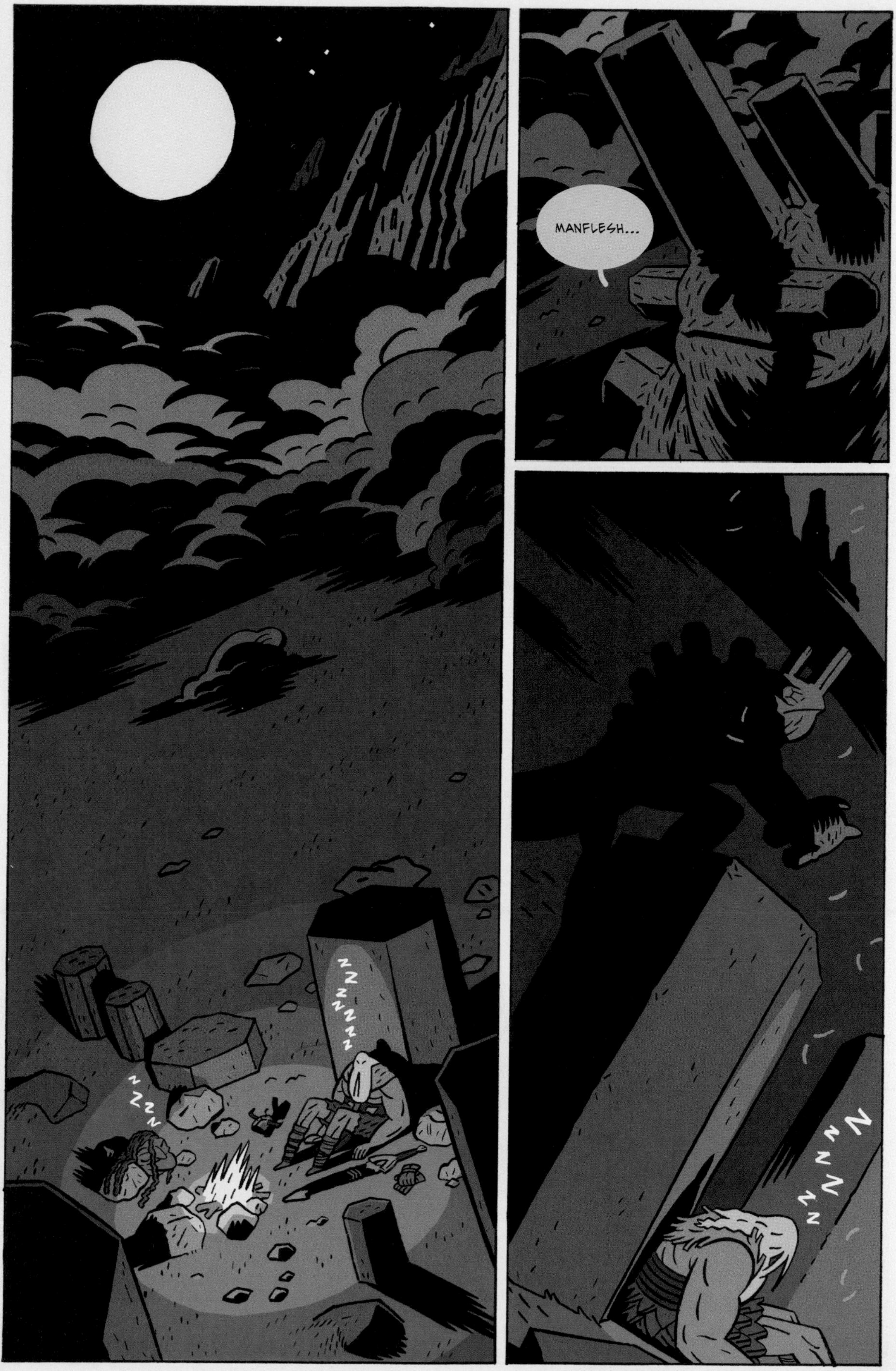
Z Z Z Z Z
Z Z Z
MANFLESH...
Z Z Z Z Z Z

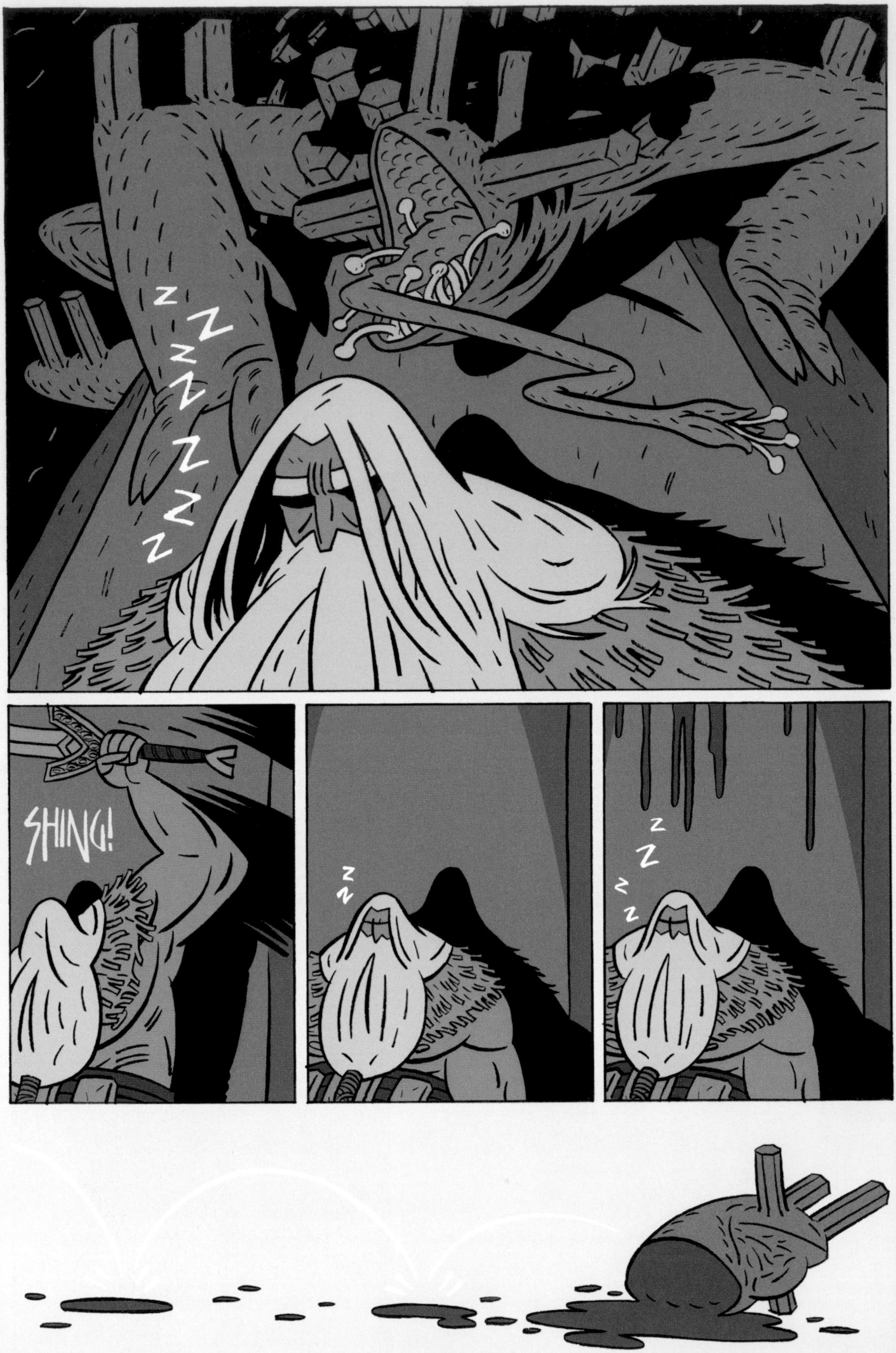
Z Z Z Z Z Z Z
SHING!
Z Z
Z Z Z Z

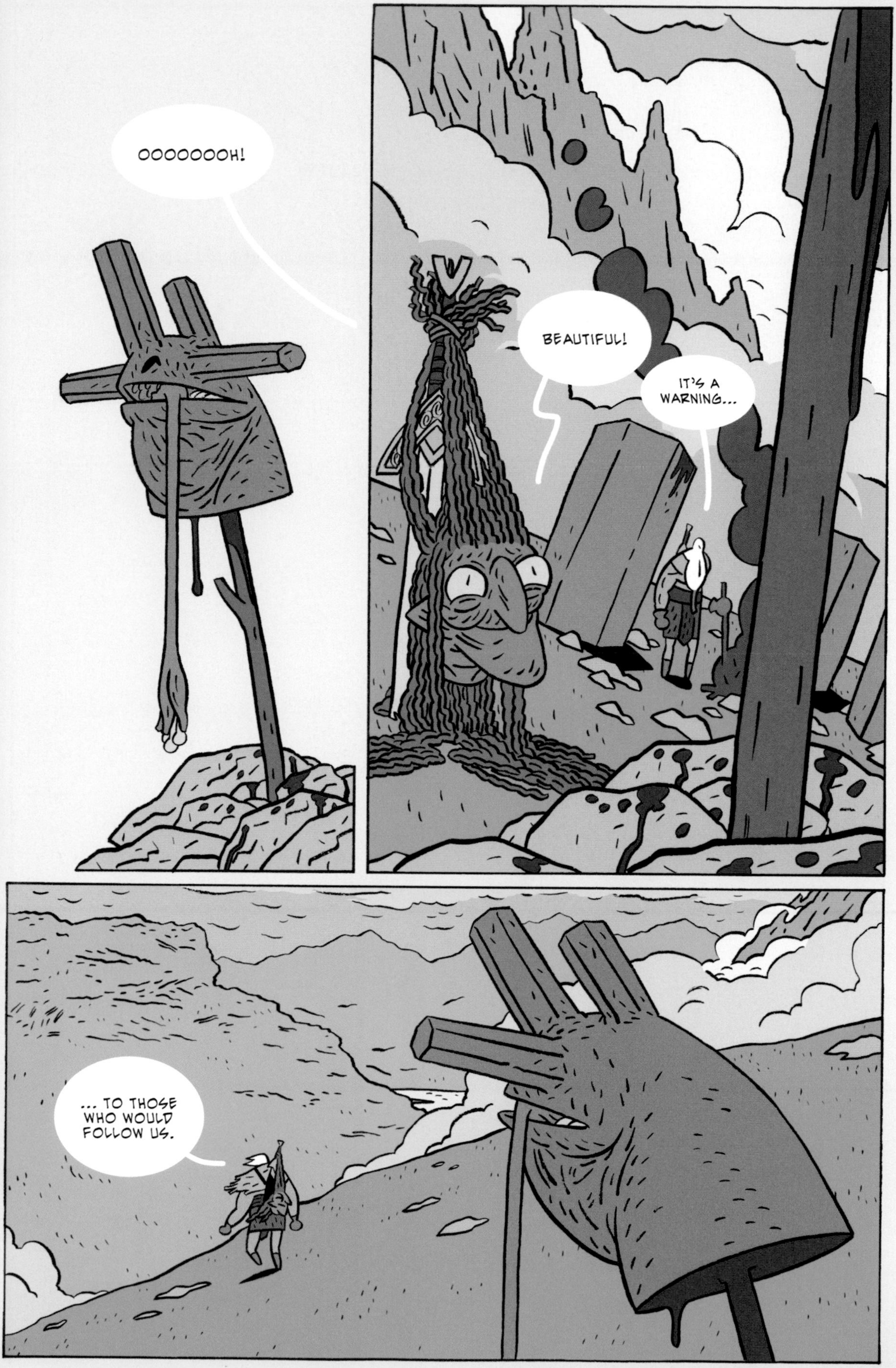
OOOOOOOH!
BEAUTIFUL!
IT'S A WARNING...
... TO THOSE WHO WOULD FOLLOW US.

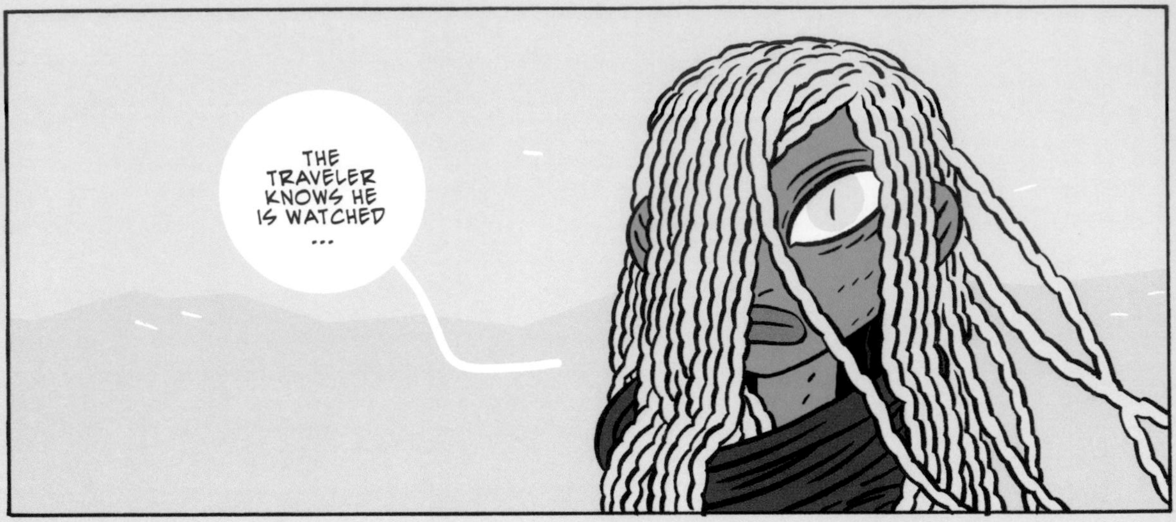
THE TRAVELER KNOWS HE IS WATCHED ...

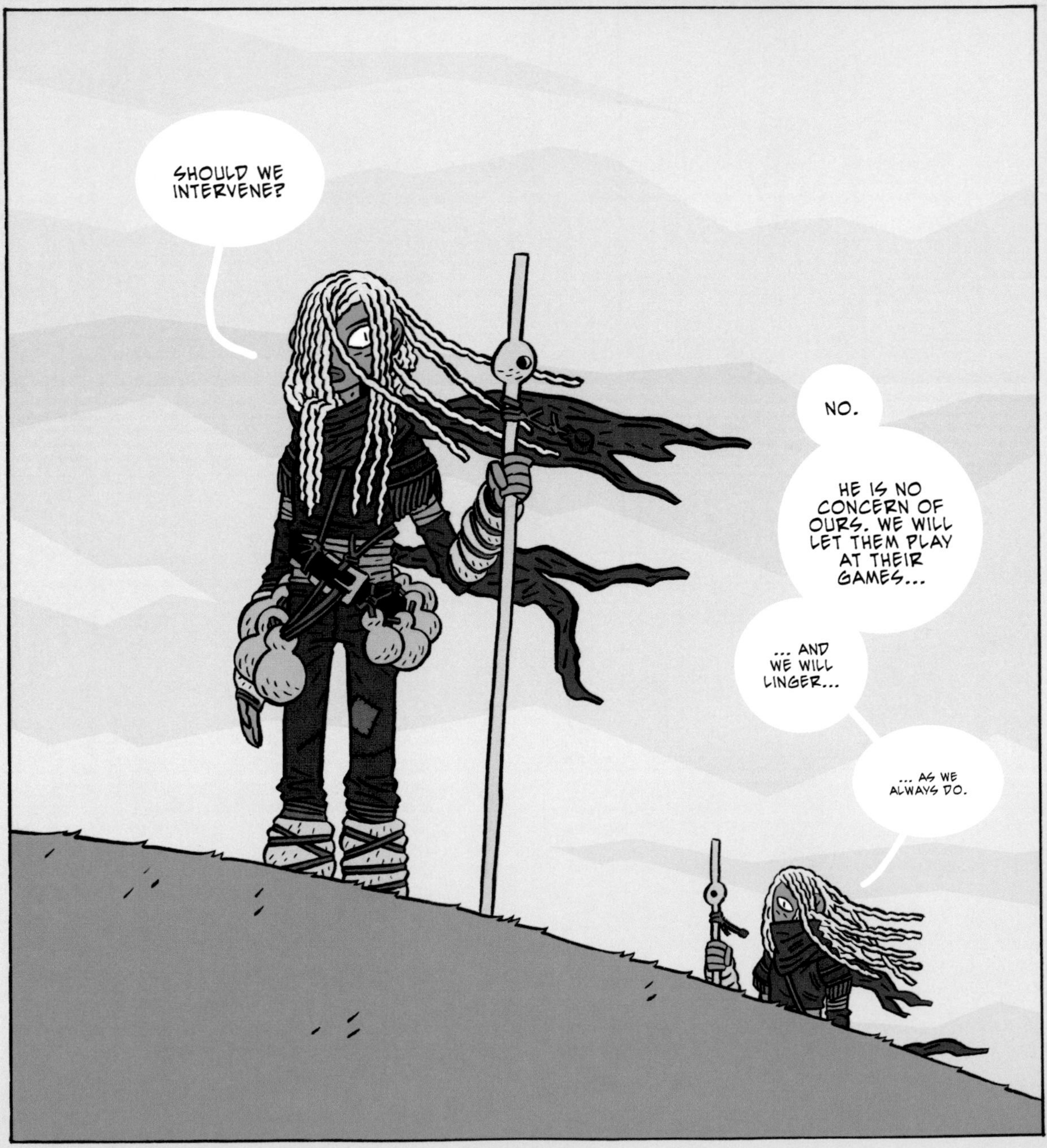
SHOULD WE INTERVENE?
NO.
HE IS NO CONCERN OF OURS. WE WILL LET THEM PLAY AT THEIR GAMES...
... AND WE WILL LINGER...
... AS WE ALWAYS DO.

CHAPTER FOUR

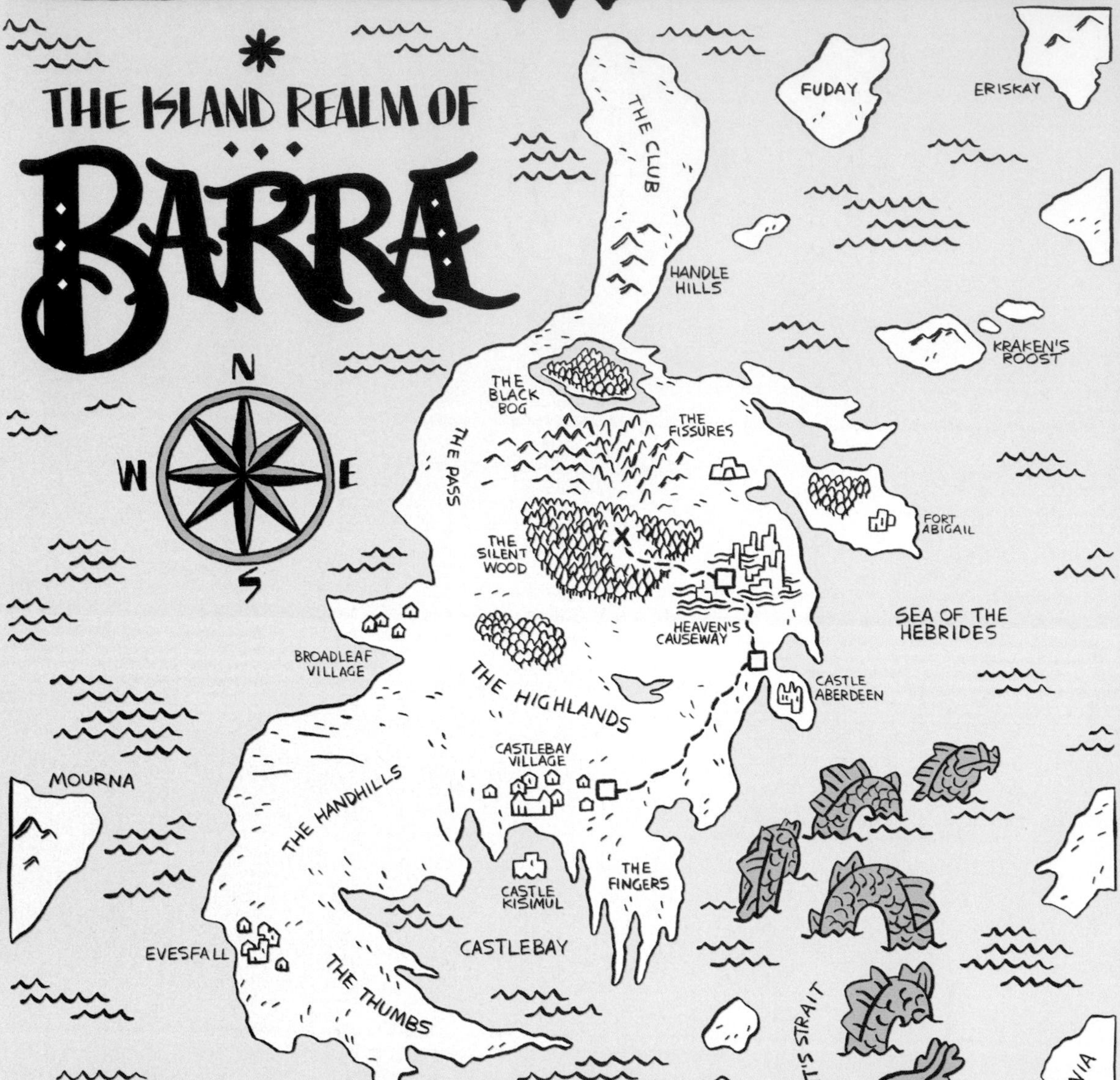
THE ISLAND REALM OF
BÄRRA
N
W
E
S
THE CLUB
HANDLE HILLS
FUDAY
ERISKAY
KRAKEN'S ROOST
THE BLACK BOG
THE FISSURES
THE PASS
FORT ABIGAIL
THE SILENT WOOD
HEAVEN'S CAUSEWAY
SEA OF THE HEBRIDES
BROADLEAF VILLAGE
THE HIGHLANDS
CASTLE ABERDEEN
CASTLEBAY VILLAGE
MOURNA
THE HANDHILLS
THE FINGERS
CASTLE KISIMUL
CASTLEBAY
EVESFALL
THE THUMBS
SERPENT'S STRAIT
ERLORNIA
ERSAY
VATERSAY
X=NORGAL & AGATHA

INTO THE SILENT WOOD

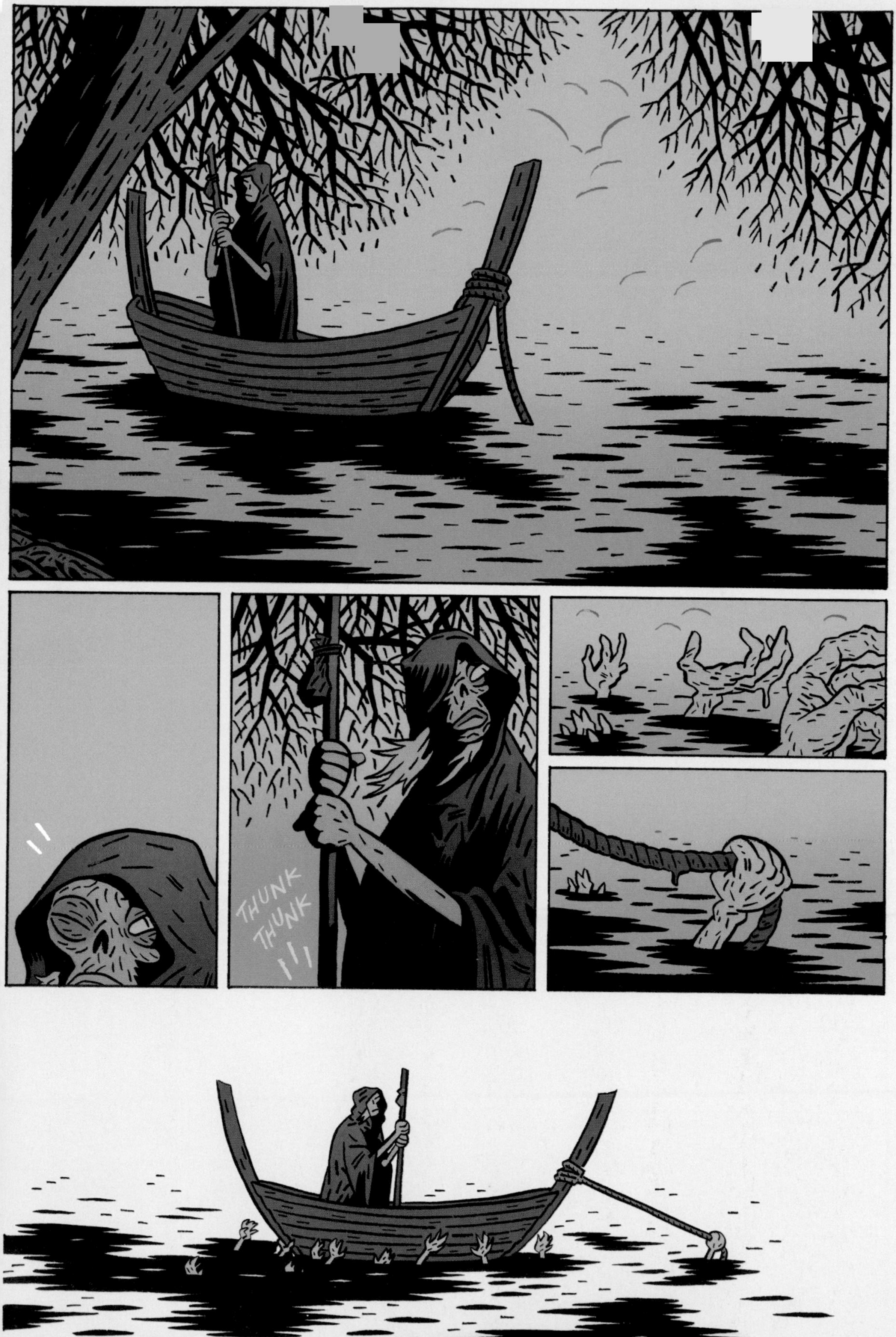
THUNK
THUNK

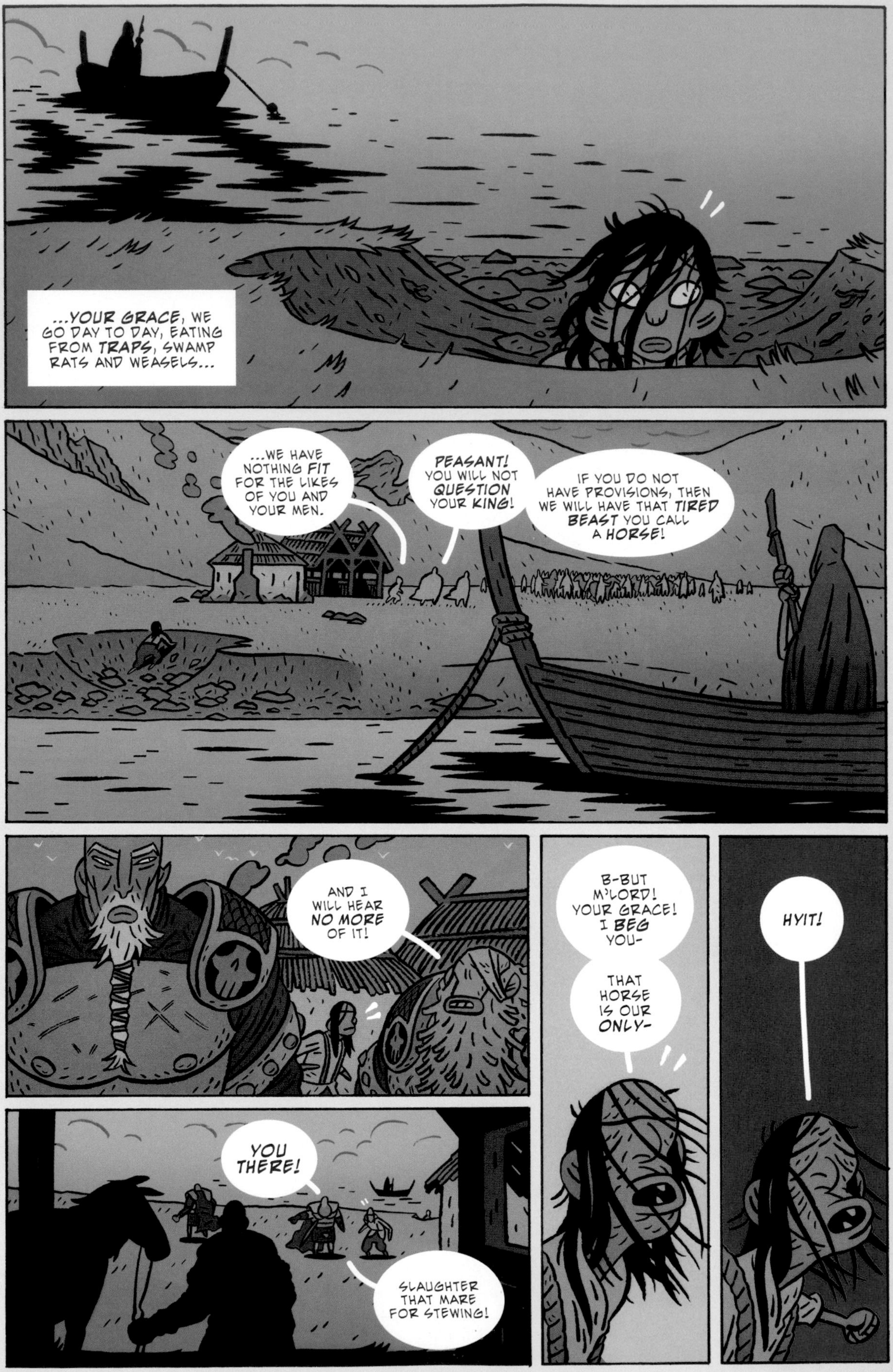
...YOUR GRACE, WE GO DAY TO DAY, EATING FROM TRAPS, SWAMP RATS AND WEASELS...
...WE HAVE NOTHING FIT FOR THE LIKES OF YOU AND YOUR MEN.
PEASANT! YOU WILL NOT QUESTION YOUR KING!
IF YOU DO NOT HAVE PROVISIONS, THEN WE WILL HAVE THAT TIRED BEAST YOU CALL A HORSE!
AND I WILL HEAR NO MORE OF IT!
YOU THERE!
SLAUGHTER THAT MARE FOR STEWING!
B-BUT M'LORD! YOUR GRACE! I BEG YOU-
THAT HORSE IS OUR ONLY-
HYIT!

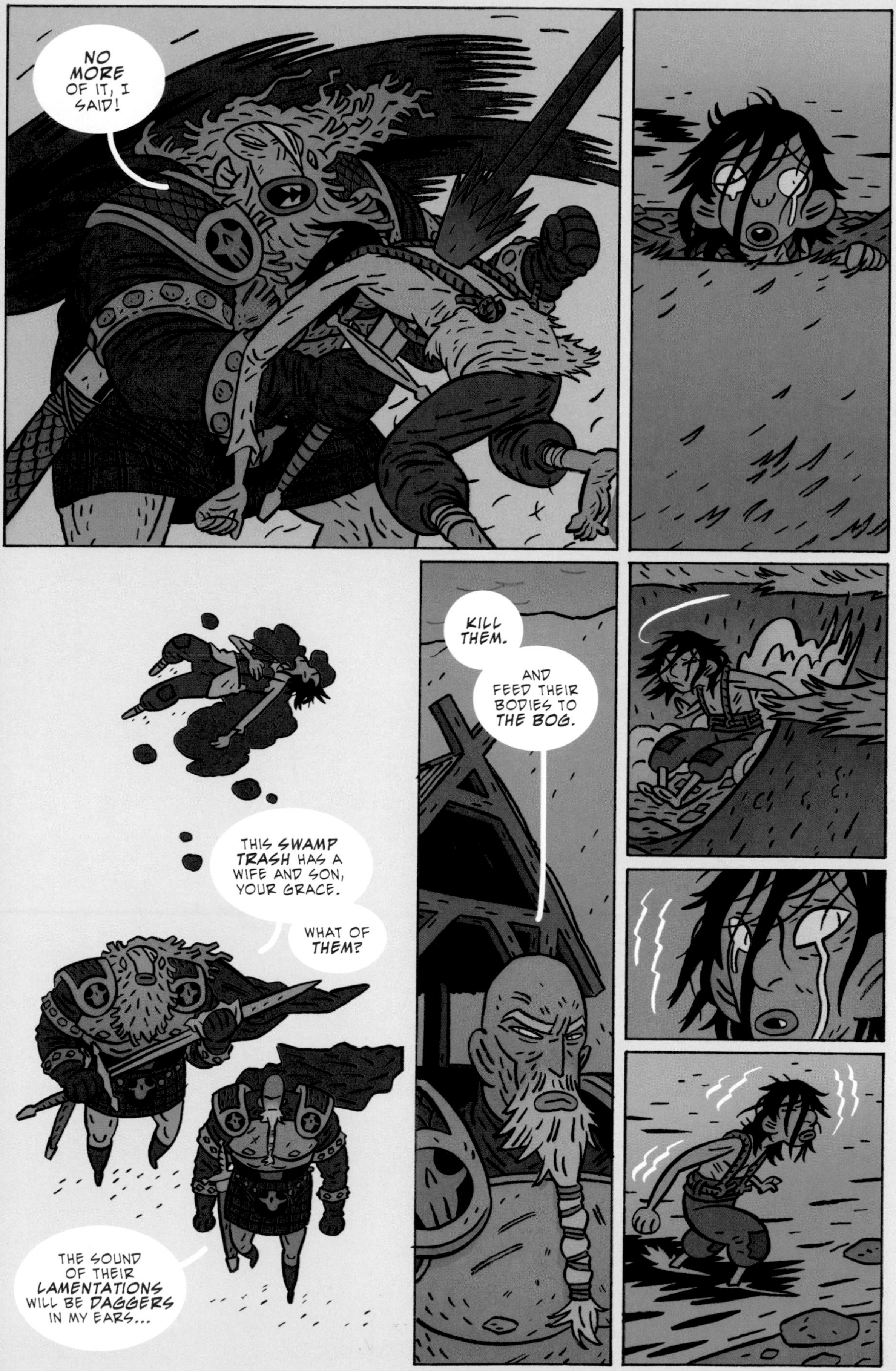
NO MORE OF IT, I SAID!
KILL THEM.
AND FEED THEIR BODIES TO THE BOG.
THIS SWAMP TRASH HAS A WIFE AND SON, YOUR GRACE.
WHAT OF THEM?
THE SOUND OF THEIR LAMENTATIONS WILL BE DAGGERS IN MY EARS...

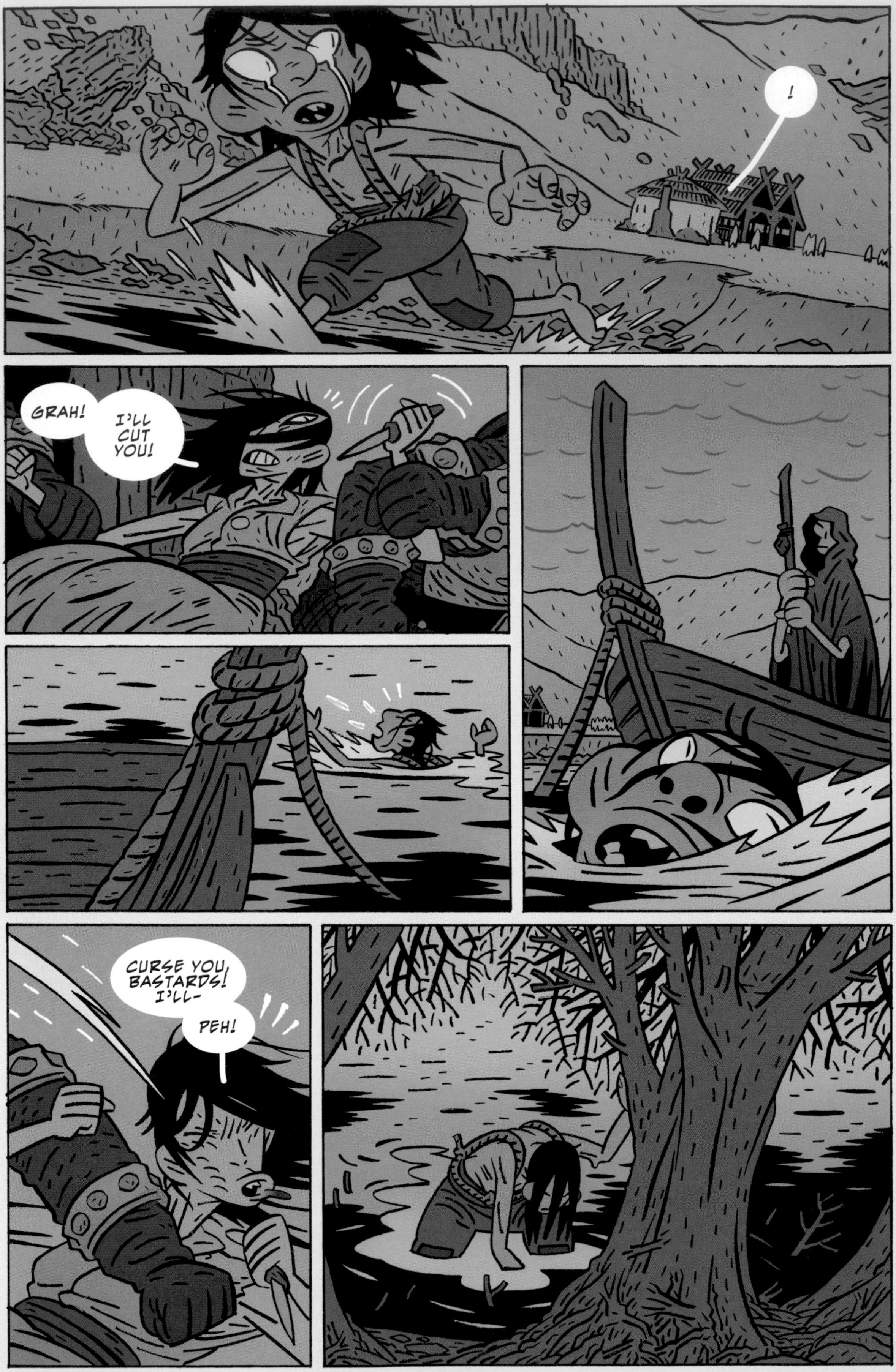
!
GRAH!
I'LL CUT YOU!
CURSE YOU, BASTARDS! I'LL-
PEH!

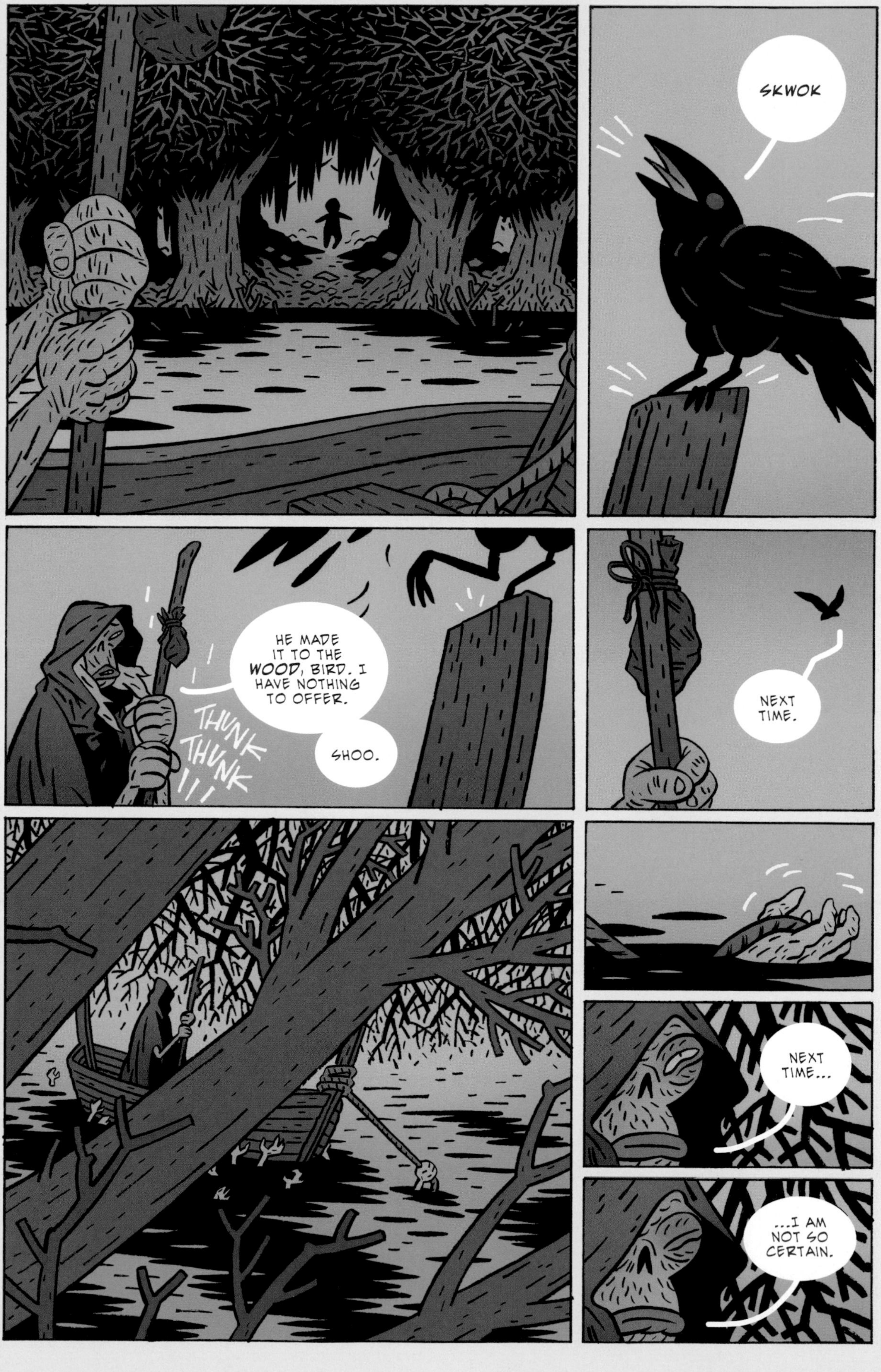
SKWOK
HE MADE IT TO THE WOOD, BIRD. I HAVE NOTHING TO OFFER.
SHOO.
THUNK THUNK !!!
NEXT TIME.
NEXT TIME...
...I AM NOT SO CERTAIN.

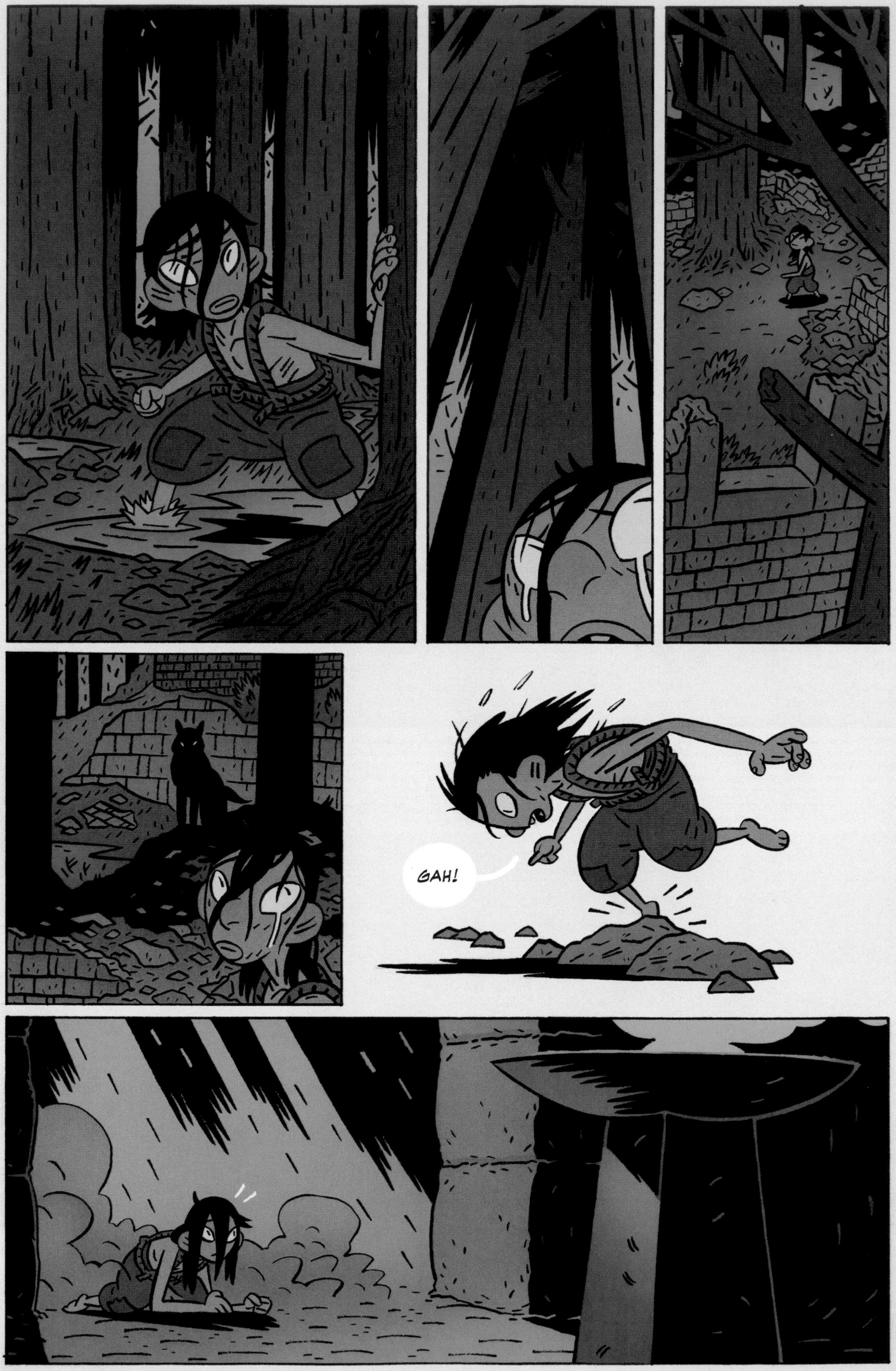
GAH!

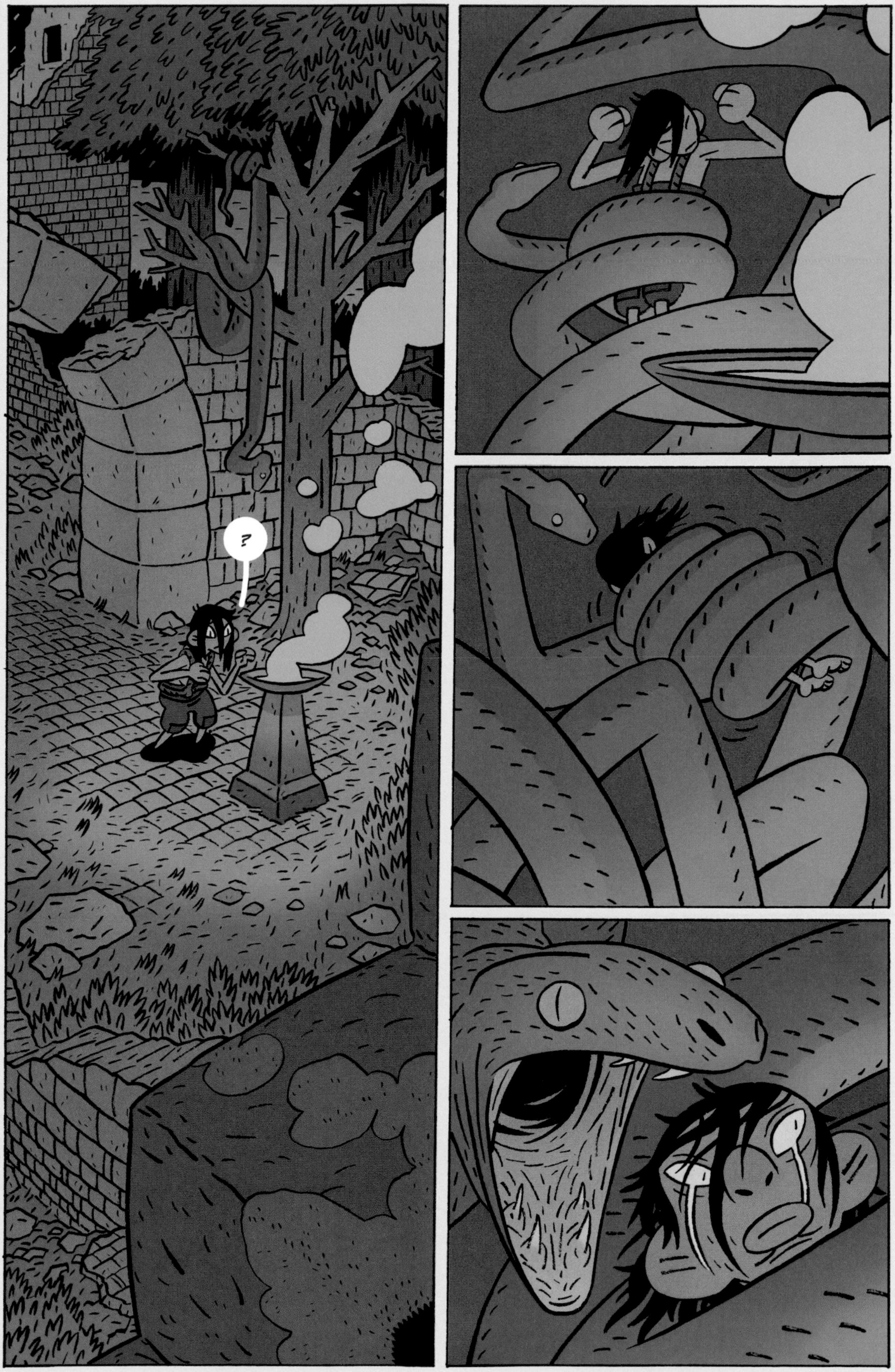
?

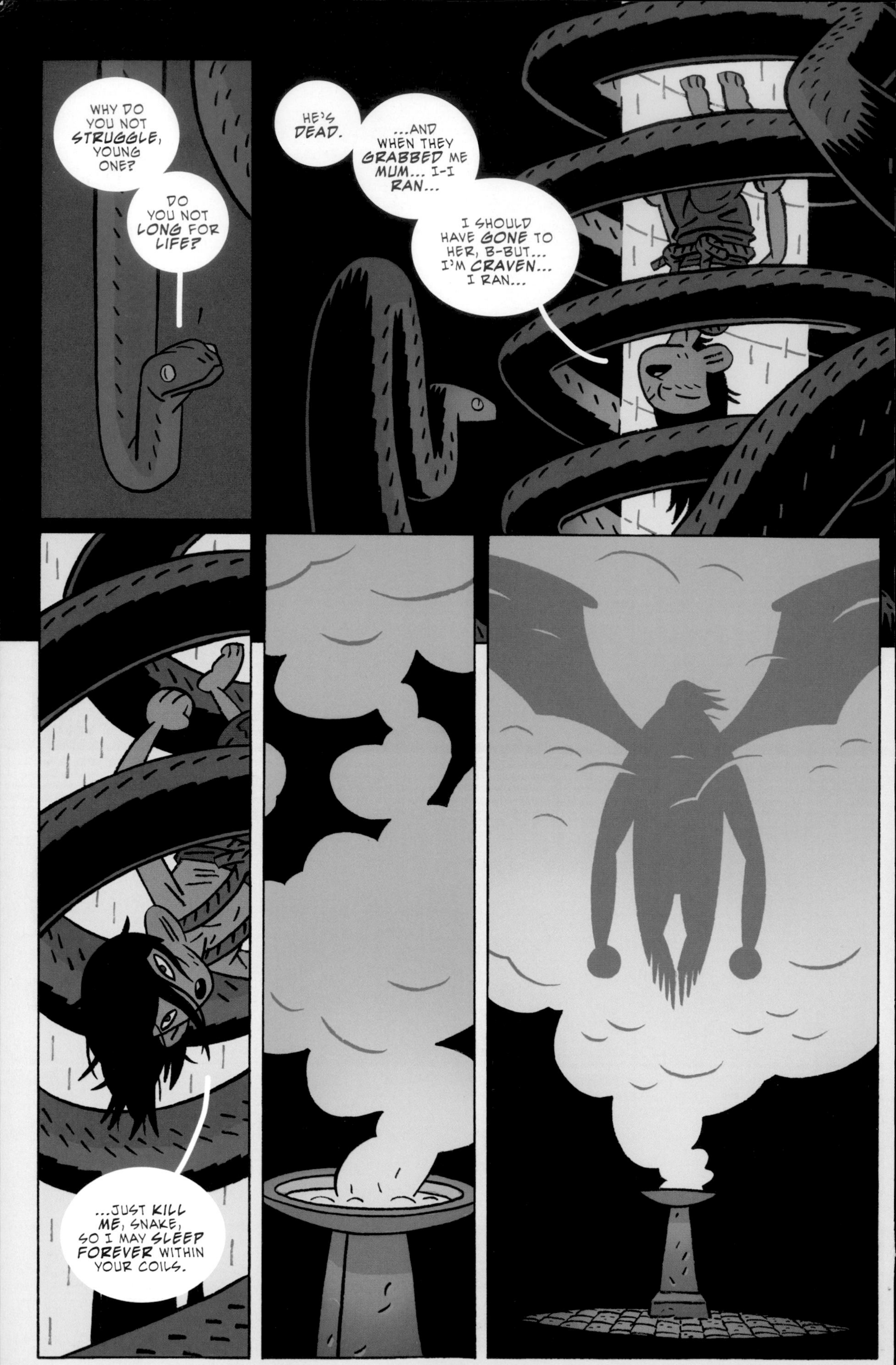
WHY DO YOU NOT STRUGGLE, YOUNG ONE?
DO YOU NOT LONG FOR LIFE?
HE'S DEAD.
...AND WHEN THEY GRABBED ME MUM... I-I RAN...
I SHOULD HAVE GONE TO HER, B-BUT... I'M CRAVEN... I RAN...
...JUST KILL ME, SNAKE, SO I MAY SLEEP FOREVER WITHIN YOUR COILS.

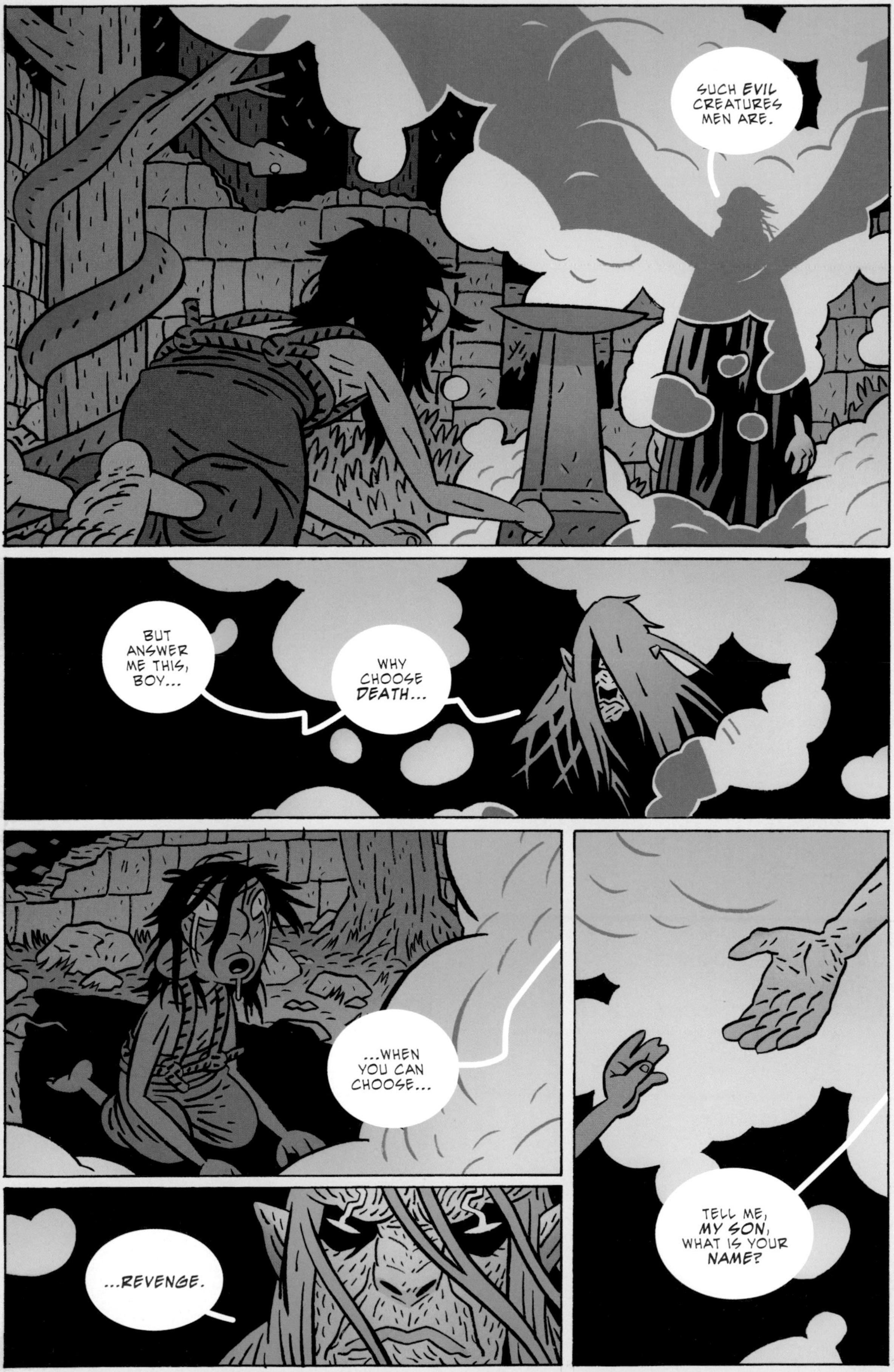

SUCH EVIL CREATURES MEN ARE.
BUT ANSWER ME THIS, BOY...
WHY CHOOSE DEATH...
...WHEN YOU CAN CHOOSE...
...REVENGE.
TELL ME, MY SON, WHAT IS YOUR NAME?

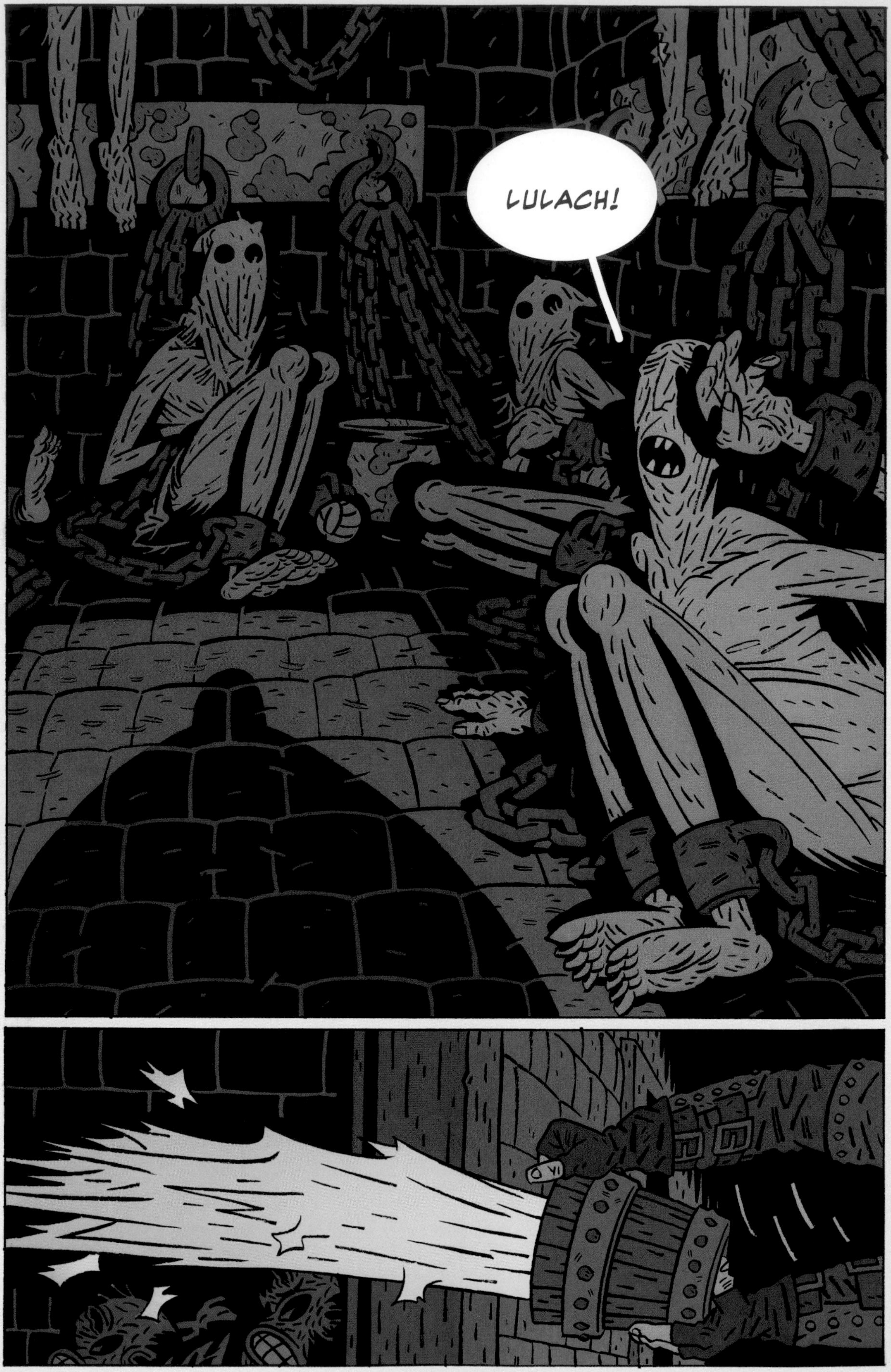
LULACH!

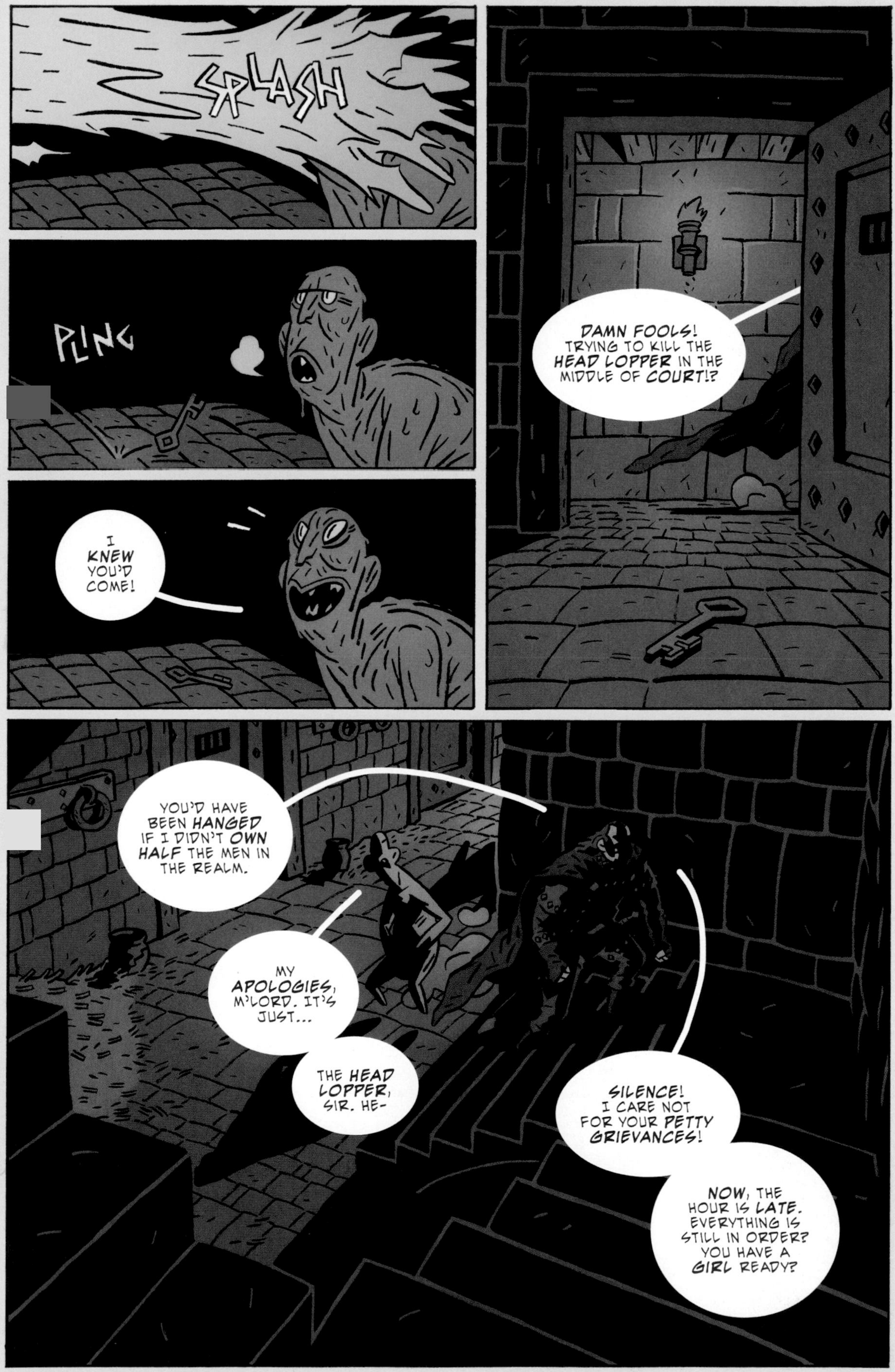
SPLASH
PLING
I KNEW YOU'D COME!
DAMN FOOLS! TRYING TO KILL THE HEAD LOPPER IN THE MIDDLE OF COURT!?
YOU'D HAVE BEEN HANGED IF I DIDN'T OWN HALF THE MEN IN THE REALM.
MY APOLOGIES, M'LORD. IT'S JUST...
THE HEAD LOPPER, SIR. HE-
SILENCE! I CARE NOT FOR YOUR PETTY GRIEVANCES!
NOW, THE HOUR IS LATE. EVERYTHING IS STILL IN ORDER? YOU HAVE A GIRL READY?

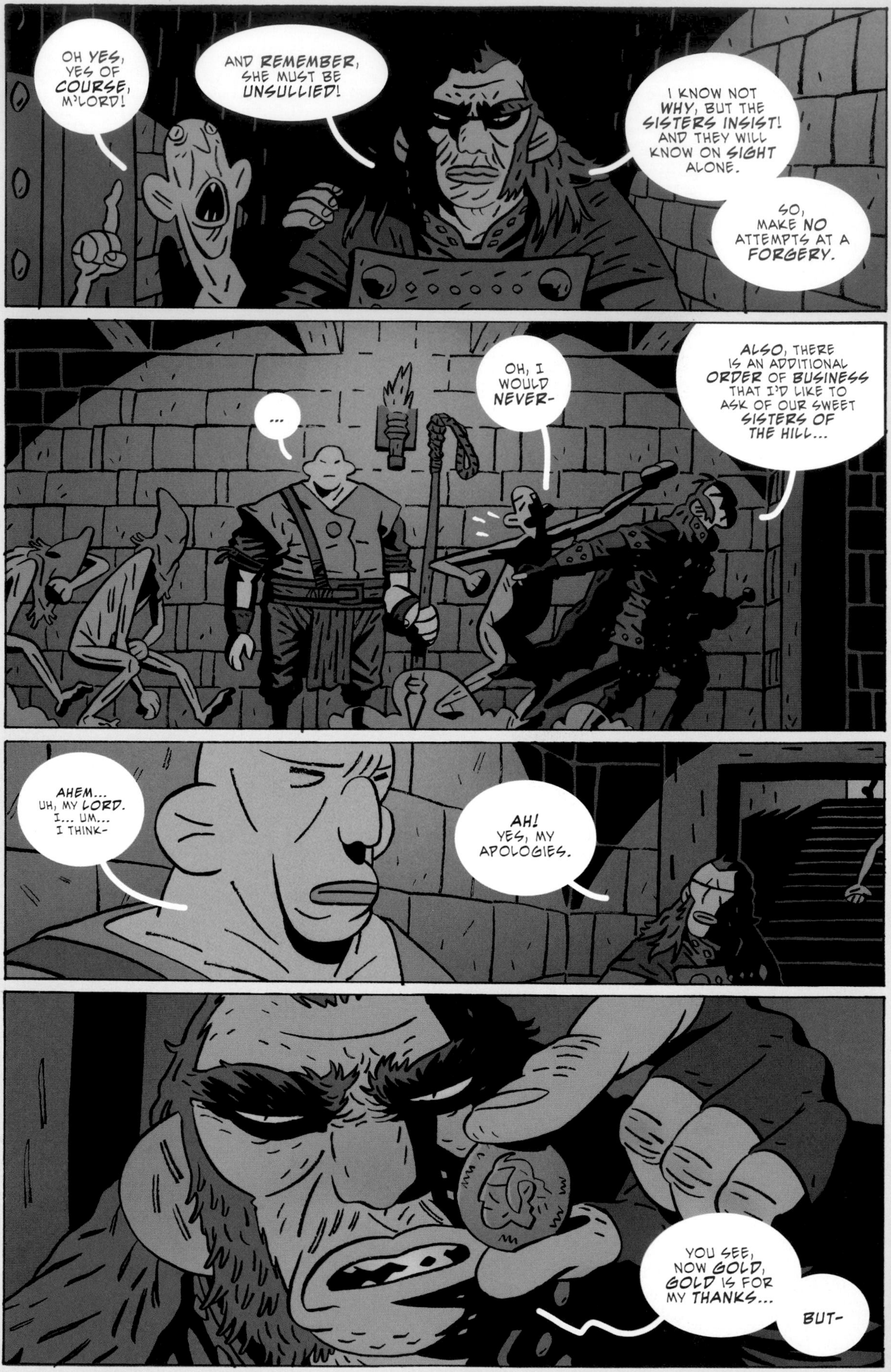
OH YES, YES OF COURSE, M'LORD!
AND REMEMBER, SHE MUST BE UNSULLIED!
I KNOW NOT WHY, BUT THE SISTERS INSIST! AND THEY WILL KNOW ON SIGHT ALONE.
SO, MAKE NO ATTEMPTS AT A FORGERY.
...
OH, I WOULD NEVER-
ALSO, THERE IS AN ADDITIONAL ORDER OF BUSINESS THAT I'D LIKE TO ASK OF OUR SWEET SISTERS OF THE HILL...
AHEM... UH, MY LORD. I... UM... I THINK-
AH! YES, MY APOLOGIES.
YOU SEE, NOW GOLD, GOLD IS FOR MY THANKS...
BUT-

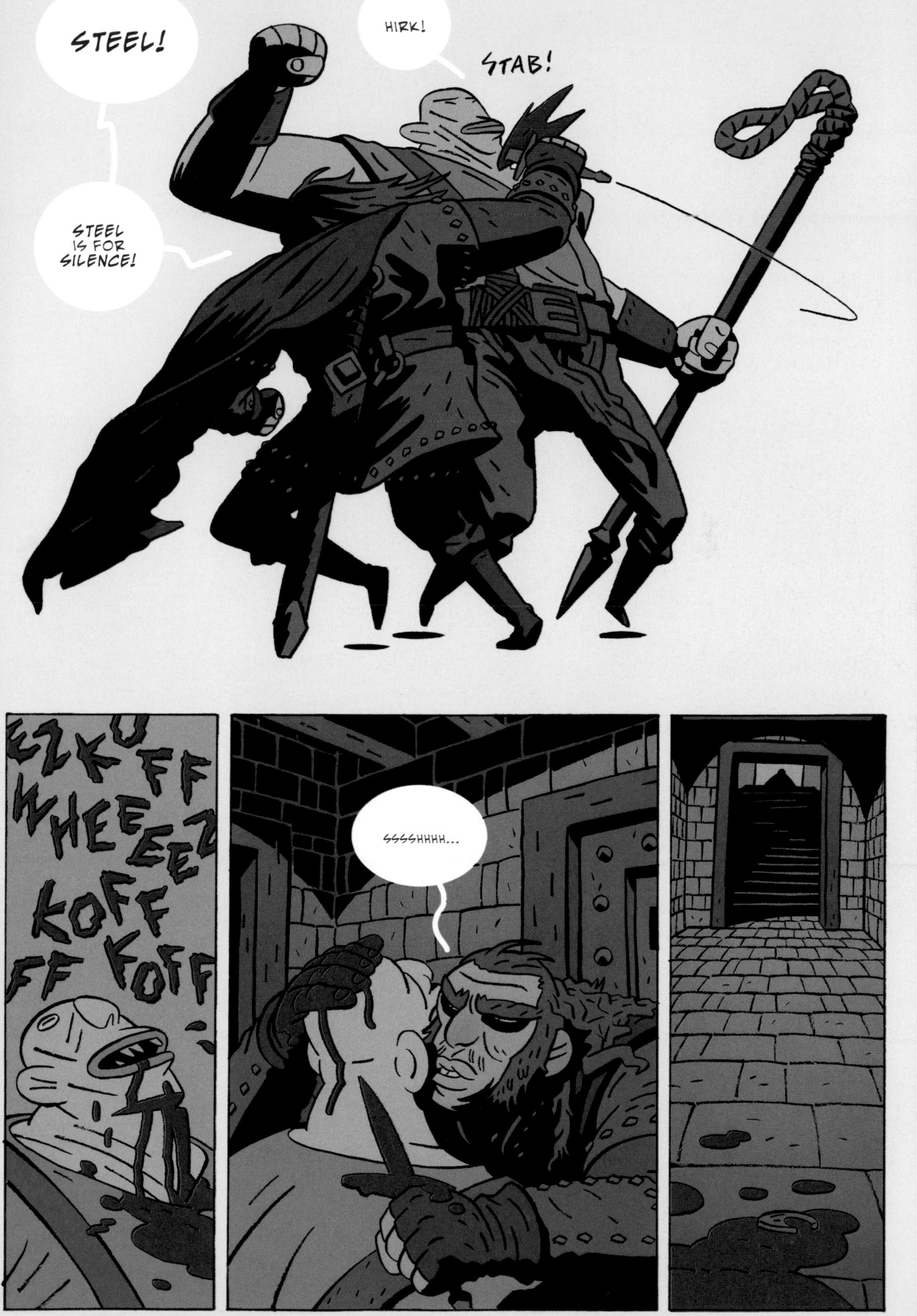
STEEL!
STEEL IS FOR SILENCE!
HIRK!
STAB!
WHEEEZ
KOFF
SSSSHHHH...

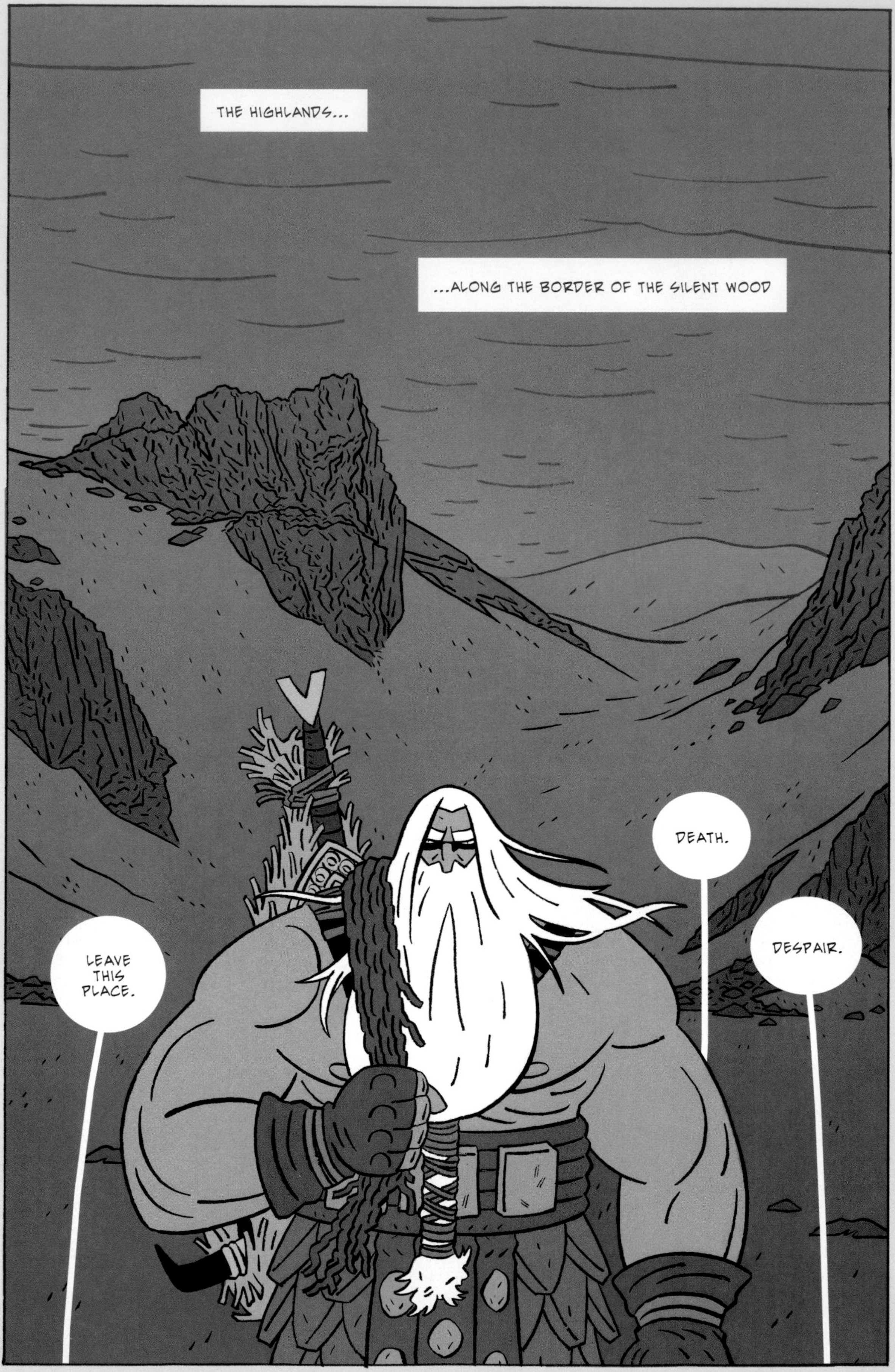
THE HIGHLANDS...
...ALONG THE BORDER OF THE SILENT WOOD
LEAVE THIS PLACE.
DEATH.
DESPAIR.

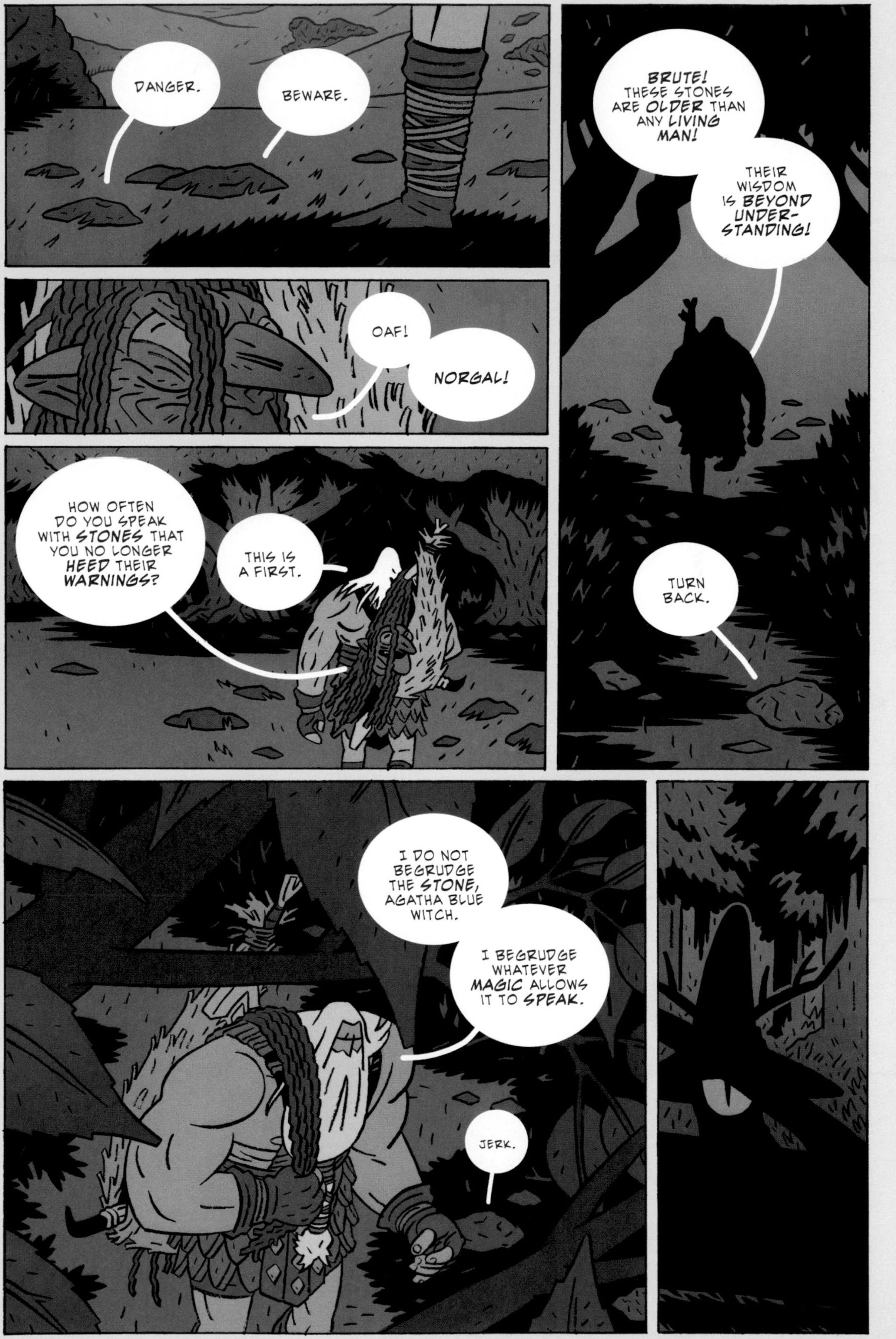
DANGER.
BEWARE.
BRUTE! THESE STONES ARE OLDER THAN ANY LIVING MAN!
THEIR WISDOM IS BEYOND UNDER-STANDING!
OAF!
NORGAL!
HOW OFTEN DO YOU SPEAK WITH STONES THAT YOU NO LONGER HEED THEIR WARNINGS?
THIS IS A FIRST.
TURN BACK.
I DO NOT BEGRUDGE THE STONE, AGATHA BLUE WITCH.
I BEGRUDGE WHATEVER MAGIC ALLOWS IT TO SPEAK.
JERK.

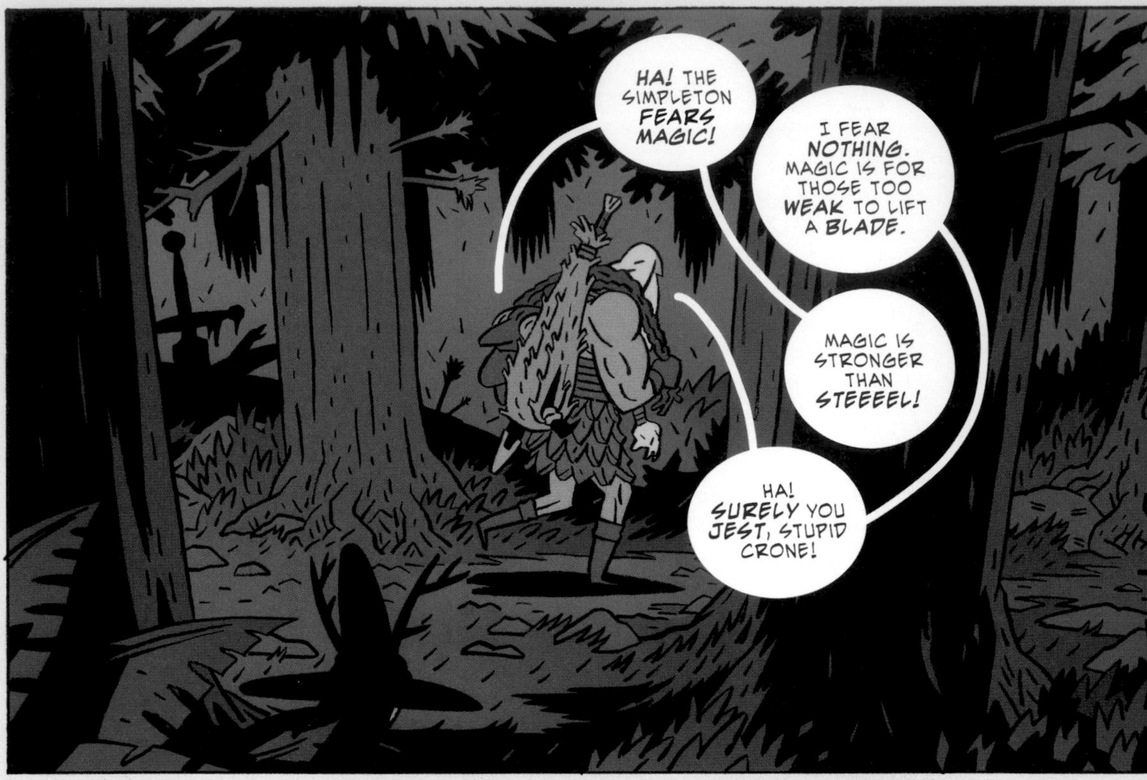
HA! THE SIMPLETON FEARS MAGIC!
I FEAR NOTHING. MAGIC IS FOR THOSE TOO WEAK TO LIFT A BLADE.
MAGIC IS STRONGER THAN STEEEEL!
HA! SURELY YOU JEST, STUPID CRONE!

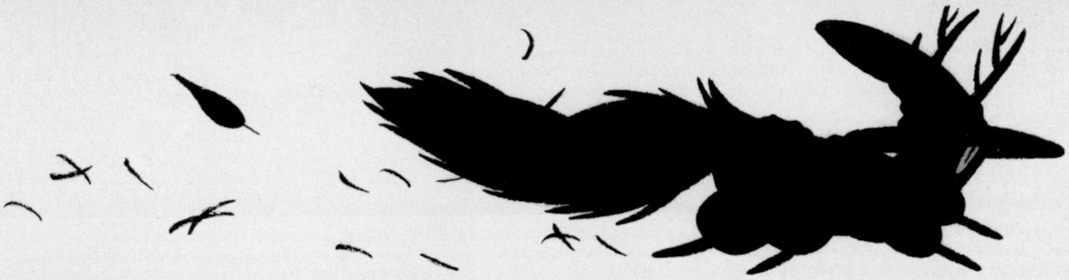

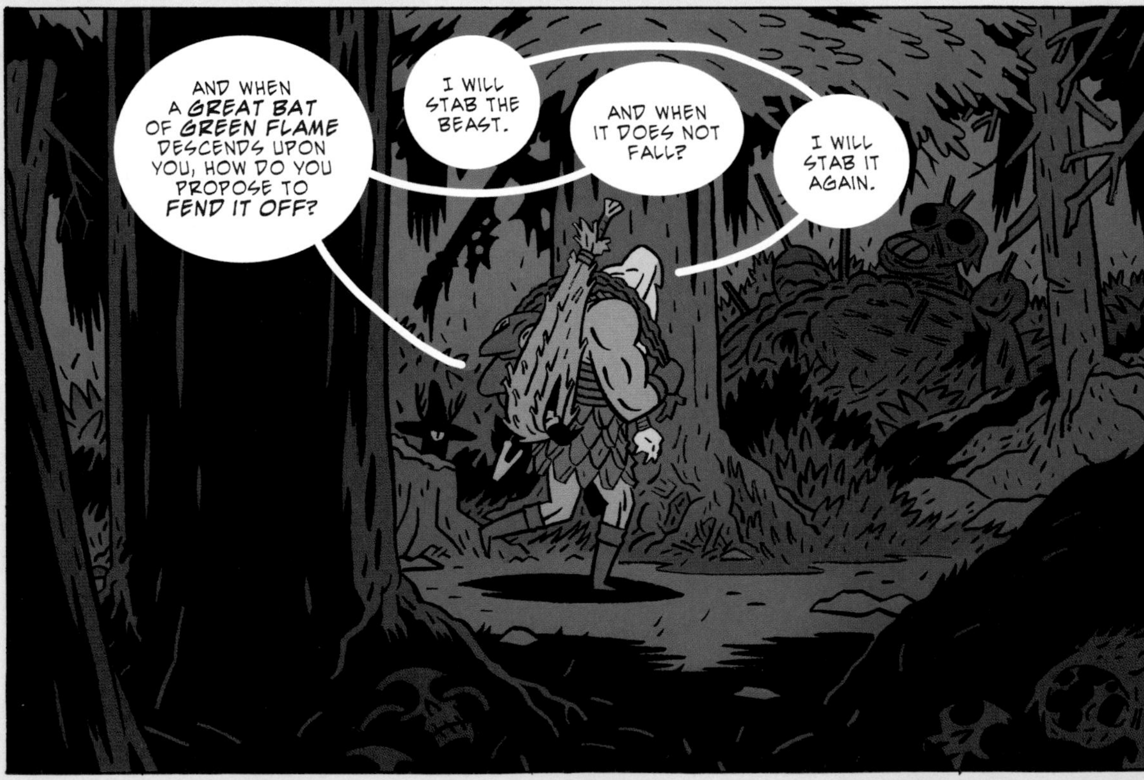
AND WHEN A GREAT BAT OF GREEN FLAME DESCENDS UPON YOU, HOW DO YOU PROPOSE TO FEND IT OFF?
I WILL STAB THE BEAST.
AND WHEN IT DOES NOT FALL?
I WILL STAB IT AGAIN.

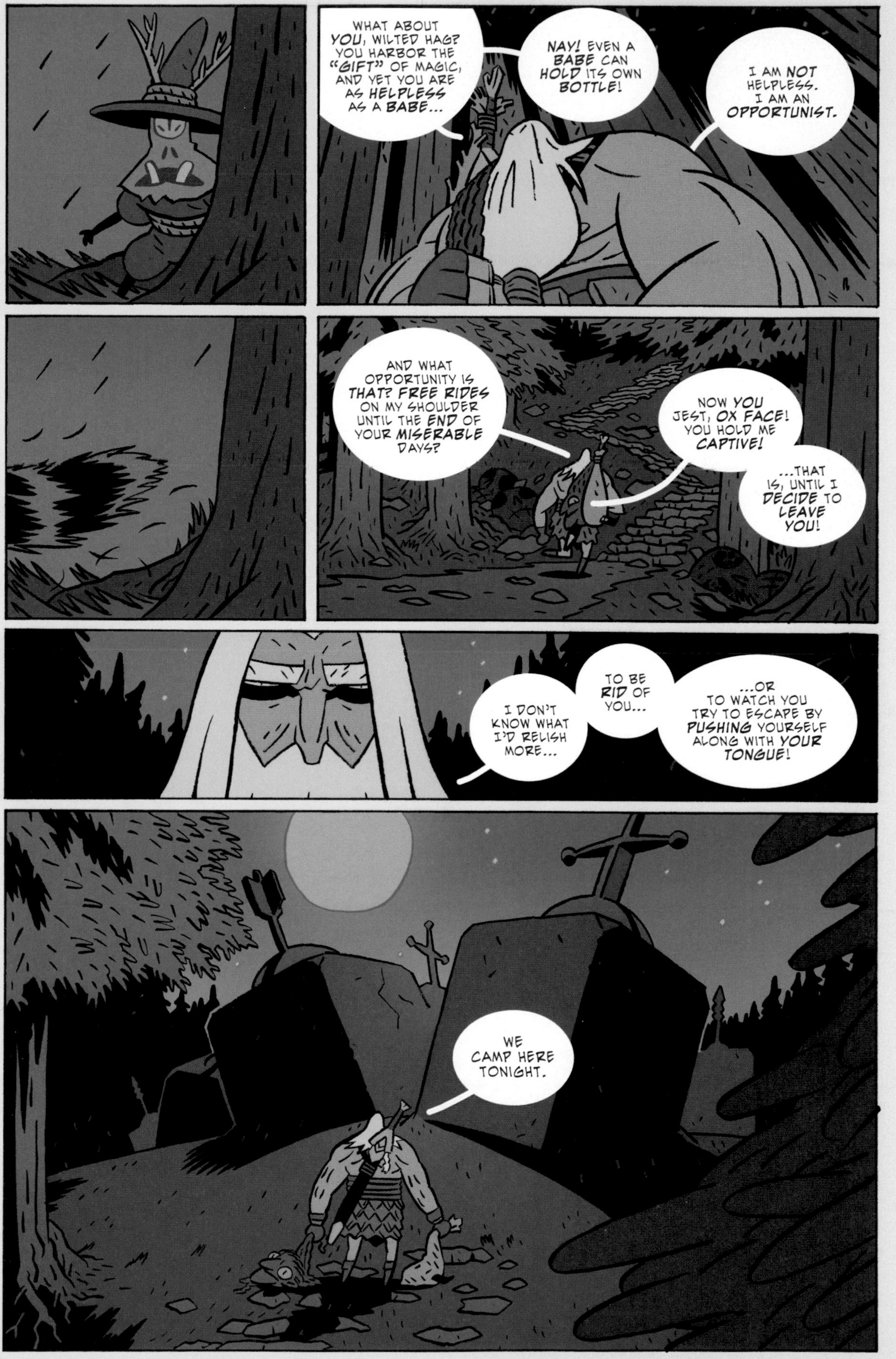

WHAT ABOUT YOU, WILTED HAG? YOU HARBOR THE "GIFT" OF MAGIC, AND YET YOU ARE AS HELPLESS AS A BABE...
NAY! EVEN A BABE CAN HOLD ITS OWN BOTTLE!
I AM NOT HELPLESS. I AM AN OPPORTUNIST.
AND WHAT OPPORTUNITY IS THAT? FREE RIDES ON MY SHOULDER UNTIL THE END OF YOUR MISERABLE DAYS?
NOW YOU JEST, OX FACE! YOU HOLD ME CAPTIVE!
...THAT IS, UNTIL I DECIDE TO LEAVE YOU!
I DON'T KNOW WHAT I'D RELISH MORE...
TO BE RID OF YOU...
...OR TO WATCH YOU TRY TO ESCAPE BY PUSHING YOURSELF ALONG WITH YOUR TONGUE!
WE CAMP HERE TONIGHT.

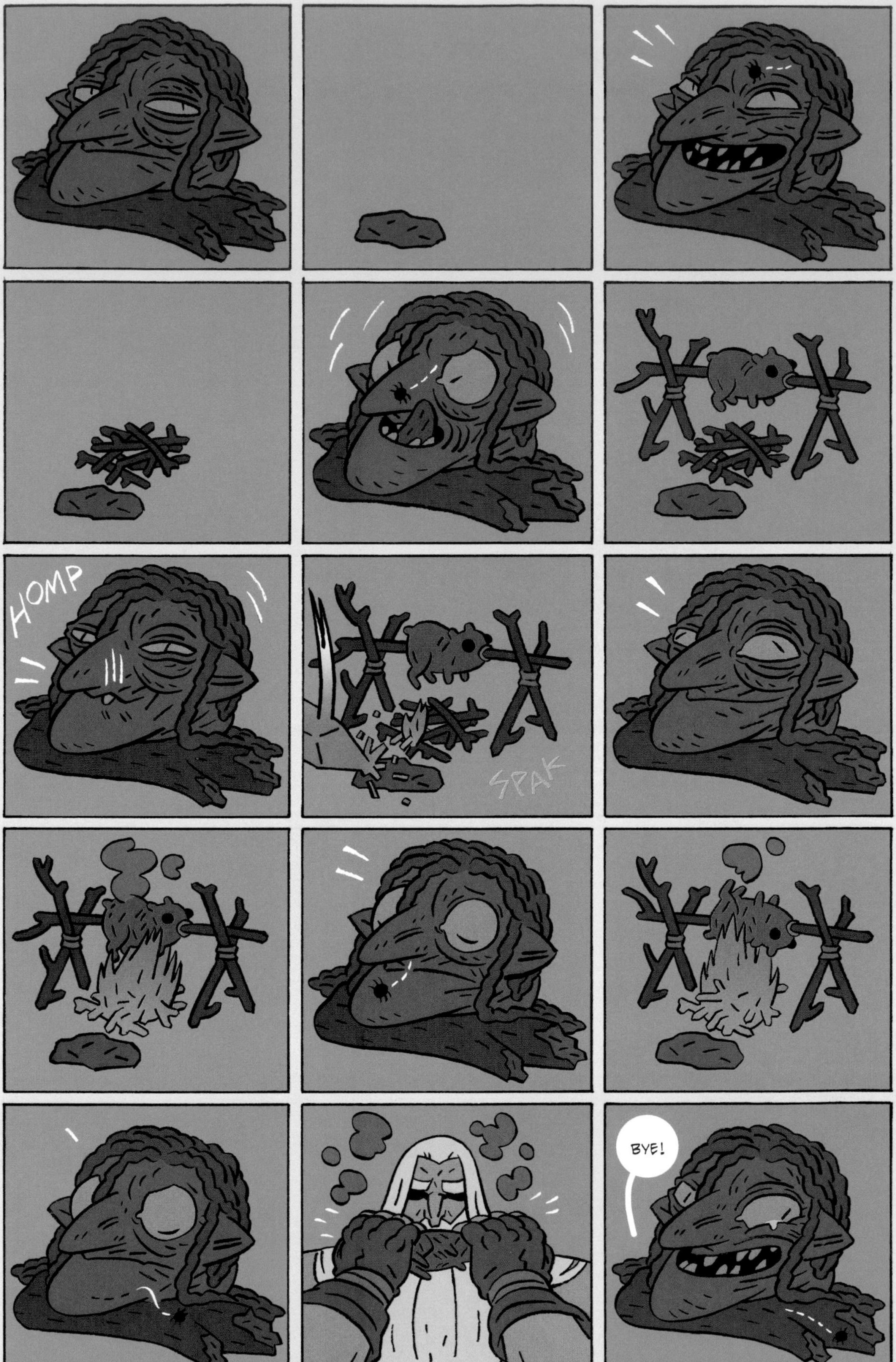
HOMP
SPAK
BYE!

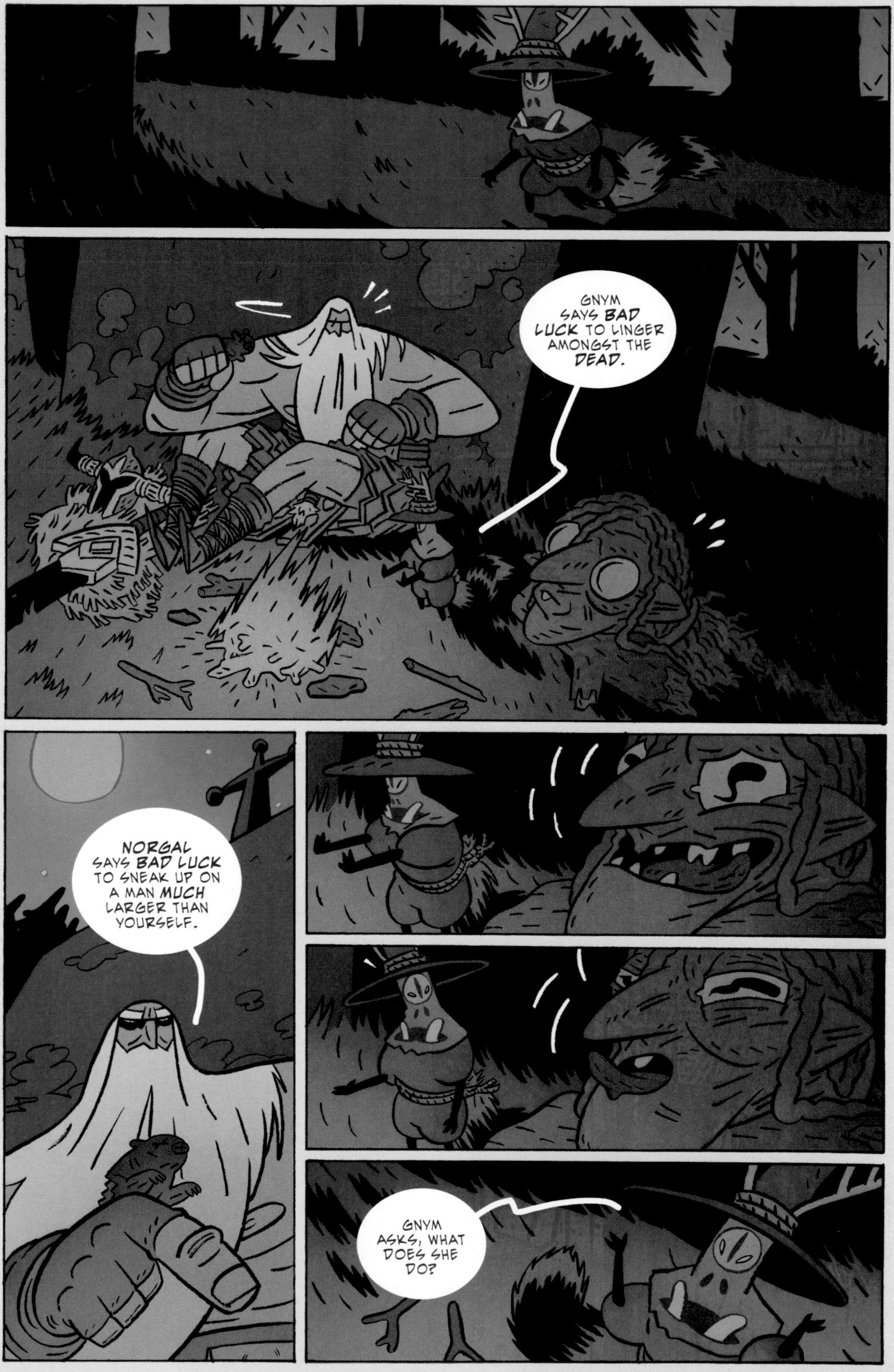
GNYM SAYS BAD LUCK TO LINGER AMONGST THE DEAD.
NORGAL SAYS BAD LUCK TO SNEAK UP ON A MAN MUCH LARGER THAN YOURSELF.
GNYM ASKS, WHAT DOES SHE DO?

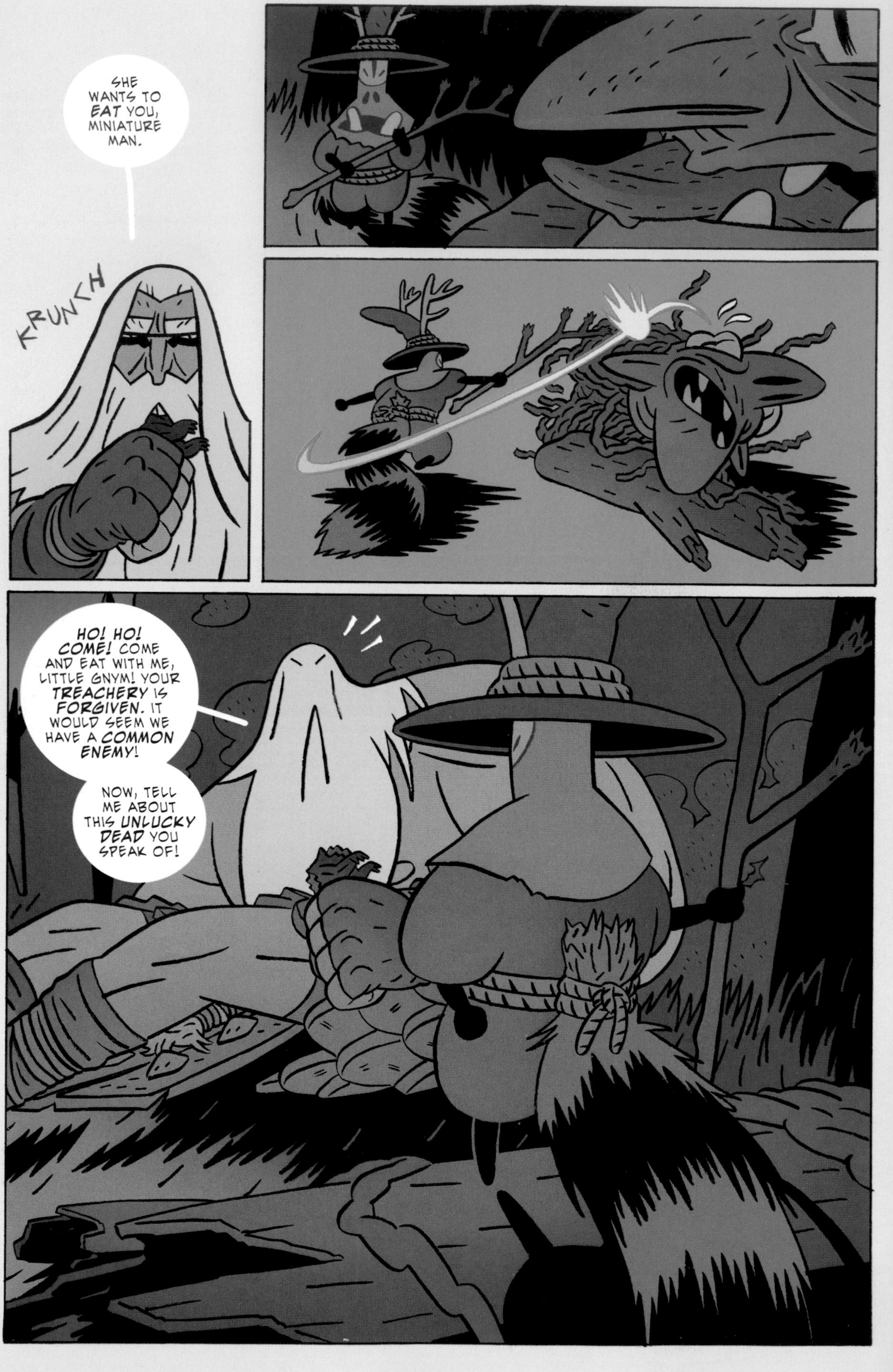
SHE WANTS TO EAT YOU, MINIATURE MAN.
KRUNCH
HO! HO! COME! COME AND EAT WITH ME, LITTLE GNYM! YOUR TREACHERY IS FORGIVEN. IT WOULD SEEM WE HAVE A COMMON ENEMY!
NOW, TELL ME ABOUT THIS UNLUCKY DEAD YOU SPEAK OF!

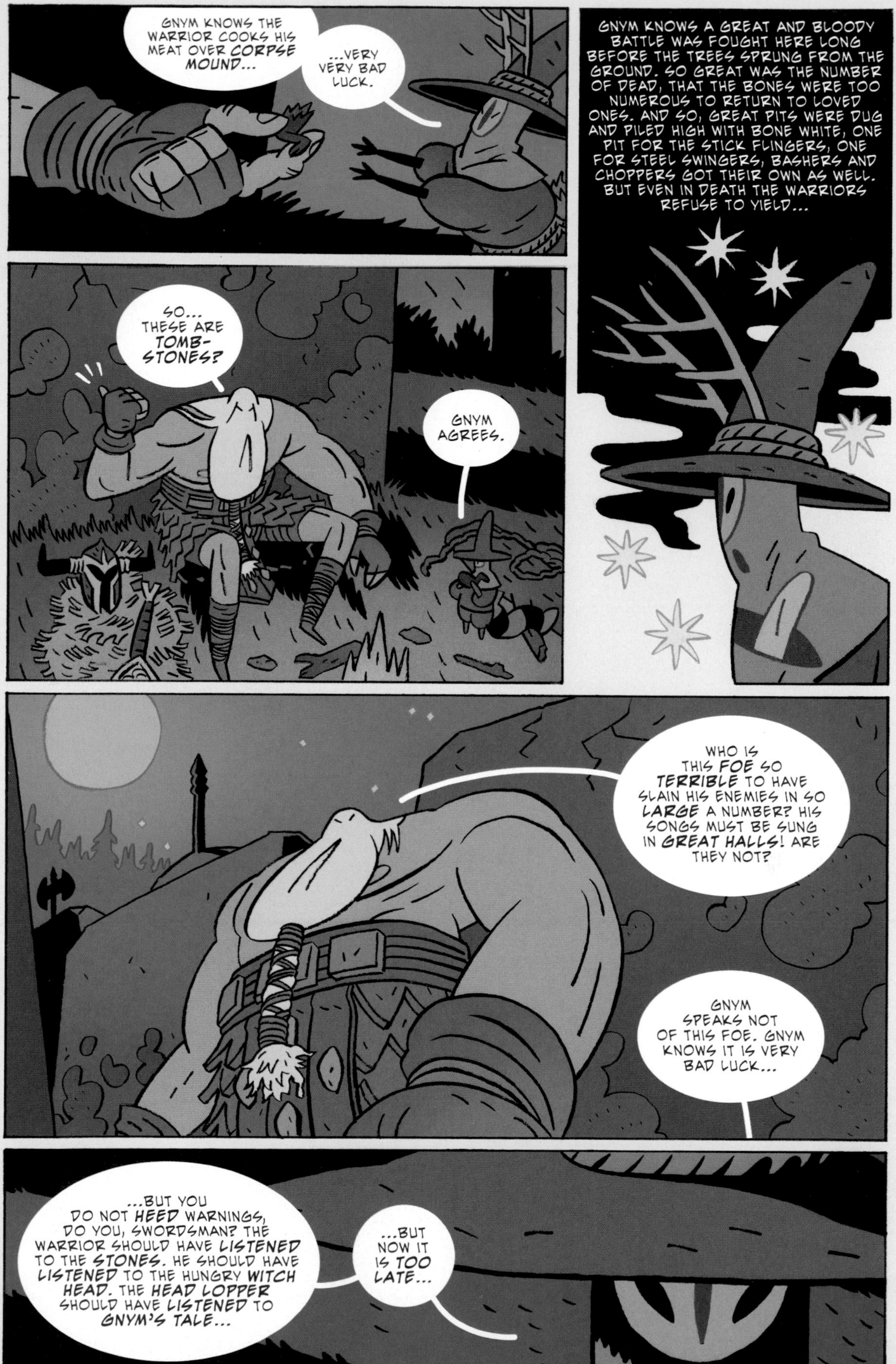
GNYM KNOWS THE WARRIOR COOKS HIS MEAT OVER CORPSE MOUND...
...VERY VERY BAD LUCK.
GNYM KNOWS A GREAT AND BLOODY BATTLE WAS FOUGHT HERE LONG BEFORE THE TREES SPRUNG FROM THE GROUND. SO GREAT WAS THE NUMBER OF DEAD, THAT THE BONES WERE TOO NUMEROUS TO RETURN TO LOVED ONES. AND SO, GREAT PITS WERE DUG AND PILED HIGH WITH BONE WHITE, ONE PIT FOR THE STICK FLINGERS, ONE FOR STEEL SWINGERS, BASHERS AND CHOPPERS GOT THEIR OWN AS WELL. BUT EVEN IN DEATH THE WARRIORS REFUSE TO YIELD...
SO... THESE ARE TOMB-STONES?
GNYM AGREES.
WHO IS THIS FOE SO TERRIBLE TO HAVE SLAIN HIS ENEMIES IN SO LARGE A NUMBER? HIS SONGS MUST BE SUNG IN GREAT HALLS! ARE THEY NOT?
GNYM SPEAKS NOT OF THIS FOE. GNYM KNOWS IT IS VERY BAD LUCK...
...BUT YOU DO NOT HEED WARNINGS, DO YOU, SWORDSMAN? THE WARRIOR SHOULD HAVE LISTENED TO THE STONES. HE SHOULD HAVE LISTENED TO THE HUNGRY WITCH HEAD. THE HEAD LOPPER SHOULD HAVE LISTENED TO GNYM'S TALE...
...BUT NOW IT IS TOO LATE...

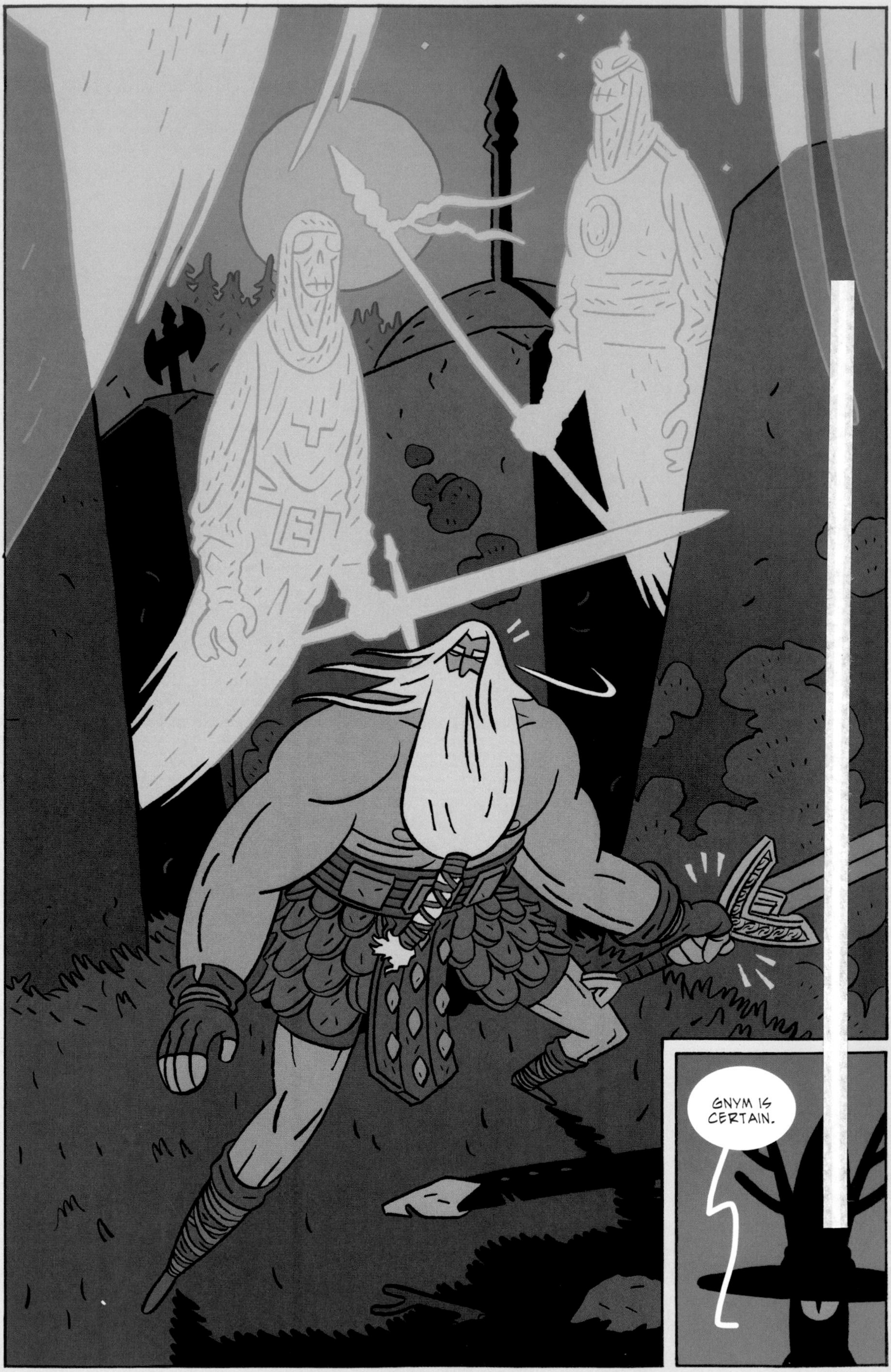
GNYM IS CERTAIN.

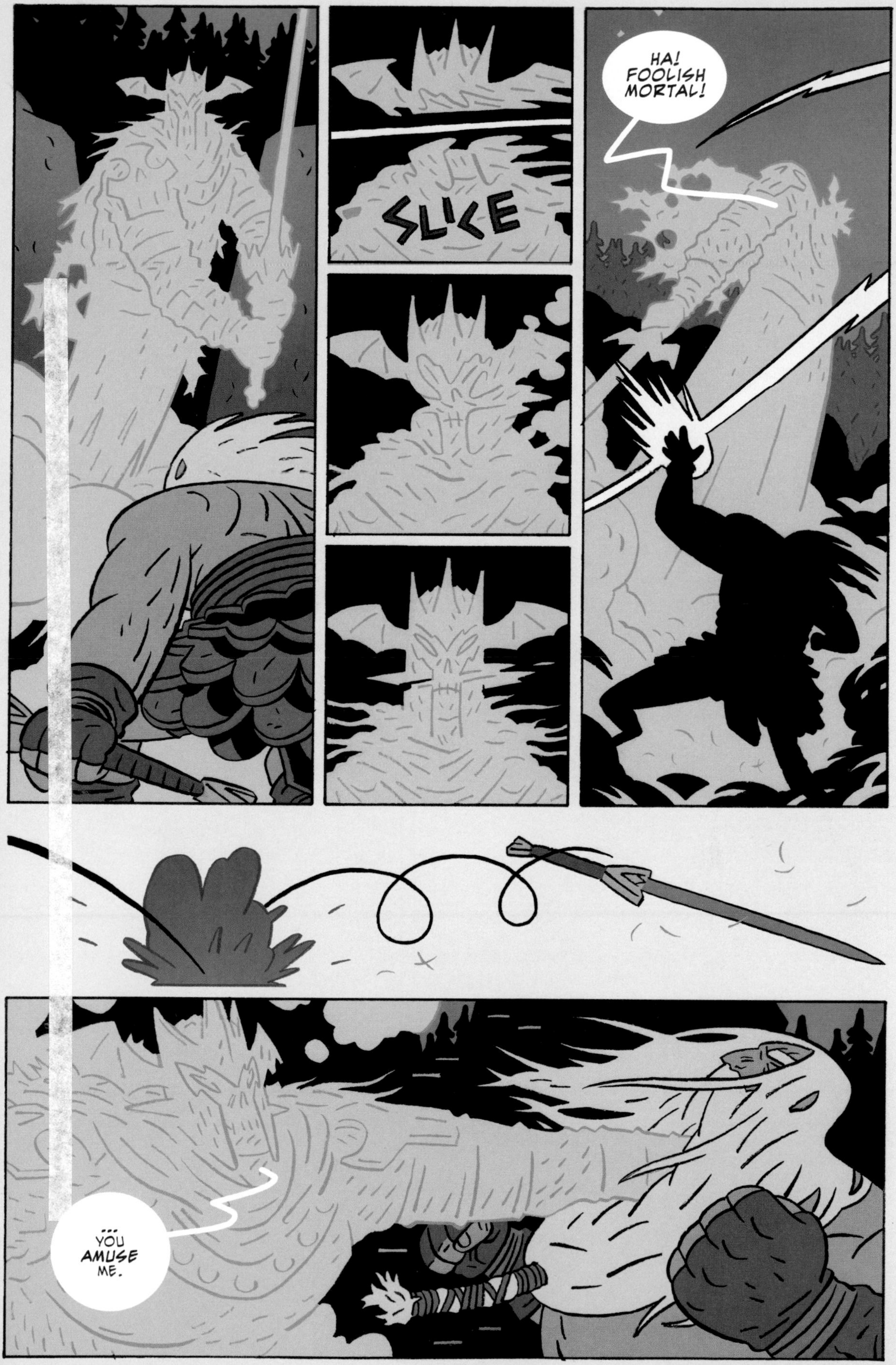
SLICE
HA! FOOLISH MORTAL!
... YOU AMUSE ME.

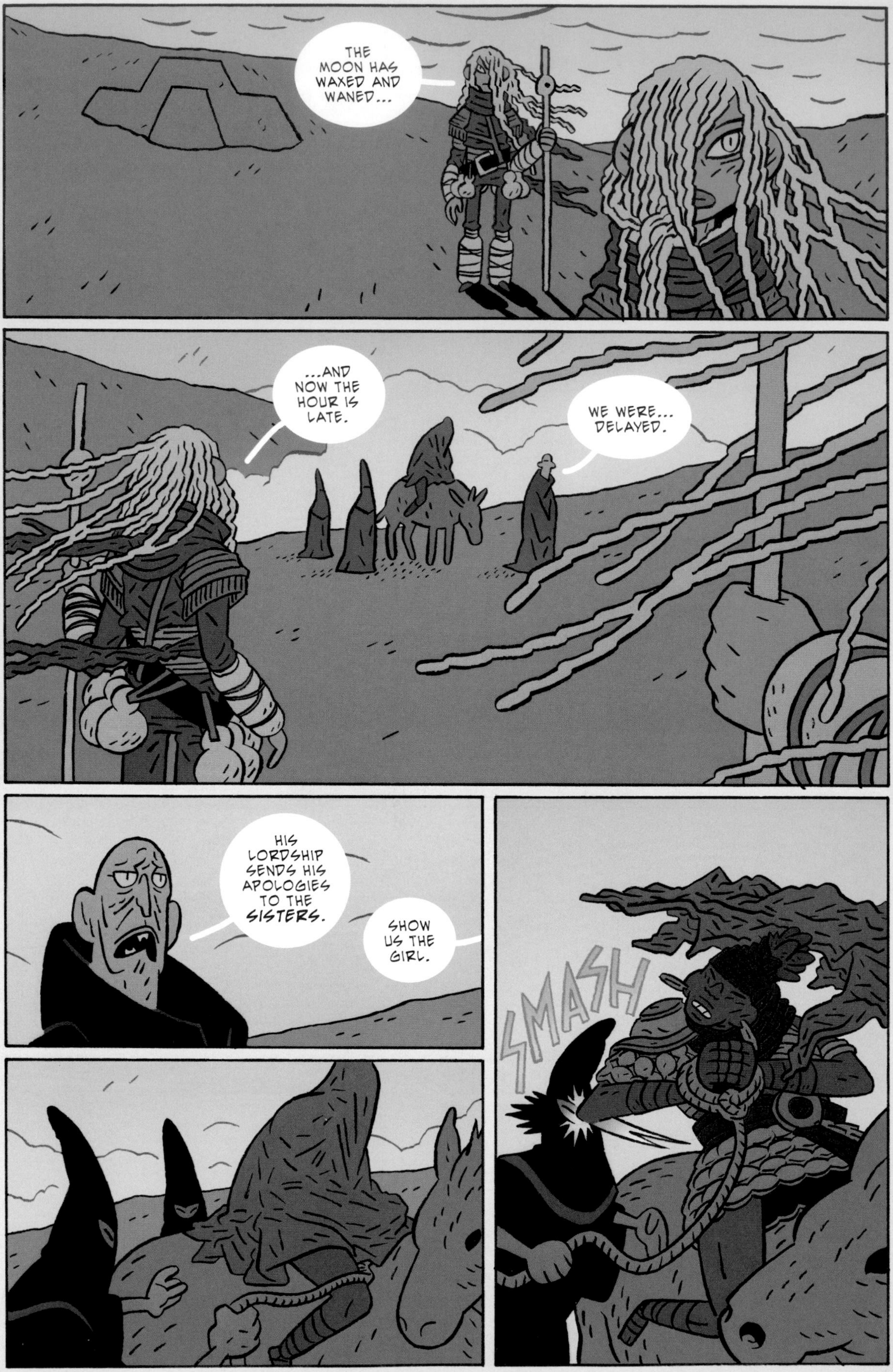
THE MOON HAS WAXED AND WANED...
...AND NOW THE HOUR IS LATE.
WE WERE... DELAYED.
HIS LORDSHIP SENDS HIS APOLOGIES TO THE SISTERS.
SHOW US THE GIRL.
SMASH

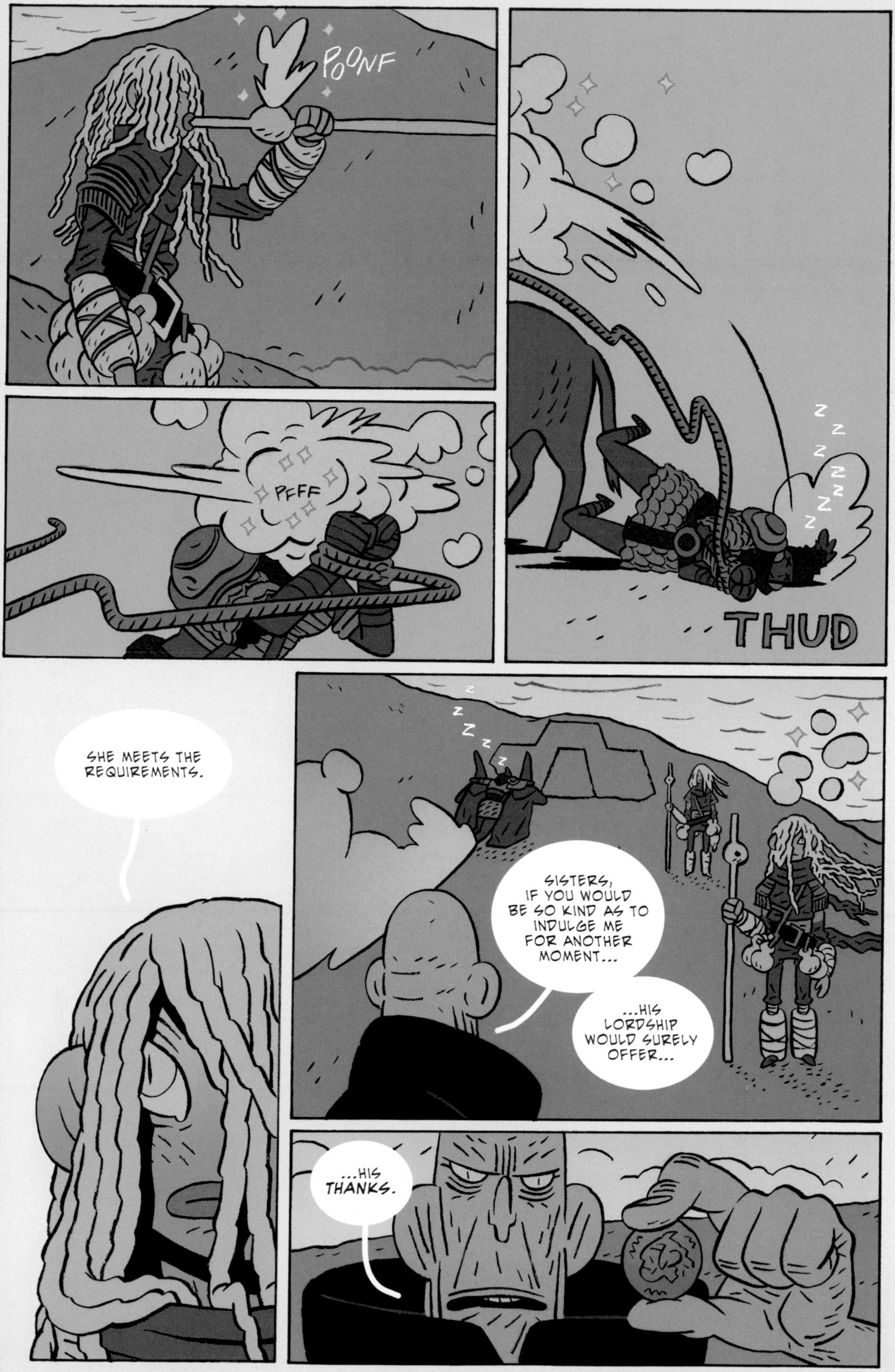
POONF
PFFF
THUD
SHE MEETS THE REQUIREMENTS.
SISTERS, IF YOU WOULD BE SO KIND AS TO INDULGE ME FOR ANOTHER MOMENT...
...HIS LORDSHIP WOULD SURELY OFFER...
...HIS THANKS.

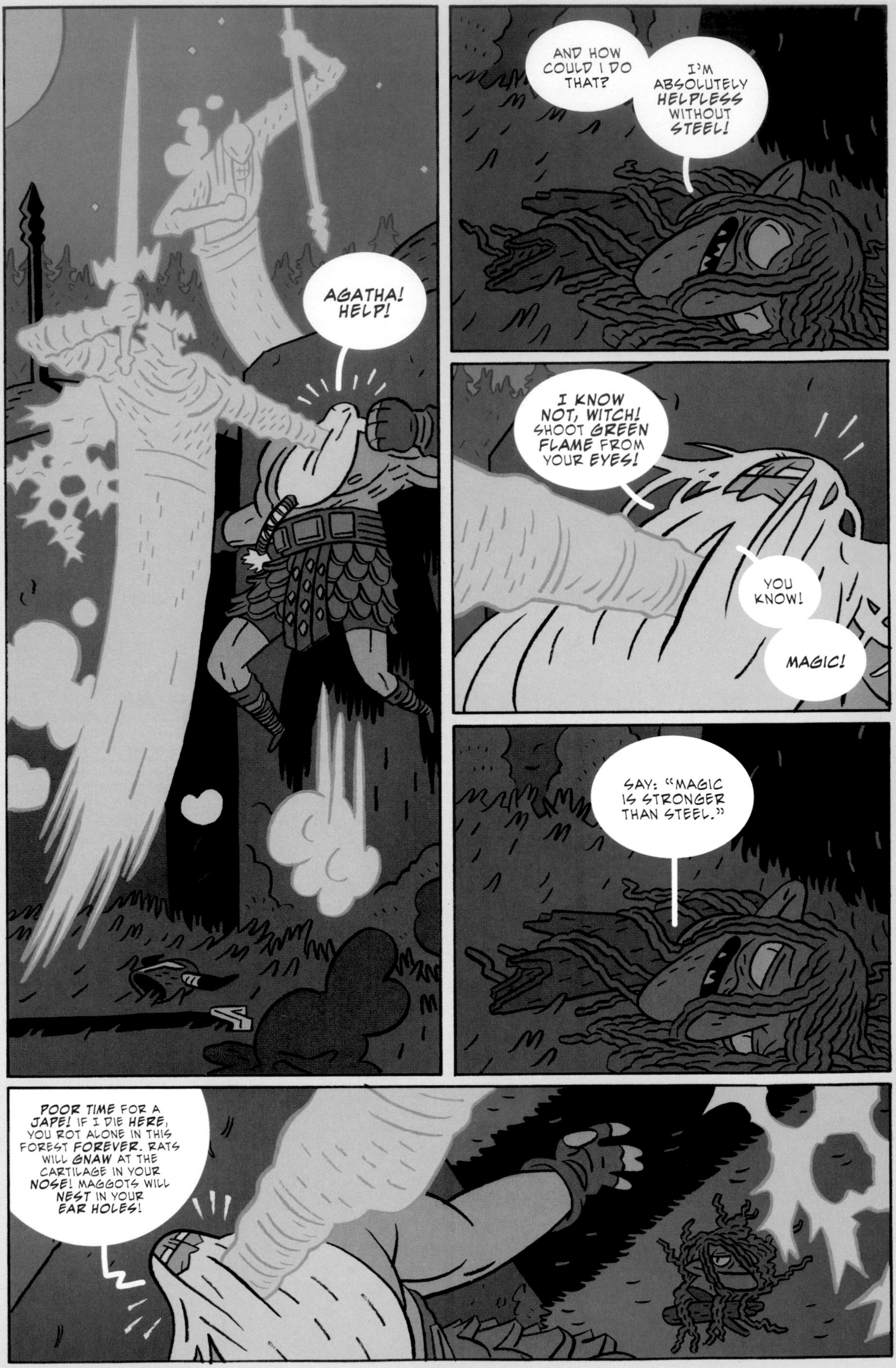
AGATHA! HELP!
AND HOW COULD I DO THAT?
I'M ABSOLUTELY HELPLESS WITHOUT STEEL!
I KNOW NOT, WITCH! SHOOT GREEN FLAME FROM YOUR EYES!
YOU KNOW!
MAGIC!
SAY: "MAGIC IS STRONGER THAN STEEL."
POOR TIME FOR A JAPE! IF I DIE HERE, YOU ROT ALONE IN THIS FOREST FOREVER. RATS WILL GNAW AT THE CARTILAGE IN YOUR NOSE! MAGGOTS WILL NEST IN YOUR EAR HOLES!

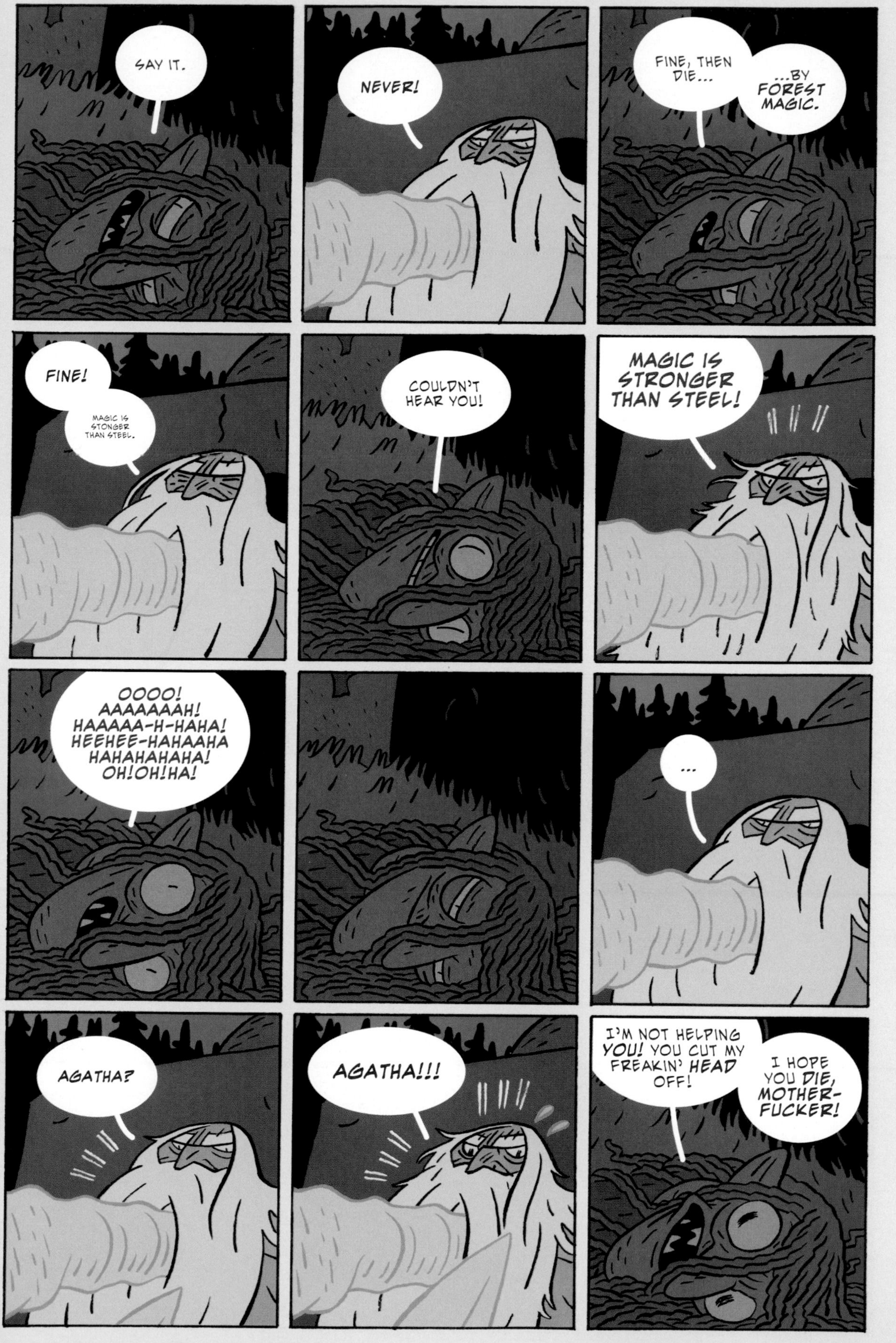
SAY IT.
NEVER!
FINE, THEN DIE...
...BY FOREST MAGIC.
FINE!
MAGIC IS STONGER THAN STEEL.
COULDN'T HEAR YOU!
MAGIC IS STRONGER THAN STEEL!
OOOO! AAAAAAAH! HAAAAA-H-HAHA! HEEHEE-HAHAAHA HAHAHAHAHA! OH!OH!HA!
...
AGATHA?
AGATHA!!!
I'M NOT HELPING YOU! YOU CUT MY FREAKIN' HEAD OFF!
I HOPE YOU DIE, MOTHER-FUCKER!

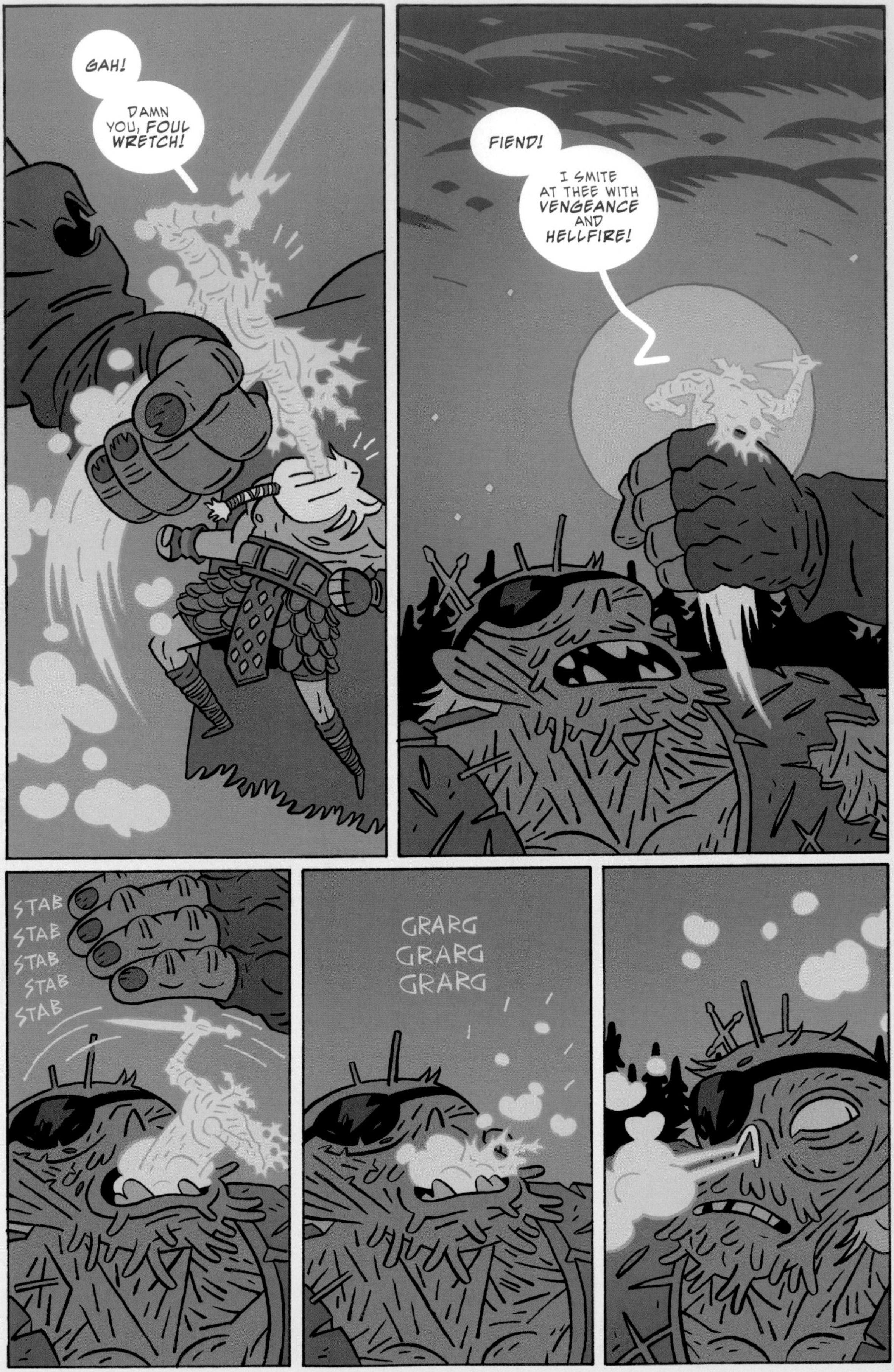
GAH!
DAMN YOU, FOUL WRETCH!
FIEND!
I SMITE AT THEE WITH VENGEANCE AND HELLFIRE!
STAB STAB STAB STAB STAB
GRARG GRARG GRARG

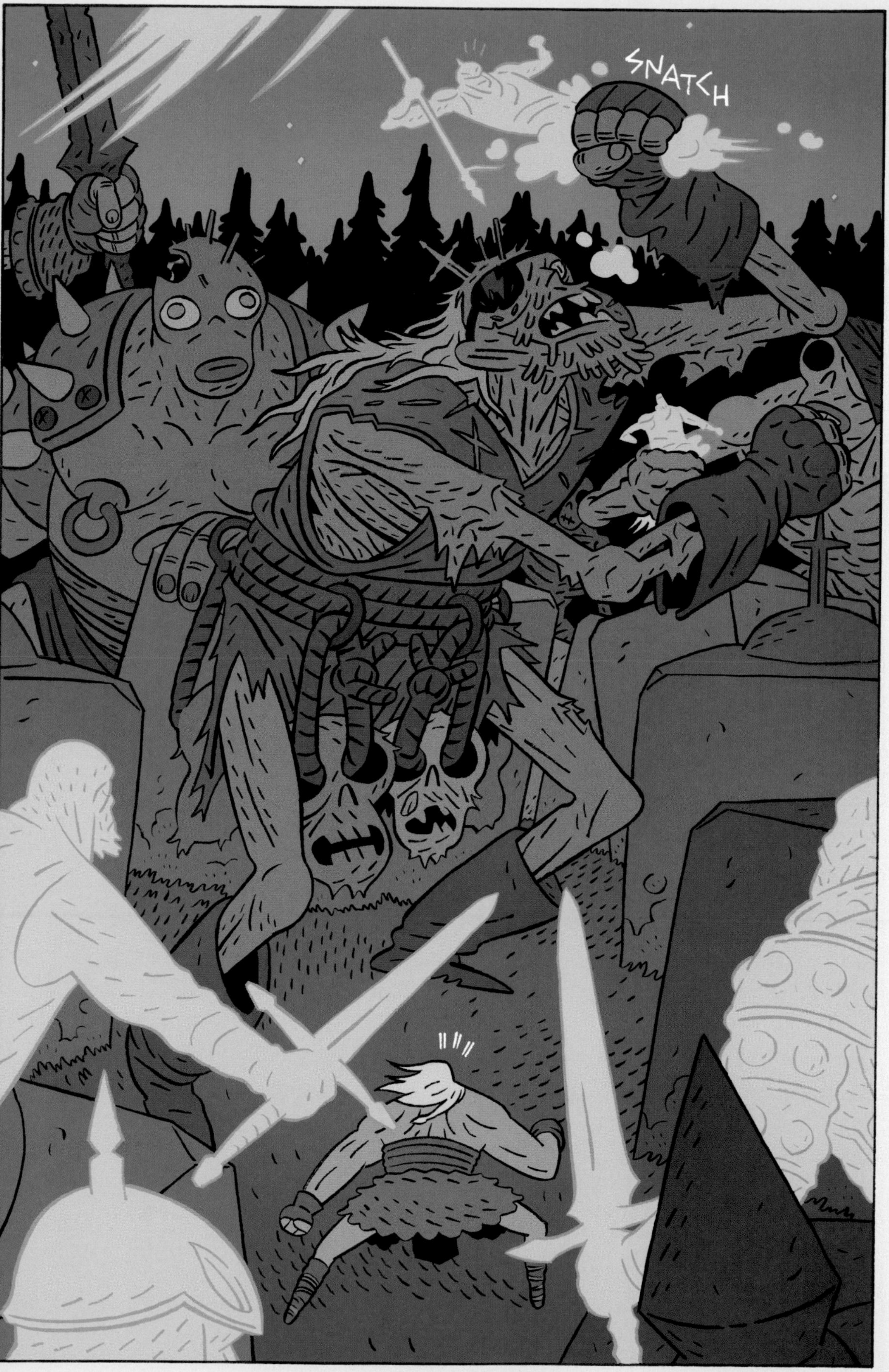
SNATCH

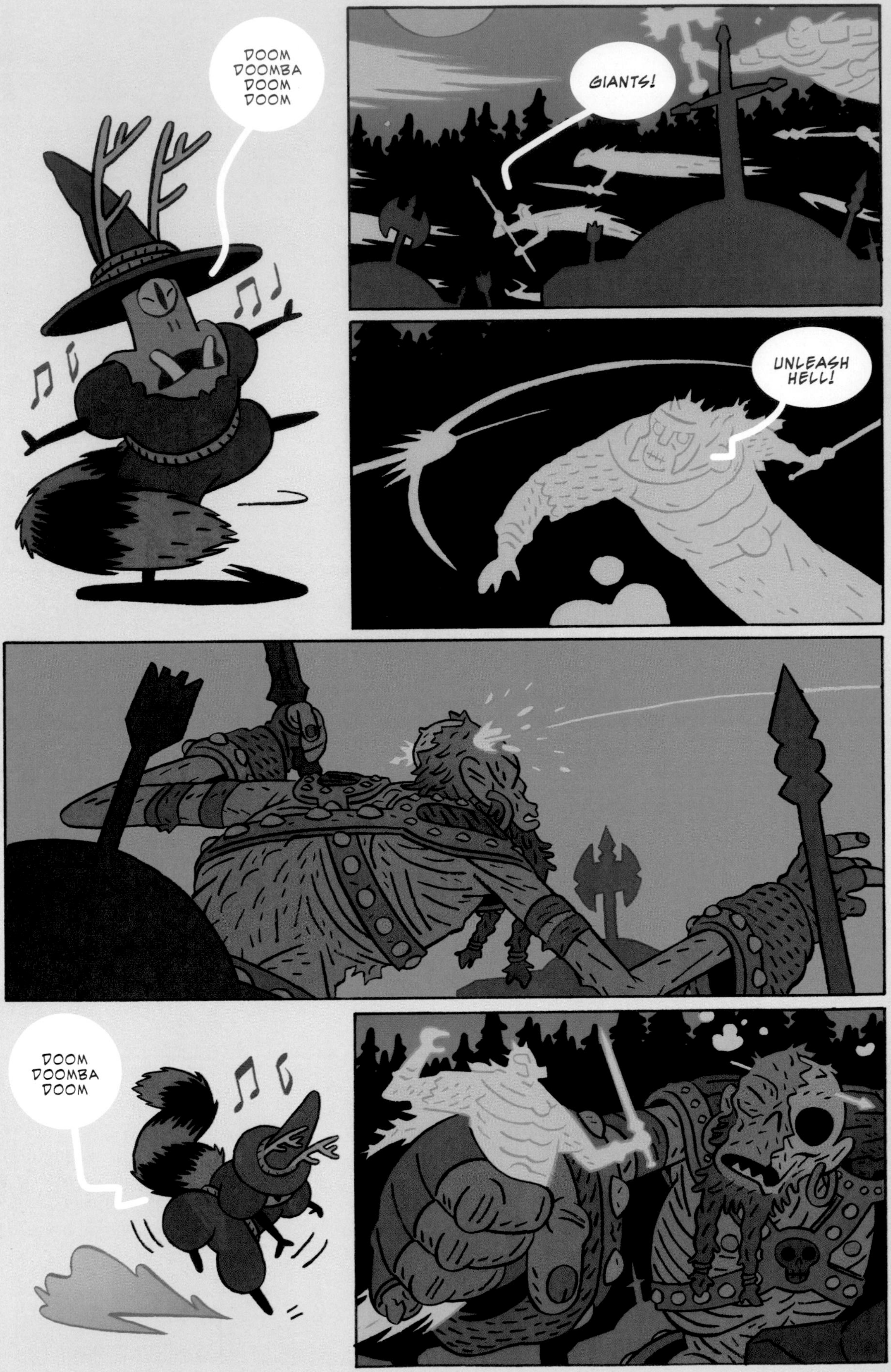
DOOM DOOMBA DOOM DOOM
GIANTS!
UNLEASH HELL!
DOOM DOOMBA DOOM

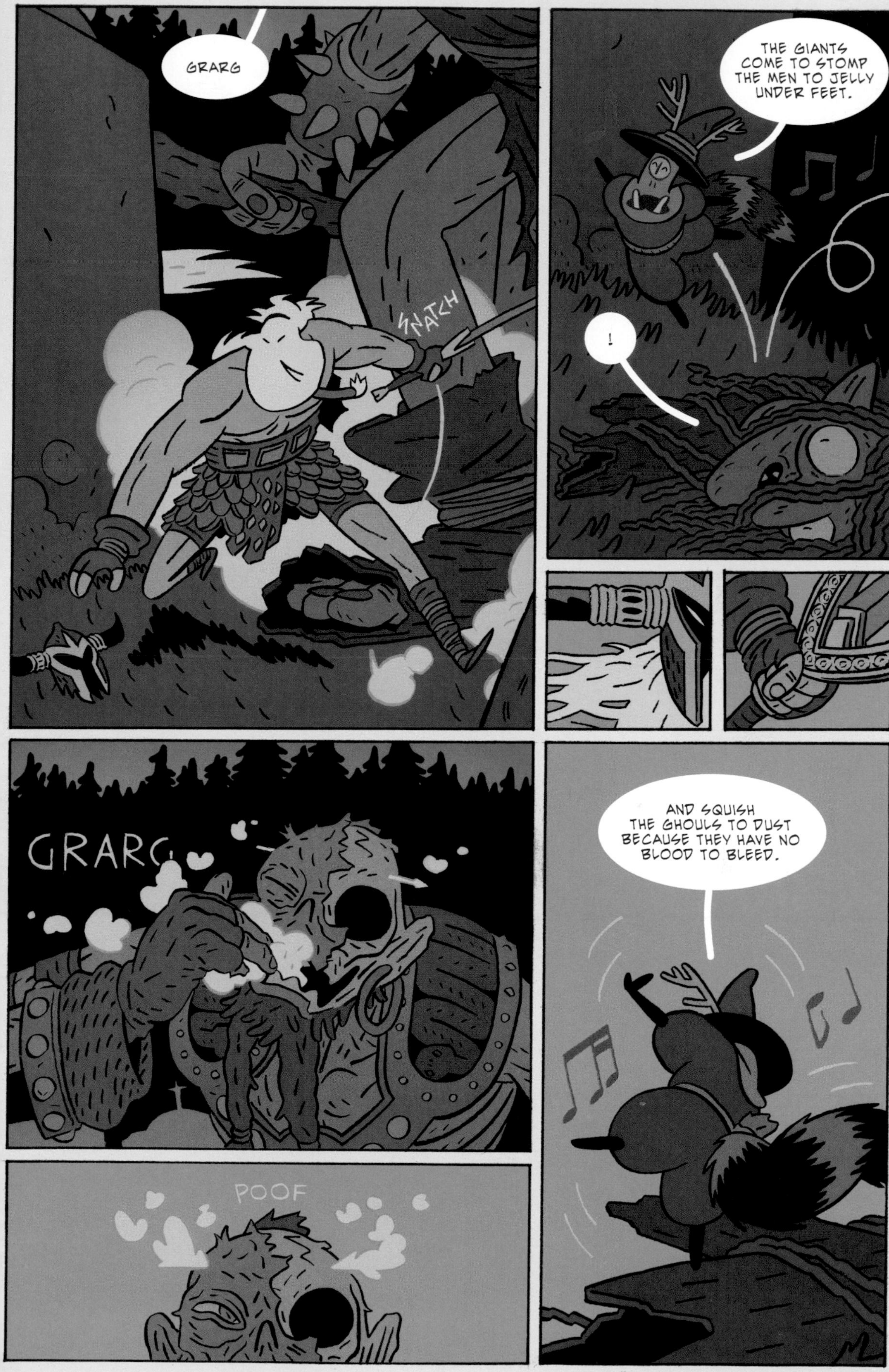
GRARG
SNATCH
THE GIANTS COME TO STOMP THE MEN TO JELLY UNDER FEET.
!
GRARG
AND SQUISH THE GHOULS TO DUST BECAUSE THEY HAVE NO BLOOD TO BLEED.
POOF

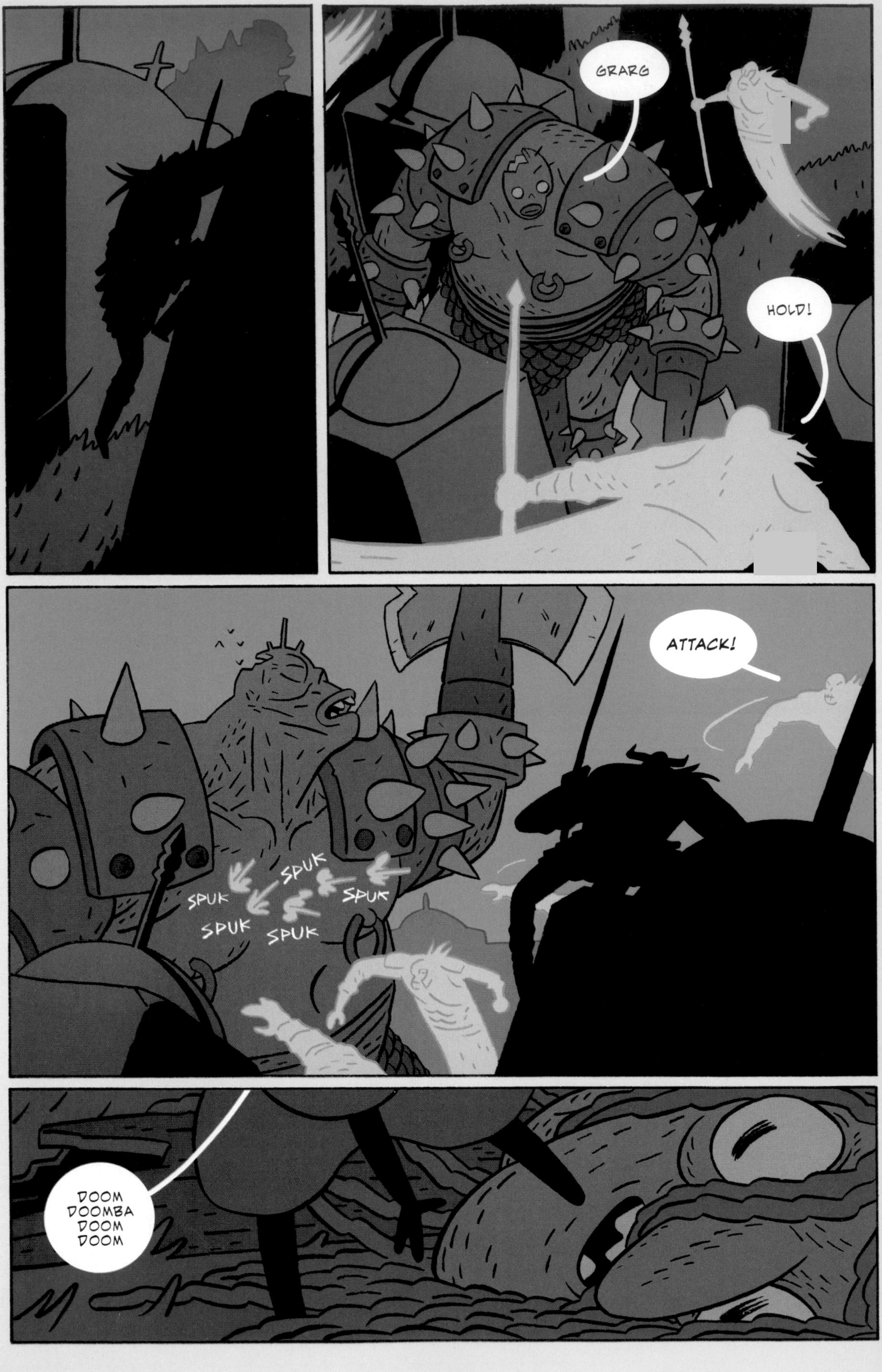
GRARG
HOLD!
ATTACK!
SPUK
SPUK
SPUK
SPUK
SPUK
DOOM DOOMBA DOOM DOOM

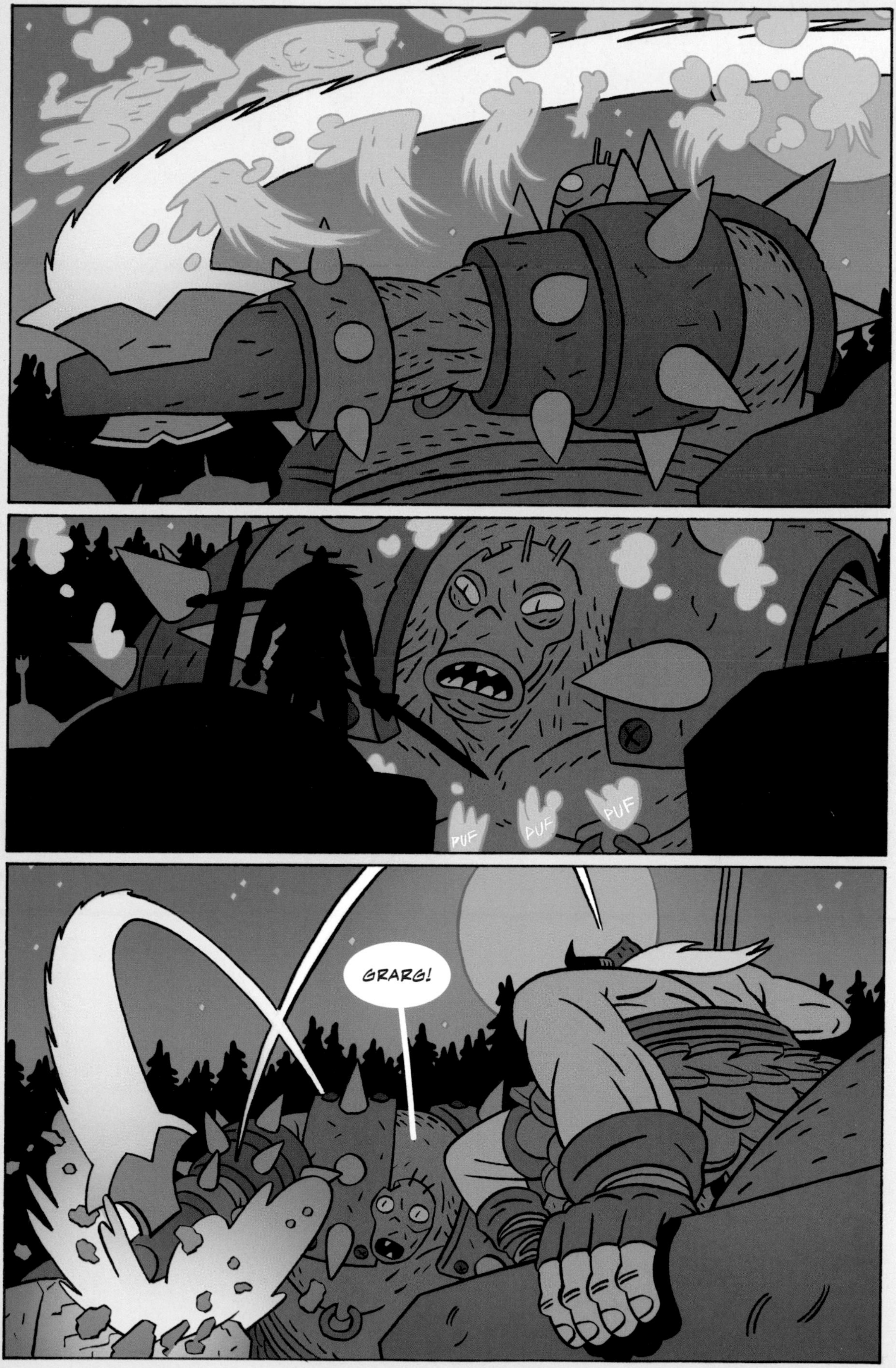
PUF
PUF
PUF
GRARG!

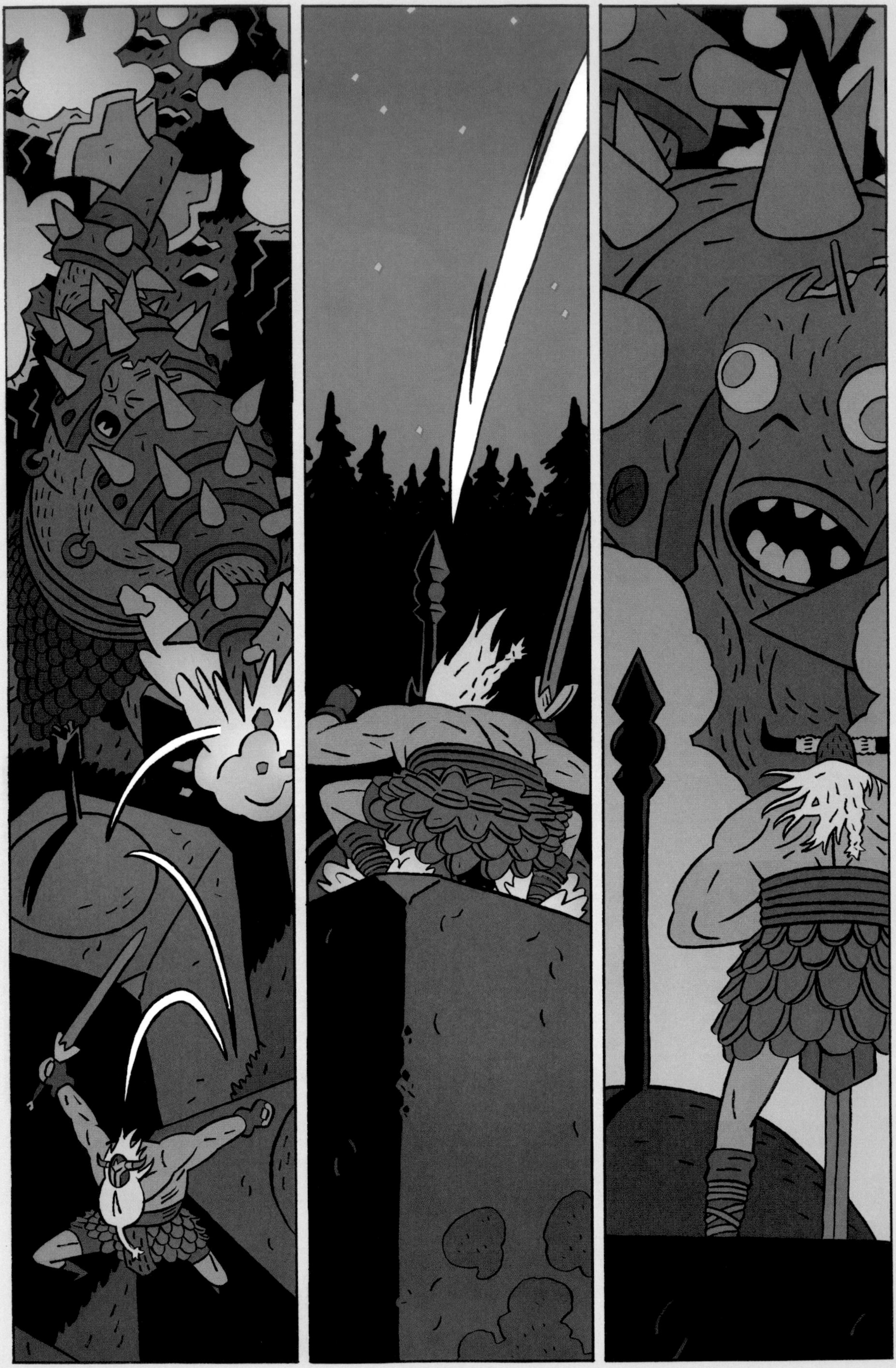

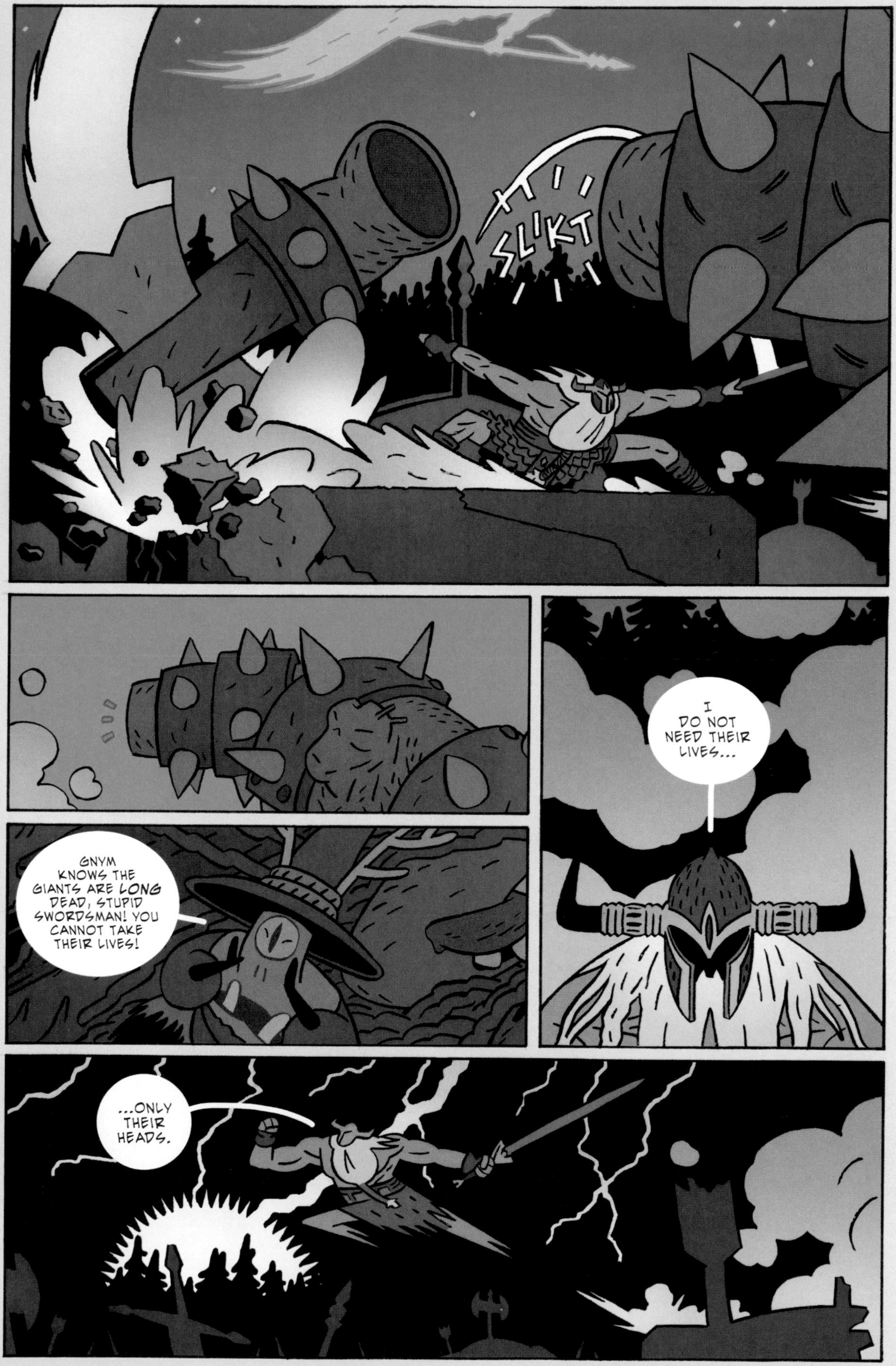
SLIKT
I DO NOT NEED THEIR LIVES...
GNYM KNOWS THE GIANTS ARE LONG DEAD, STUPID SWORDSMAN! YOU CANNOT TAKE THEIR LIVES!
...ONLY THEIR HEADS.

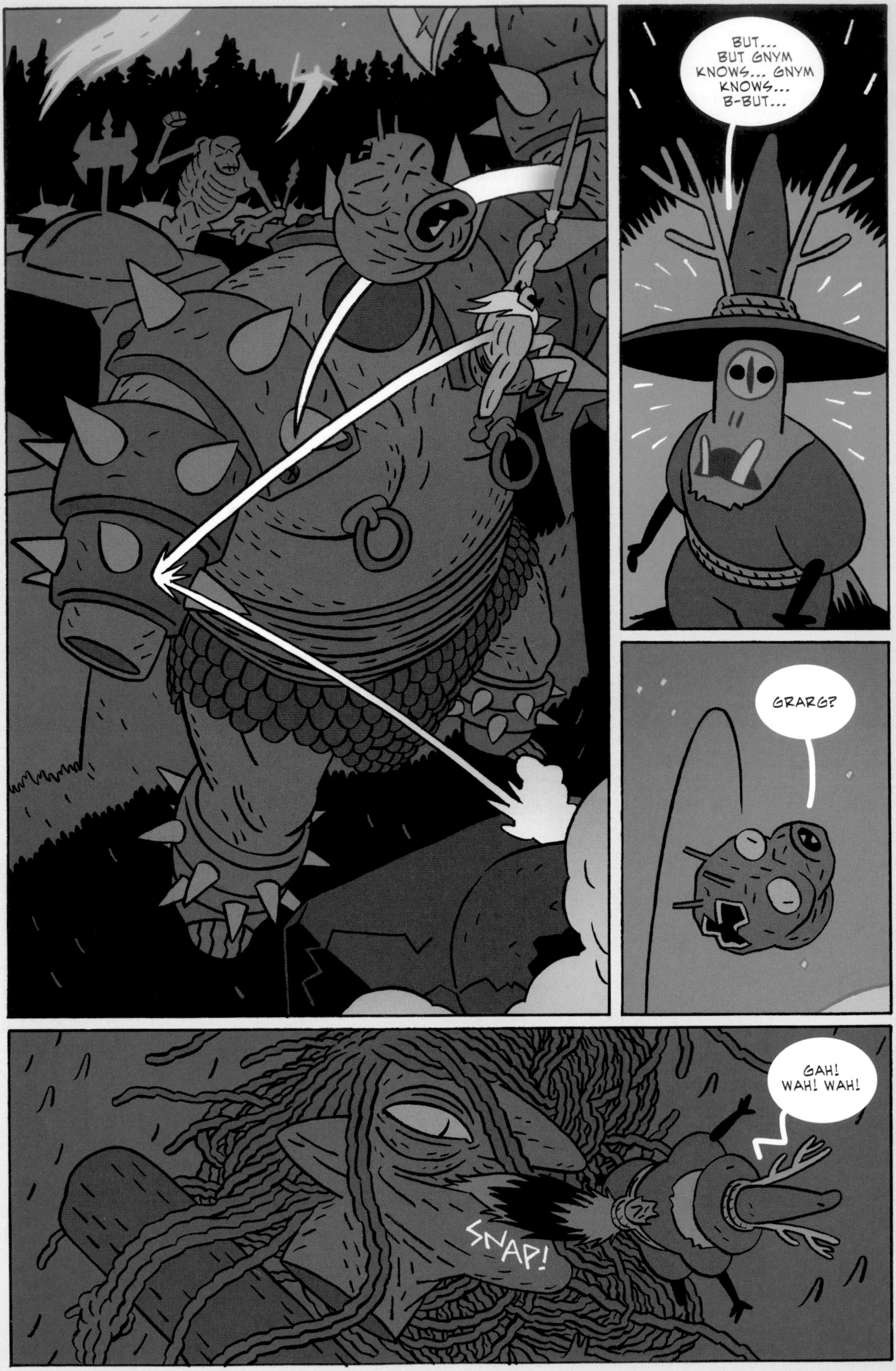
BUT... BUT GNYM KNOWS... GNYM KNOWS... B-BUT...
GRARG?
GAH! WAH! WAH!
SNAP!

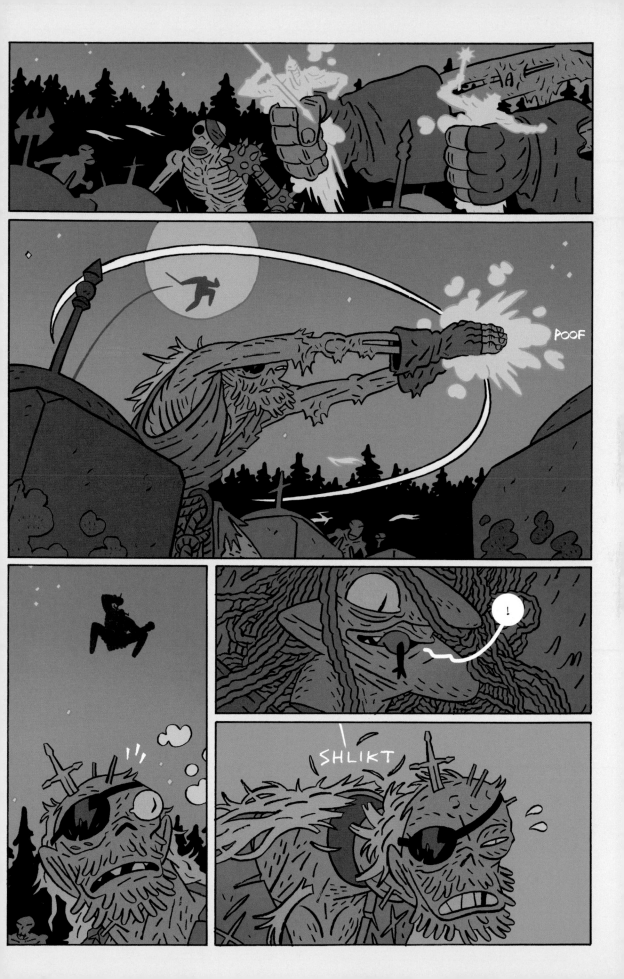

POOF

SHLIKT

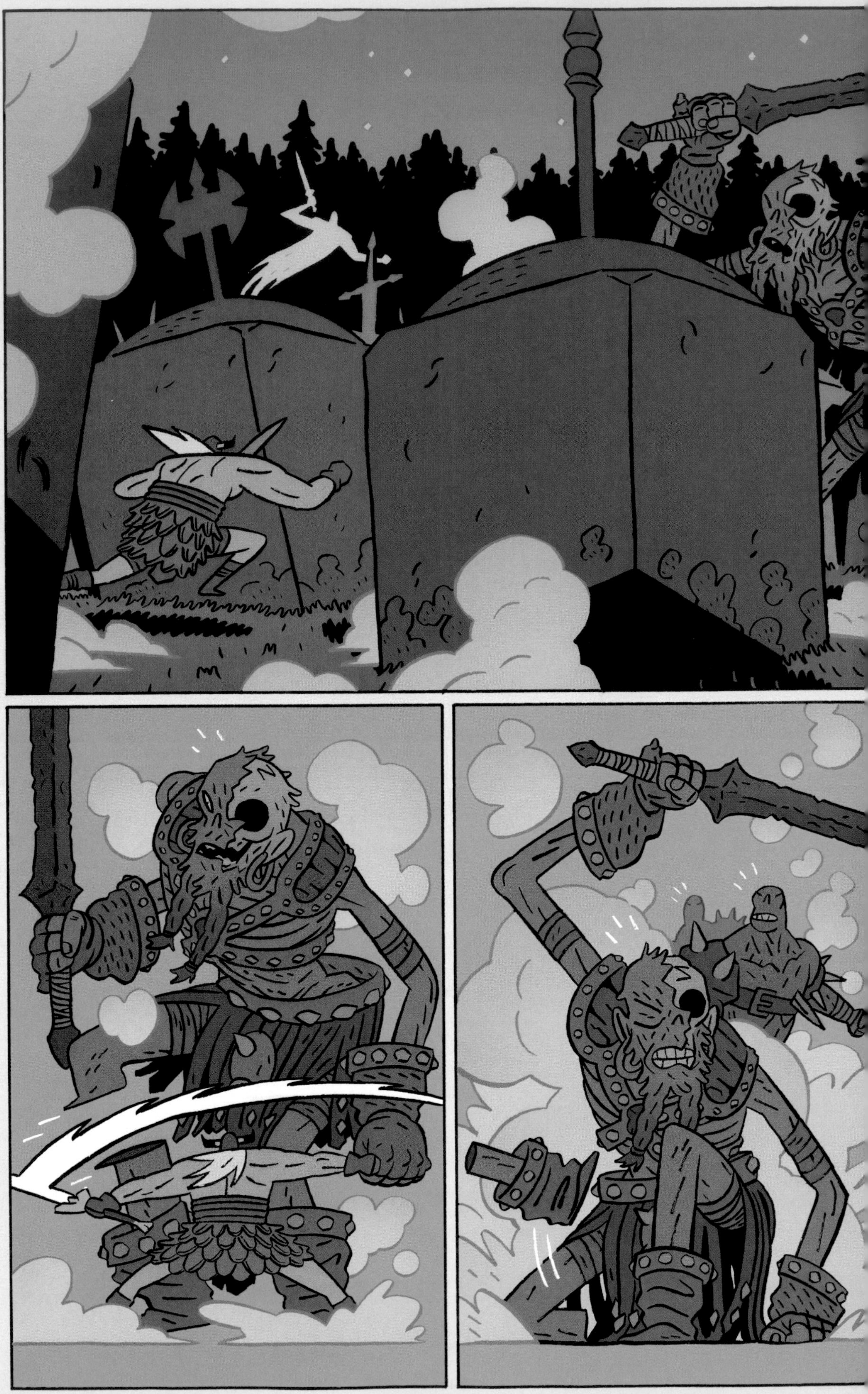

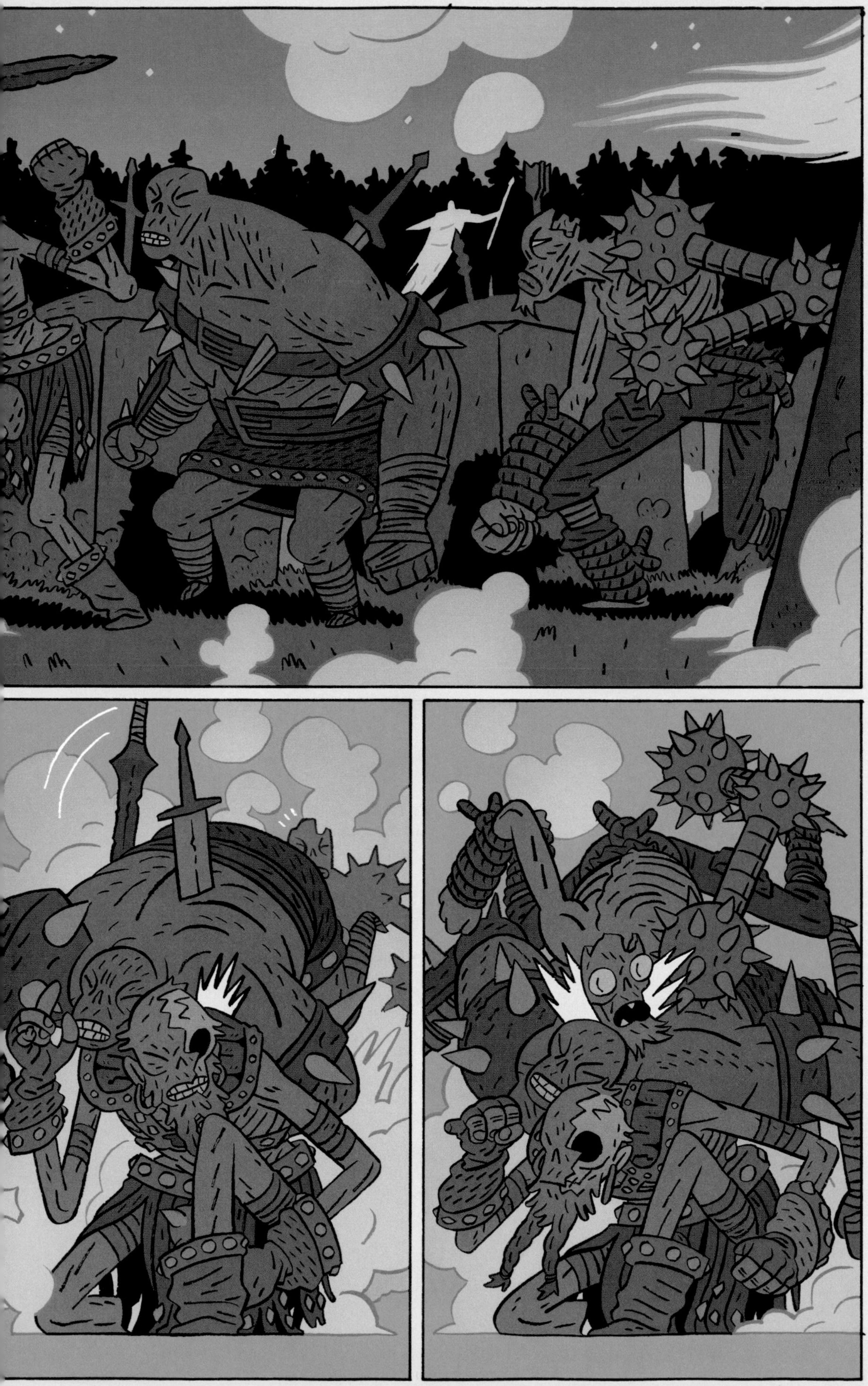

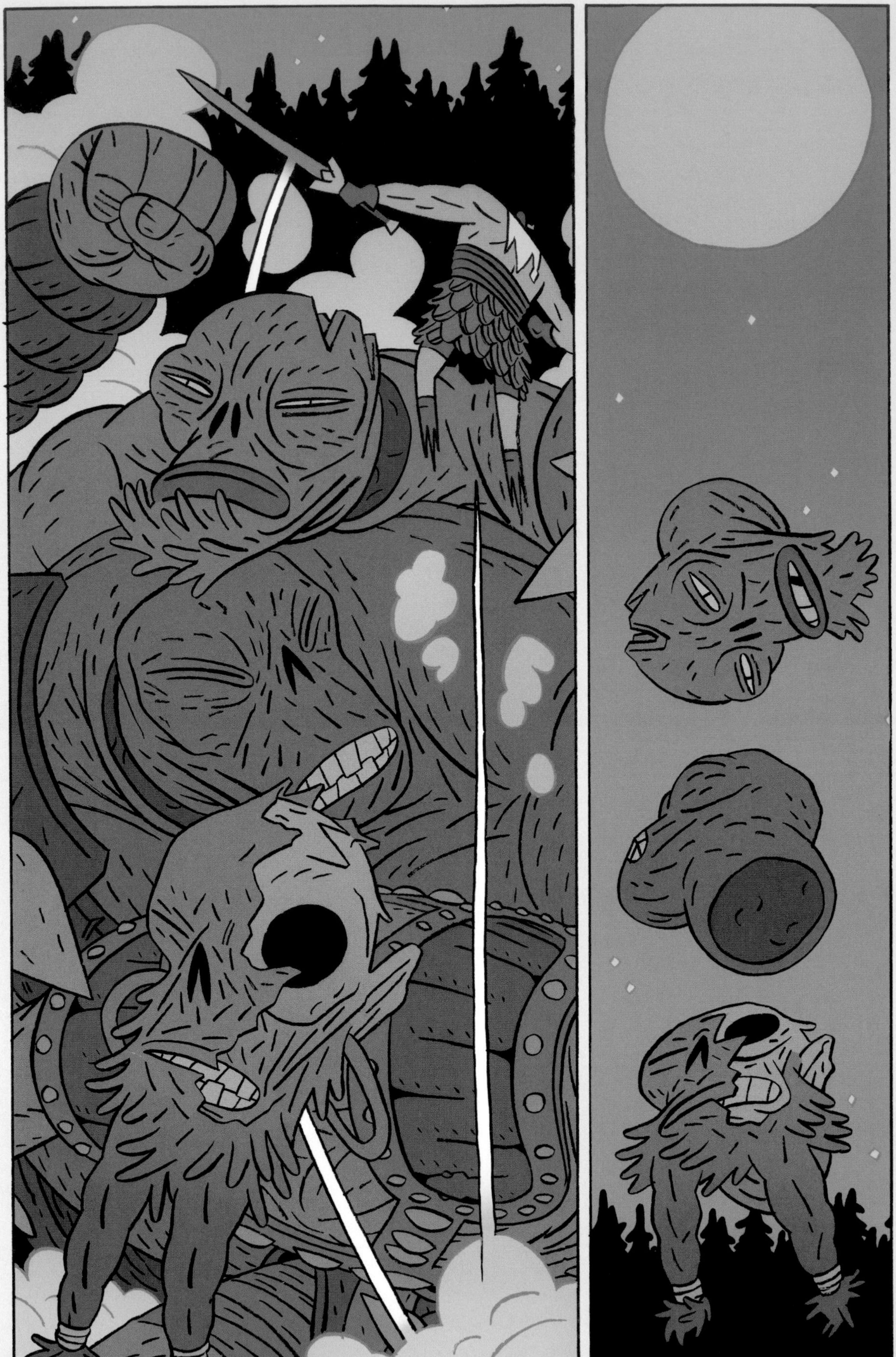

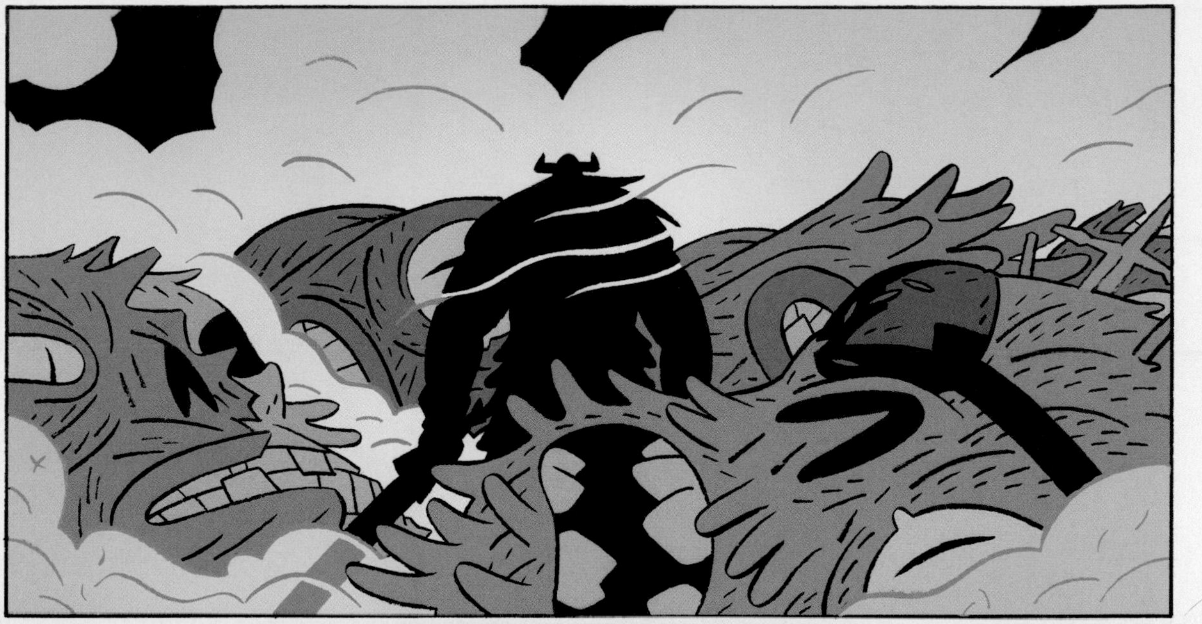

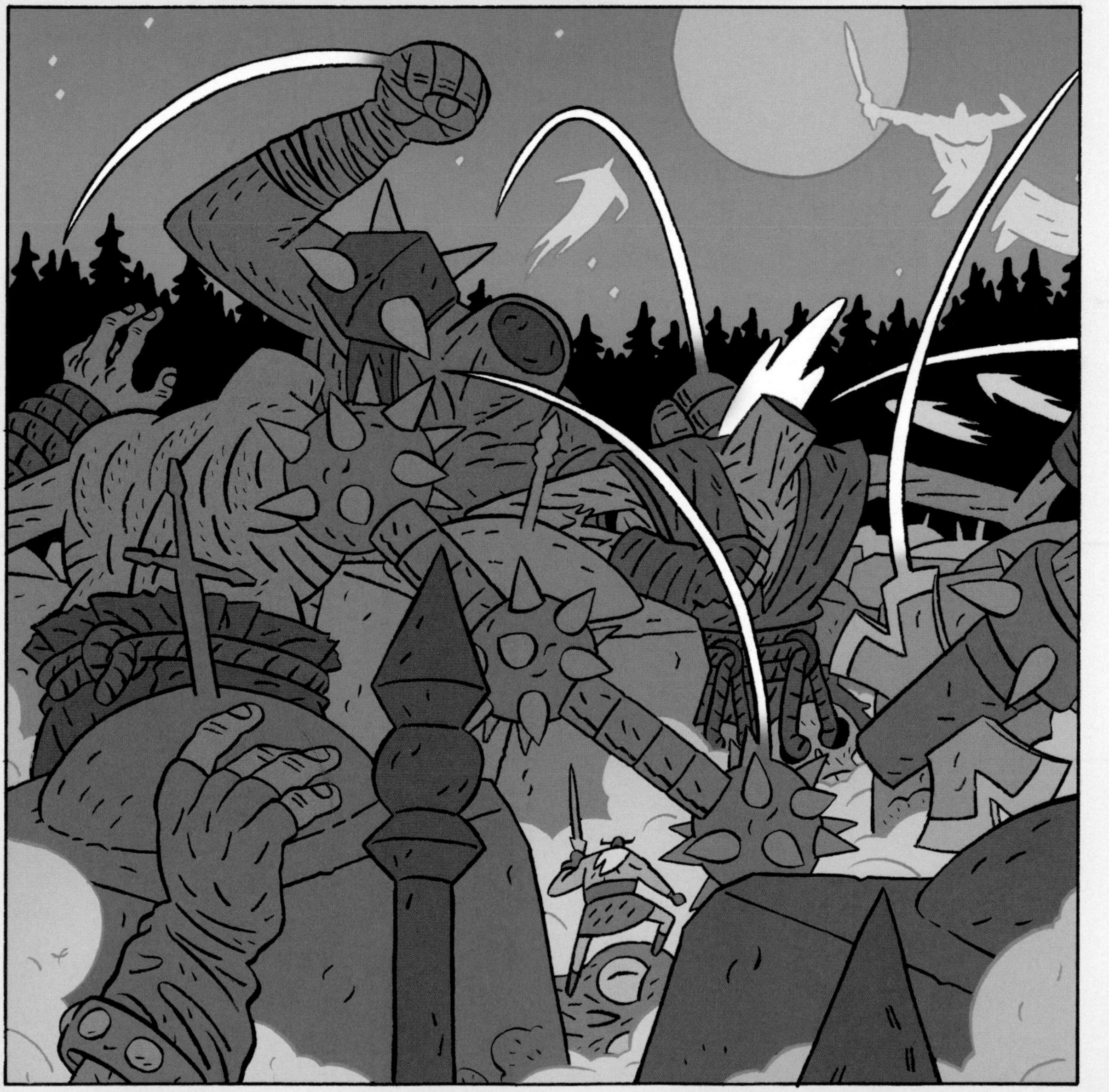

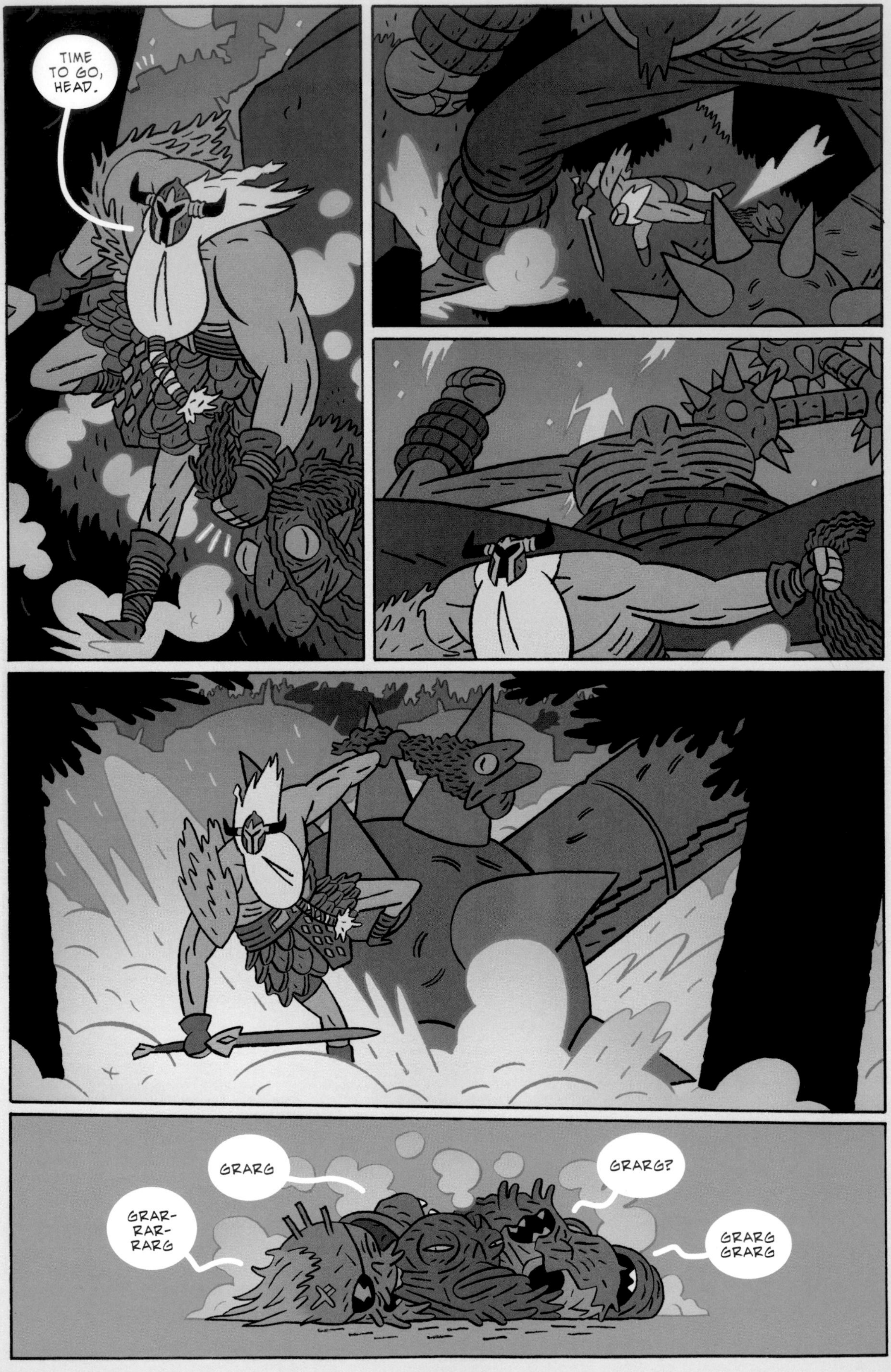
TIME TO GO, HEAD.
GRARG
GRARG?
GRAR-RAR-RARG
GRARG GRARG

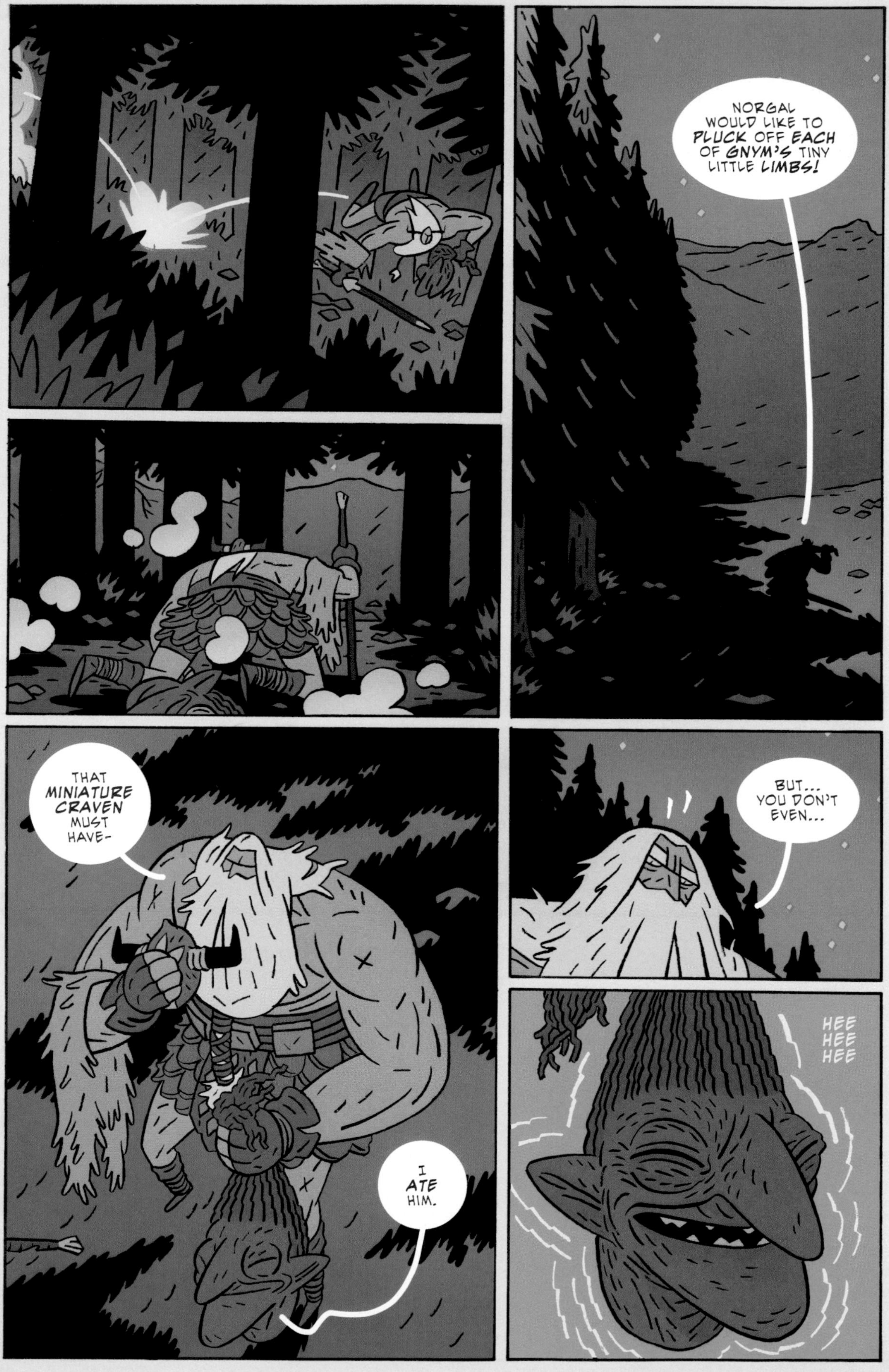
NORGAL WOULD LIKE TO PLUCK OFF EACH OF GNYM'S TINY LITTLE LIMBS!
THAT MINIATURE CRAVEN MUST HAVE-
I ATE HIM.
BUT... YOU DON'T EVEN...
HEE HEE HEE

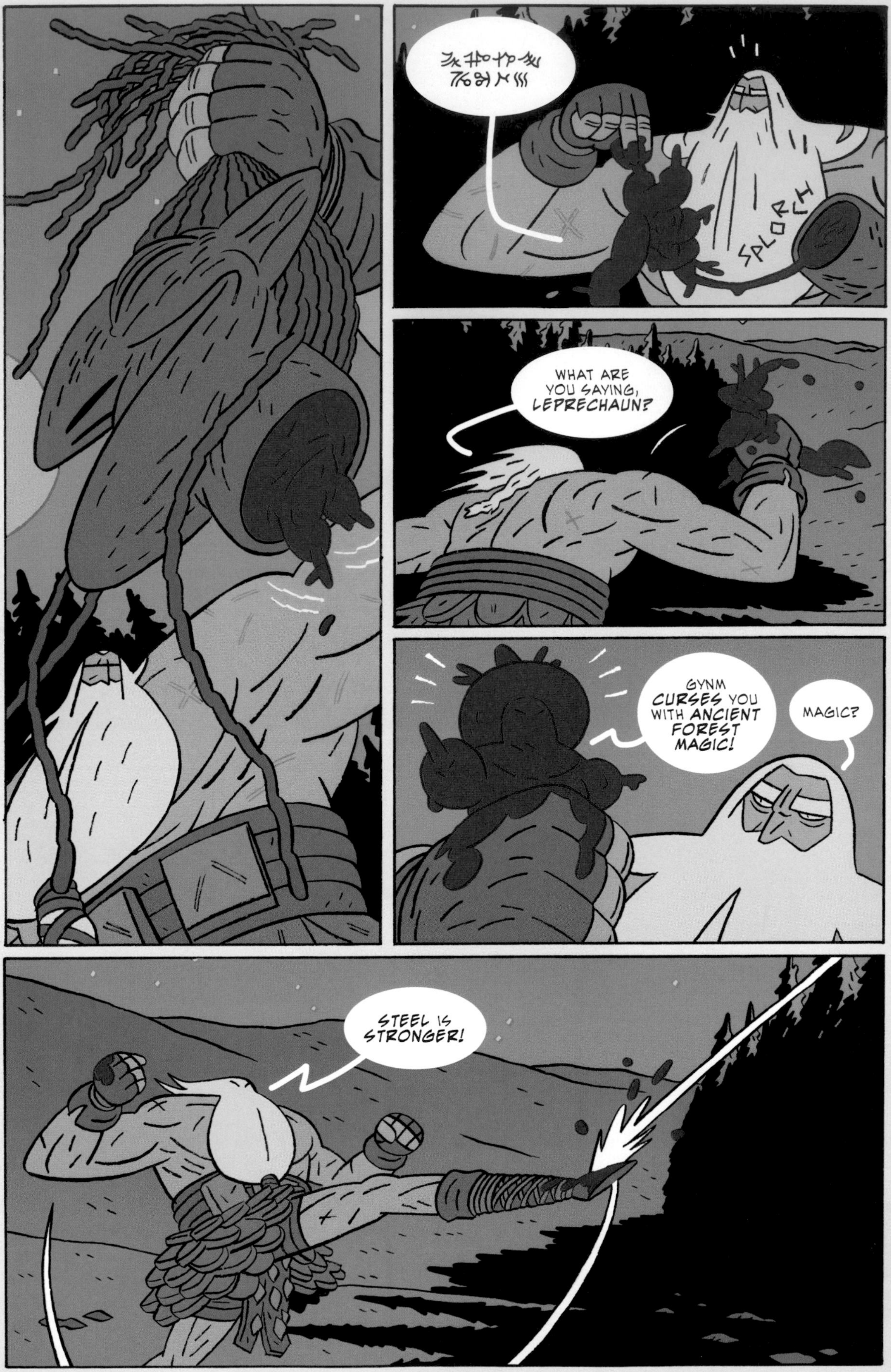
SPLORCH
WHAT ARE YOU SAYING, LEPRECHAUN?
GYNM CURSES YOU WITH ANCIENT FOREST MAGIC!
MAGIC?
STEEL IS STRONGER!

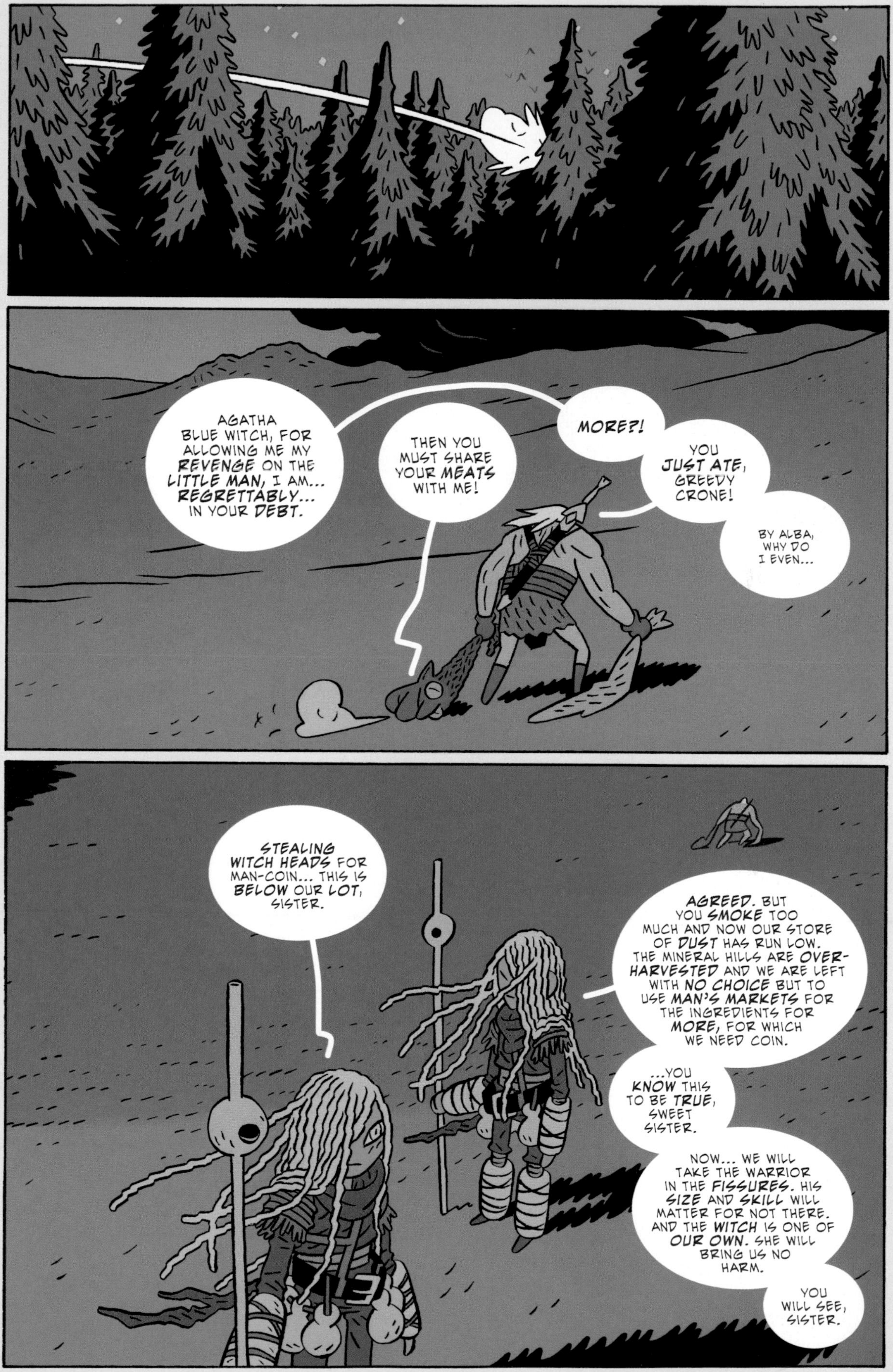
AGATHA BLUE WITCH, FOR ALLOWING ME MY REVENGE ON THE LITTLE MAN, I AM... REGRETTABLY... IN YOUR DEBT.
THEN YOU MUST SHARE YOUR MEATS WITH ME!
MORE?!
YOU JUST ATE, GREEDY CRONE!
BY ALBA, WHY DO I EVEN...
STEALING WITCH HEADS FOR MAN-COIN... THIS IS BELOW OUR LOT, SISTER.
AGREED. BUT YOU SMOKE TOO MUCH AND NOW OUR STORE OF DUST HAS RUN LOW. THE MINERAL HILLS ARE OVER-HARVESTED AND WE ARE LEFT WITH NO CHOICE BUT TO USE MAN'S MARKETS FOR THE INGREDIENTS FOR MORE, FOR WHICH WE NEED COIN.
...YOU KNOW THIS TO BE TRUE, SWEET SISTER.
NOW... WE WILL TAKE THE WARRIOR IN THE FISSURES. HIS SIZE AND SKILL WILL MATTER FOR NOT THERE. AND THE WITCH IS ONE OF OUR OWN. SHE WILL BRING US NO HARM.
YOU WILL SEE, SISTER.

CHAPTER FIVE

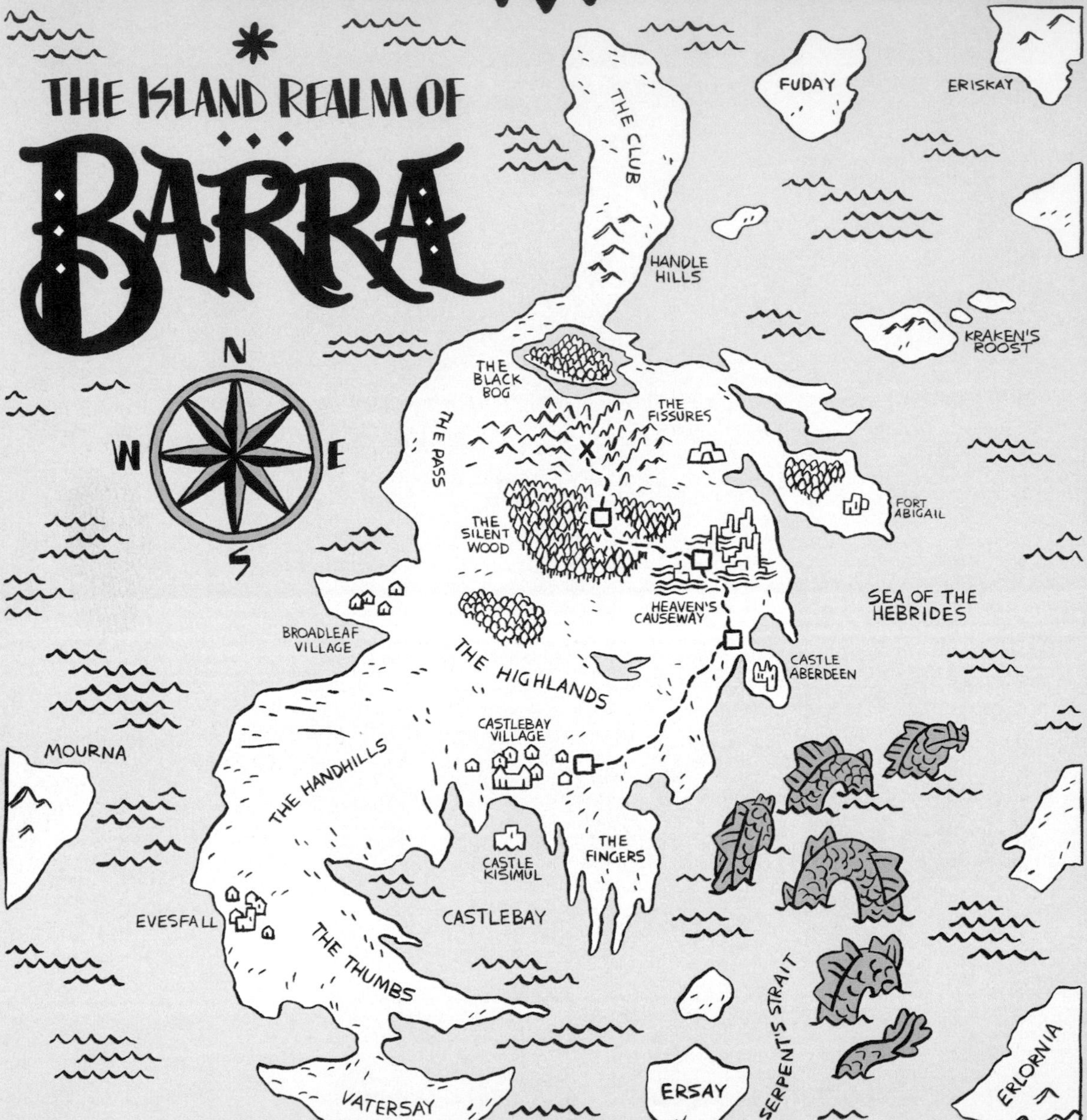
THE ISLAND REALM OF
BARRA
N
W
E
S
THE CLUB
HANDLE HILLS
FUDAY
ERISKAY
KRAKEN'S ROOST
THE BLACK BOG
THE PASS
THE FISSURES
FORT ABIGAIL
THE SILENT WOOD
HEAVEN'S CAUSEWAY
SEA OF THE HEBRIDES
BROADLEAF VILLAGE
THE HIGHLANDS
CASTLE ABERDEEN
CASTLEBAY VILLAGE
MOURNA
THE HANDHILLS
THE FINGERS
CASTLE KISIMUL
EVESFALL
CASTLEBAY
THE THUMBS
SERPENT'S STRAIT
ERLORNIA
VATERSAY
ERSAY
X=NORGAL & AGATHA

SISTERS OF THE HILL

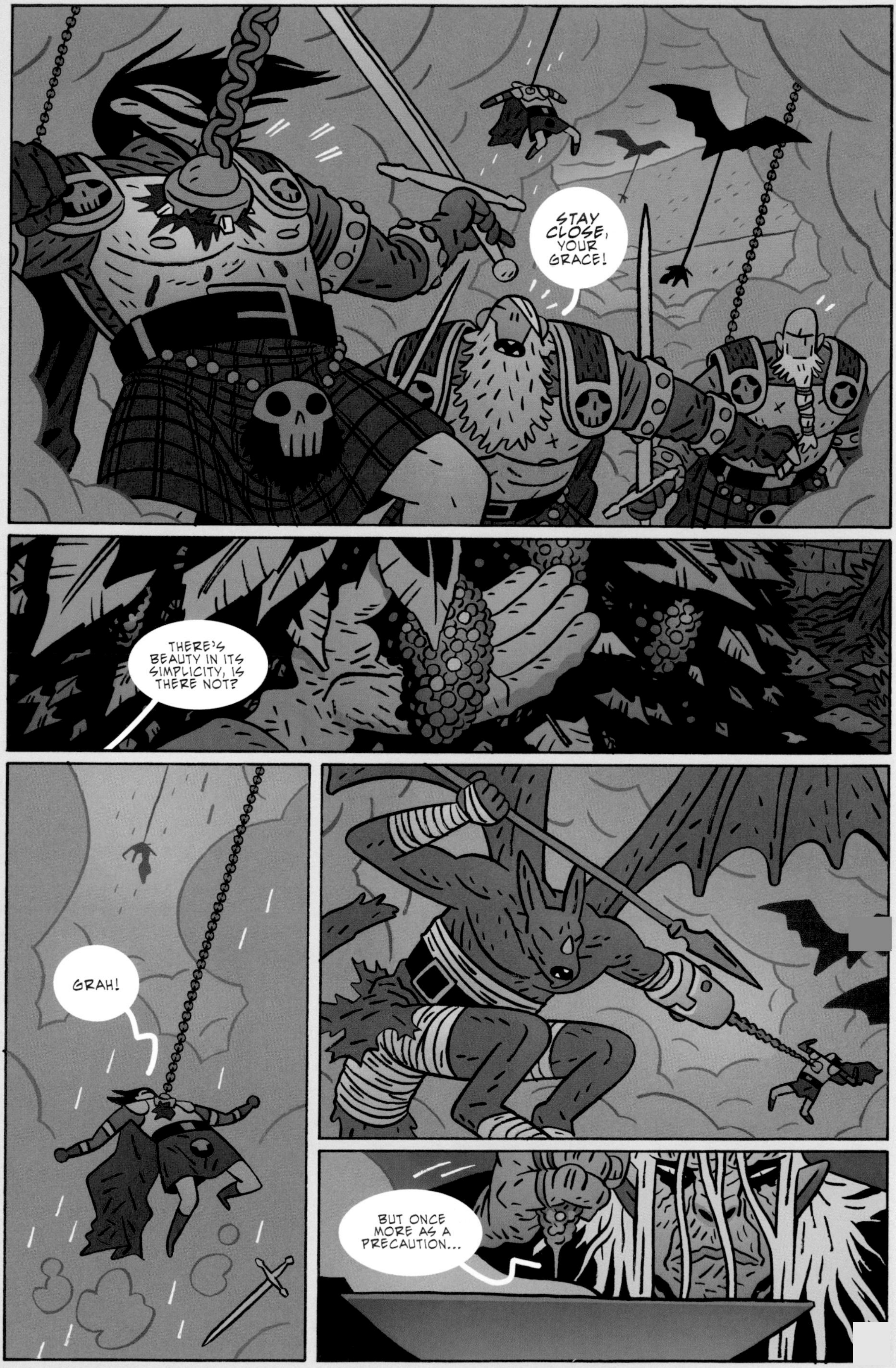
STAY CLOSE, YOUR GRACE!
THERE'S BEAUTY IN ITS SIMPLICITY, IS THERE NOT?
GRAH!
BUT ONCE MORE AS A PRECAUTION...

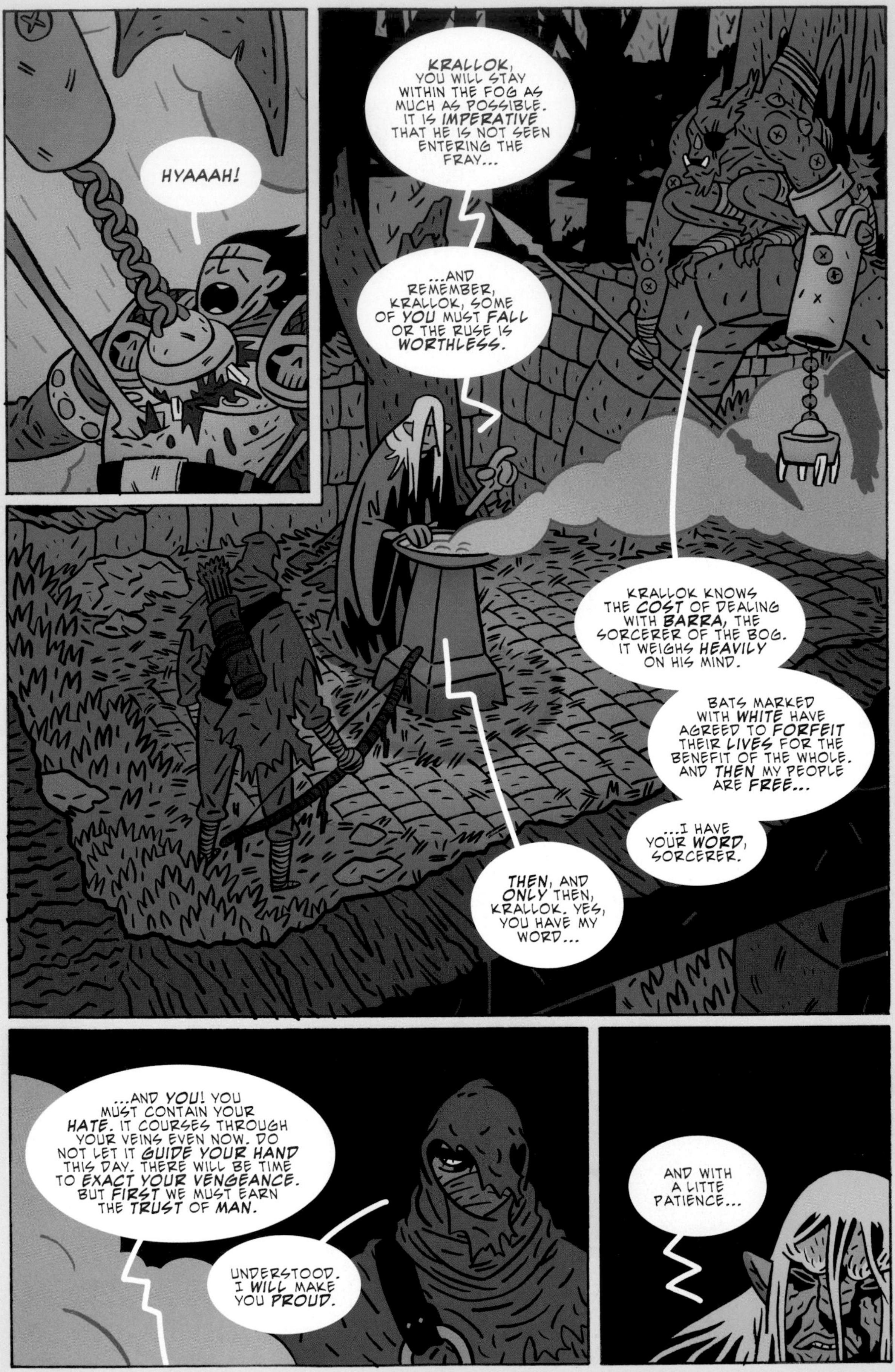
HYAAAH!
KRALLOK, YOU WILL STAY WITHIN THE FOG AS MUCH AS POSSIBLE. IT IS IMPERATIVE THAT HE IS NOT SEEN ENTERING THE FRAY...
...AND REMEMBER, KRALLOK, SOME OF YOU MUST FALL OR THE RUSE IS WORTHLESS.
KRALLOK KNOWS THE COST OF DEALING WITH BARRA, THE SORCERER OF THE BOG. IT WEIGHS HEAVILY ON HIS MIND.
BATS MARKED WITH WHITE HAVE AGREED TO FORFEIT THEIR LIVES FOR THE BENEFIT OF THE WHOLE. AND THEN MY PEOPLE ARE FREE...
...I HAVE YOUR WORD, SORCERER.
THEN, AND ONLY THEN, KRALLOK. YES, YOU HAVE MY WORD...
...AND YOU! YOU MUST CONTAIN YOUR HATE. IT COURSES THROUGH YOUR VEINS EVEN NOW. DO NOT LET IT GUIDE YOUR HAND THIS DAY. THERE WILL BE TIME TO EXACT YOUR VENGEANCE. BUT FIRST WE MUST EARN THE TRUST OF MAN.
UNDERSTOOD. I WILL MAKE YOU PROUD.
AND WITH A LITTE PATIENCE...

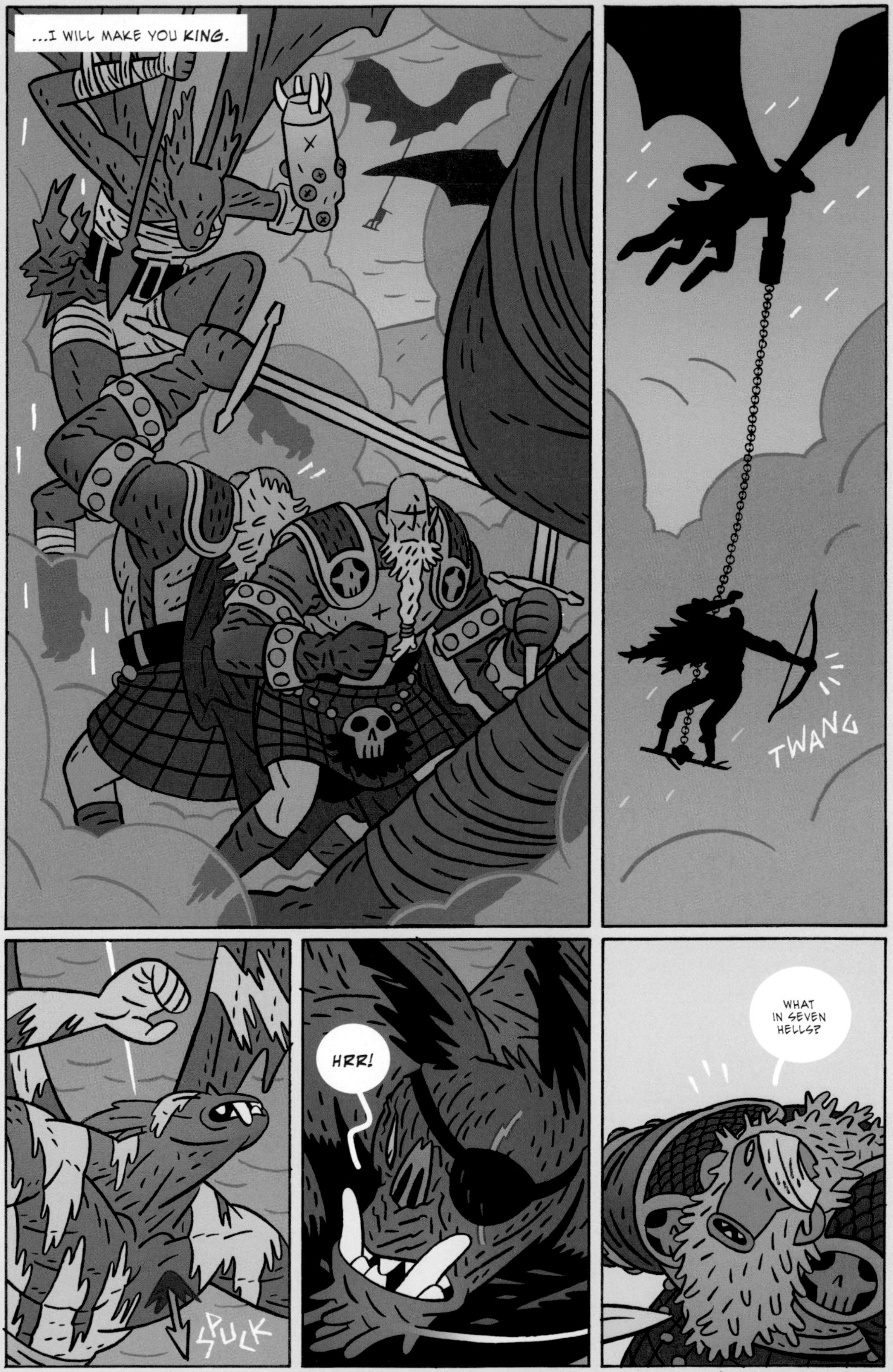

...I WILL MAKE YOU KING.
TWANG
SPULK
HRR!
WHAT IN SEVEN HELLS?

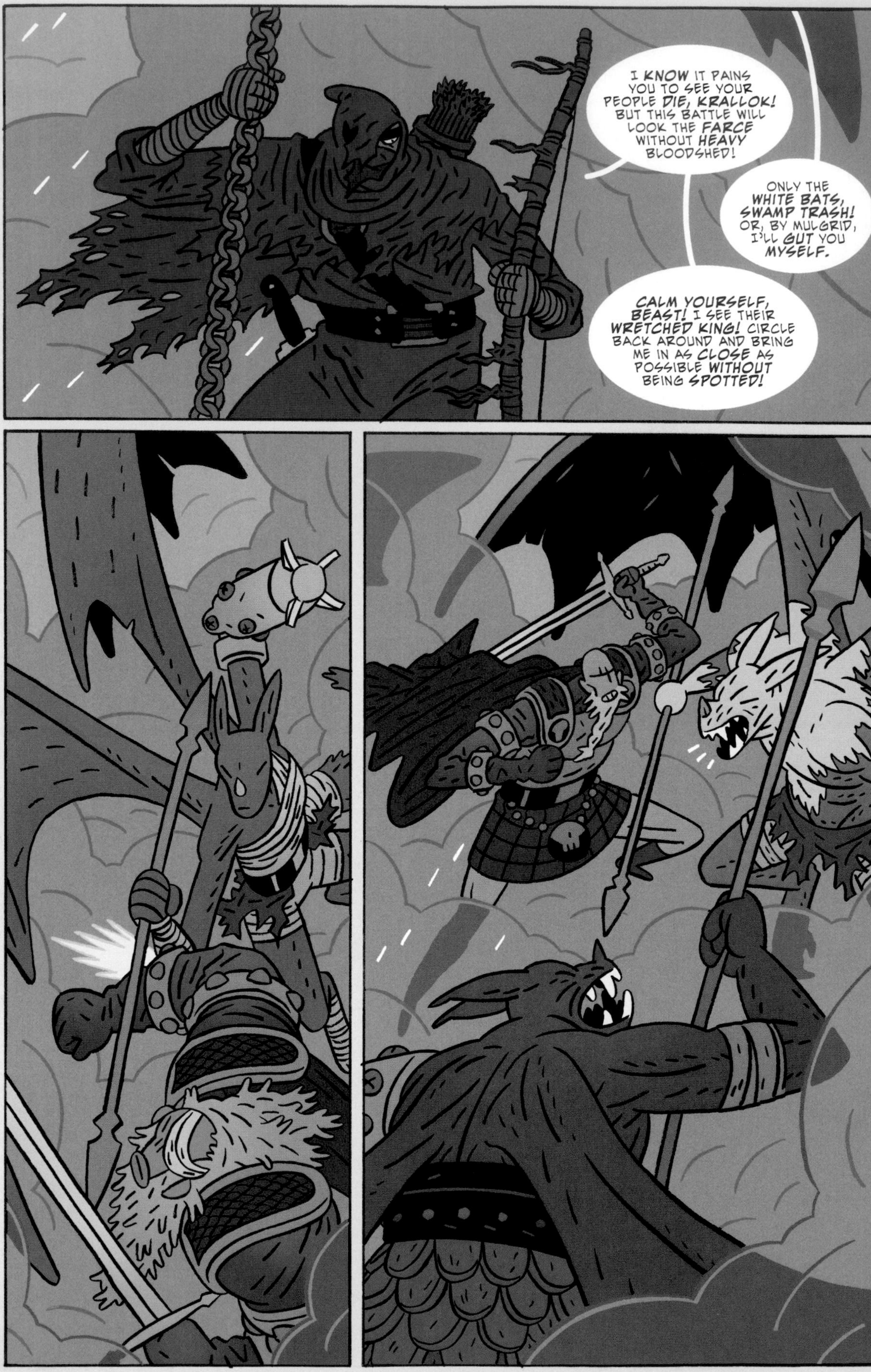
I KNOW IT PAINS YOU TO SEE YOUR PEOPLE DIE, KRALLOK! BUT THIS BATTLE WILL LOOK THE FARCE WITHOUT HEAVY BLOODSHED!
ONLY THE WHITE BATS, SWAMP TRASH! OR, BY MULGRID, I'LL GUT YOU MYSELF.
CALM YOURSELF, BEAST! I SEE THEIR WRETCHED KING! CIRCLE BACK AROUND AND BRING ME IN AS CLOSE AS POSSIBLE WITHOUT BEING SPOTTED!

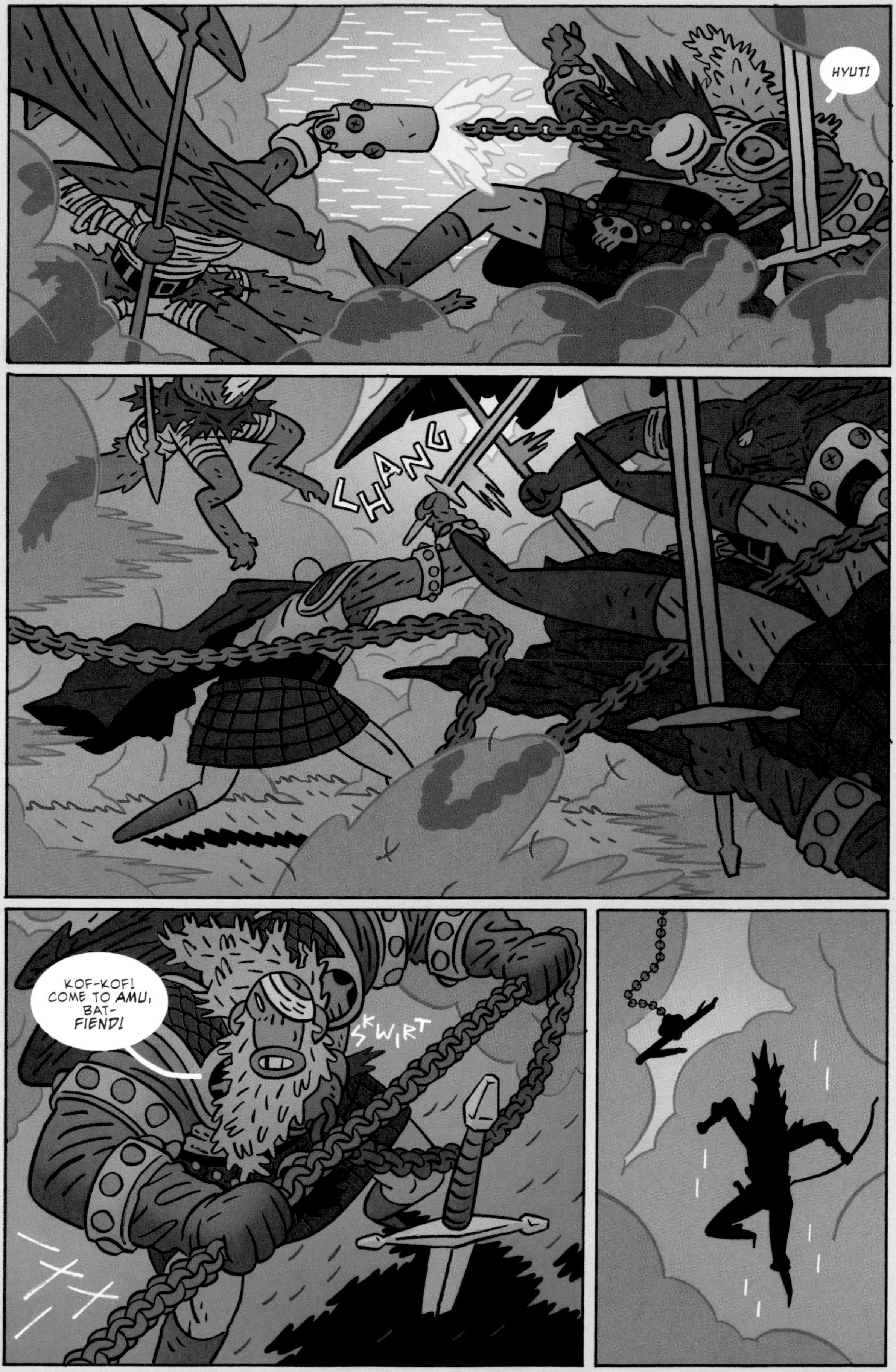
HYUT!
CHANG
KOF-KOF! COME TO AMU, BAT-FIEND!
SKWIRT

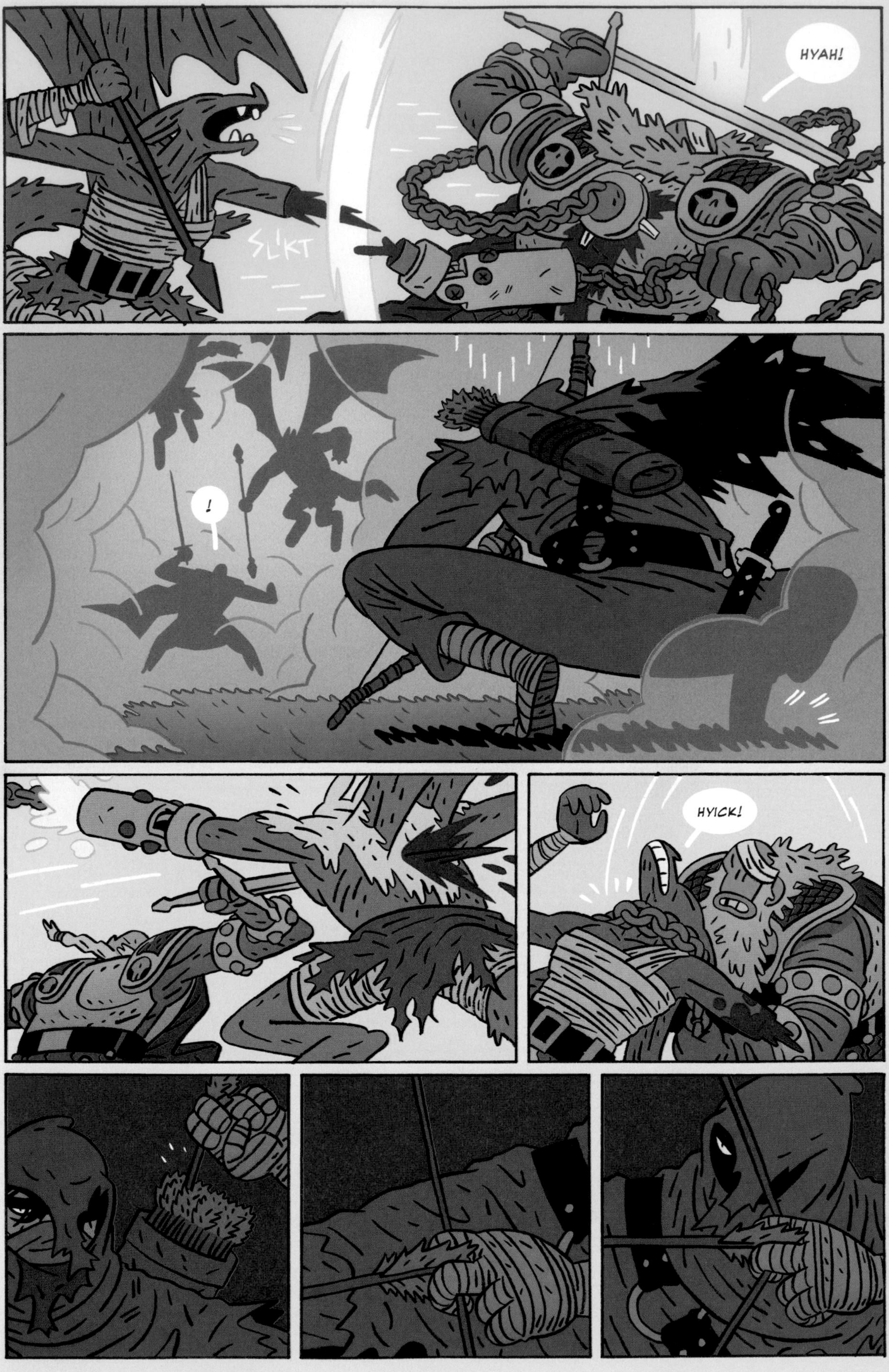
HYAH!
SLIKT
!
HYICK!

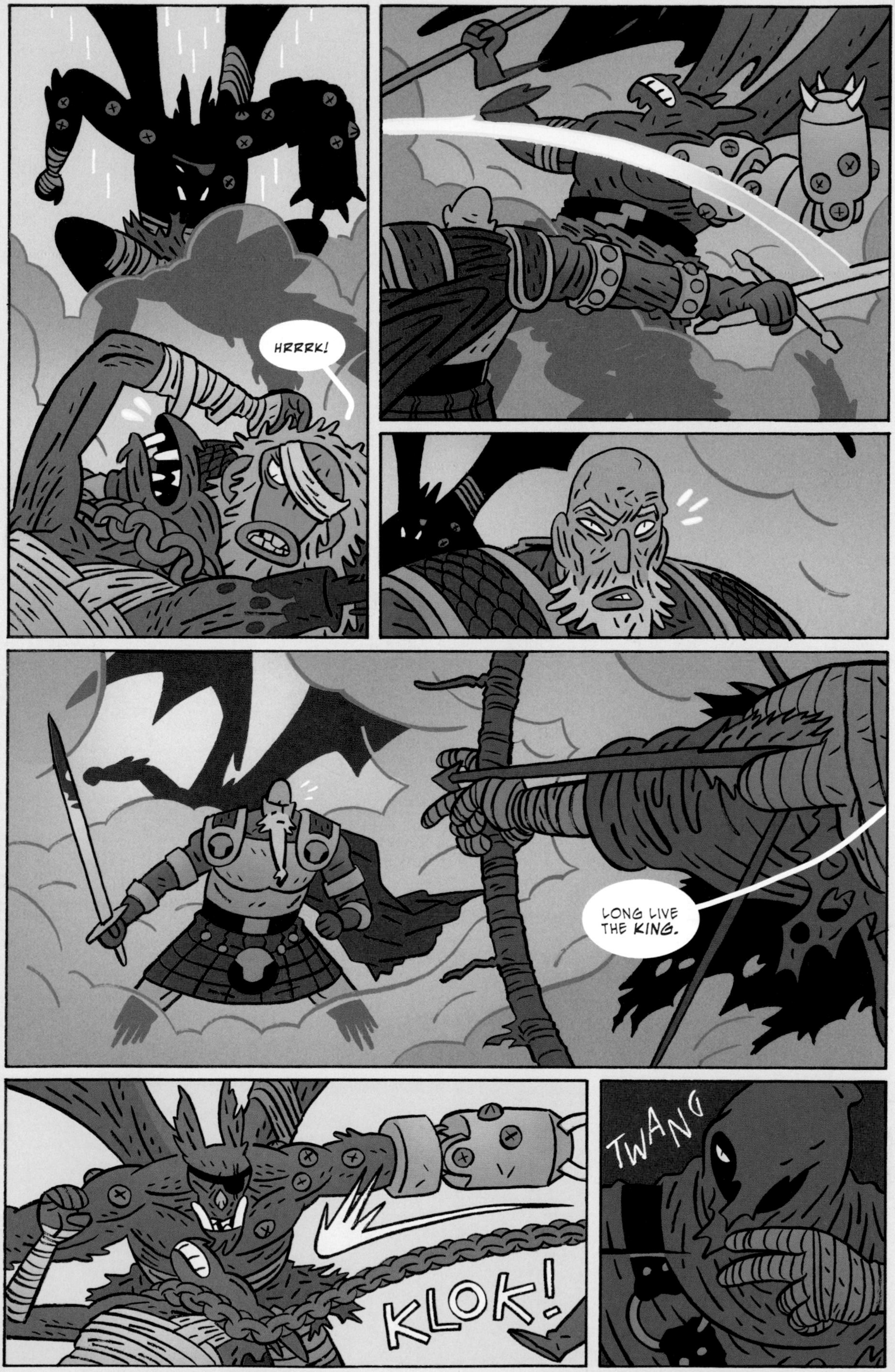
HRRRK!
LONG LIVE THE KING.
TWANG
KLOK!

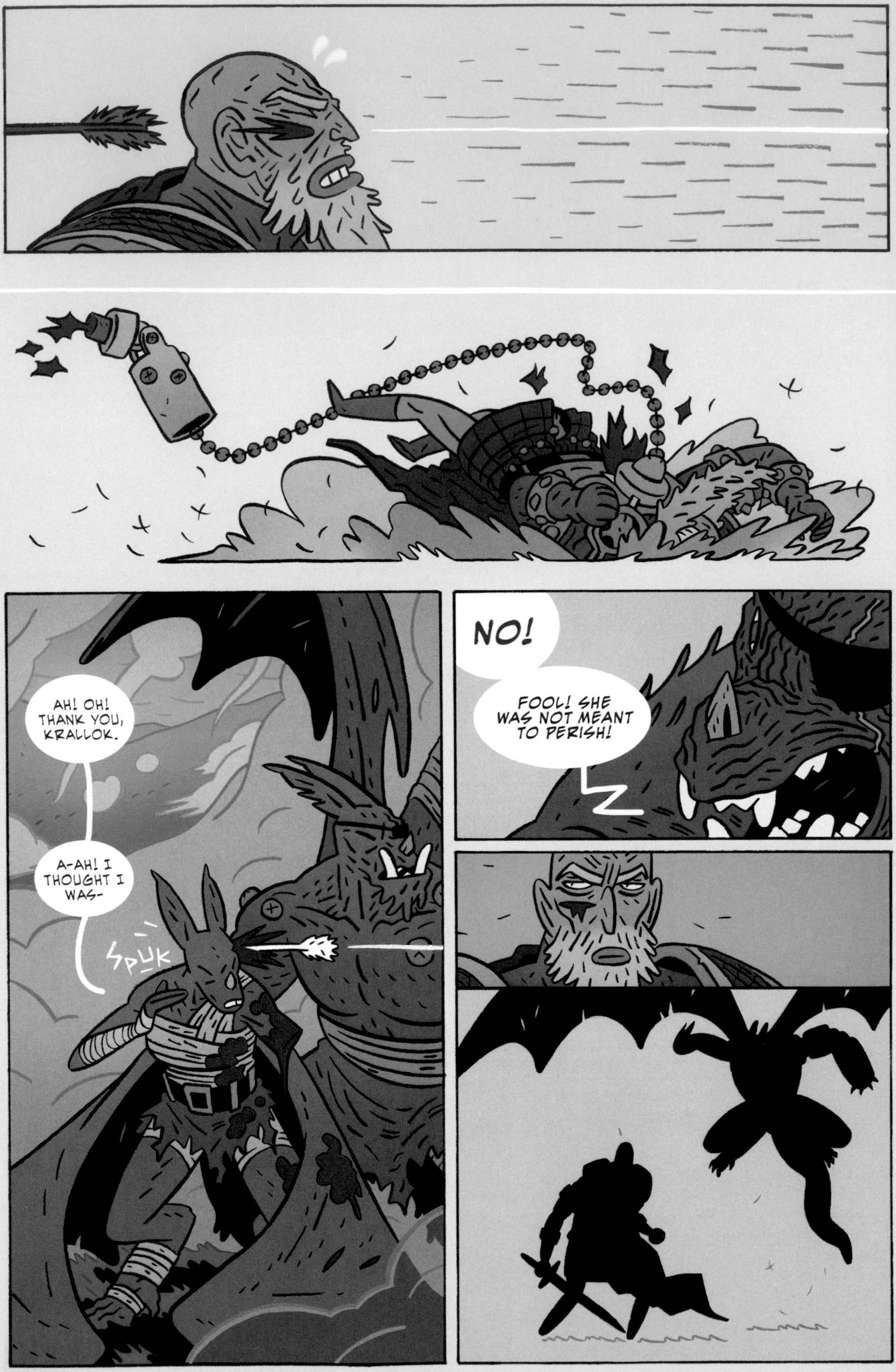

AH! OH! THANK YOU, KRALLOK.
A-AH! I THOUGHT I WAS-
SPUK
NO!
FOOL! SHE WAS NOT MEANT TO PERISH!

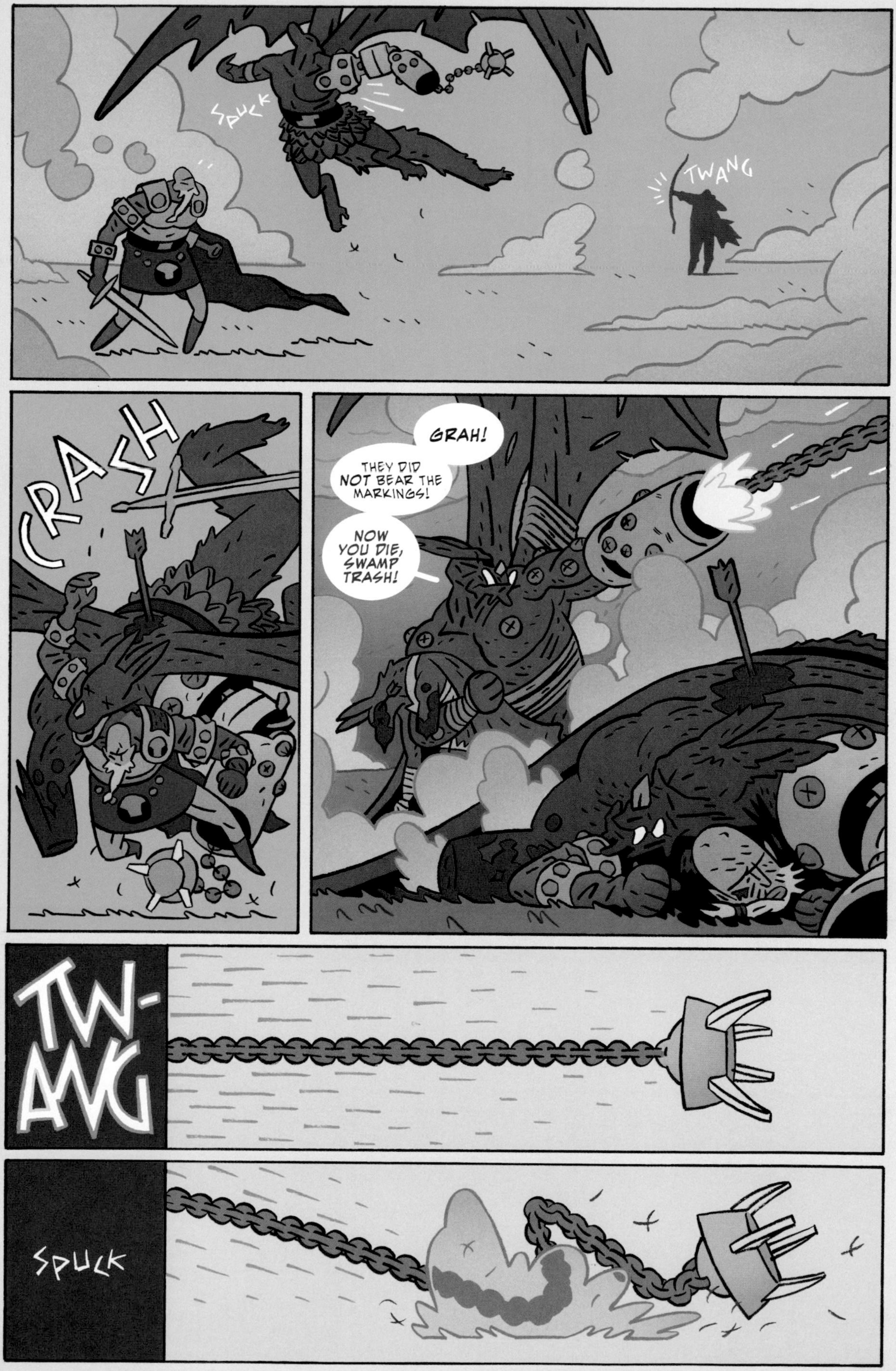
SPUCK
TWANG
CRASH
GRAH!
THEY DID NOT BEAR THE MARKINGS!
NOW YOU DIE, SWAMP TRASH!
TW-ANG
SPUCK

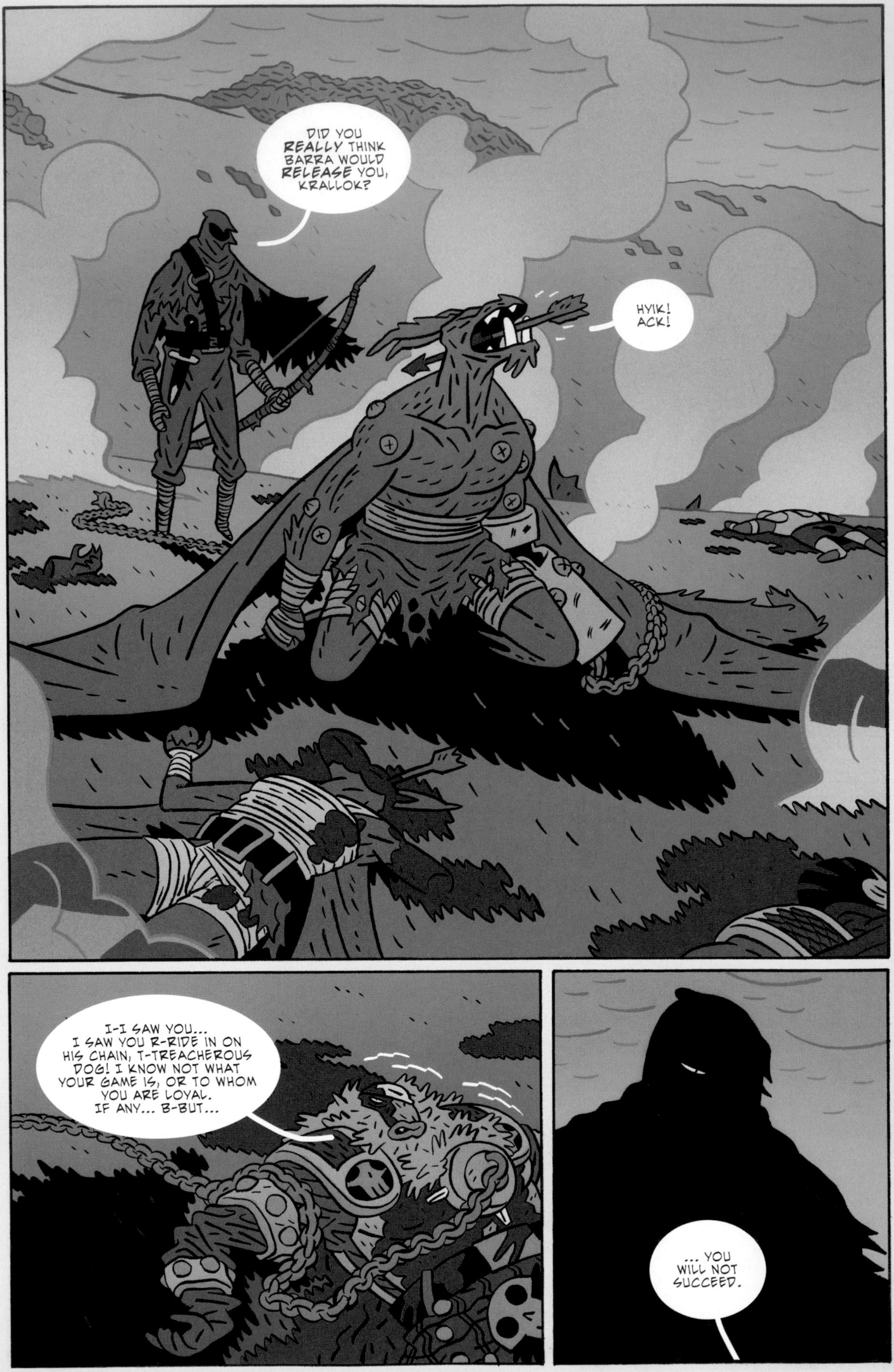
DID YOU REALLY THINK BARRA WOULD RELEASE YOU, KRALLOK?
HYIK! ACK!
I-I SAW YOU... I SAW YOU R-RIDE IN ON HIS CHAIN, T-TREACHEROUS DOG! I KNOW NOT WHAT YOUR GAME IS, OR TO WHOM YOU ARE LOYAL. IF ANY... B-BUT...
...YOU WILL NOT SUCCEED.

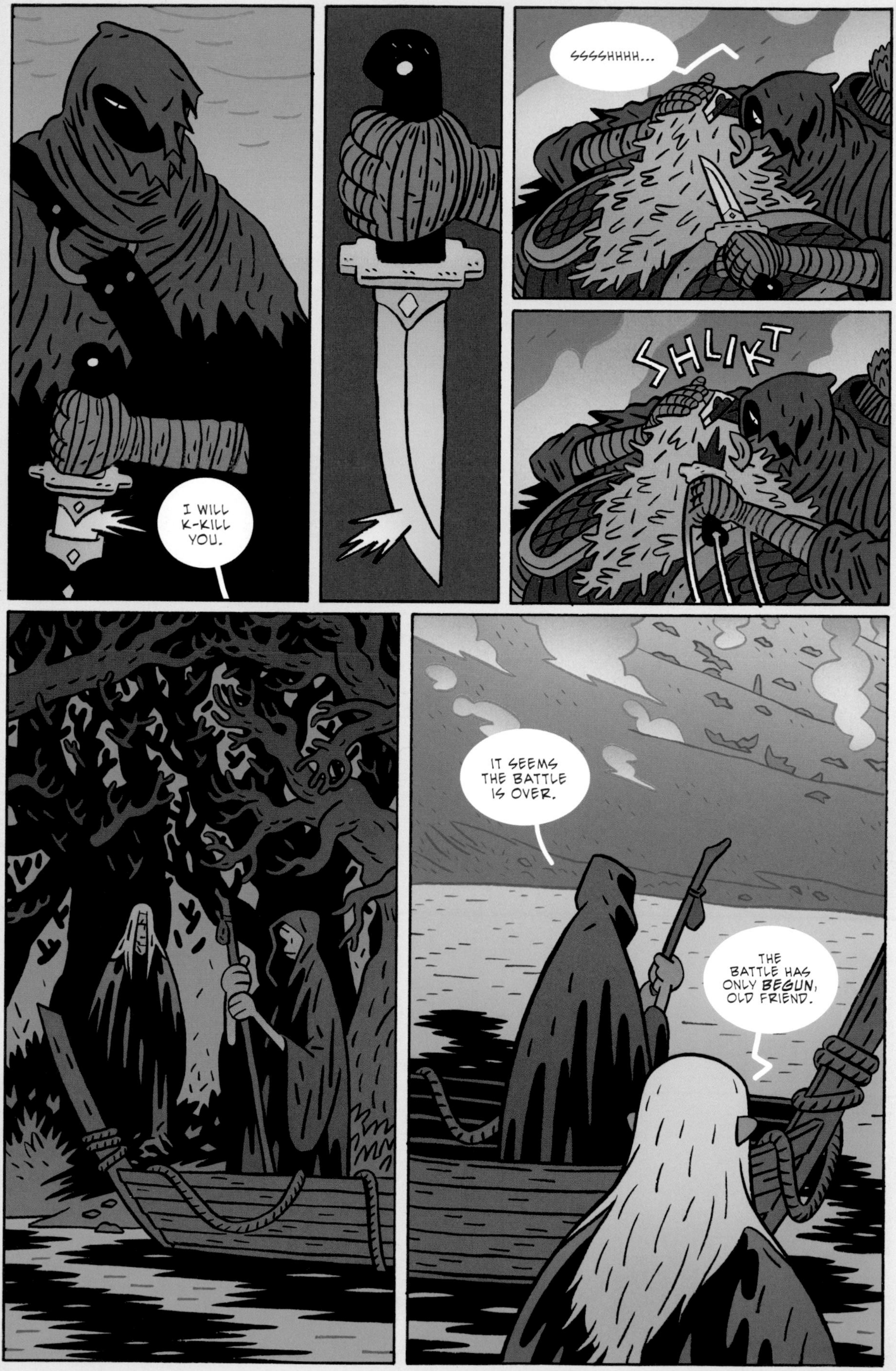

I WILL K-KILL YOU.
SSSSHHHH...
SHLIKT
IT SEEMS THE BATTLE IS OVER.
THE BATTLE HAS ONLY BEGUN, OLD FRIEND.

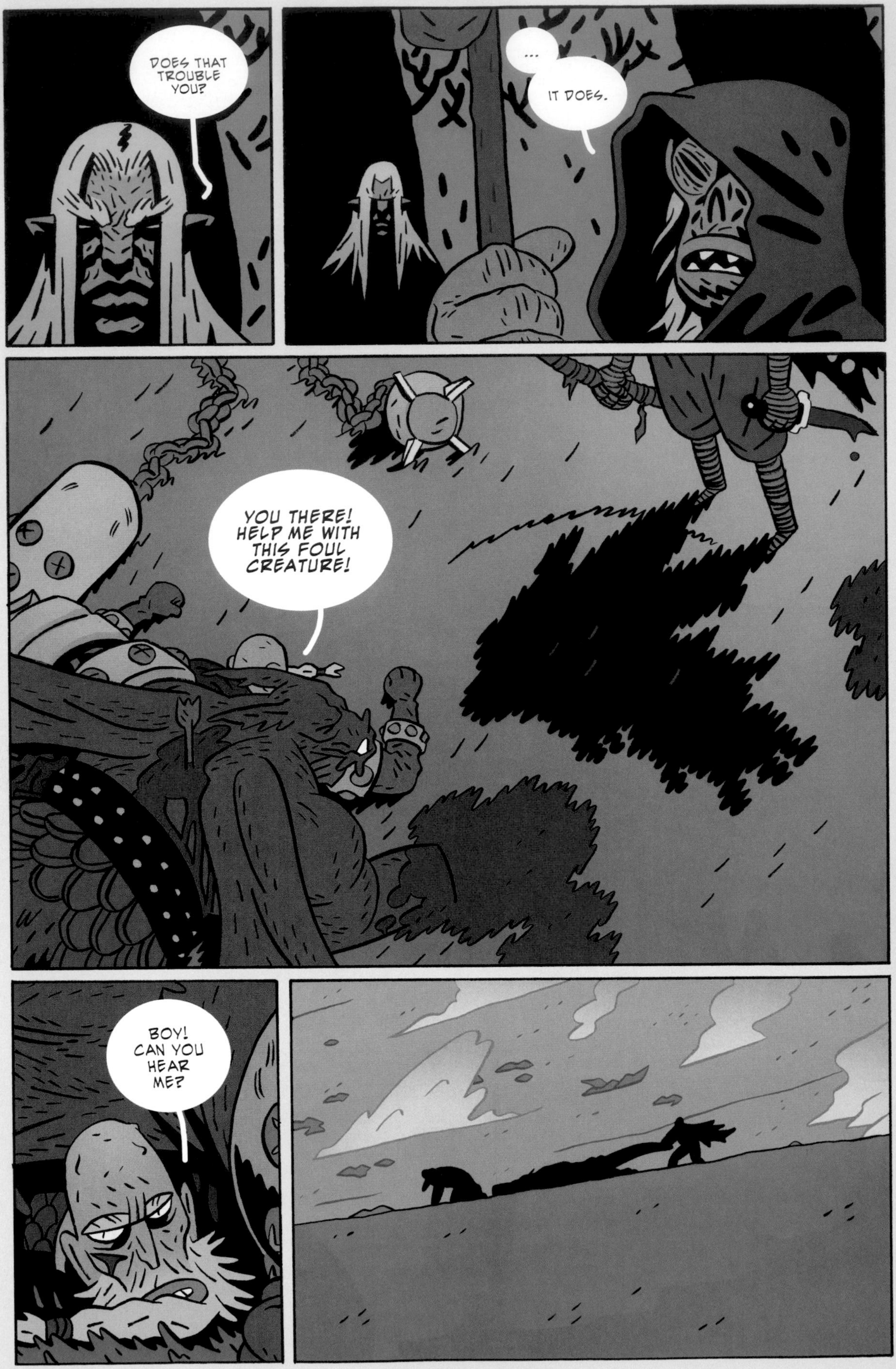
DOES THAT TROUBLE YOU?
...
IT DOES.
YOU THERE! HELP ME WITH THIS FOUL CREATURE!
BOY! CAN YOU HEAR ME?

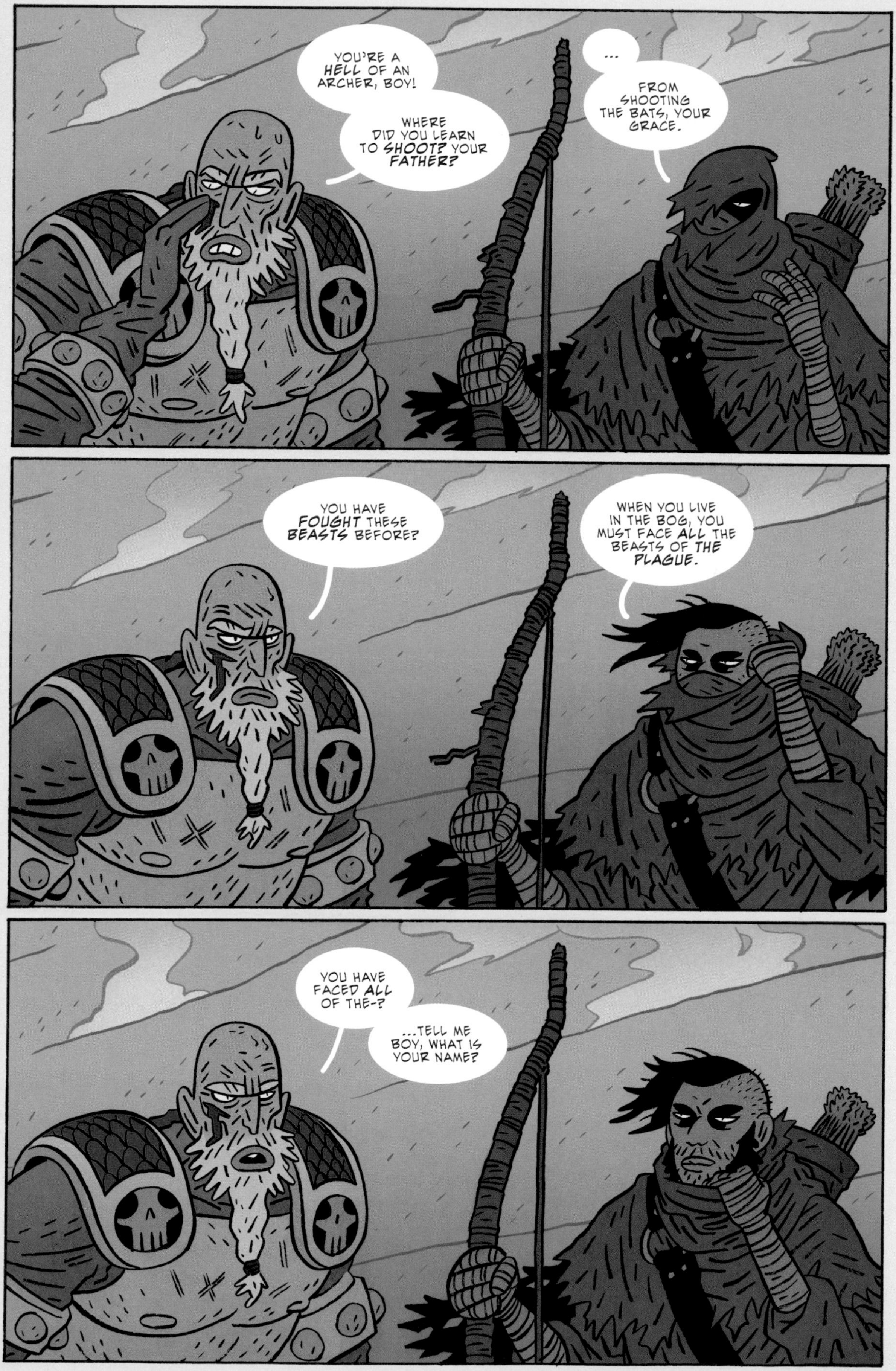
YOU'RE A HELL OF AN ARCHER, BOY!
WHERE DID YOU LEARN TO SHOOT? YOUR FATHER?
...
FROM SHOOTING THE BATS, YOUR GRACE.
YOU HAVE FOUGHT THESE BEASTS BEFORE?
WHEN YOU LIVE IN THE BOG, YOU MUST FACE ALL THE BEASTS OF THE PLAGUE.
YOU HAVE FACED ALL OF THE-?
...TELL ME BOY, WHAT IS YOUR NAME?

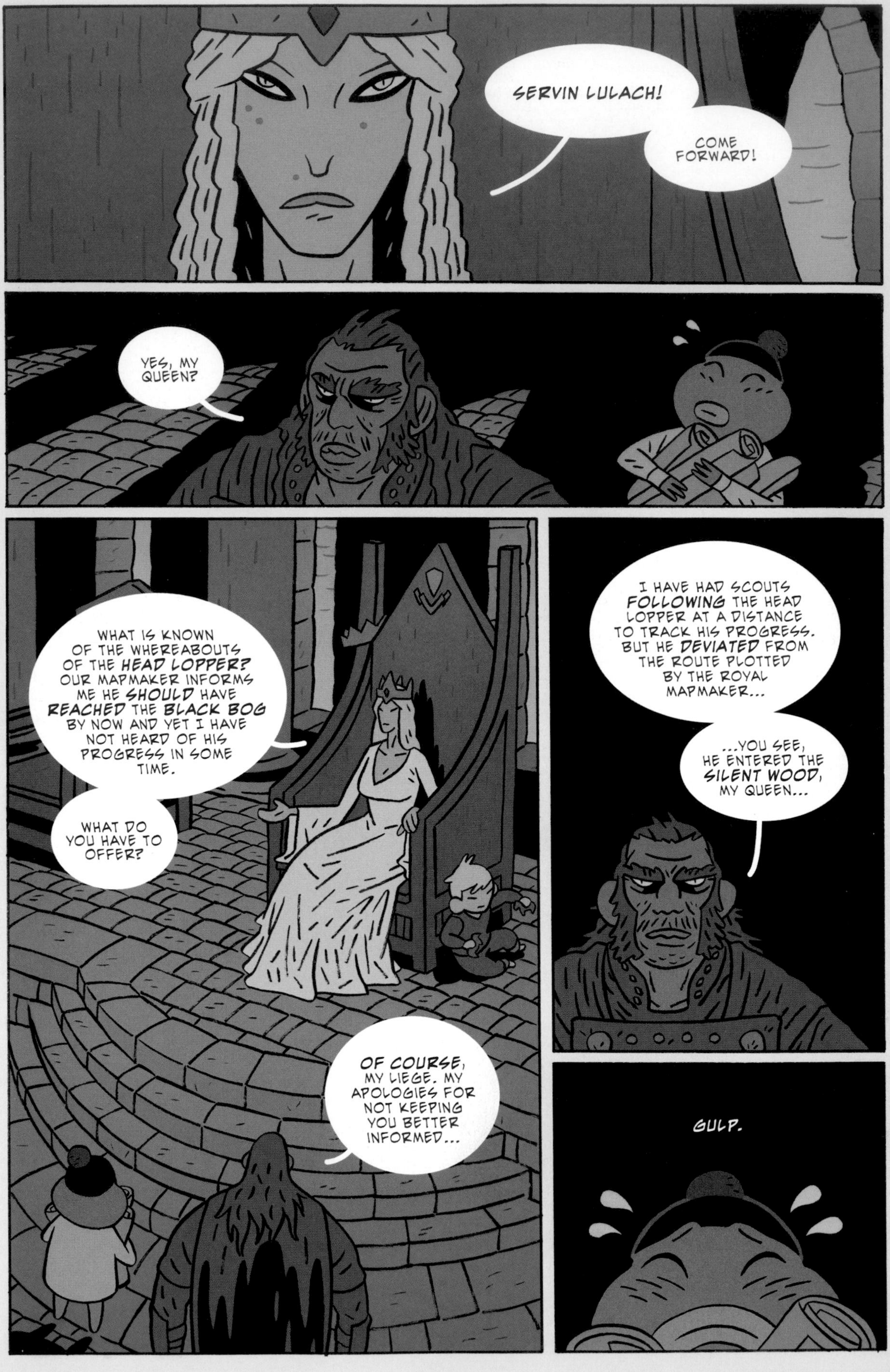
SERVIN LULACH!
COME FORWARD!
YES, MY QUEEN?
WHAT IS KNOWN OF THE WHEREABOUTS OF THE HEAD LOPPER? OUR MAPMAKER INFORMS ME HE SHOULD HAVE REACHED THE BLACK BOG BY NOW AND YET I HAVE NOT HEARD OF HIS PROGRESS IN SOME TIME.
WHAT DO YOU HAVE TO OFFER?
OF COURSE, MY LIEGE. MY APOLOGIES FOR NOT KEEPING YOU BETTER INFORMED...
I HAVE HAD SCOUTS FOLLOWING THE HEAD LOPPER AT A DISTANCE TO TRACK HIS PROGRESS. BUT HE DEVIATED FROM THE ROUTE PLOTTED BY THE ROYAL MAPMAKER...
...YOU SEE, HE ENTERED THE SILENT WOOD, MY QUEEN...
GULP.

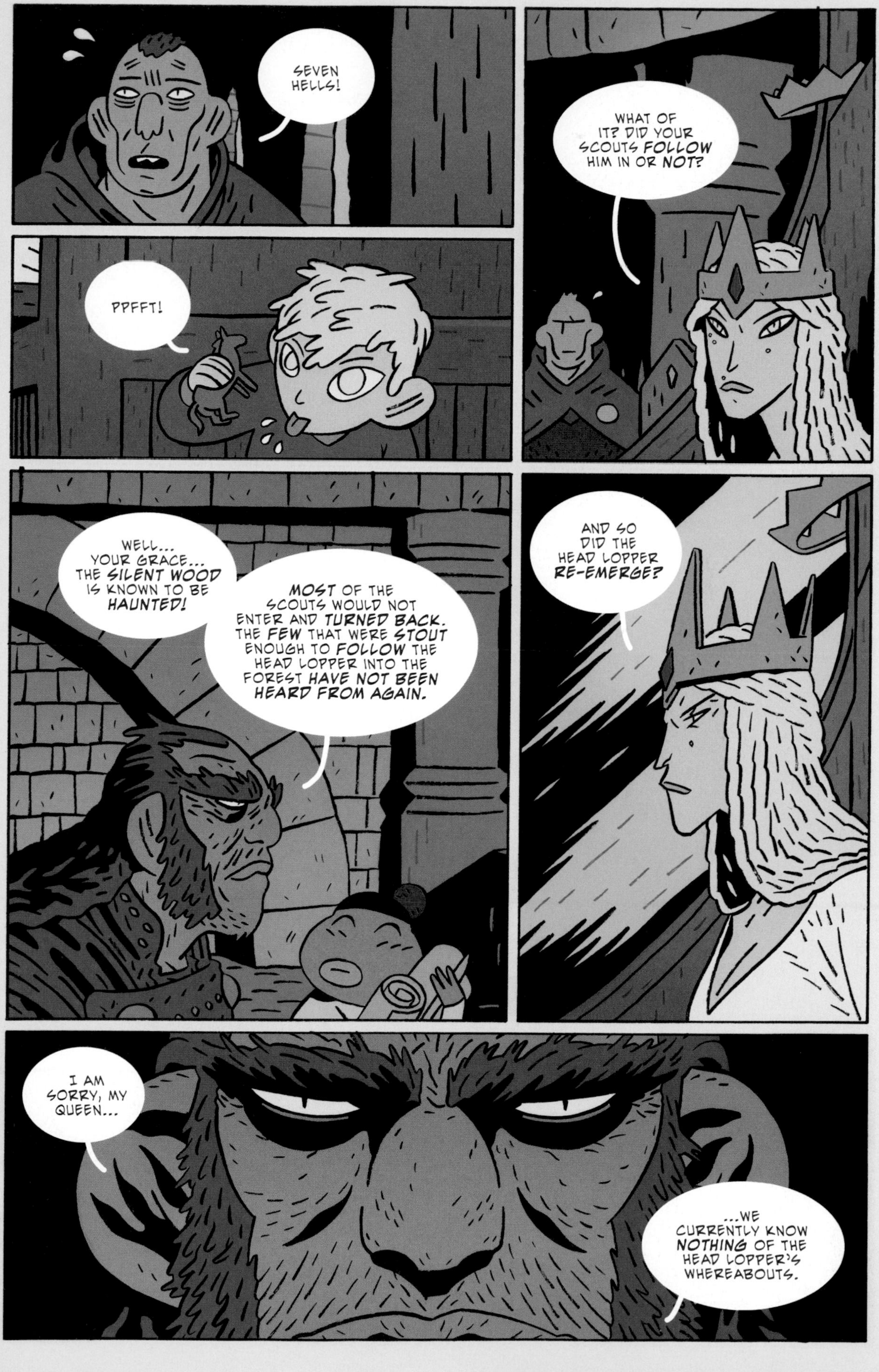
SEVEN HELLS!
WHAT OF IT? DID YOUR SCOUTS FOLLOW HIM IN OR NOT?
PPFFT!
WELL... YOUR GRACE... THE SILENT WOOD IS KNOWN TO BE HAUNTED!
MOST OF THE SCOUTS WOULD NOT ENTER AND TURNED BACK. THE FEW THAT WERE STOUT ENOUGH TO FOLLOW THE HEAD LOPPER INTO THE FOREST HAVE NOT BEEN HEARD FROM AGAIN.
AND SO DID THE HEAD LOPPER RE-EMERGE?
I AM SORRY, MY QUEEN...
...WE CURRENTLY KNOW NOTHING OF THE HEAD LOPPER'S WHEREABOUTS.

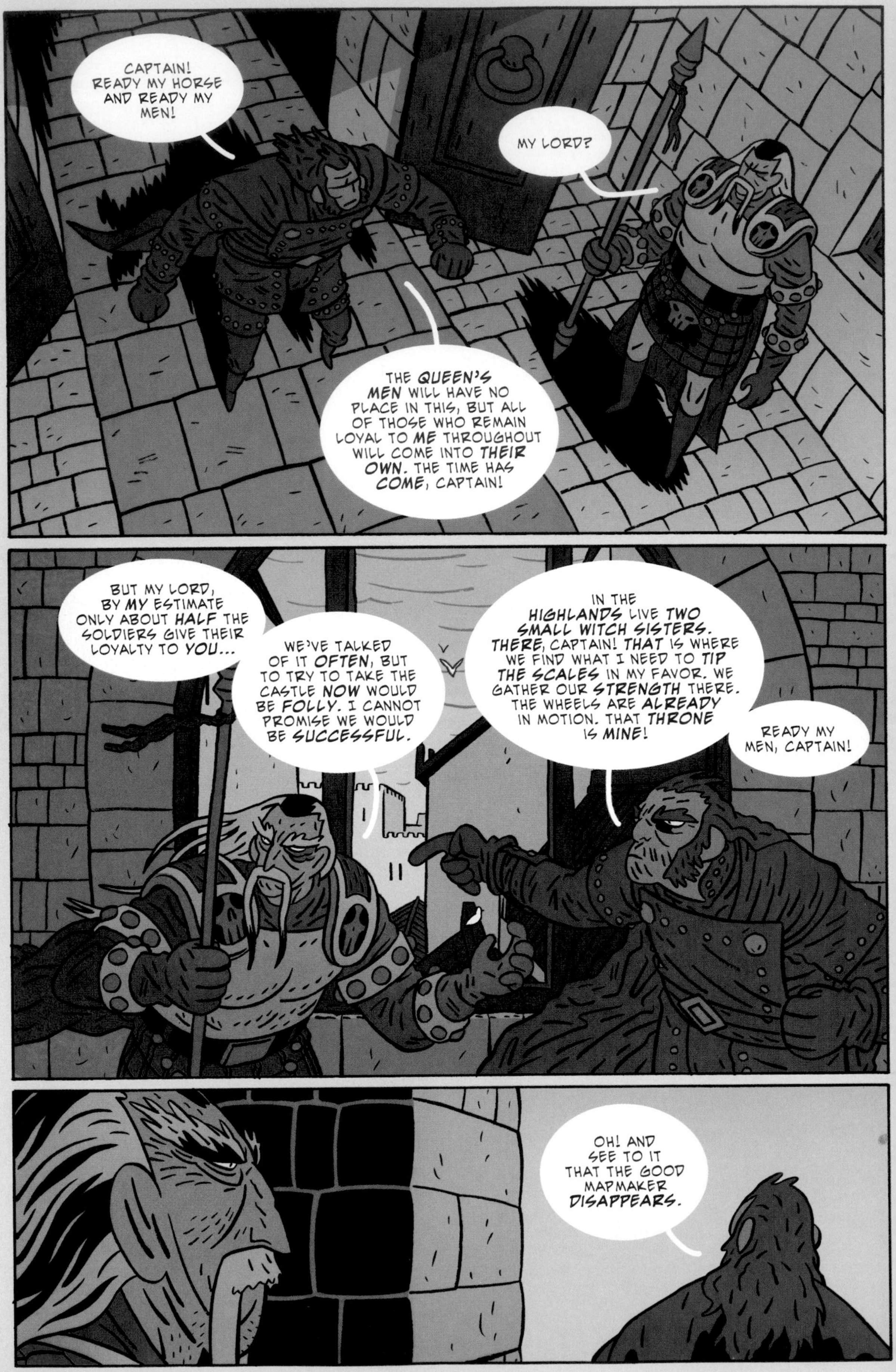
CAPTAIN! READY MY HORSE AND READY MY MEN!
MY LORD?
THE QUEEN'S MEN WILL HAVE NO PLACE IN THIS, BUT ALL OF THOSE WHO REMAIN LOYAL TO ME THROUGHOUT WILL COME INTO THEIR OWN. THE TIME HAS COME, CAPTAIN!
BUT MY LORD, BY MY ESTIMATE ONLY ABOUT HALF THE SOLDIERS GIVE THEIR LOYALTY TO YOU...
WE'VE TALKED OF IT OFTEN, BUT TO TRY TO TAKE THE CASTLE NOW WOULD BE FOLLY. I CANNOT PROMISE WE WOULD BE SUCCESSFUL.
IN THE HIGHLANDS LIVE TWO SMALL WITCH SISTERS. THERE, CAPTAIN! THAT IS WHERE WE FIND WHAT I NEED TO TIP THE SCALES IN MY FAVOR. WE GATHER OUR STRENGTH THERE. THE WHEELS ARE ALREADY IN MOTION. THAT THRONE IS MINE!
READY MY MEN, CAPTAIN!
OH! AND SEE TO IT THAT THE GOOD MAPMAKER DISAPPEARS.

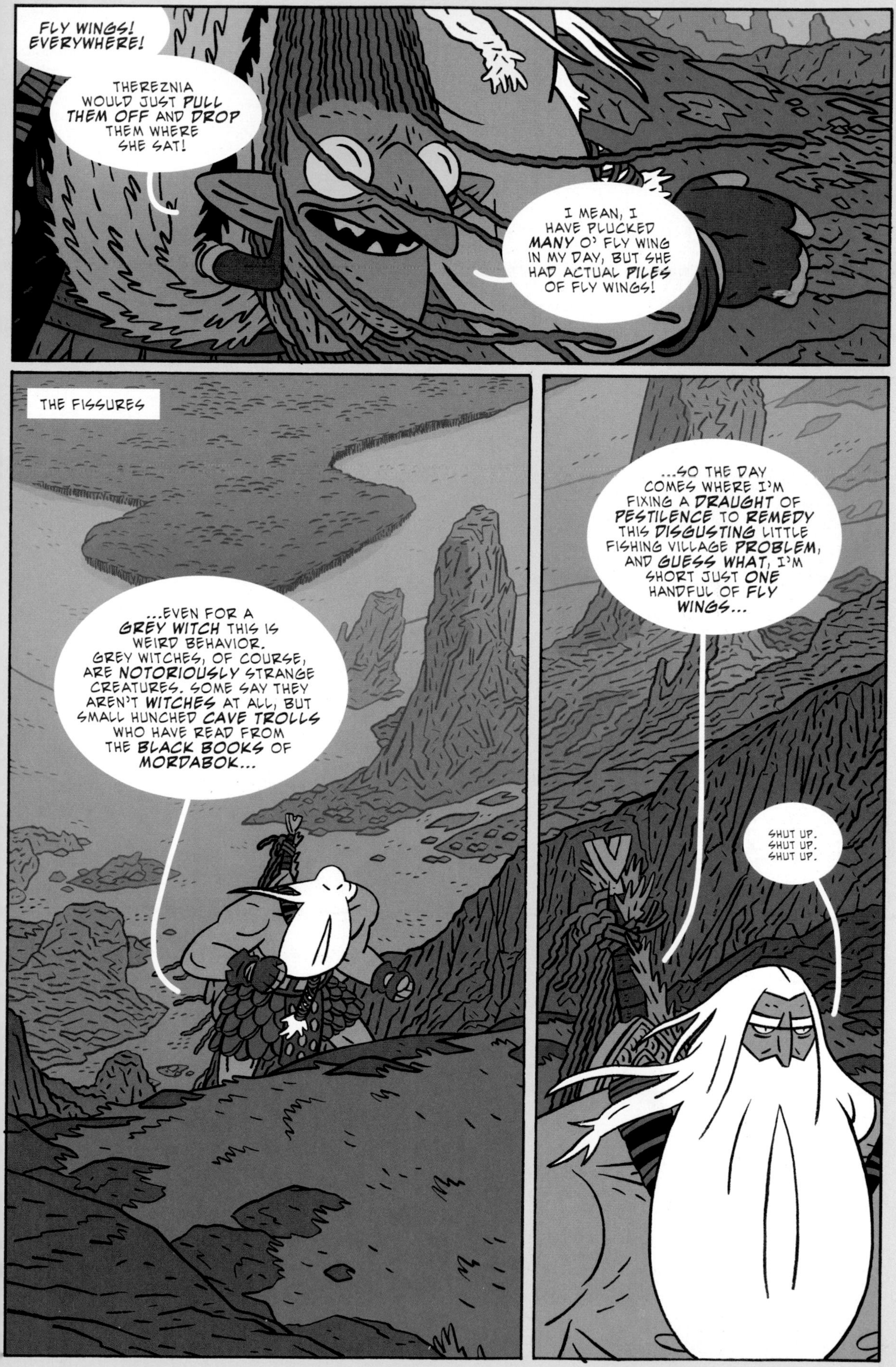
FLY WINGS! EVERYWHERE!
THEREZNIA WOULD JUST PULL THEM OFF AND DROP THEM WHERE SHE SAT!
I MEAN, I HAVE PLUCKED MANY O' FLY WING IN MY DAY, BUT SHE HAD ACTUAL PILES OF FLY WINGS!
THE FISSURES
...EVEN FOR A GREY WITCH THIS IS WEIRD BEHAVIOR. GREY WITCHES, OF COURSE, ARE NOTORIOUSLY STRANGE CREATURES. SOME SAY THEY AREN'T WITCHES AT ALL, BUT SMALL HUNCHED CAVE TROLLS WHO HAVE READ FROM THE BLACK BOOKS OF MORDABOK...
...SO THE DAY COMES WHERE I'M FIXING A DRAUGHT OF PESTILENCE TO REMEDY THIS DISGUSTING LITTLE FISHING VILLAGE PROBLEM, AND GUESS WHAT, I'M SHORT JUST ONE HANDFUL OF FLY WINGS...
SHUT UP. SHUT UP. SHUT UP.

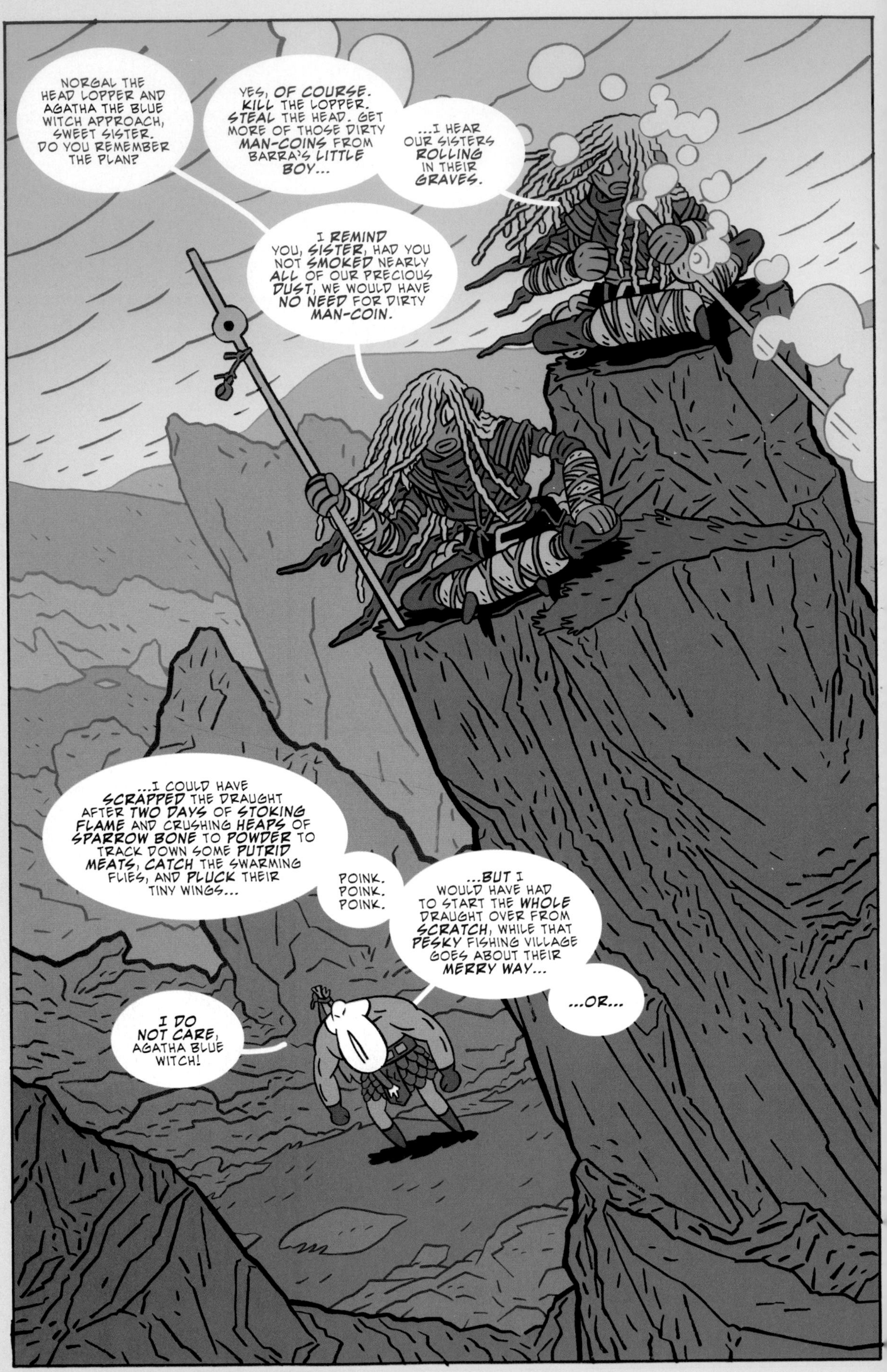
NORGAL THE HEAD LOPPER AND AGATHA THE BLUE WITCH APPROACH, SWEET SISTER. DO YOU REMEMBER THE PLAN?
YES, OF COURSE. KILL THE LOPPER. STEAL THE HEAD. GET MORE OF THOSE DIRTY MAN-COINS FROM BARRA'S LITTLE BOY...
...I HEAR OUR SISTERS ROLLING IN THEIR GRAVES.
I REMIND YOU, SISTER, HAD YOU NOT SMOKED NEARLY ALL OF OUR PRECIOUS DUST, WE WOULD HAVE NO NEED FOR DIRTY MAN-COIN.
...I COULD HAVE SCRAPPED THE DRAUGHT AFTER TWO DAYS OF STOKING FLAME AND CRUSHING HEAPS OF SPARROW BONE TO POWDER TO TRACK DOWN SOME PUTRID MEATS, CATCH THE SWARMING FLIES, AND PLUCK THEIR TINY WINGS...
POINK. POINK. POINK.
...BUT I WOULD HAVE HAD TO START THE WHOLE DRAUGHT OVER FROM SCRATCH, WHILE THAT PESKY FISHING VILLAGE GOES ABOUT THEIR MERRY WAY...
...OR...
I DO NOT CARE, AGATHA BLUE WITCH!

...OR I COULD JUST WALK THE SIX STONE-THROW TO WHERE *THEREZNIA* HAD *SO* MANY FLY WINGS THEY *SWIRLED* ABOUT HER FEET WITH EVERY STEP.

GROAN

...SO I MADE LIKE I HAD BEEN PASSING THROUGH THE AREA AND STOPPED BY FOR A CASUAL VISIT. I ASKED HER SOME *STUPID* QUESTIONS LIKE; "WHEN IS THE NEXT COMMUNE? WAS IT THREE TURNS OF THE MOON OR FOUR? DO GREY WITCHES MEET SEPARATELY?"

MARK MY WORDS, AGATHA, IF I COULD KILL YOU AGAIN...

...WHEN *OF COURSE* THEY DON'T! EVERYONE KNOWS GREY WITCHES ARE *SOLITARY* CREATURES. BUT I HAD TO FEIGN INTEREST, NOT THAT IT EVEN *MATTERED*. SHE NEVER LOOKED UP FROM HER FLY-WING PLUCKING AND ONLY MADE THE OCCASIONAL GRUNT. WHICH *MAY* OR *MAY NOT* HAVE EVEN BEEN A RESPONSE TO A QUESTION. HELL! I'M NOT EVEN CONVINCED SHE KNEW I WAS *THERE*! JUST POINK, POINK, POINK, *AAAAAAAAALLL* DAY WITH THOSE *FLY WINGS!* SO I SNATCHED UP A HANDFUL WHEN SHE...

...

OH, THANK VENORA.

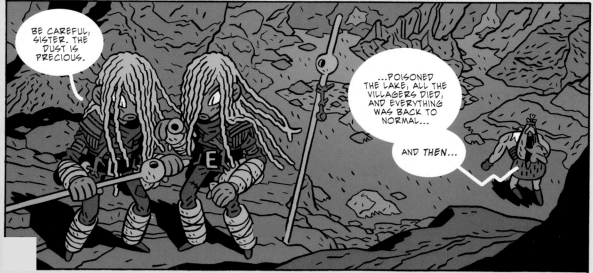

BE CAREFUL, SISTER. THE DUST IS PRECIOUS.

...POISONED THE LAKE, ALL THE VILLAGERS DIED, AND EVERYTHING WAS BACK TO NORMAL...

AND *THEN*...

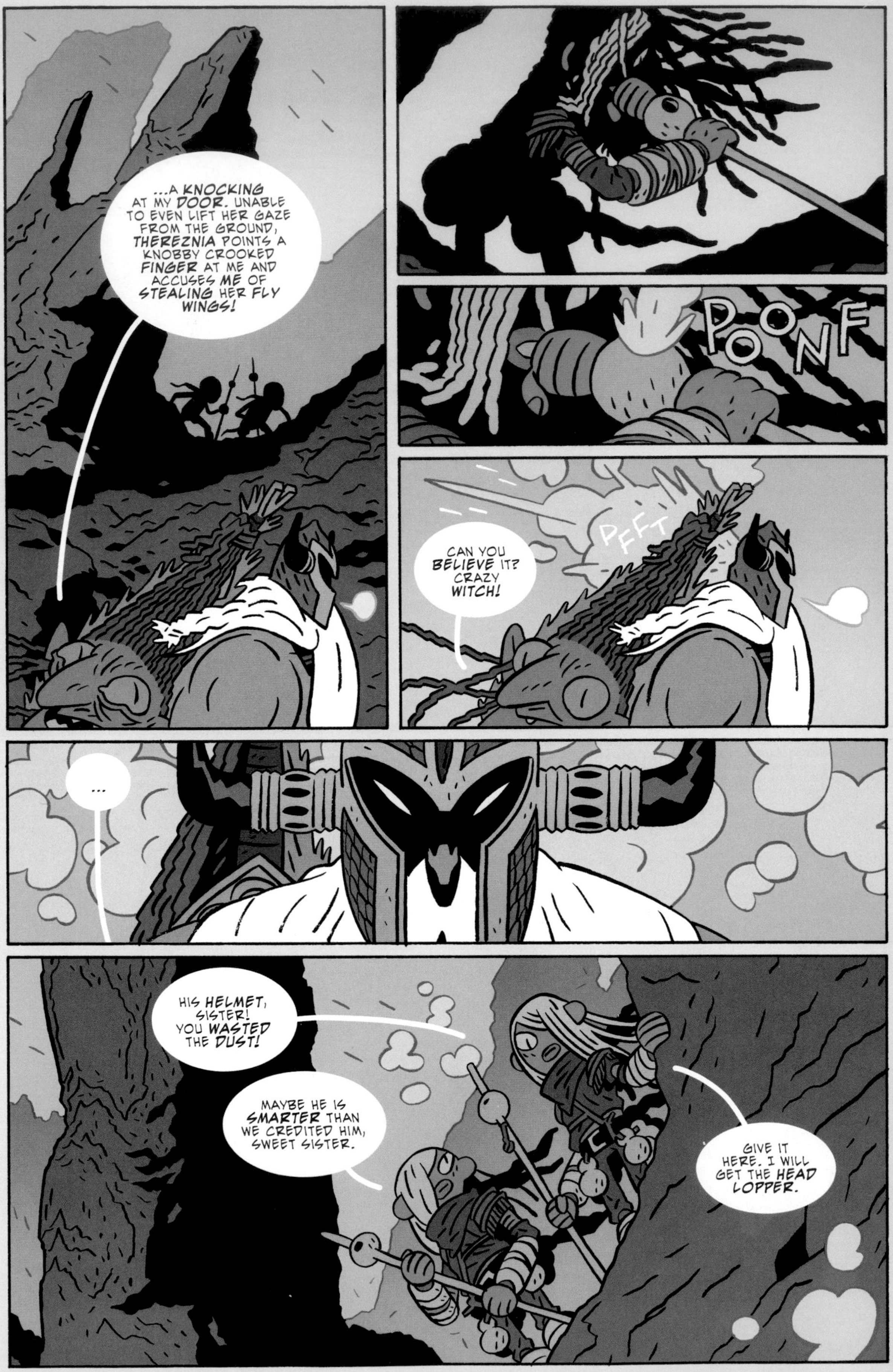
...A KNOCKING AT MY DOOR. UNABLE TO EVEN LIFT HER GAZE FROM THE GROUND, THEREZNIA POINTS A KNOBBY CROOKED FINGER AT ME AND ACCUSES ME OF STEALING HER FLY WINGS!
POONF
PFFT
CAN YOU BELIEVE IT? CRAZY WITCH!
...
HIS HELMET, SISTER! YOU WASTED THE DUST!
MAYBE HE IS SMARTER THAN WE CREDITED HIM, SWEET SISTER.
GIVE IT HERE. I WILL GET THE HEAD LOPPER.

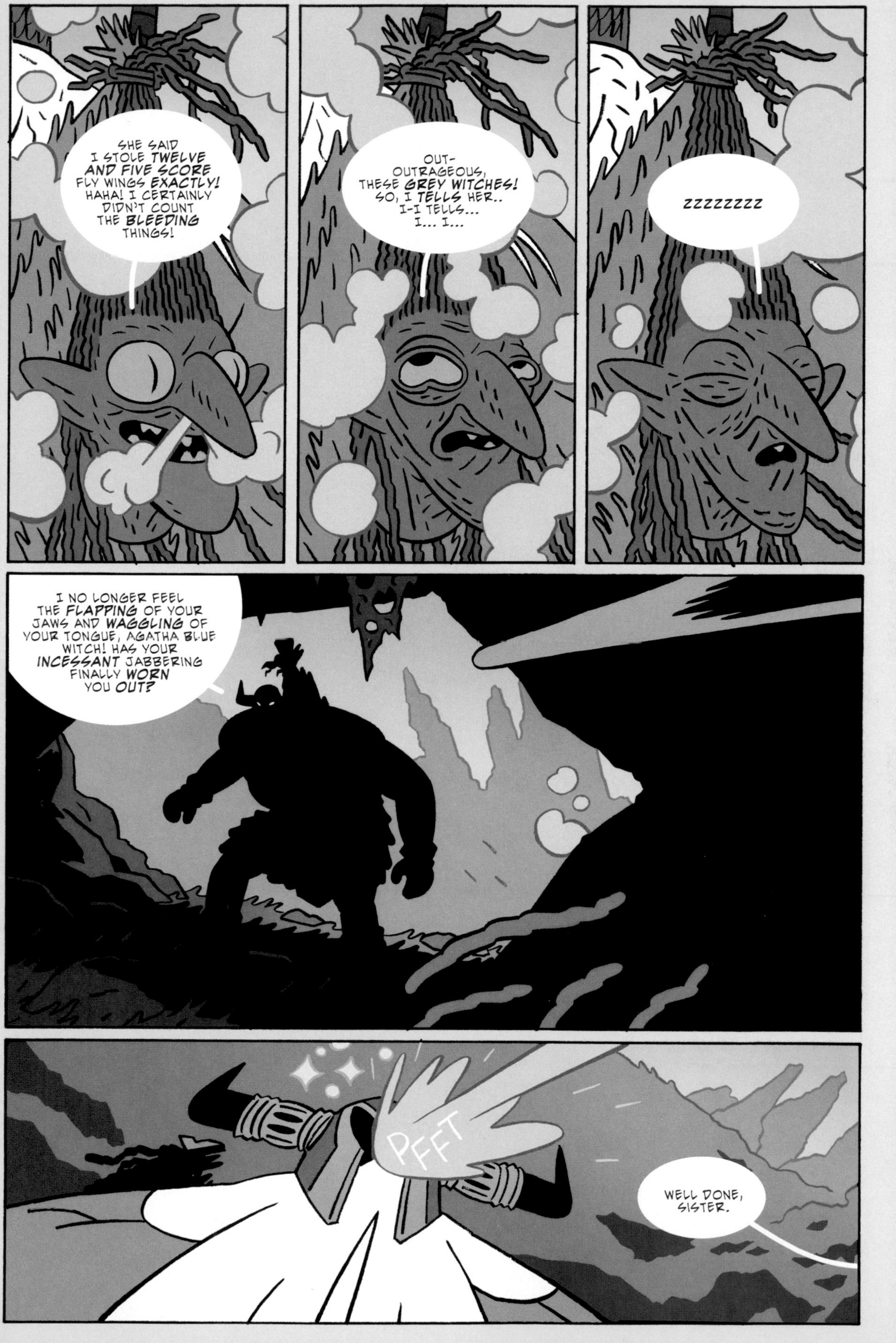
SHE SAID I STOLE TWELVE AND FIVE SCORE FLY WINGS EXACTLY! HAHA! I CERTAINLY DIDN'T COUNT THE BLEEDING THINGS!
OUT- OUTRAGEOUS, THESE GREY WITCHES! SO, I TELLS HER.. I-I TELLS... I... I...
ZZZZZZZZ
I NO LONGER FEEL THE FLAPPING OF YOUR JAWS AND WAGGLING OF YOUR TONGUE, AGATHA BLUE WITCH! HAS YOUR INCESSANT JABBERING FINALLY WORN YOU OUT?
PFFT
WELL DONE, SISTER.

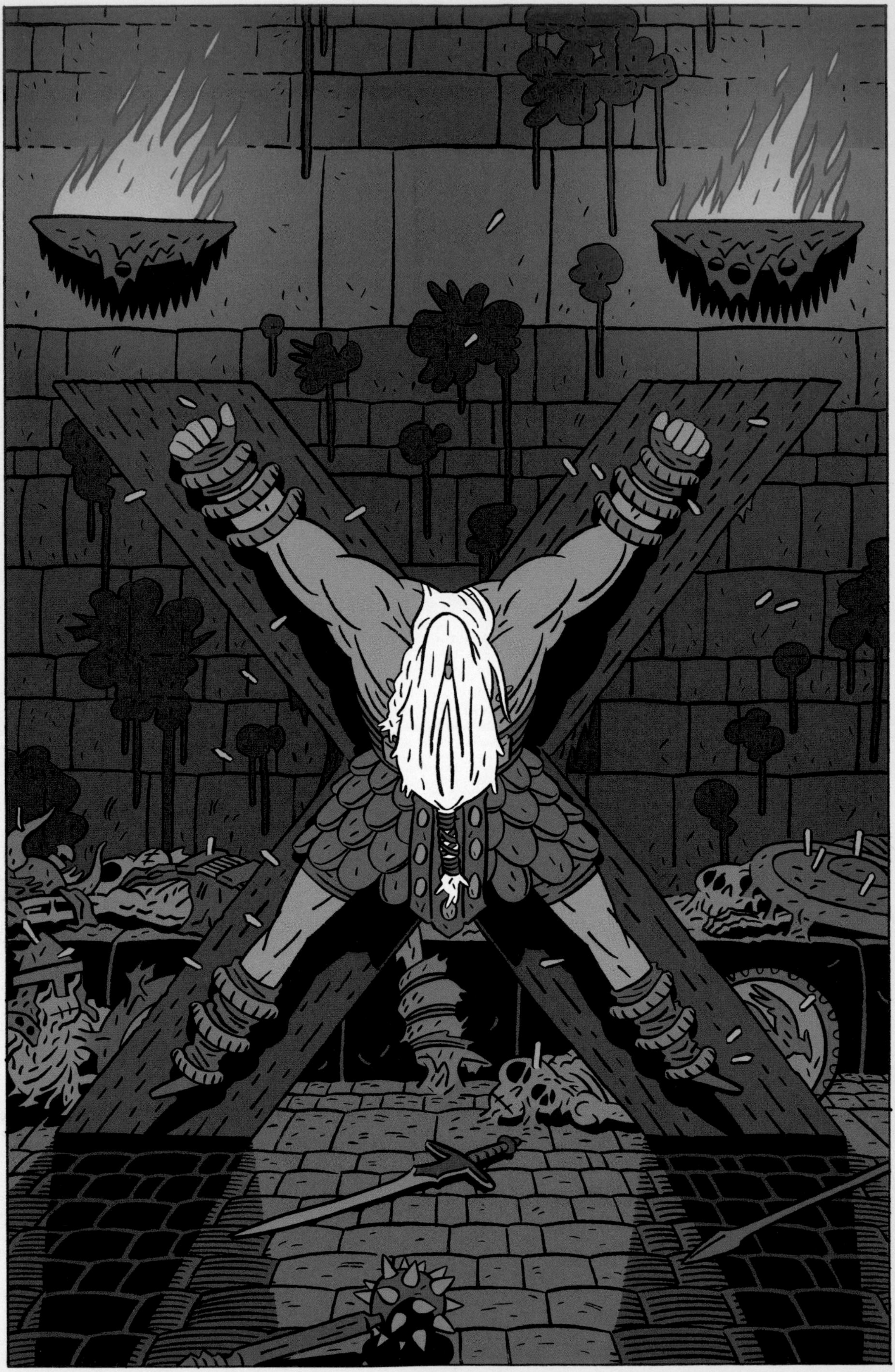

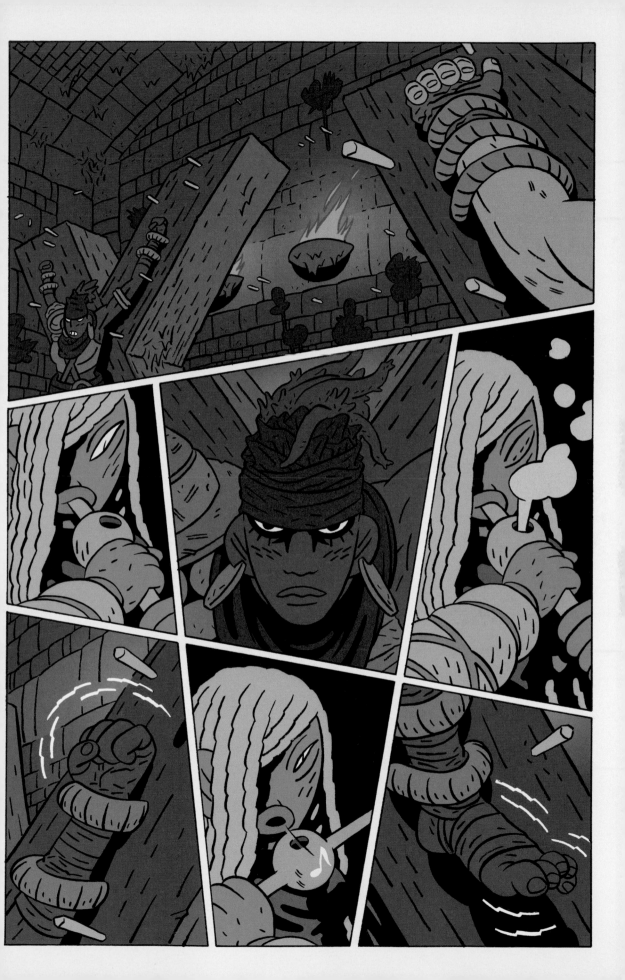

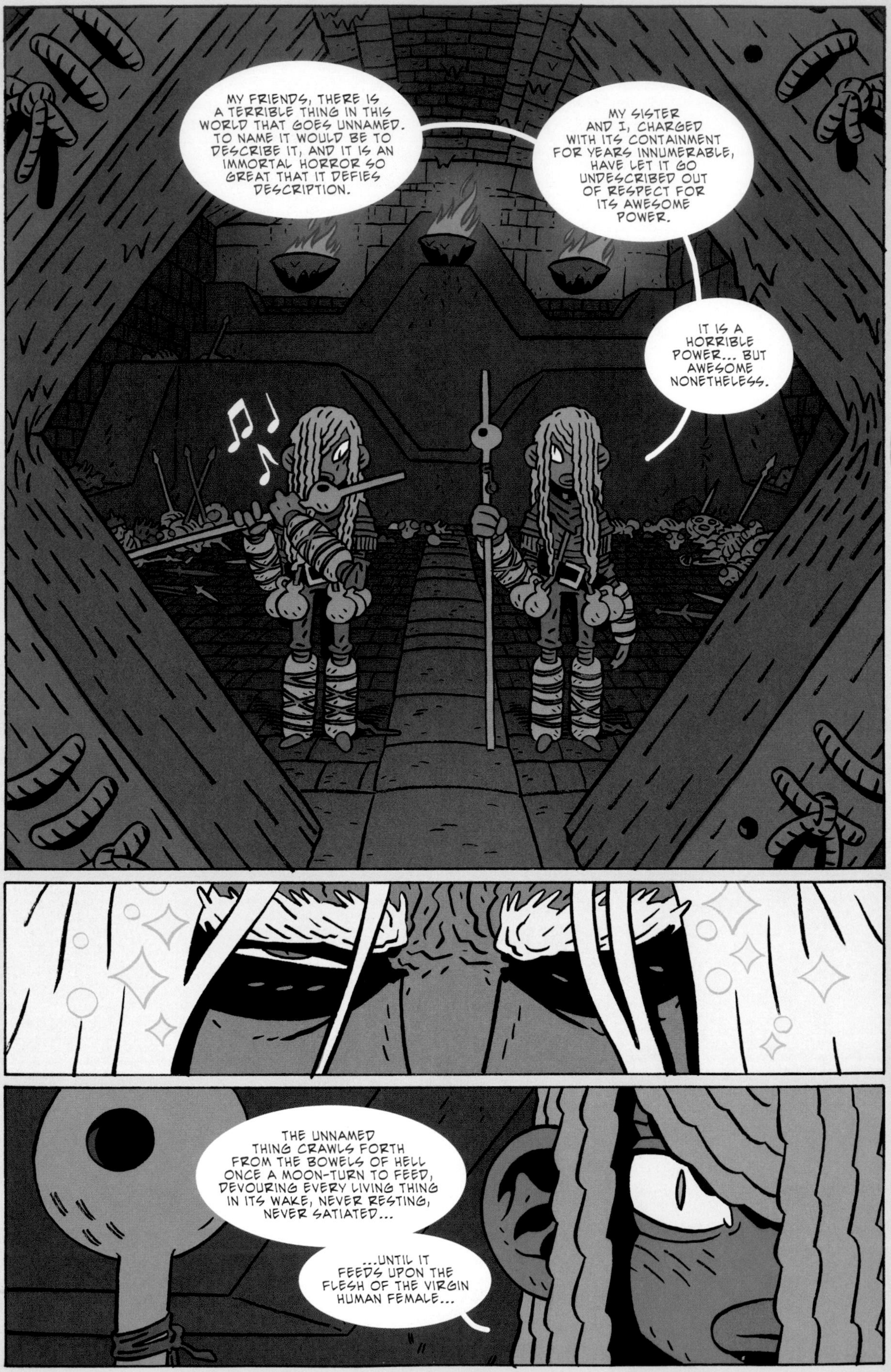
MY FRIENDS, THERE IS A TERRIBLE THING IN THIS WORLD THAT GOES UNNAMED. TO NAME IT WOULD BE TO DESCRIBE IT, AND IT IS AN IMMORTAL HORROR SO GREAT THAT IT DEFIES DESCRIPTION.
MY SISTER AND I, CHARGED WITH ITS CONTAINMENT FOR YEARS INNUMERABLE, HAVE LET IT GO UNDESCRIBED OUT OF RESPECT FOR ITS AWESOME POWER.
IT IS A HORRIBLE POWER... BUT AWESOME NONETHELESS.
THE UNNAMED THING CRAWLS FORTH FROM THE BOWELS OF HELL ONCE A MOON-TURN TO FEED, DEVOURING EVERY LIVING THING IN ITS WAKE, NEVER RESTING, NEVER SATIATED...
...UNTIL IT FEEDS UPON THE FLESH OF THE VIRGIN HUMAN FEMALE...

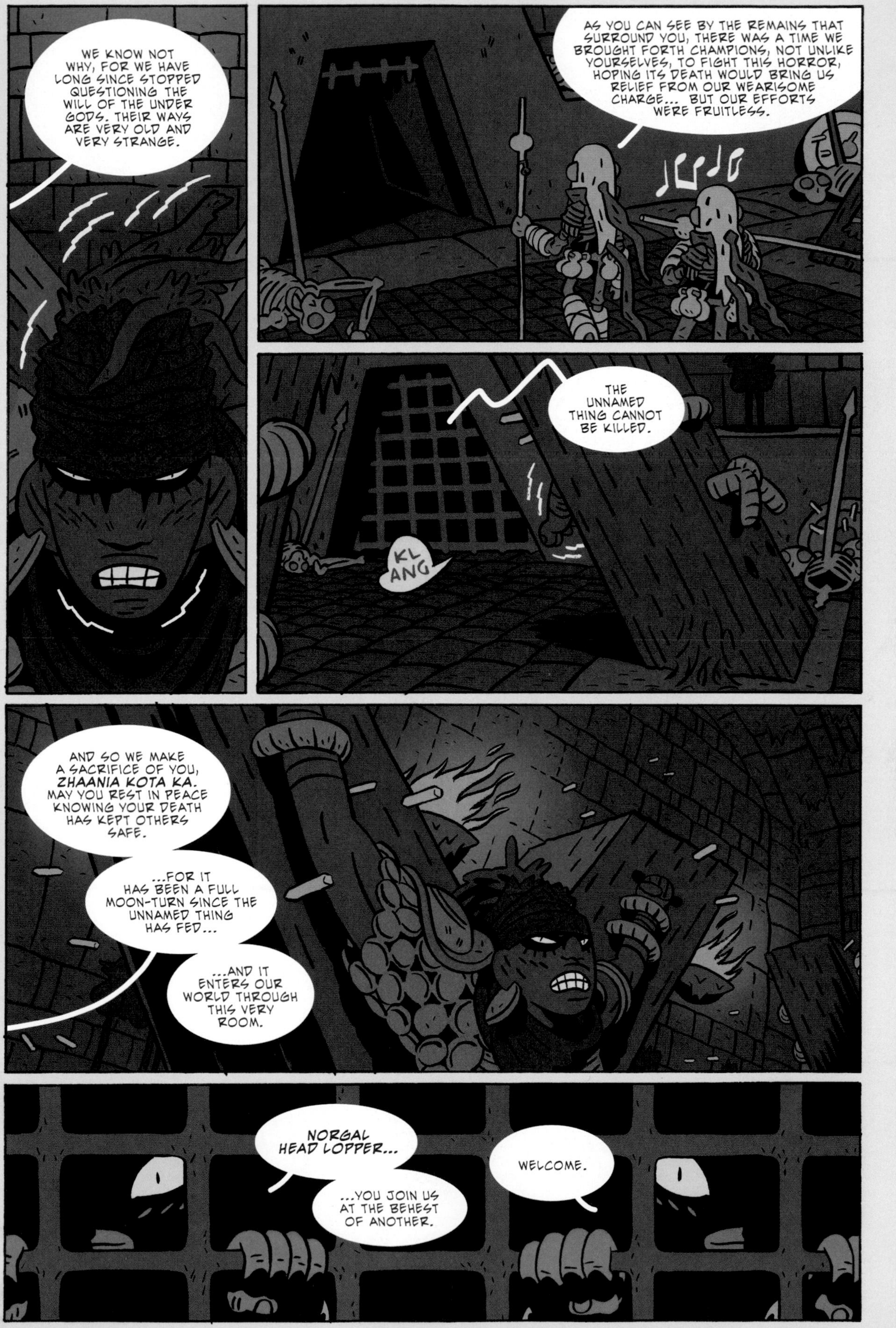
WE KNOW NOT WHY, FOR WE HAVE LONG SINCE STOPPED QUESTIONING THE WILL OF THE UNDER GODS. THEIR WAYS ARE VERY OLD AND VERY STRANGE.
AS YOU CAN SEE BY THE REMAINS THAT SURROUND YOU, THERE WAS A TIME WE BROUGHT FORTH CHAMPIONS, NOT UNLIKE YOURSELVES, TO FIGHT THIS HORROR, HOPING ITS DEATH WOULD BRING US RELIEF FROM OUR WEARISOME CHARGE... BUT OUR EFFORTS WERE FRUITLESS.
THE UNNAMED THING CANNOT BE KILLED.
KLANG
AND SO WE MAKE A SACRIFICE OF YOU, ZHAANIA KOTA KA. MAY YOU REST IN PEACE KNOWING YOUR DEATH HAS KEPT OTHERS SAFE.
...FOR IT HAS BEEN A FULL MOON-TURN SINCE THE UNNAMED THING HAS FED...
...AND IT ENTERS OUR WORLD THROUGH THIS VERY ROOM.
NORGAL HEAD LOPPER...
...YOU JOIN US AT THE BEHEST OF ANOTHER.
WELCOME.

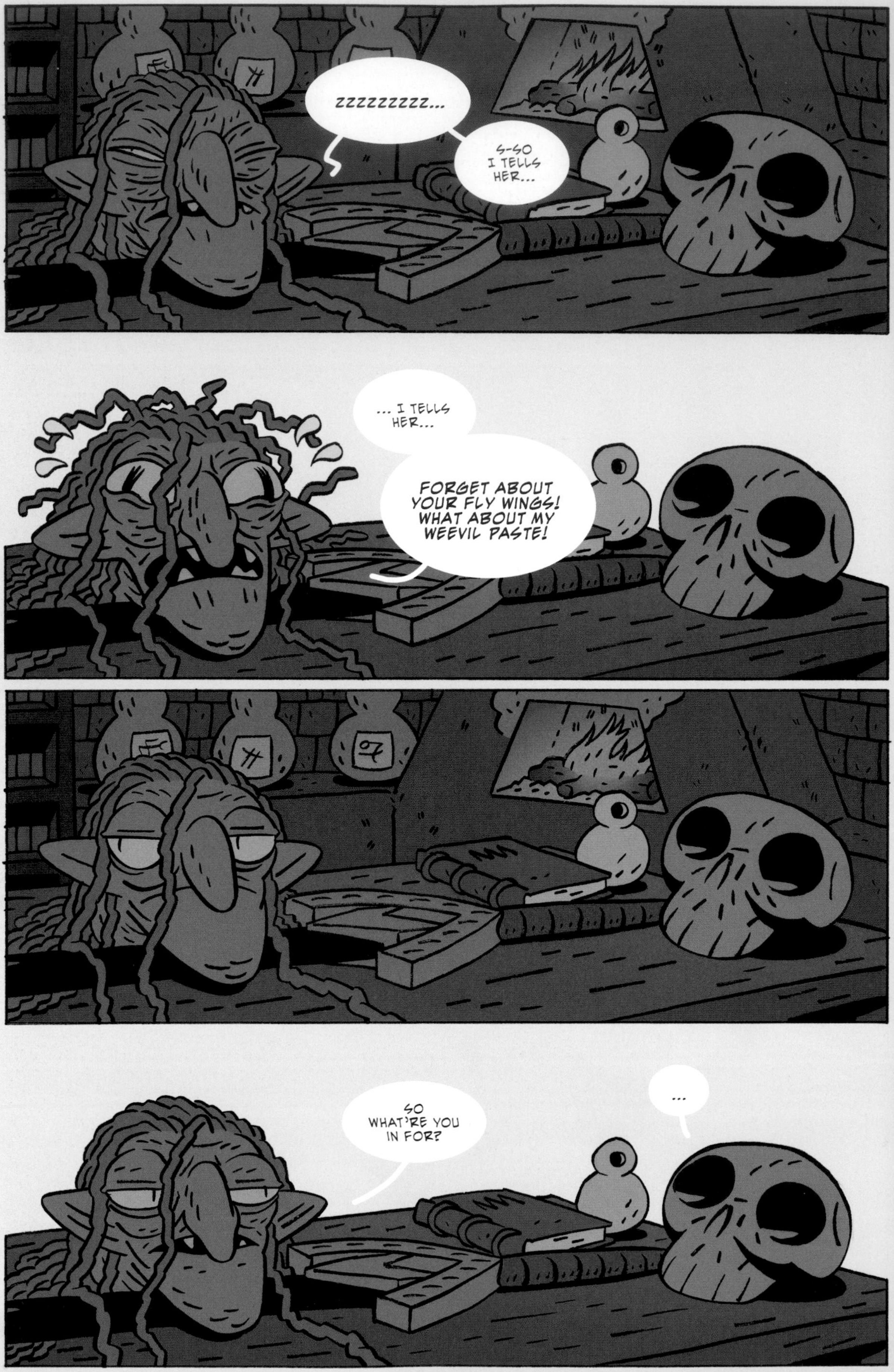
ZZZZZZZZZ...
S-SO I TELLS HER...
... I TELLS HER...
FORGET ABOUT YOUR FLY WINGS! WHAT ABOUT MY WEEVIL PASTE!
SO WHAT'RE YOU IN FOR?
...

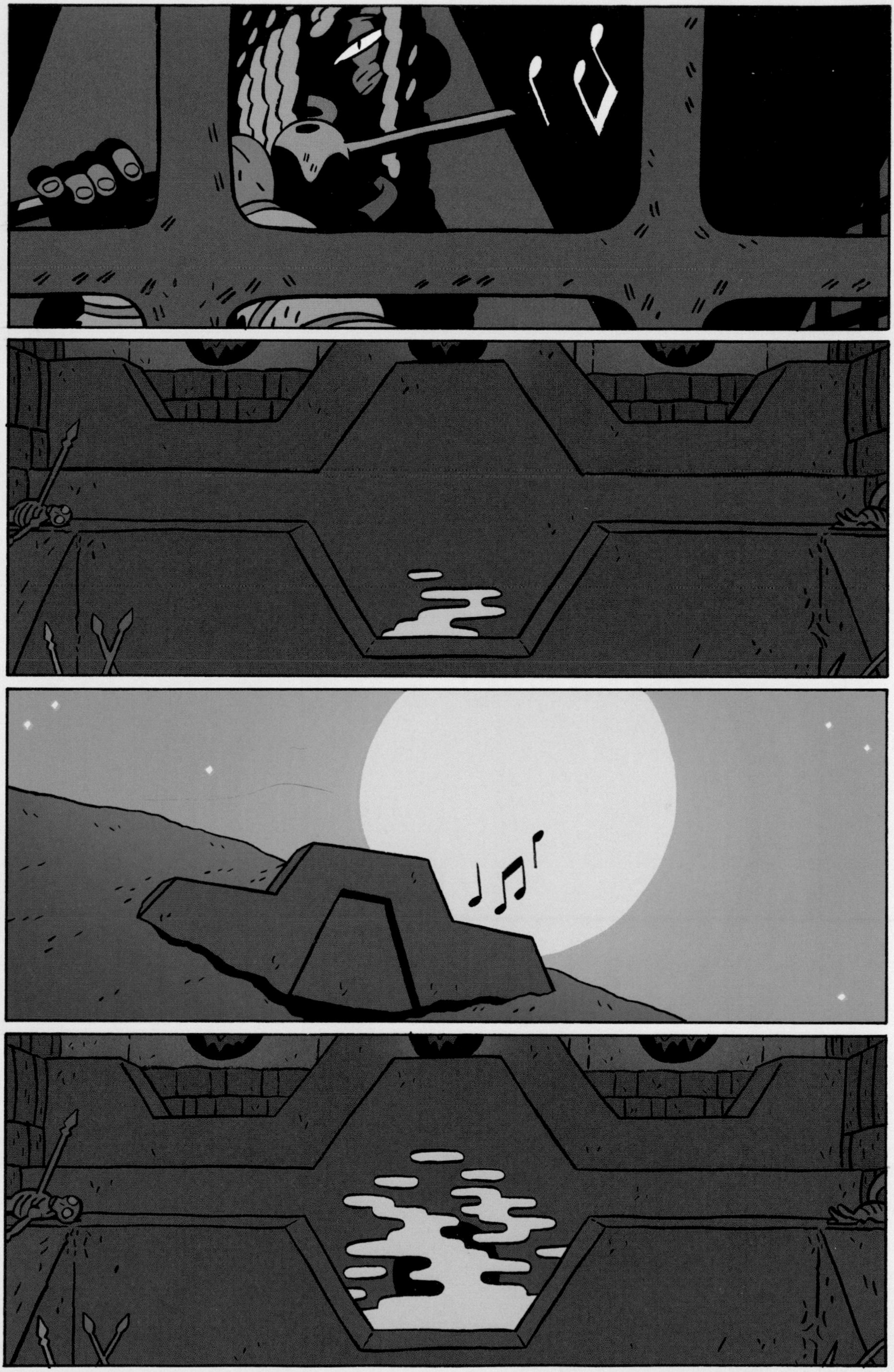

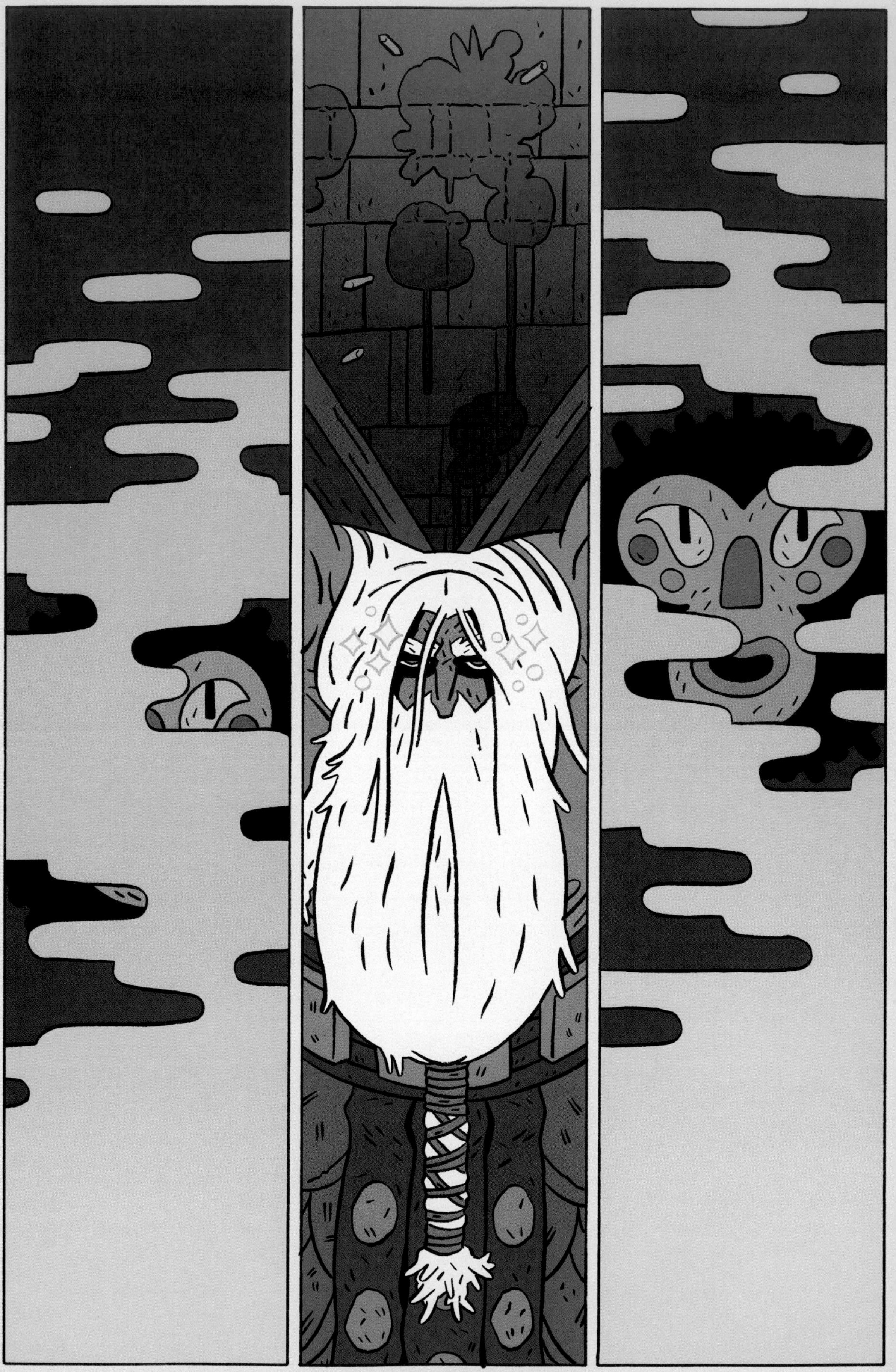

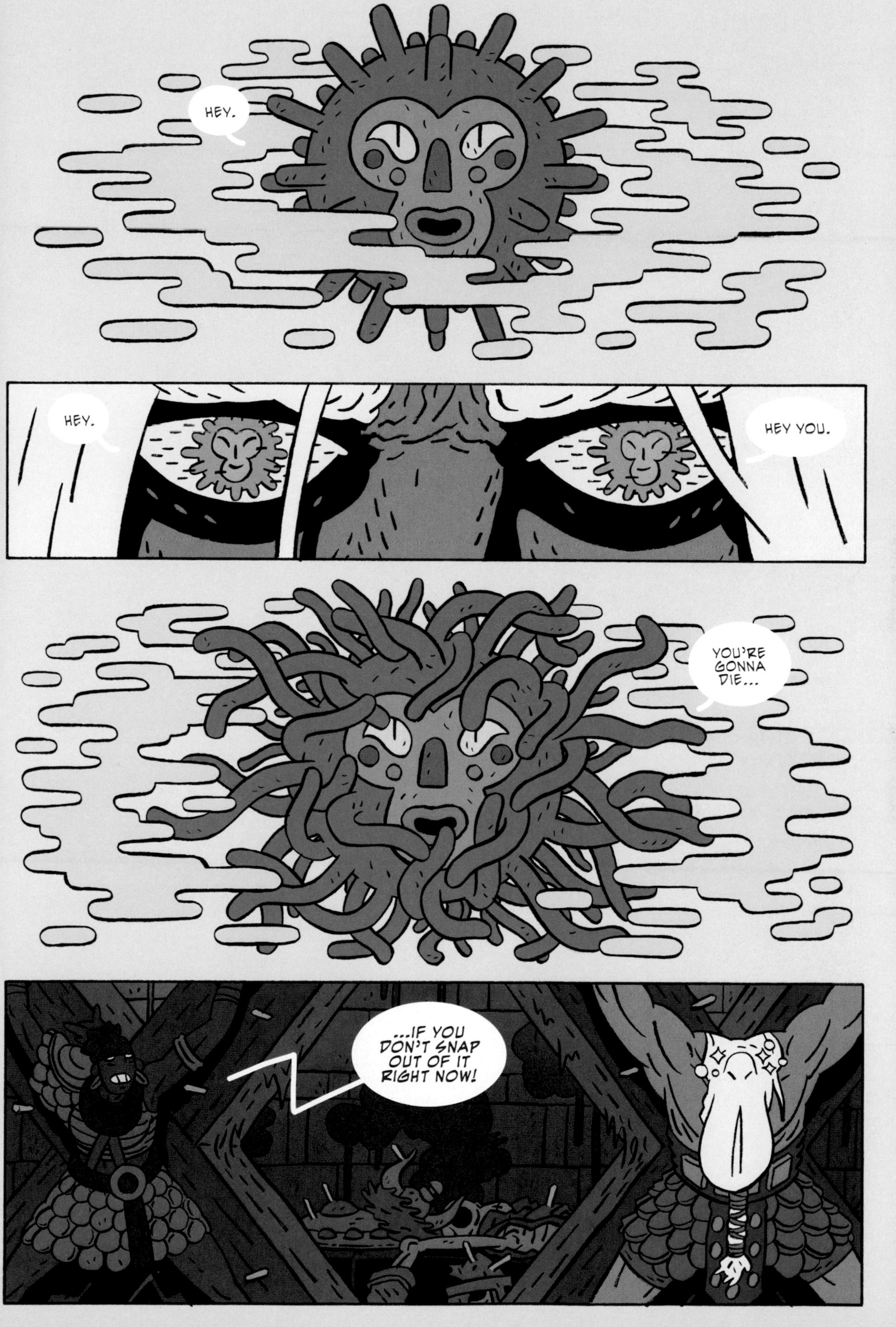
HEY.
HEY.
HEY YOU.
YOU'RE GONNA DIE...
...IF YOU DON'T SNAP OUT OF IT RIGHT NOW!

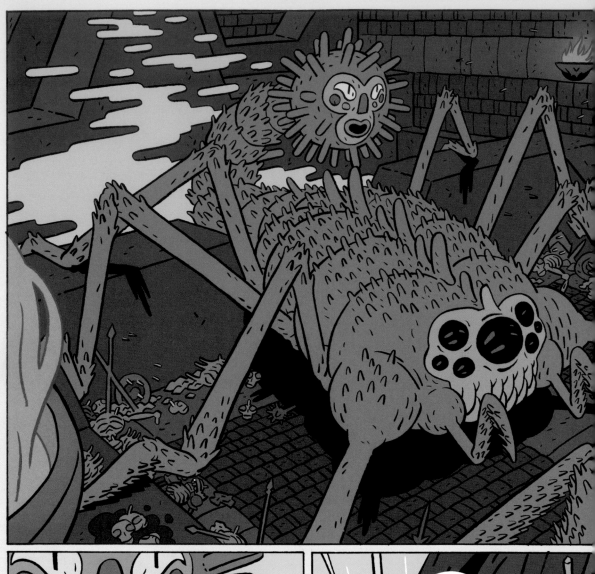

FINE!

SUIT YOURSELF, BRAVE WARRIOR!

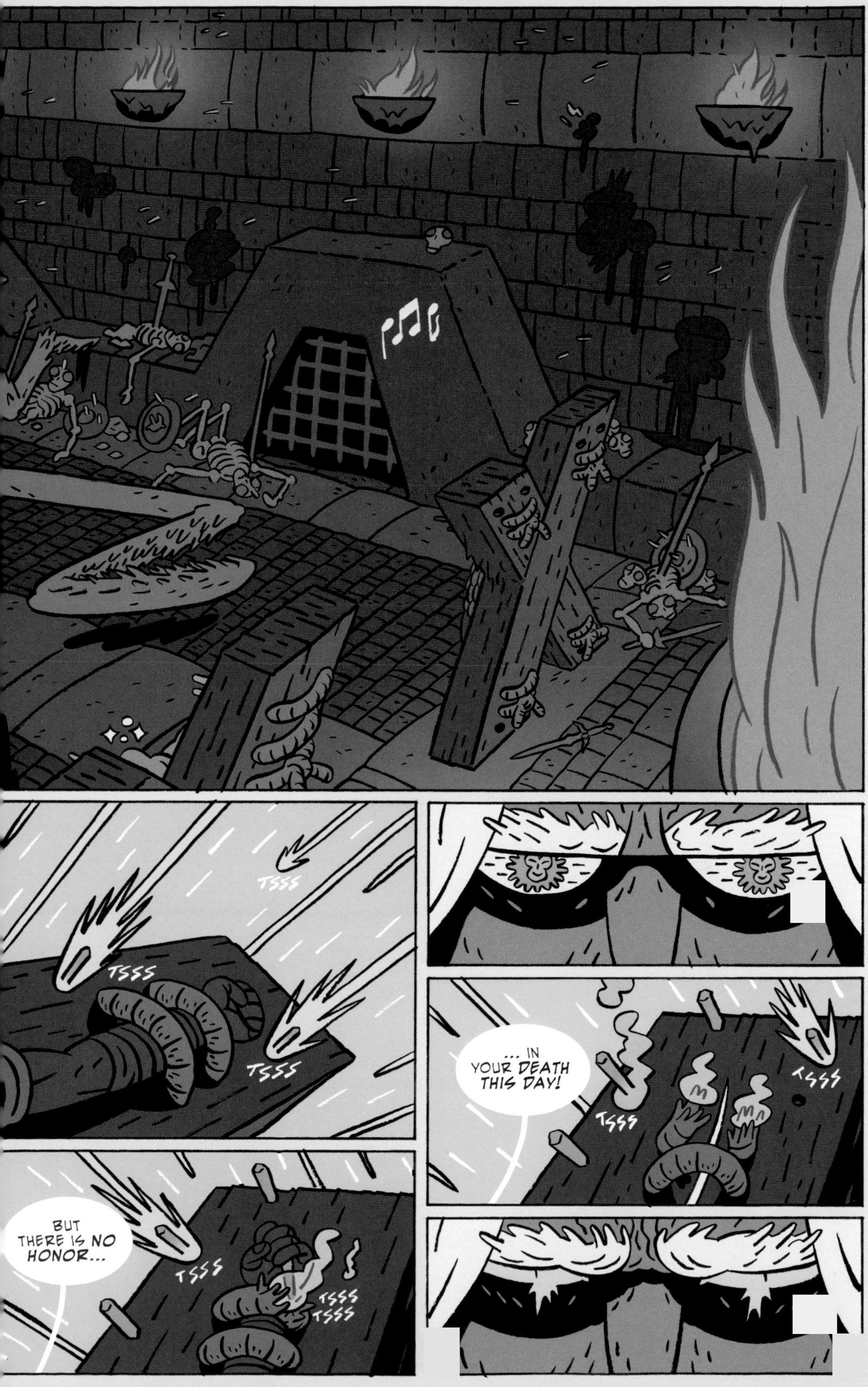
TSSS
TSSS
TSSS
... IN YOUR DEATH THIS DAY!
TSSS
TSSS
BUT THERE IS NO HONOR...
TSSS
TSSS TSSS

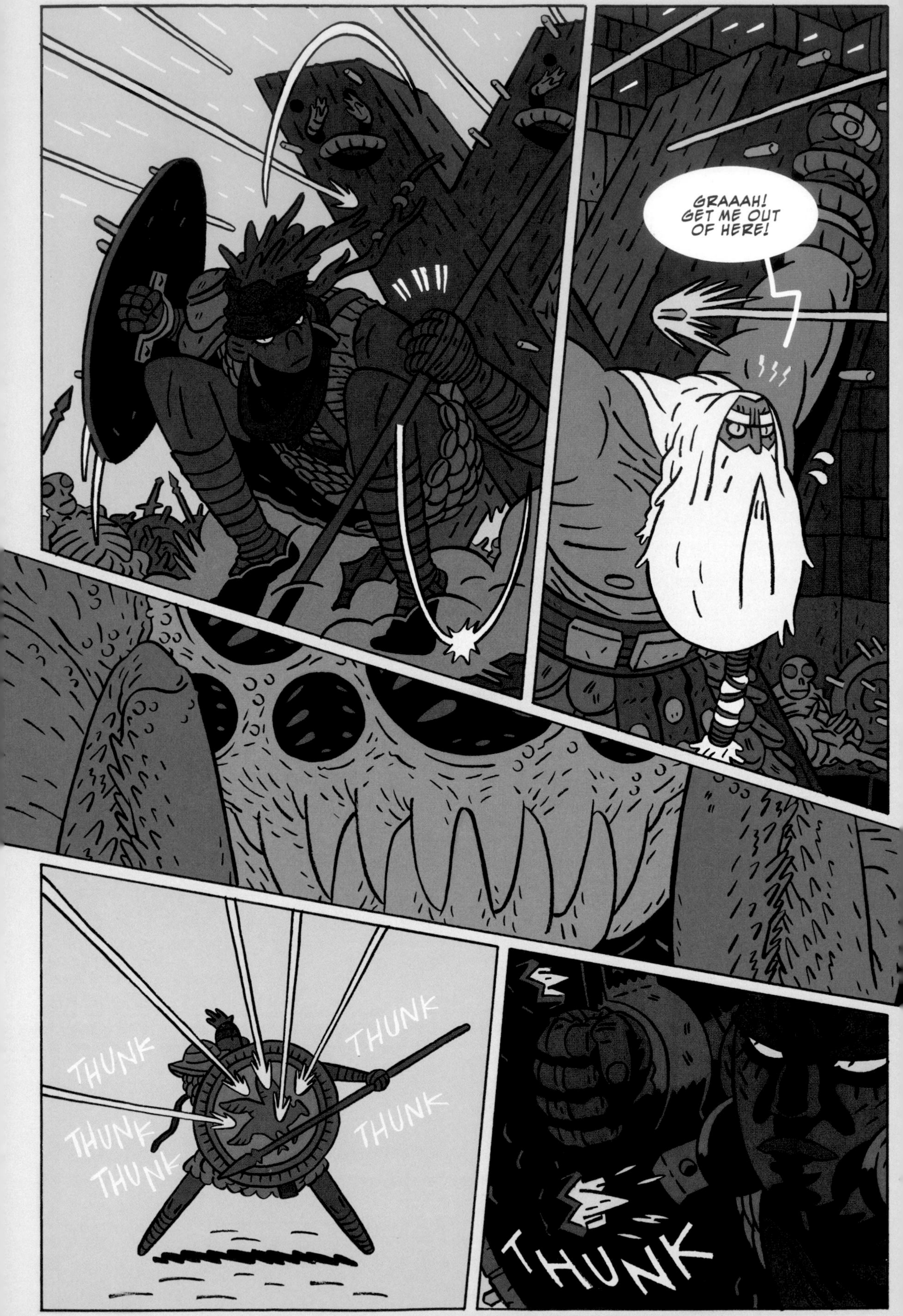
GRAAAH! GET ME OUT OF HERE!
THUNK
THUNK
THUNK
THUNK
THUNK
THUNK

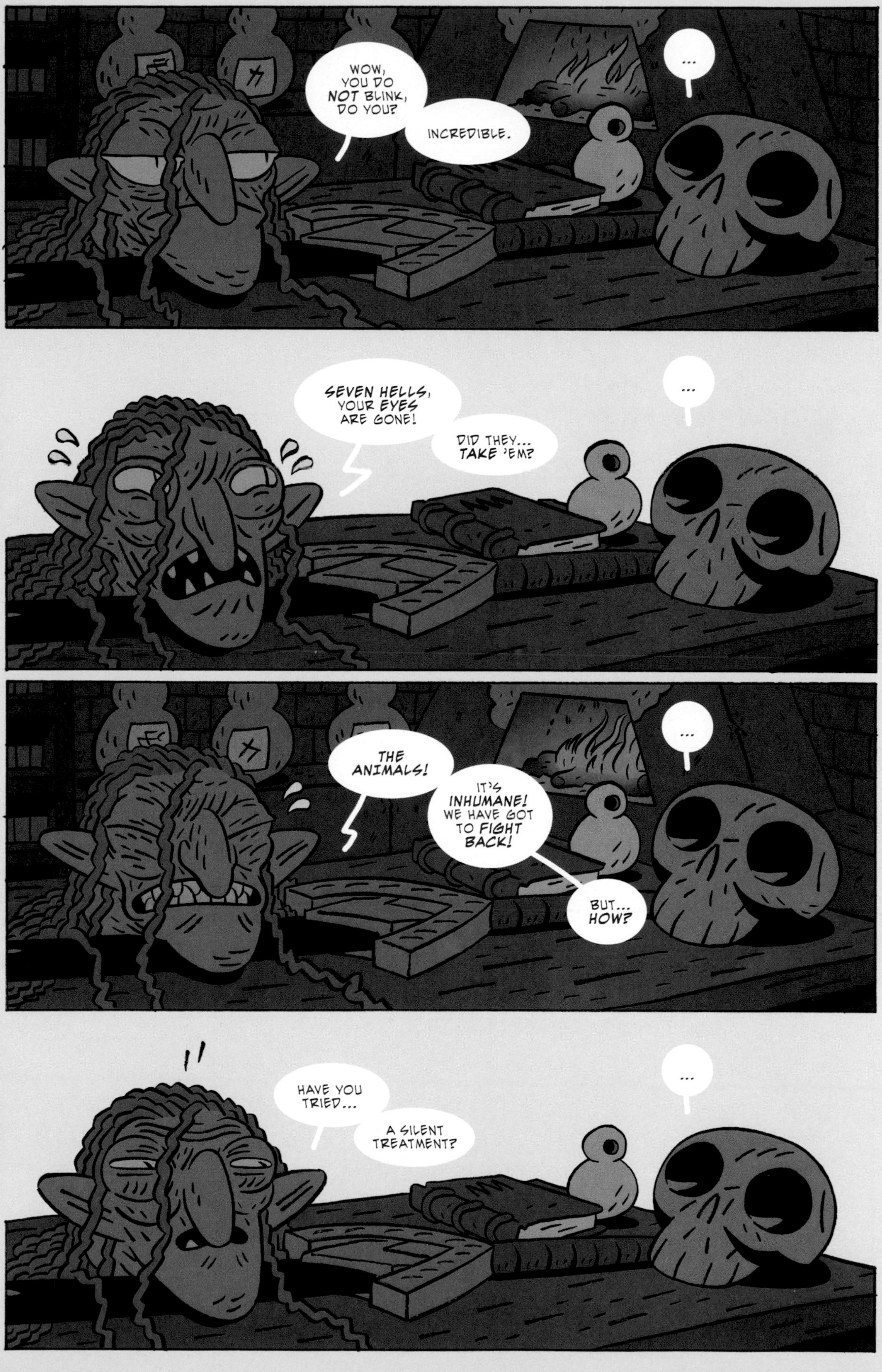
...
WOW, YOU DO NOT BLINK, DO YOU?
INCREDIBLE.
...
SEVEN HELLS, YOUR EYES ARE GONE!
DID THEY... TAKE 'EM?
...
THE ANIMALS!
IT'S INHUMANE! WE HAVE GOT TO FIGHT BACK!
BUT... HOW?
...
HAVE YOU TRIED...
A SILENT TREATMENT?

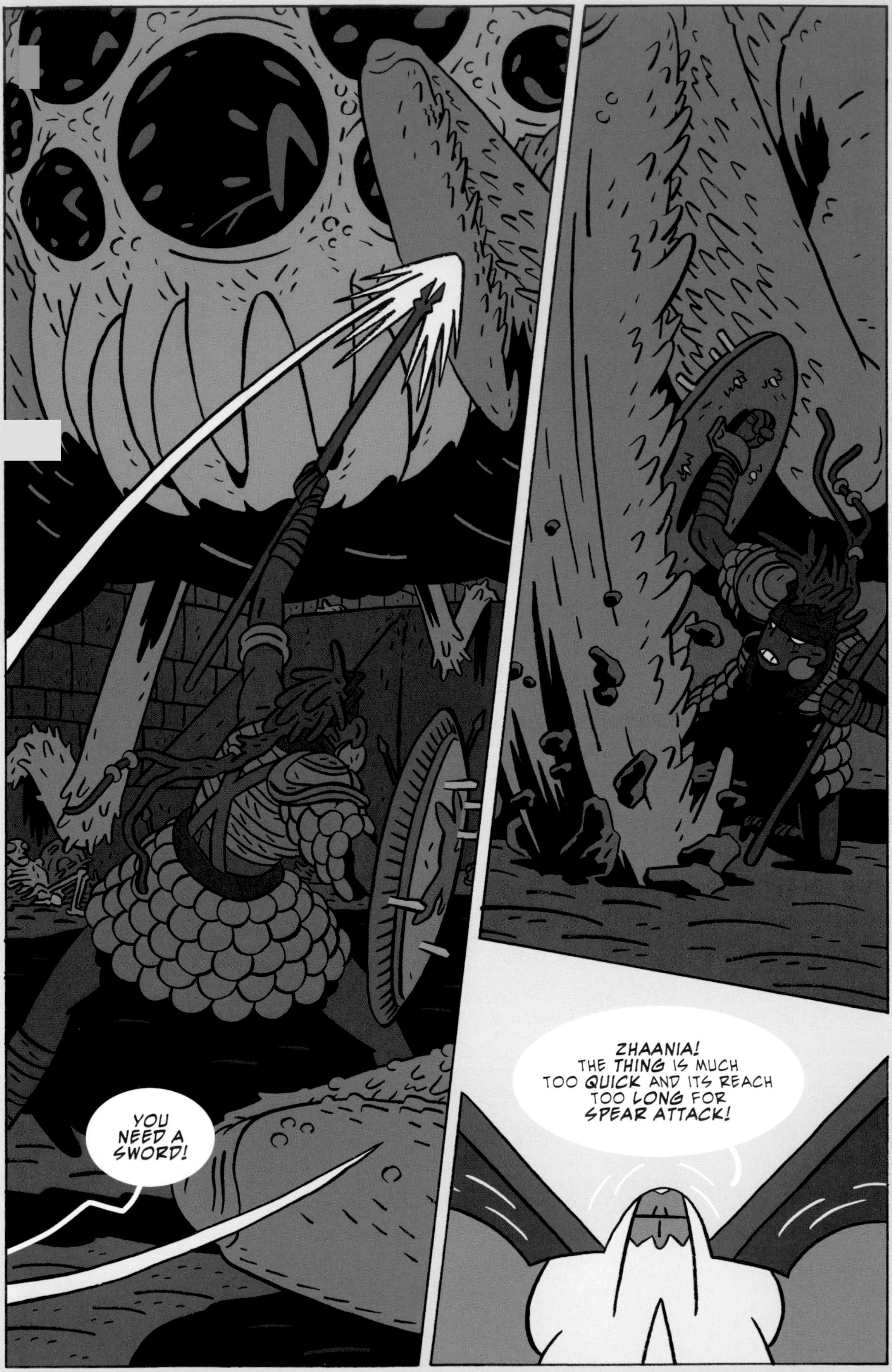
YOU NEED A SWORD!
ZHAANIA! THE THING IS MUCH TOO QUICK AND ITS REACH TOO LONG FOR SPEAR ATTACK!

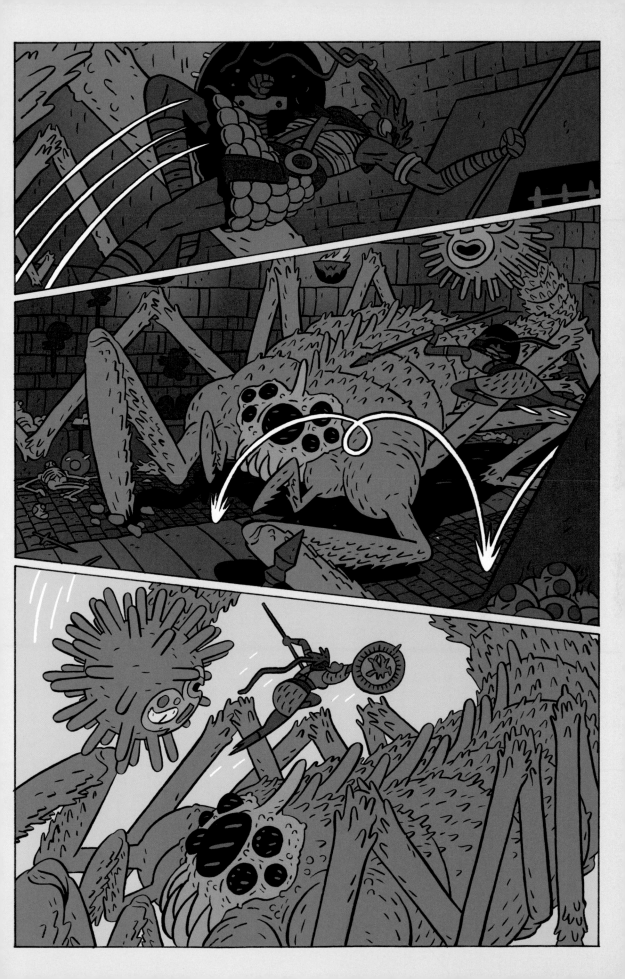

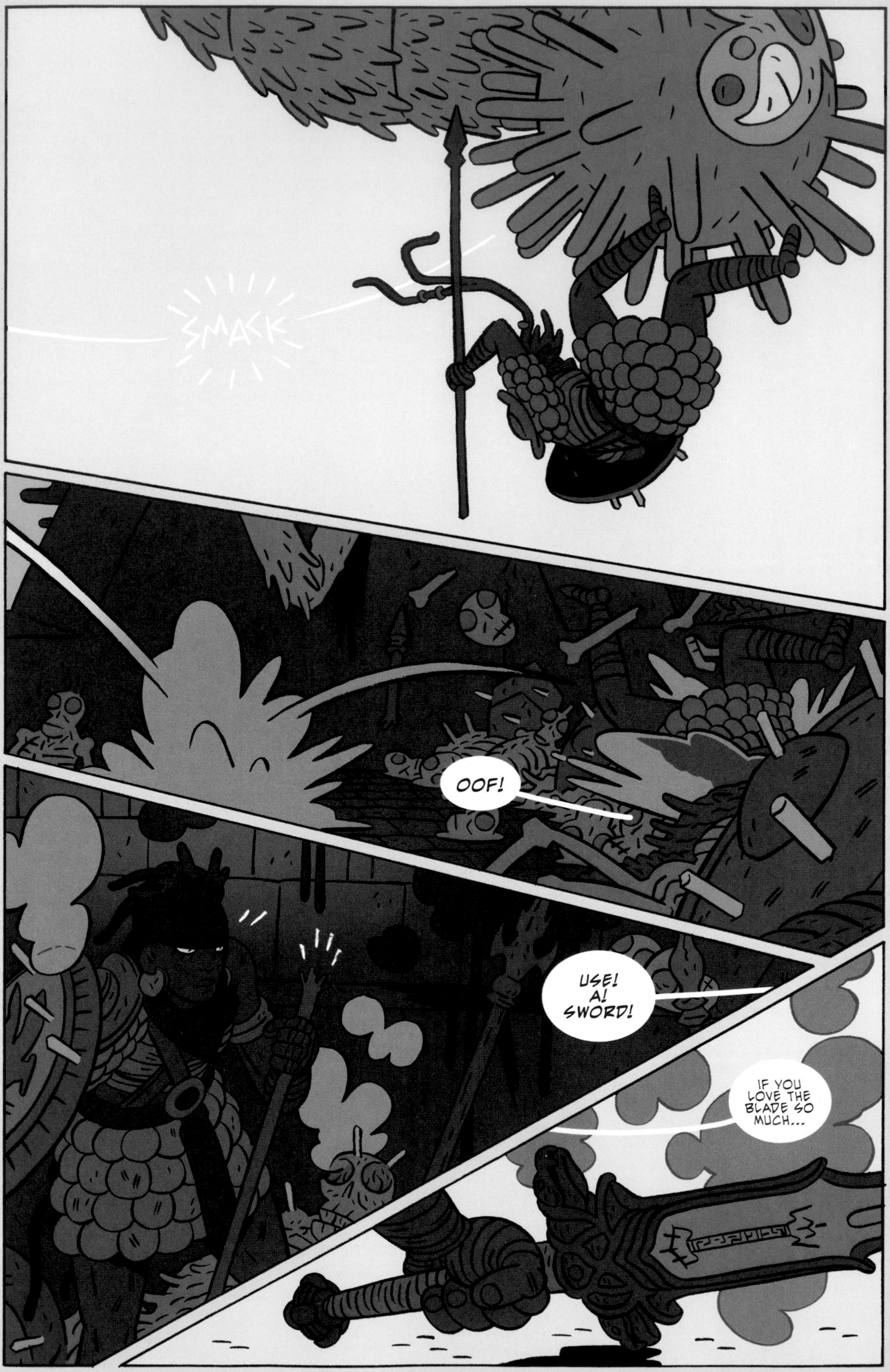
SMACK
OOF!
USE! A! SWORD!
IF YOU LOVE THE BLADE SO MUCH...

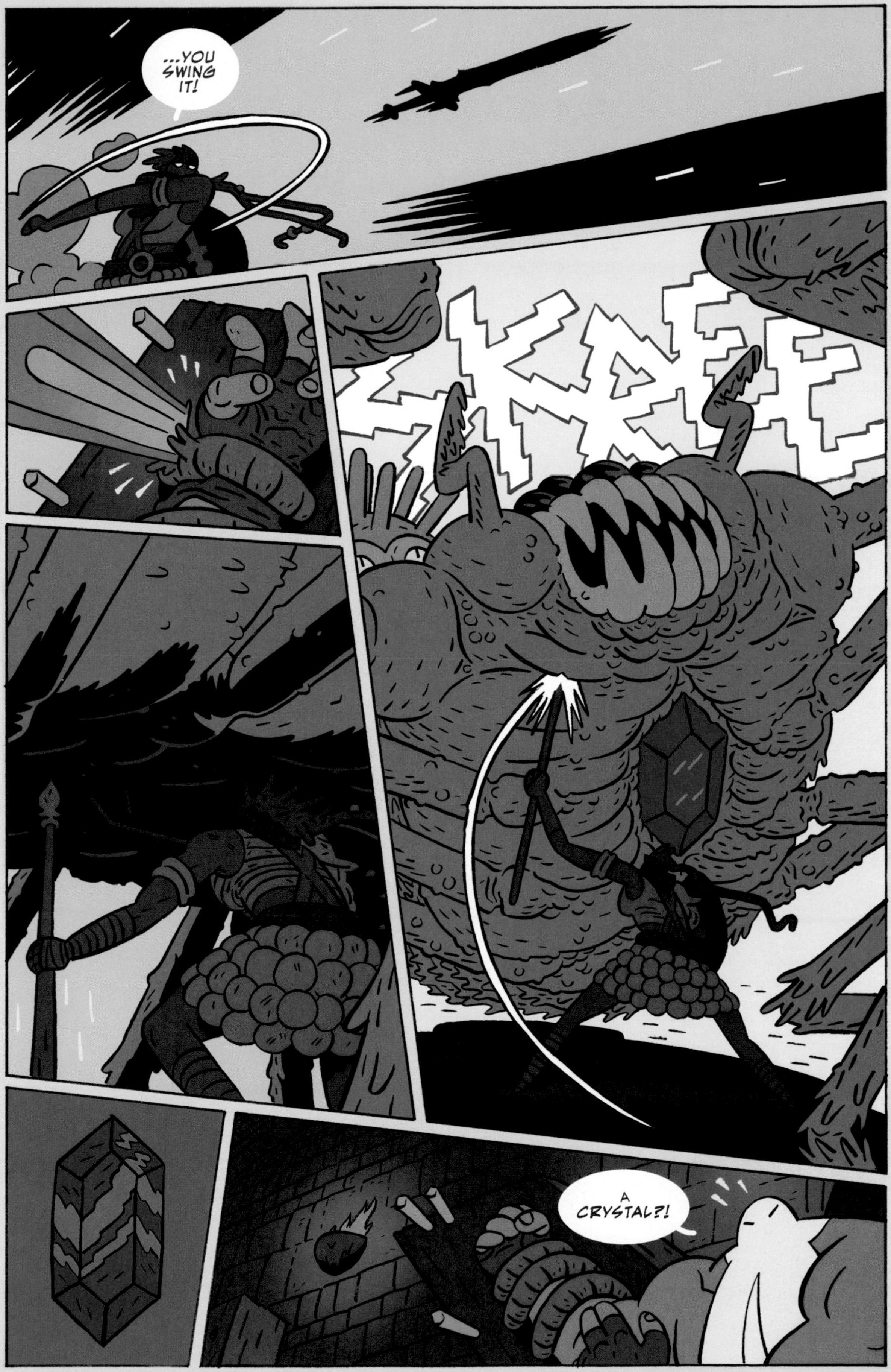
...YOU SWING IT!
A CRYSTAL?!

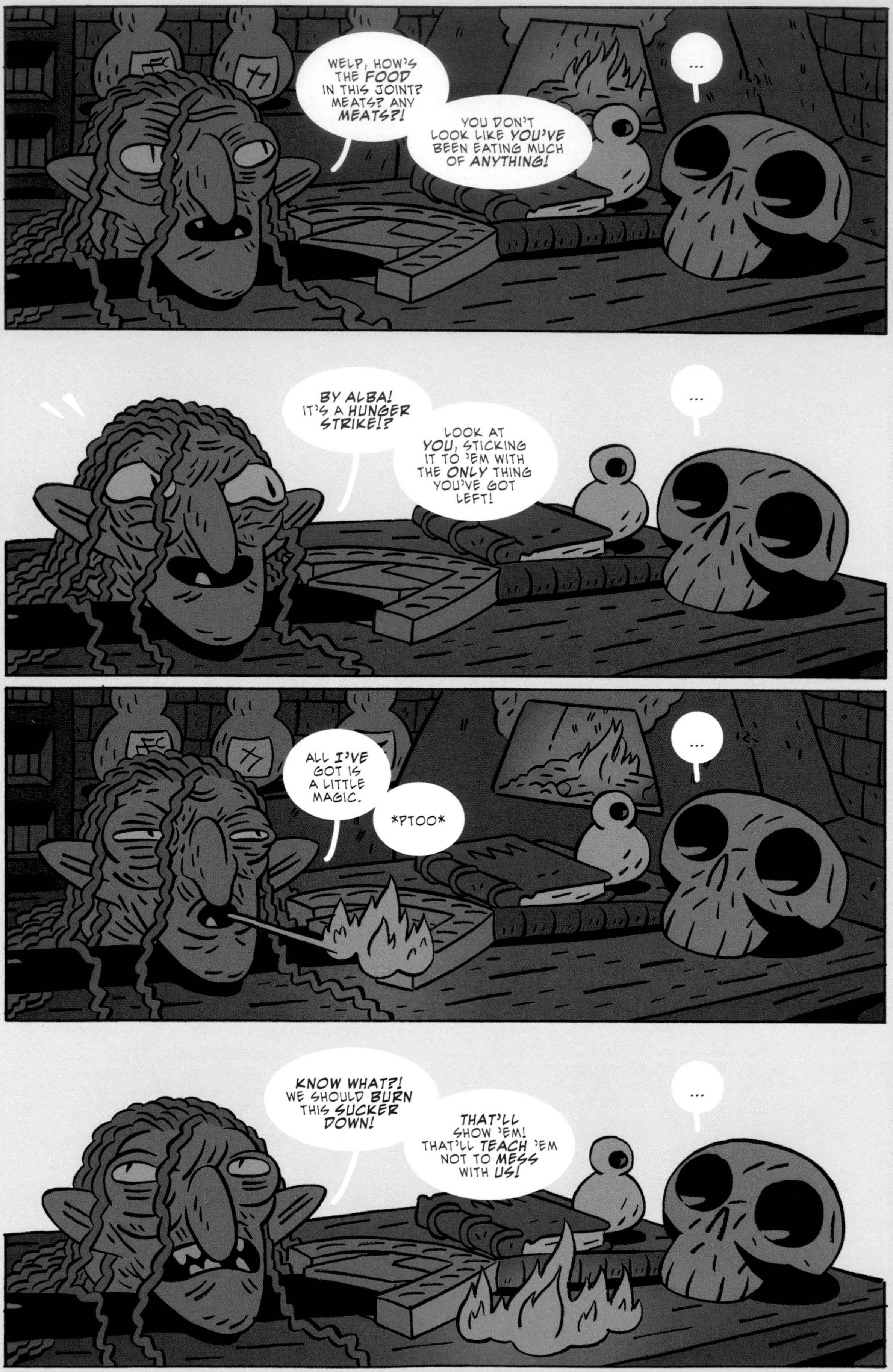
WELP, HOW'S THE FOOD IN THIS JOINT? MEATS? ANY MEATS?!
YOU DON'T LOOK LIKE YOU'VE BEEN EATING MUCH OF ANYTHING!
...
BY ALBA! IT'S A HUNGER STRIKE!?
LOOK AT YOU, STICKING IT TO 'EM WITH THE ONLY THING YOU'VE GOT LEFT!
...
ALL I'VE GOT IS A LITTLE MAGIC.
PTOO
...
KNOW WHAT?! WE SHOULD BURN THIS SUCKER DOWN!
THAT'LL SHOW 'EM! THAT'LL TEACH 'EM NOT TO MESS WITH US!
...

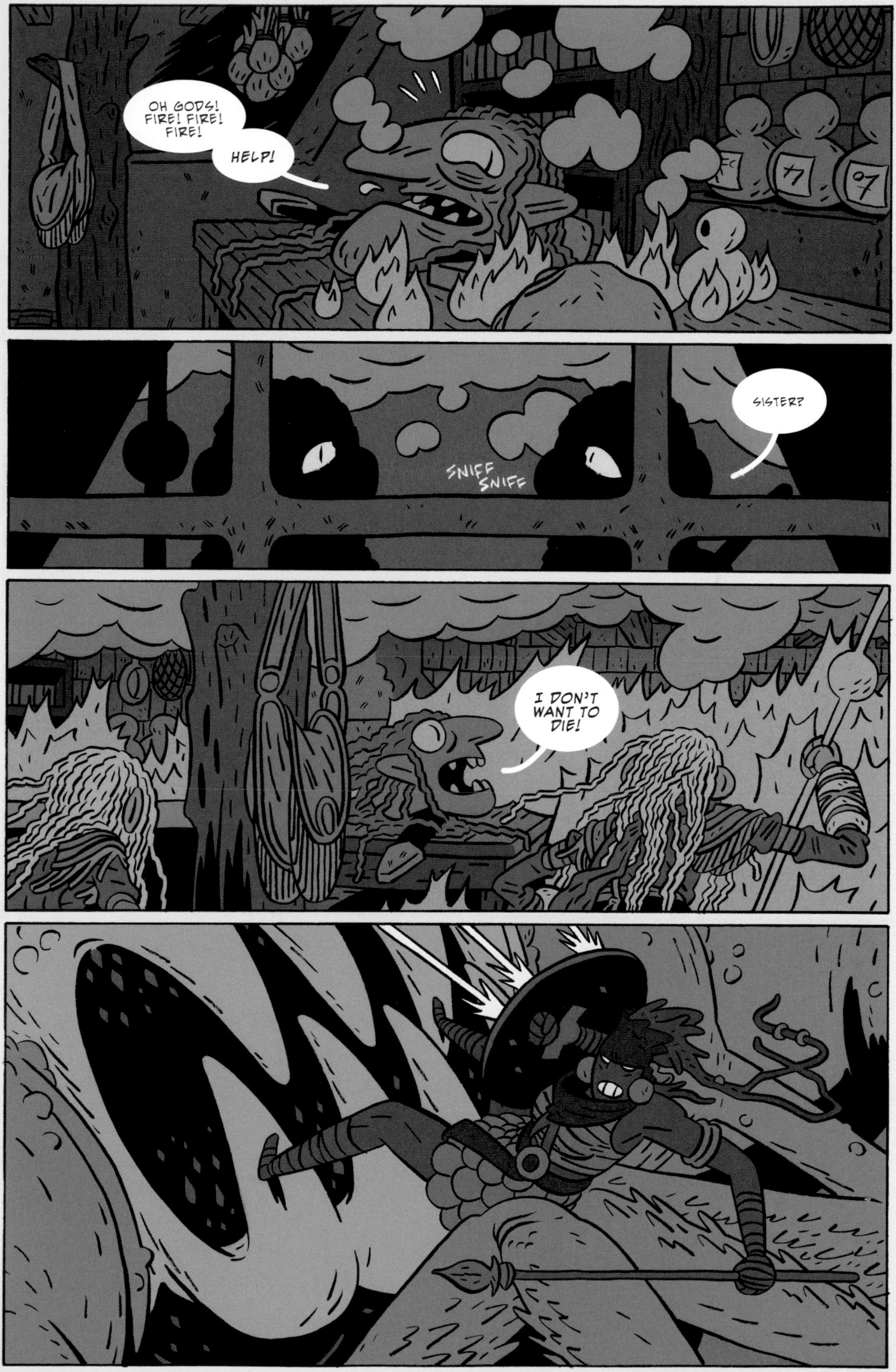
OH GODS! FIRE! FIRE! FIRE!
HELP!
SISTER?
SNIFF SNIFF
I DON'T WANT TO DIE!

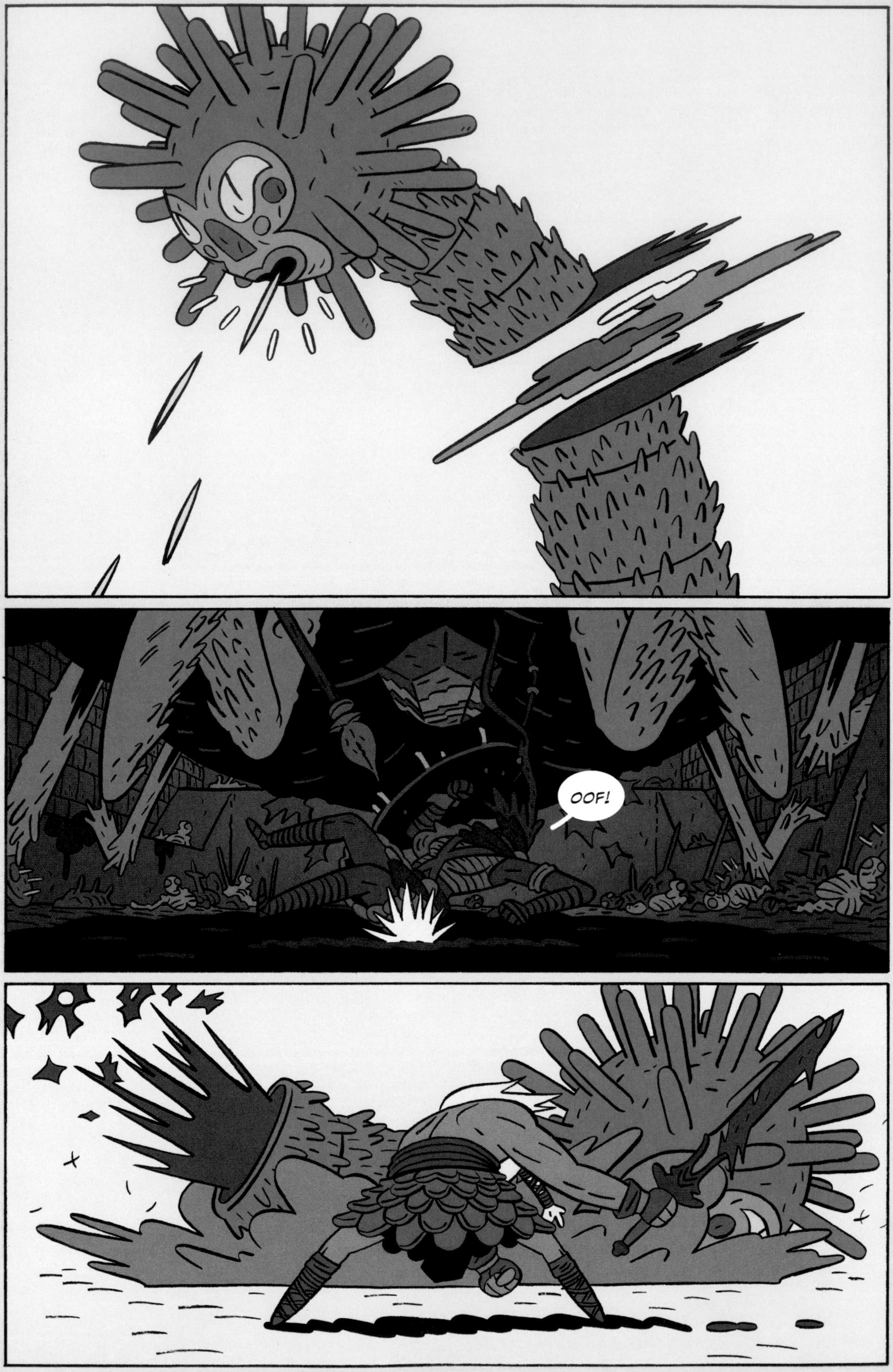
OOF!

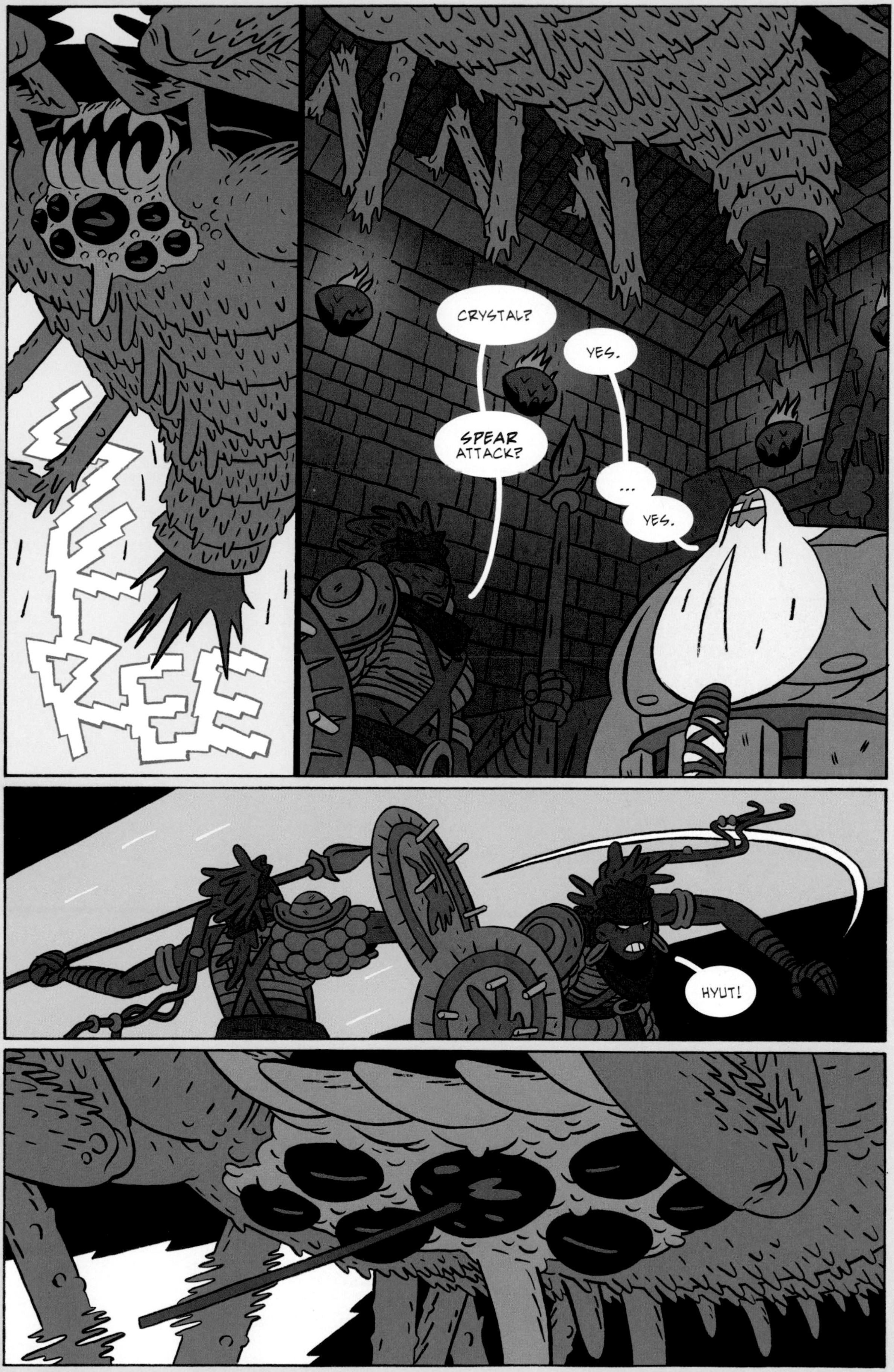
SKREE
CRYSTAL?
YES.
SPEAR ATTACK?
...
YES.
HYUT!

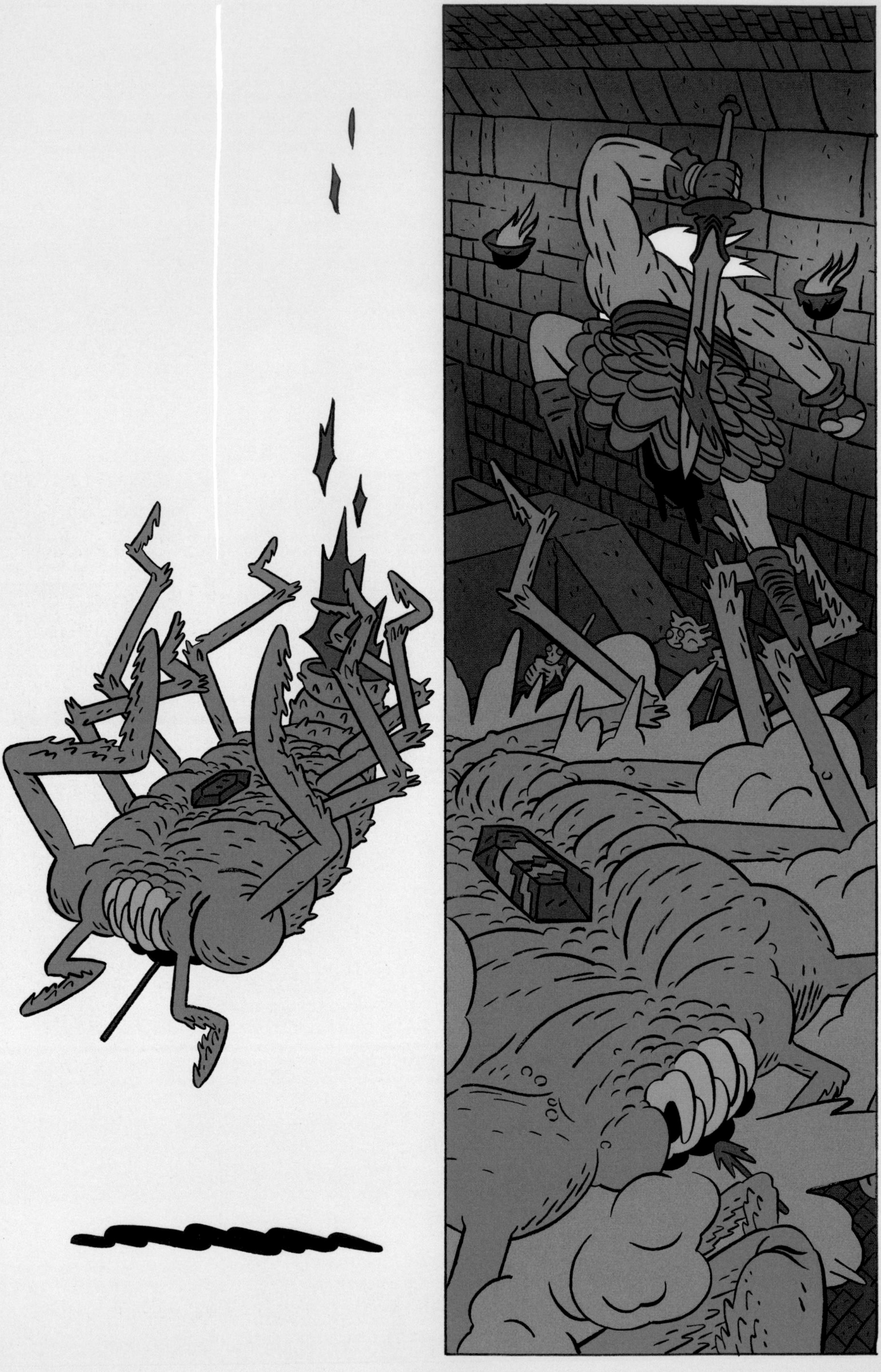

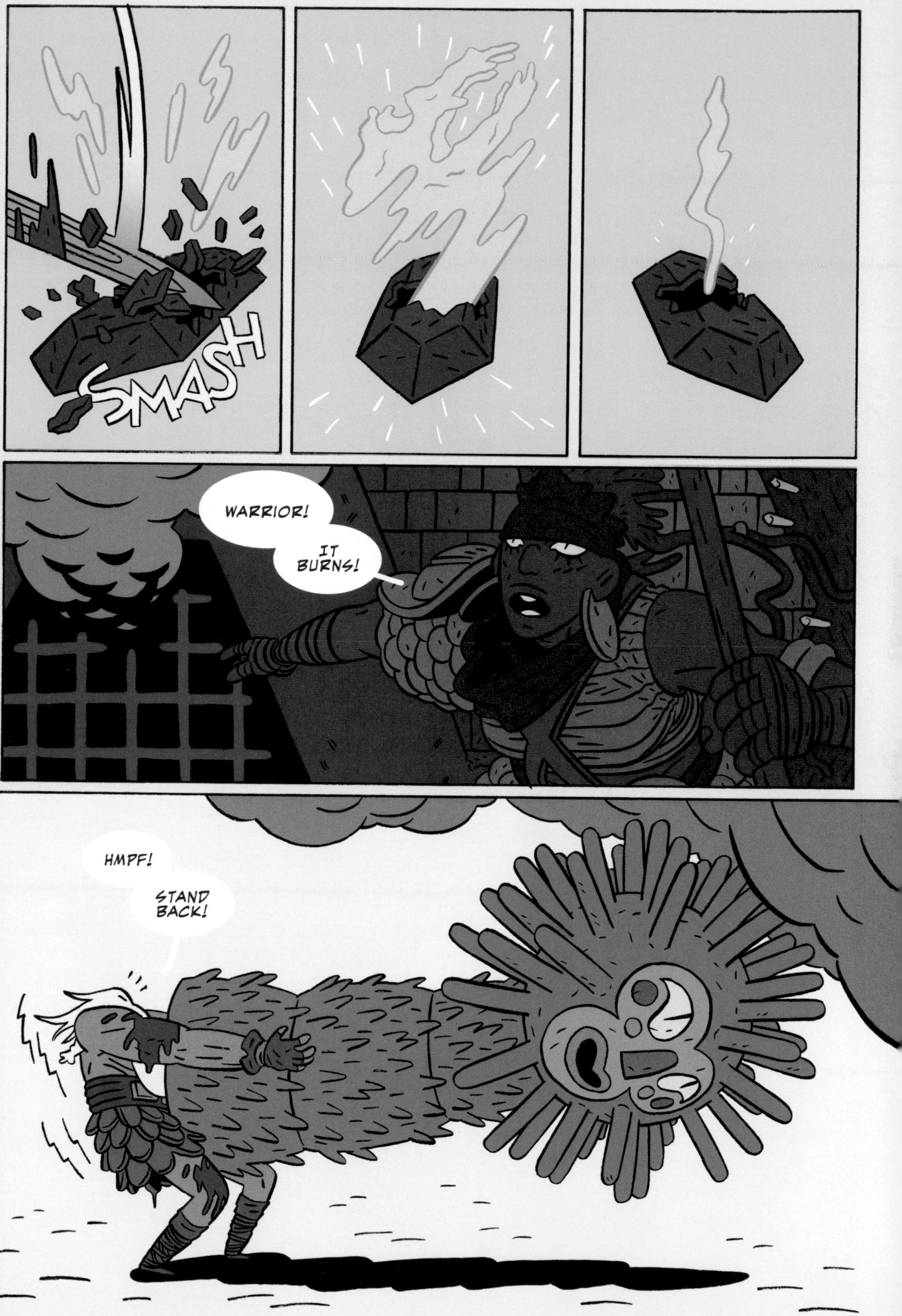
SMASH
WARRIOR!
IT BURNS!
HMPF!
STAND BACK!

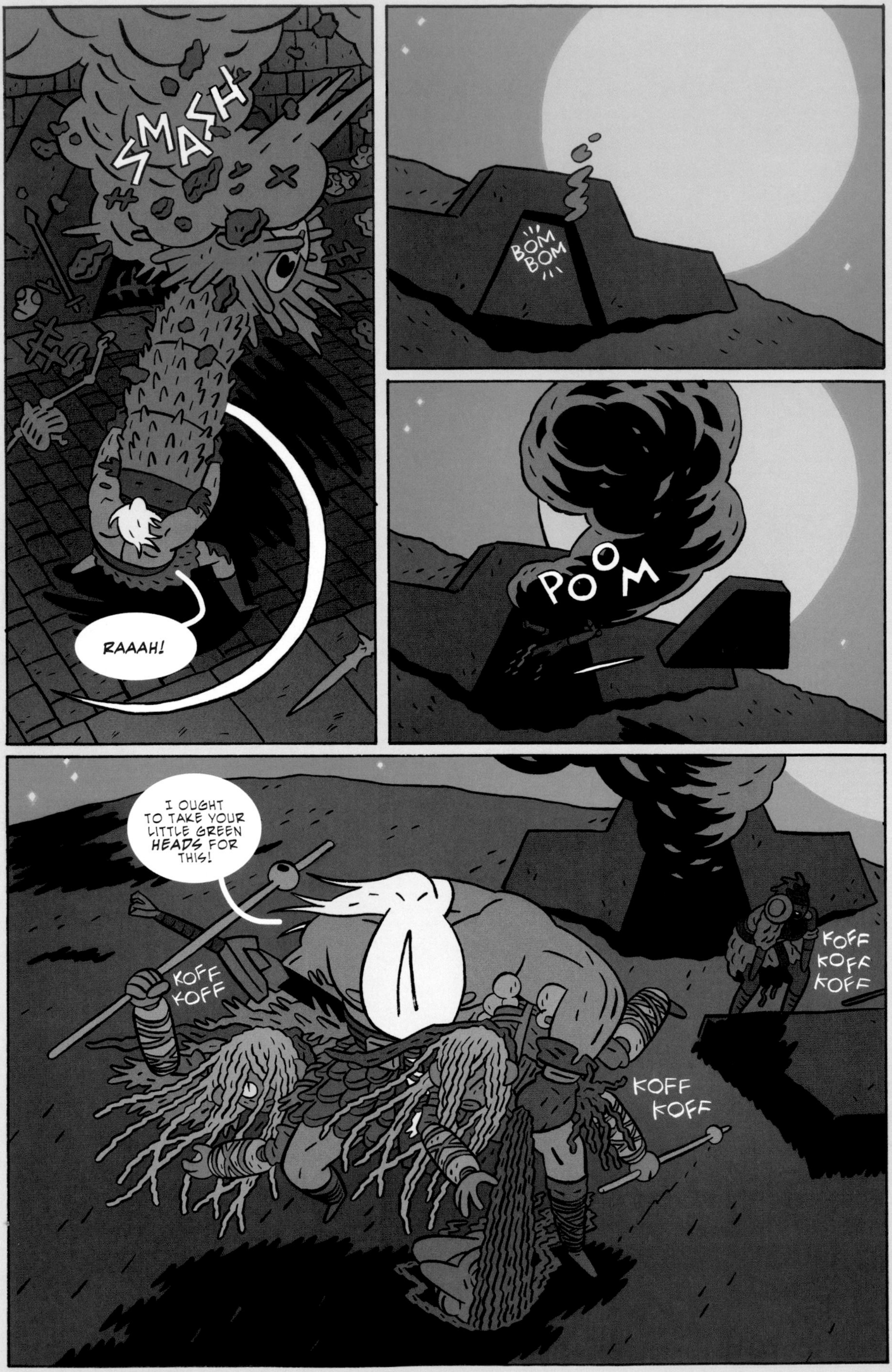
SMASH
RAAAH!
BOM BOM
POOM
I OUGHT TO TAKE YOUR LITTLE GREEN HEADS FOR THIS!
KOFF KOFF
KOFF KOFF KOFF
KOFF KOFF

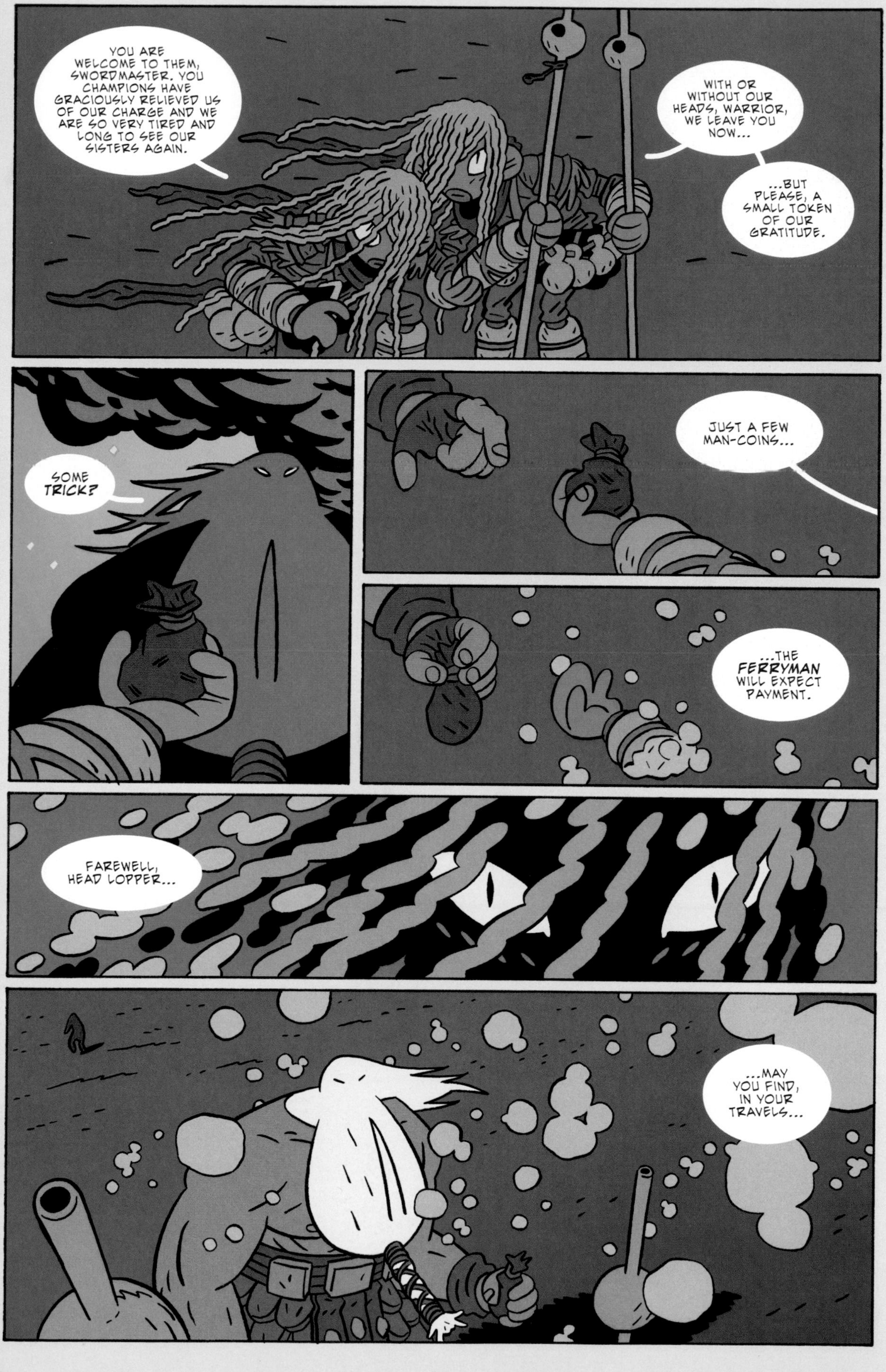
YOU ARE WELCOME TO THEM, SWORDMASTER. YOU CHAMPIONS HAVE GRACIOUSLY RELIEVED US OF OUR CHARGE AND WE ARE SO VERY TIRED AND LONG TO SEE OUR SISTERS AGAIN.
WITH OR WITHOUT OUR HEADS, WARRIOR, WE LEAVE YOU NOW...
...BUT PLEASE, A SMALL TOKEN OF OUR GRATITUDE.
SOME TRICK?
JUST A FEW MAN-COINS...
...THE FERRYMAN WILL EXPECT PAYMENT.
FAREWELL, HEAD LOPPER...
...MAY YOU FIND, IN YOUR TRAVELS...

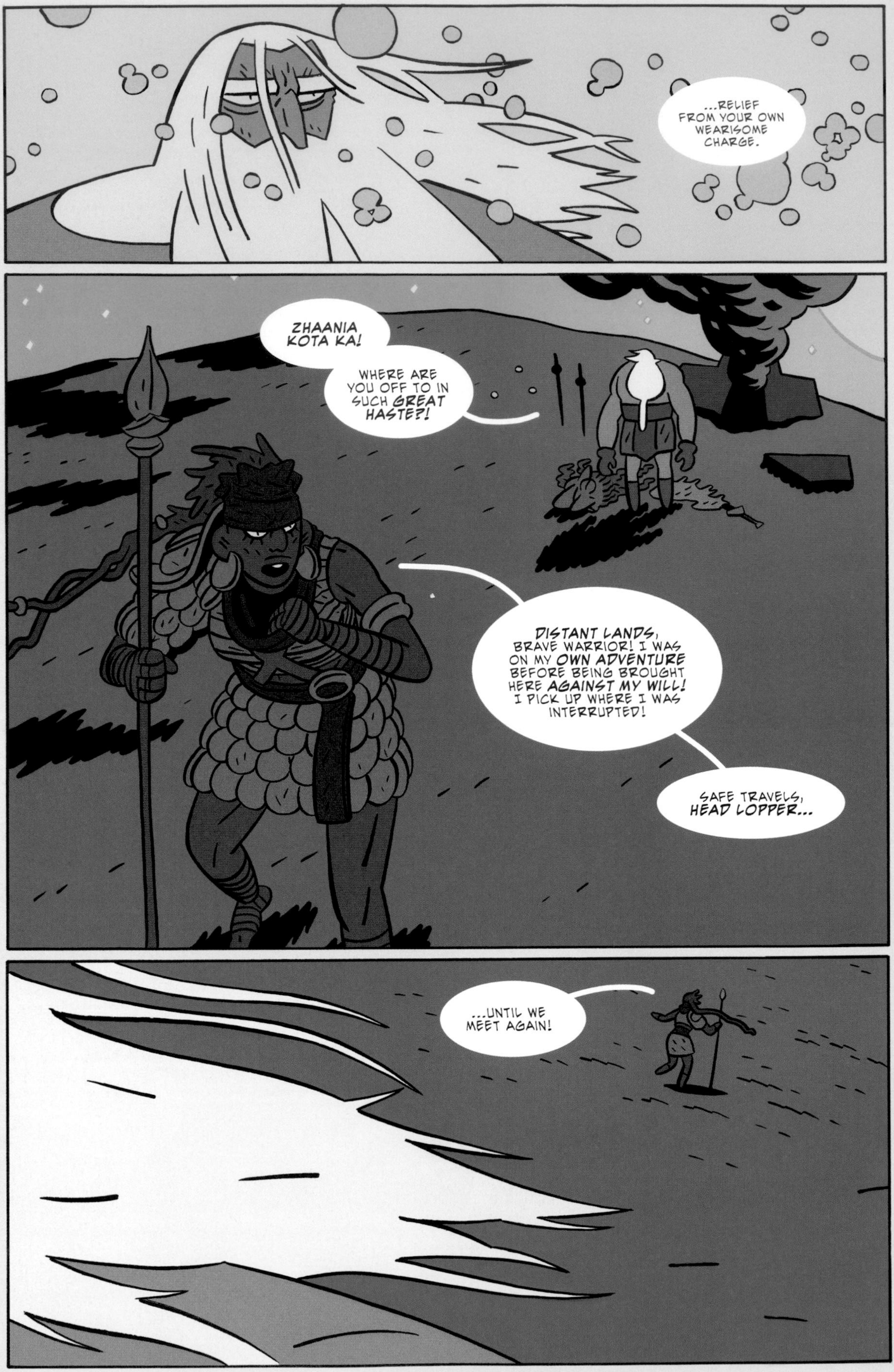
...RELIEF FROM YOUR OWN WEARISOME CHARGE.
ZHAANIA KOTA KA!
WHERE ARE YOU OFF TO IN SUCH GREAT HASTE?!
DISTANT LANDS, BRAVE WARRIOR! I WAS ON MY OWN ADVENTURE BEFORE BEING BROUGHT HERE AGAINST MY WILL! I PICK UP WHERE I WAS INTERRUPTED!
SAFE TRAVELS, HEAD LOPPER...
...UNTIL WE MEET AGAIN!

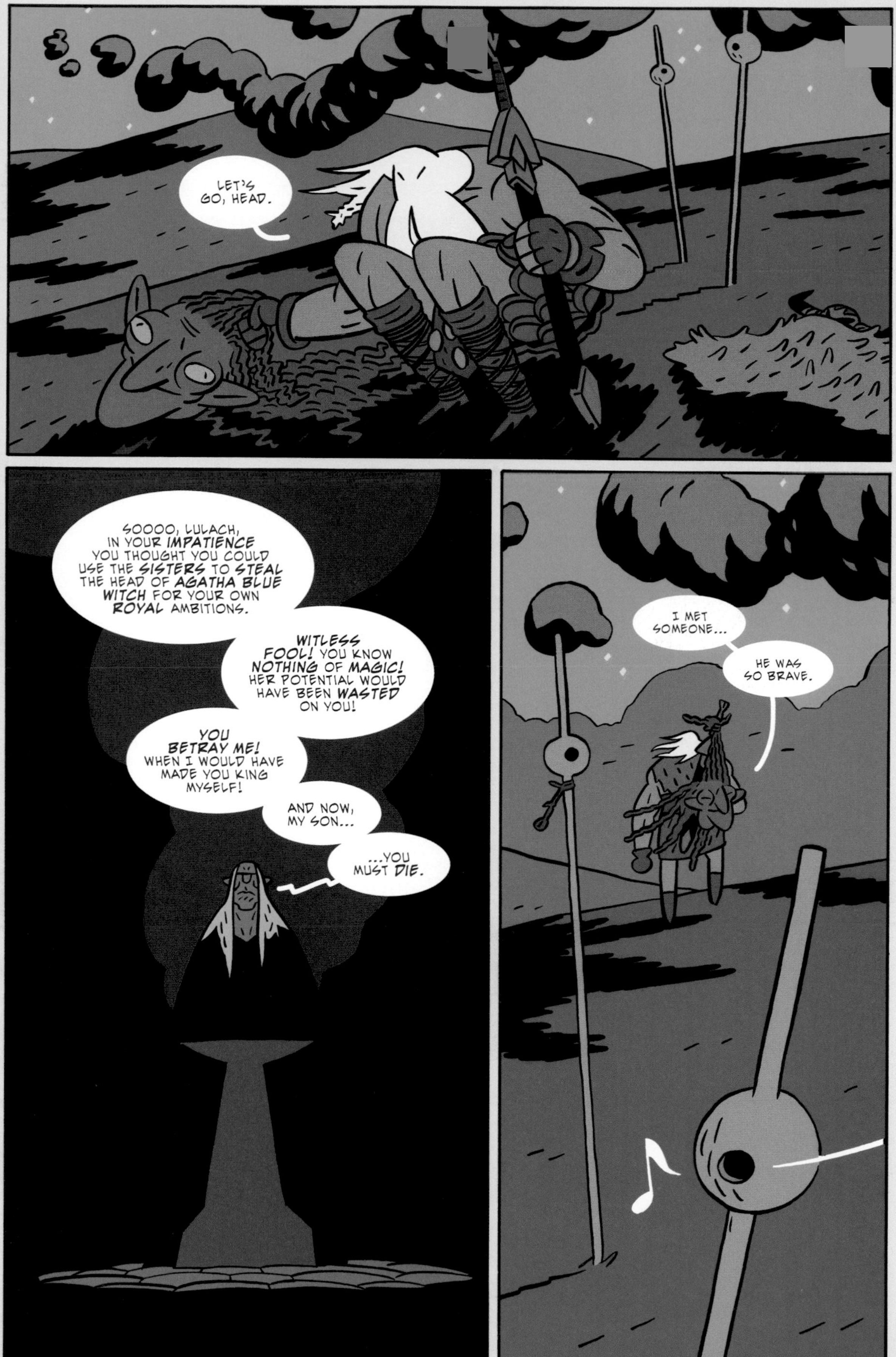
LET'S GO, HEAD.
SOOOO, LULACH, IN YOUR IMPATIENCE YOU THOUGHT YOU COULD USE THE SISTERS TO STEAL THE HEAD OF AGATHA BLUE WITCH FOR YOUR OWN ROYAL AMBITIONS.
WITLESS FOOL! YOU KNOW NOTHING OF MAGIC! HER POTENTIAL WOULD HAVE BEEN WASTED ON YOU!
YOU BETRAY ME! WHEN I WOULD HAVE MADE YOU KING MYSELF!
AND NOW, MY SON...
...YOU MUST DIE.
I MET SOMEONE...
HE WAS SO BRAVE.

CHAPTER SIX

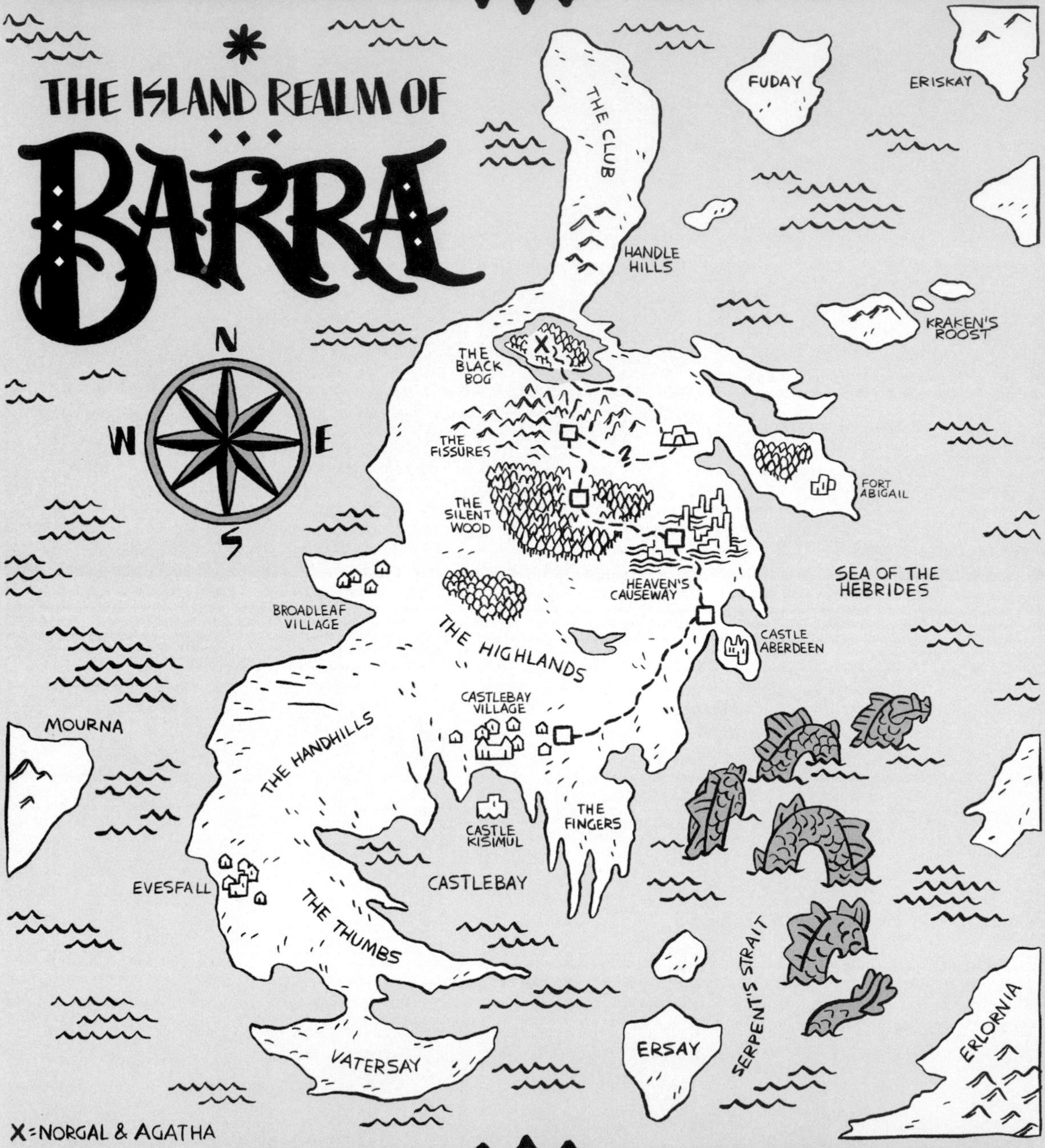

THE ISLAND REALM OF
BARRA
N
E
S
W
THE CLUB
HANDLE HILLS
FUDAY
ERISKAY
KRAKEN'S ROOST
THE BLACK BOG
THE FISSURES
THE SILENT WOOD
FORT ABIGAIL
HEAVEN'S CAUSEWAY
SEA OF THE HEBRIDES
BROADLEAF VILLAGE
CASTLE ABERDEEN
THE HIGHLANDS
CASTLEBAY VILLAGE
MOURNA
THE HANDHILLS
THE FINGERS
CASTLE KISIMUL
CASTLEBAY
EVESFALL
THE THUMBS
SERPENT'S STRAIT
ERLORNIA
ERSAY
VATERSAY
X=NORGAL & AGATHA

THE BLACK BOG

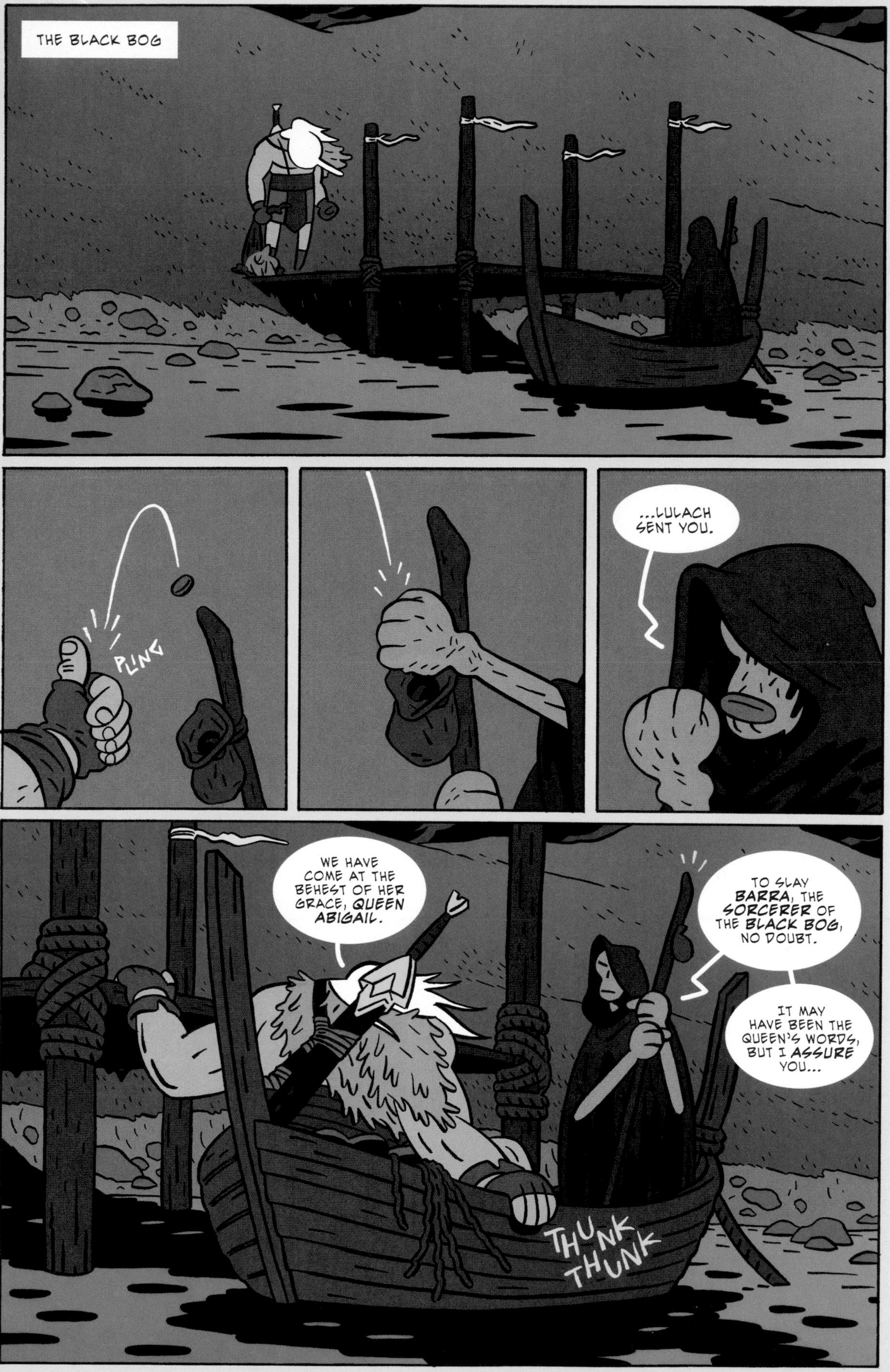
THE BLACK BOG
PLING
...LULACH SENT YOU.
WE HAVE COME AT THE BEHEST OF HER GRACE, QUEEN ABIGAIL.
TO SLAY BARRA, THE SORCERER OF THE BLACK BOG, NO DOUBT.
IT MAY HAVE BEEN THE QUEEN'S WORDS, BUT I ASSURE YOU...
THUNK THUNK

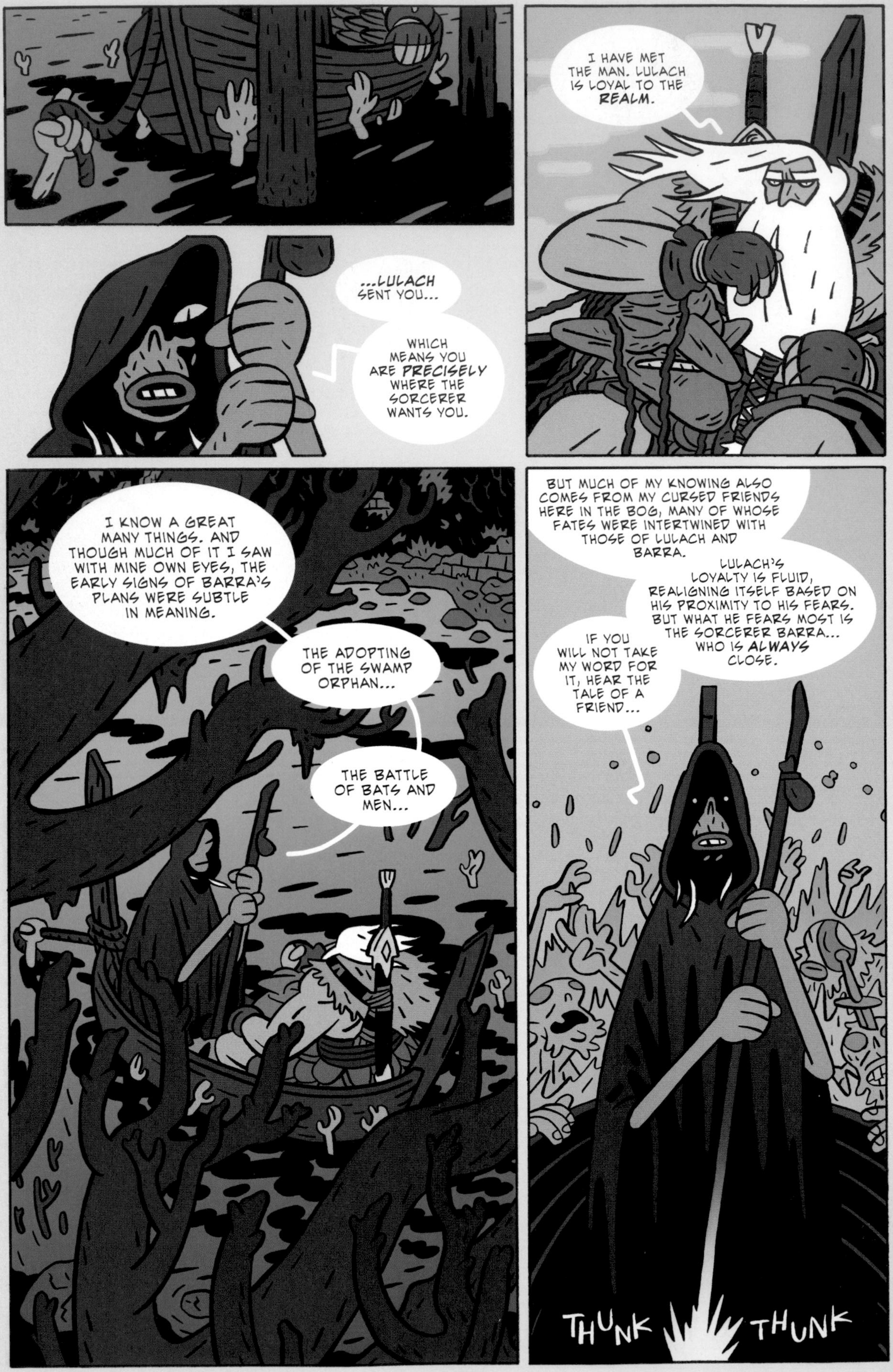
I HAVE MET THE MAN. LULACH IS LOYAL TO THE REALM.
...LULACH SENT YOU...
WHICH MEANS YOU ARE PRECISELY WHERE THE SORCERER WANTS YOU.
I KNOW A GREAT MANY THINGS. AND THOUGH MUCH OF IT I SAW WITH MINE OWN EYES, THE EARLY SIGNS OF BARRA'S PLANS WERE SUBTLE IN MEANING.
THE ADOPTING OF THE SWAMP ORPHAN...
THE BATTLE OF BATS AND MEN...
BUT MUCH OF MY KNOWING ALSO COMES FROM MY CURSED FRIENDS HERE IN THE BOG, MANY OF WHOSE FATES WERE INTERTWINED WITH THOSE OF LULACH AND BARRA.
LULACH'S LOYALTY IS FLUID, REALIGNING ITSELF BASED ON HIS PROXIMITY TO HIS FEARS. BUT WHAT HE FEARS MOST IS THE SORCERER BARRA... WHO IS ALWAYS CLOSE.
IF YOU WILL NOT TAKE MY WORD FOR IT, HEAR THE TALE OF A FRIEND...
THUNK THUNK

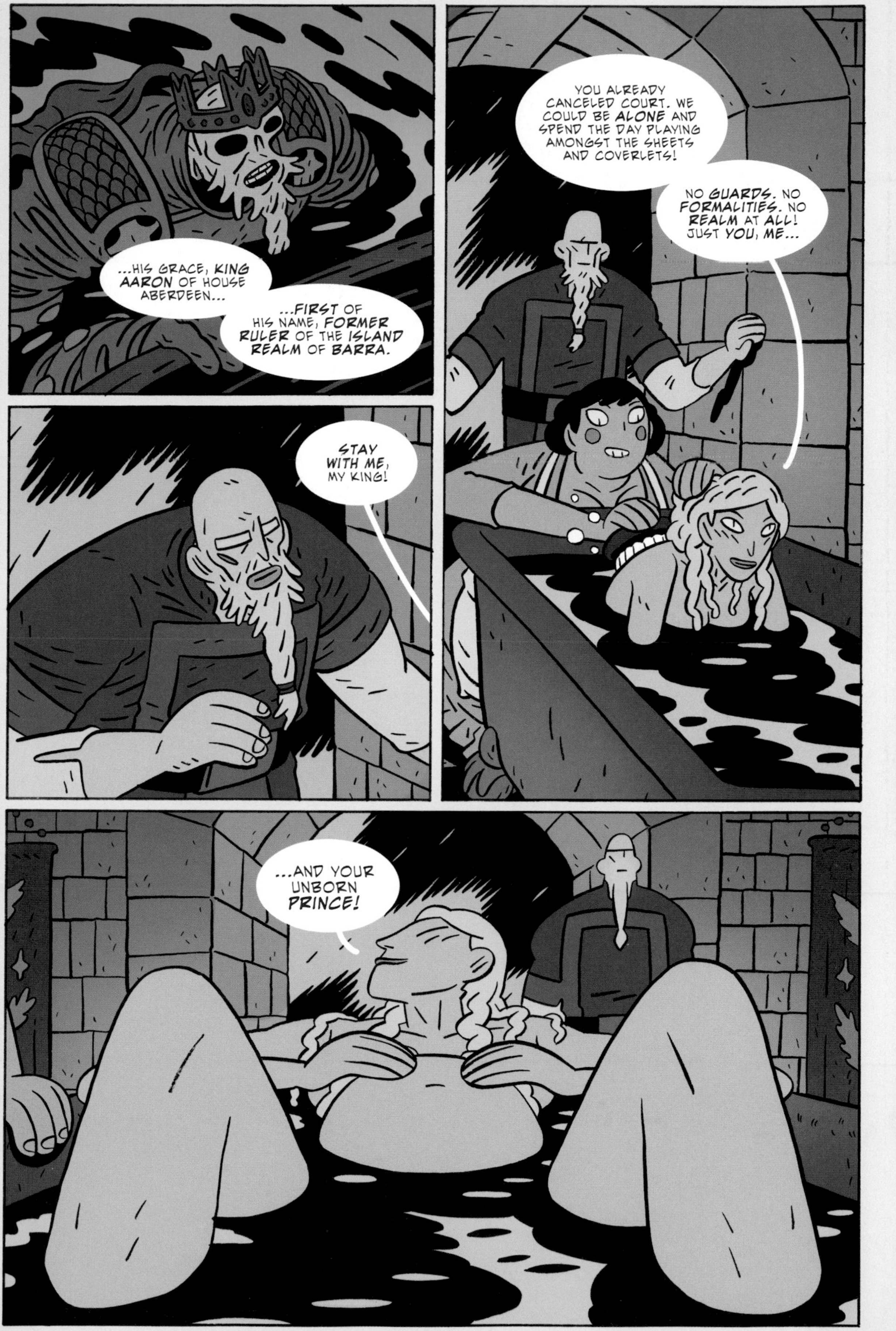
...HIS GRACE, KING AARON OF HOUSE ABERDEEN...
...FIRST OF HIS NAME, FORMER RULER OF THE ISLAND REALM OF BARRA.
YOU ALREADY CANCELED COURT. WE COULD BE ALONE AND SPEND THE DAY PLAYING AMONGST THE SHEETS AND COVERLETS!
NO GUARDS. NO FORMALITIES. NO REALM AT ALL! JUST YOU, ME...
STAY WITH ME, MY KING!
...AND YOUR UNBORN PRINCE!

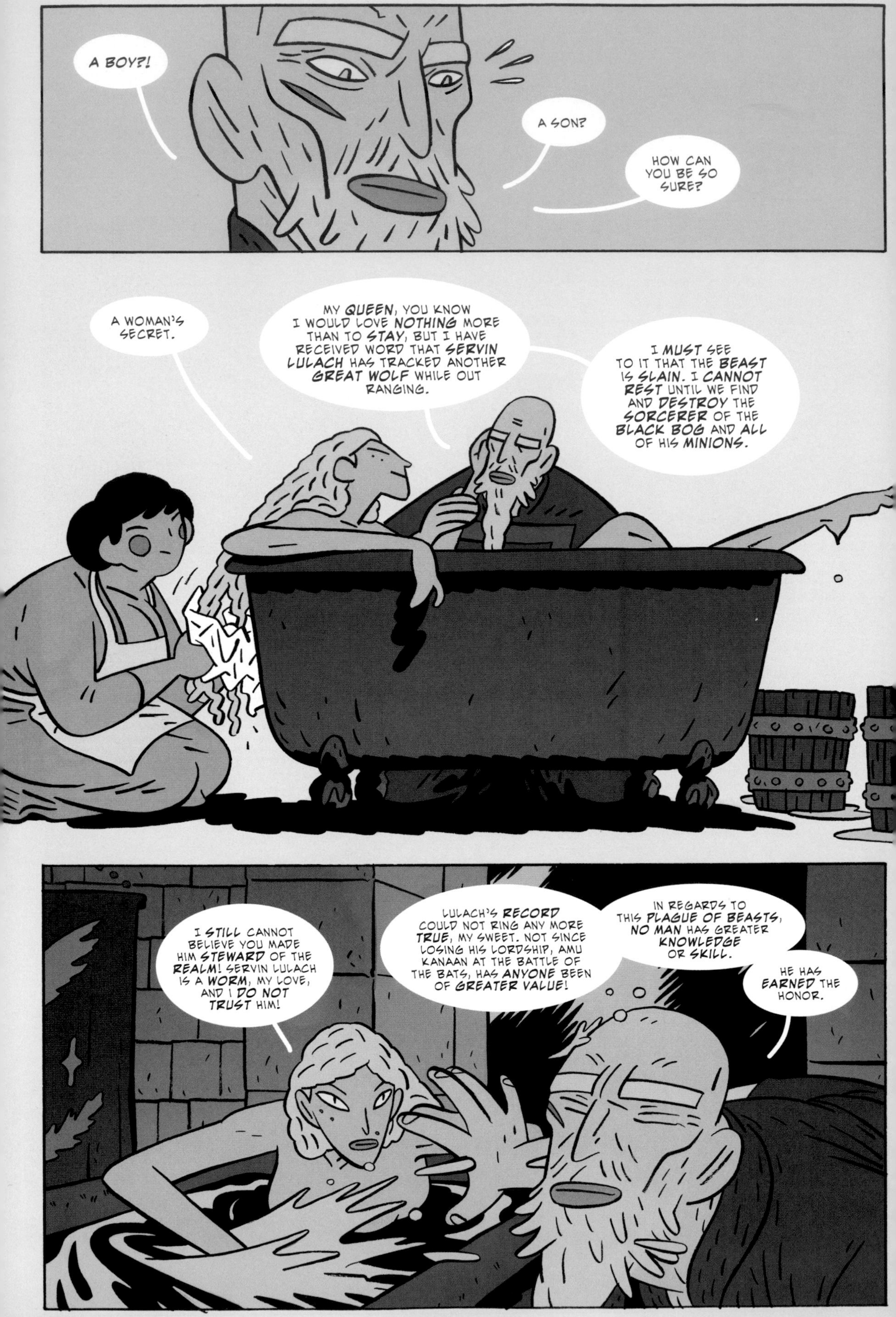
A BOY?!
A SON?
HOW CAN YOU BE SO SURE?
A WOMAN'S SECRET.
MY QUEEN, YOU KNOW I WOULD LOVE NOTHING MORE THAN TO STAY, BUT I HAVE RECEIVED WORD THAT SERVIN LULACH HAS TRACKED ANOTHER GREAT WOLF WHILE OUT RANGING.
I MUST SEE TO IT THAT THE BEAST IS SLAIN. I CANNOT REST UNTIL WE FIND AND DESTROY THE SORCERER OF THE BLACK BOG AND ALL OF HIS MINIONS.
I STILL CANNOT BELIEVE YOU MADE HIM STEWARD OF THE REALM! SERVIN LULACH IS A WORM, MY LOVE, AND I DO NOT TRUST HIM!
LULACH'S RECORD COULD NOT RING ANY MORE TRUE, MY SWEET. NOT SINCE LOSING HIS LORDSHIP, AMU KANAAN AT THE BATTLE OF THE BATS, HAS ANYONE BEEN OF GREATER VALUE!
IN REGARDS TO THIS PLAGUE OF BEASTS, NO MAN HAS GREATER KNOWLEDGE OR SKILL.
HE HAS EARNED THE HONOR.

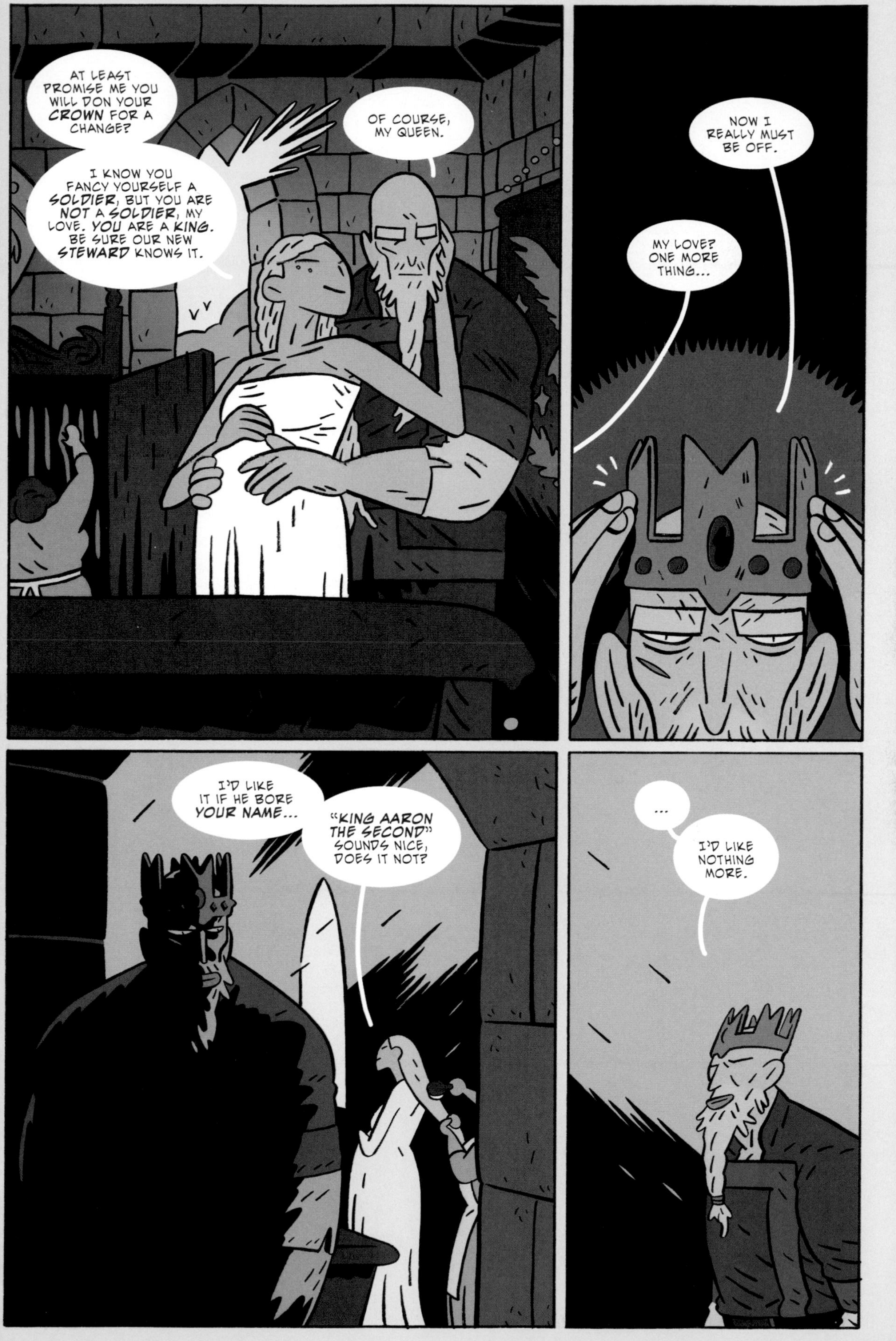
AT LEAST PROMISE ME YOU WILL DON YOUR CROWN FOR A CHANGE?
I KNOW YOU FANCY YOURSELF A SOLDIER, BUT YOU ARE NOT A SOLDIER, MY LOVE. YOU ARE A KING. BE SURE OUR NEW STEWARD KNOWS IT.
OF COURSE, MY QUEEN.
NOW I REALLY MUST BE OFF.
MY LOVE? ONE MORE THING...
I'D LIKE IT IF HE BORE YOUR NAME...
"KING AARON THE SECOND" SOUNDS NICE, DOES IT NOT?
...
I'D LIKE NOTHING MORE.

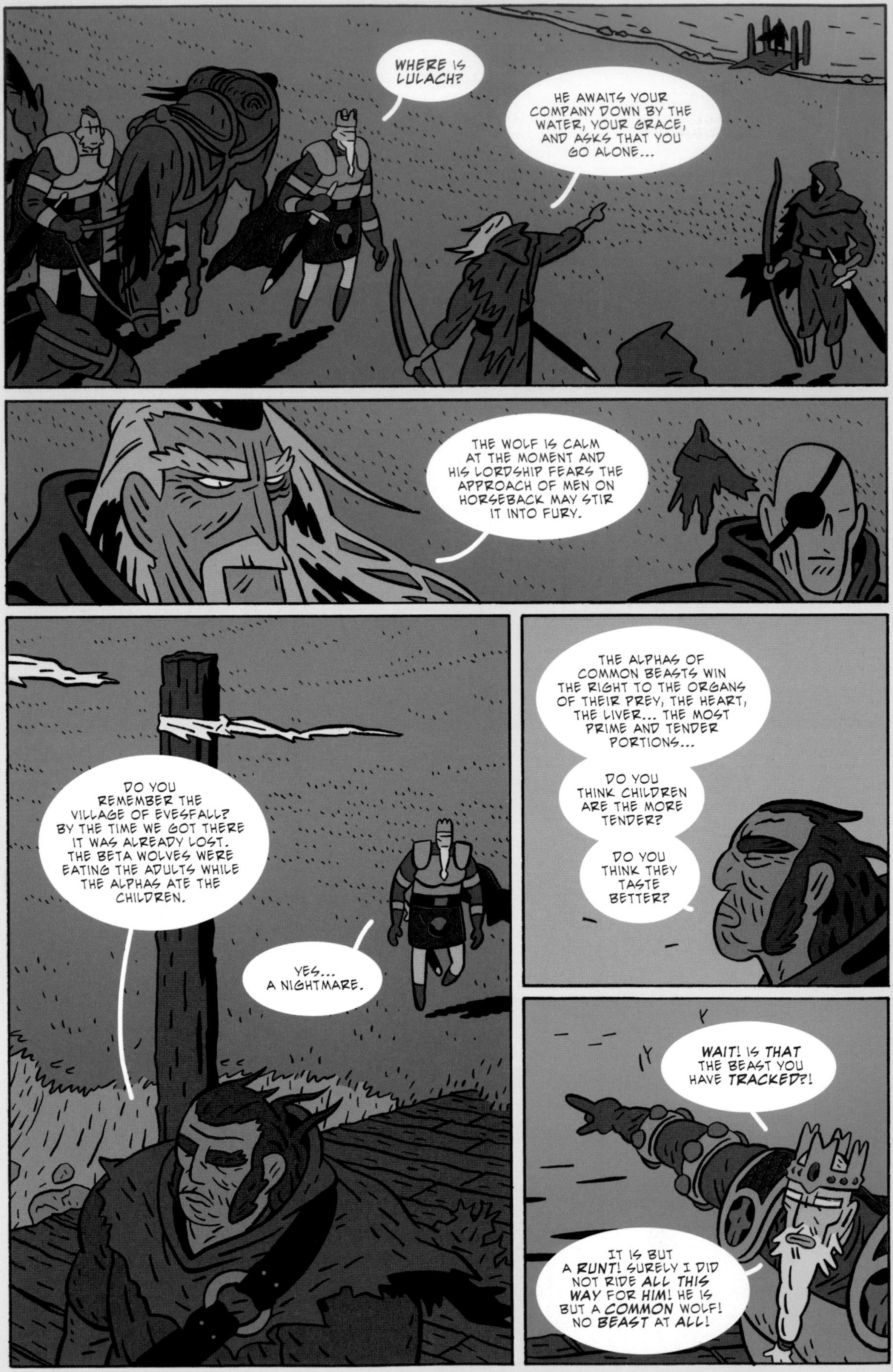
WHERE IS LULACH?
HE AWAITS YOUR COMPANY DOWN BY THE WATER, YOUR GRACE, AND ASKS THAT YOU GO ALONE...
THE WOLF IS CALM AT THE MOMENT AND HIS LORDSHIP FEARS THE APPROACH OF MEN ON HORSEBACK MAY STIR IT INTO FURY.
DO YOU REMEMBER THE VILLAGE OF EVESFALL? BY THE TIME WE GOT THERE IT WAS ALREADY LOST. THE BETA WOLVES WERE EATING THE ADULTS WHILE THE ALPHAS ATE THE CHILDREN.
YES... A NIGHTMARE.
THE ALPHAS OF COMMON BEASTS WIN THE RIGHT TO THE ORGANS OF THEIR PREY, THE HEART, THE LIVER... THE MOST PRIME AND TENDER PORTIONS...
DO YOU THINK CHILDREN ARE THE MORE TENDER?
DO YOU THINK THEY TASTE BETTER?
WAIT! IS THAT THE BEAST YOU HAVE TRACKED?!
IT IS BUT A RUNT! SURELY I DID NOT RIDE ALL THIS WAY FOR HIM! HE IS BUT A COMMON WOLF! NO BEAST AT ALL!

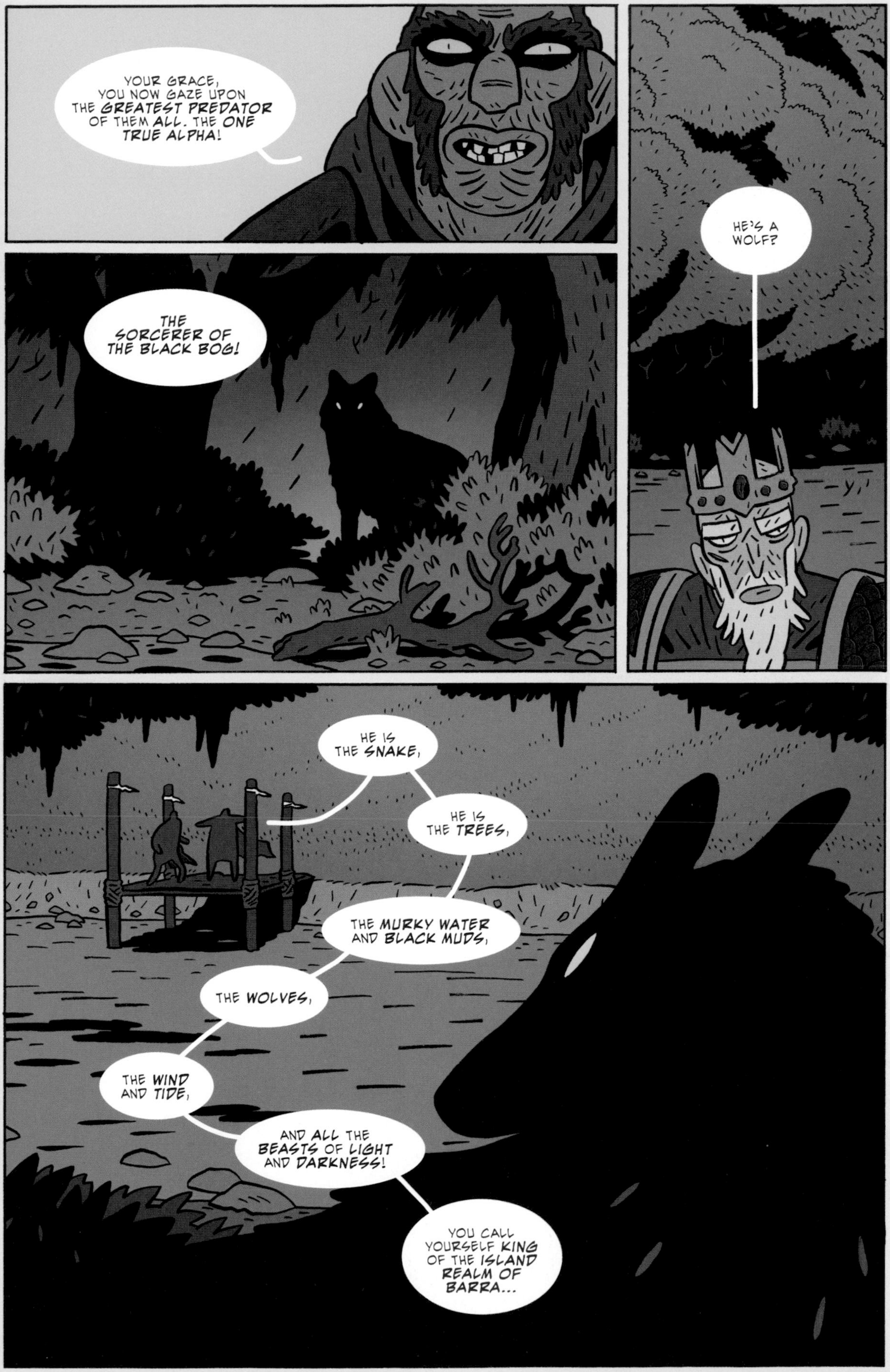
YOUR GRACE, YOU NOW GAZE UPON THE GREATEST PREDATOR OF THEM ALL. THE ONE TRUE ALPHA!
THE SORCERER OF THE BLACK BOG!
HE'S A WOLF?
HE IS THE SNAKE,
HE IS THE TREES,
THE MURKY WATER AND BLACK MUDS,
THE WOLVES,
THE WIND AND TIDE,
AND ALL THE BEASTS OF LIGHT AND DARKNESS!
YOU CALL YOURSELF KING OF THE ISLAND REALM OF BARRA...

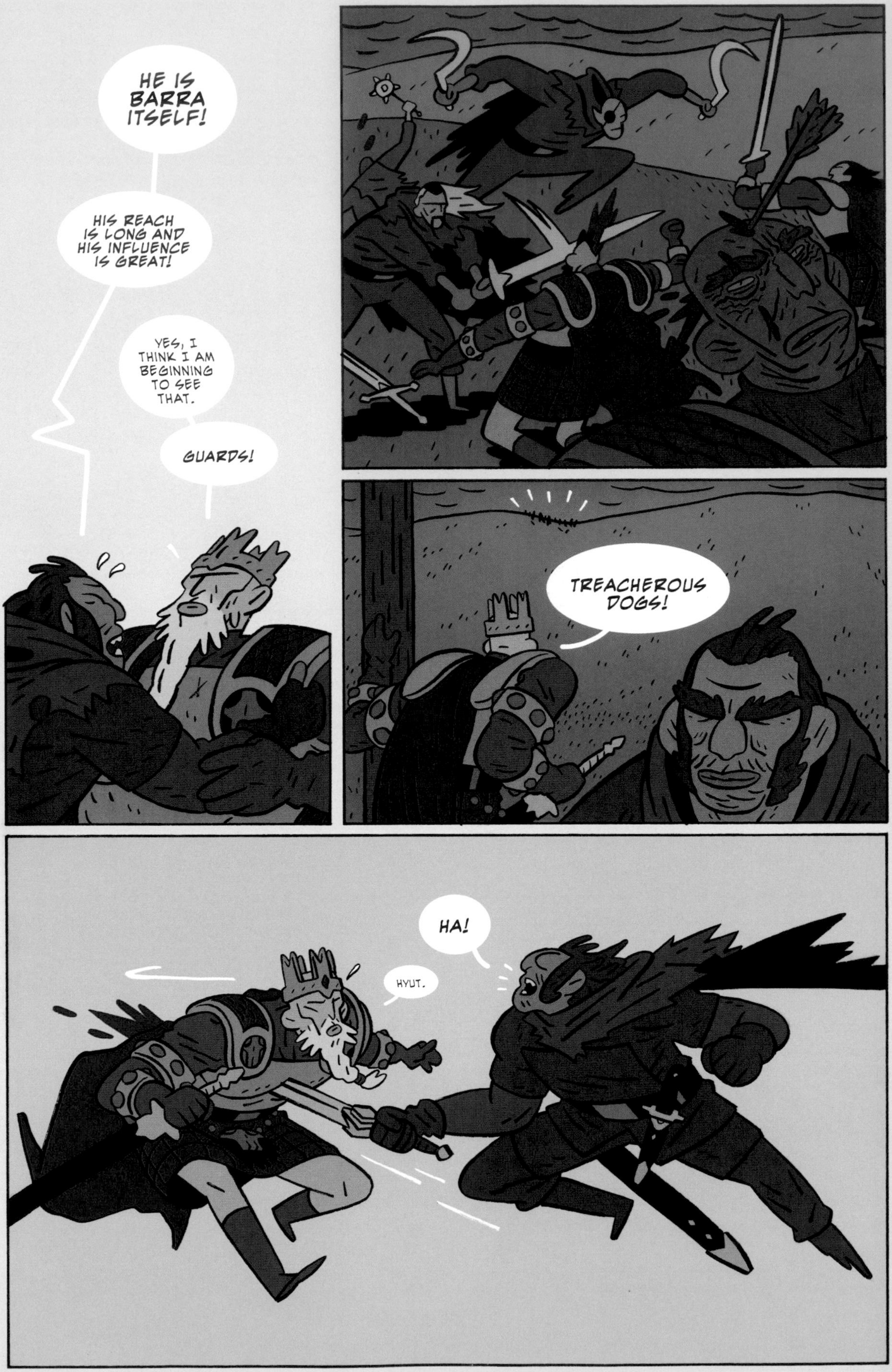
HE IS BARRA ITSELF!
HIS REACH IS LONG AND HIS INFLUENCE IS GREAT!
YES, I THINK I AM BEGINNING TO SEE THAT.
GUARDS!
TREACHEROUS DOGS!
HA!
HYUT.

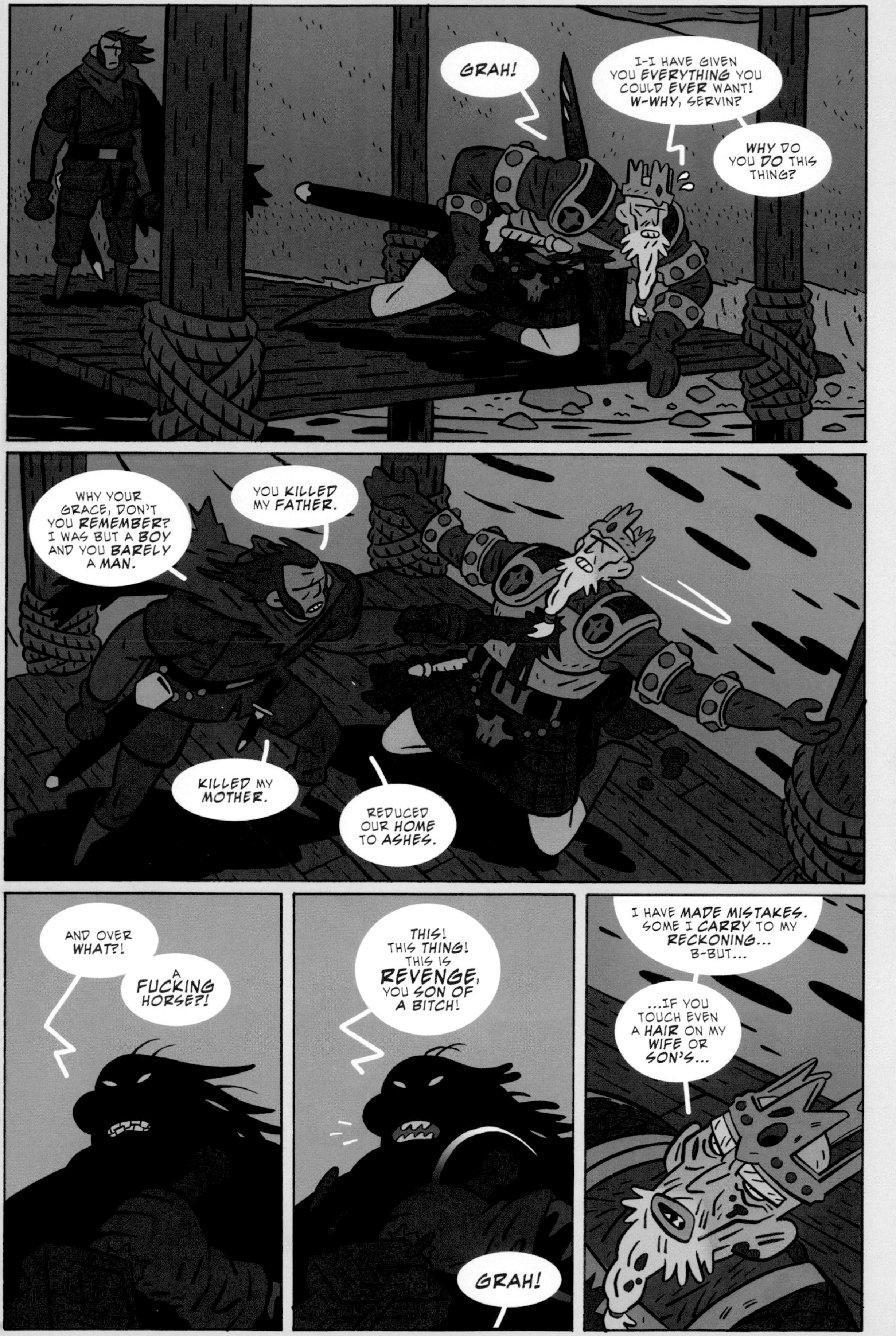
GRAH!
I-I HAVE GIVEN YOU EVERYTHING YOU COULD EVER WANT! W-WHY, SERVIN?
WHY DO YOU DO THIS THING?
WHY YOUR GRACE, DON'T YOU REMEMBER? I WAS BUT A BOY AND YOU BARELY A MAN.
YOU KILLED MY FATHER.
KILLED MY MOTHER.
REDUCED OUR HOME TO ASHES.
AND OVER WHAT?!
A FUCKING HORSE?!
THIS! THIS THING! THIS IS REVENGE, YOU SON OF A BITCH!
GRAH!
I HAVE MADE MISTAKES. SOME I CARRY TO MY RECKONING... B-BUT...
...IF YOU TOUCH EVEN A HAIR ON MY WIFE OR SON'S...

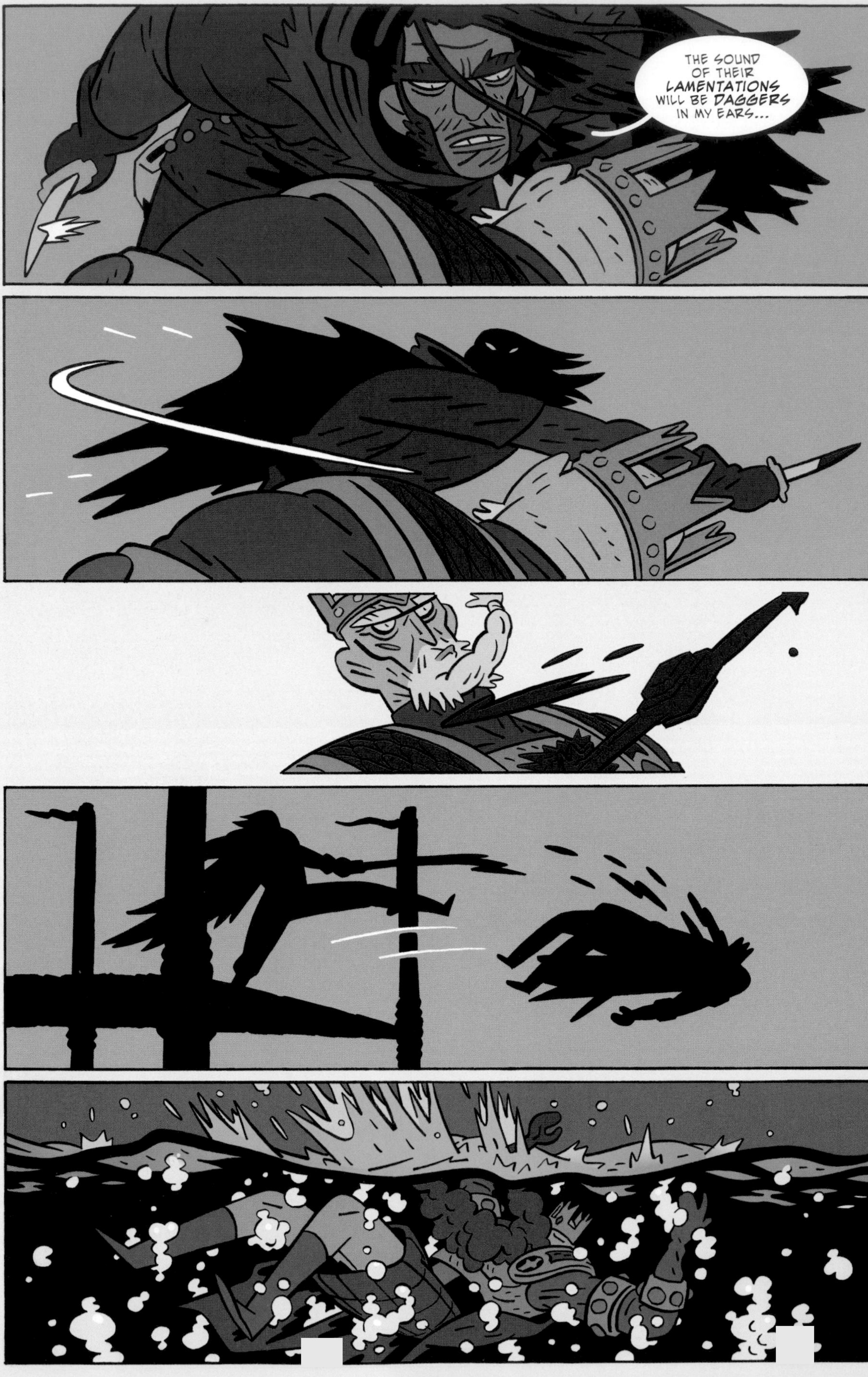
THE SOUND OF THEIR LAMENTATIONS WILL BE DAGGERS IN MY EARS...

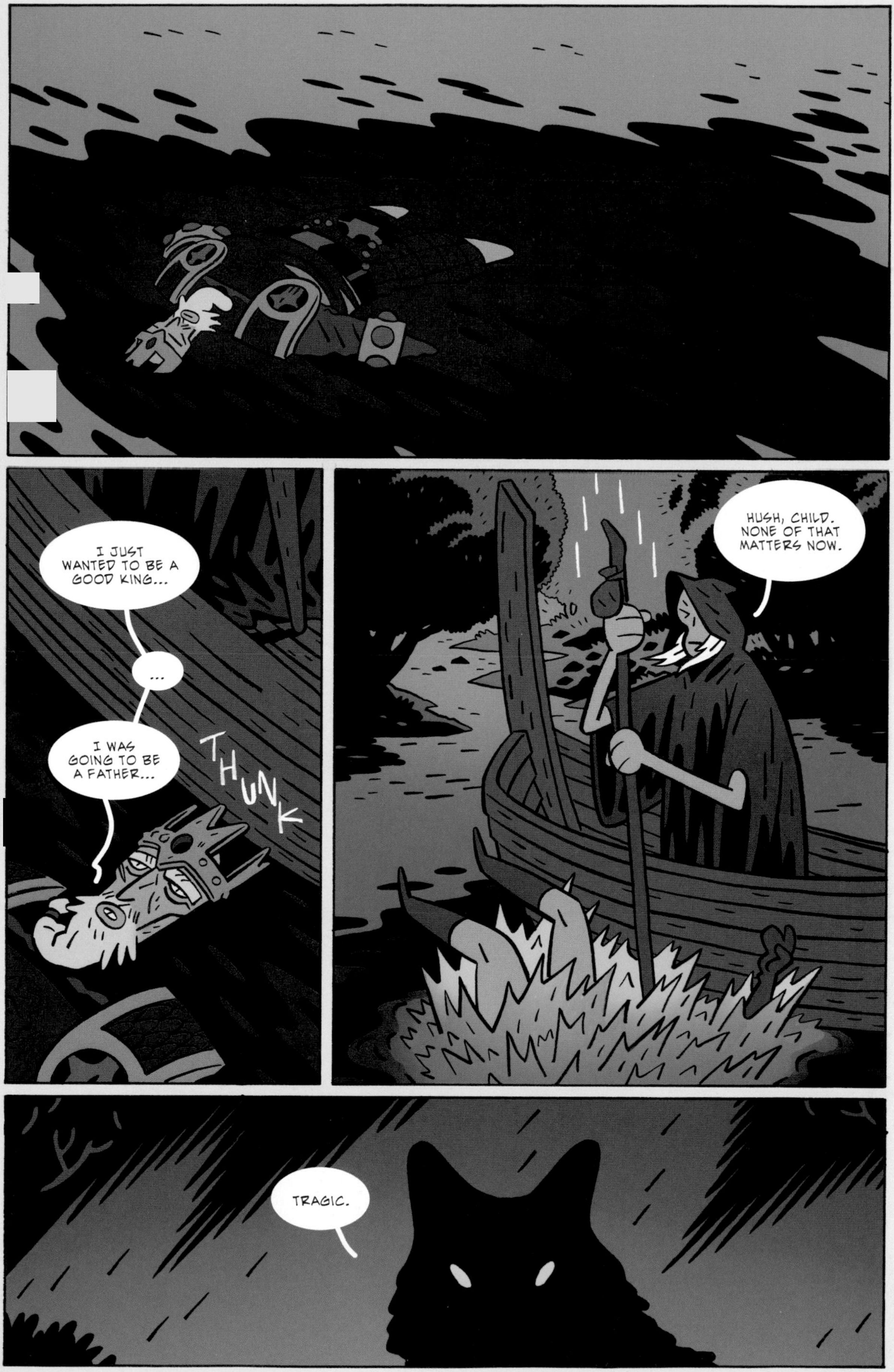
I JUST WANTED TO BE A GOOD KING...
...
I WAS GOING TO BE A FATHER...
THUNK
HUSH, CHILD. NONE OF THAT MATTERS NOW.
TRAGIC.

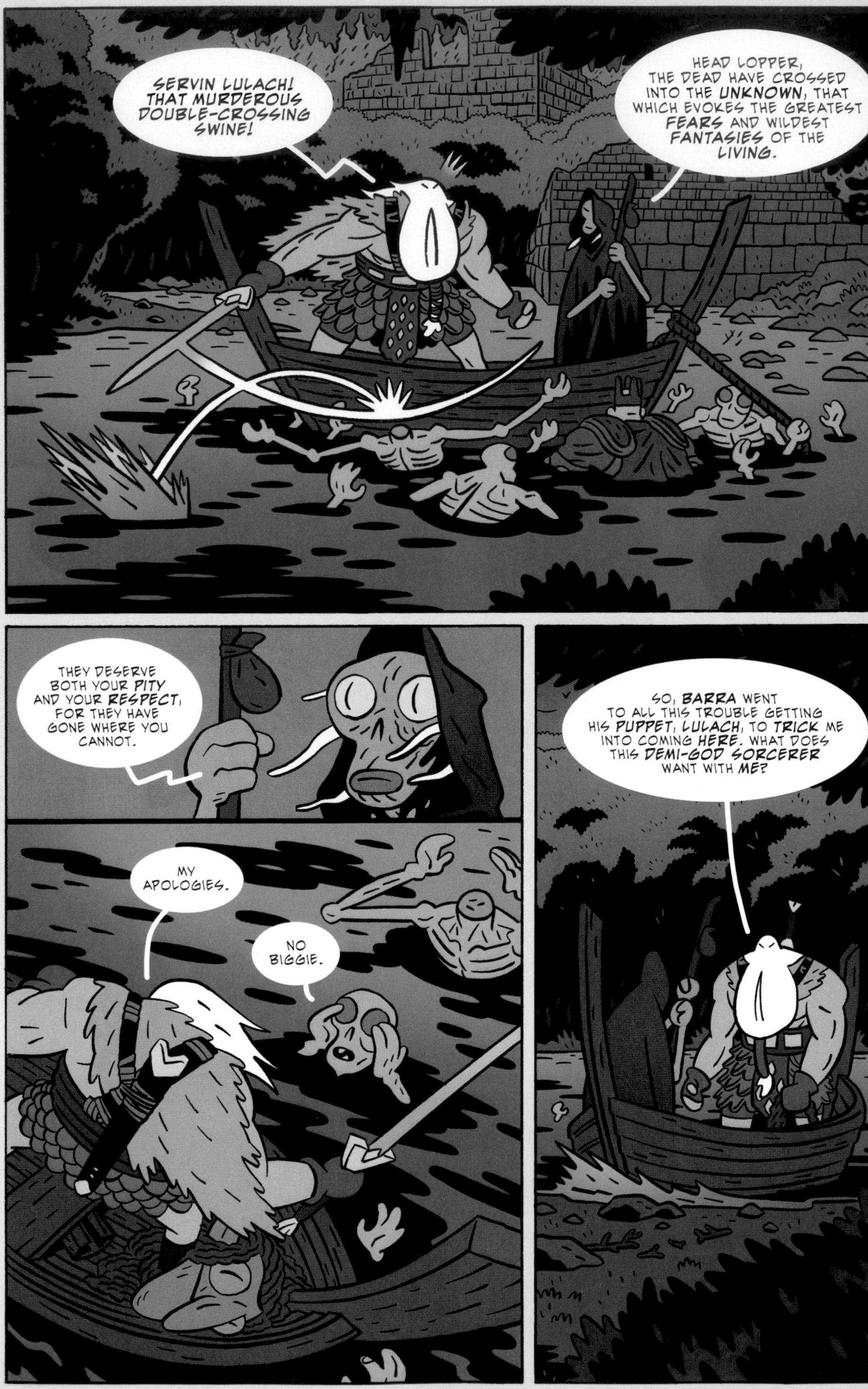
SERVIN LULACH! THAT MURDEROUS DOUBLE-CROSSING SWINE!
HEAD LOPPER, THE DEAD HAVE CROSSED INTO THE UNKNOWN, THAT WHICH EVOKES THE GREATEST FEARS AND WILDEST FANTASIES OF THE LIVING.
THEY DESERVE BOTH YOUR PITY AND YOUR RESPECT, FOR THEY HAVE GONE WHERE YOU CANNOT.
MY APOLOGIES.
NO BIGGIE.
SO, BARRA WENT TO ALL THIS TROUBLE GETTING HIS PUPPET, LULACH, TO TRICK ME INTO COMING HERE. WHAT DOES THIS DEMI-GOD SORCERER WANT WITH ME?

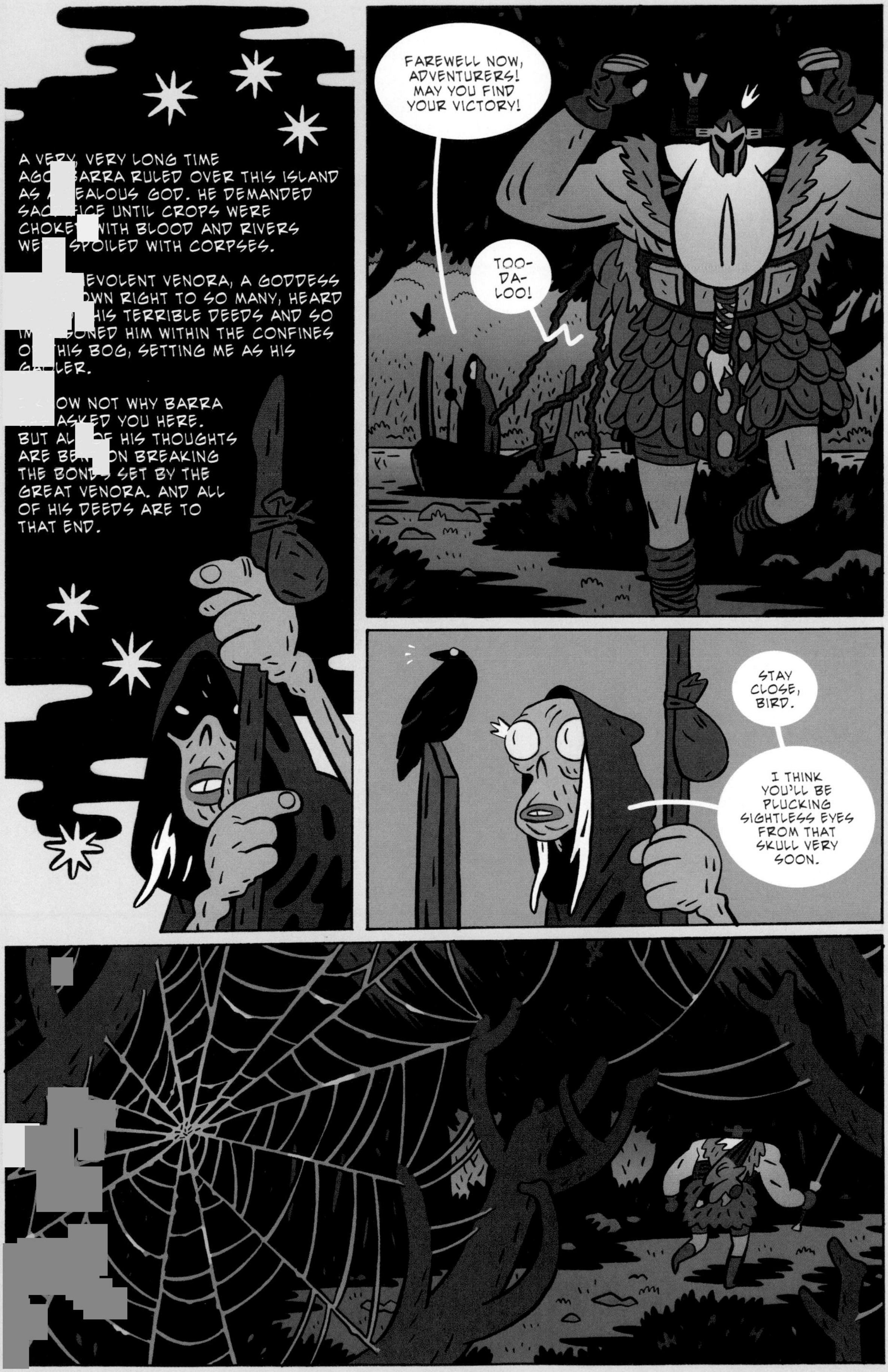
A VERY, VERY LONG TIME
AGO BARRA RULED OVER THIS ISLAND
AS A EALOUS GOD. HE DEMANDED
SAC FICE UNTIL CROPS WERE
CHOKE WITH BLOOD AND RIVERS
WE SPOILED WITH CORPSES.
EVOLENT VENORA, A GODDESS
OWN RIGHT TO SO MANY, HEARD
HIS TERRIBLE DEEDS AND SO
IM GONED HIM WITHIN THE CONFINES
O THIS BOG, SETTING ME AS HIS
G LER.
OW NOT WHY BARRA
ASKED YOU HERE.
BUT AL F HIS THOUGHTS
ARE BE ON BREAKING
THE BOND SET BY THE
GREAT VENORA. AND ALL
OF HIS DEEDS ARE TO
THAT END.
FAREWELL NOW, ADVENTURERS! MAY YOU FIND YOUR VICTORY!
TOO-DA-LOO!
STAY CLOSE, BIRD.
I THINK YOU'LL BE PLUCKING SIGHTLESS EYES FROM THAT SKULL VERY SOON.

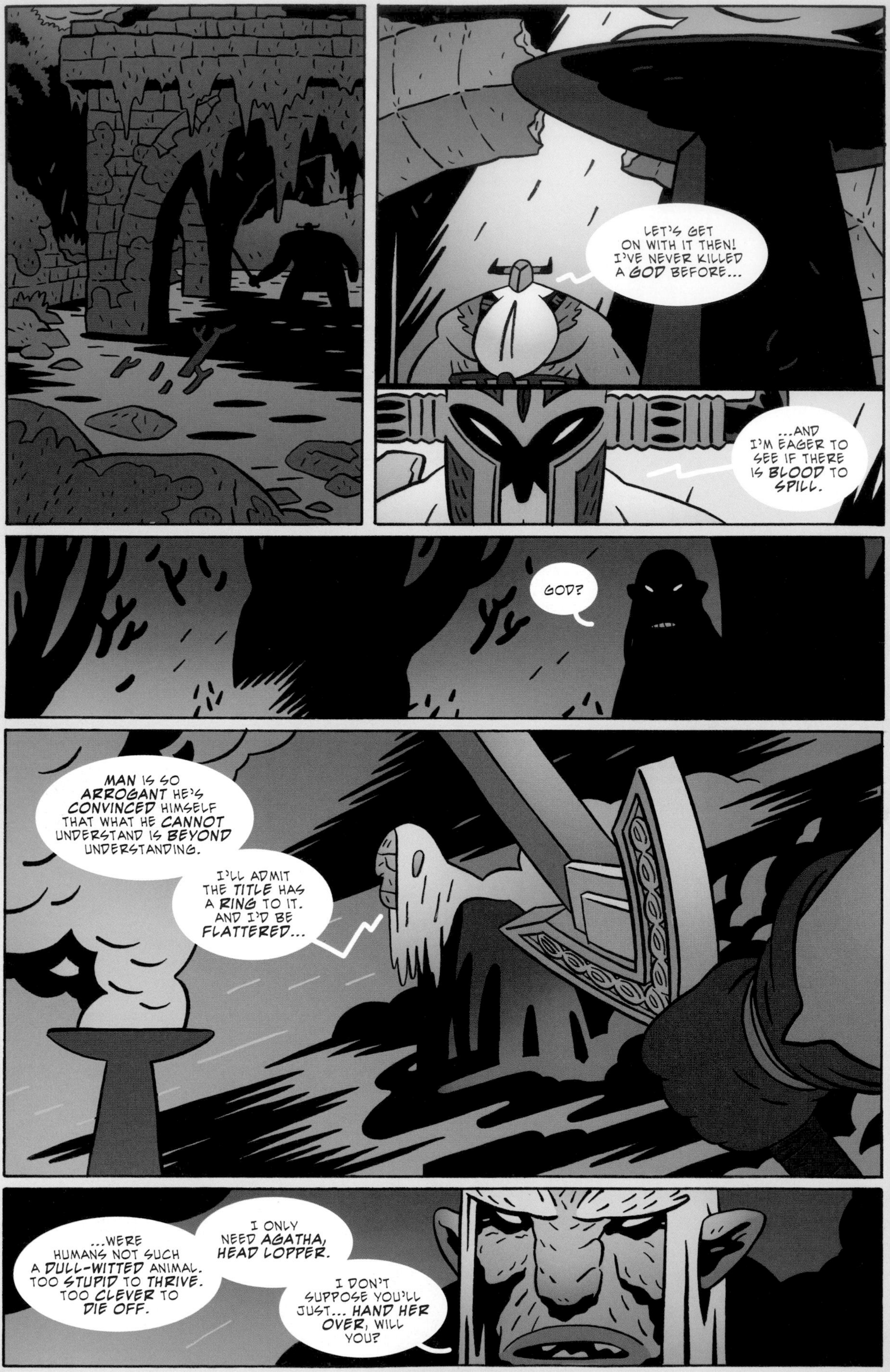
LET'S GET ON WITH IT THEN! I'VE NEVER KILLED A GOD BEFORE...
...AND I'M EAGER TO SEE IF THERE IS BLOOD TO SPILL.
GOD?
MAN IS SO ARROGANT HE'S CONVINCED HIMSELF THAT WHAT HE CANNOT UNDERSTAND IS BEYOND UNDERSTANDING.
I'LL ADMIT THE TITLE HAS A RING TO IT. AND I'D BE FLATTERED...
...WERE HUMANS NOT SUCH A DULL-WITTED ANIMAL. TOO STUPID TO THRIVE. TOO CLEVER TO DIE OFF.
I ONLY NEED AGATHA, HEAD LOPPER.
I DON'T SUPPOSE YOU'LL JUST... HAND HER OVER, WILL YOU?

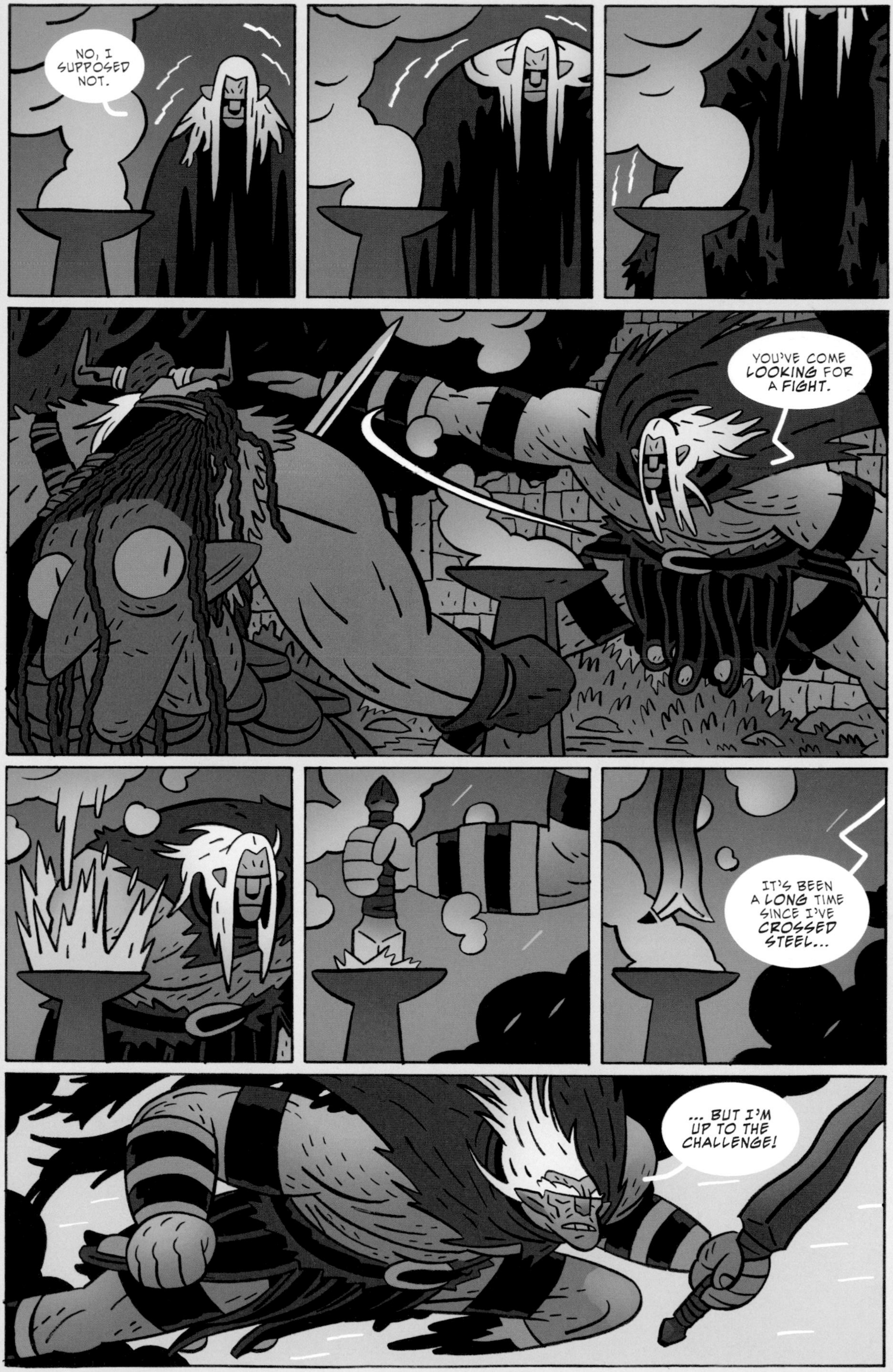
NO, I SUPPOSED NOT.
YOU'VE COME LOOKING FOR A FIGHT.
IT'S BEEN A LONG TIME SINCE I'VE CROSSED STEEL...
... BUT I'M UP TO THE CHALLENGE!

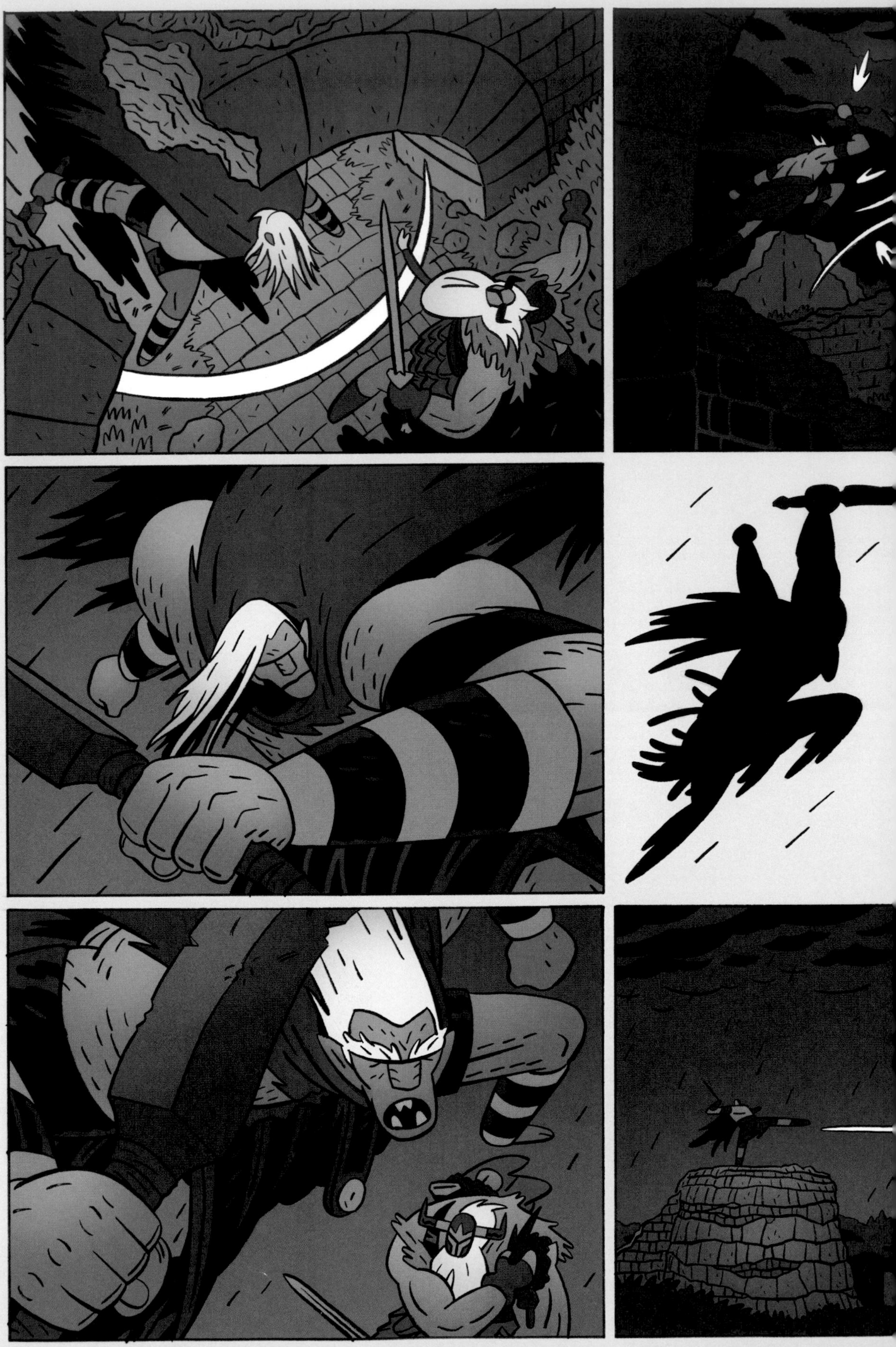

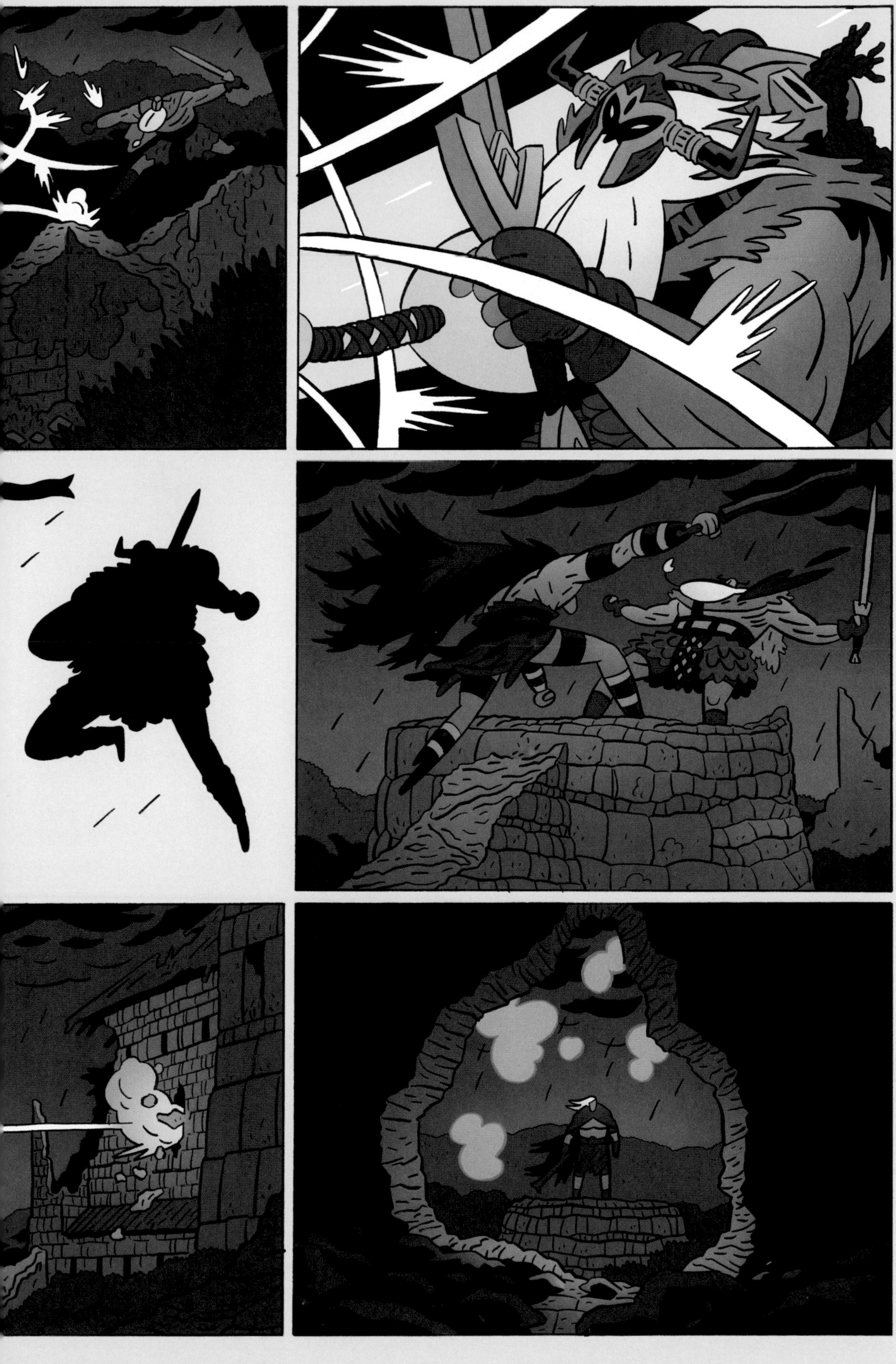

MY LORD, THERE IS MUCH IN THE WAY OF *CHARRED HUMAN REMAINS* AND THAT WHICH LOOKS LIKE AN *ENORMOUS BUG* - BUT WE HAVE FOUND *NOTHING* THAT LOOKS LIKE THE OVER-LARGE *SKULL* OF A *BLUE WITCH.*

THEN THE HEAD LOPPER MUST STILL LIVE.

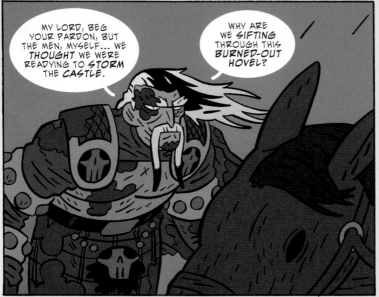

MY LORD, BEG YOUR PARDON, BUT THE MEN, MYSELF... WE *THOUGHT* WE WERE READYING TO *STORM* THE CASTLE.

WHY ARE WE *SIFTING* THROUGH THIS *BURNED-OUT HOVEL?*

THE HEAD OF THE *BLUE WITCH* CARRIED BY THE *HEAD LOPPER* IS *POWERFUL* BEYOND BELIEF, A *MAGICAL WEAPON!* I ARRANGED TO HAVE THE *LOPPER KILLED* AND THE HEAD *STOLEN* SO WE COULD USE ITS *POWER* TO TAKE THE *THRONE.* BUT IT WOULD SEEM THE HEAD LOPPER *BESTED* MY *ASSAILANTS.*

MEN! WE RIDE FOR THE *BLACK BOG!* THE HEAD LOPPER HOLDS THE KEY TO THE THRONE. WE MUST OVERTAKE HIM - OR ALL IS LOST!

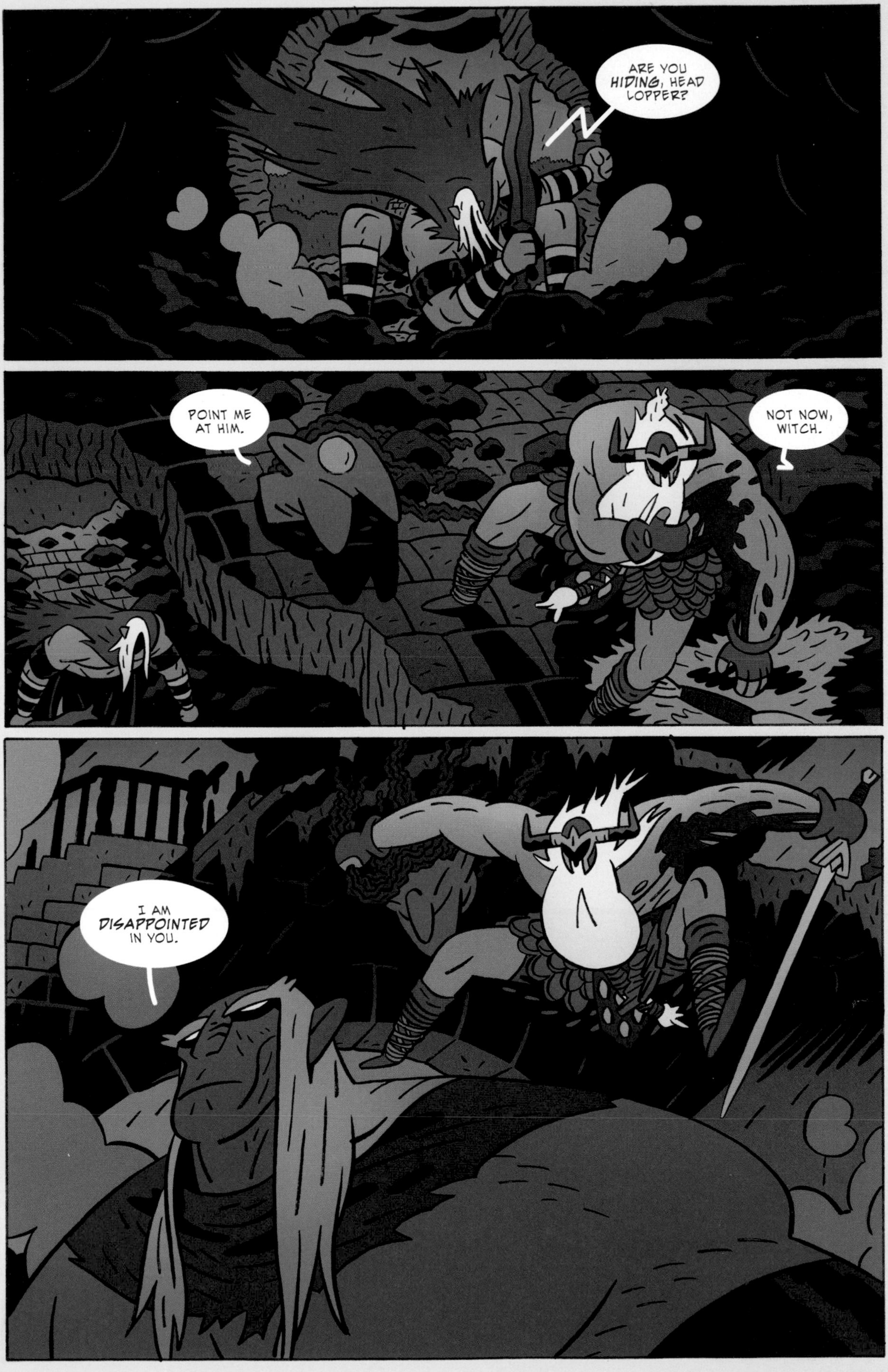
ARE YOU HIDING, HEAD LOPPER?
POINT ME AT HIM.
NOT NOW, WITCH.
I AM DISAPPOINTED IN YOU.

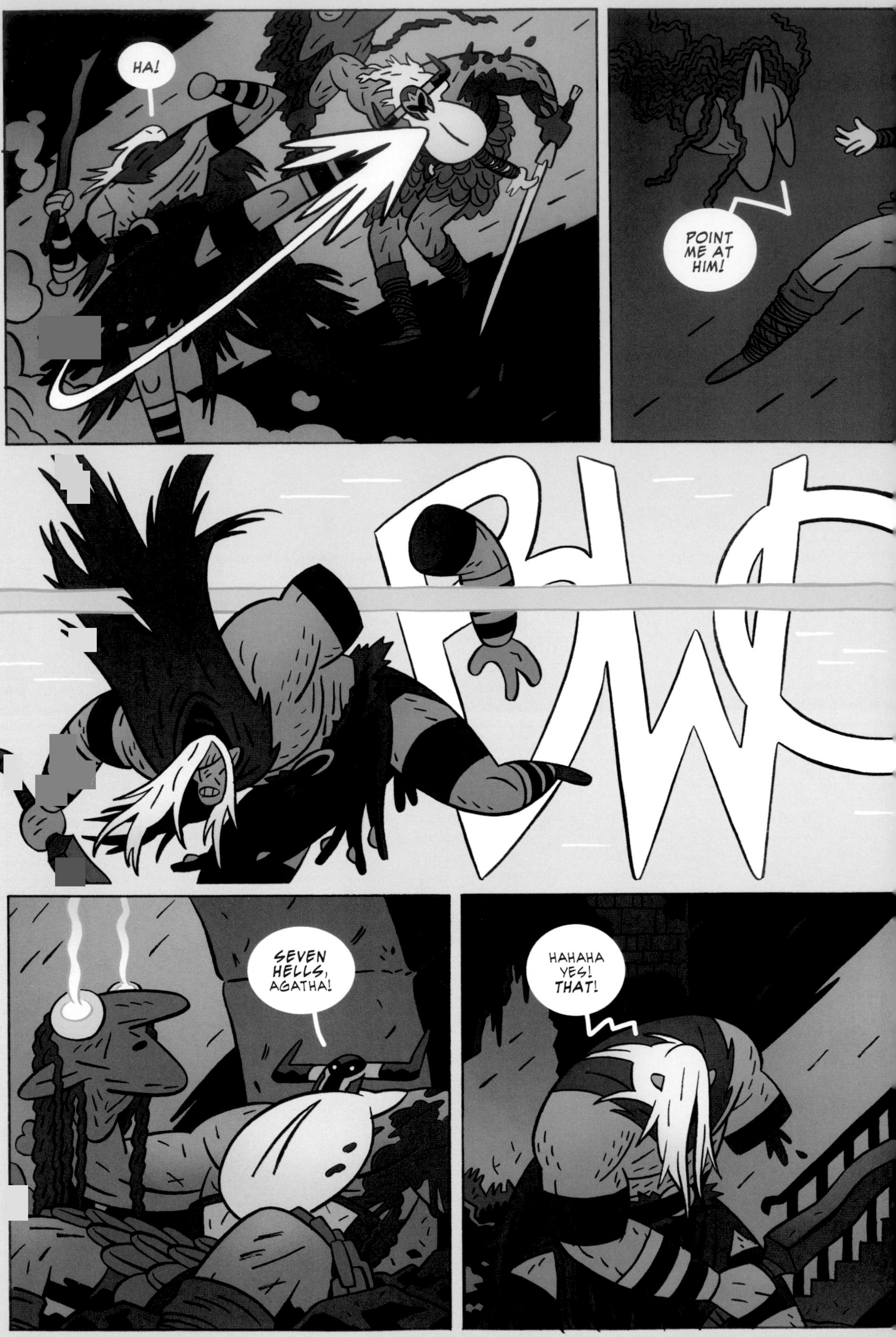
HA!
POINT ME AT HIM!
SEVEN HELLS, AGATHA!
HAHAHA YES! THAT!

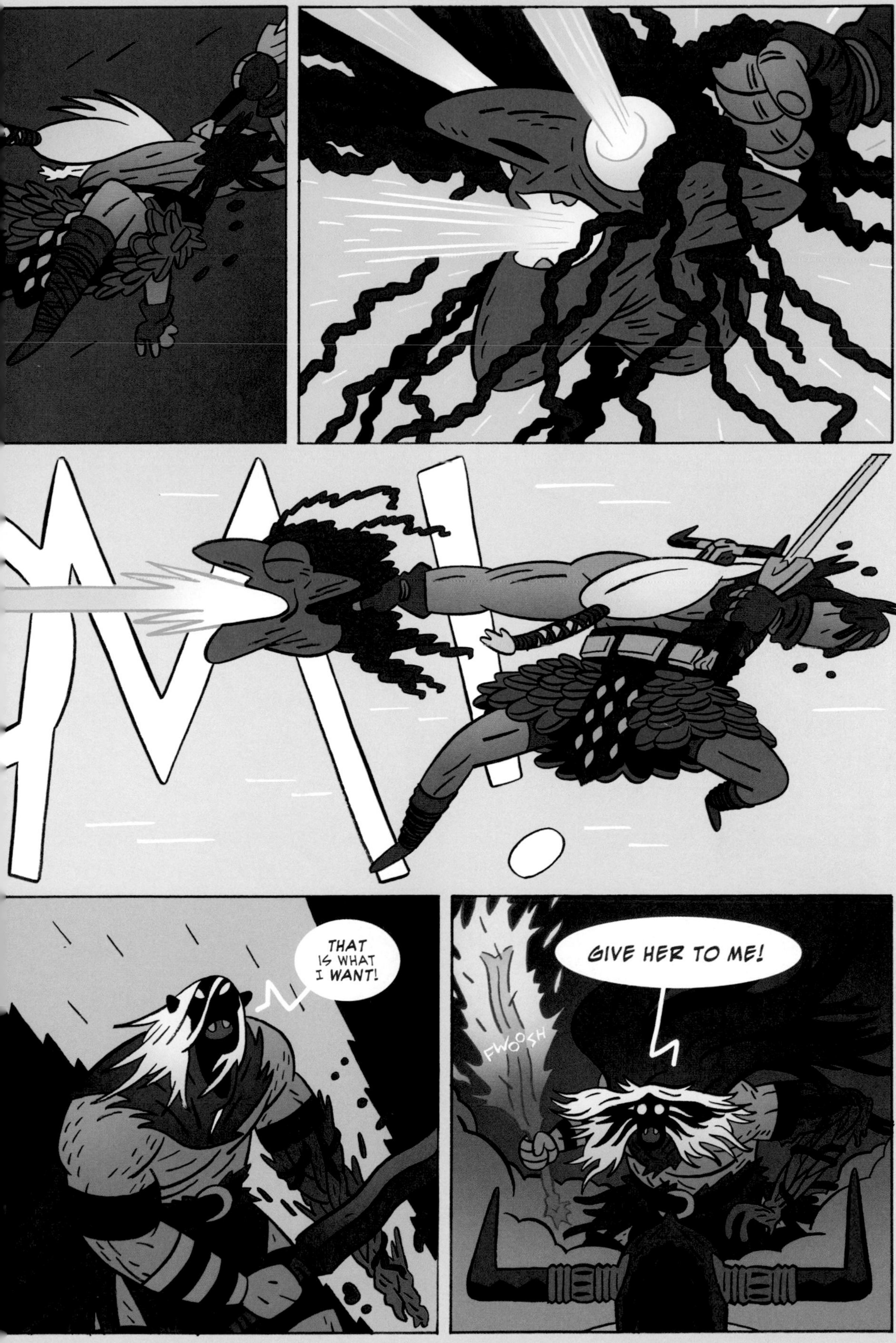
THAT IS WHAT I WANT!
GIVE HER TO ME!
FWOOSH

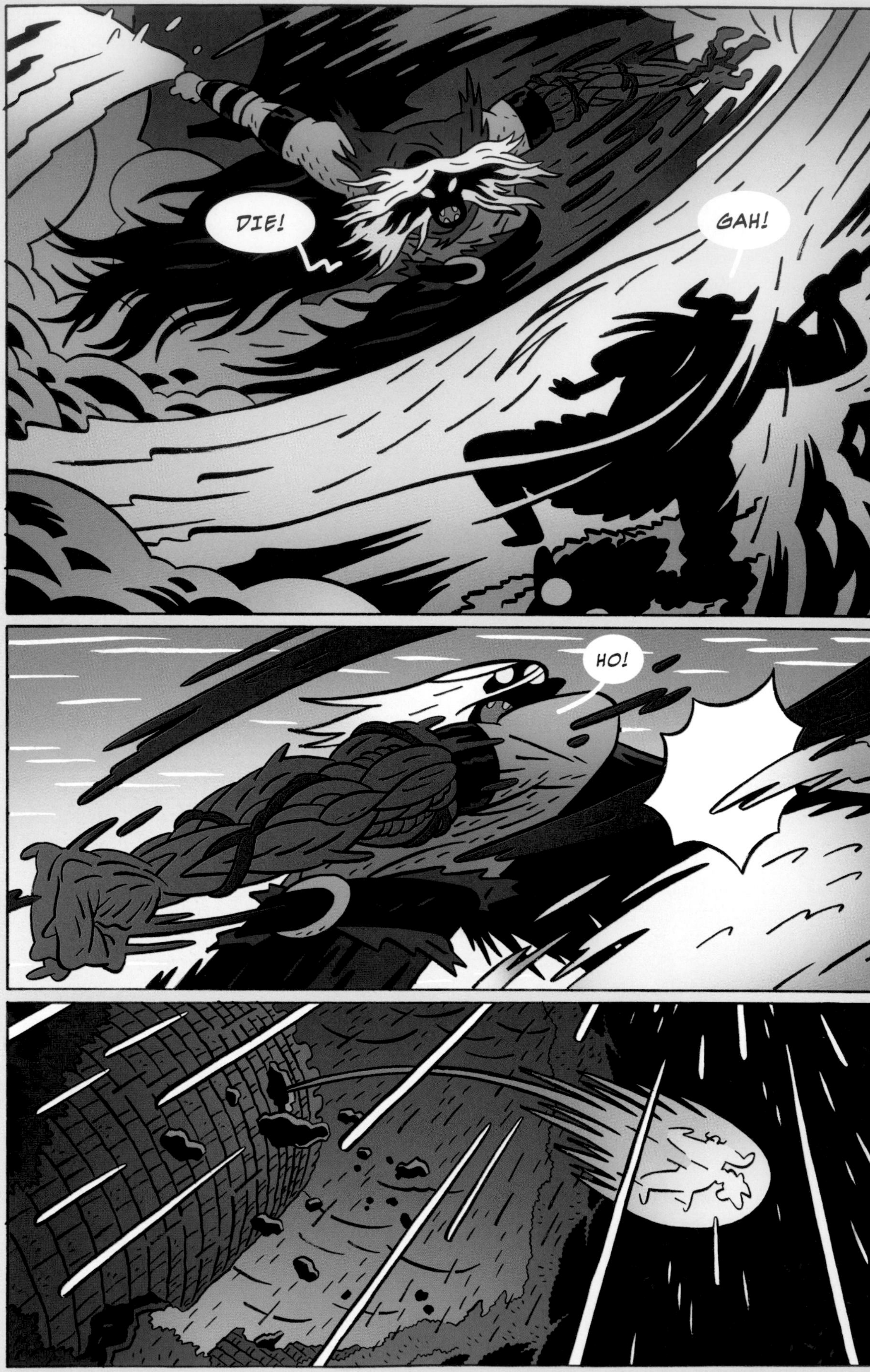
DIE!
GAH!
HO!

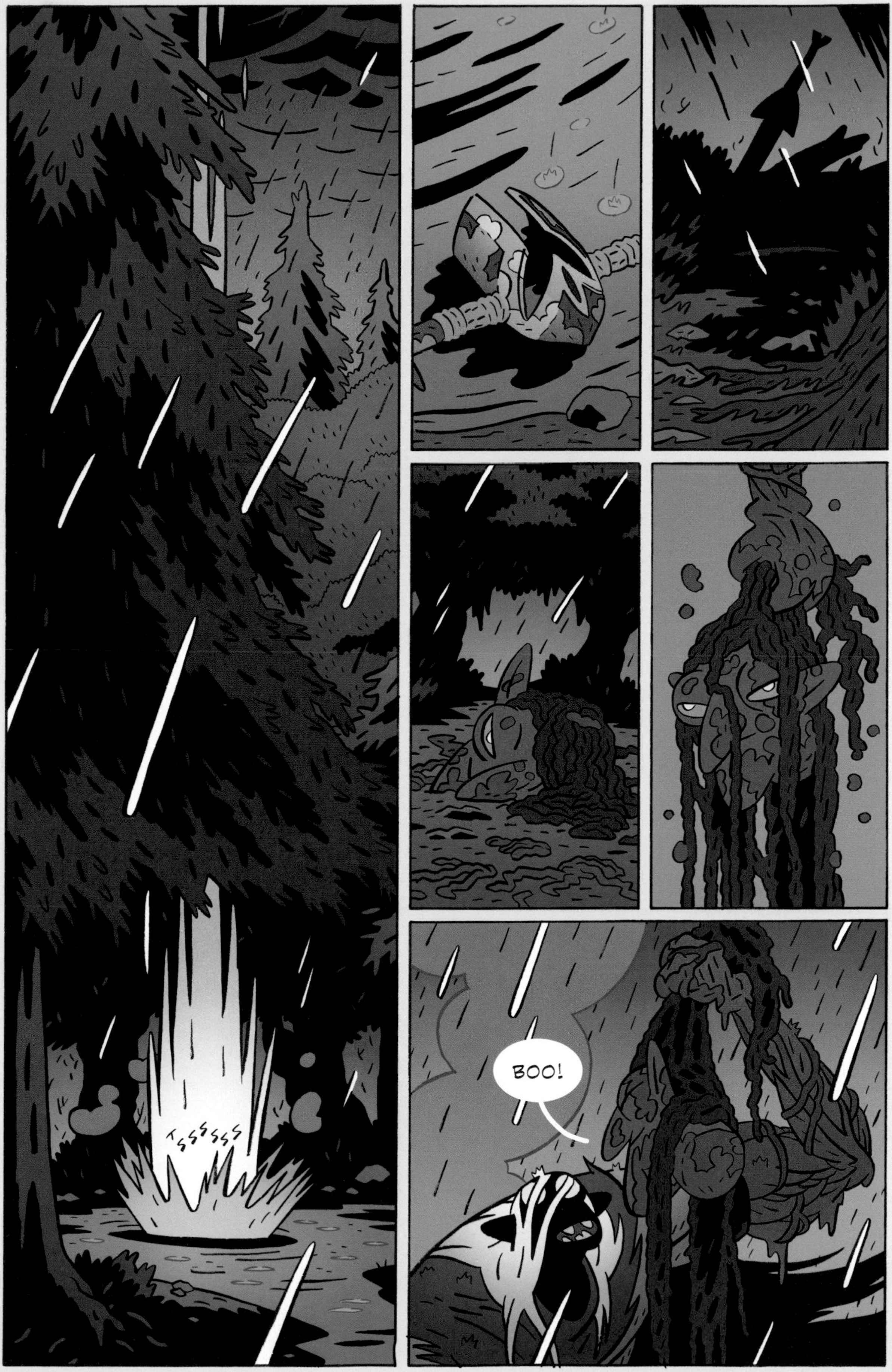
TSSSSSSS
BOO!

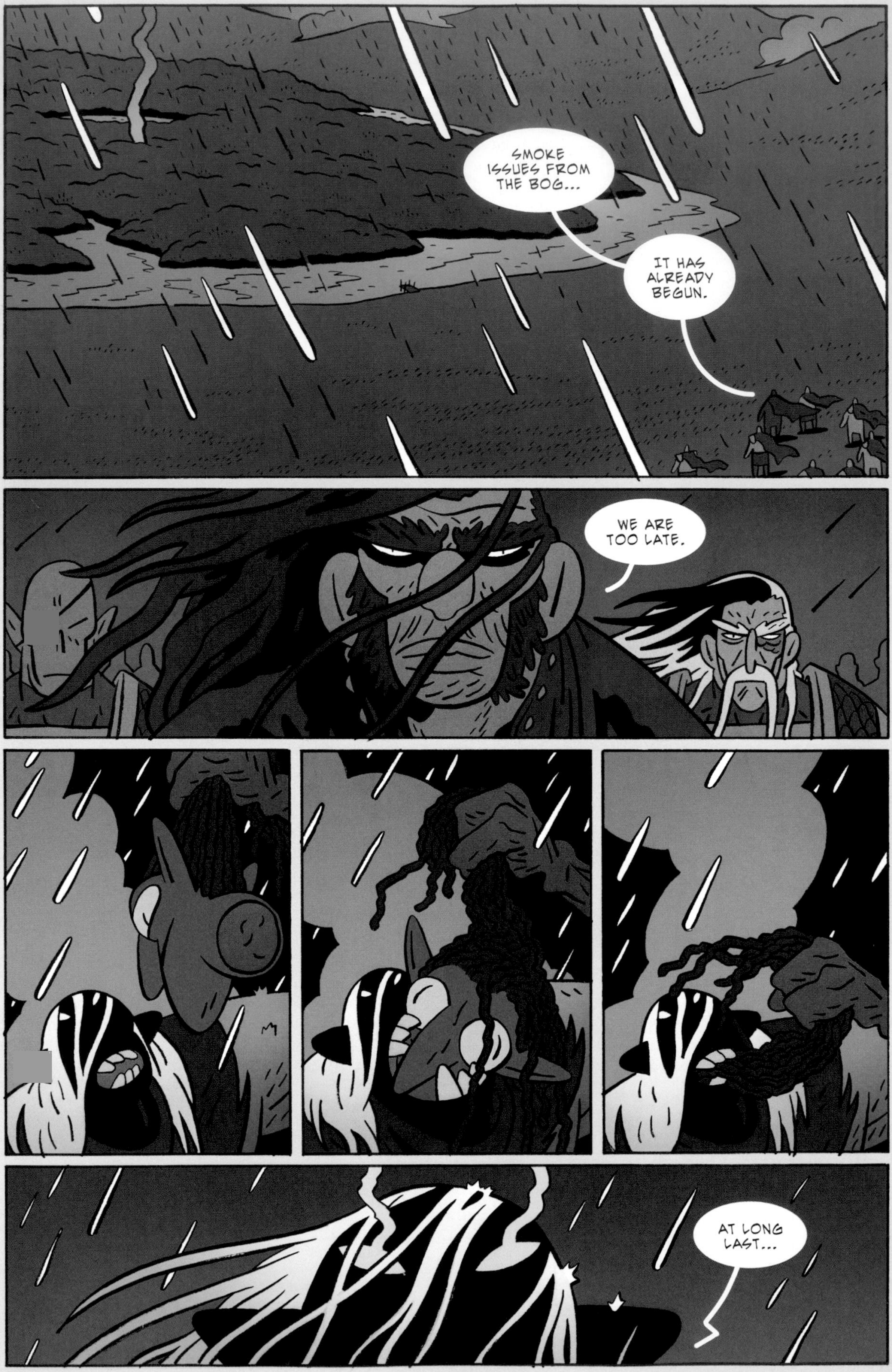
SMOKE ISSUES FROM THE BOG...
IT HAS ALREADY BEGUN.
WE ARE TOO LATE.
AT LONG LAST...

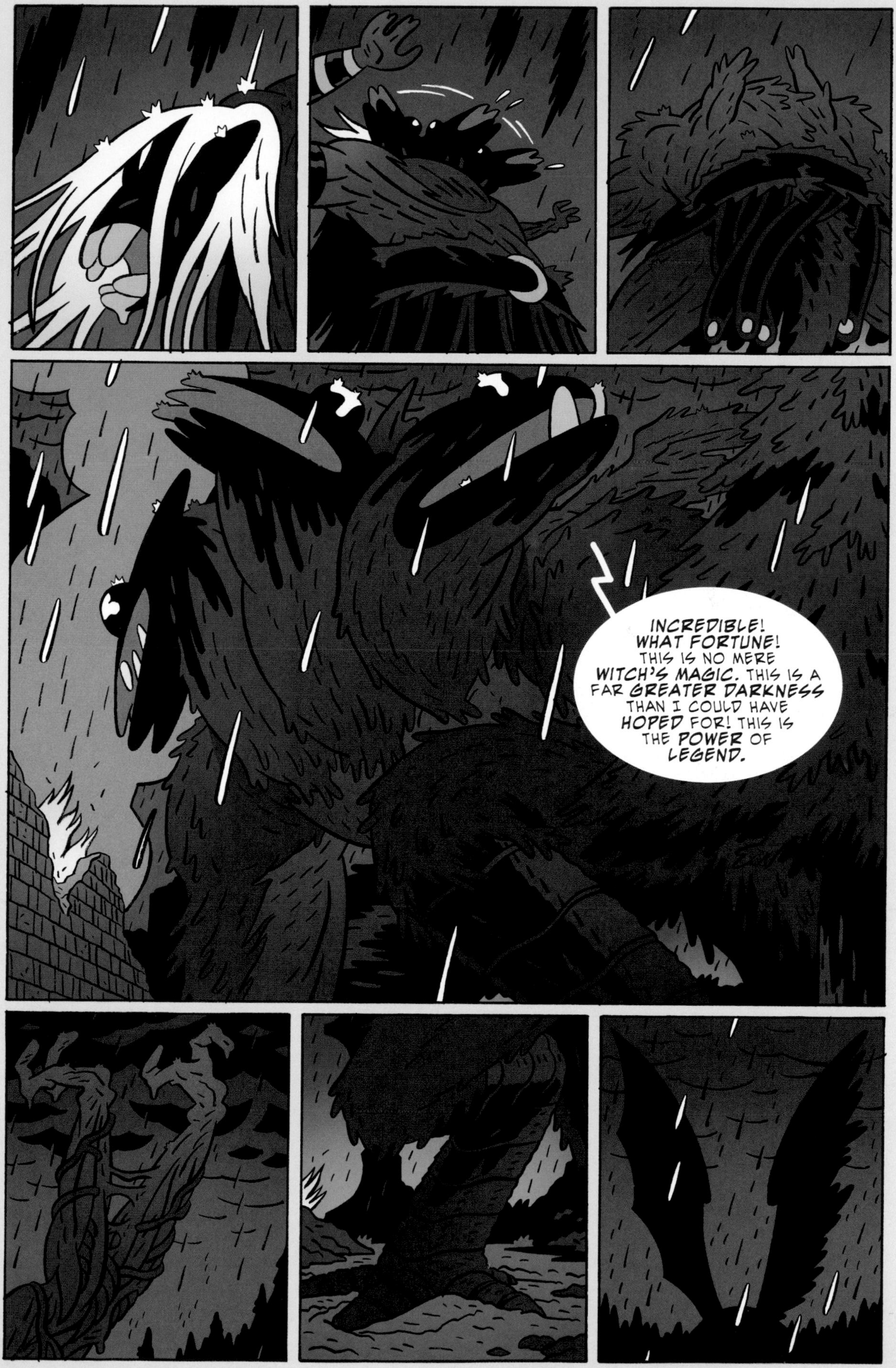
INCREDIBLE! WHAT FORTUNE! THIS IS NO MERE WITCH'S MAGIC. THIS IS A FAR GREATER DARKNESS THAN I COULD HAVE HOPED FOR! THIS IS THE POWER OF LEGEND.

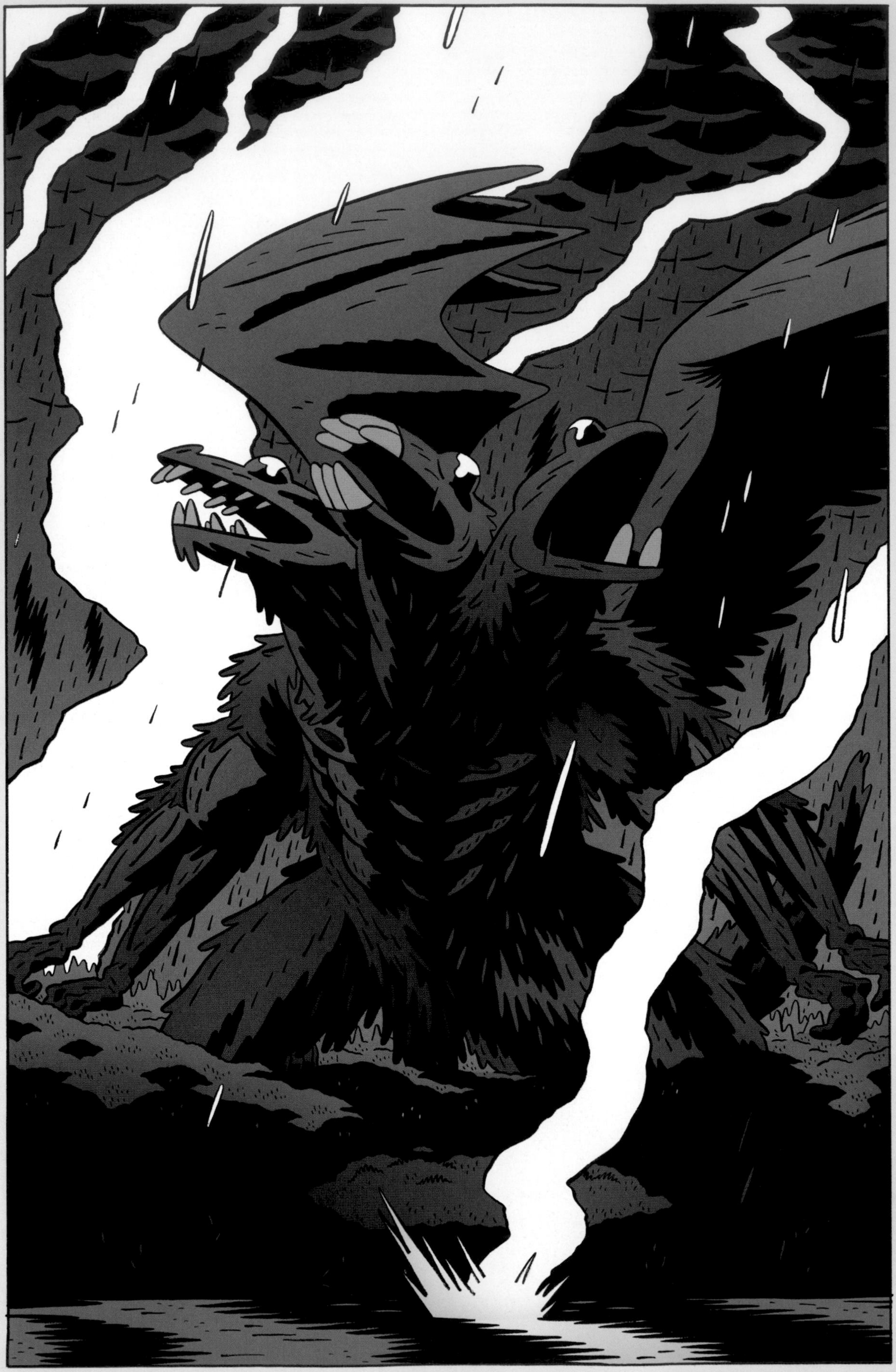

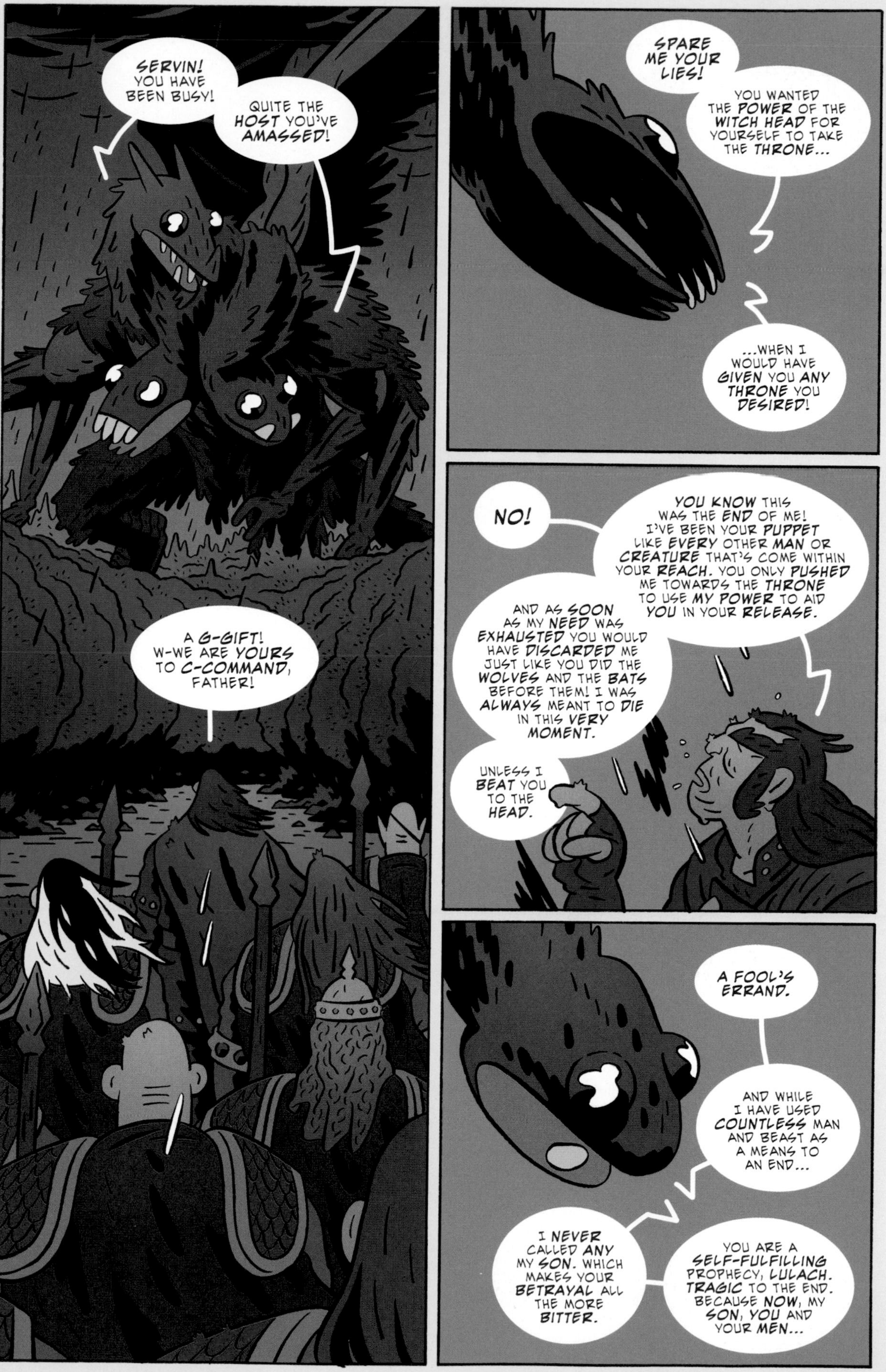
SERVIN! YOU HAVE BEEN BUSY!
QUITE THE HOST YOU'VE AMASSED!
A G-GIFT! W-WE ARE YOURS TO C-COMMAND, FATHER!
SPARE ME YOUR LIES!
YOU WANTED THE POWER OF THE WITCH HEAD FOR YOURSELF TO TAKE THE THRONE...
...WHEN I WOULD HAVE GIVEN YOU ANY THRONE YOU DESIRED!
NO!
YOU KNOW THIS WAS THE END OF ME! I'VE BEEN YOUR PUPPET LIKE EVERY OTHER MAN OR CREATURE THAT'S COME WITHIN YOUR REACH. YOU ONLY PUSHED ME TOWARDS THE THRONE TO USE MY POWER TO AID YOU IN YOUR RELEASE.
AND AS SOON AS MY NEED WAS EXHAUSTED YOU WOULD HAVE DISCARDED ME JUST LIKE YOU DID THE WOLVES AND THE BATS BEFORE THEM! I WAS ALWAYS MEANT TO DIE IN THIS VERY MOMENT.
UNLESS I BEAT YOU TO THE HEAD.
A FOOL'S ERRAND.
AND WHILE I HAVE USED COUNTLESS MAN AND BEAST AS A MEANS TO AN END...
I NEVER CALLED ANY MY SON. WHICH MAKES YOUR BETRAYAL ALL THE MORE BITTER.
YOU ARE A SELF-FULFILLING PROPHECY, LULACH. TRAGIC TO THE END. BECAUSE NOW, MY SON, YOU AND YOUR MEN...

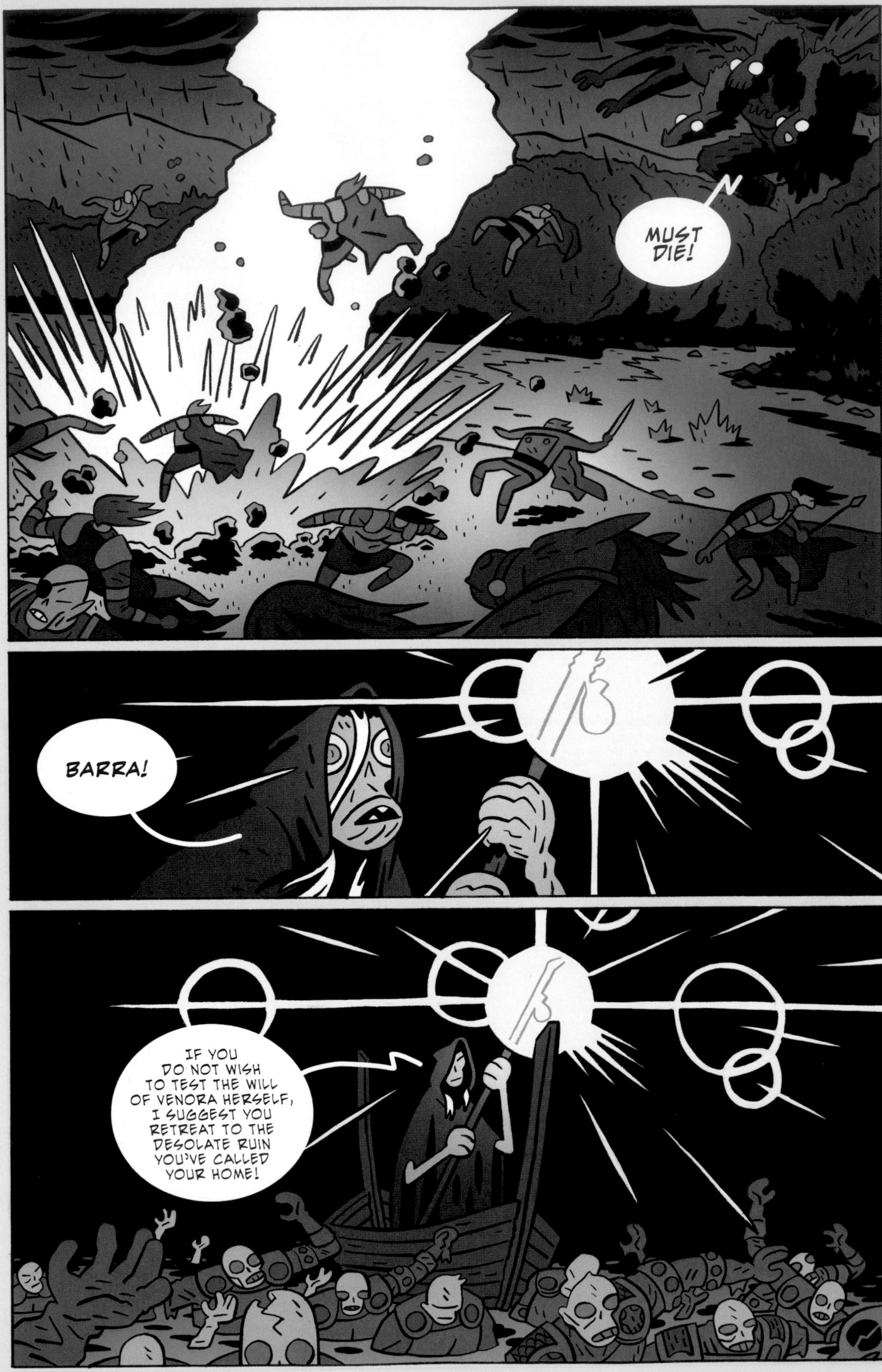
MUST DIE!
BARRA!
IF YOU DO NOT WISH TO TEST THE WILL OF VENORA HERSELF, I SUGGEST YOU RETREAT TO THE DESOLATE RUIN YOU'VE CALLED YOUR HOME!

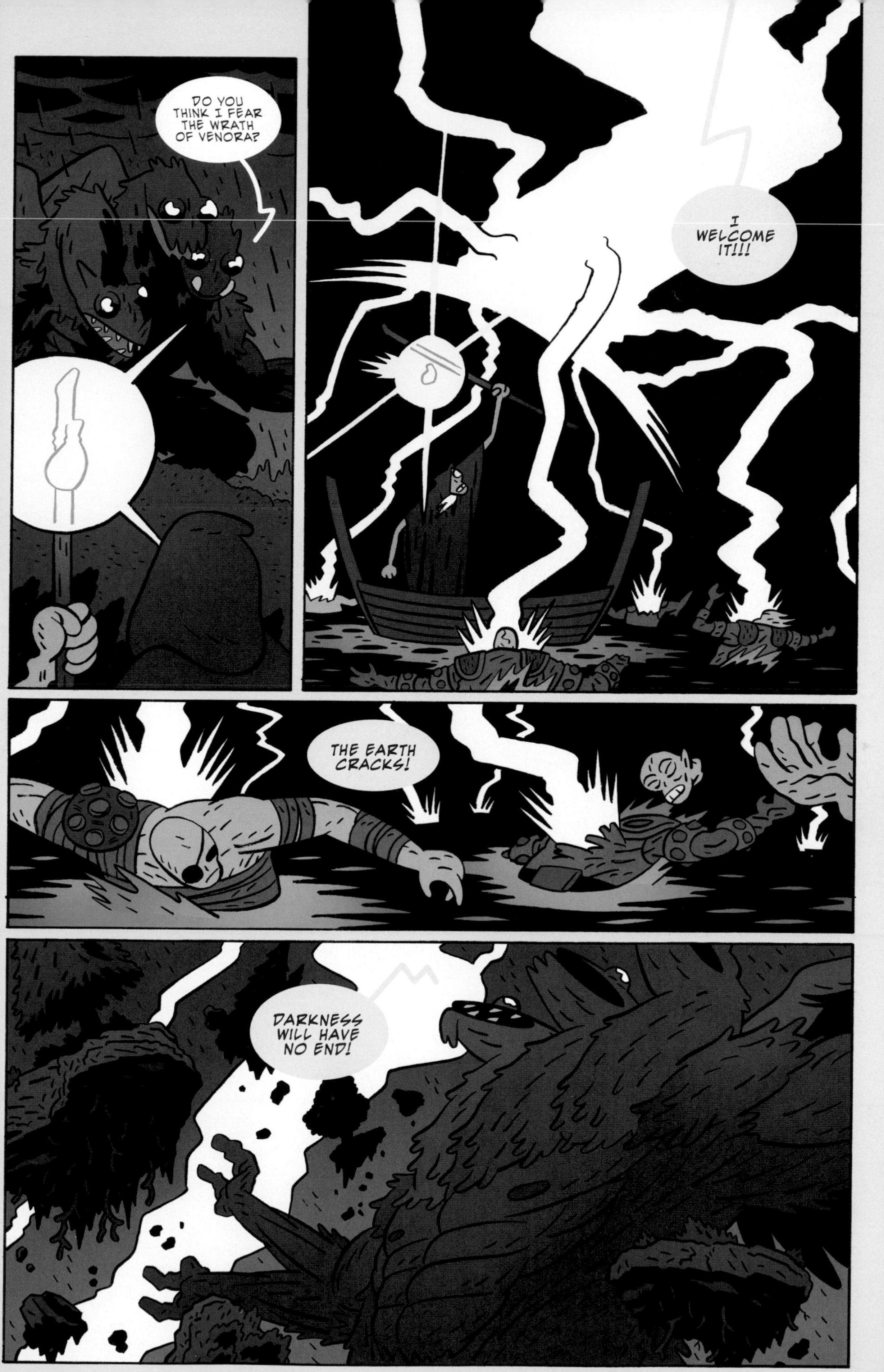
DO YOU THINK I FEAR THE WRATH OF VENORA?
I WELCOME IT!!!
THE EARTH CRACKS!
DARKNESS WILL HAVE NO END!

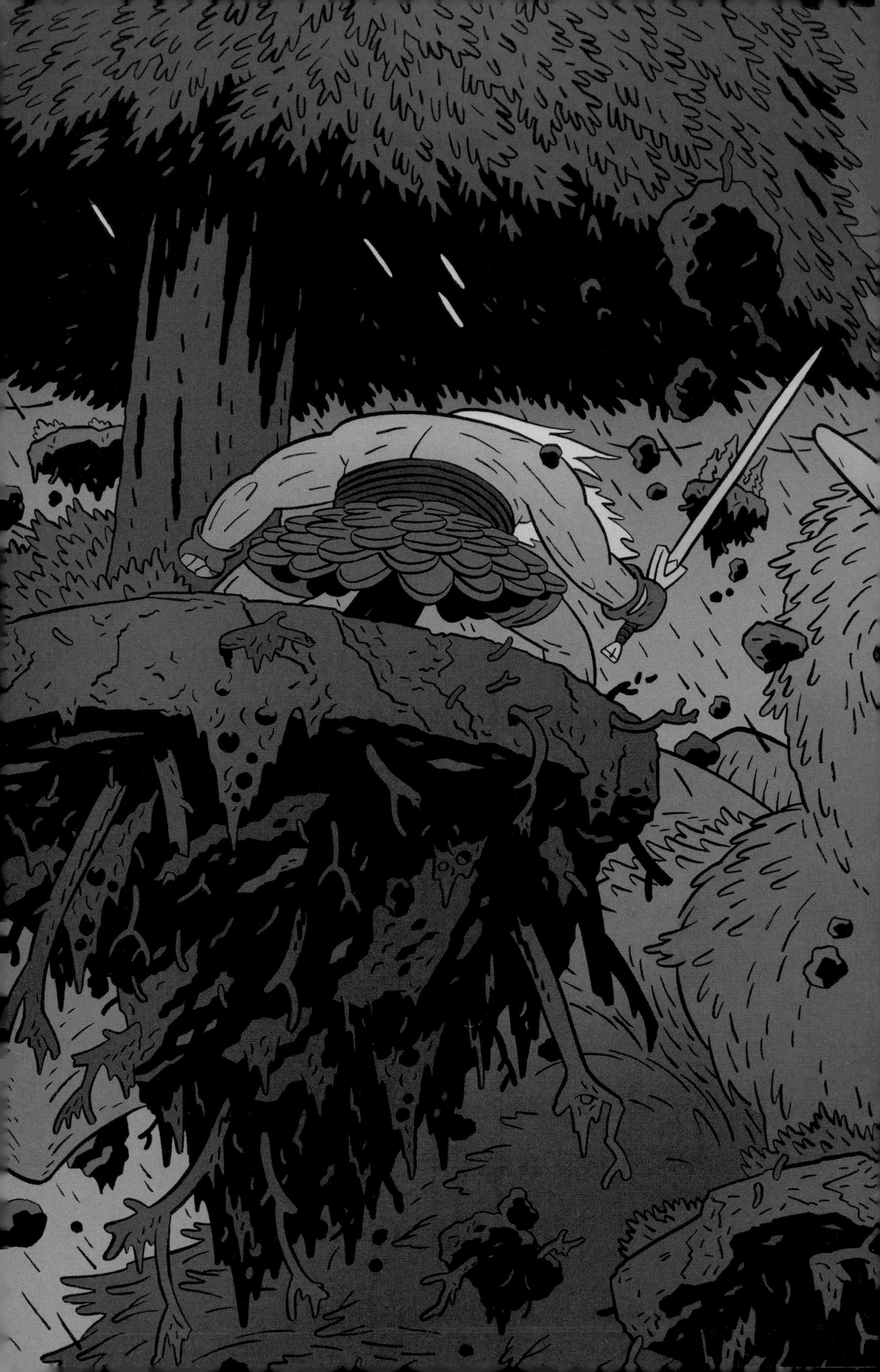

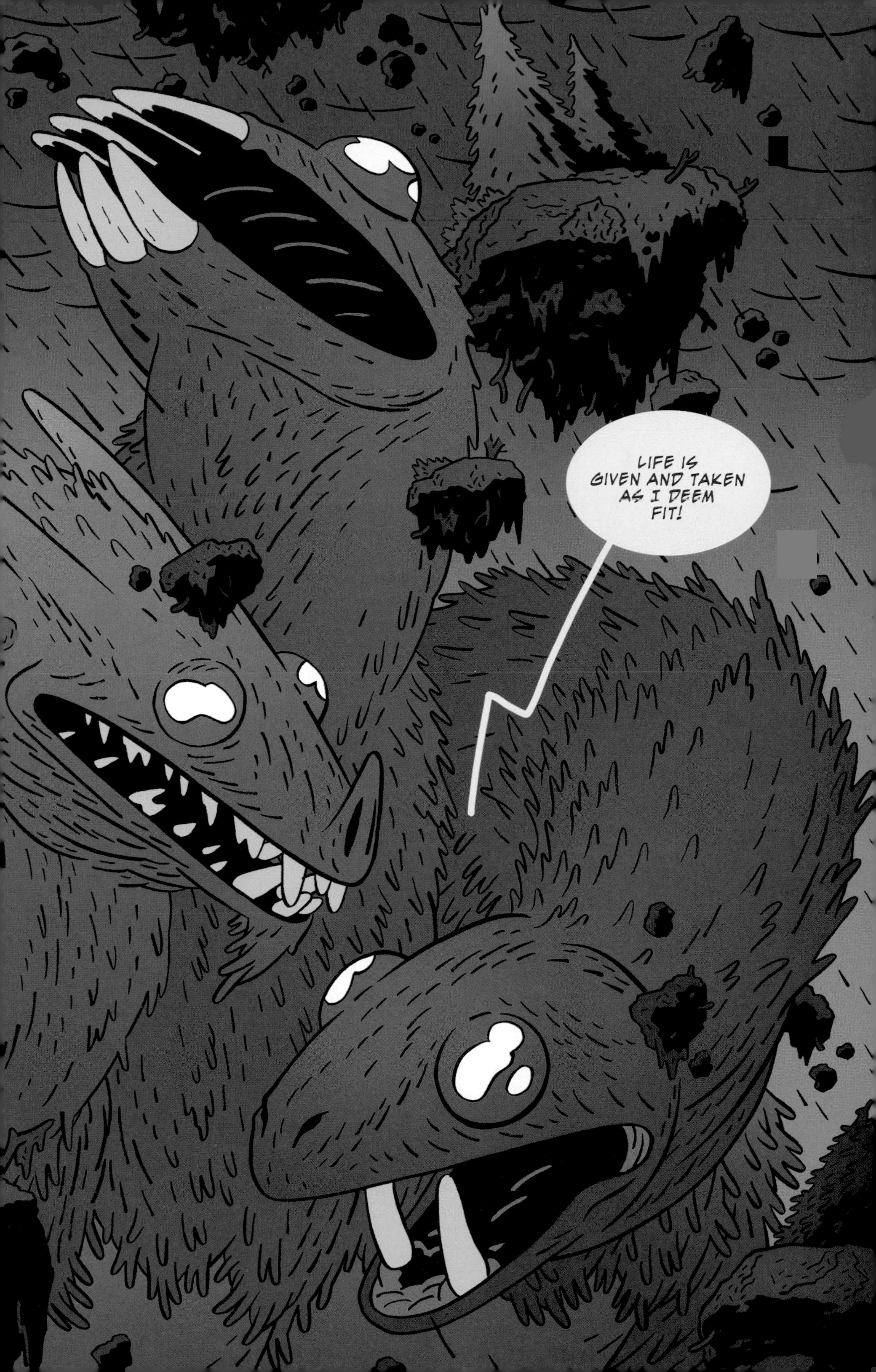
LIFE IS GIVEN AND TAKEN AS I DEEM FIT!

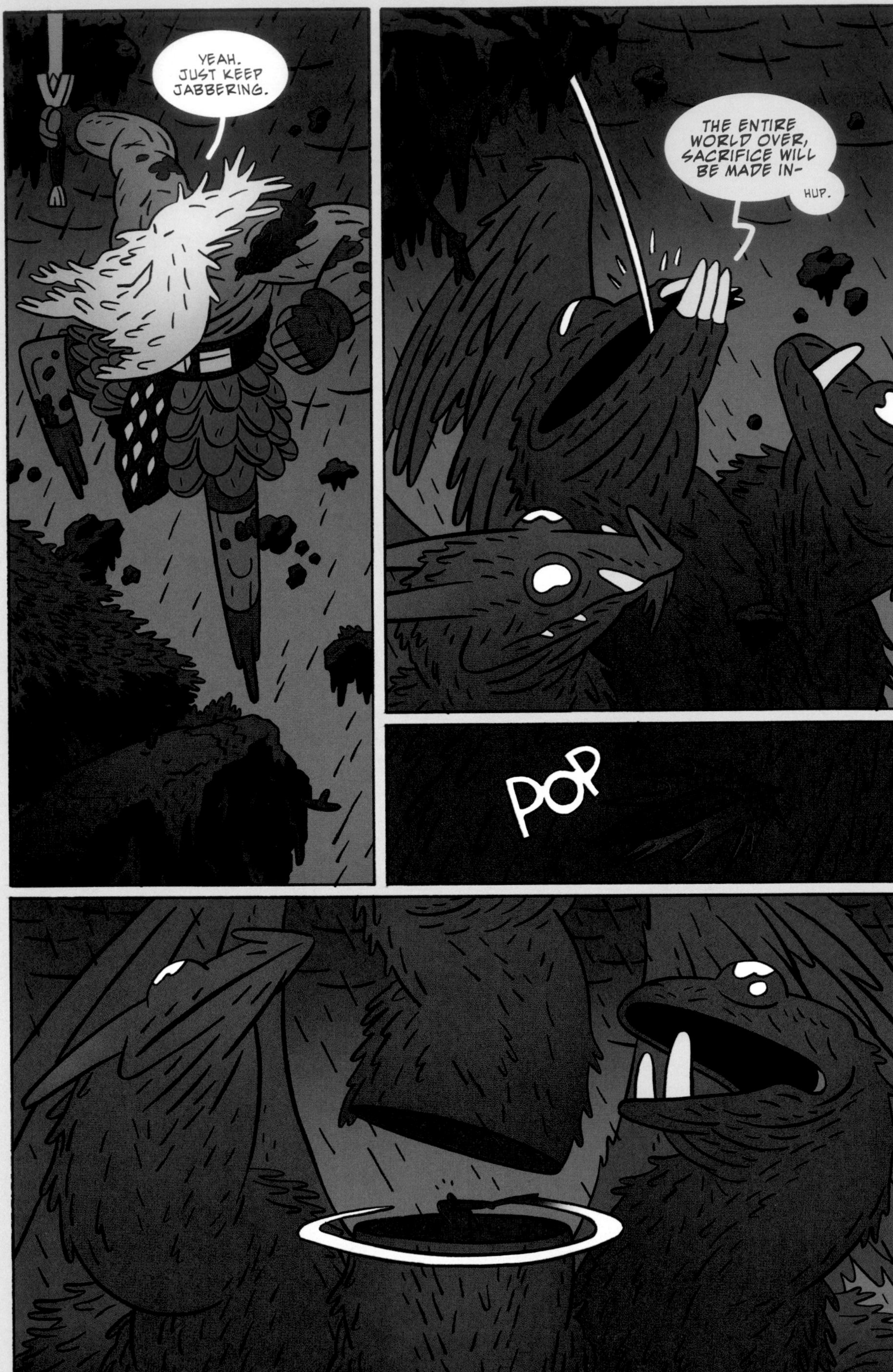
YEAH. JUST KEEP JABBERING.
THE ENTIRE WORLD OVER, SACRIFICE WILL BE MADE IN-
HUP.
POP

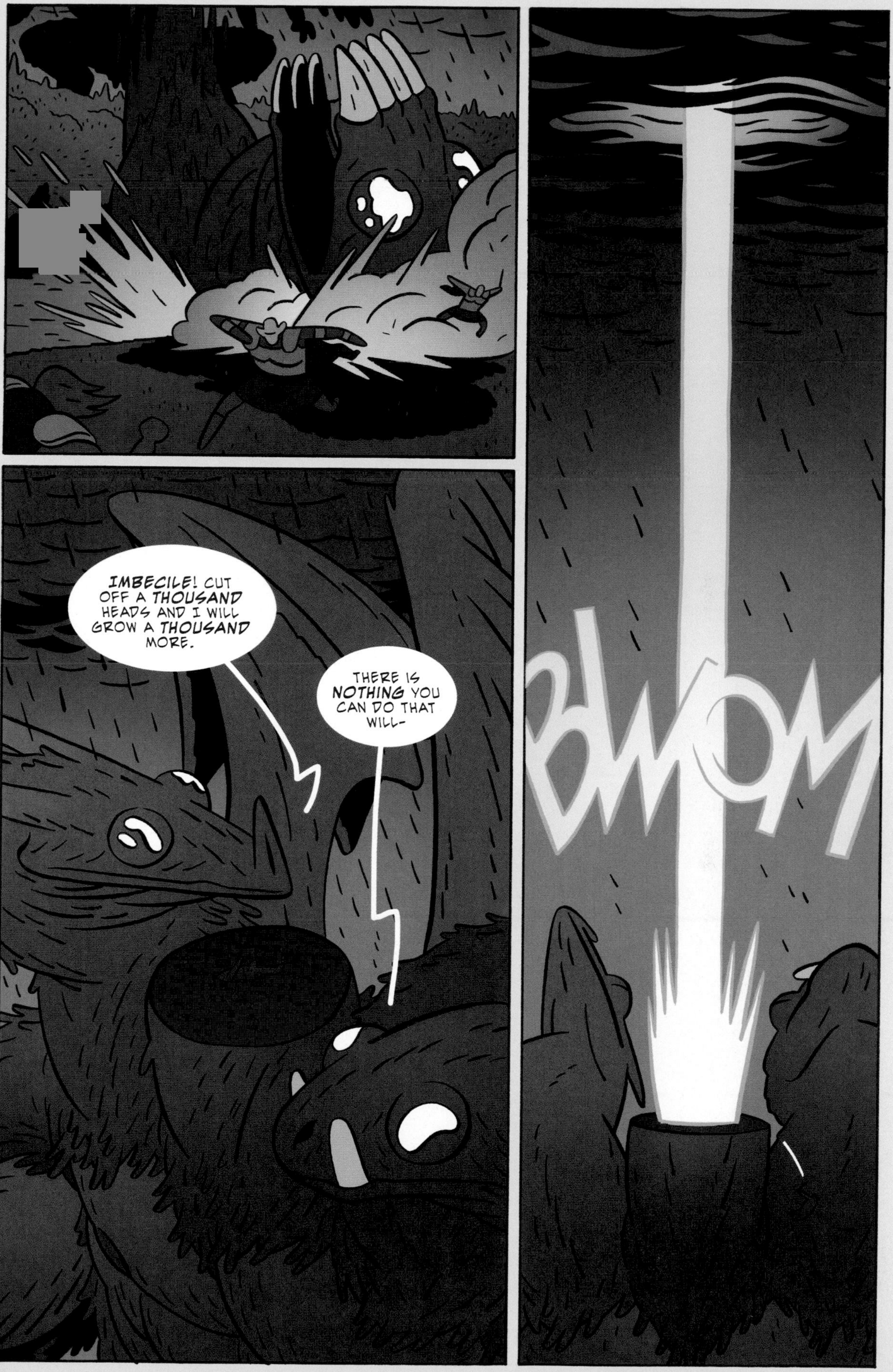
IMBECILE! CUT OFF A THOUSAND HEADS AND I WILL GROW A THOUSAND MORE.
THERE IS NOTHING YOU CAN DO THAT WILL-
BWOM

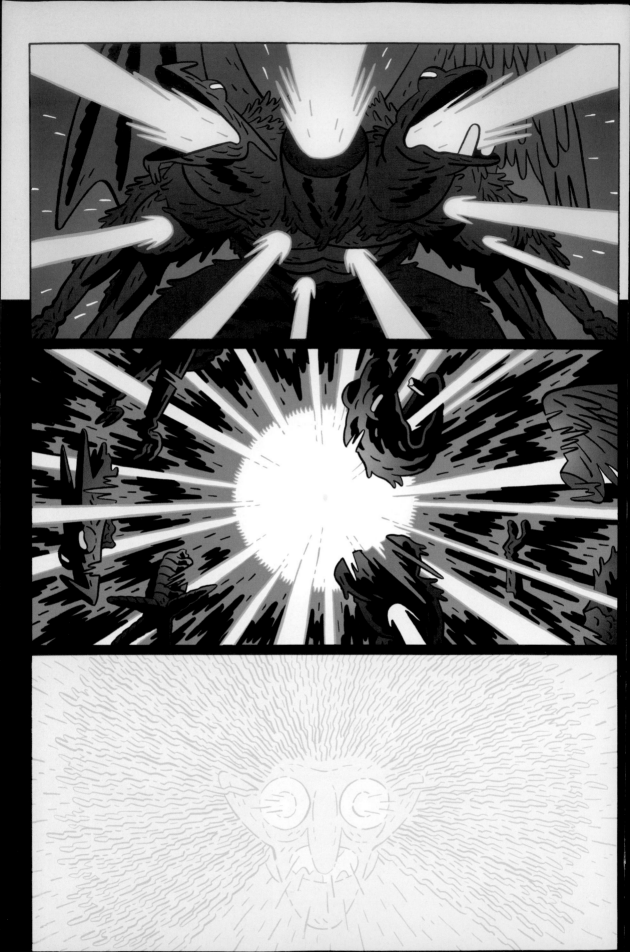

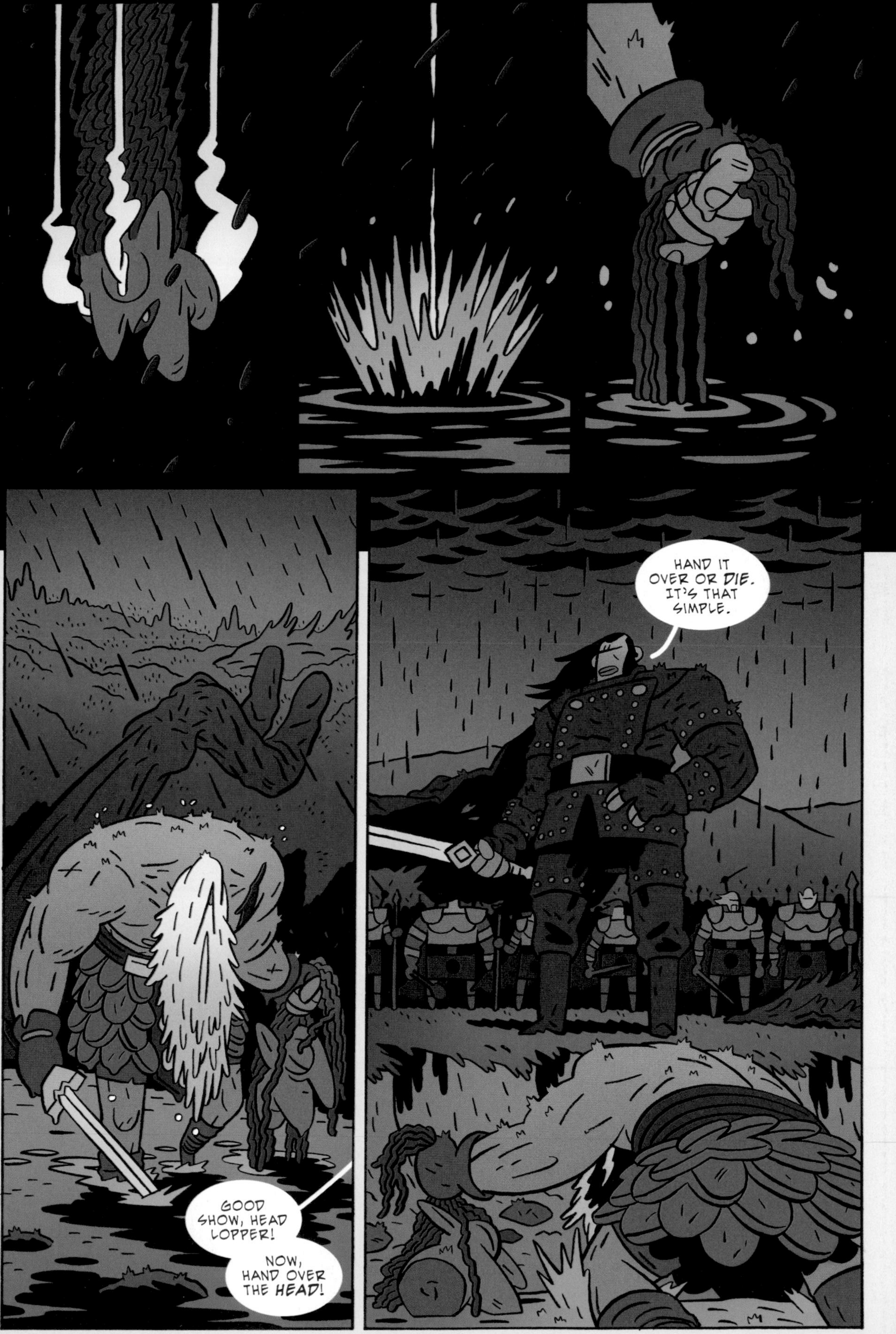
GOOD SHOW, HEAD LOPPER!
NOW, HAND OVER THE HEAD!
HAND IT OVER OR DIE. IT'S THAT SIMPLE.

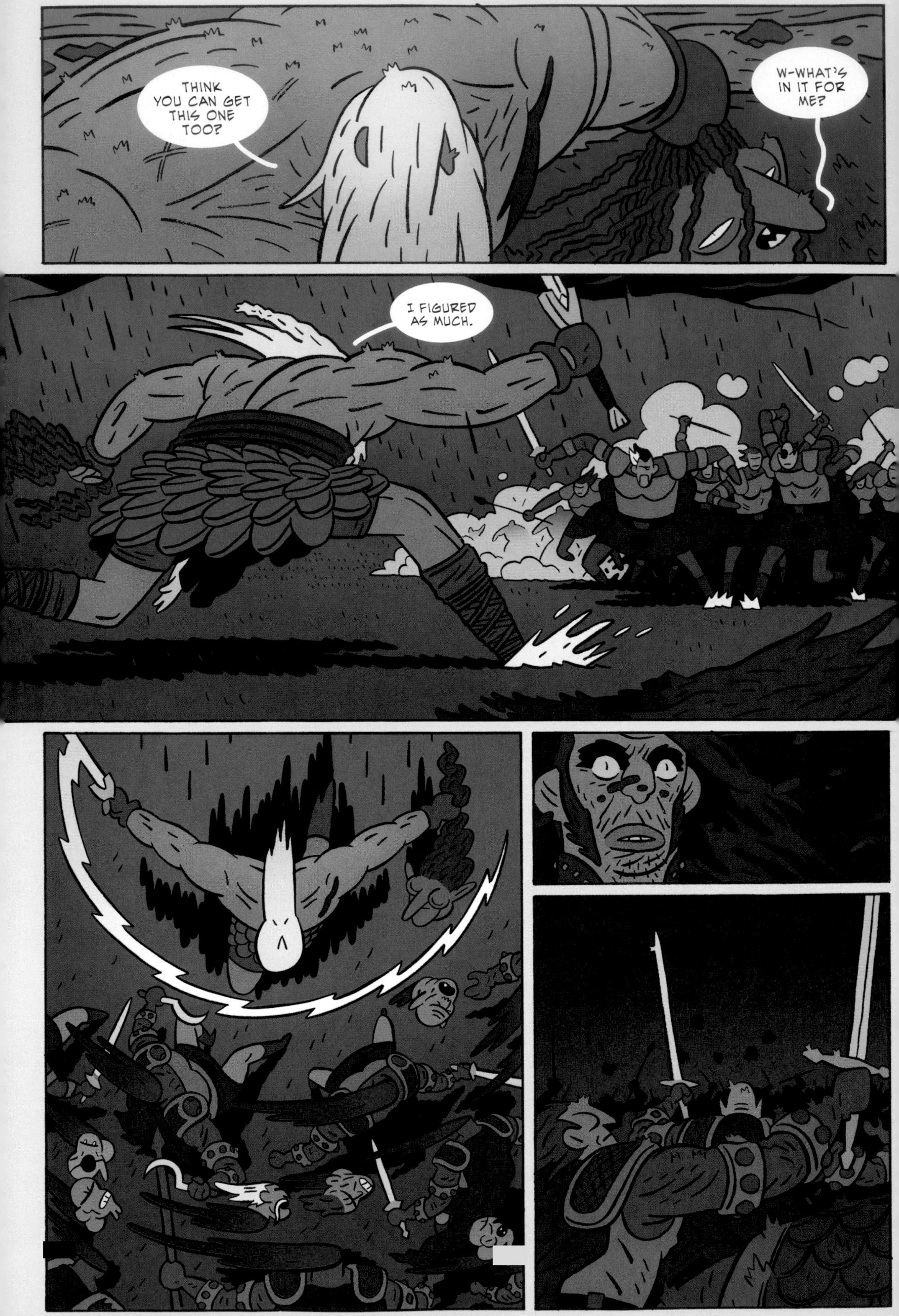
THINK YOU CAN GET THIS ONE TOO?
W-WHAT'S IN IT FOR ME?
I FIGURED AS MUCH.

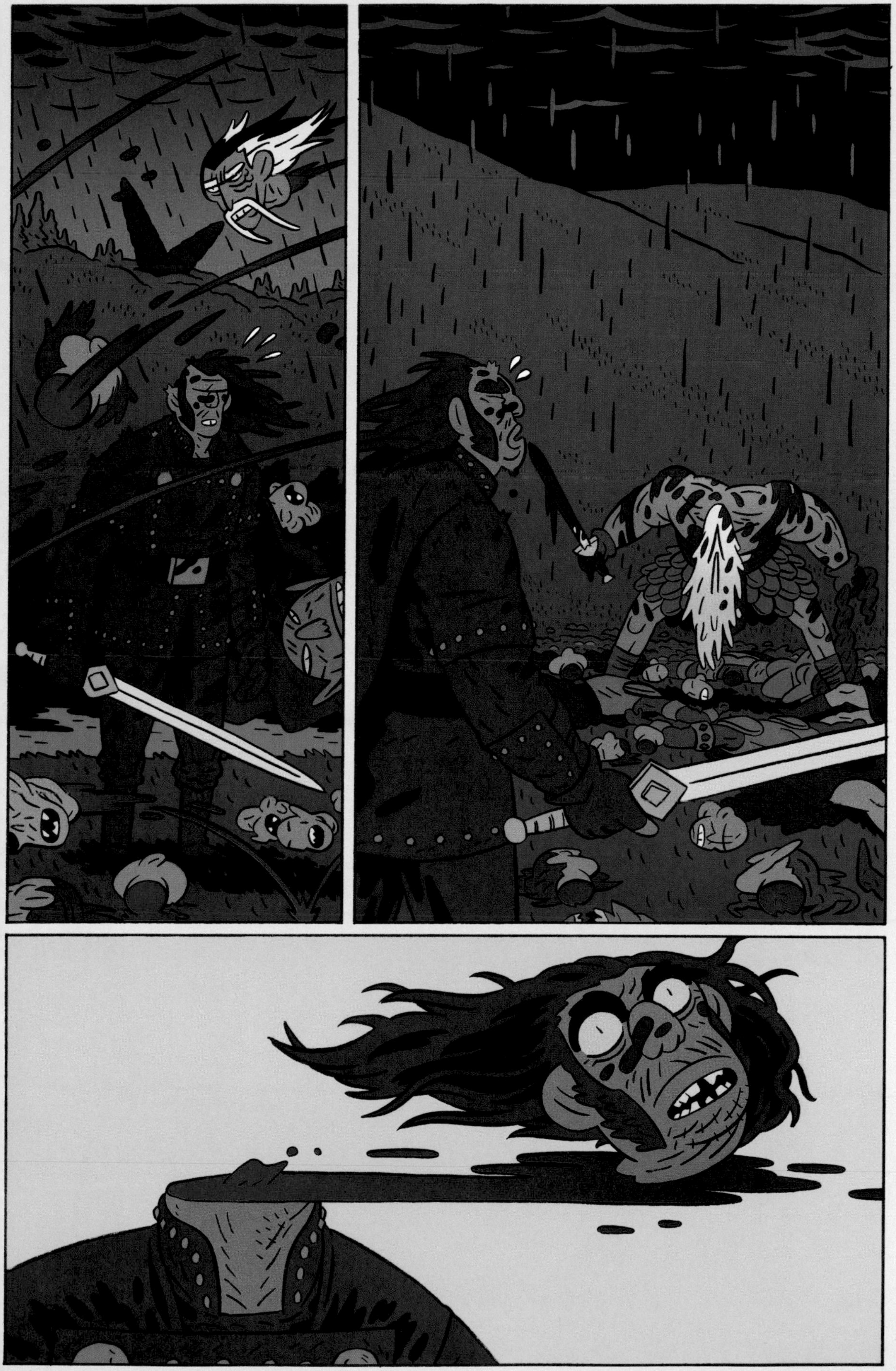

WHAT IS THE MEANING OF THIS?!

EXPLAIN YOURSELF AT ONCE!

BEASTS HAVE PLAGUED YOUR ISLAND REALM FOR COUNTLESS YEARS, YOUR GRACE. YOU ASKED FOR THE HEAD OF THE ONE RESPONSIBLE.

I HAVE BROUGHT IT TO YOU.

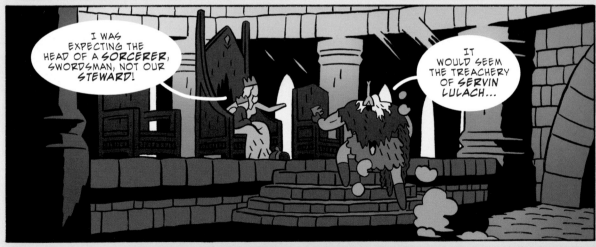

I WAS EXPECTING THE HEAD OF A SORCERER, SWORDSMAN, NOT OUR STEWARD!

IT WOULD SEEM THE TREACHERY OF SERVIN LULACH...

GOES BACK MANY YEARS, YOUR GRACE.

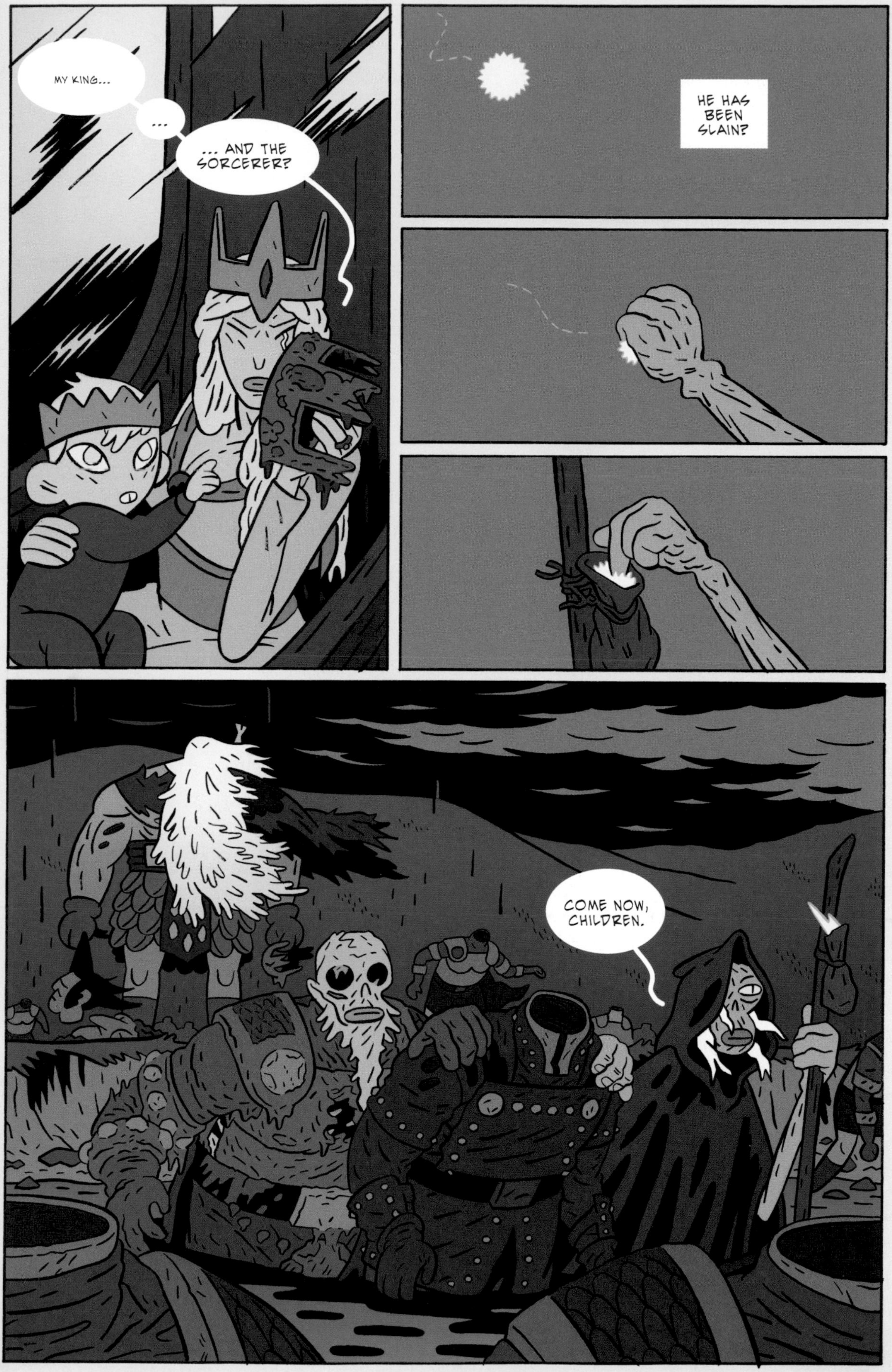
MY KING...
...
... AND THE SORCERER?
HE HAS BEEN SLAIN?
COME NOW, CHILDREN.

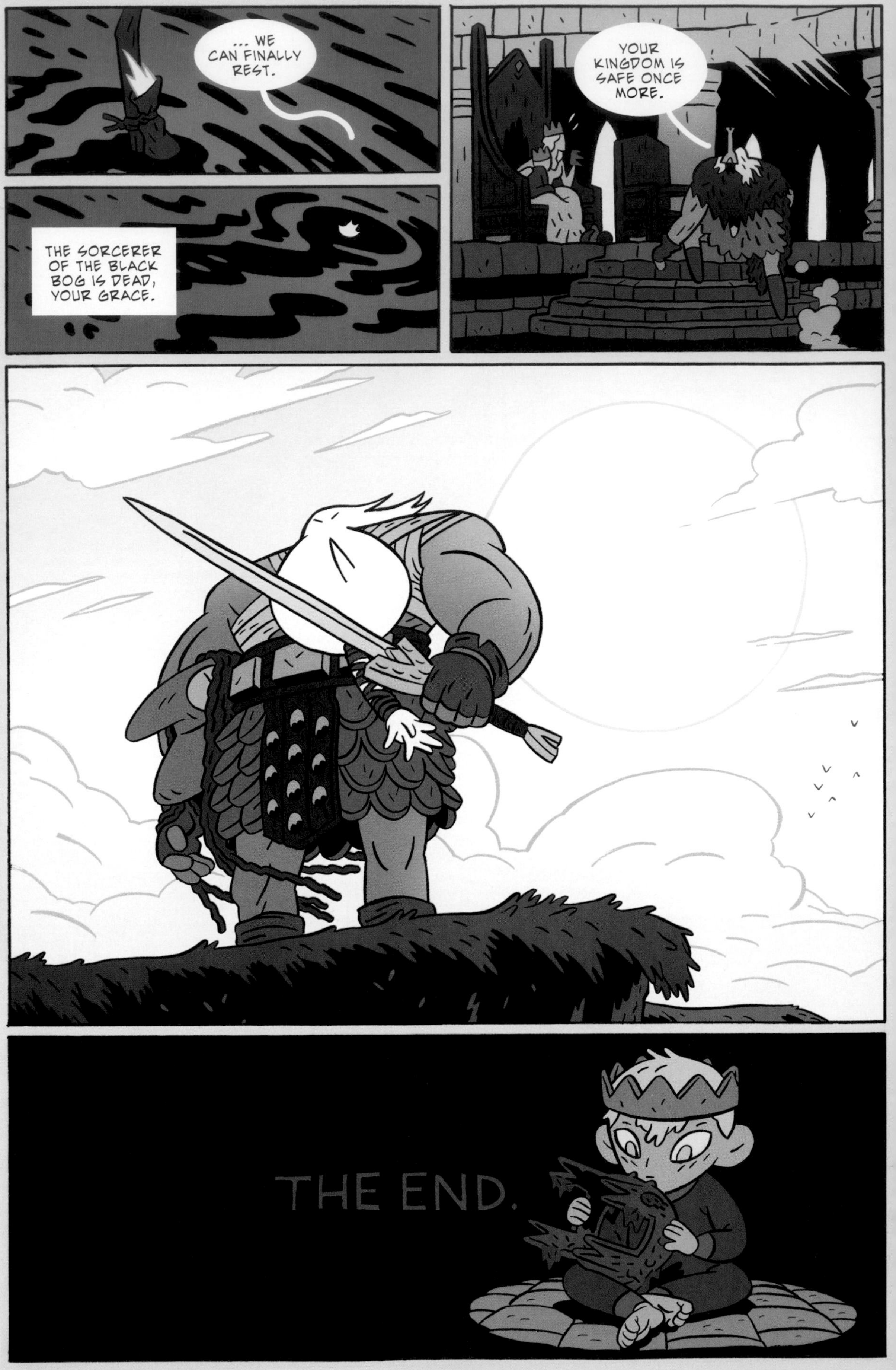
... WE CAN FINALLY REST.
YOUR KINGDOM IS SAFE ONCE MORE.
THE SORCERER OF THE BLACK BOG IS DEAD, YOUR GRACE.
THE END.

EPILOGUE

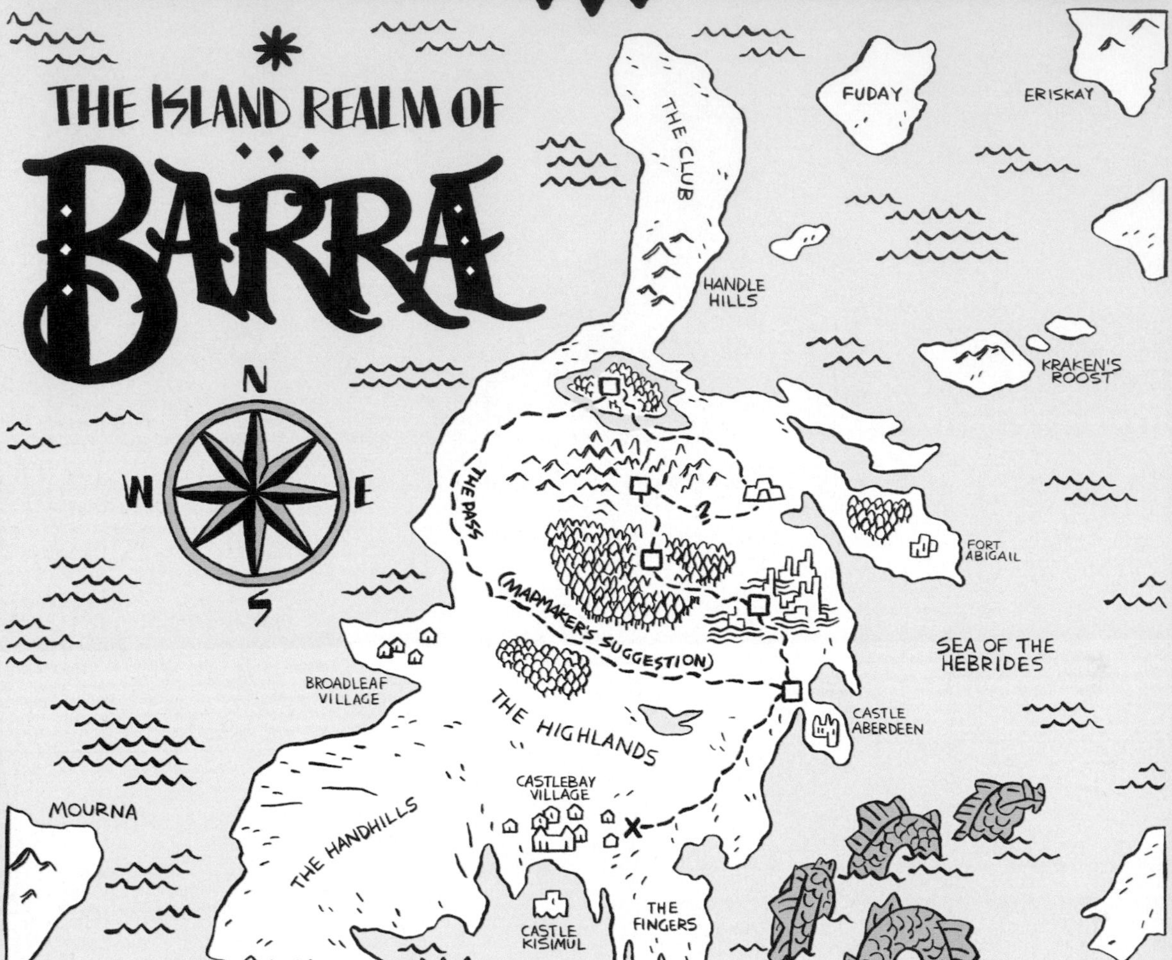

THE ISLAND REALM OF
BARRA
N
W
E
S
THE CLUB
HANDLE HILLS
FUDAY
ERISKAY
KRAKEN'S ROOST
THE PASS
(MAPMAKER'S SUGGESTION)
FORT ABIGAIL
SEA OF THE HEBRIDES
BROADLEAF VILLAGE
THE HIGHLANDS
CASTLE ABERDEEN
CASTLEBAY VILLAGE
MOURNA
THE HANDHILLS
THE FINGERS
CASTLE KISIMUL
EVESFALL
CASTLEBAY
THE THUMBS
SERPENT'S STRAIT
ERSAY
ERLORNIA
VATERSAY
X=NORGAL & AGATHA

RETURN TO CASTLEBAY

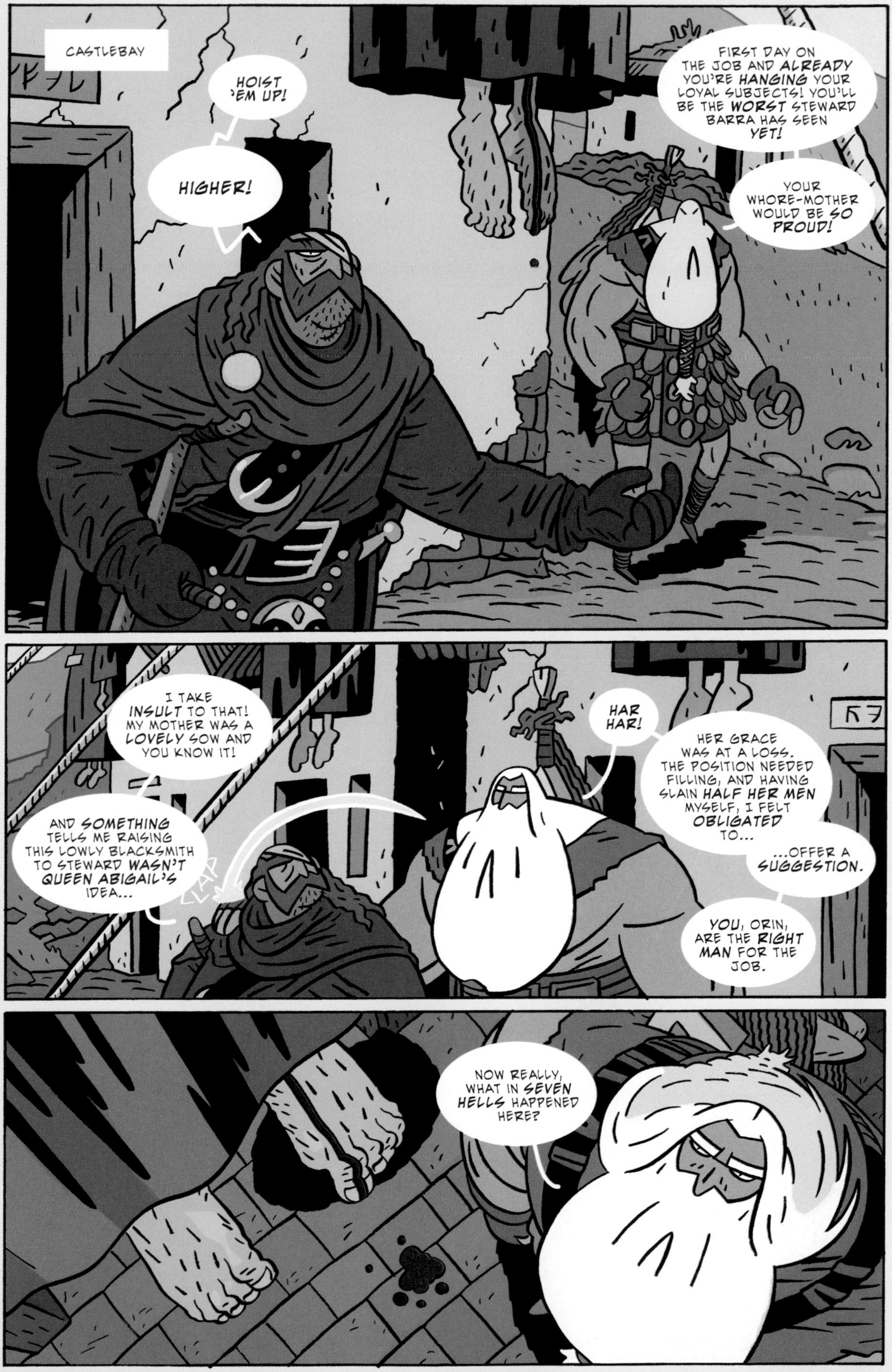
CASTLEBAY
HOIST 'EM UP!
HIGHER!
FIRST DAY ON THE JOB AND ALREADY YOU'RE HANGING YOUR LOYAL SUBJECTS! YOU'LL BE THE WORST STEWARD BARRA HAS SEEN YET!
YOUR WHORE-MOTHER WOULD BE SO PROUD!
I TAKE INSULT TO THAT! MY MOTHER WAS A LOVELY SOW AND YOU KNOW IT!
AND SOMETHING TELLS ME RAISING THIS LOWLY BLACKSMITH TO STEWARD WASN'T QUEEN ABIGAIL'S IDEA...
HAR HAR!
HER GRACE WAS AT A LOSS. THE POSITION NEEDED FILLING, AND HAVING SLAIN HALF HER MEN MYSELF, I FELT OBLIGATED TO...
...OFFER A SUGGESTION.
YOU, ORIN, ARE THE RIGHT MAN FOR THE JOB.
NOW REALLY, WHAT IN SEVEN HELLS HAPPENED HERE?

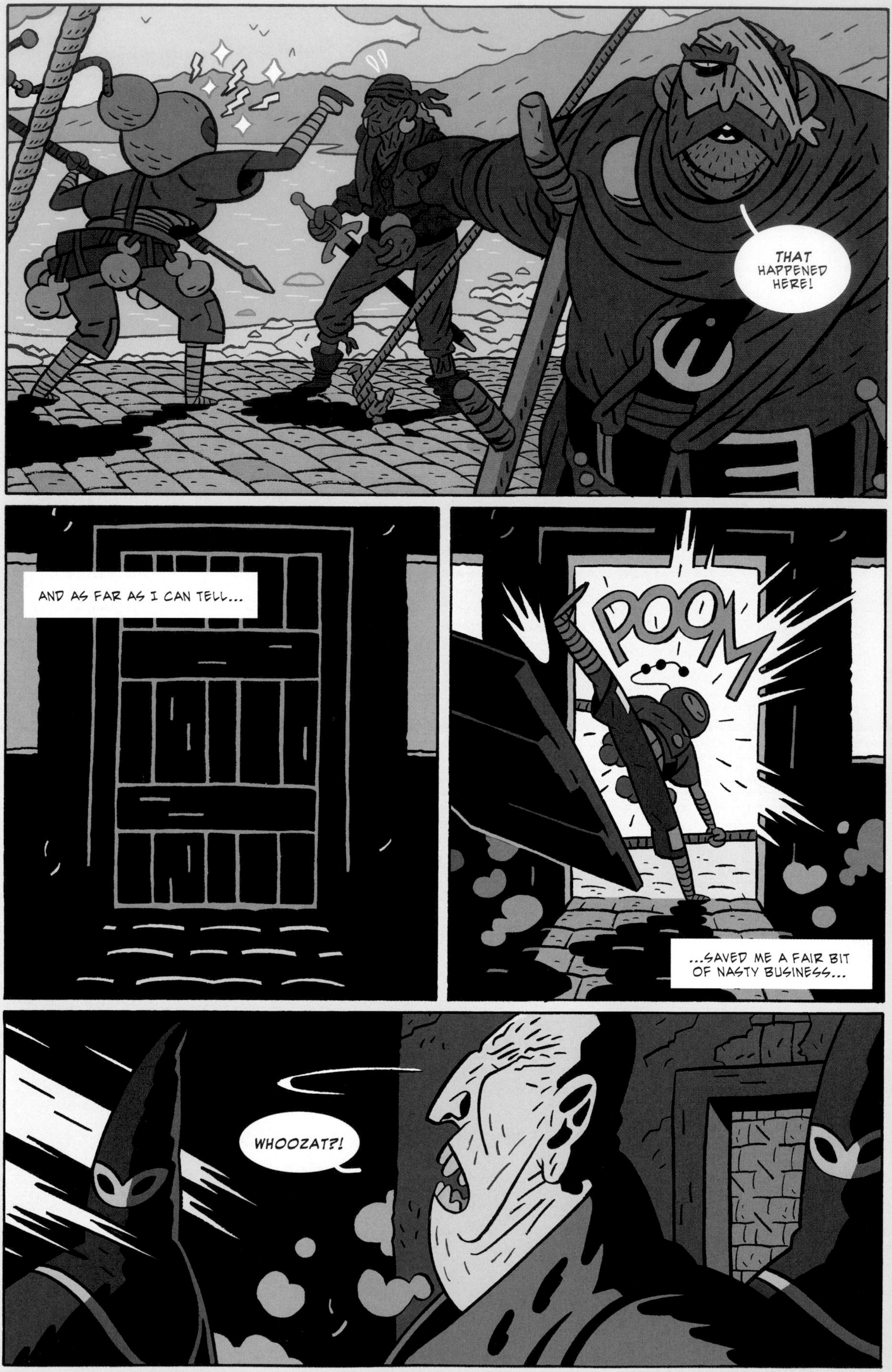
THAT HAPPENED HERE!
AND AS FAR AS I CAN TELL...
POOM
...SAVED ME A FAIR BIT OF NASTY BUSINESS...
WHOOZAT?!

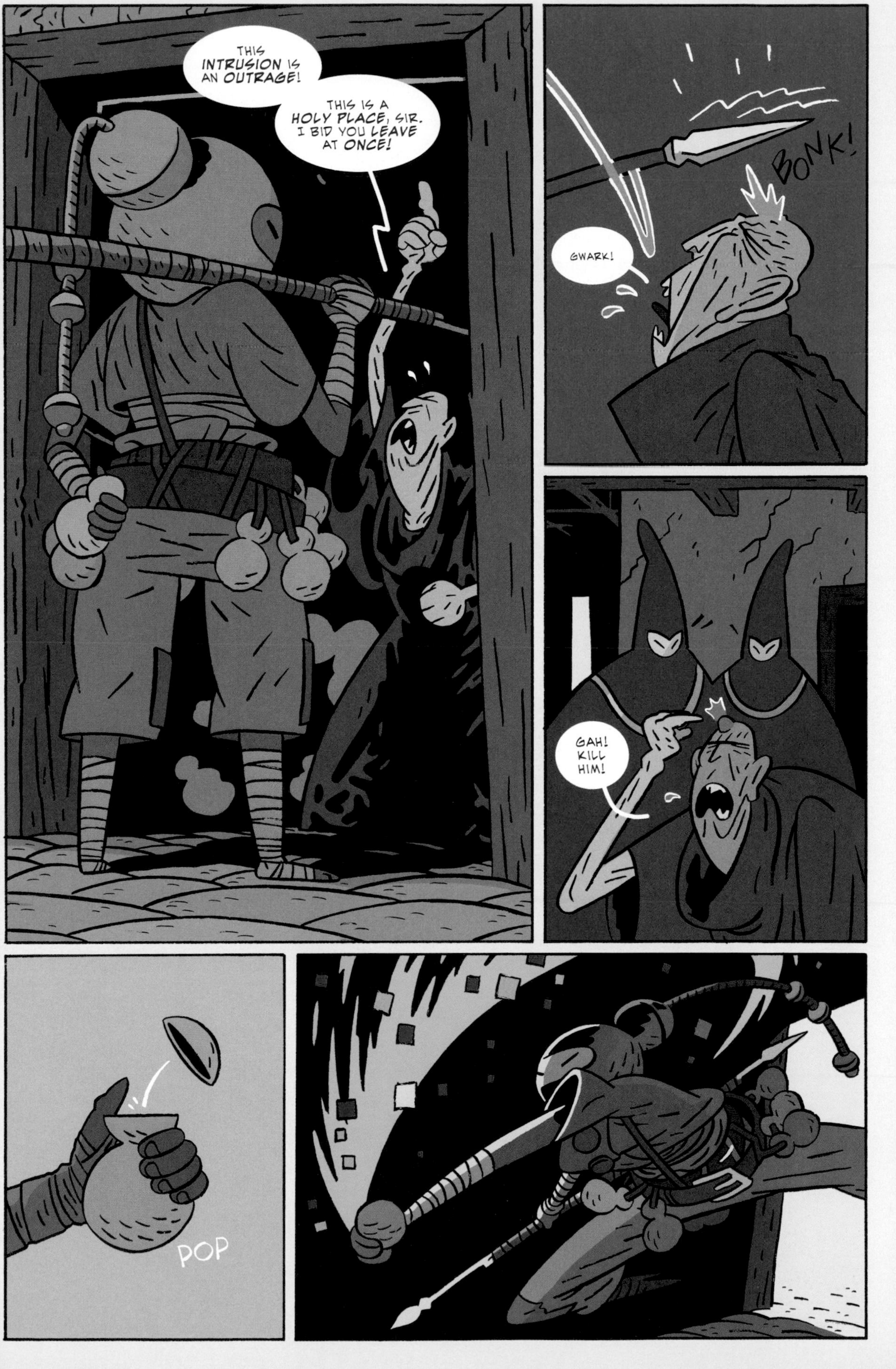
THIS INTRUSION IS AN OUTRAGE!
THIS IS A HOLY PLACE, SIR. I BID YOU LEAVE AT ONCE!
BONK!
GWARK!
GAH! KILL HIM!
POP

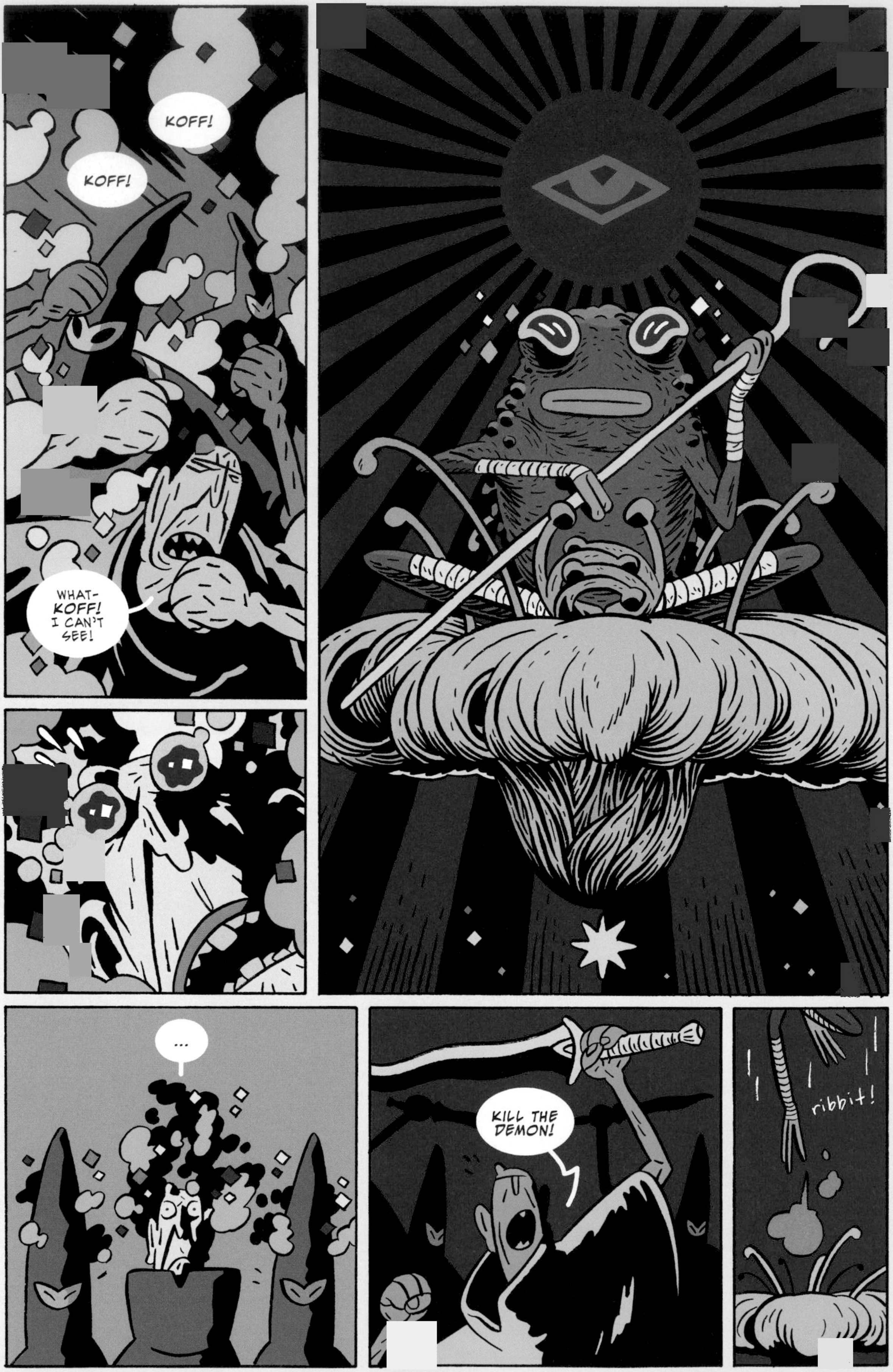
KOFF!
KOFF!
WHAT- KOFF! I CAN'T SEE!
...
KILL THE DEMON!
ribbit!

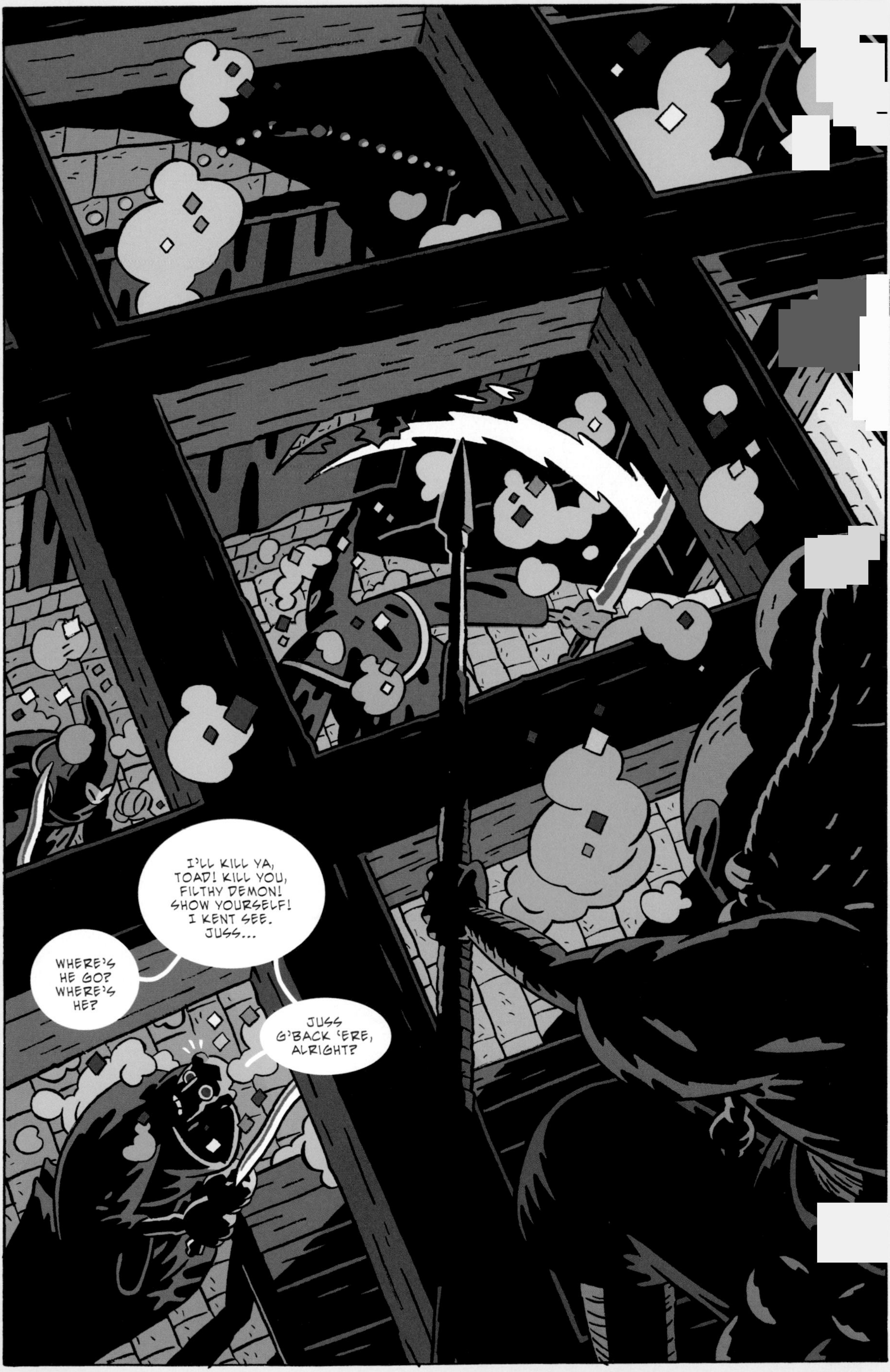
I'LL KILL YA, TOAD! KILL YOU, FILTHY DEMON! SHOW YOURSELF! I KENT SEE. JUSS...
WHERE'S HE GO? WHERE'S HE?
JUSS G'BACK 'ERE, ALRIGHT?

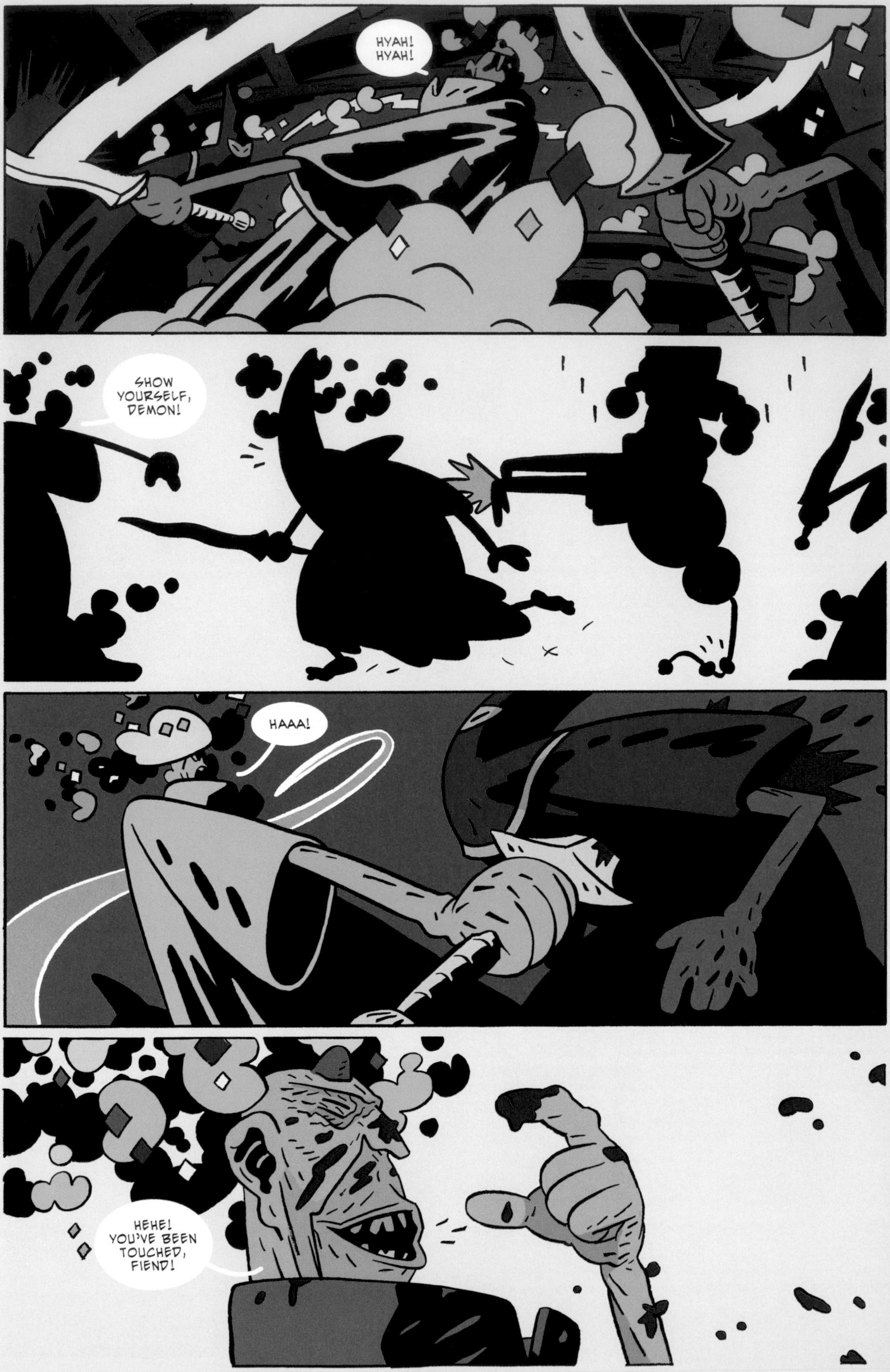
HYAH! HYAH!
SHOW YOURSELF, DEMON!
HAAA!
HEHE! YOU'VE BEEN TOUCHED, FIEND!

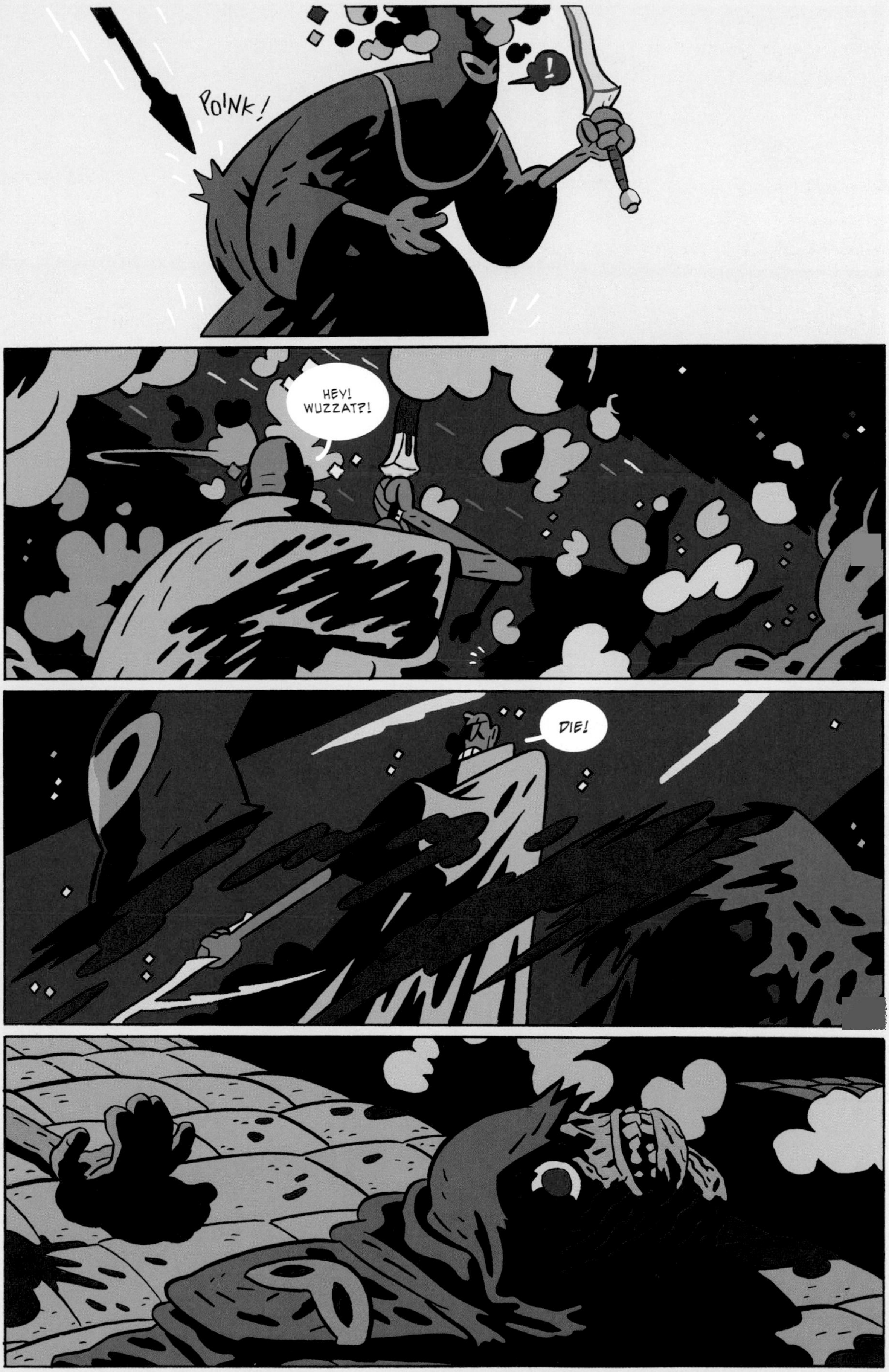
POINK!
HEY! WUZZAT?!
DIE!

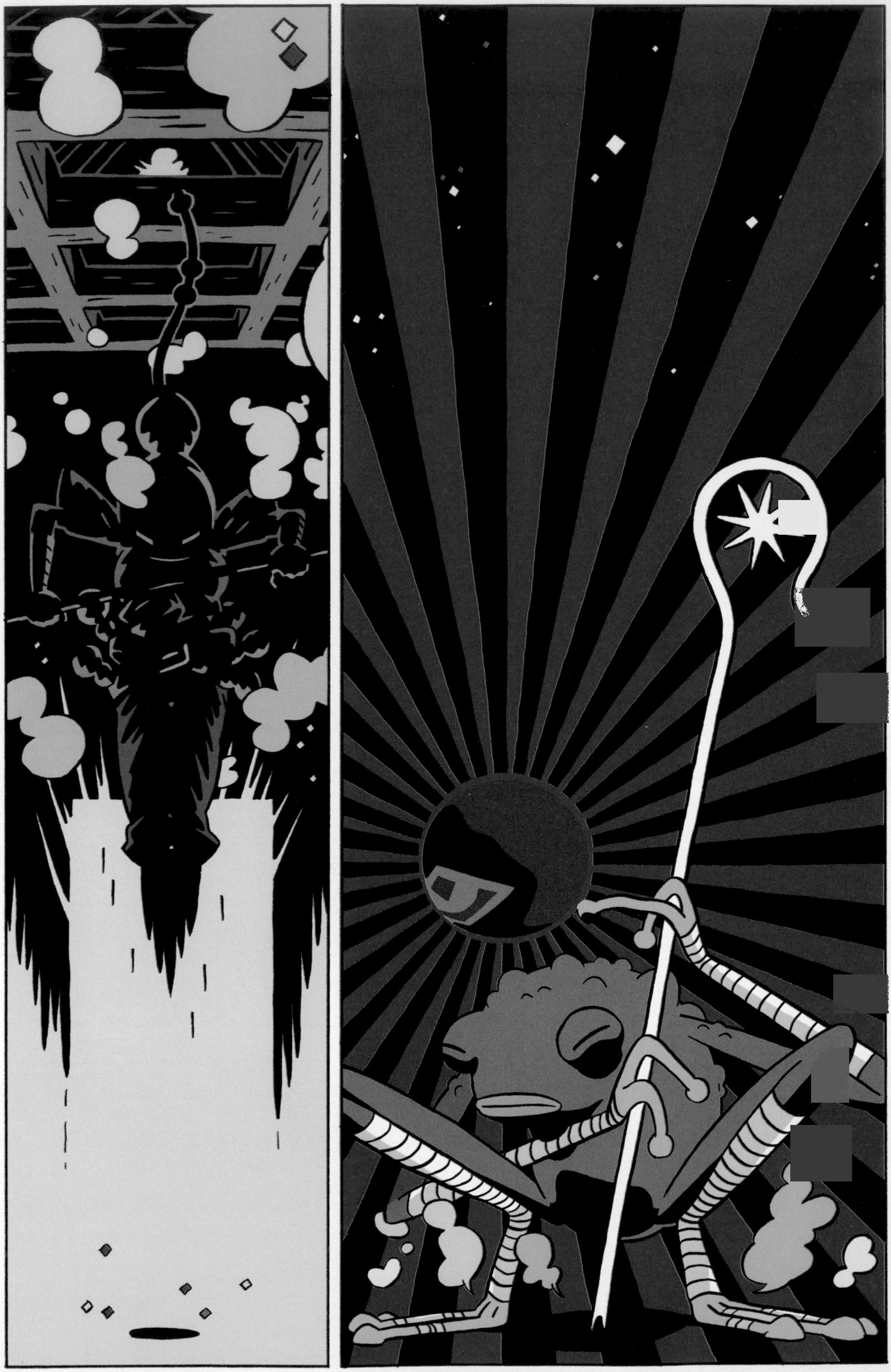

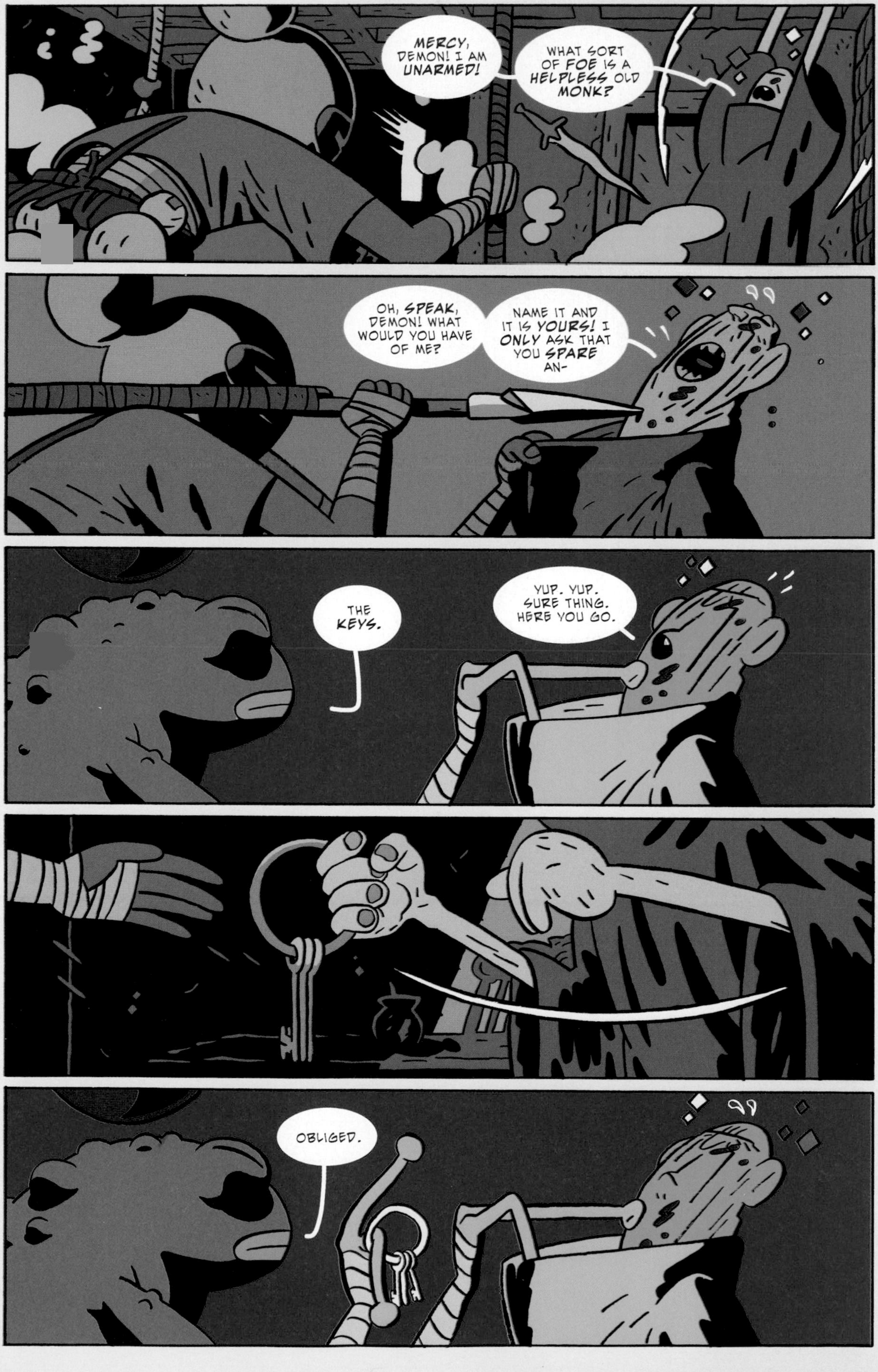
MERCY, DEMON! I AM UNARMED!
WHAT SORT OF FOE IS A HELPLESS OLD MONK?
OH, SPEAK, DEMON! WHAT WOULD YOU HAVE OF ME?
NAME IT AND IT IS YOURS! I ONLY ASK THAT YOU SPARE AN-
THE KEYS.
YUP. YUP. SURE THING. HERE YOU GO.
OBLIGED.

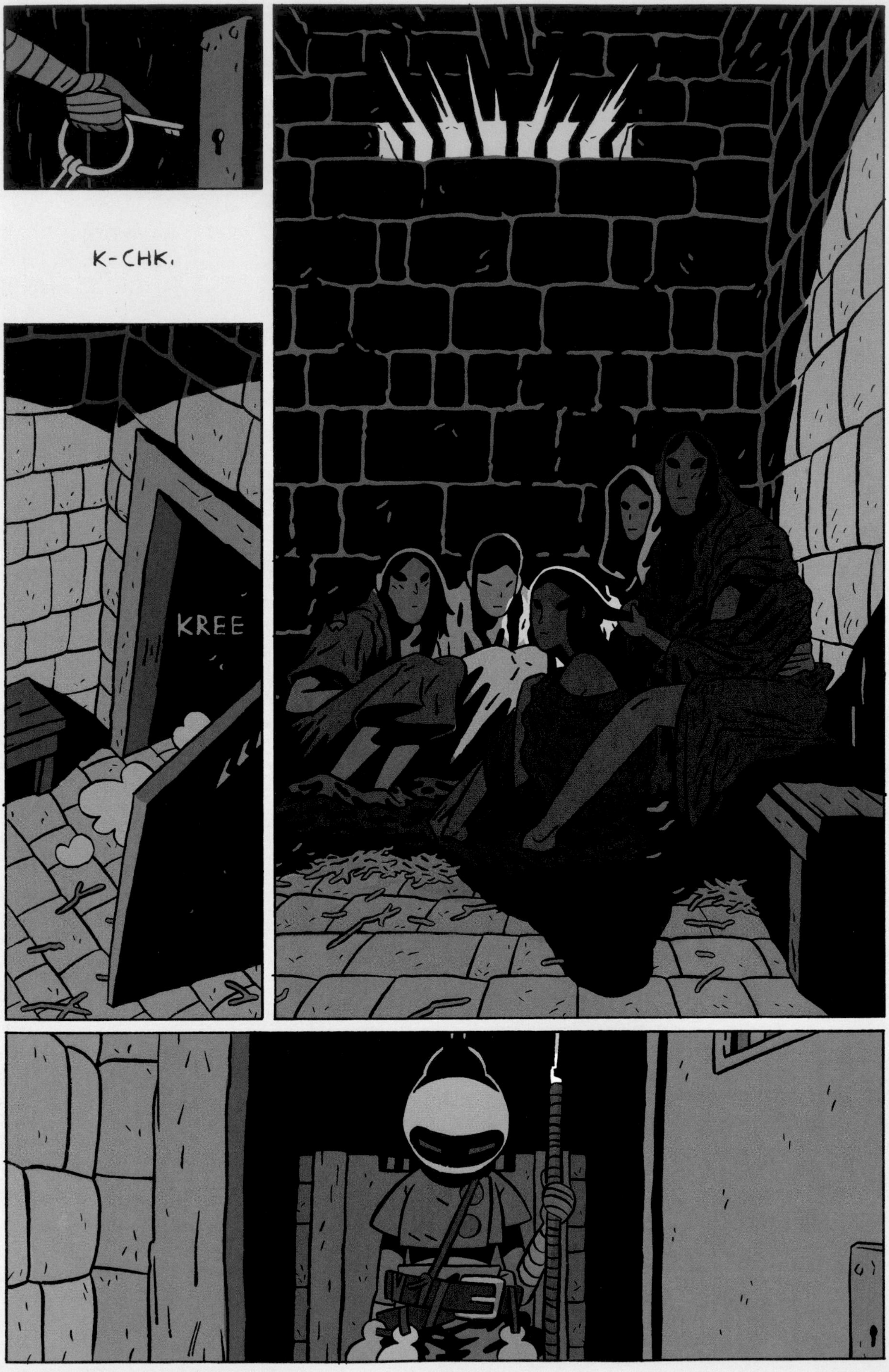
K-CHK.
KREE

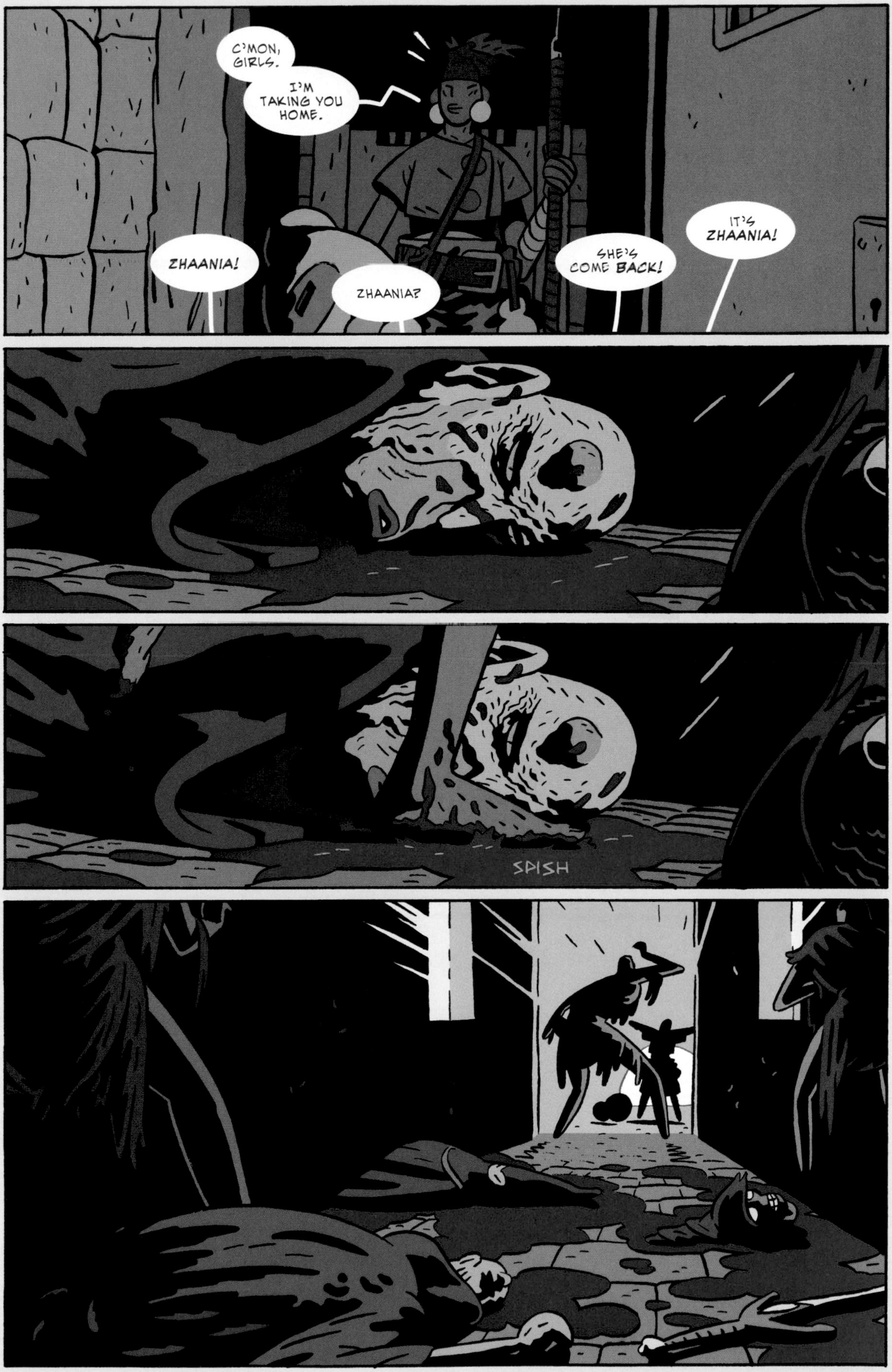
C'MON, GIRLS.
I'M TAKING YOU HOME.
ZHAANIA!
ZHAANIA?
SHE'S COME BACK!
IT'S ZHAANIA!
SPISH

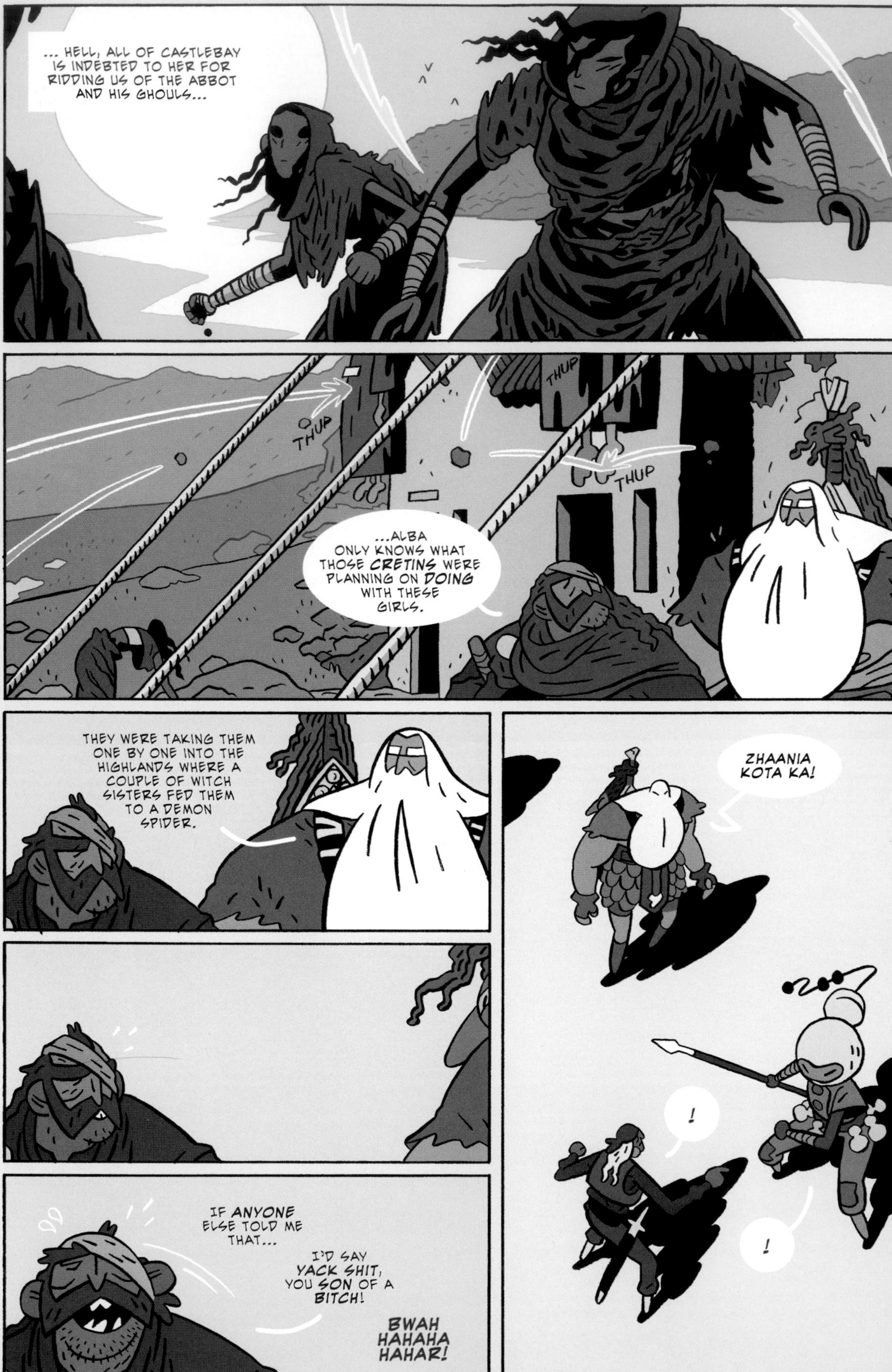
... HELL, ALL OF CASTLEBAY IS INDEBTED TO HER FOR RIDDING US OF THE ABBOT AND HIS GHOULS...
THUP
THUP
THUP
...ALBA ONLY KNOWS WHAT THOSE CRETINS WERE PLANNING ON DOING WITH THESE GIRLS.
THEY WERE TAKING THEM ONE BY ONE INTO THE HIGHLANDS WHERE A COUPLE OF WITCH SISTERS FED THEM TO A DEMON SPIDER.
IF ANYONE ELSE TOLD ME THAT...
I'D SAY YACK SHIT, YOU SON OF A BITCH!
BWAH HAHAHA HAHAR!
ZHAANIA KOTA KA!
!
!

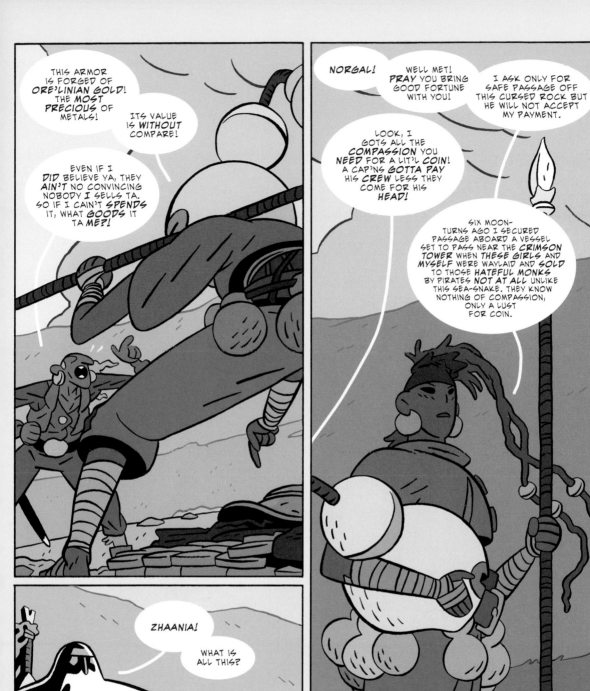

THIS ARMOR IS FORGED OF *ORE?LINIAN GOLD!* THE *MOST PRECIOUS* OF METALS!

ITS VALUE IS *WITHOUT* COMPARE!

EVEN IF I *DID* BELIEVE YA, THEY *AIN'T* NO CONVINCING NOBODY I SELLS TA. SO IF I CAIN'T *SPENDS* IT, WHAT *GOODS* IT TA ME?!

NORGAL!

WELL MET! *PRAY* YOU BRING GOOD FORTUNE WITH YOU!

I ASK ONLY FOR SAFE PASSAGE OFF THIS CURSED ROCK BUT HE WILL NOT ACCEPT MY PAYMENT.

LOOK, I GOTS ALL THE *COMPASSION* YOU *NEED* FOR A LIT?L *COIN!* A CAP?NS *GOTTA PAY* HIS *CREW* LESS THEY COME FOR HIS *HEAD!*

SIX MOON-TURNS AGO I SECURED PASSAGE ABOARD A VESSEL SET TO PASS NEAR THE *CRIMSON TOWER* WHEN *THESE GIRLS* AND *MYSELF* WERE WAYLAID AND *SOLD* TO THOSE *HATEFUL MONKS* BY PIRATES *NOT AT ALL* UNLIKE THIS SEA-SNAKE. THEY KNOW NOTHING OF COMPASSION, ONLY A LUST FOR COIN.

ZHAANIA!

WHAT IS ALL THIS?

CAPTAIN! THAT IS YOUR SHIP THERE, MOORED NEAR THE CASTLE IN THE BAY, IS IT NOT?

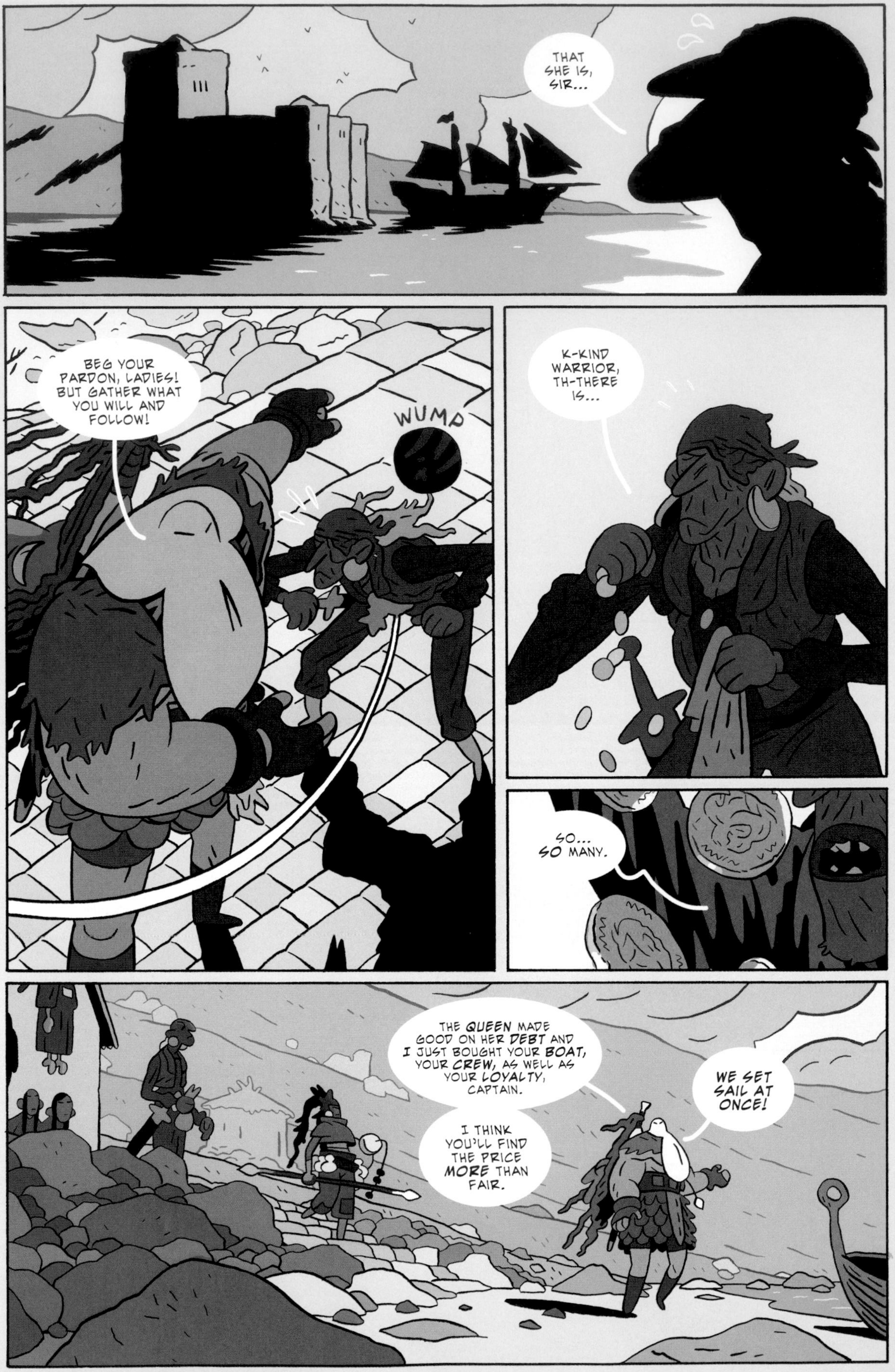
THAT SHE IS, SIR...
BEG YOUR PARDON, LADIES! BUT GATHER WHAT YOU WILL AND FOLLOW!
WUMP
K-KIND WARRIOR, TH-THERE IS...
SO... SO MANY.
THE QUEEN MADE GOOD ON HER DEBT AND I JUST BOUGHT YOUR BOAT, YOUR CREW, AS WELL AS YOUR LOYALTY, CAPTAIN.
I THINK YOU'LL FIND THE PRICE MORE THAN FAIR.
WE SET SAIL AT ONCE!

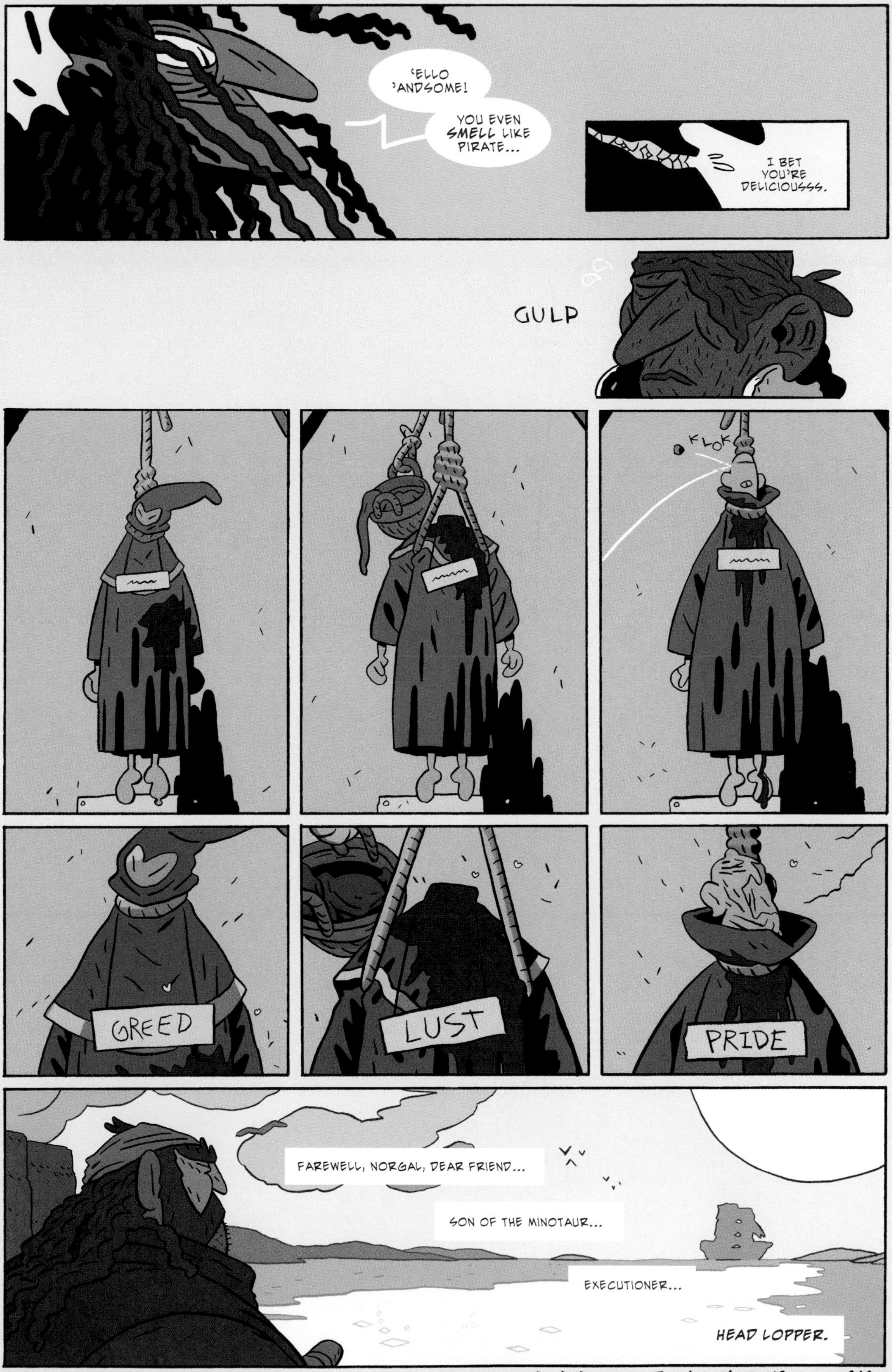

'ELLO 'ANDSOME!
YOU EVEN SMELL LIKE PIRATE...
I BET YOU'RE DELICIOUSSS.
GULP
KLOK
GREED
LUST
PRIDE
FAREWELL, NORGAL, DEAR FRIEND...
SON OF THE MINOTAUR...
EXECUTIONER...
HEAD LOPPER.

TO WHEREVER WIND AND FORTUNE MAY TAKE US... -AM

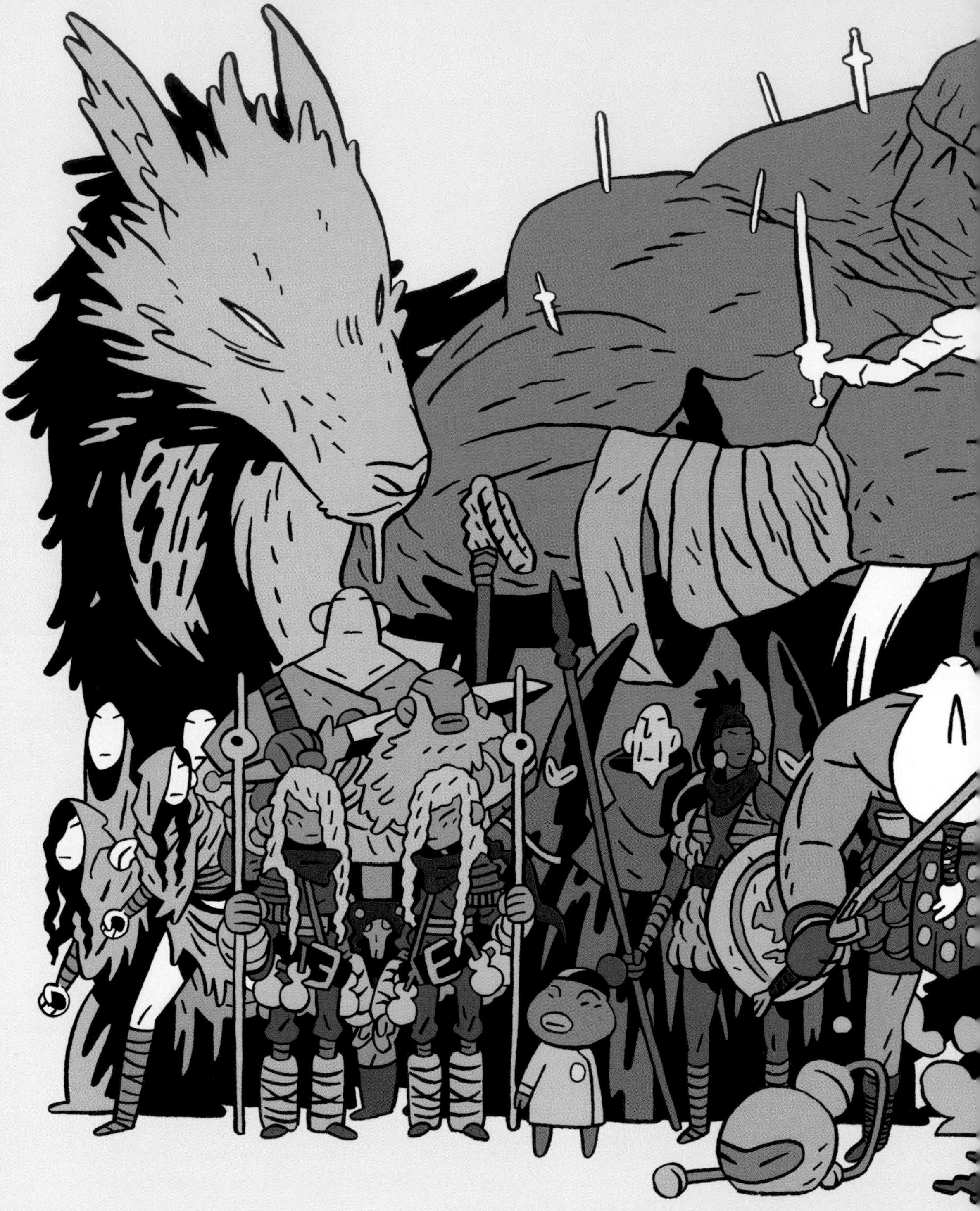

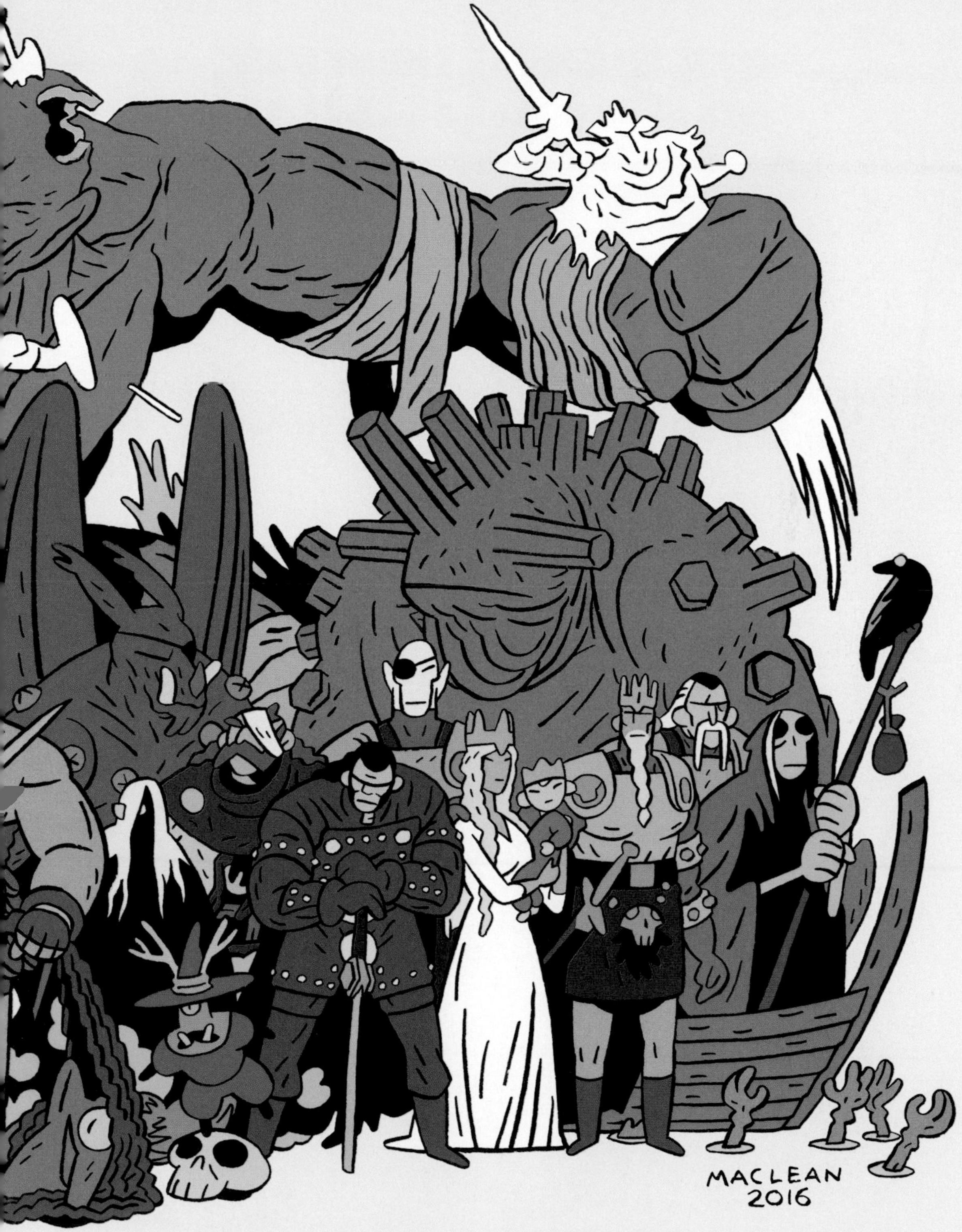
MACLEAN
2016

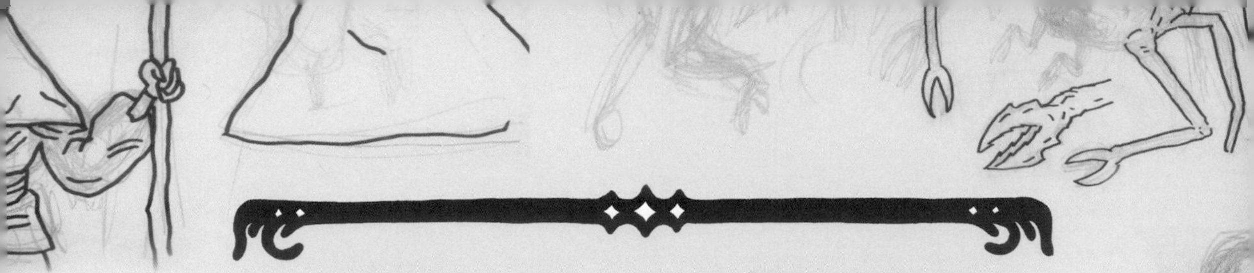

SKETCHBOOK

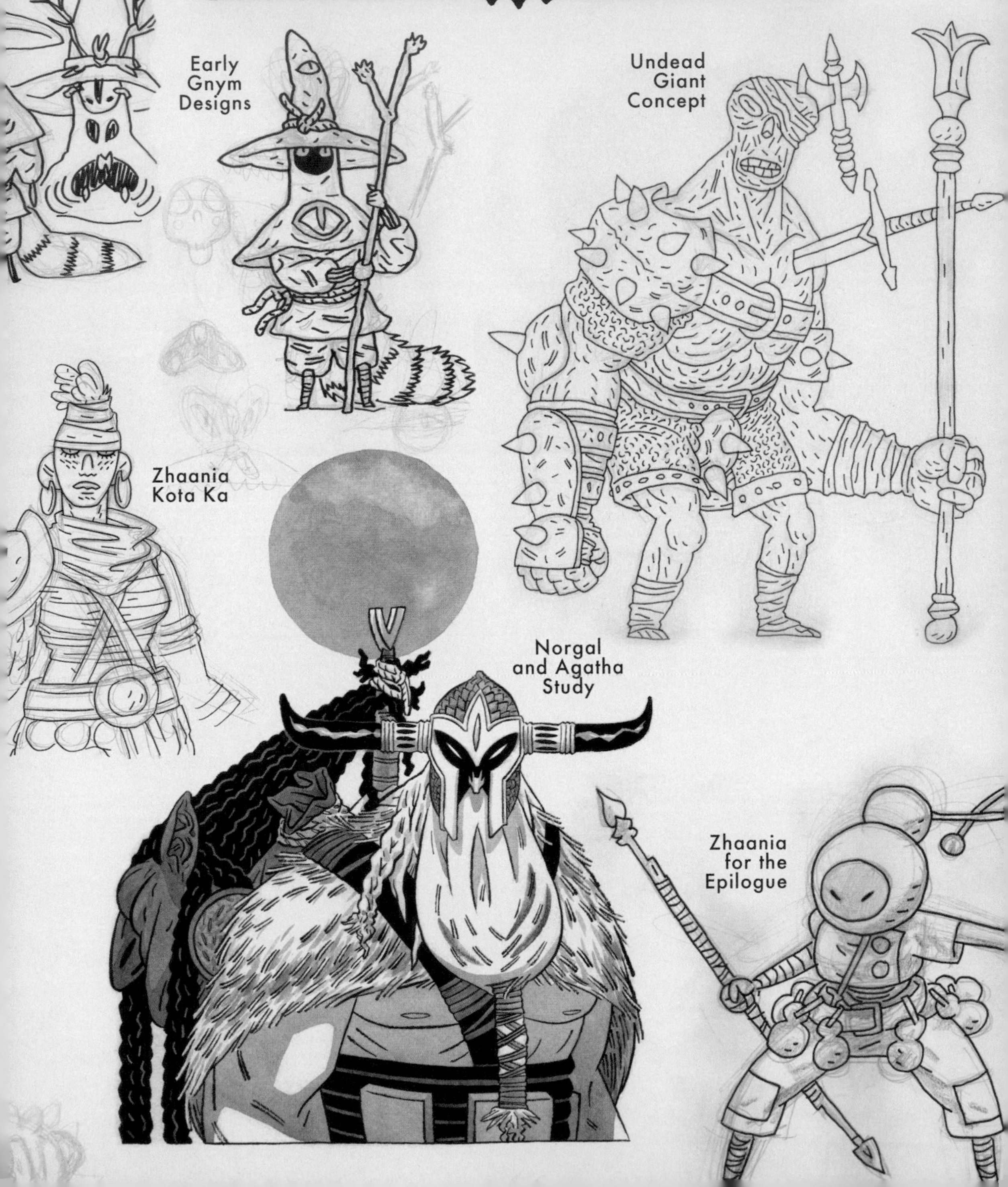

Early Gnym Designs
Undead Giant Concept
Zhaania Kota Ka
Norgal and Agatha Study
Zhaania for the Epilogue

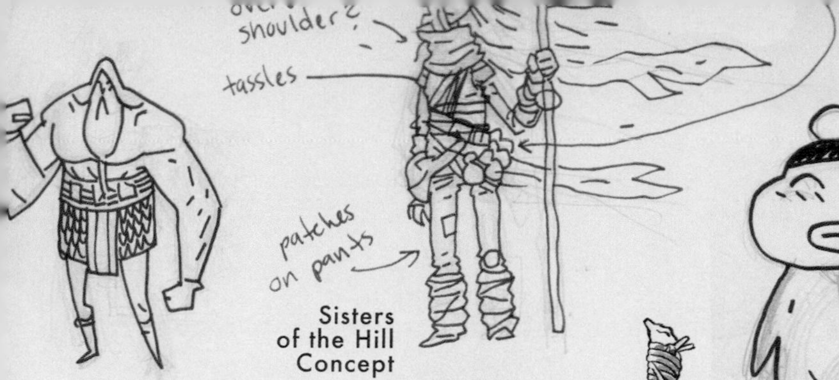
shoulder?
tassles
patches on pants

Sisters of the Hill Concept

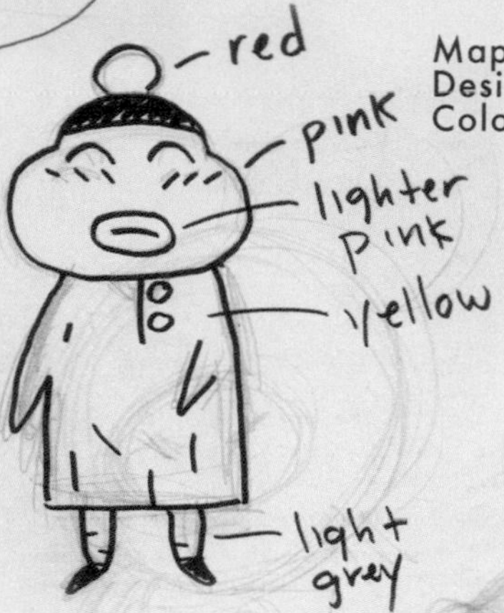
red
pink
lighter pink
yellow
light grey

Mapmaker Design with Color Notes

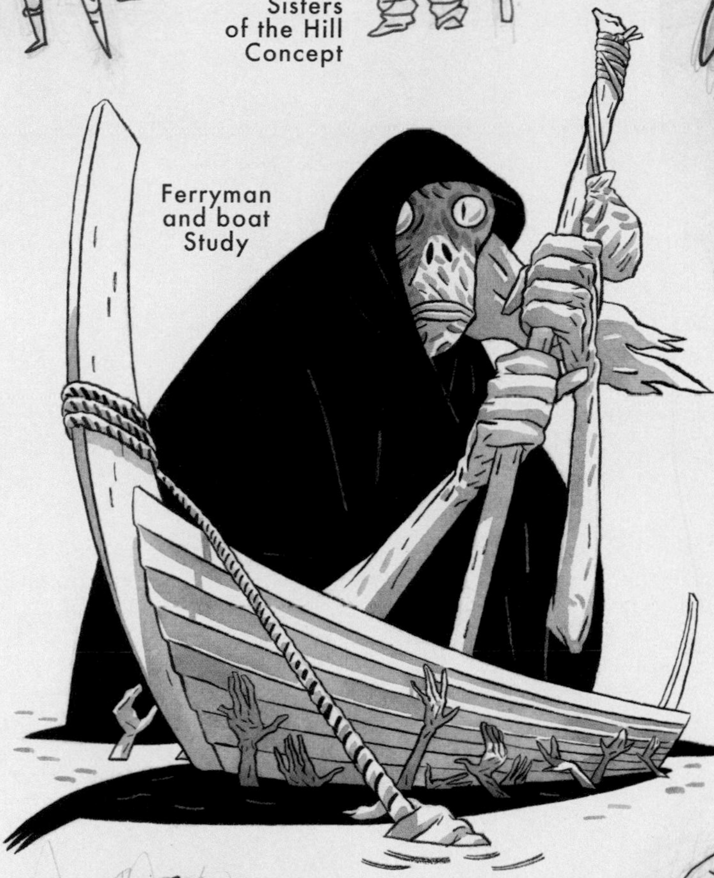

Ferryman and boat Study

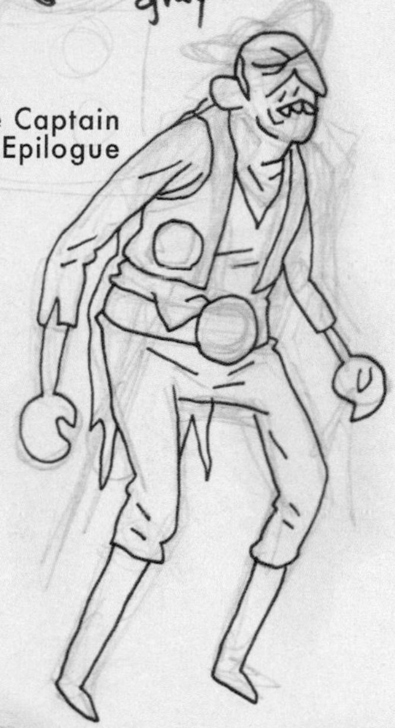

Pirate Captain in the Epilogue

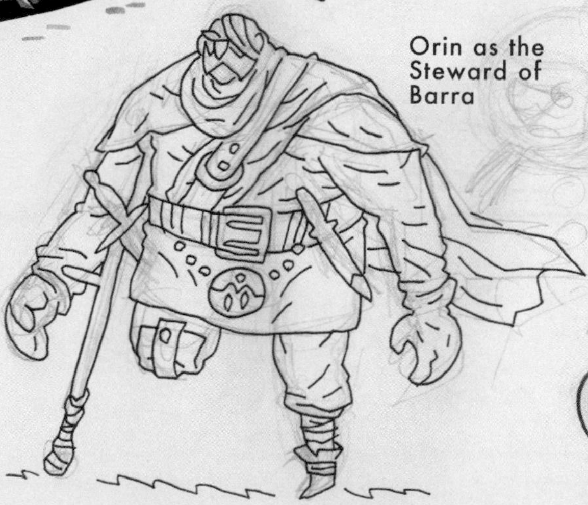

Orin as the Steward of Barra

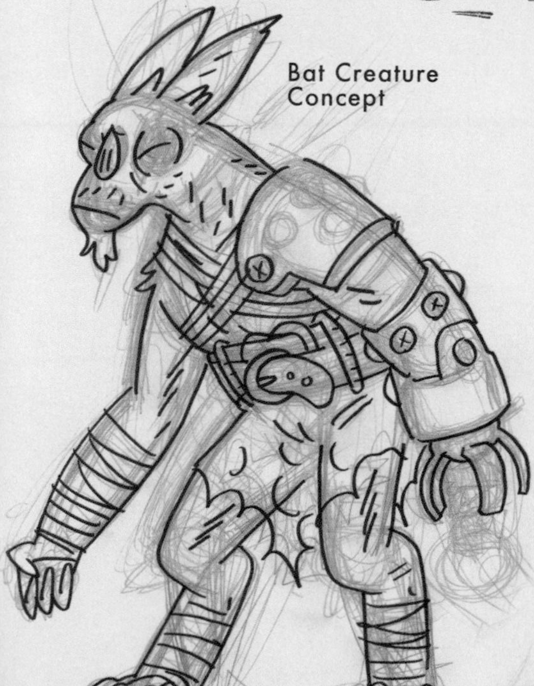

Bat Creature Concept

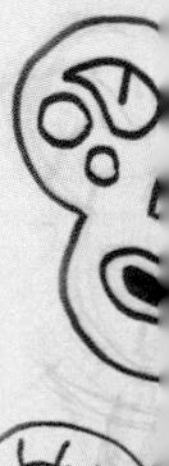

Possible faces for the Mega-Arachnid's tail

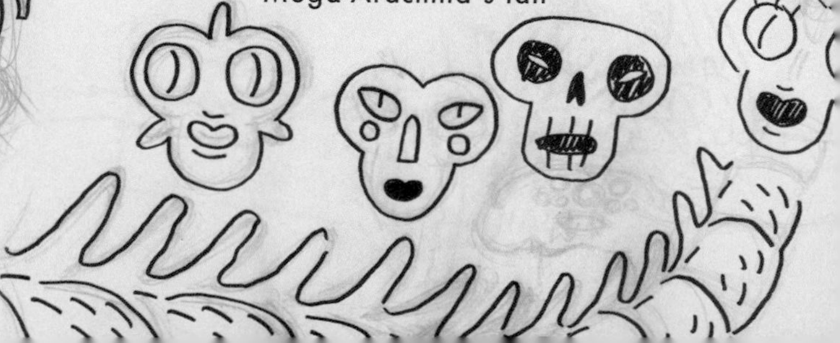

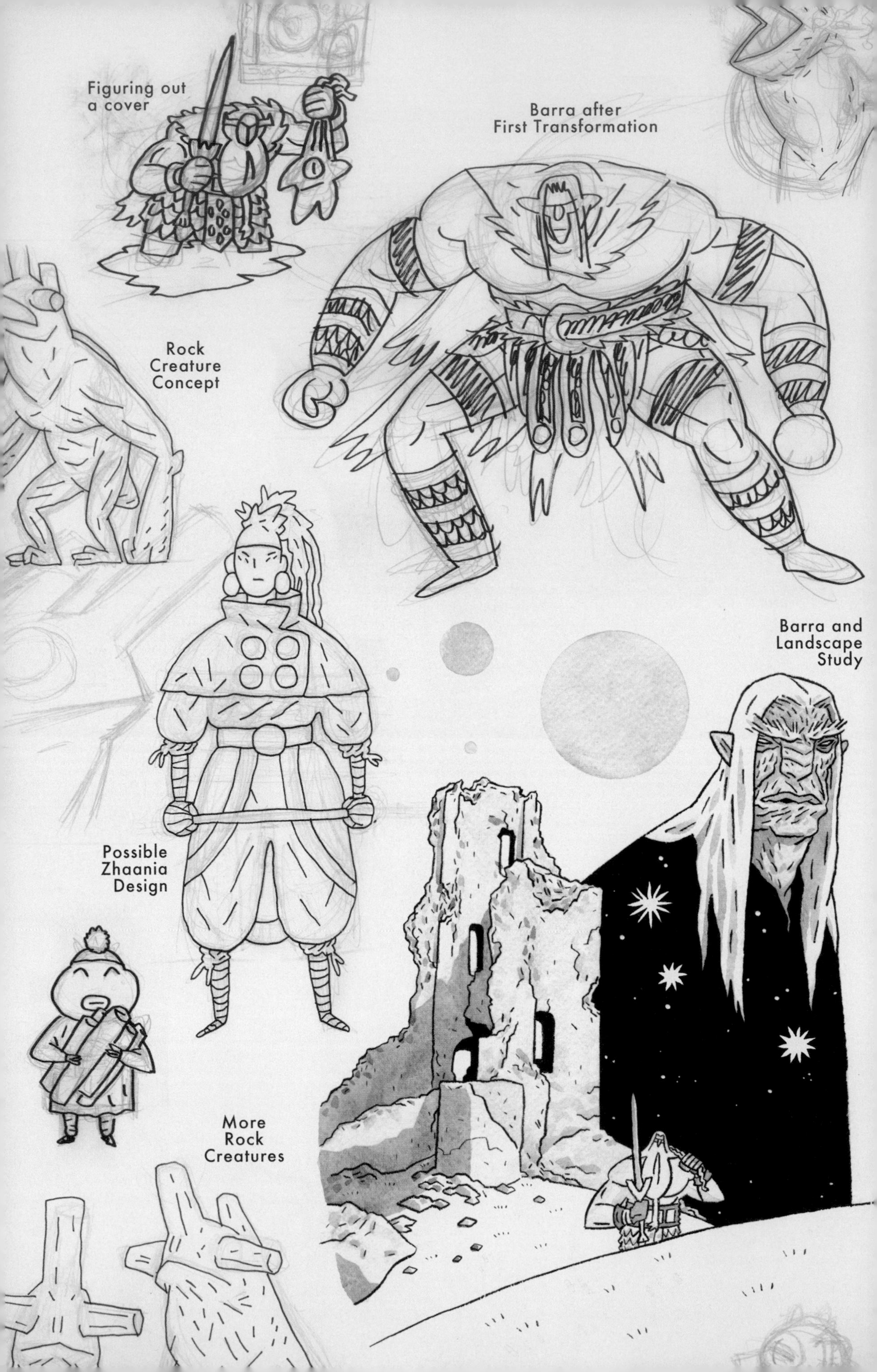
Figuring out a cover
Barra after First Transformation
Rock Creature Concept
Barra and Landscape Study
Possible Zhaania Design
More Rock Creatures

Adolescent
Servin Lulach

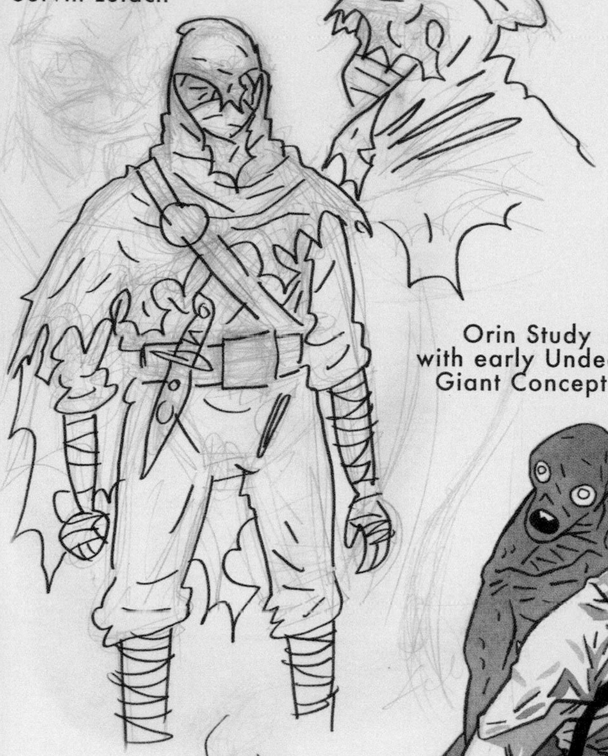

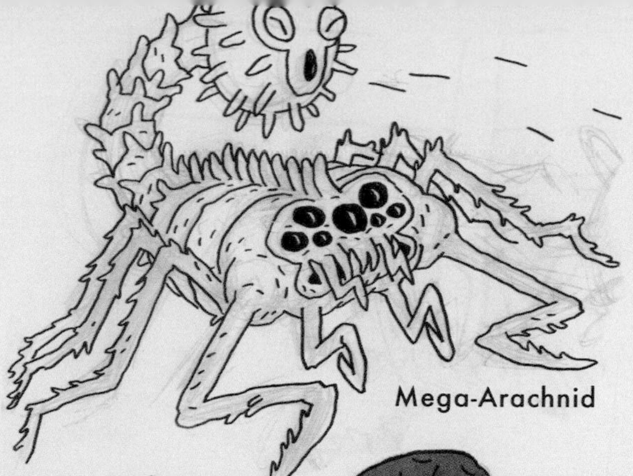

Mega-Arachnid

Orin Study
with early Undead
Giant Concepts

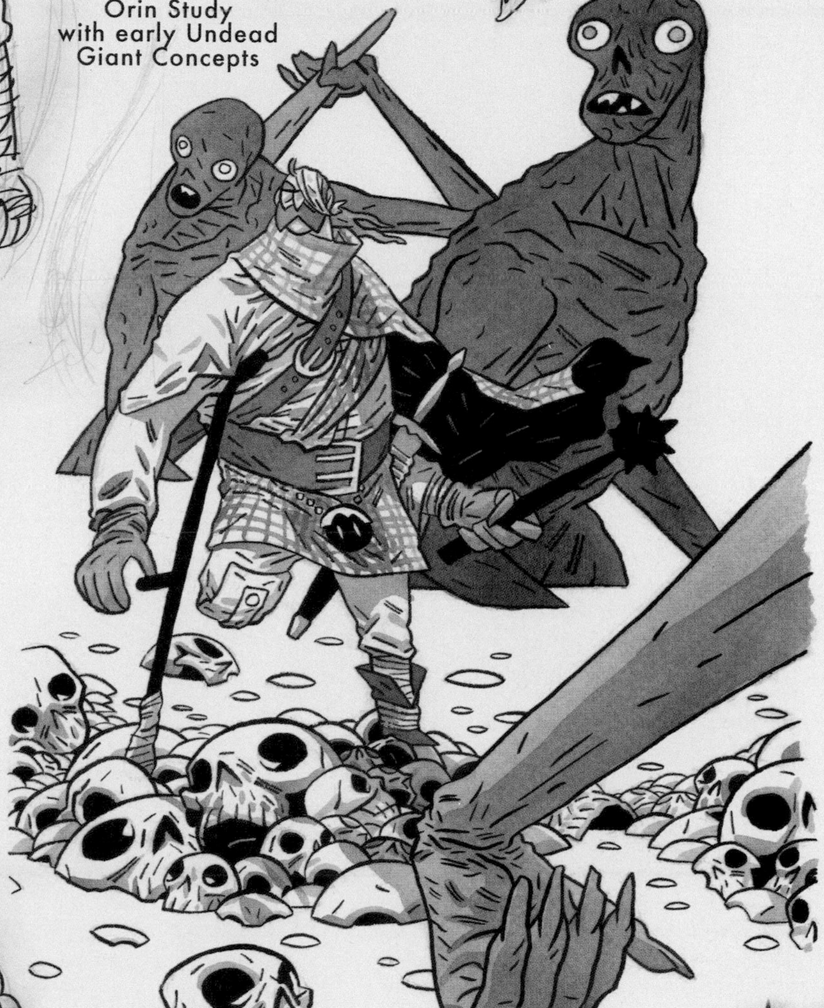

Bats

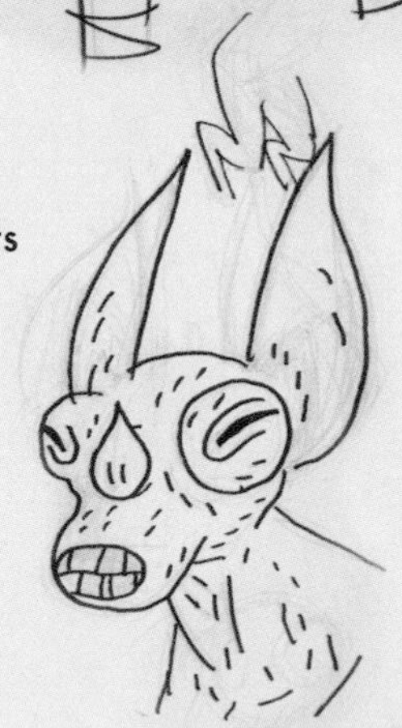

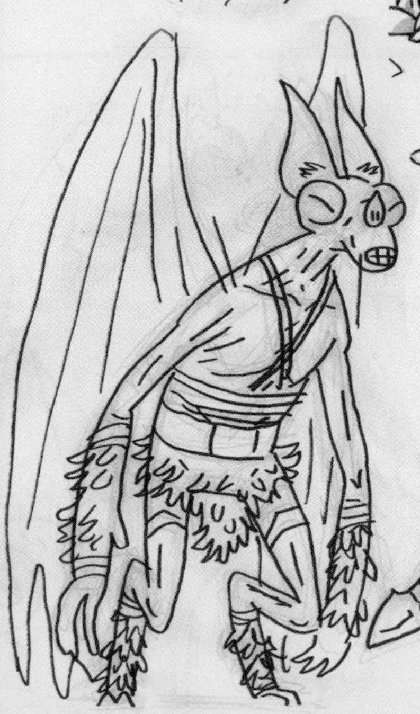

Bats

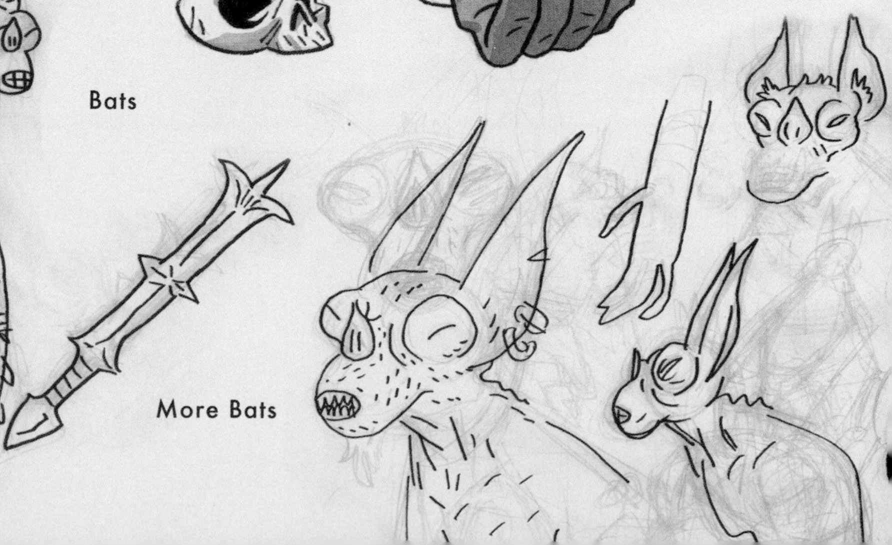

More Bats

Barra's Second Transformation

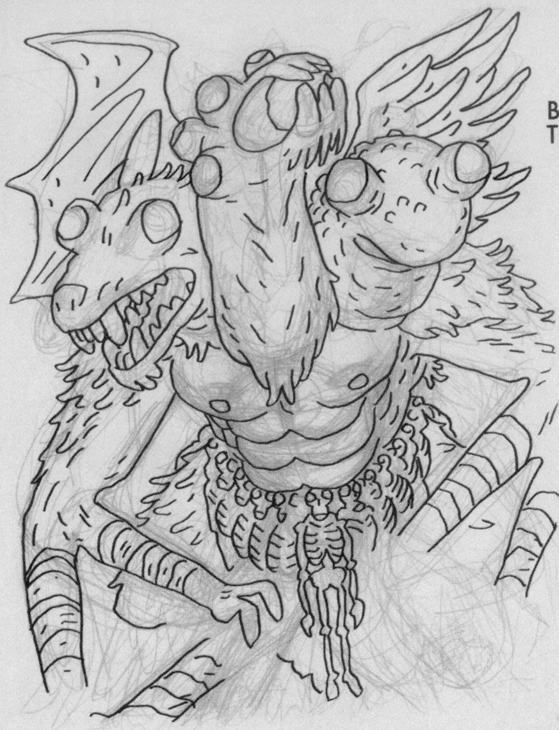

The Mega-Arachnid had many iterations...

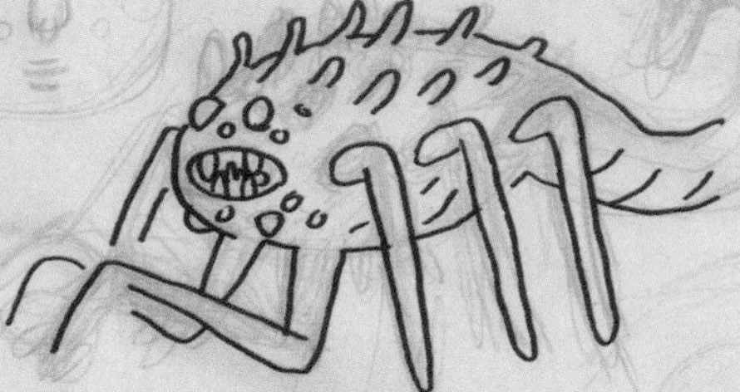

Servin Lulach Study

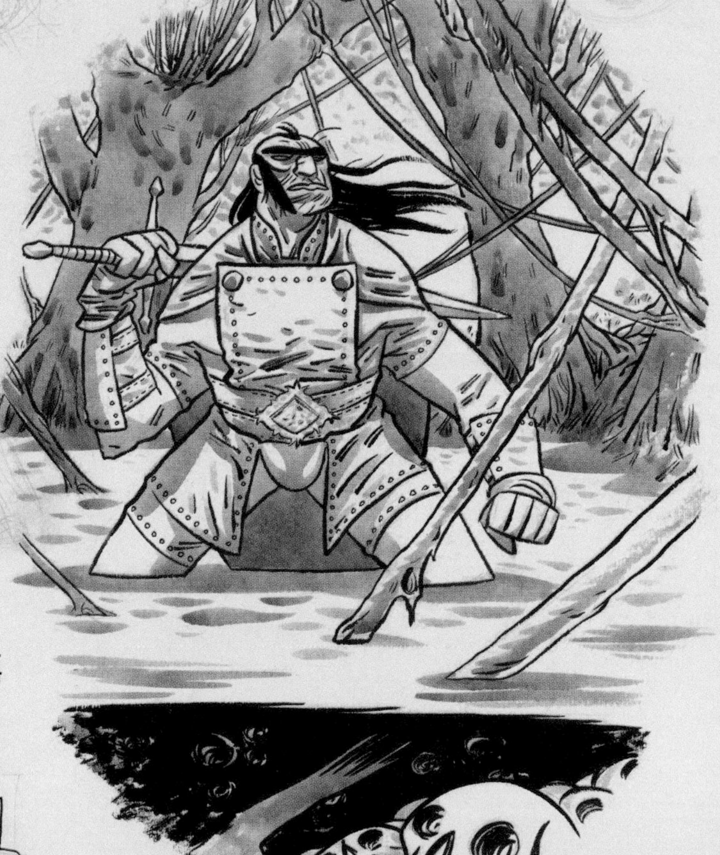

...so many iterations

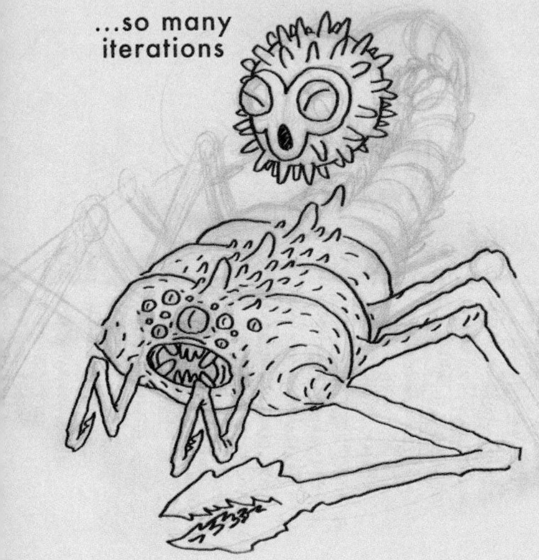

Issue 4 Cover Concept

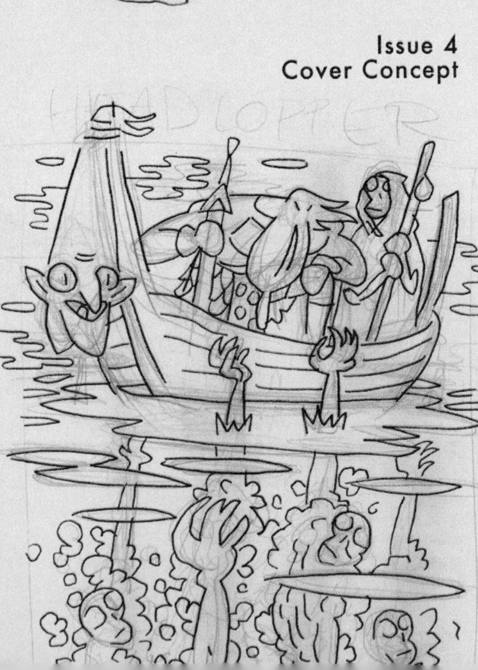
HEADLOPPER

Even More Bats

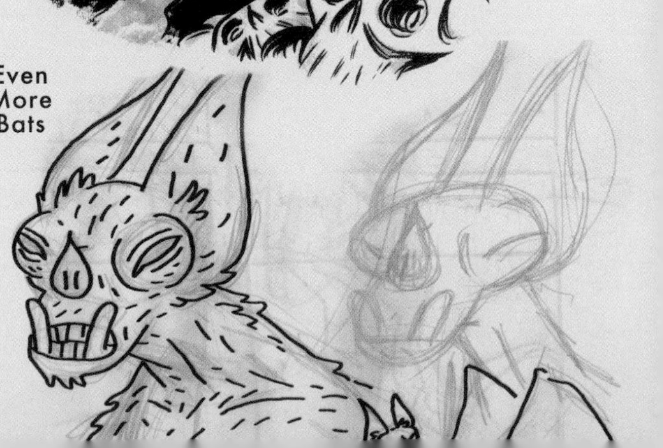

PINUP GALLERY

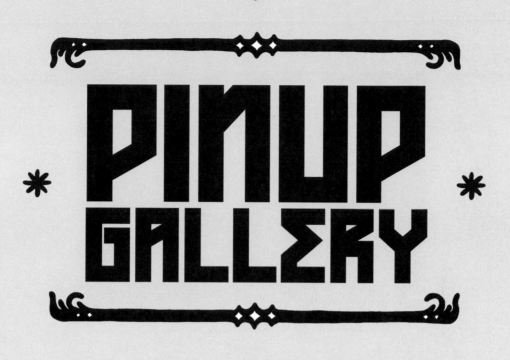

BOB FINGERMAN

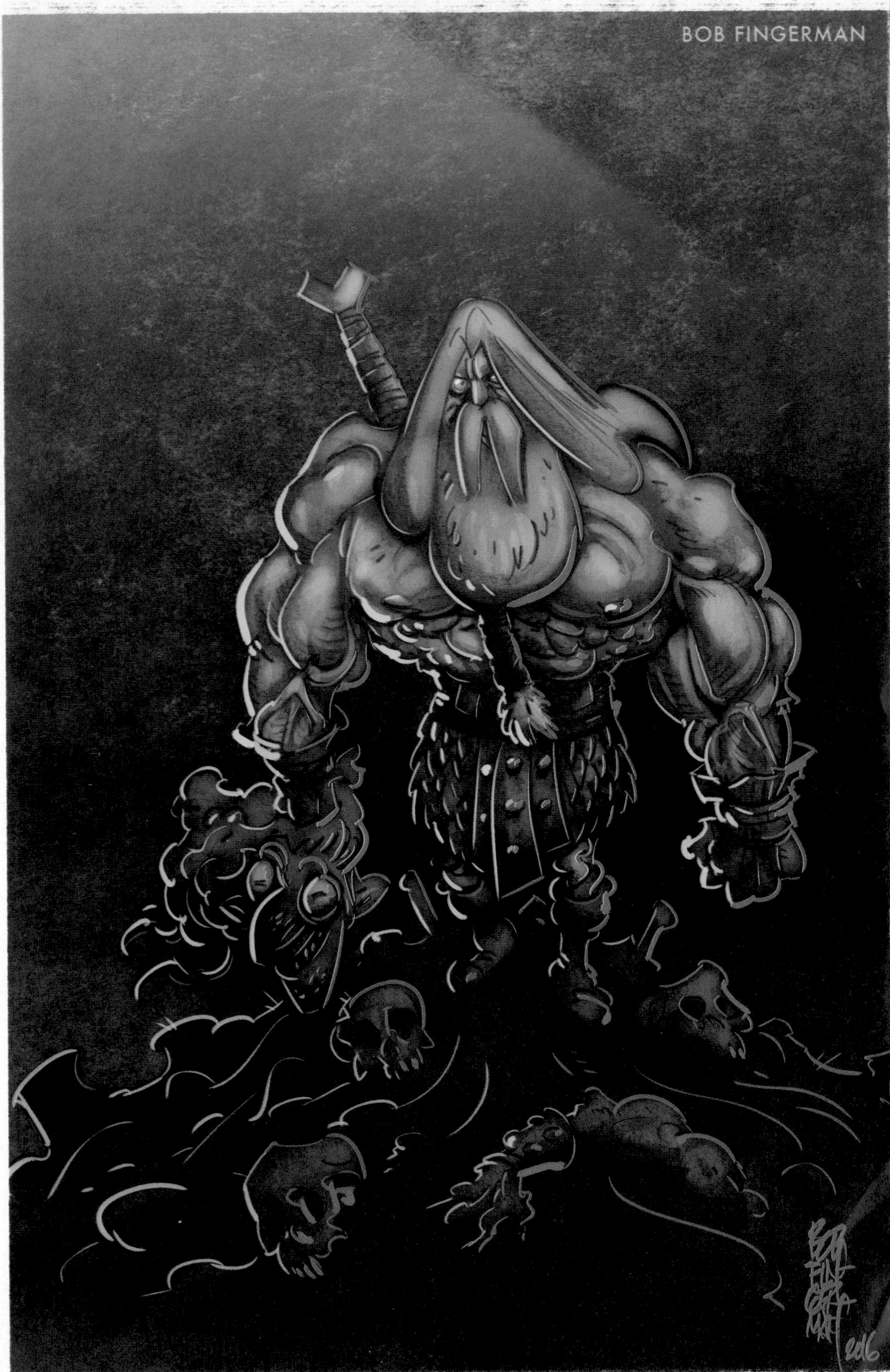

ENRIQUE FERNANDEZ

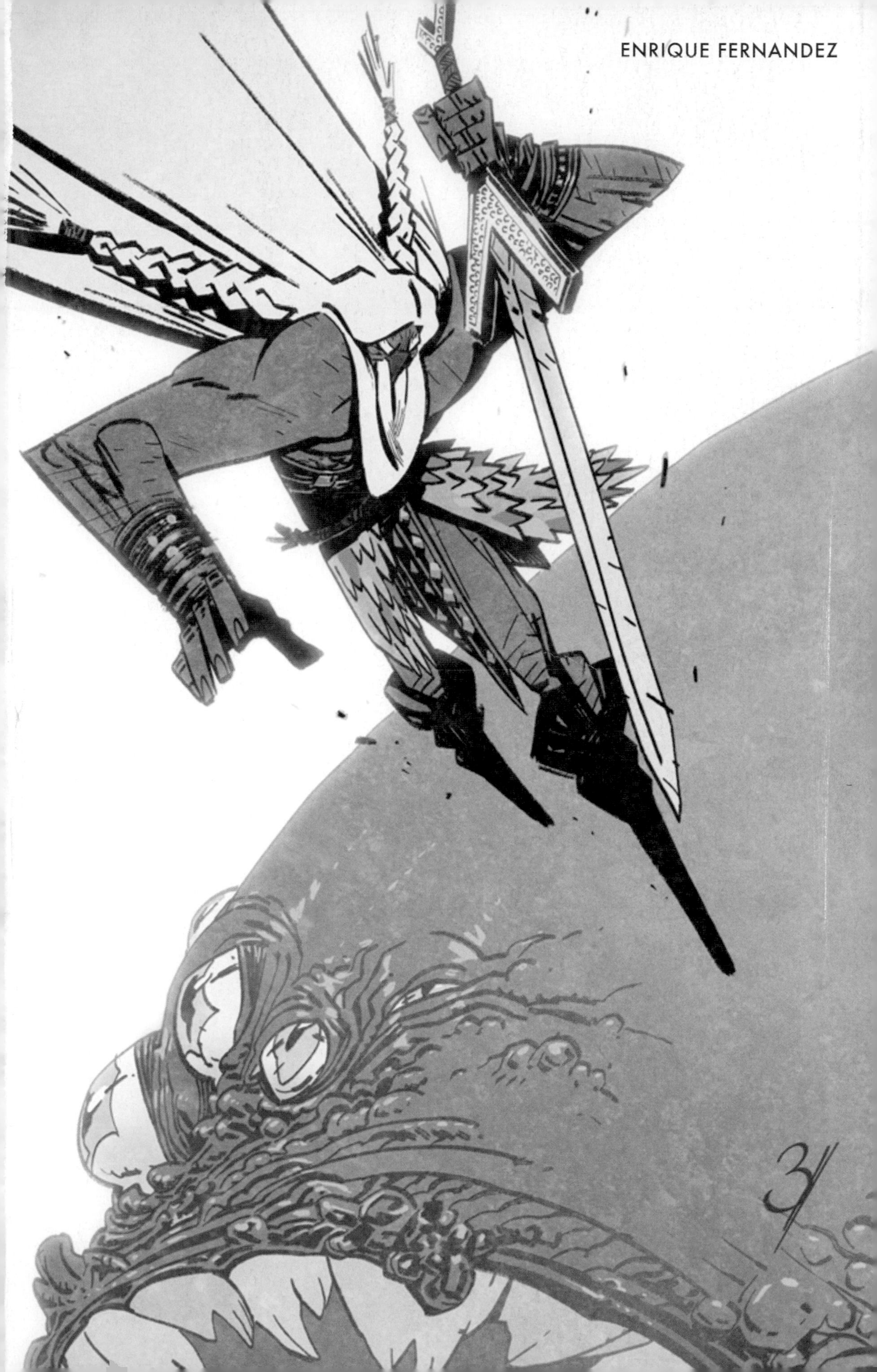

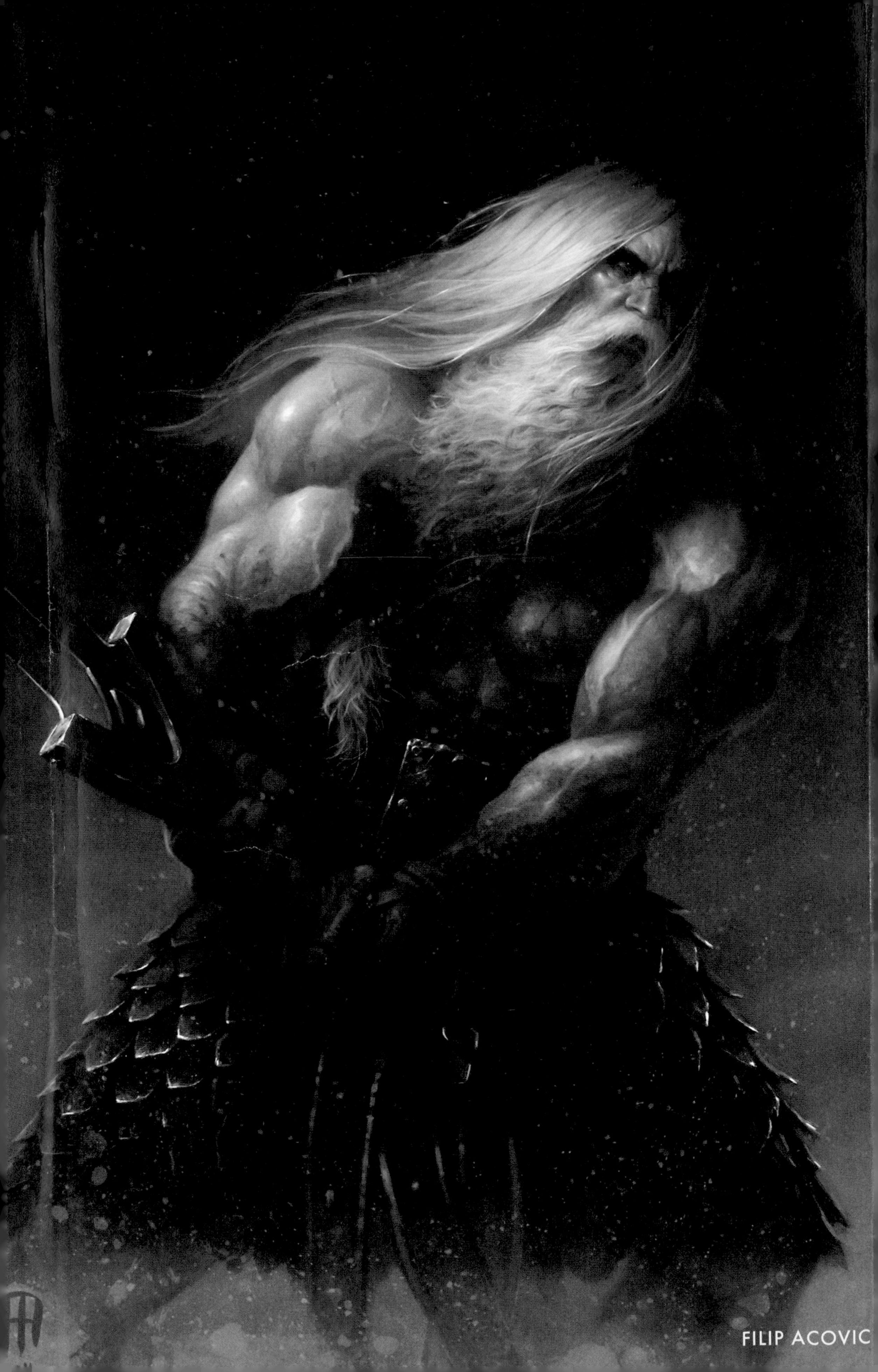

FILIP ACOVIC

JOE DELLAGATTA

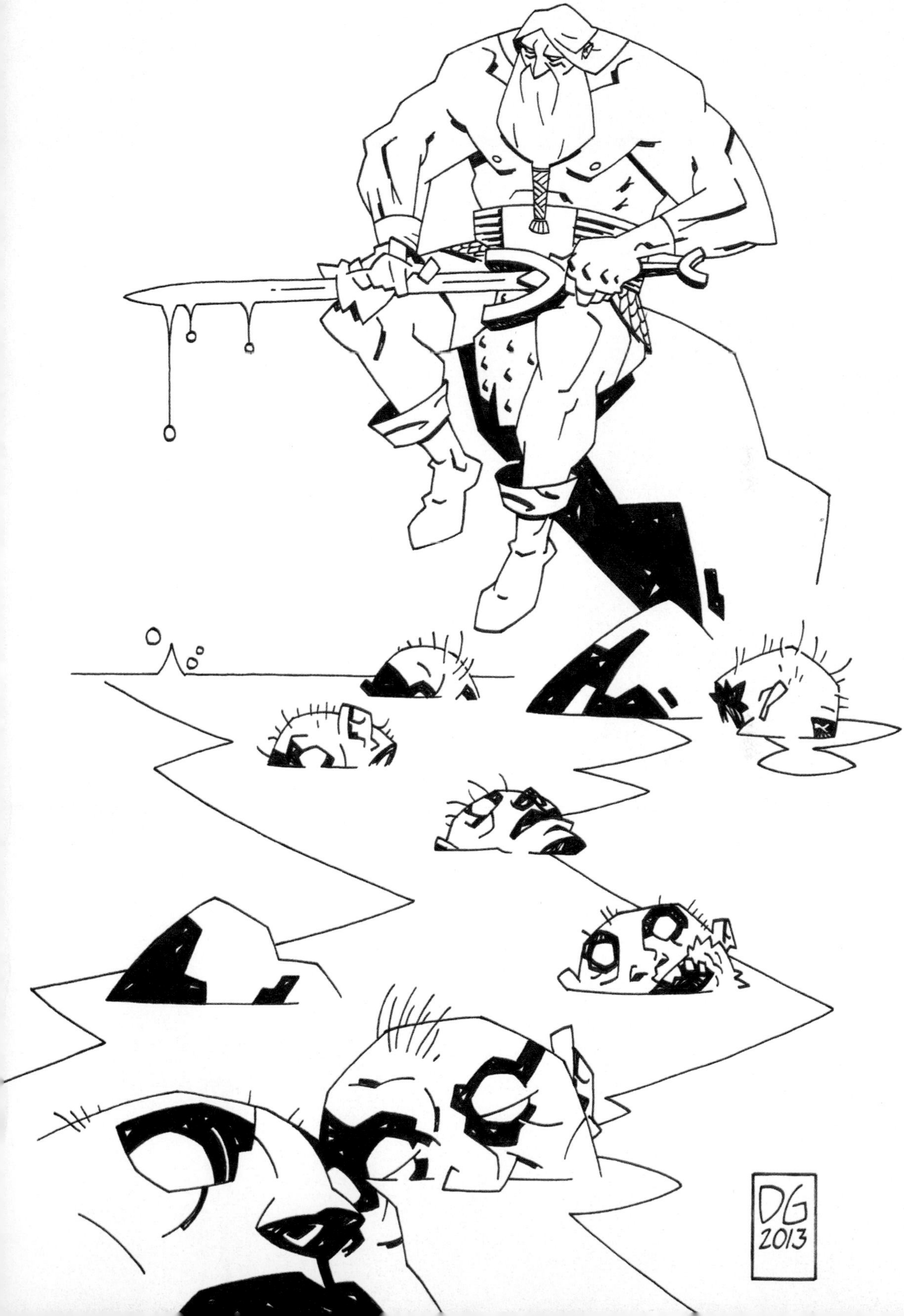
DG
2013

MAX FIUMARA

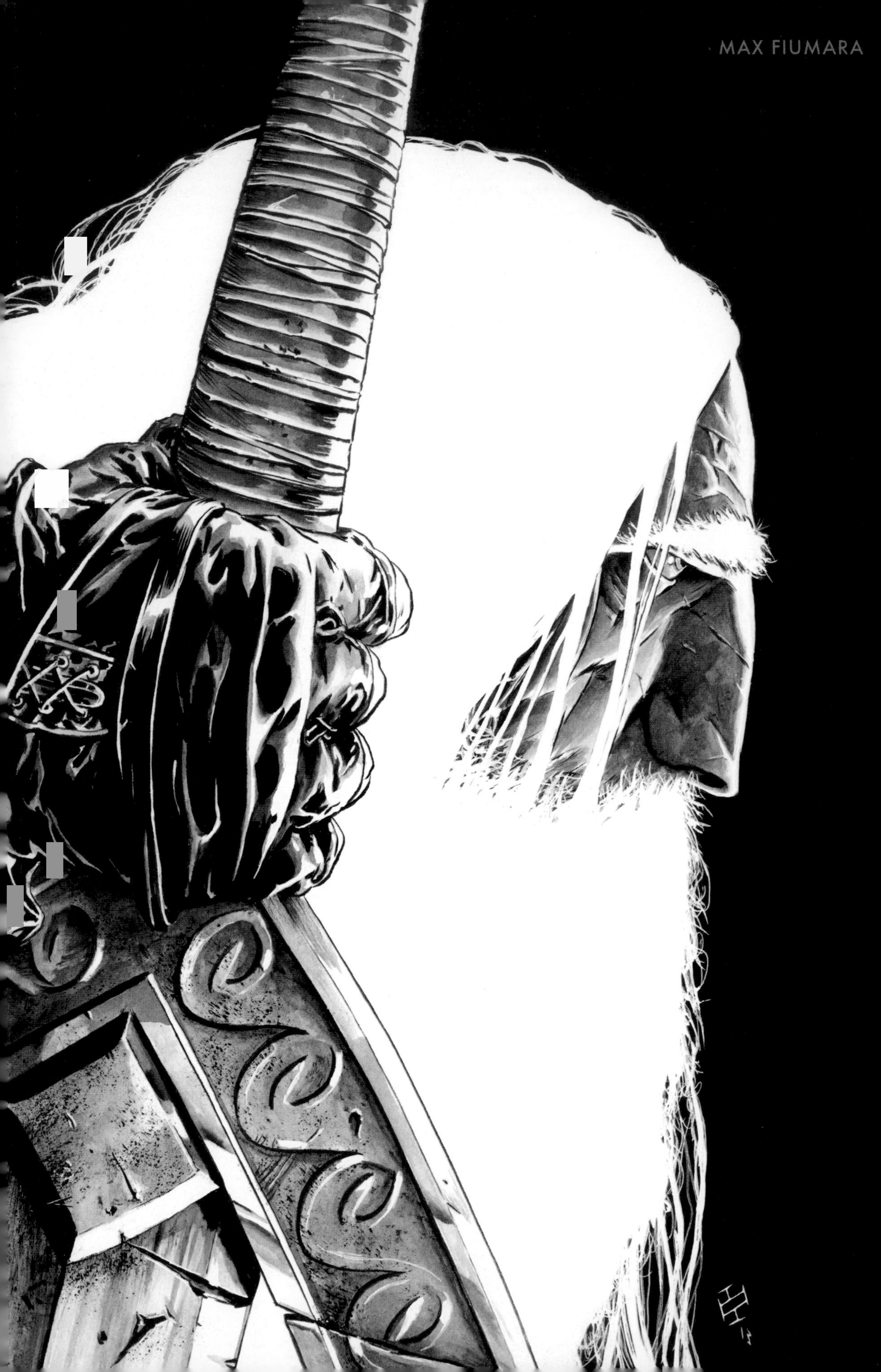

JAMES HARREN

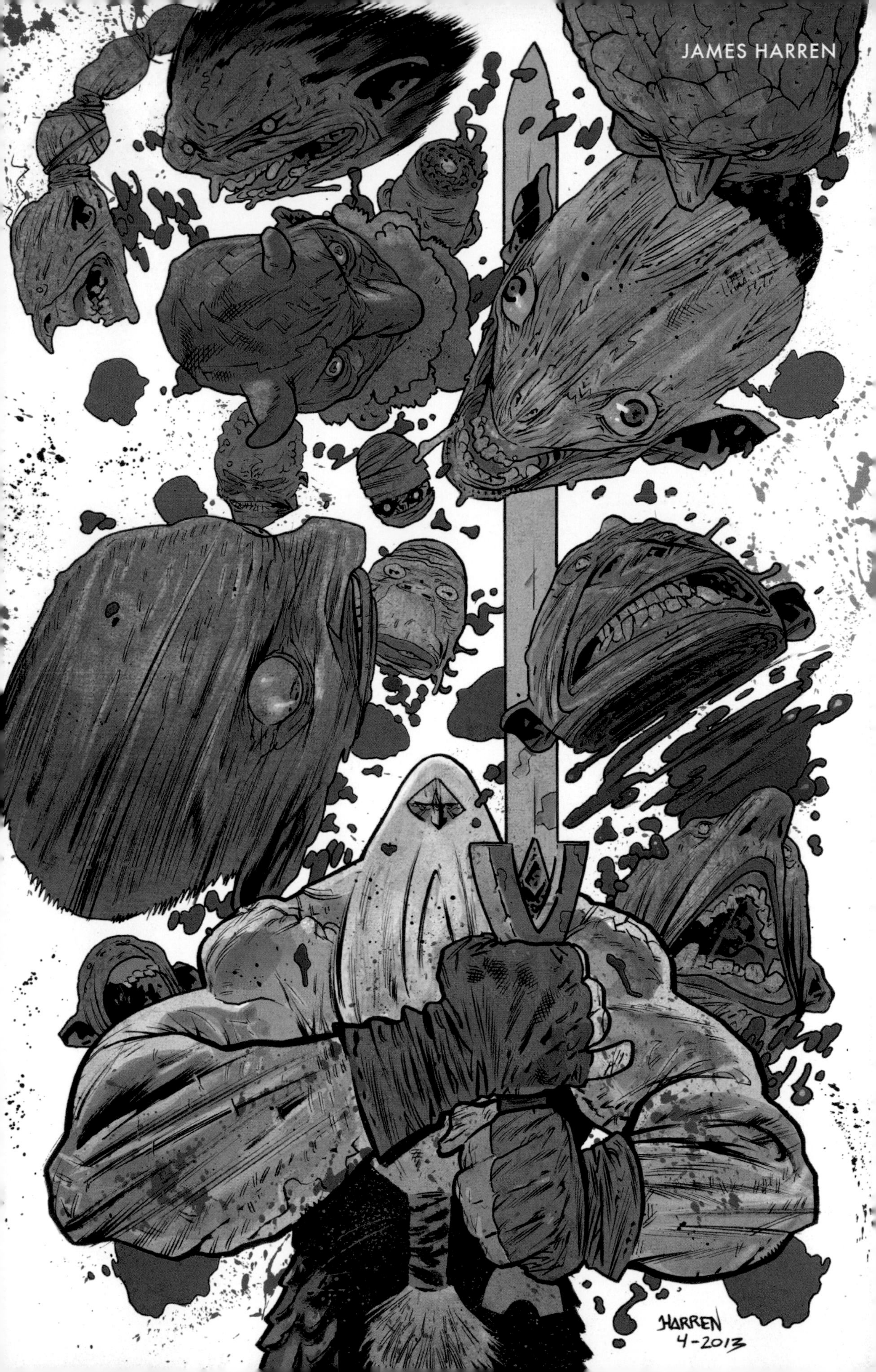
HARREN
4-2013

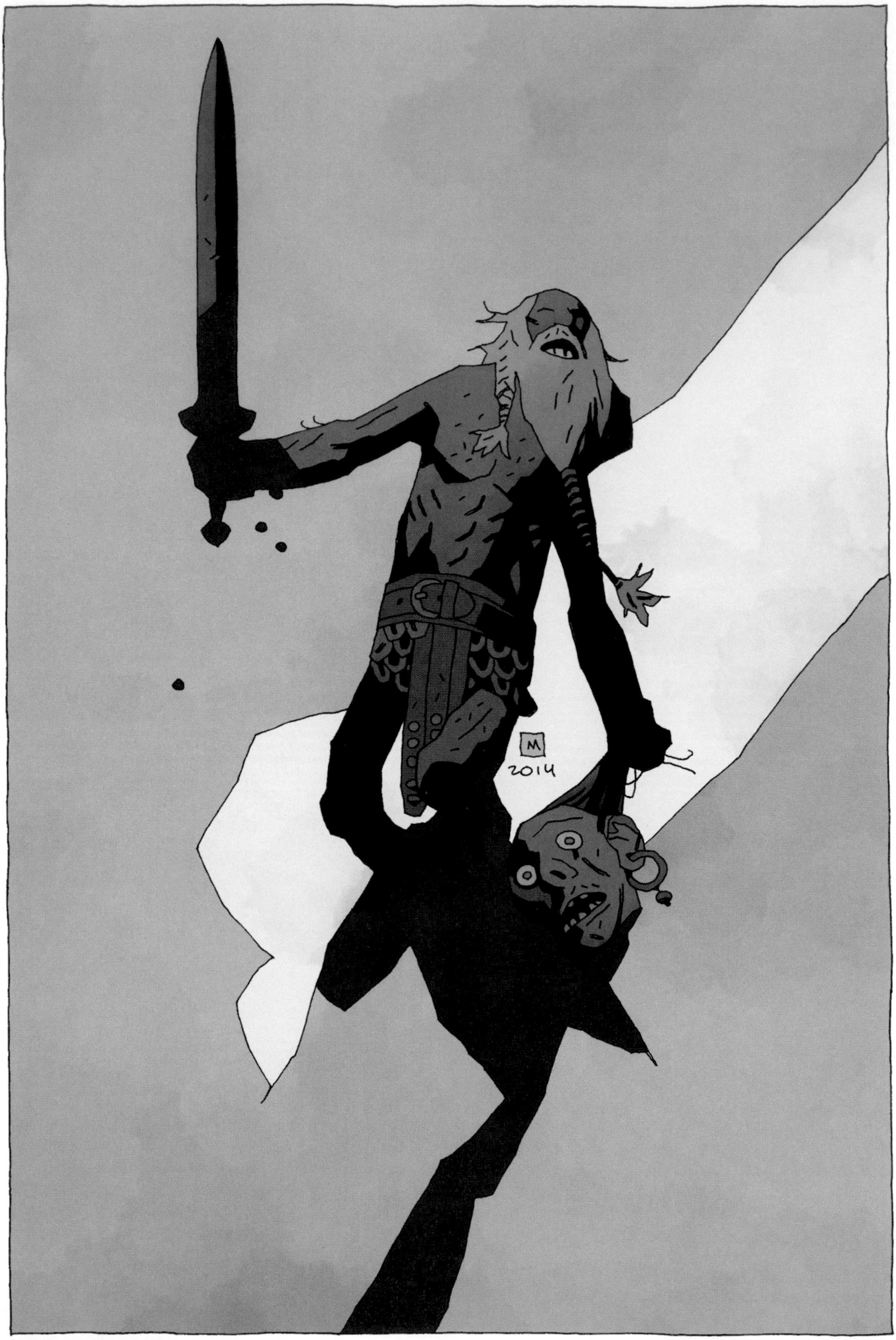
M
2014
MIKE MIGNOLA
& DAVE STEWART

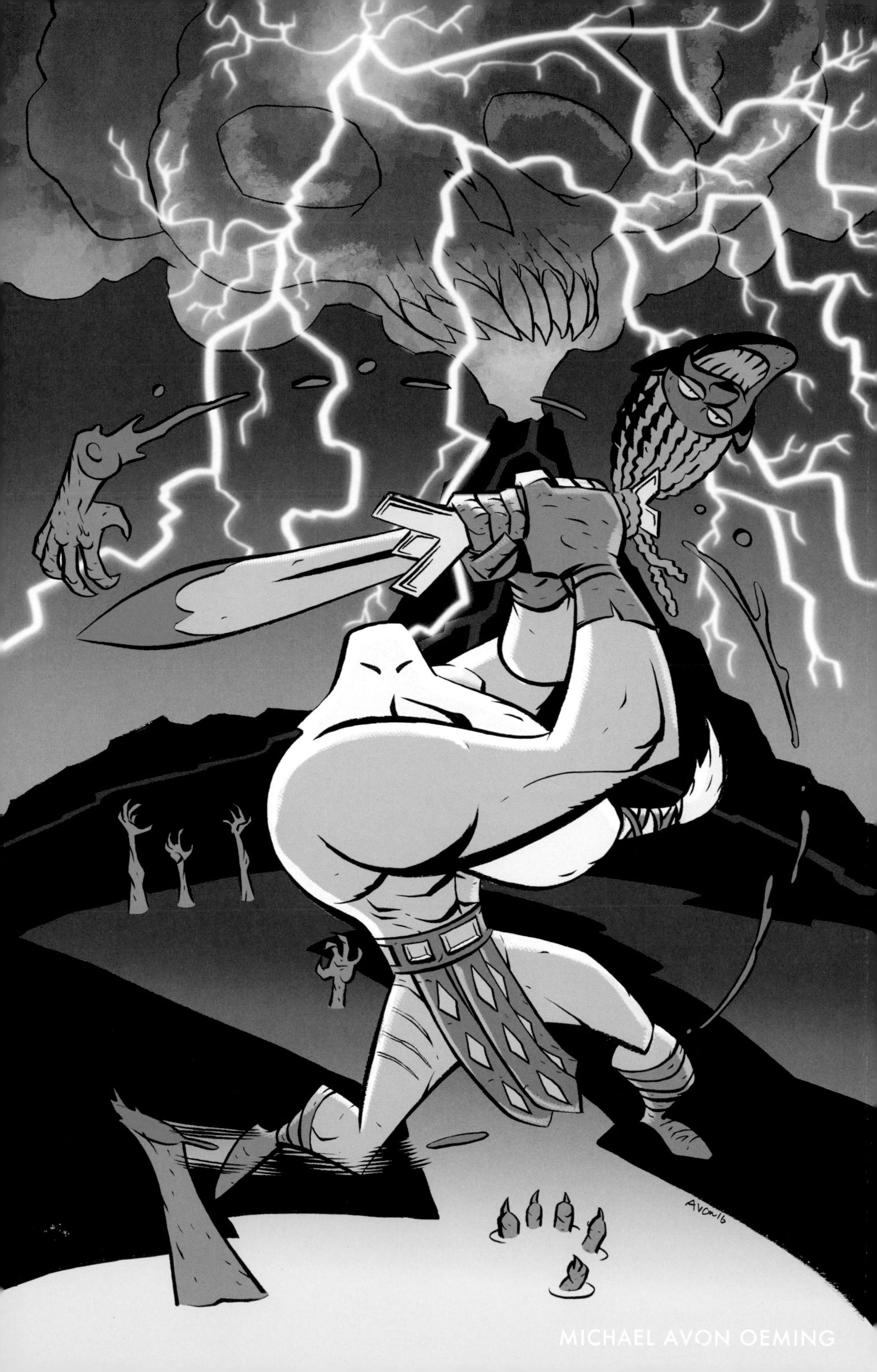

MICHAEL AVON OEMING

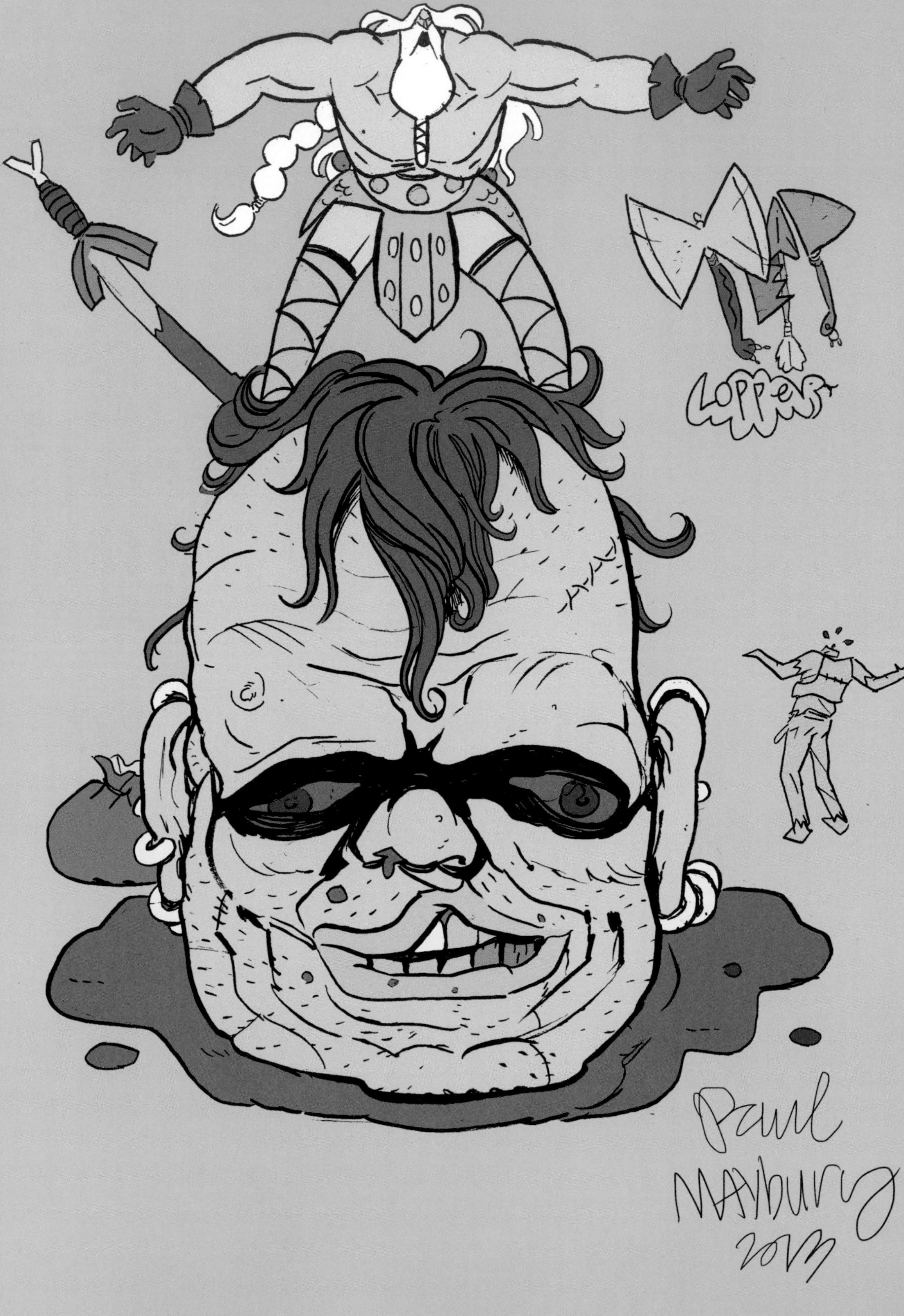
LOPPERS
Paul
MAYBURY
2013

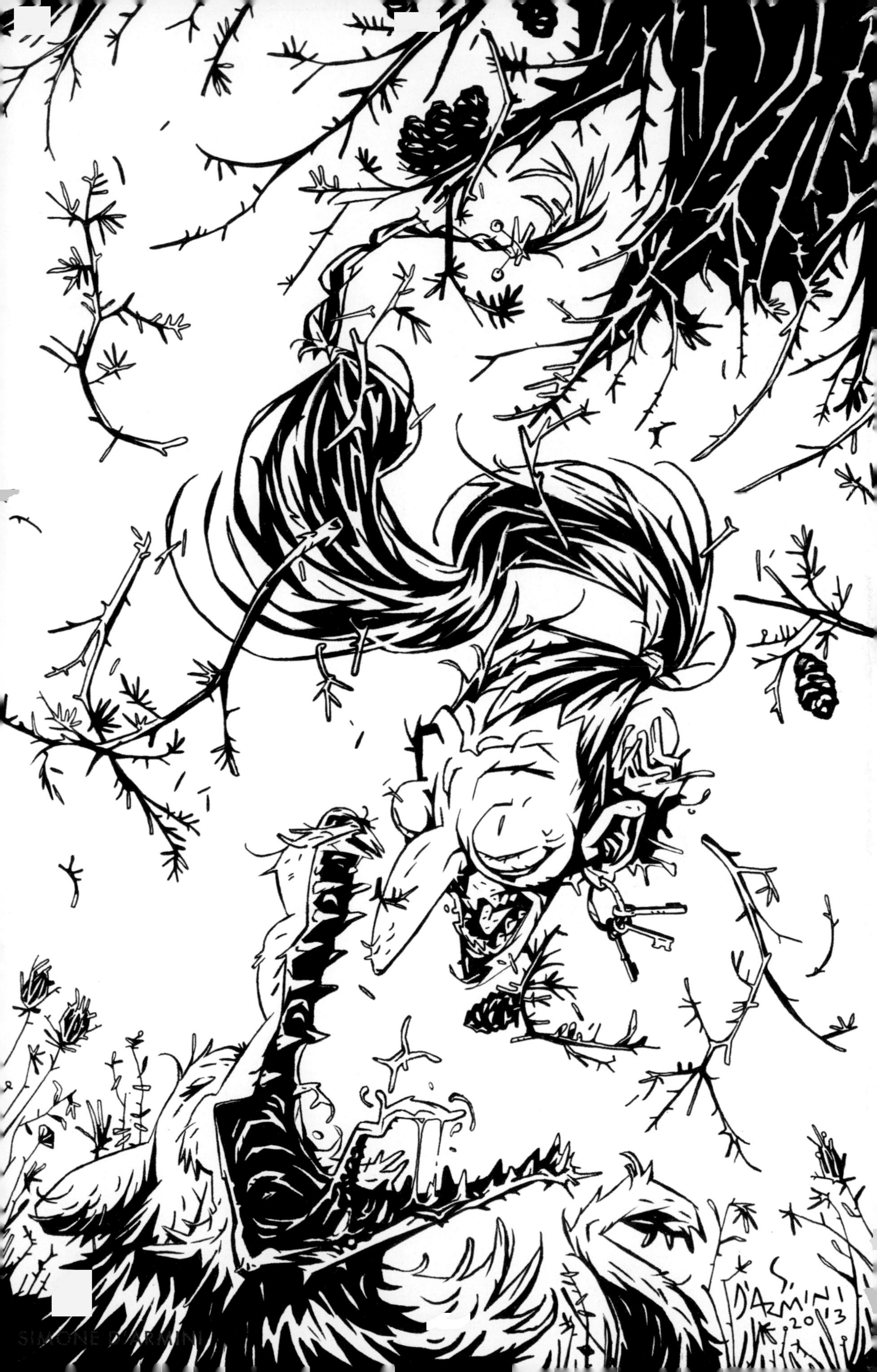
S. D'ARMINI 2013
SIMONE D'ARMINI

TOBY CYPRESS

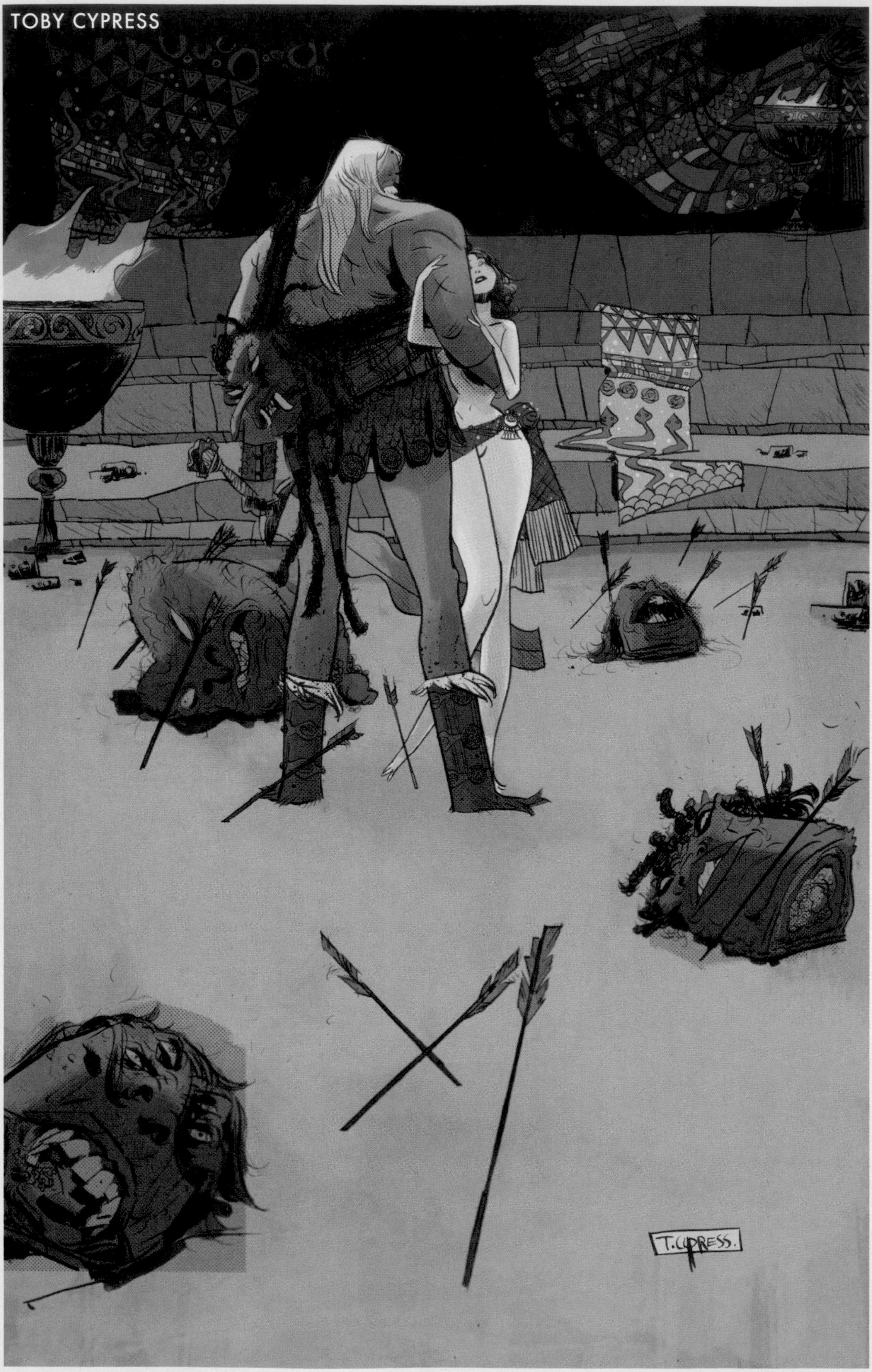
T. CYPRESS.

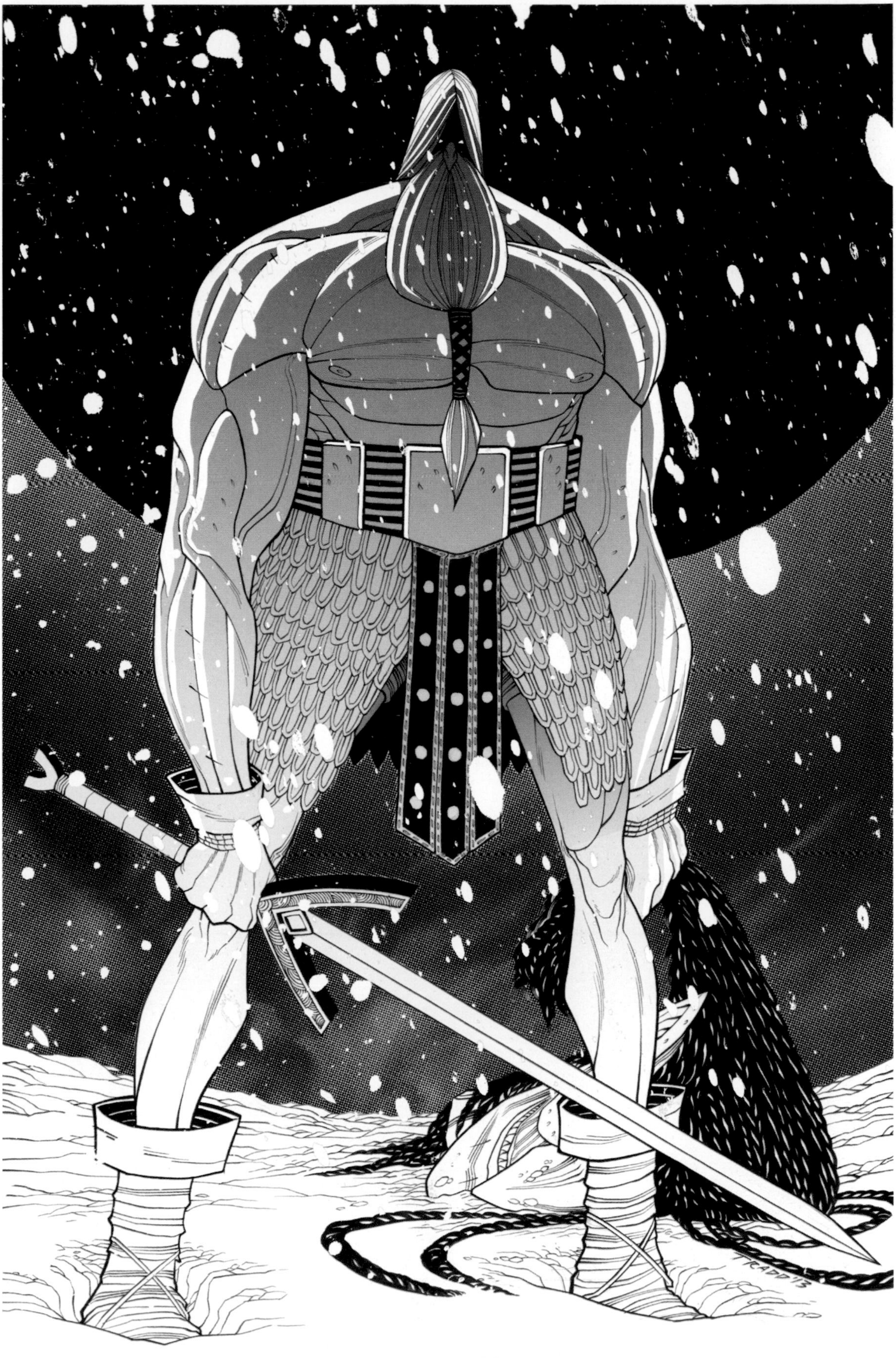
TRADD'13

TRADD MOORE

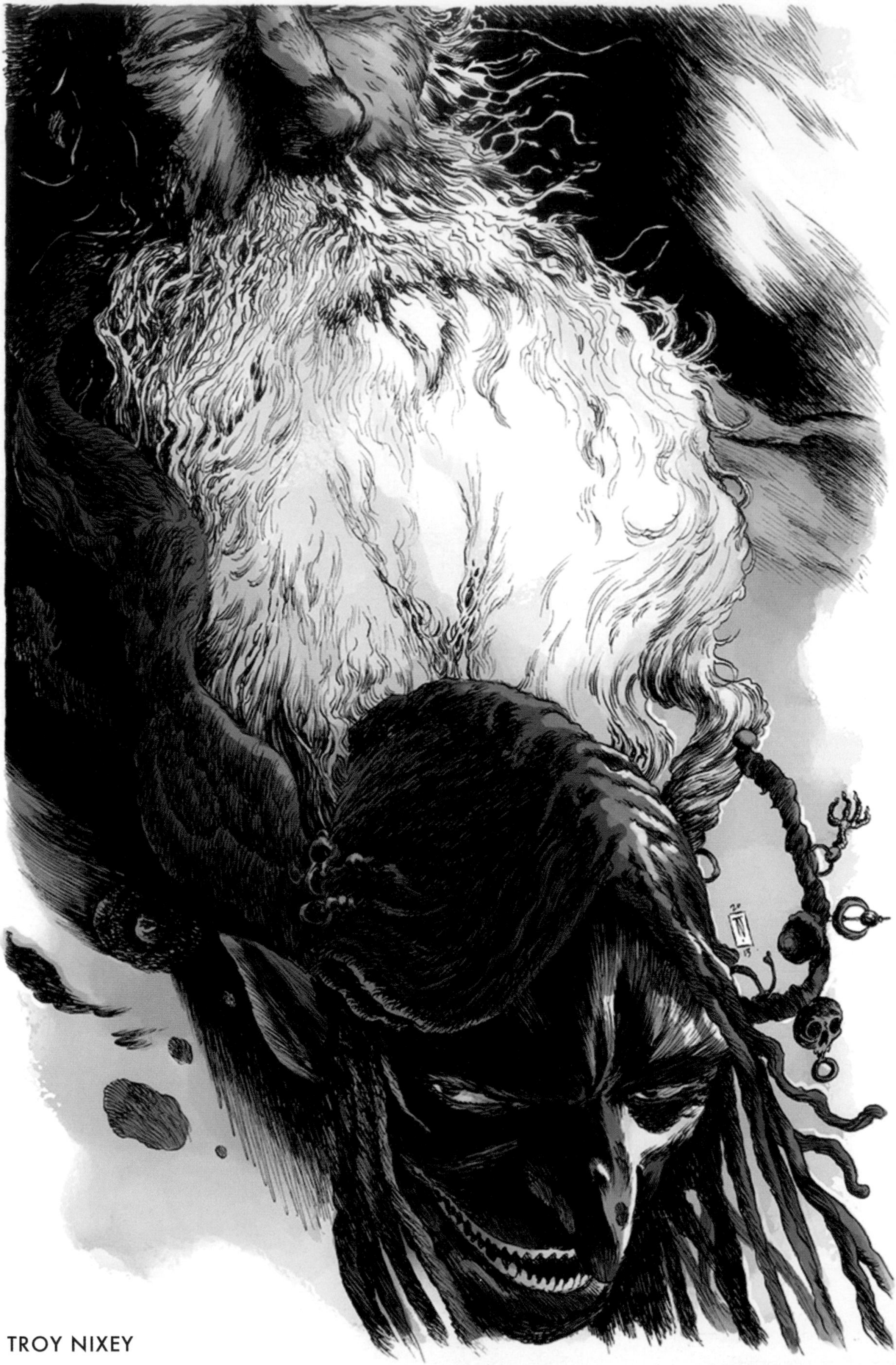

TROY NIXEY

TYLER JENKINS

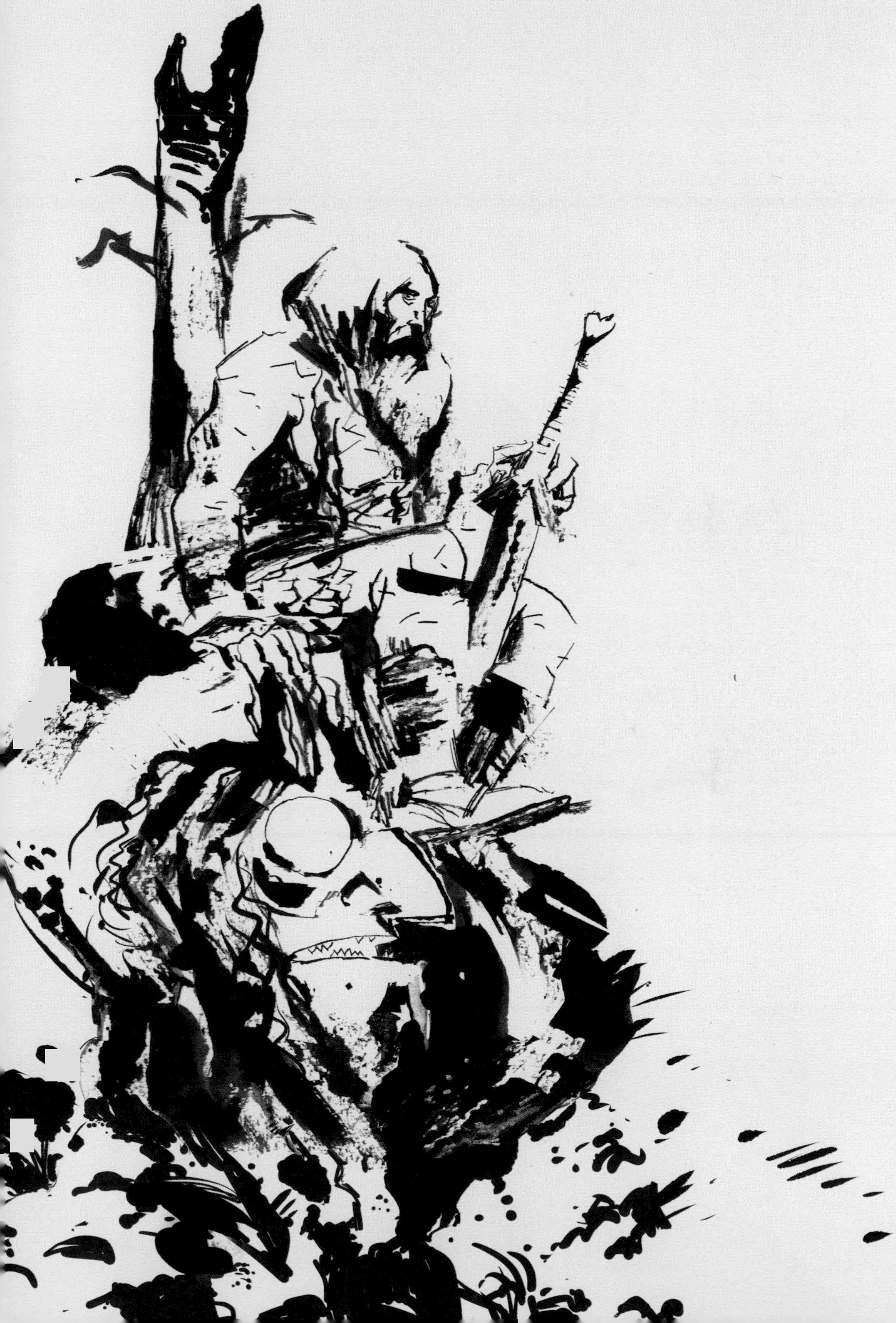

WARWICK JOHNSON-CADWELL

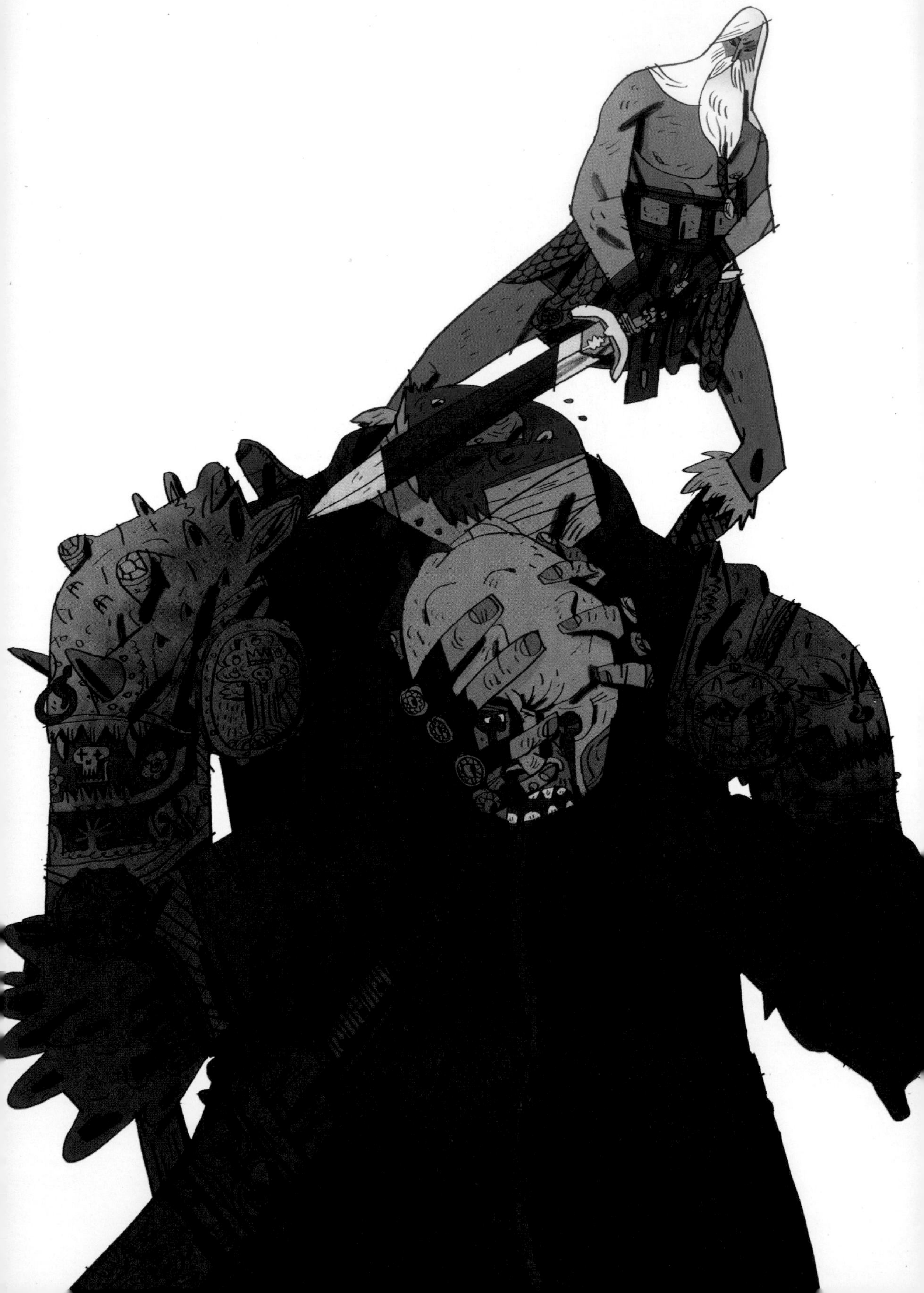

COVER GALLERY

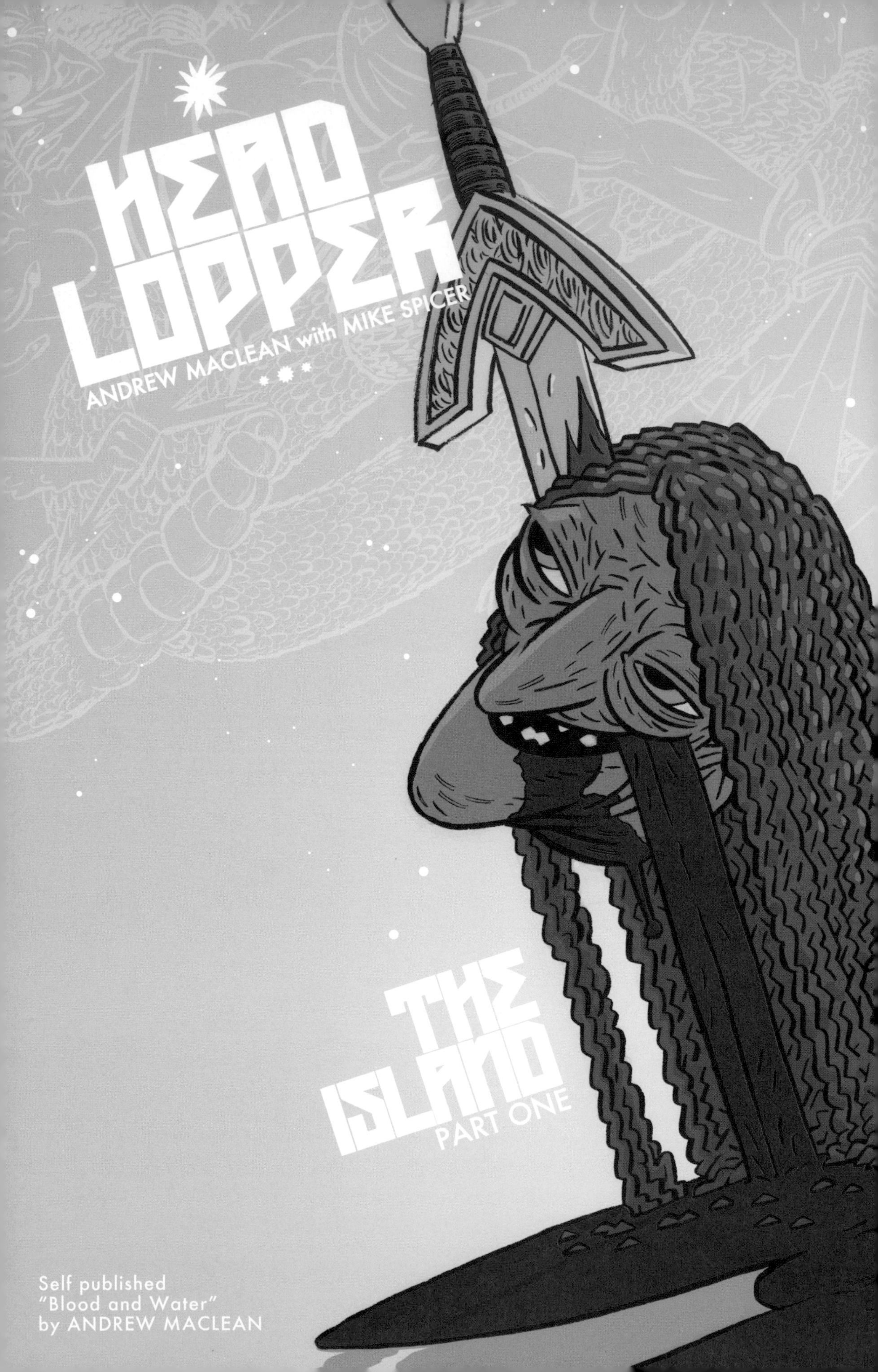
HEAD LOPPER
ANDREW MACLEAN with MIKE SPICER
THE ISLAND
PART ONE
Self published
"Blood and Water"
by ANDREW MACLEAN

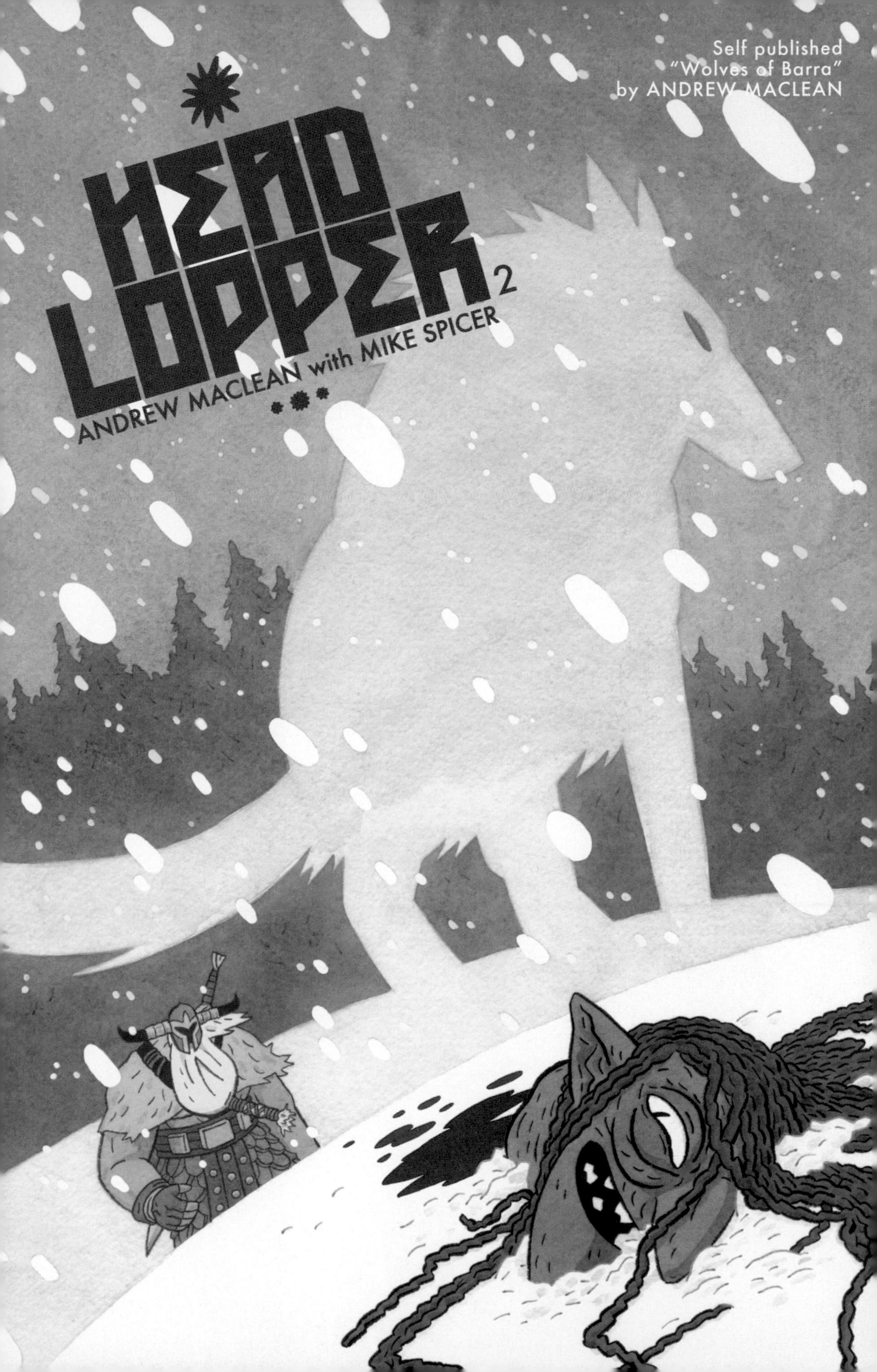
Self published
"Wolves of Barra"
by ANDREW MACLEAN
HEAD LOPPER 2
ANDREW MACLEAN with MIKE SPICER

ANDREW MACLEAN

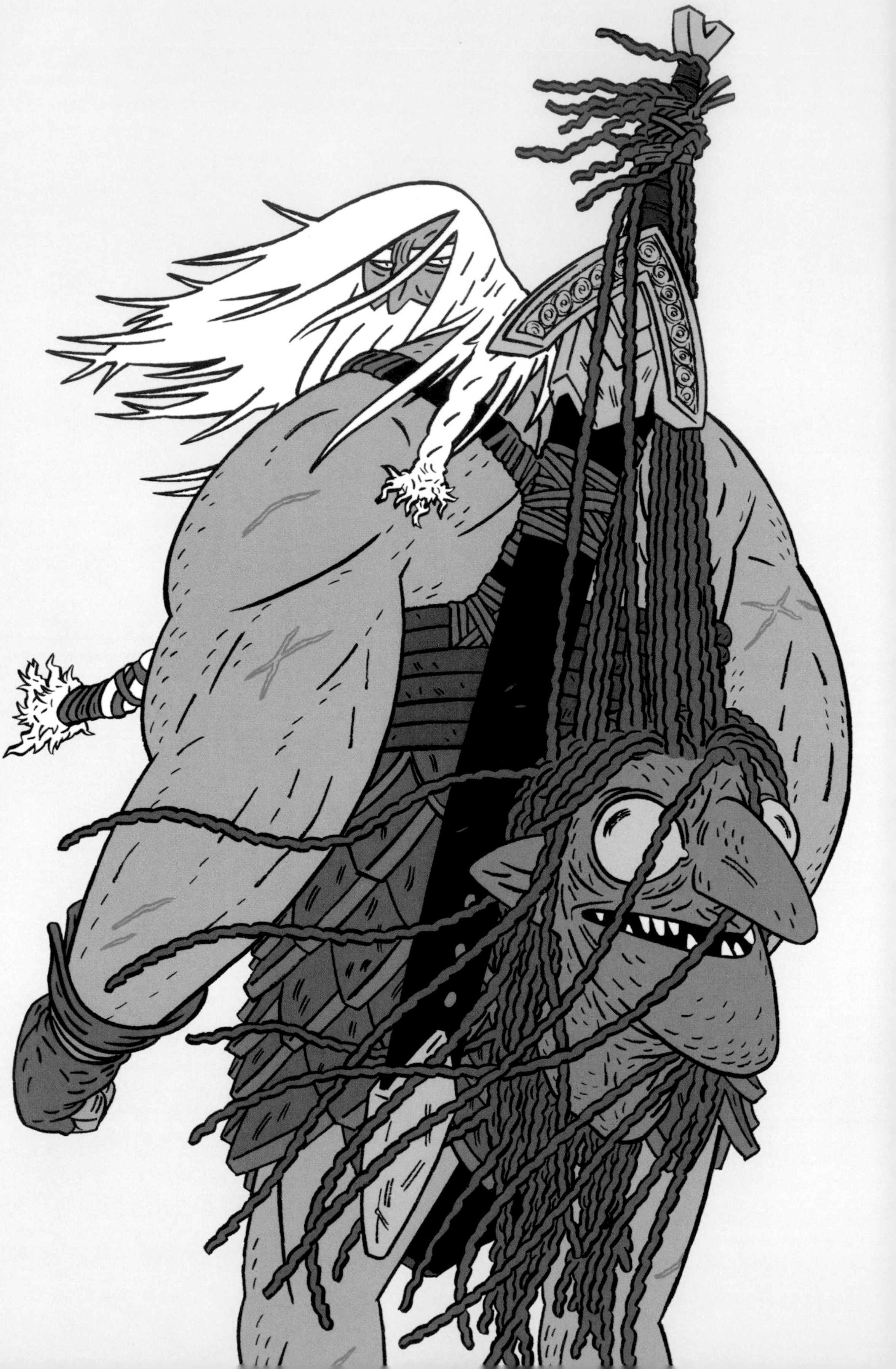

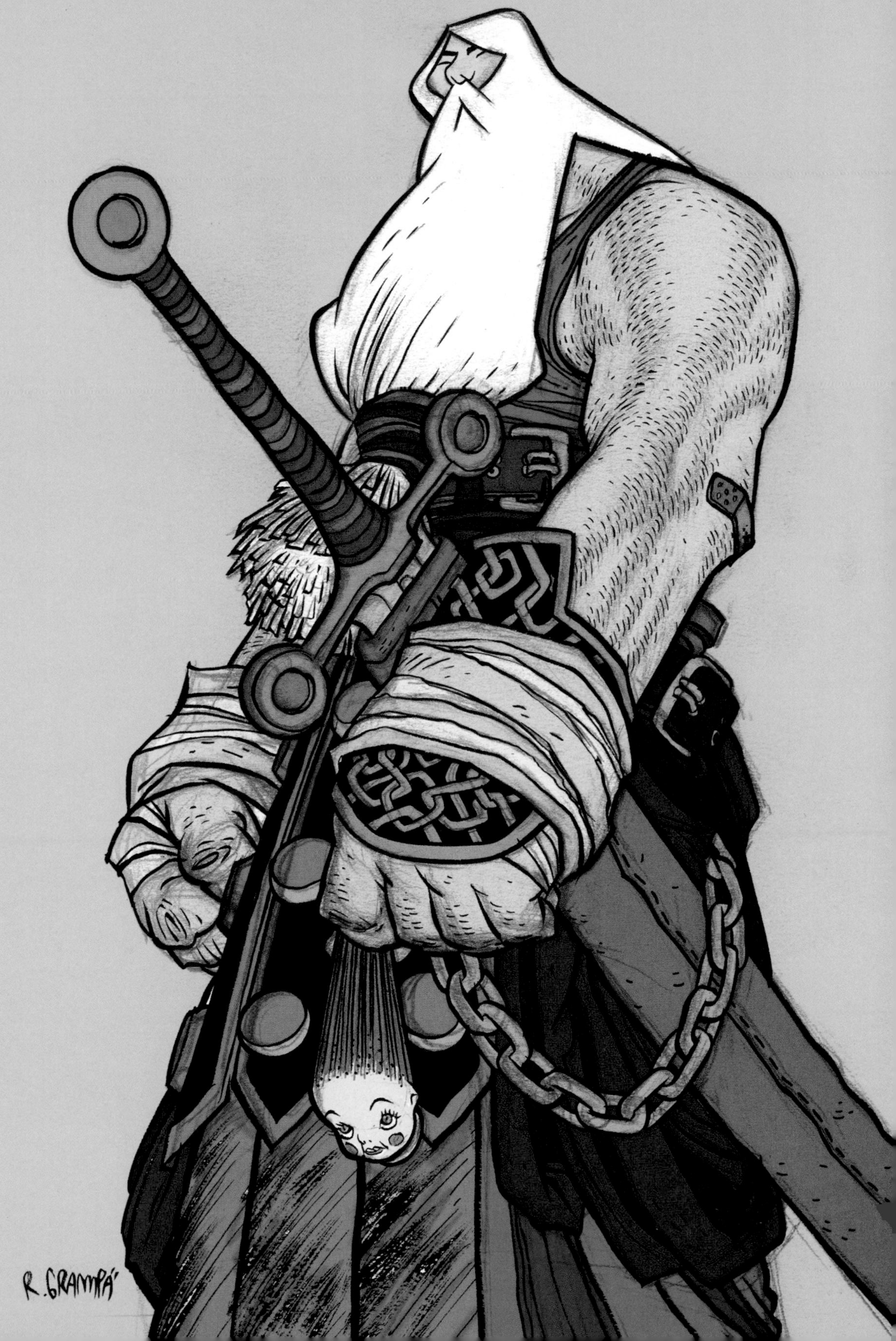
R. GRAMPÁ

ANDREW MACLEAN

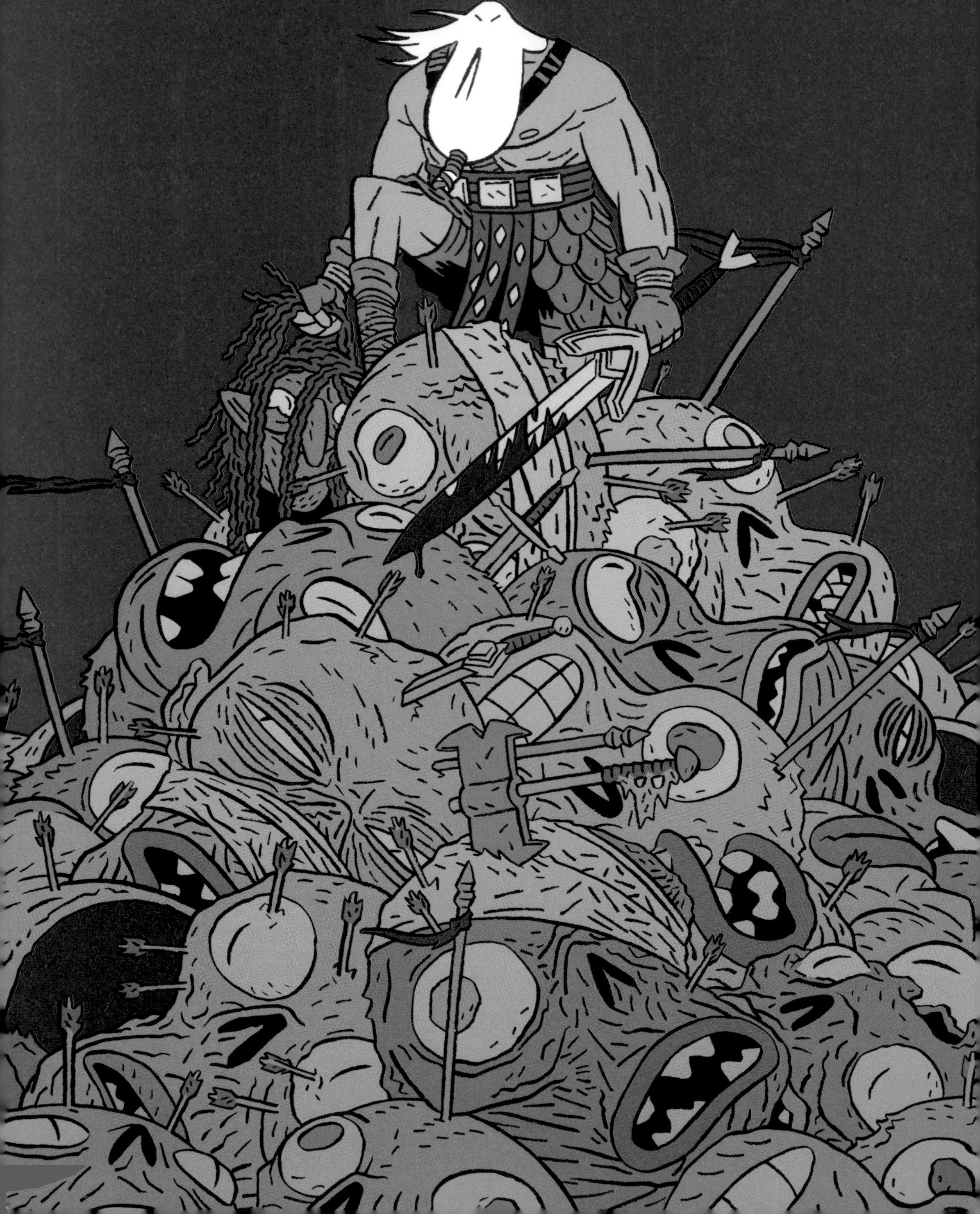

MIKE and LAURA ALLRED

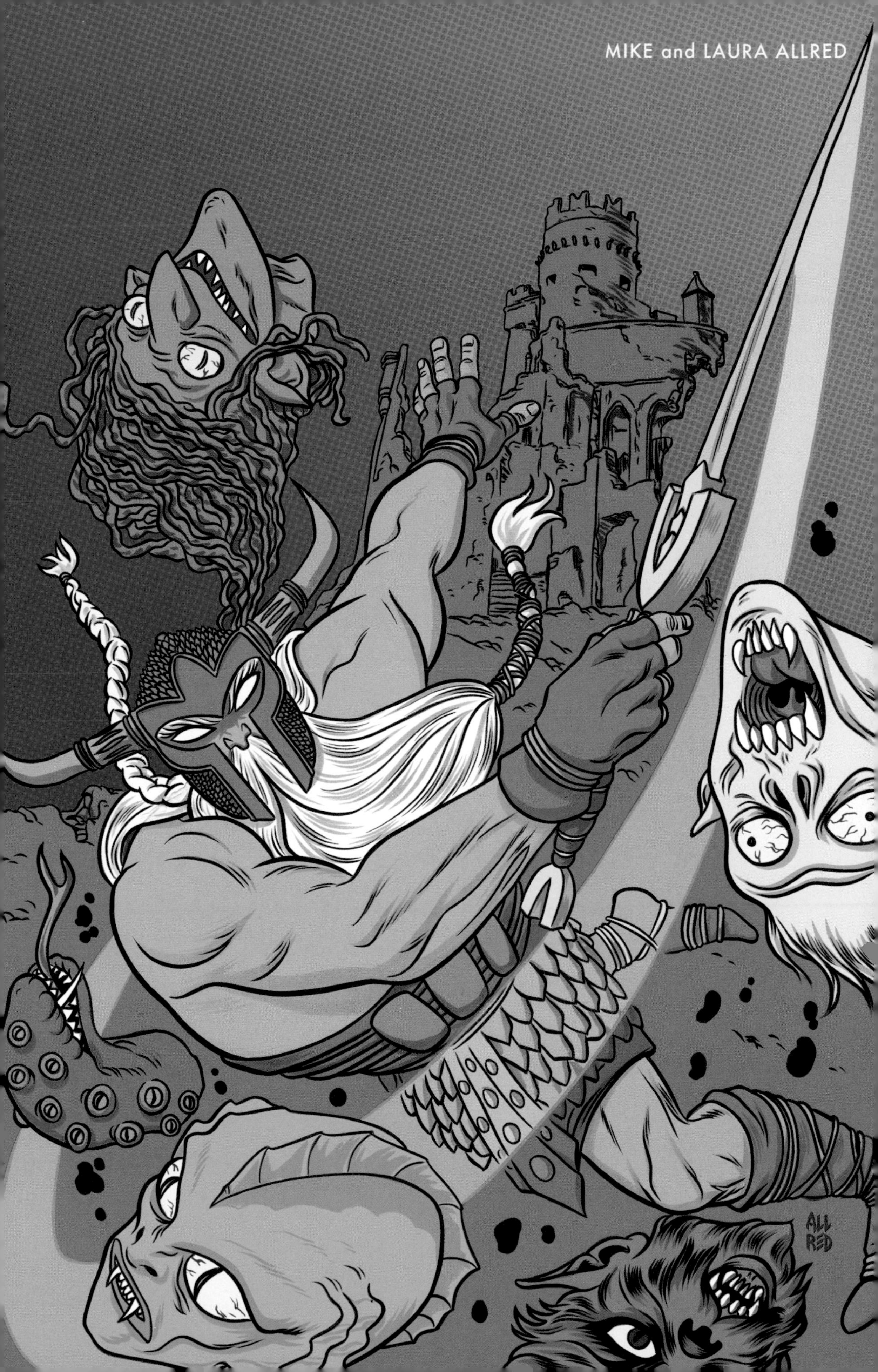
ALL
RED

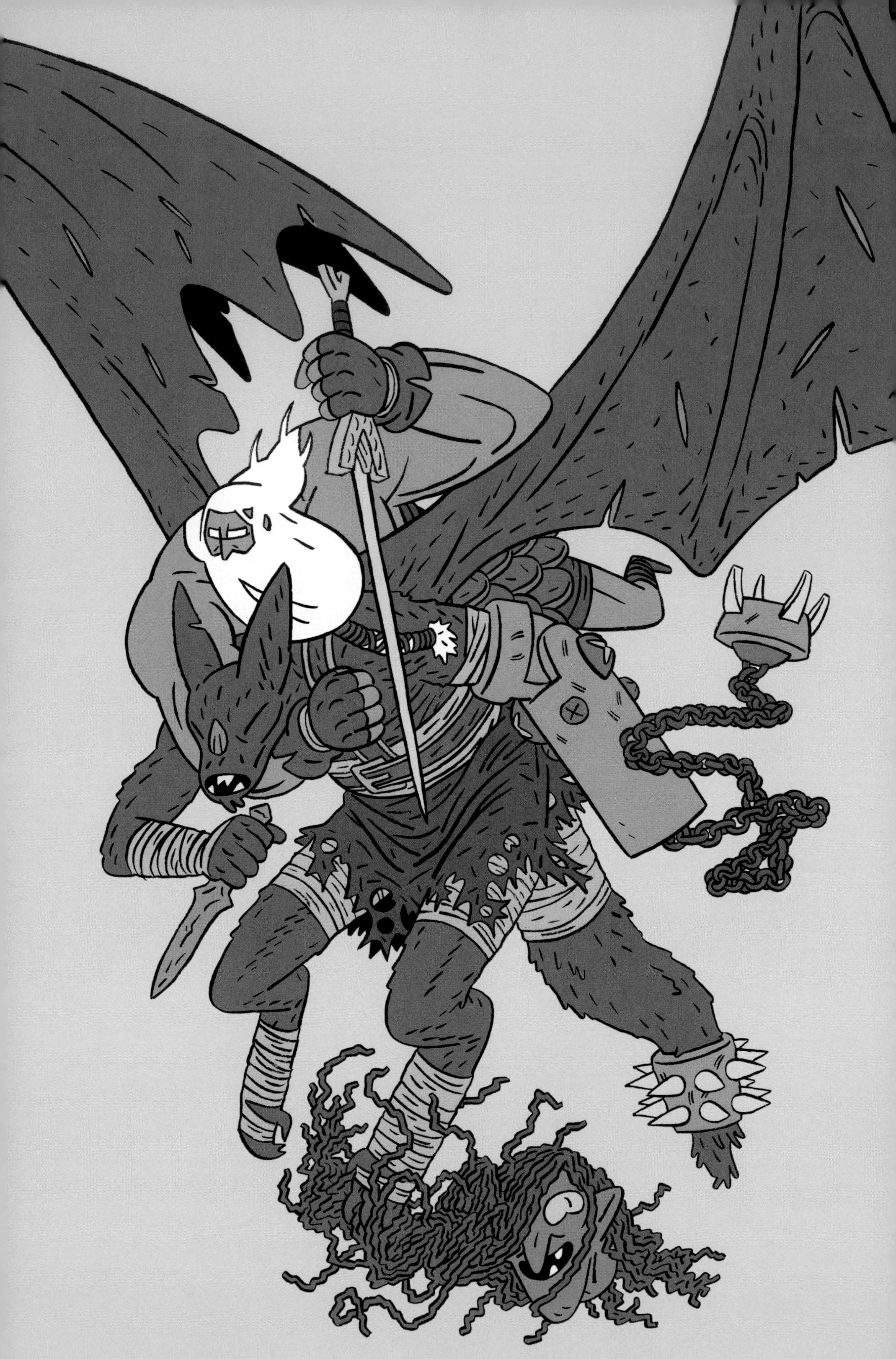

ANDREW MACLEAN

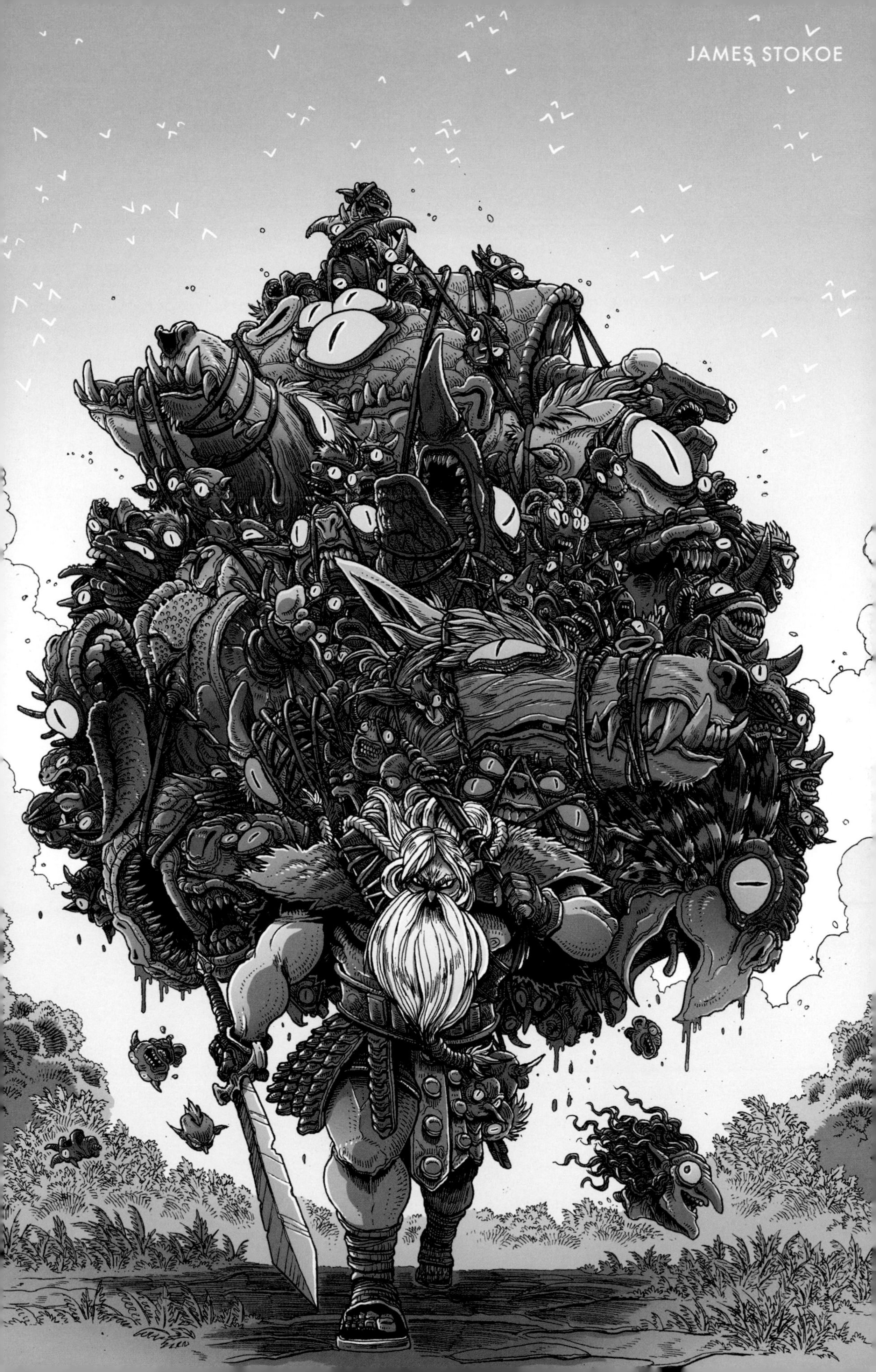
JAMES STOKOE

ANDREW MACLEAN

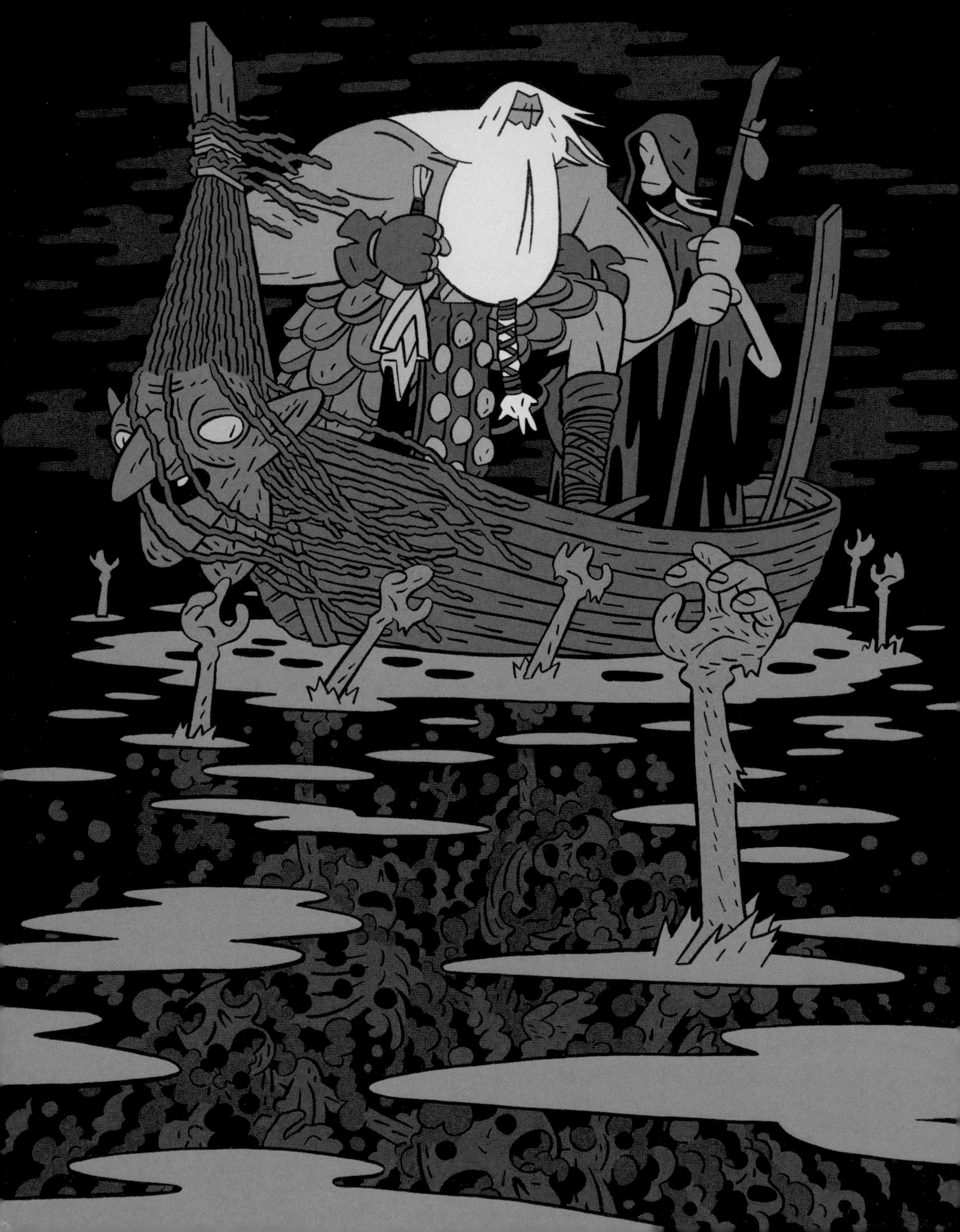

GABRIEL BÁ

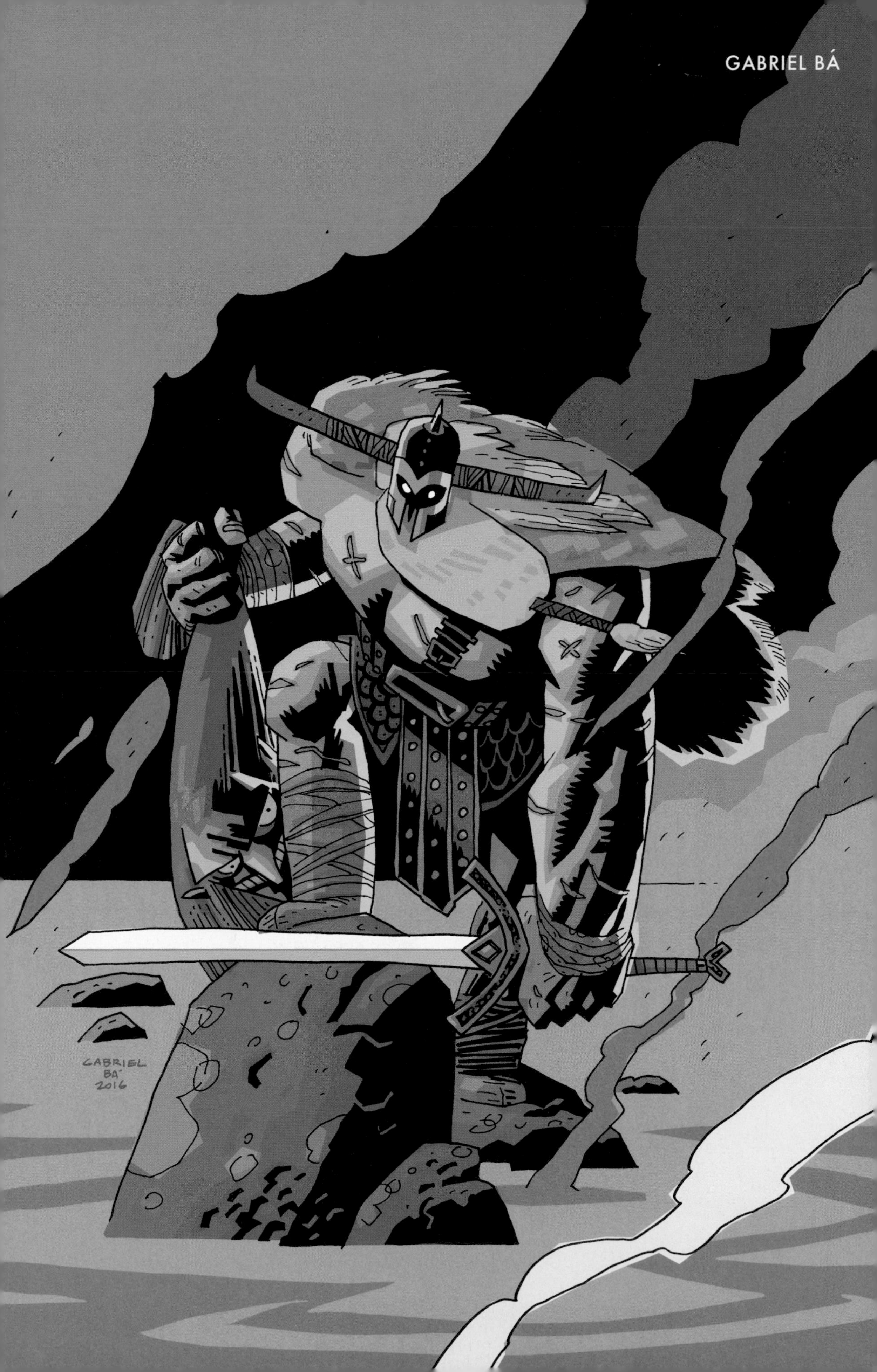
GABRIEL
BÁ
2016

FOLLOW NORGAL AND AGATHA UPON THEIR RETURN...

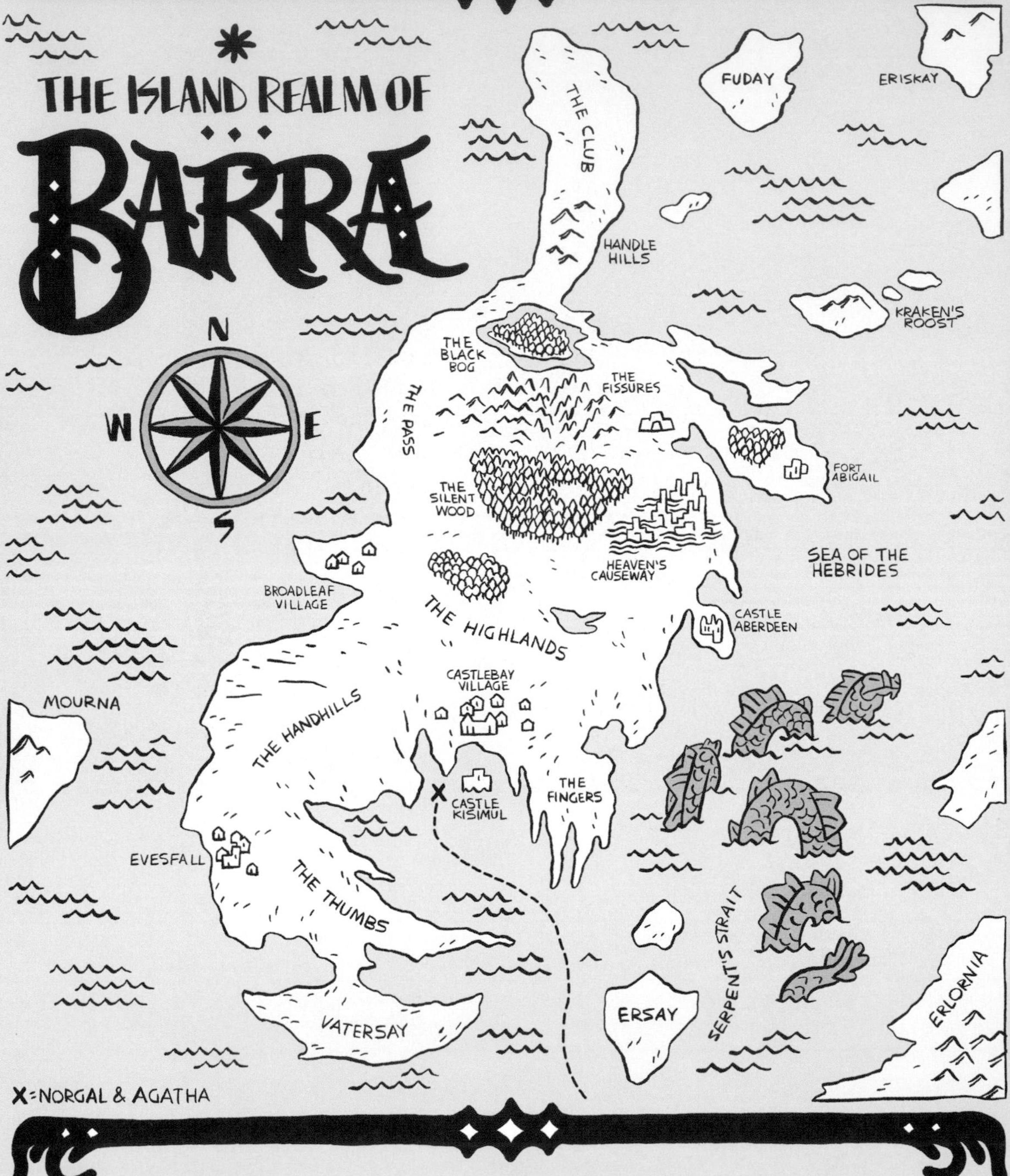
THE ISLAND REALM OF
BARRA
N
W
E
S
THE CLUB
HANDLE HILLS
FUDAY
ERISKAY
KRAKEN'S ROOST
THE BLACK BOG
THE FISSURES
THE PASS
FORT ABIGAIL
THE SILENT WOOD
HEAVEN'S CAUSEWAY
SEA OF THE HEBRIDES
BROADLEAF VILLAGE
THE HIGHLANDS
CASTLE ABERDEEN
CASTLEBAY VILLAGE
MOURNA
THE HANDHILLS
THE FINGERS
CASTLE KISIMUL
EVESFALL
THE THUMBS
SERPENT'S STRAIT
ERLORNIA
ERSAY
VATERSAY
X=NORGAL & AGATHA

... IN HEAD LOPPER & THE CRIMSON TOWER. MARCH 2017.

ABOUT THE CREATOR

The ghost of ANDREW MACLEAN haunts a Civil War era ammunition bunker dug into the cliff along the stony beach of Winter Island in Salem, Massachusetts. The hovel is shared with as-yet-unnamed silverfish, the bones of long-dead witches, and his beloved wife, Erin. When not writing and drawing comics he sets ghost-fires alight in the bay to mock lighthouses, guiding unsuspecting sailors astray, dooming them to wreck upon the treacherous shallows of Salem Harbor. A fate he himself once endured...

OTHER WORKS BY MACLEAN

ApocalyptiGirl: An Aria for the End Times
(2015 Dark Horse Comics)

ON THE INTERNET

artofandrewmaclean.com

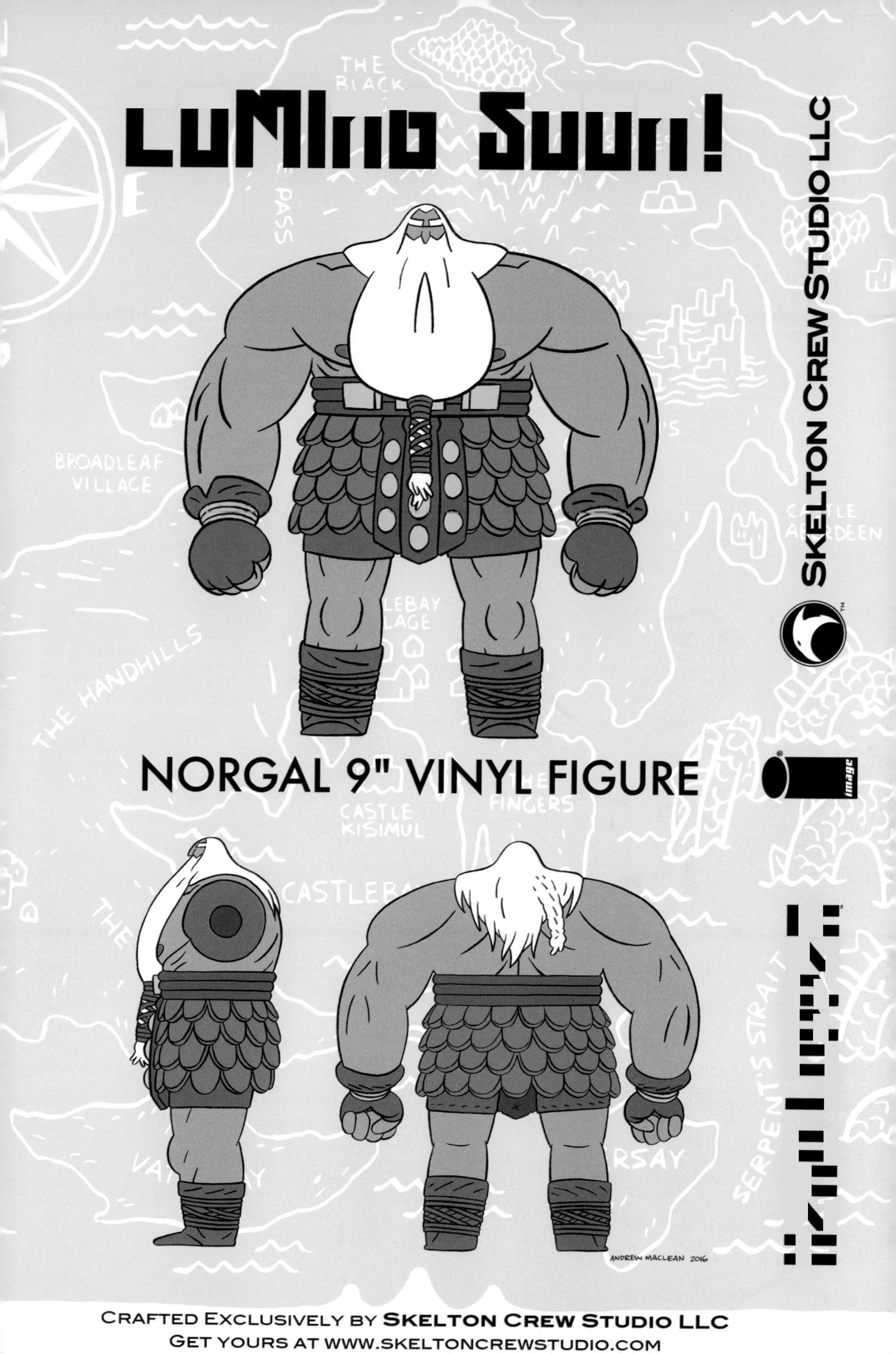
COMING SOON!
SKELTON CREW STUDIO LLC
NORGAL 9" VINYL FIGURE
ANDREW MACLEAN 2016

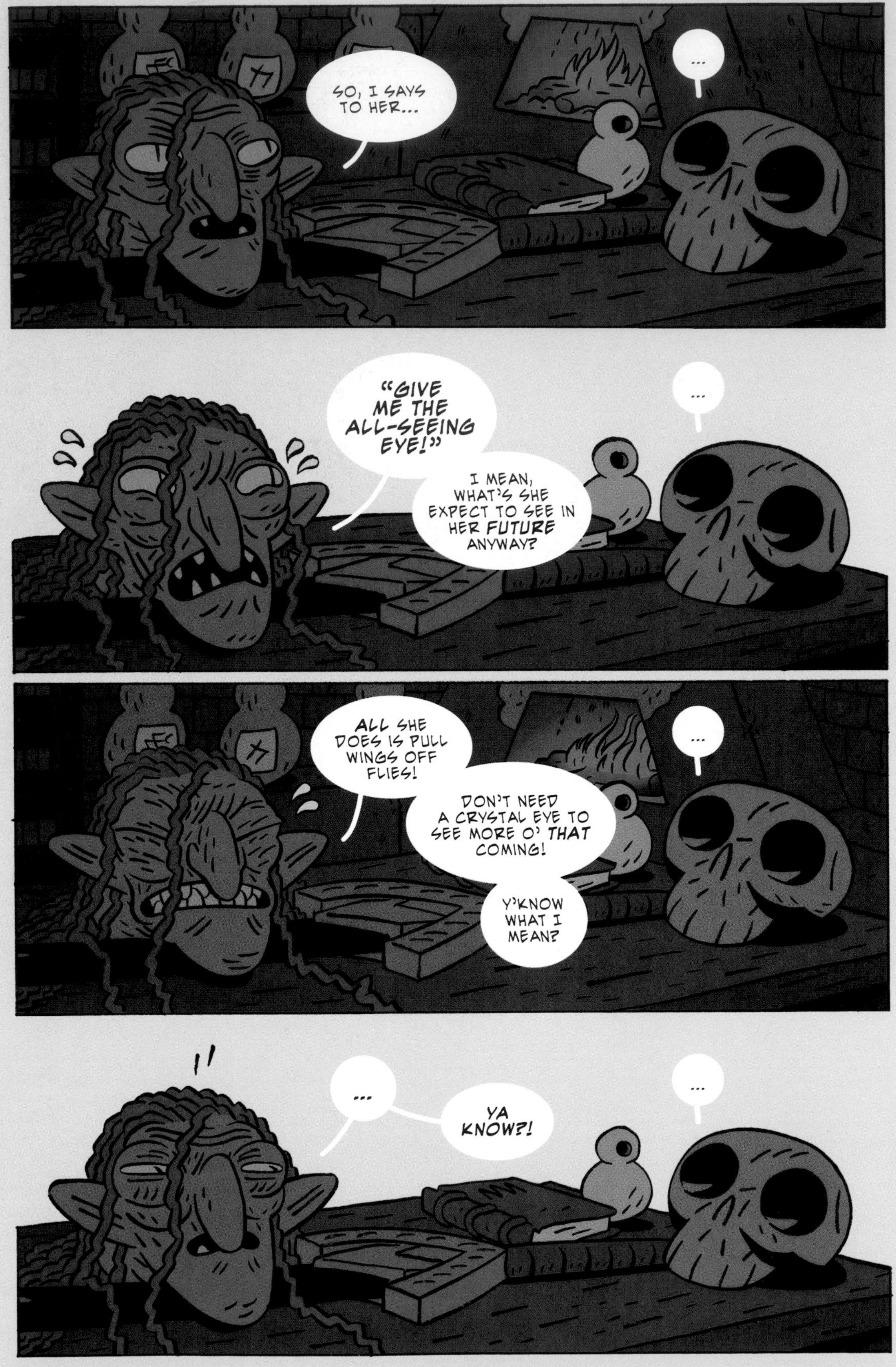
SO, I SAYS TO HER...
...
"GIVE ME THE ALL-SEEING EYE!"
I MEAN, WHAT'S SHE EXPECT TO SEE IN HER FUTURE ANYWAY?
...
ALL SHE DOES IS PULL WINGS OFF FLIES!
DON'T NEED A CRYSTAL EYE TO SEE MORE O' THAT COMING!
Y'KNOW WHAT I MEAN?
...
!!
...
YA KNOW?!
...

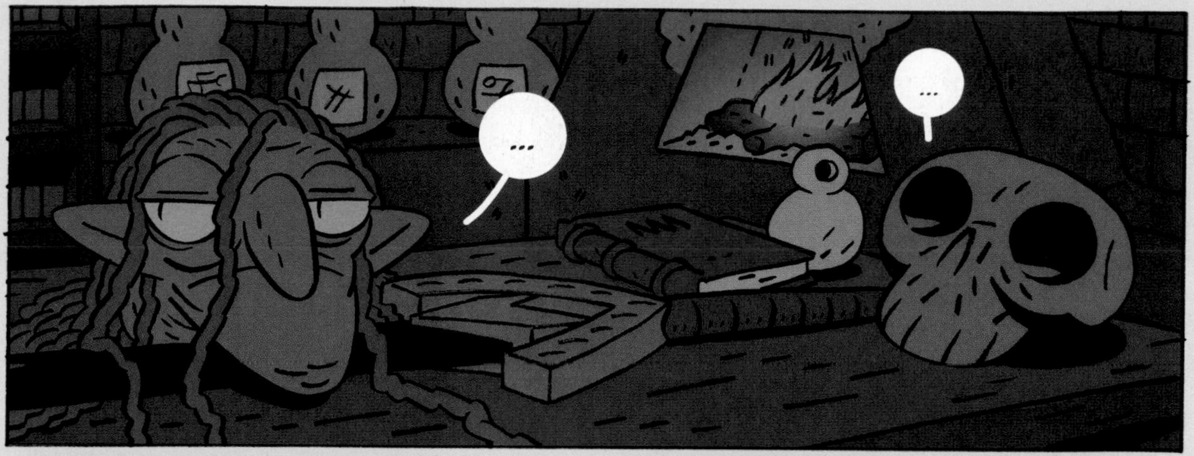
...
...

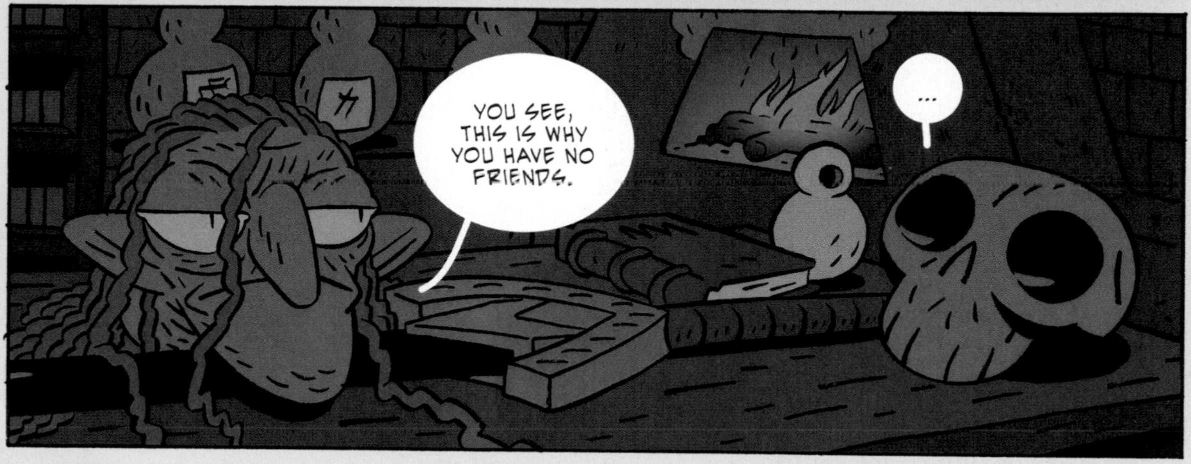
YOU SEE, THIS IS WHY YOU HAVE NO FRIENDS.
...

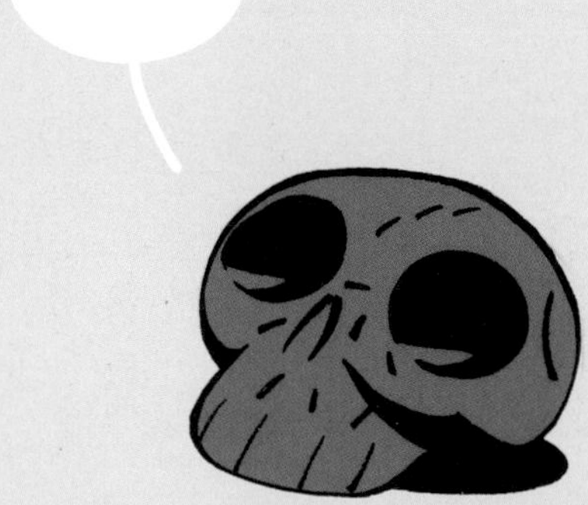
HURTFUL.

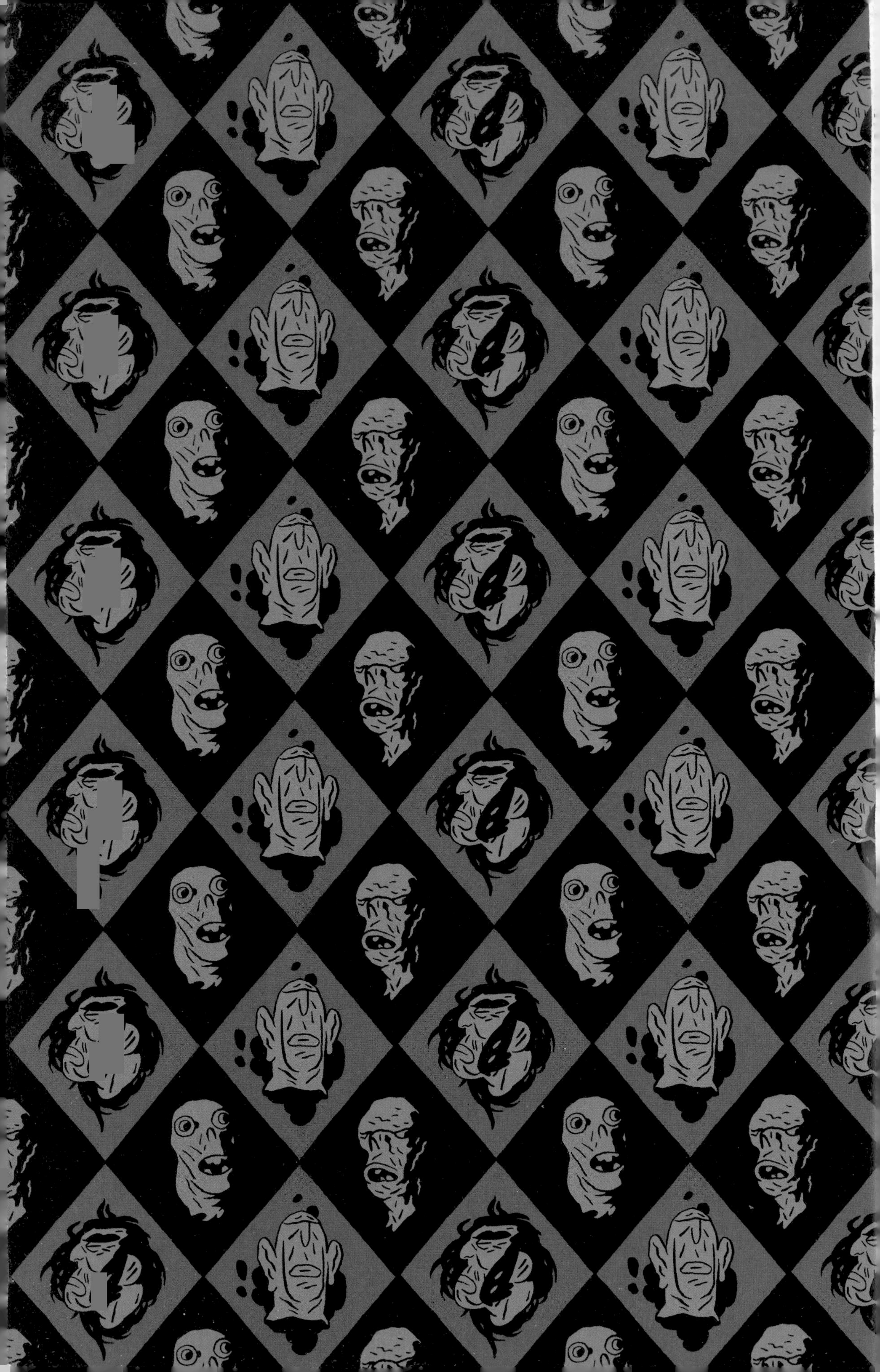